WICKED GAMES

FANG AND DAGGER
BOOK 3

JS HARKER

Developmental editing done by Sue Brown-Moore.

Copyediting done by One Love Editing.

Cover art by Reese Dante.

Cover art is for illustrative purposes only.

Please do not load this work into an AI machine. It's 180,000 words of sweat, tears, and sleepless nights. Don't let a machine rob me and other artists like me of our passion for creation.

CONTENT DISCRETION

The purpose of a story is to provide the reader with an exploration. All journeys come with risks, but in order for my readers to properly prepare, I'm providing this content discretion. You can only decide if this story is right for you if you're given the knowledge. It is out of an abundance of caution that I've labeled one event graphic and given a fuller description.

Referenced: physical abuse, sexual abuse, child abuse.

Depicted: violence, main characters who are held hostage, vampire mcs drinking blood, vampire mcs draining people of blood, and there's a very kinky sex scene.

Graphic: This book contains domestic abuse between Seamus and Anton, two villains, and at one point, Seamus beats Anton. Zack is aware of the inner emotional state of both, and Anton's fear draws a more depicted recollection of an instance of abuse within his own life. This occurs in Chapter 29, and there will be a warning at the beginning of that chapter as well.

This book is part of the middle of a longer narrative, and

our heroes struggle to reunite. And we have another cliffhanger, though of an entirely different sort than the last book.

For the readers and dreamers

PROLOGUE

The truck rumbled down the highway. The low vibrations of the engine tickled Zack's fingertips as he hung on to the edge of his seat. He was getting to ride in the front, which was the only upside of no one else coming to his blade ritual. Dad was with him, but only because Zack was ten and couldn't drive himself.

It wasn't fair. Everyone had been at his brother Cal's ceremony, and he'd had a big birthday party after. But Zack's birthday was Halloween, one of the busiest nights of the year for monster hunting. Even worse, the grown-ups had been whispering for the last three weeks. They'd ordered Zack, Cal, and his sister, Amber, to bed, but Zack and Cal had snuck out of their windows and hid near the kitchen door. The situation was Serious, possibly Apocalyptic, and Grandpa Wright had suggested that they push Zack's ceremony back until he was sixteen. Sixteen! That was forever.

Mom had stood up for Zack. She'd pointed out that everyone else had gotten their blades at ten, so Zack deserved his. Well, the everyone else that were Wrights. Both sides of Zack's family tree were legendary hunters, but the enchanted blade was a tradition from his father's side, not the Gladwells of his mother's. She'd gotten one on her wedding night.

Dad had agreed with her, and that'd been the end of the argument. So Zack was a little surprised when Dad said, "This ritual's a big deal. You sure you want to do this?"

"I *have* to," Zack said.

"Plenty of hunters fight every day without magic tied to their souls," Dad replied.

"And lots of them call us to help with dangerous stuff because we're armed with better resources, like our daggers."

"Suppose that's true." Dad turned onto a country road. The gravelly path was almost smoother than the highway had been. "But this is a big responsibility. If you're not ready—"

"I *am*," Zack insisted. "And it has to be tonight."

"Your great-great-great grandfather didn't have a blade until his twenty-first birthday, and he took down a seven-hundred-year-old vampire."

Zack rolled his eyes. He knew all the family stories by heart, so he knew the details Dad had skipped. "Great-great-great Grandpa Wright also had a squad of soldiers and burnt the vampire's plantation house down in the middle of the day. All he had to do was make sure the vampire couldn't hide in a shadow and regenerate."

"You should always choose the smart path when taking on evil," Dad said.

"And it would be smarter if I had a magical dagger," Zack replied. "Cal got his when he was ten. Why doesn't anyone want me to have mine?"

Dad was quiet for a long moment. When he spoke, he had that extra-stern tone in his voice that meant he was being ultra-serious. "Getting one because you're jealous of your brother is not the reason to do this."

Zack could get serious, too. He puffed up and folded his arms over his chest. "That doesn't answer the question!"

They pulled onto a long driveway, and Dad not only stopped the truck but put it in park. The witch's house seemed miles away, and the little porchlight didn't reach them. Out in the darkness, his father was a shadow with a weighty parental presence. He turned in his seat, and the dim lights of the dashboard barely dented the shadows around him.

Dad didn't usually grow a beard, but he had some stubble. A few days' worth, Zack figured. His parents always seemed *old*—Dad more than Mom whenever a crisis hit. Mom always got way too much energy, and Dad seemed to lose all of his. Whatever had been happening the past few nights was *huge*.

When Zack was older, he'd be able to help. He wouldn't need anyone to take care of him, and he'd be able to kill the monsters and make his family proud. The sooner he had a magical dagger, the sooner he wasn't as big of a burden.

"Zack, do you understand what the ritual will do?" Dad asked.

"The witches will bind a silver dagger to me, and that will give me a magical weapon to fight the forces of darkness," Zack recited.

"You know what has to happen, don't you?" Dad put his hand on Zack's shoulder. "A piece of your soul will be outside of your body forever. Do you know what that means?"

"It means that I should never lose the dagger because a clever monster could find a way to tear out the rest of my soul," Zack replied. "But I'll also always know where my dagger is because we're bound together. Like a Jedi and their lightsaber."

"It also means a part of you will be *gone*."

"If it's in the dagger, then it's not really gone."

Dad stared out into the night. Sometimes, Dad needed the silence to think out the rest of his point, especially when he was arguing with Mom or Zack. He never seemed to take extra time when he had to yell at Cal about something.

Zack figured that meant he always had a better argument. He was smarter than Cal, though no one ever said it. But Zack had the better grades and did the best research for what he was allowed to work with. Grandma Bonnie said his mind was a blessing, and she had *never* called anything about Cal a blessing.

"A piece of yourself will always be just out of reach," Dad said slowly, bringing his gaze back to Zack. "You won't know what's missing, but you'll know there's this bit that's just gone. And you won't know who you could've been if it was still inside you. You could be giving up your courage, your heart. Anything."

Since Dad had taken a moment, Zack decided thinking before he spoke was a good thing. He usually didn't need to because he was pretty smart, but he wanted to make sure Dad took him seriously. "The soul doesn't work like that. You can't just give up all your courage. Grandma Bonnie made me write a whole essay about the ritual, and I had to read all these books. A person's soul has a huge amount of energy. It's more like our skin and blood. It's always shedding and regenerating. The dagger is like ... Dad, do you know about amber?"

"I would make a dad joke about the fact that that's your sister's name, but I'm a bit too tired," Dad replied.

Duh, stupid, a voice in Zack's mind teased him. It sounded like Cal. Zack hated that voice. It had been popping up in his head lately. "Okay, so, I think this ritual is like taking a piece of my soul that would flake off and putting it in amber. But, like, not totally like amber because I'll be able to reach out and connect with it. I'm not losing anything. I'm keeping something *forever.* I'll always know who I am no matter what."

Dad was silent so long that Zack was afraid he'd said

something wrong. Then he shook his head. "I worry about you, kiddo."

"Why?" Zack asked.

With a sigh, Dad put the truck in gear, and they gently rolled on toward the witch's house. "Because the smart hunters are the ones that die young."

Zack snorted. "Mom says dumb hunters are the ones that die early."

"Them too," Dad replied.

"Then you should be worried about Cal," Zack said.

"I worry about all my kids." As Dad parked the truck in front of the witch's house, he said, "Just promise me one thing, Zack. Promise me that you won't lose your heart in this business."

That seemed like a weird thing to ask. But hunters sometimes did worse than die. Sometimes, they became the creatures they hunted. Cal had certainly been changing lately. He was meaner. Zack wanted to be like him but not entirely like him. "I promise I won't turn into a monster, Dad. I'm going to be the greatest hunter since Mary Gladwell."

Dad ruffled Zack's hair and smiled at him. "All right. Guess we should get you that blade."

CHAPTER 1

L'Hotel Monde De Nuit, Chicago, Illinois, 2021

"Roger, please! I can't do this on my own!"

The pleading voice sliced through the oblivion that clouded Roger's sight all the way through to his soul. Pain so intense that it scalded, froze, and then thawed him shattered the shreds of reality attempting to stitch themselves into consciousness. Every nerve and fragment of his body ached with an agony that threatened to pin him to a wall in an abyss of unknowing.

"Roger!"

Grasping for the waking world was like groping for a loose rope in a storm, the length rain-slick and constantly bandying about in the wind. He was reaching, but it kept slipping away from him. The harder he tried, the further life seemed to be, until finally, *finally*, he saw a bit of carpet beneath him. His hand was pressed against it. He had a body.

With consciousness came the fragments of memories. Pieces tumbled away from him, but he fought to form a picture of himself. He had been in a fight. In a hotel room.

Before a ball? No, after going to a ball. He'd walked into a party with Takashi on his arm. Spun Zack around the dance floor in an elegant waltz. Then fled. Ran to the hotel room because Seamus was angry. Because Anton had declared that the gamble was settled.

Strange that the thought of the flaxen-haired ancient vampire was what brought focus to the downpour of memories flooding through Roger. For over three hundred years, he had believed that he survived the cruelty of his sire because he had become someone that his sire at least tolerated, if not liked. That he had cut away enough bits of himself that Seamus didn't hate him, that he had spent night after night smiling away his pains because that was the only way to stay alive.

But he had been nothing more than a plaything. Seamus and Anton had been competing with each other to see whose sireling would live longer, Roger or Dmitri. Their lives had been a damn game for their sires.

Even now, he was coming back to consciousness because their bet wasn't over. At the Grand Winter's Ball, he'd shown off his ability to incite desire in others in order to shut down the fear that Seamus had been spreading. He'd humiliated Seamus in what he'd thought was a coy move, but he hadn't survived because of any skill or talent of his own. He'd lived as long as he had because *Seamus* willed it.

Seamus couldn't stand for the humiliation to go unpunished. He would have ripped them to shreds inside the Chateau de Vampire, except the Lady Belladonna, an Unseelie noble, had interrupted and demanded he remain civil as it was a party to honor the fey.

Roger and his group had fled the party. On their way out, Roger had scooped up Vincent into his arms. The boy had been one of Seamus's pets, and Seamus had beaten him. Roger wasn't sure he could save the boy's life in the end.

He wasn't sure of anything anymore except that someone was calling to him.

"*Roger*!" The voice was unfamiliar, climbing in pitch with desperation.

The sharp pain in Roger's neck was subsiding. The last wound Anton had dealt was to snap his neck. Not deadly for a vampire, but inconvenient. How long had he been out?

Roger pushed himself to his hands and knees. His vision swayed like the world was the deck of a ship before settling. The blades he'd wielded from the fight were gone. The one he'd made of shadows must have melted away when he lost consciousness, but he didn't spot Callum Wright's magical Bowie knife either.

Callum Wright. The name of that monster was the key to unlocking another flood of memories. Bits of Zack appeared, fragments of visions. Now, Roger could hear the echo of his laugh, remember the feel of him in his arms.

Was the voice calling out to him Zack's?

No.

Did Zack need his help?

Roger's vision settled, and he took in his surroundings. How odd that the hotel suite that had been the home for the five of them for weeks was in nearly the order they'd left it in. The couches were pushed out from the center of the living room because they'd practiced their ballroom dances one last time before the party. Where the lights had dimmed during the fight, they were back to their usual brightness. The bar and large television remained untouched from the fight.

But the glass doors leading to the balcony were broken. A gaping hole and the scent of blood on the air were evidence that part of the fight had gone that way.

Zack had been fighting Seamus, and Roger had been too busy with Anton to help him.

Takashi had fought at Roger's side until Anton had

snapped his neck to knock him out. Where was he? He had been close.

Kit and Carver had to be somewhere nearby. They were vulnerable mortals, made more so by Roger's decision to exclude them from his true mission.

Where were his friends? His lovers? Were any of them still alive? Who was calling to him?

Moving was a mistake. Roger had fought with every ounce of his spirit with the belief that he might not live another moment. Doing so had torn through his stored energy, and without that power in his veins, his hunger became a thirst so fierce that his throat was rougher than the barnacles caked onto the underside of a hull that hadn't been cleaned in three decades. He ground his teeth. The pain of his fangs pricking his gums was minor compared to the rest of his aches.

There was blood. He smelled a pool of it behind him, and he turned toward it.

Carver was lying in the doorway, his body keeping the exit open. Another flash of memory sparked for Roger. Seamus had torn Carver's throat open.

The blood would be no good for Roger.

That the realization came before the first pang of grief drove a dagger deep into Roger's heart. Carver had been a friend and someone who had shared his blood with Roger. He had been a mortal boy with a broad smile and an easygoing love for life.

And he was dead because of Roger. Because Roger couldn't see that he hadn't been acting the part of a fool but been one.

He staggered to his feet. *Migraine* was a mundane word for the agony threatening to shred his mind. A whine filled his ears, some indiscernible pitch that had to be a concoction of his inner senses rather than something real. Every thought was sluggish, especially when memories danced in front of his vision. Nearby was a source of fresh, wondrous blood. He wanted to lap it up.

No, that's the life draining from someone I care about. I don't want to kill them. Roger struggled out of the remnants of his tuxedo jacket and dropped the ruined silver fabric to the floor. "Where are you?"

"Over here!"

Fuck, there was a lot of "here" in the suite. The pitched note in his ears moved to a higher frequency and stopped blocking the deeper sounds. He could pick out heartbeats. Two pulses pounded away, one fast while the other was weaker but steady.

Two? There should have been *four*. Wait, no. Carver was already gone. Three. He should have heard three.

Roger stumbled toward the source of the heartbeats. On the floor, he discovered a white-gold dagger pendant on a beautiful, broken chain. It had a pink tourmaline gem— Zack's birthstone—set in the tiny pommel and little diamonds on either side of the hilt and in a line down the center of the two-inch pendant. Takashi had given it to Zack for his birthday. Though it took far too much energy, Roger scooped it up from the floor and slid it into his pocket. *He'll want this back.*

A muffled cry drew his attention. Whoever was alive was hiding behind the bar. He was moving closer to the fresh blood, but he throttled his hunger and choked it into submission. He was over three hundred years old and would not fall into a blood frenzy.

A smear of blood across the floor led him through the furniture and to his destination.

Kit lay on the floor. Deep red soaked their beautiful silver dress, the light failing to illuminate any of the sparkles. Their eyes were closed, and they lacked tension in their body, dangerously close to having the sort of stillness that only came to the dead. Against the pallor of their skin, their dyed red hair was a brilliant shock of color. They had shifted into their hybrid form, and they had long foxlike ears, a tail, and claws on the tips of their fingers.

Holding a blanket to the largest of Kit's wounds, Vincent trembled as he continued to press down. His right eye was puffy, and the red marks on his arms were more bruises than welts. His lip was split anew from his shouts. Every mortal Roger met anymore felt young, but Vincent couldn't be older than Zack. Besides the hallmarks of youth clinging to Vincent, Roger knew what sort of mortal Seamus claimed. The young and helpless.

As Vincent choked on tears while trying to staunch Kit's bleeding, Roger's mental winds shifted, and his sails snapped into place. He had to step up for Kit's and Vincent's sakes. He had to take action before Kit was lost.

Roger went to his knees beside Kit. "They're a shifter. We need to reposition the blanket before it heals into the wound."

Immediately, Vincent lifted the cloth. Rather than sticking, blood welled too quickly.

I could lap it up. Suck it down.

NO.

Darting forward, Roger snatched the blanket from Vincent and pressed it back onto Kit. "They should have been healing."

"Zack." Vincent coughed on the name and started again, wiping tears from his eyes. "They were helping Zack fight Seamus, and ... and Seamus blurred out of the way and made Zack cut them."

"They were cut with the enchanted silver." Roger fought the urge to clench his hands. He had to keep the pressure steady. But was there a point?

Yes. Kit's heart was still beating. In theory, Roger could use a few of the blood bags that he'd kept for himself and Takashi as emergency supplies and pump them into Kit to give them a better shot. But the wound …

His long life had given Roger too many opportunities to smell the dead and dying. Having been the cause of much of it, he knew the scents. He ignored his hunger and sifted through the odors of blood around him. Kit's was overpowering, but only in the most delicious of ways. No trace of foulness polluted the smell of them. No organs were nicked.

"Can you move?" Roger asked Vincent.

"Yes?"

"I need you to go into the bedroom across the living room," Roger said firmly. "Underneath the bed are three duffle bags. You want the one that has C.W. on it. There's a dark green pouch. Bring it to me. *Hurry.*"

Vincent scrambled to his feet and dashed for it.

Left alone with blood covering his hands while more soaked into the blanket beneath his fingertips, Roger had to focus on the world outside himself. If he let himself think of the blood so close to him, he might lick his fingers clean. He might lose himself to feeding on Kit.

But blood was only part of feeding. The sustenance from blood truly came from its connection to a mortal's spirit. Kit was fighting for their life. They couldn't afford to lose an ounce of their essence.

Breathing wasn't necessary for a vampire, so Roger slid out of the habit to cut off his sense of smell as much as possible and relied on his hearing and psychic senses. He didn't hear anyone else in the suite. Kit was unconscious, so they had no wants or fears. The only source of emotion that Roger felt outside himself was the bubble of fear that was Vincent.

Darling, I said you weren't going to die tonight. I said nothing about anyone else, Anton had said before snapping his neck and leaving him unconscious.

Was everyone he loved dead or gone?

Not everyone. He had people he cared about outside the suite. But were they safe? Was anywhere safe?

"Got it!" Vincent ran back toward them. "Is this a first aid kit, master?"

"A hunter's med kit," Roger replied. "It has suture supplies."

"You think that'll work?"

"If it couldn't, they'd already be dead." Roger held out his hand for the med kit.

Vincent looked over at Roger, and his features hardened, sliding from panicked to determined. His blue eyes were the color of storm clouds, and he shook his head. "I've got this."

"I—"

"You're hanging on to the edge. I've seen it before. Last thing they need is for you to start hoovering up their blood." Vincent set the kit down on the counter and washed his hands in the sink. He took a second to wet a towel and wipe his face as well.

When he settled down next to Kit again, he was no less young, but Roger knew the mantle on his shoulders. A survivor's weight. It didn't tear away his youth by adding the burden of years but created that odd juxtaposition of an old soul in a young body.

"You've done this before," Roger murmured.

"Yes, master. Do you have a water bottle?"

"Don't bother with calling me that." Cracking the small bar fridge open in their current setup was hard, but Roger managed to dig out two bottles of water.

Vincent peeled away the blanket and set to work flushing the wound and closing it. Rather than steeping in his guilt, Roger let it make him steadier. He tore open Kit's beautiful dress farther so that Vincent would have easier access to the wound. He sifted through the scent of Kit's blood after Vincent washed the wound to ensure he was right that nothing serious had been nicked. If anything deeper had been damaged, Kit had healed the worst of it. They might live.

The last conversation Roger had had with them, they were wishing that Roger had been more for them. Roger paid them and Carver to be exclusive donors for him and Takashi, but that wasn't what Kit had dreamed of having with a vampire. The words felt like they'd been spoken months ago instead of hours. Another eternity passed while Vincent worked to stitch the wound closed. His movements were precise, practiced.

Roger had to close his eyes. Not because of his hunger. Seeing Vincent stitch another's flesh while his own was marred caused an echo reaching back into the earliest of Roger's nights. Seamus had always had a collection of pets. He had always treated them abysmally.

Abused them, Roger corrected himself. He had avoided words like that. Manipulated. Abused. Raped. Those and more applied to him just as much as others. He was certain they applied to Vincent. Roger had seen Seamus do so to other pets and done nothing for fear of his own life.

Bloody tears colored his vision, and he had to sit back against the bar. Vincent had Kit's wound handled. But Roger was passing off responsibility *again*, he was becoming useless *again*, and worse yet was the way his heart ached for Zack or Takashi to miraculously appear, hold his hand, and tell him what he needed to do next. For anyone to give him guidance because his own wisdom was fucking terrible.

Centuries doing nothing but partying and pretending that the world couldn't be changed when the truth was he could have done anything. His fucking monster of a sire would've fought to keep him alive just to spite his lover.

No, no, his pain was his own fault because he let his fear pen him in.

Others would have suffered. Like they did tonight.

He had a fraction of solace before his mind countered,

Others did suffer. You simply chose to ignore their pain because it wasn't yours.

"I'm sorry," Roger murmured to the boy before him. "I am so sorry that I did nothing for so long."

Vincent frowned. He finished taping a bandage over the stitches. "Huh?"

"I know what he's like better than anyone other than perhaps you," Roger continued. He wasn't speaking to just the boy but to all of them. The long-ago ones whose faces he couldn't recall. "I am so fucking sorry."

"You got me out, master," Vincent said quietly. Carefully.

Because they didn't know each other and Vincent was scared he was treading into dangerous waters. Roger could feel that pulse of fear in him, feel as Vincent attempted to morph it into some sort of desire. Because he had lived for years with a monster who would be able to sense those inner workings and make demands of him.

Roger's only respite had been his months away in Taliville. He'd had freedom only to come back to this wretched coven and realize just how awful this corner of the globe was. Instead of taking his loved ones and running as far as he could, he had stayed and waited and played his fucking part and attempted to scheme for coven leadership, and now … now his plans were nothing.

Kit's pulse was becoming stronger, steadier. Their breathing was deeper. They were still too pale—a full recovery from the wound might take days—but they weren't in more danger than Roger and Vincent were.

Which left Roger to face the other horrors waiting for him in the suite.

"Vincent, what happened to them?" Roger asked.

"I told you. Seamus drove Zack's blade into them."

"Not Kit," Roger rasped. "Zack. Takashi. I need to know where I'll find their bodies."

Vincent stilled like a mouse hoping a cat hadn't spotted

him. The fear emanating from him became an electric, salty mixture that was alluring to the thirst burning in Roger. *I will never hurt another innocent.*

"Please," Roger whispered.

"They took them," Vincent replied.

The answer was harsher than a slap. Roger was stunned into silence, left with the beating of Kit's and Vincent's hearts. A glimpse of waking in bed with his lovers—Zack between him and Takashi—came to mind, and he held on to it. They were his stars. His wind.

And they had been abducted.

The meaning slithered into Roger and coiled around his chest. It compressed his spirit and bound it in iron and threw it to the bottom of the sea. Zack and Takashi weren't dead, but that would have been a mercy because Seamus and Anton had perfected the cruelties of torture in their eight hundred years together. Roger had seen them at it over and over. Had been forced to participate. Had pretended he'd liked what was happening so that his mind might believe he was all right. But even he had suffered under those hands.

Now, they had his lovers.

A resounding note of anger cleared the storm from Roger's mind. Grief was too new a thing. Anger, oh, that had been buried in him, but he knew it from his mortal years. He had smothered it in his early decades as a vampire, but it had never truly died. It had waited for him to open the chest and pull out the sharp sword of rage.

A bottle rattled off the shelf beside Roger's shoulder, and he let it hit the floor with a thud. He picked it up. It was a bottle of Dolorous Rum, an Unseelie liquor made in the fey realm and brought to the mortal plane. One of his least favorites because it always brought out a drinker's sorrows.

He wondered if he could find some way to set Seamus alight with it. *I could burn that fucking mansion.* Perhaps it was a flash of madness, perhaps it was the rage pouring through him, but new wants were forming.

Roger would find his lovers.

Then he would repay Seamus for the painful centuries by burning everything he cared for into ashes.

And then maybe, *maybe*, he would grant the bastard his well-deserved death.

CHAPTER 2

They couldn't remain in the hotel suite. Besides the damage done, it was an exposed location. Seamus had come for them once. He might return.

Roger drank two blood bags. The cold food barely dented his hunger, but he gained enough strength to push forward. Though his anger was a steady presence, he had to approach his situation with clarity and precision. Lives were counting on him.

In theory, he could attempt anything. He could stride up to the gates of Seamus's mansion and plead for Zack's and Takashi's lives. He could abandon the mortals counting on him and run to the farthest corner of the Earth. He could carry on with his attempt to take the Great Lakes Coven from Seamus.

His choices hadn't felt this infinite since he ran away from his mortal home. What he had done then was escape as far as he could. That path had led him all the way to a dingy tavern in the Caribbean and into Seamus's fangs.

He had to do better. Vincent, Kit, Zack, Takashi—they all deserved whatever strength he could muster. He had led them into this disaster. He would get them out of it.

There wasn't time to pack the entire suite. Roger focused on the important parts. He filled a suitcase with clothing for Kit, grabbing what seemed sentimental and in easy reach. Since Carver was gone, Roger didn't step into his room.

The suite was lush enough to have its own office. Zack had spent countless hours at the desk. Part of his hunter training had been research, and he devoted himself to thorough notetaking. Roger went for the notebooks he'd written about the Great Lakes Coven and other supernaturals. The information would be vital to developing a plan.

But they were gone. So was Takashi's laptop and Zack's. Their tablets, too.

Briskly, he crossed the living room to the master bedroom. Memories bubbled, but this time, he stamped them down and remained in the present. His grief would have to wait.

Drawers hung out from the dresser, and the wardrobe door was wide open. The room had been searched, ripped apart, and abandoned. The safe where Roger had kept a wad of cash, along with the bullets and Cal's handgun, was empty. Takashi had broken the shotgun during the fight, but next to the safe had been a short sword and a crossbow. Both of those weapons were missing as well. Under the bed should have been three duffle bags, but only the one with Callum's initials remained. One had been Zack's; the other had been Callum's weapon bag.

They were hoping to leave me defenseless.

I've started with less.

A phone began to ring. Roger sought the source of the sound and discovered it on the floor under the dresser. The screen read, "Dad."

Zack had mentioned that he'd spoken to his father and sister. After five months, the man was finally giving a damn about his son again.

Roger began to fill Callum's duffle with necessities. His own journal had been hiding in the bag, and he added a few changes of his own clothes, five sets of Zack's clothes since he and Vincent were a similar size, and even a change of clothes for Takashi. Much of their jewelry was missing, as was Roger's.

Absentmindedly, he put his hand to his ear to check his earring. It was a white-gold stud with four sapphires dangling from it. Takashi had given it to him to represent his lovers and his donors. At least he still had it. And he had Zack's dagger pendant.

The last thing he grabbed was Zack's smart phone, which had begun to ring again. Roger threw it into the bottom of the bag.

Kit was stable enough that Roger picked them up. He handed off the bags to Vincent, who managed the two pieces of luggage without issue. Then the three of them left the suite.

Their trip took them through the lobby. No one was in it, which was odd for that hour in a vampire hotel on one of the busiest social nights of the year. Others should have been coming and going. Even the concierge desk was empty. Did the staff know what had happened upstairs? Had Seamus told them to clear out before he struck?

Vincent nabbed a taxi from the stand outside before the driver could realize their group was covered in blood. The driver swore something about never picking up at the freaky hotel again but didn't throw them out of the vehicle.

The problem was where to go. Candide was still hosting the ball at her extravagant donor house, and many of the vampires Roger knew were there. His trusted inner circle had been shattered, except for Nell and Josefina. But they were the leaders of a different domain in Tennessee. Roger couldn't leave the city without freeing Zack and Takashi first.

Dmitri would have helped him, but Roger's blood brother and former lover had been captured weeks ago. Until the attack in the hotel, Roger had thought he was probably dead. Anton's words made him believe otherwise, but that didn't mean Dmitri could help him. Anton likely had him in the basement of the mansion he shared with Seamus.

There was a vampire he might turn to. The chances were high that he'd spit in Roger's face and call him a disappointment of a grand-sire, but Nathaniel might take pity on Kit and Vincent at the least. Getting the two of them to safety was his first priority.

Roger had the taxi driver drop them off a block from the Last Deal and handed over a reasonable wad of cash from his wallet. Takashi had teased him that no one used physical currency anymore, but Roger hadn't been able to let go of the habit, especially since the Wrights had tracked Zack down using his credit card purchases at one point. Cash simply made sense, and he was grateful to have enough on hand to last a short while.

Stepping out into the cold night, Roger lifted Kit into his arms again. Kit remained unconscious, but they curled instinctively toward Roger. *I'll take any good sign I can get.* Instead of walking through the front, Roger led the way around to the bar's back door.

Roger had turned Ezra into a vampire, and about thirty years later, Ezra had turned Nathaniel. In the mid-1770s, Roger and Nathaniel had had a night of drinking where they bonded over drinking songs of the English peasantry. He instructed Vincent to knock the rhythm of one on the door.

It swung open. Nathaniel was a stockier man; his fingertips were blunt from years as a blacksmith in his mortal life. A scar ran through his clouded right eye. Hunters had managed to inflict that on him. Almost eighty years had passed, and his eye had never fully healed. But his gruff attitude was older than his scars. Ezra had fallen in love with his brusqueness.

The love hadn't lasted, but Nathaniel had.

Nathaniel glanced from Roger to Kit in his arms, then to Vincent, before finally settling back on Roger. His glare was unreadable. "You did what they're talking about?"

"Depends on what they're saying," Roger replied carefully.

"You out-magicked him in a crowded ballroom, then snatched his head pet," Nathaniel said.

"I threw away my collar, master," Vincent said quickly and quietly. Only at this point did Roger realize that the boy was still wearing Zack's bow tie loosely tied around his throat. The fabric had Roger's crest, a kraken, on it.

"Don't bother with that master shit around here." Nathaniel eyed Roger as he said it.

"I told him that before," Roger said.

"Habit, ma—therfucker," Vincent replied.

Nathaniel snorted and cracked a grin, which was rare for him. The mirth lasted only the flash of an instant. He opened the door wider and stepped out of the way. Handing off a set of keys to Vincent, he said, "I've got an apartment upstairs. Aluminum key opens the door at the top of the steps here, brass is for my door. It's third floor, door on the left. Quick and quiet as you can."

Vincent took the keys and headed up the staircase just inside the door.

Roger stepped inside and was about to thank Nathaniel, but Nathaniel shook his head sharply. He hooked his thumb over his shoulder toward the door leading from the kitchen to the bar. "Place is full up. I'll come up in an hour to check on you. Should be slower then."

The kitchen wasn't empty either. Determined not to fall for false safety again, Roger dipped down into his deeper senses.

Something odd was going on with how he could perceive the world. His hunger remained where it was, the burning, grating sensation in his throat, but he could feel out the others in the room. But not their emotions, what they were.

It was like running his hand across fabric and discerning the shape hiding underneath. The woman coming to the window and gathering an order was a shifter; the boy washing dishes was human; Nathaniel was a vampire, and so was the cook, a Black girl who looked like a teenager, working the grill.

Nathaniel shivered and narrowed his eyes. "What was that? No. Never mind. Get going."

Withdrawing his new odd sense, Roger trucked up the stairs behind Vincent. They made their way up to Nathaniel's apartment. It was a humble place compared to the lap of luxury that Roger had been living in for two and a half centuries. Yet there was a comfort in the lack of ostentatious furniture. Nathaniel's couch had a threadbare corner on an armrest, otherwise it was in fine shape. The chair next to it didn't match, but it was low and solid. Two large bookcases held scores of books. Most of them were paperbacks, and many had well-worn spines. A few beer bottles were strewn across the coffee table, along with a copy of *Over My Grave*, one of Ezra's books written under the pen name HT Moss.

The kitchen was connected to the living room, with only a small table to declare it a new space. One counter was crowded with bottles of alcohol. The sink had a few dishes in it. Altogether, the small open area was about the size of the master bedroom of Roger's hotel suite.

"What do we do?" Vincent asked as he shut the door behind Roger.

"We clean up Kit, then you, then me. After that, the two of you try to get some sleep."

Since stitching up Kit, Vincent had remained in a more methodical demeanor. He no longer radiated an intense fear. He set down the luggage in the living room and began to investigate the apartment. Poking around in the kitchen/living room didn't take him long, even though he gave a cursory glance through the cabinets.

Roger carried Kit into the bathroom and flicked on the light with his elbow. Luckily, Nathaniel had a tub, which suited Roger's purposes. He set Kit down in it and began to undress them. Their beautiful dress was already ruined, but he carefully removed it and the tuxedo half-jacket. After stripping them, Roger turned on the faucet to begin filling the tub.

A soft shimmer danced across Kit's skin, and their foxlike features melted away into their human ones. Their breath became ragged on the ends, and their eyes fluttered open. They croaked, "Wh-what happened?"

"Don't worry, sweetheart," Roger murmured as he leaned in closer so they could see him without straining. "We're safe now. You're still healing. Try not to move."

"Hurts."

"I'll find something for the pain." Roger planted a kiss on their forehead and then stood.

A medicine cabinet sat above the sink. Its door had edges like it'd held a mirror at some point, but Nathaniel had removed it. Most vampires didn't like the reminder that they lacked reflections.

Inside were a few packaged toothbrushes, a stack of soap bars, and a top shelf lined with opaque prescription bottles. The maker's logo belonged to Coldwell Apothecary, a small chain of mage-run pharmacies. Mundane mortals didn't know about the stores' secret magical offerings.

Vampires and shifters shared a weakness to healing, and both had quickened healing speeds, but certain herbs could dull a vampire's pain while harming a shifter. Zack and Takashi would've known which of these drugs would hurt Kit. Roger swallowed the drop of grief before it could swell and drown him. "Vincent, come here, please."

The apartment was so small it took Vincent only seconds to arrive at his side. "Yes, master?"

"How many times do I have to tell you not to call me that?" Roger said sternly.

The thin layer of Vincent's calm cracked, and fragility seeped into his blue eyes. He stepped to the side of the doorway, as if he intended to duck behind the wall if Roger moved the wrong way. But his voice was firm as he said, "You claimed me."

"To protect you from him. When we get through this night, we can talk about what you need from me, but I will never demand anything of you, Vincent. I didn't get you out to make you my boy." Roger handed him the bottles. "Do you know if any of these would be safe for Kit?"

"He goes to Coldwell's? Classy." Vincent took the bottles from him and sorted through them. "This one is like emergency anti-anxiety, this one's a daily antidepressant. No wonder Nathaniel always seems so well-adjusted. He's actually doing something for his mental health."

"You know him?" Roger asked.

"Only by reputation. Met him a couple of times. He's kicked me out of his bar for being too young. Other vampires claim he's 'weak on mortals,' but that just means he's not a dick." Vincent started putting away the bottles that wouldn't be of any use.

That brought him into close proximity with Roger. With the remnants of fear-filled sweat dried to his skin, Vincent smelled *delicious*. His heartbeat began to echo through Roger, overwhelming the sound of rushing water from the bathtub. And though Roger had dismissed the idea of keeping him as a pet, he was a beautiful boy. The left side of his neck had a few scar marks from previous bites. Did he ever enjoy it?

Doesn't matter. He is weak and he is hurt, and I will not be the monster Seamus forced me to be. Never again. Roger cleared his throat and took a step back. If Vincent realized how close Roger had been to giving in to his hunger, he didn't show it. After a quick pause, he continued putting away the bottles they wouldn't need, leaving one out.

"What of my reputation?" Roger asked.

"You want to know what the coven says or what Seamus

was saying behind your back?" Vincent held up a bottle. "Give them one of these every six hours."

"Can you get me a glass of water?" Roger said. He'd left Vincent's question unanswered on purpose. He wasn't sure that he wanted to know either answer after all. Before the attack, he would have needed to know both. He would've turned to Takashi and wondered if he could confirm whatever Vincent had to say.

But he was on his own.

I should have worked with Dmitri. I should have struck in the middle of the day and burned the bastard to ash. Roger knelt beside Kit and turned off the water. The water had risen over their hips. Not wanting to soak the stitches, he let a little of it out before hunting down a washcloth and a bar of soap.

Vincent returned with a glass of water, and Roger coaxed Kit into taking the pill.

"So which do you want to know?" Vincent asked, once more hanging on to the doorframe rather than standing in it.

"Fuck it," Roger replied. "Fuck the coven, and fuck Seamus. I don't need to know."

"Can I ... can I say it?" Vincent's voice dropped to a whisper.

Roger frowned. "Say what?"

"Fuck ... *you know*." Vincent leaned his head against the doorframe. "You seem cool, but he's your sire."

"He's my nightmare," Roger said. "The only good of becoming his sireling has been immortality."

"Really?"

As gently as he could, Roger began to wash Kit clean of the blood clinging to their skin. "I didn't realize until tonight how utterly I had been fooling myself, but it's true. He ... he forced me into the worst version of myself. While I don't hate everything about that side of me, at least not tonight I don't, I can see him for what Zack named him in the Chateau.

Abuser. Rapist. Murderer. And so much more. Nightmare is the only word that sums him in entirety. I intend to wake up."

"But you like being a vampire," Vincent said.

"I do. I have watched the world evolve and yet can trace some things back to their roots within my own experience. I have been able to nurture artists and witness technological advancements that would've seemed like magic when I was a mortal. And I could be much more than what I've been." Roger frowned to himself as he continued cleaning Kit. Though he'd begun to write his long life down in a journal, he hadn't opened his emotions like this, not even to himself. The truth of his words felt like a ray of sunlight, but he had lived in the dark too long for that to remain comfortable. "Anyway, yes. You can say fuck Seamus. You can wish him ill. You can tell me how you'd love to stake him down in the middle of the desert, douse him with holy water, and then stand back while the sun slowly rises to fry him inch by inch."

"Thrown into a vat of molten silver blessed by a dozen different religious leaders, which is then used for solar panels," Vincent replied quickly. A bead of desire—a pressure of a will for vengeance and violence—rolled out from him. It was compressed and small despite the eagerness in Vincent's voice.

God, why had Roger never cared about what happened to those outside of his care? *Because you were too busy guarding your own.* He cleared his throat. "That's a good one."

"Should I have not said that?" Vincent asked.

"It's not you." Roger sank onto his ass, his back hitting the toilet. The bathroom was tiny, not much larger than a coffin, really. The weight of the night, of his life, continued to press on him. No wonder Dmitri had struggled with his depression. The reality they'd both lived in had no beacons of light, only the joy they made.

A joy that was often ripped away.

What were Seamus and Anton doing to Zack and Takashi? What did they have planned? Were they going to kill them? Takashi belonged to Nell's bloodline, and though she had released him from her coven, she still cared for him. Would they use that? Or would that protect him from the worst?

For Zack, the answer was too easy. He was descended from two lines of infamous vampire hunters, the Wrights and the Gladwells. If Seamus wanted to hurt Roger and Zack and all those hunters, he would turn Zack into a vampire. Force the blood upon him. Zack had told Roger that he never wanted to become an immortal. What if he didn't have a choice?

But that lacked poetry, and Seamus always looked for the severest cut. He had taken Zack and Takashi to punish Roger for his humiliation. He would hurt them in order to continue hurting him.

"Fuck Seamus," he said because the only rope he could hold on to in this storm was his anger. His rage. His grief would swallow him and leave him inactive. He'd spent too long waiting for the right time, the right action, the right idea. He couldn't afford to waste more.

"Are you ... all right?" Vincent asked slowly.

"I'm weaker than I thought."

"Nate's got some blood in the fridge."

"He's Nate now?" Roger asked with a wry grin.

Vincent almost blushed. Roger could see the slightest pinking of his cheeks around the growing bruises of his right eye. "Nathaniel's a mouthful."

"Mm. Please get me a bag."

"On it, ma—therfucker," Vincent replied.

Roger finished bathing Kit and wondered how long it would take to wash the blood and pain from his own soul. *I have eternity to find out.*

CHAPTER 3

Three hours passed. Kit and Vincent were clean and settled in. Kit slept on the couch while Vincent did the same on the floor beside them. Thankfully, Nathaniel had a heap of extra blankets and pillows to make them comfortable.

Roger took up a spot by the window. His anger cooled into a lingering rage, a yearning for retribution that settled into his bones. The strength of it kept him on his feet, though the ache of exhaustion threatened to overtake him.

Nathaniel rapped on the door in the same rhythm Vincent had done before letting himself into his apartment. After taking in the sight of his fairly full living room, he wandered over to his fridge and took out two beers and a bag of blood. He crossed the room to where Roger stood and offered him a beer.

Nathaniel's voice had a natural timbre that worked well for a grouchy barkeep, and like many vampires, he'd adopted the local accent rather than keeping his original. "I should thank you for the extra business. We'll be open until dawn, assuming the cops don't shut us down."

"You worry about mortal authorities?" Roger asked.

Nathaniel snorted. "You've been sitting next to the throne

too long, former captain. You forget how the rest of us live. Not everyone's made of billions of dollars that they can use to pay off troublesome mortals."

"You've had the bar for decades. Isn't business—"

"The business is fine, though the pandemic's put a crunch on it." Nathaniel motioned around them. "I own the damn building. But there's this thing called taxes. And another thing known as coven dues. Not just for my drinking privileges but the bar."

"Hadn't considered that," Roger murmured. He wrenched off the beer's bottlecap but wound up watching the bubbles rather than taking a sip. Alcohol was a way to forget his pains, though one mortal-made beer wouldn't be enough to dampen any of his senses. He set it down on the window ledge. "You said former captain."

"I did." Nathaniel took out his phone and read a text aloud. "'The vampire known as Roger, Gentleman Pirate of the Seven Seas, is no longer my captain. Henceforth, he shall not be welcomed in the territory of the Great Lakes Coven. Anyone who gives him aid will find themselves incurring my wrath. Your Master, Seamus.'"

"Fuck." Roger wiped a hand down his face. Passing up on a beer felt foolish now. He grabbed it and took a swig. Shaking his head, he said, "If you can provide safety for Kit and Vincent, I would be grateful. I can—"

"Hold on there." Nathaniel nodded at the door. "Come with me a moment, yeah?"

Roger wanted to say no. He longed to wake and discover that the last several hours had been nothing but a terrible dream. *That would be the easy way out and leave me caught in Seamus's web. Long for this moment. Need this.* He set the bottle down and gestured for Nathaniel to lead the way.

Nathaniel locked the apartment on their way out and tromped down the stairs to the first floor. He pulled a hairband and a black baseball cap with the name *Last Deal* embroidered onto it out of a locker beside the staircase. "Could use your help clearing dishes. Had to send Phil home."

Roger took the hairband and baseball cap. "I'm exiled, and you want me to walk through your bar?"

"Everyone's drunk off their asses and believe you're too busy to show up in a bar no one's seen you enter in forty years. Pull up your hair, keep the hat low, don't look anyone in the eye, and they're not going to notice shit." They'd reached the kitchen. Nathaniel took a busboy tray and shoved it into Roger's hands. "Try not to break anything."

The girl who'd been at the grill was busy at the dishwasher, pulling free a clean batch of dishes before shoving in a set of dirty. Her gaze lingered on Roger. She was sizing him up with a scrutiny in her eyes that spoke to an older age than she appeared. "Just bring it back here and hand it off when it's full."

"Right," Roger muttered. He still wasn't certain this was the smart course of action. But Nathaniel had taken him in when he could have slammed the door in his face. Roger did as Nathaniel instructed with his hair and the hat, let his shoulders droop, and hung his head a little as he followed Nathaniel into the bar.

The Last Deal was packed from wall to wall despite the late hour. Each of the wooden tables seemed overflowing with empty glasses and plates. The floorboards creaked under the weight of a large demon who wasn't bothering with a human disguise at the pool table. A set of tables had been pushed together nearer to the pool tables, and clamoring patrons were impatiently waiting on their turn at a table. What had been a fireplace in the 1970s was now a faux mantle with a fake fire crackling on an HD screen. Which was a good thing because two guests pushed each other, and one tumbled back against the screen.

Nathaniel handled the rowdiness. The large demon with

curling horns that scraped the ceiling helped him. Roger began his task of gathering dishes.

The task was needling Roger. Instead of taking the threat of Seamus seriously, Nathaniel wanted him in public removing dirty silverware? Why? What was the point? He should be finding a discreet hotel with what cash he had left. Candide might be done with her party. She might be willing to help him. *But not likely. I'm on my own, and I'm fucked.*

"So then, get this," a drunk patron was saying to a table of friends. "I'm like three weeks a vampire. Three weeks. Or was it three months?"

"Get *on* with it," a friend demanded.

Roger dipped around the sway of the drunk and plucked up another empty glass. But the tray was almost full, and he had to figure out how to put it in without cracking anything beneath it.

"Fine, fine. I'm a fledgling baby vampire," the drunk continued, "and my sire drags me in front of Seamus to show me off like a fucking doll. Oh, he thought he was doing something special. Like somehow, I was this unique marvel. Seamus is like ready to stake me right there. He's yelling at my sire that he hadn't gotten permission and he wasn't strong enough. That I was nothing more than a human with sharper teeth. And Roger, Roger's just *sitting* there, like he did, you know? Just sitting all calm while Seamus rants about the dilution of his sire line, and Roger *yawns*. Like what vampire needs to yawn, you know? But it catches Seamus's attention, and suddenly, Roger's looking at me with those eyes. I swear those eyes can see your soul, you know? Deep brown like the woods. Anyway, Roger scans me over and says, 'You're that singer, aren't you? Lovely voice. We should see if Dempsey has a song for you.' And it turns out that Seamus had been looking to launch a recording studio and wanted some of his own vamps to use it."

"Didn't Seamus burn the studio down?" a friend asked the drunk.

The drunk waved off the question. "I was in a cooldown period at the time. Can't go too long in the public eye, you know?"

Roger carried the tray off to another table and nabbed a few of the empty glasses there. One of the patrons was talking about Seamus's recent Halloween party. "I mean, Seamus had a fucking siren onstage—"

"My cousin's a fucking siren, thank you very much, bitch," another replied.

"Well, if your cousin's making humans grind on each other for the amusement of my kind, then kick their fucking ass," the first patron replied. "But shit was about to get real, and all of the older vamps were just standing around with their thumbs up their asses, and Roger leaps onto the railing like he's fucking Batman, and then *hiiiiisssss*—" The patron imitated the way Roger had snarled at the crowd as if daring them to join him. "—and the elders are all leaping over the railing and joining their mortals. Could've been a bloodbath. Seamus has done it that way before. 1995. Remember?"

"More times than that," another replied.

Other stories drifted past Roger while he worked. Unrelated tales cropped up here and there, but there was a common theme. Fuck Seamus. Roger was one of the admirable ones.

Roger filled the first tray and a second and was onto a third. Nathaniel and his waitress were still passing out the drink orders. A level of unruliness, brought on by drunkenness and camaraderie, began to brew. Finally, Nathaniel rang for last call, though the crowd attempted to cajole him into another hour.

They were genuinely giddy that Roger had metaphorically flipped his middle finger in Seamus's face. They wondered where he had been for thirty years. More than one hoped they'd develop some sort of powers similar to his soon. The belief had been that only vampires closer to Seamus's age could have any sort of real power, but that hadn't been true of Roger. He was only three hundred. There were younger vampires boasting that they could take off their gold rings.

The rings were another of Anton's lies. He'd claimed that it'd only come off when a vampire was ready to be their own master, but he'd revealed to Roger that the charm ended after fifty years.

With the third tray full, Roger carried it into the kitchen and set it on the counter beside the girl. She was struggling to keep up with the amount he'd already dragged in, so he took a moment to help her reorganize the dishes onto trays that would go into the washer.

"The Great Roger doing dishes," the girl muttered.

Roger wasn't sure what to think of the crowd praising him. Part of him had sought that adulation, hadn't he? He'd wanted to be the savior of the GLC, to kill Seamus and take his place as the ruler and lead everyone into a brighter future. But he'd never had a real plan to enact. He'd come up with a few ideas, but most of them were Candide's.

Rather than spiral into whatever abyss waited for him, he leaned against the counter and smiled warmly at the girl. He tugged on one of his old facades to ease the pain of self-inspection. A joker's tone slipped into his voice. "Not impressed?"

"Not in the least," she replied.

Winning people over was one of Roger's talents. He let his charm thicken his voice, though he withheld flirtier notes. Girls didn't interest him, and though she could be a hundred years old, she looked like a child, putting her firmly in the category he had no desire to flirt with. Brightening his smile, he said, "Come now. How often do you have the chance to speak with a legend?"

"Every goddamn night." She narrowed her eyes and

shouldered him out of her way while she corrected the tray of dishes. Then she shoved them into the washer and pulled down the lever.

"You mean Nathaniel," Roger replied, dropping his charmer act for another tact: the honest vampire. He relaxed and nodded toward the bar. "Suppose he does have a certain level of renown."

"Who said I was talking about a vampire?" the girl said shortly. She shoved an empty busboy tray into his hands. "Aren't you supposed to be cleaning tables?"

Roger took the tray but remained where he was and studied the girl's face. So many people had filtered in and out of his life. Had he forgotten this girl? Was that why she was upset with him? Teenage vampires weren't entirely uncommon—Roger had made Ezra when he was eighteen, which technically qualified him as one—but she appeared on the younger side of the teen spectrum. A few months ago, Zack had killed Quinn Turner, Roger's sireling. Maybe she was blaming him for that death.

"Are you descended from Quinn?" Roger asked. "Is that how I've upset you? I sired him, and he was attempting to kill what was mine. I was within my rights to watch him die."

The girl rolled her eyes and carried a tray of dry dishes across the kitchen to put them in their place.

"Wait," Roger said sharply.

"You're not a coven captain anymore. I don't have to listen to you," the girl replied.

She knew who he was. If she spoke to anyone about him, then Nathaniel would be in trouble, which would jeopardize Kit and Vincent. Roger couldn't let that happen. He tossed down the busboy tray and stormed over toward her. When she didn't acknowledge his closeness, he started to reach for her.

I suppose I should expect more of the same once you take over for

Seamus, Dmitri had said when Roger first returned to the city. *Another violent tyrant.*

I won't be him. Roger clenched his fist and dropped his hand back to his side. "I care for Nathaniel's safety. I won't allow someone to compromise it."

The girl paused and finally glanced up at him. She was almost a foot shorter than him, but she had a fierceness in her brown eyes that negated their height difference. "Neither will I."

"If you have a problem with me, I'd like to know what I've done," Roger said.

"I bet you would," she replied.

Then she went back to her work.

Roger could reach into her desires and make her want to tell him what was bothering her, but that wasn't like him. Besides, she had a layer of desire that was a flame, and Roger recognized the reflection of it in himself. She wanted to protect someone—likely Nathaniel, as she'd said.

Since she clearly didn't want to talk to him, Roger picked up the busboy tray and went back to gathering dishes. Patrons settled their tabs and began to depart. Their numbers dwindled. Roger gathered one last tray's worth of dishes and remained in the kitchen rather than risk discovery. He lingered near the serving window, using the wall as cover from view of the main room. Bits of conversation drifted.

"No one's *ever* going to be able to do it," an extremely drunk voice proclaimed. Their words were slurred so drastically that Roger barely understood them. "He's too fucking powerful. I bet he puts a bounty on Roger's head, or—or—or I bet Roger's already fucking dead. Don't tell me to shut up. I don't care what everyone else's been saying. Everyone was all 'fuck Seamus' tonight, but tomorrow, they'll be kissing his ass again. I bet *Roger* will be."

If I thought I could get Zack and Takashi back that way, I would. Roger closed his eyes to prevent them from leaking. *Fuck me.*

I'm no hero. Takashi. Zack. They would have comforted him. They would have held him close, told him he was doing his best, and helped him figure out what to do.

Terror had dragged him down too many centuries. He'd been terrified that Seamus would lash out. Terrified that he'd say the wrong word and wind up with a stake in his heart. Terrified that no matter where he went, Seamus would find him and drag him back. So he had stayed. He had obeyed.

All for *nothing*.

Not nothing. Not if he could save others like he had managed to save Vincent. Zack and Takashi needed him. He couldn't afford to wallow.

But how could he free them? Seamus would have taken them back to his mansion.

Dawn was too close, and Roger didn't have the time or strength to infiltrate the fortress of a house. Maybe, if he could come up with a plan, he might be able to find a way in and out. Seamus had a coven to run. He wouldn't be able to stay holed up in his mansion all night, every night. Roger simply needed to wait for an opportunity.

No, not wait. Zack had taken the lead in the fight in the hotel suite, and Roger needed to be more like him.

An idea began to form, but Roger couldn't do it on his own.

People were moving about the kitchen, though Roger wasn't in anyone's way. He ignored them until Nathaniel said, "Janiyah, stop trying to light him on fire with your glares."

"I would never do that to your bar," the girl declared. She muttered, "But we could toss him out onto the street."

"I don't know what I've done to incur your wrath," Roger said hollowly, "but I doubt it was intentional."

"It's like four hours past the end of my shift. Can I be done?" Janiyah asked sharply.

"Go on," Nathaniel replied.

After she tromped up the stairs, Roger finally cracked one eye open. Nathaniel was alone with the piles of dishes, so Roger began to help him. A long time had passed since Roger had settled into performing mundane chores. The actions didn't soothe him. Instead, he was left spinning on his own anger and the animosity Janiyah had shown him. Everyone else in the Last Deal had been ecstatic, though they didn't know what Roger's actions had cost him. Her reaction had been hostile, but in retrospect, he preferred it. He deserved everyone's anger.

"Why did you bring me down here?" Roger asked after he and Nathaniel had been cleaning for a solid hour.

"Was hoping it'd cheer you up," Nathaniel replied. He tossed a dry towel to Roger and then slid a tray of glasses toward him.

For the most part, the glasses were dry, but they had droplets of water here and there. With a sigh as he dried, Roger admitted, "That's not possible. Not until I have Zack and Takashi back."

Nathaniel stilled. "What?"

Roger explained what had happened at the ball and the hotel to Nathaniel, but he left out the part about Seamus and Anton's bet and the fact that he had intended to kill Seamus at New Year's and take the role of coven master.

Nathaniel wiped at his own jaw and scowled. "I see. Explains the doom and gloom. Figured something must have happened to the boy since he wasn't with you. Guess I was hoping he and Takashi were somewhere else. A divided camp so you couldn't be attacked again."

"Nothing so intelligent," Roger murmured.

After a long moment, Nathaniel grunted, shook his head, then said, "I brought you down here because I wanted you to see the impact you've been having. I know I'm on the low rung of coven notables, and I prefer it that way. But people've been whispering about you for a while. I don't know what they're saying at the upper levels, but these people adore you."

Did the upper levels of leadership give a damn? Roger had shown them his power as well, but there wasn't one among them that he trusted. He knew them, but like him, they had found ways to hide their hurts. How many enjoyed being the cruel, sadistic vampire Seamus molded them into, and how many longed for a new life?

Dmitri was right. The coven should fall to ash. "I appreciate your concern, but we know what Seamus will do. He's exiled me, which means anyone who brings my head to him will earn favor. They may have lauded my 'accomplishments' tonight, but they would climb over each other in a heartbeat if they believed they could gain his goodwill."

"Ezra said you were looking to put him down," Nathaniel said.

I need to remind Ezra not to run his mouth. Roger set down another dry glass. "I tried tonight. I failed. He and Anton are too strong."

"Then you—"

"The two people on this planet who may have been able to outsmart him are already his prisoners," Roger snapped, his voice carrying more than he meant. The echo of it came back to him, and the rage bubbling in his depths roiled toward the surface.

But Nathaniel had been exceedingly kind.

Roger couldn't afford to be tossed to the street or to ruin Kit's chance to recover. Though he had only promised Vincent what he could, he had taken him under his protection as well. The boy deserved a life of peace after everything he had gone through. They all did. He had to smooth over the turbulence with Nathaniel before it became an excuse to rescind his help.

"I'm sorry," Roger said. His rage wasn't so easily packaged away, but he tried. "I have to get them back. Until I do … I can't think of doing anything else. Seamus will find ways to torture them that would make a devil pause. I have to save them before he breaks them. If I move against him before I have them back, he will use their safety against me."

"All right," Nathaniel said slowly. "What do you need from me?"

"A place to stay. A car if you have one."

Nathaniel leaned against the bar. "I remind you that I'm over two hundred and served on a few frontlines."

"I don't need a soldier," Roger replied. "I need a brilliant SWAT team, and I think I know who to call. I only hope they answer."

CHAPTER 4

The light of the tent barely touched the heights of the trapeze act. Takashi stepped onto his platform and lifted his hand as the ring-leader continued his long speech about the performers' pedigree. All of it bullshit. All of it just a lie for the audience. Takashi hadn't brought any "mystic arts" to their act; he had learned everything from Sergei and his family when he joined the circus at twelve.

But he acknowledged the crowd, then his fellow performer, and waited for his cue. The circus's musician hit a gong, and Takashi was off, flying through the air on the trapeze.

Memory took on the elements of dream; what had been warped with what his mind concocted. Instead of Sergei, Takashi clapped hands with Zack at the end of a flip. Zack nodded to him and held on to him with a strength that eased Takashi's worry. When the time came, as they soared through the air to the next maneuver, Zack released him on cue.

Takashi flew, twisting as he had in practice a thousand upon a thousand times, and stretched for his next partner. Nothing brushed his fingertips. He searched the sky and saw Roger grasping for him but failing. Takashi was sinking, plummeting, becoming a comet for the hard-packed earth that made the ring of the circus. It was dozens of feet that morphed to hundreds, the fall ever continuing.

He knew what came at the end of the fall. He didn't want it. Didn't want to remember. Didn't want the memory to morph further. He wanted to wake.

He landed with a crack against the dirt. Shattered. Broken. Forsaken. Until Nell gave her blood and he became a vampire.

She never came in the nightmare. Instead, he began again, stepping onto the platform. The crowd cheering. The ringleader lying.

"Evigilas," a voice whispered in Takashi's ear.

Details of the dream world slipped away as Takashi shuddered out of his sleep. Urgency struck him, but he couldn't pinpoint whether that was the remnant of the nightmare or a reminder of reality. A groan worked its way up from his core, and he fought to lift his head.

"Seems you put him under a little too far, love," Seamus said.

"You wanted him out, I put him out," Anton replied.

Anton had whispered that first word to Takashi. Recent memory sparked, fanning his panic into a brighter light. Anton and Seamus had attacked the suite. Takashi had fired a shotgun loaded with silver pellet at Anton. That hadn't slowed him down, and though Takashi had struggled, Anton had snapped his neck.

Takashi attempted to move, but his wrists were bound to a heavy wooden chair. He was a captive.

The rest of his grogginess cleared. He was in a well-appointed study with all the trappings of a long-acquired wealth. The rug was a plush Persian in deep reds with black, gold, and blue weaved into scrolling patterns. Seamus's desk was a heavy Victorian monstrosity. He had an arrangement of notebooks, a leather-bound journal, and two laptops across its surface.

Zack's notes. And mine. Takashi fought to keep his expression neutral. This wasn't the first time a coven master had hauled him into a study and demanded to know more of him.

But this was the first one that Takashi had been actively plotting to kill.

Takashi swallowed his urge to demand answers. Seamus had brought him here for a reason when he could have killed him outright. Before Takashi played any of his remaining cards, he needed to know what the damn game was.

Seamus met his gaze. The tales of his evil deeds tended to leave out how ordinarily handsome he was. If not for the muddled red in his blue eyes and his ice-cold aura, he would have fit into human society without a problem. He kept his brown hair to modern style, he could turn on a smile that disguised the nature of his soul, and he had a preternatural grace that made him a pleasure to watch. His current attire was simpler than his formal tuxedo; a white dress shirt and black slacks gave him a professional air, though he had rolled the sleeves of his shirt. He stood behind his desk and exuded a level of command Takashi had come to expect of ancient vampires.

Anton stood before the desk, though he leaned his backside against the heavy furniture. His pale blond hair hung past his shoulders, and he still had on the white tuxedo he'd worn to the ball. His jacket was missing, and dried blood marred his clothing. He was the sort of rare vampire whose skin seemed to glow porcelain white, and his eyes remained a darkened red that spoke to his power as a vampire. Along with that magic, he was proficient in the arcane arts.

The two of them were among the most terrifying creatures Takashi had ever known—possibly worse than the dragon lord of Lake Michigan. They had been together for over eight hundred years. Takashi admired that their relationship had lasted and was envious of the years of living, but he hated nearly everything else about them.

"Welcome back to the waking world," Seamus said amicably. He approached Takashi with a silver Bowie knife in his right hand. Runes were etched into the blade. It belonged to Callum Wright. The last person Takashi had seen wielding it was Roger.

Now, Seamus stepped around his desk and brought the blade closer and closer. Takashi steeled himself for the burn of silver, schooled his features into a blank mask devoid of any emotion, and put a mental wall around his emotions. He would not let these creatures know that he was terrified of what would become of him, of what might have already befallen his lovers.

Seamus cut the ropes binding Takashi's wrists to the chair and smiled at him.

Warily, Takashi rubbed his wrists. He still wore the black wool tuxedo pants that had been part of his outfit for the ball, but his captors had changed his shirt. This blue dress shirt was one from his closet and one he liked.

When he glanced down at his shirt, Seamus said, "The other was covered in blood. We took no liberties other than removing it and the jacket. Both ruined, I'm afraid. Combat will do that, even to Unseelie finery."

"Unfortunate," Takashi said dryly. "I rather liked that jacket."

"It was beautiful." Seamus handed off the silver knife to Anton as he circled back around to stand behind his desk.

Anton played with the point of the dagger, pushing it against his fingertip. Its sharpness drew blood, and the silver singed him. The slightest whiff of burning flesh mingled with the potent scents of the grave the ancient vampires had. Old blood, dirt, dust, and death created an odd perfume, especially since there was a hint of roses in the air. Takashi glanced over his shoulder and spotted two large vases of flowers beside the study door.

So he's a little vain about his smell. Takashi tucked the information away. Hopefully, he would live long enough to make use of the knowledge.

"Any particular reason you put me under a sleep spell?" Takashi asked conversationally. Balancing a tone between deferential and confident had taken decades to master, but he fell into the habit easily. Panic would only get him killed; making demands would only incite his captors' anger. Clearly, they had a plan if they were going to this much effort.

"My love wasn't ready for you," Anton replied. He set the blade down on the desk, though he kept his hand on top of the hilt. "We've had a busy night. A ball, an attack, and—"

"And much to Roger's dismay, I have a coven to run." Seamus closed one of Zack's notebooks. "Unlike Nell, I don't sequester myself away and rely upon others to ensure my territory remains well governed."

"I noticed," Takashi said.

"You and Zack notice quite a bit, don't you?" Seamus asked.

Takashi pretended to relax into his seat. Whatever the game, he had to win. "A vampire ambassador would be dead if they couldn't make a few obvious observations."

"I suppose that's true," Seamus said thoughtfully. "Which makes me wonder, how could one as clever as you fall in with a pissant with delusions of grandeur?"

"Love convinces one of foolish notions," Takashi said.

"Was love truly your reason?" Anton asked. He had a far-off quality to his voice, and his question brought Takashi's attention to him. His eyes were deep red, slightly glowing, and he leaned forward to put his hands on Takashi's wrists, trapping him against the chair.

Vampires were a proud, arrogant species that boasted more power than they had. They tended to squabble over territory like dogs barking at strangers, loud and without impact. They fucked and fed and wasted away their immortal lives becoming *nothing*. Takashi had long lost count of the number of vampires who claimed they could charm anyone with a glance.

As Anton cinched his grip around Takashi's wrists, he flooded his mind with power. Takashi braced the best he could. Others had attempted to use their ability to sense desire on him before. Roger had even plumed his mental depths, something that had been a violation. Takashi had forgiven him; Roger had been acting out of his own fears.

But each time before had been like a shoelace coming undone, a quiet loosening of his mind that he easily remedied by taking a moment to fix his mental ward.

Anton shoved into his mind with the force of a sledge-hammer and began to root around in intimate places. He slid forward and sat on Takashi's lap. Takashi growled and dipped his head. His efforts to block Anton weren't working. Each mental wall was instantly shattered. Anton was reaching in, not only sensing his mind but taking hold of desires and heightening them.

"What is going on in here?" Anton whispered. He grabbed Takashi tightly by the back of his hair and wrenched his head back.

I love Roger. I do. But that wasn't the real reason he had agreed to join him. Nell had given an order, and he had taken advantage of the opportunity. Takashi had been the one she sent to interface with hundreds of other vampires, and he had built a reputation for himself. One that was always overshad-owed by being an ambassador to a vampire whose only goal was a status quo. Seventy years as someone else's errand boy had been grueling.

Takashi wanted *more*. He fought not to name it while Anton dug in his mind. Fought not to feel the true source of it. But trying to stop Anton's magic was like shoving his hands against a burst pipe. Even as he managed to stem the worst, the pressure created another leak, and a stream dripped from what he'd hoped to close off.

"Oh, you aren't a good little boy at all." Anton grinned wickedly. He stroked Takashi's cheek. "I see you."

The desire that he had crafted mask after mask after mask to hide rushed to the surface. Self-denial, excuses, everything he had laid on top of it to quash it down so even he might not embrace it was cast off as Anton heightened Takashi's desires.

I want power.

Not for anyone else's sake, not to help or to soothe or to negotiate. He longed to be the one people turned to for a favor—out of desperation or simply because he was the one who could accomplish it. He wanted people to owe *him*, to seek *him*. The spotlight no longer mattered. The spotlight had been a mortal fascination. He wanted the power behind a throne.

And he wanted to touch and be touched. He wanted to tear into another's throat and drink blood until he was too full. He wanted to feel his own flesh break and heal and become whole and do it all again. Wanted pain that thoroughly ruined him for anyone else. Wanted to bind someone to him so they never wanted to leave him. Needed to use someone and be used in return. Wanted wanted wanted …

"You don't have to fight it," Anton crooned. "You can have it all. Just let yourself fall."

Falling.

The dream. His memory. The sudden recollection, the flash of memory that overwhelmed the present from time to time, claimed him. He fell from the trapeze. Smashed his body against the ground. Was dying, there on the dirt. Betrayed because Roger—*no*, in the memory, it was Sergei— had failed him. Hadn't been there. Had let him fall.

The fear mingled with the desire. He couldn't breathe. He had been a vampire more than a century, had long schooled himself out of the habit, but he needed air and couldn't get it. He had to get free. But Anton was on his lap and holding him down, and some part of him *wanted* to be stuck beneath him. *No. No. No.*

"You could be ours," Anton murmured.

"S-s-stop," Takashi managed. His eyes were leaking bloody tears.

"Lover," Seamus said, the warning in his tone deepening his voice.

"I could break him. He'd give us all his secrets, and then we'd have a new toy. A fresh one." Anton stroked Takashi's cheek and leaned upward, over him, like he was about to plant a kiss on his trembling lips.

Suddenly, he was gone. His presence became nothing but cold air. A resounding crack and a sharp, pained whimper filled Takashi's ears before he realized that Anton had stopped his constant magical pressure. Reclaiming his senses with a wave of relief, Takashi used his abilities on his own mind to diminish his desires and cleared the residual haze in his mind.

Anton was on the floor, cradling his head with one hand. A bloody gash in his head was deep, bone and brain showing, but was already healing. A corner of Seamus's desk had blood on it.

Seamus glowered down at Anton, the red in his eyes flaring brighter. "Out."

Pouting, Anton pawed at Seamus's leg, but Seamus kicked his hand. With tears in his eyes, Anton got to his feet, swayed, and then staggered out of the room.

Once the door was closed, Seamus strode over to it and locked it. He stood beside it for a long moment.

Takashi seized that moment to finish collecting himself. Somewhere in the midst of Anton's magic, his cock had grown hard, but the reality of his situation siphoned that lust away. Anton had turned him into simpering putty, and for the briefest, impossible fraction of a second, Takashi had wanted to give in. Had that been a forced injection, something of Anton's mind? A vampire could only encourage what existed within their target, but Anton was also a warlock. Did he have skills others didn't?

Or was there some part of Takashi that craved a dominant partner so badly that even Anton would do? *Not the time to think about what I want in the bedroom. He was using me.*

But what would have happened if Seamus hadn't stepped in?

Takashi clasped the arms of his chair so his hands wouldn't tremble.

"I apologize for him," Seamus said, his tone calm and cordial. Slowly, he walked over to his desk and leaned his backside against it. On his left was the Bowie knife, and on his right was the bloody corner.

Seamus had stopped Anton, but he'd also allowed him to get that far in the first place.

This conversation isn't some card game. It's a four-dimensional chess match. The only reason Takashi was still in the game was because Seamus willed it. That was the point behind his course of action, wasn't it? Or was Anton stronger than Seamus? Did Seamus want Takashi's loyalty, or did he suspect that Takashi would know that everything was a setup?

"Thank you," Takashi said softly, layering on as much respect as he could muster past the shiver in his veins. "I do appreciate the mercy. Considering what I've done these last ten weeks, you would have been within your rights to let him break me."

Seamus grinned, a glimmer of triumph in his muddy red eyes. "I can admire a clever man."

But can you tolerate his presence? Allow him to thrive? Takashi gave a small smile, playing up a pensive attitude. "My cleverness is simply an ability to perceive the world around me and come to a conclusion."

"And what conclusion have you reached about your current situation?" Seamus asked.

Takashi had walked him into asking that question. Ancient vampires had schemes upon schemes, and he had long ago learned that the more he knew, the more he could survive them. Nell had intimated that Seamus planned on ruling over the vampires of North America, uniting them in a single coven and claiming it a kingdom.

But he would face stiff complications. International vampires might not care if Seamus stole so much territory, but they wouldn't tolerate someone with an army of vampires that could outdo them. Mundane means of travel didn't take as long as they used to. One could cross the globe in a day without the aid of magic at all. That made an army of vampires *very* dangerous.

A vampire like Takashi, who had connections all over the world, could be useful to someone planning to become a vampire king.

If he behaved. What Anton had done was a warning, and Takashi was meant to know that.

Takashi did his best to relax into his seat. "I am a guest at your mansion until you have no use for me, and if I am … disruptive, then I may find my status downgraded. At that point, I'll likely wish for a stake in my heart rather than what will happen."

"Intelligence, such a rare and beautiful thing. You've gathered the gist of the situation." Seamus moved to his chair behind the desk and sat. "Zack's notes about international covens are sparse. I was hoping you might confirm a few details for me."

Most international vampires were pains in the ass that only wanted to further subjugate humans, and several masters were rampant racists that were gleefully funding the resurgence of fascism. Takashi didn't owe those bastards a damn bit of his loyalty.

But he did have lines. Likely, Seamus wouldn't respect him if he didn't. *Just as likely that he'll kill me for them.*

Yet what Anton had dragged to the surface had left him shaken. He wanted power. When he was alone, he couldn't deny that.

But he wanted love. *Had* love. And he wouldn't forsake it.

"May I ask a question?" Takashi said.

"I may not answer it."

"That's within your rights." Rather than swallowing his fear for his loved ones, Takashi let it bubble upward, making it obvious. "Are they dead?"

Seamus watched him for a long moment. Takashi didn't budge, didn't blink. He waited.

"You wouldn't betray them even if they were," Seamus replied.

"I would not."

"I can appreciate loyalty, even to a traitorous bastard such as Roger, when it's born out of love." Seamus flipped through one of the pages before him. "The heart cannot help what it wants. No one knows that better than I."

An odd piece of information. Takashi examined its place on the chess board and made note of it. His question wasn't answered, but the expectation was set. Keeping his head level, he said, "Since we have an understanding, I have no qualms discussing our international brethren. You are my coven master, after all."

"Wonderful," Seamus said happily. "Dawn is nearing, so we'll keep tonight's session short."

"Thank you," Takashi said with a slight nod of his head. *I will find out what happened to you Roger, Zack. Kit. If you are dead, then I will orchestrate this bastard's burning by his own fucking hand.* "Where would you like to start?"

CHAPTER 5

The abandoned house in the middle of the empty cornfields was silent except for the distant sounds of passing trucks on the highway. Darkness enveloped Roger where he stood beside one of the upper-floor windows.

The solitary company of the stars was a boon. He'd woken at dusk, and Vincent had promptly offered his blood. When Roger had turned the boy down, a glimmer of a vague and violent desire had swept through him. The shape of that desire had remained unfathomable, and that had left Roger wondering about the boy he'd taken in.

Nathaniel had offered a mage friend a clean tab if she provided Roger with a fresh feeding. Her blood had been perfectly all right, but Roger's heart remained a lump in his chest.

Holes in the walls of the house allowed for an icy wind that would've been rough for a human or shifter but suited Roger's mood fine.

He had fucked up so many times, but he didn't know of any other path he could've tread. If he hadn't returned to Chicago, then Seamus would have sent someone after him. If he hadn't convinced Zack to accompany him, then Zack would have continued trying to kill him. And if he'd killed Zack? If he'd never known him? Zack would be safe from whatever torture he currently suffered, but he would've died uselessly.

Monstrous memories played out. Zack practically dragging Vincent down the hall. Another boy, his name long forgotten, who had belonged to Seamus but had died in the middle of Devil's Cove back in 1969 because Seamus had fed too long from him. The smell of the Gladwell Manor that fateful night in 1755 and the sight of Anton reveling in the destruction of a family. Ezra's grief, crying out. And only once did Roger lift a finger. Only for Vincent, who was so jaded by vampires he didn't seem to understand that Roger wouldn't demand his blood.

Even though a part of him hungered for blood now.

Roger clenched his fists in his jacket pockets. He'd never doubted becoming a vampire, but he'd never had a choice in it. Feeding was something one did, and humans were hardly an innocent species.

But without Seamus to dictate behavior, Roger could redraw his boundaries. No, he could unearth them, find the root and shape of who he was when he didn't have to pretend to be a foolish playboy.

Who was that? After centuries, was there anything left of the mortal man he'd been? Did Roger even want any part of that bastard who had been too stupid to realize he was walking toward death without a fucking care?

I can't be that coward anymore.

From the second-story window, he had a clear vantage for well over an acre down the gravel road. He'd parked his borrowed vehicle behind the house to obscure it. Five minutes before his first meeting was scheduled, a sleek black luxury sedan crawled down the road, eventually turning onto the short drive.

The car came to a stop closer to the road, and the engine

turned off, though the headlights remained on. The driver's door opened, and a woman stepped out. Her long braid swung as she strode. Rock and dirt crunched under her feet until she veered her path onto a patch of lawn before the house. The dry, frozen grass bent in rustles and snaps.

"Roger," Josefina called out, "you're being incredibly dramatic, and it better be for a damn good reason."

Roger dropped from the window to land several feet ahead of her. She jumped, and he couldn't help the ghost of a smile. Apparently, she hadn't spotted him. That meant his attempt to pull a loose shadow around him had worked. Doing so had been easy in the darkness, but it was a skill he had to practice. "Forgive me for a few precautions. Last night has put me on edge."

"So the rumors are true," Josefina said. "You've been exiled."

"How do you know already?" Roger asked. "Taliville is hundreds of miles from Chicago."

"It's called the internet." Josefina tched and shook her head. "Reed has been glued to social media since the video of your waltz with Zack went viral on the Fang app. You countered Seamus's ability right in front of him, didn't you?"

"I was showing off a bit, yes," Roger replied.

"You should've staked the bastard weeks ago."

"You, more than anyone, should know how delicate a game politics can be."

Josefina slid her hands into her coat pockets and stilled as only a vampire could. With no reason to breathe or to fidget, she could stand motionless for an age if she wanted. She'd been a member of the Great Lakes Coven when she was first made. A descendant of Anton's had turned her, and she had hated her lot in life. In 1921, Roger had introduced her to Nell, a master vampire with a coven based in Tennessee, in an effort to save her from a worse fate. Roger had watched the way Seamus and Anton would begin to circle around a victim before draining a vampire of their life force. They were always careful, always certain to take a loner, and Josefina had been one until Nell.

Roger's matchmaking had worked. Seamus hadn't wanted to let her leave the GLC, but Roger had convinced him that Josefina would become a spy in Nell's court. His lie had gotten her to safety, and he'd swallowed another round of Seamus's anger. Seamus had chalked up his "miscalculation" to Roger's lack of intelligence rather than a purposeful deception.

At least I've managed one good deed in my life. Roger matched her neutral expression, glad to suppress his worries instead of giving in to them.

"People were supposed to welcome you back," Josefina said.

"About that. Dmitri had his own plan," Roger replied.

Josefina scowled. Roger told her what had happened since his return to Chicago as precisely as he could. As he spoke about the night that Dmitri was dragged out onto the stage, he found a hollow part inside himself and pulled it forth. He didn't have time for his emotions. The information mattered. He barreled forward into recounting the previous night's ball and attack.

When he had woken from his cursed coma, she had been the first vampire he encountered. And out of everyone he knew, she was one of the few that he had broken down and admitted his deepest need. He had to rid himself of Seamus so that he could finally have a life. A real one. She'd agreed to help.

He'd failed her, too.

"In the 1680s, Seamus and Anton made a wager between themselves," Roger said. "They'd been going through a patch of killing each other's sirelings, so they made a bet over whose would live longest."

"So they made you and Dmitri the same night," Josefina said.

"My life's a fucking game to them," Roger said hoarsely. "Now, they've taken Zack and Takashi. I have to get them back."

The wind gusted past them, and Josefina stared off into the distance. Her car's headlights finally snapped off and plunged them into darkness. Both of them could see well enough not to need the light source.

Josefina nodded tightly. "That explains a lot. Do you know where they took Zack and Takashi?"

"Likely his mansion northwest of the city," Roger replied. "I'm planning a strike to free them. After I get them back, I am ruining everything Seamus holds dear."

"I hope you're not expecting me to be part of a raid. If anyone spots me, that will mean a war between the GLC and my love's coven. That's the opposite of our goals."

"I have a part for you to play." Roger heard the rumble of a vehicle turning onto the gravel road. "But I'll have to tell you later. Do me a favor. Hide in the shadows and make sure my second appointment doesn't kill me."

Josefina opened her mouth to ask the question, but she must have heard the growing sounds of the truck's engine. She darted into the house with a burst of vampiric speed.

Roger braced himself, keeping his hands loose at his sides.

Eventually, the truck swerved around Josefina's car and came to a stop in the yard. Its headlights illuminated Roger. He squinted into the bright light but remained still. *Hopefully, they aren't planning to run over me.*

The engine remained on, though the headlights dipped from high intensity to a regular glow. Both doors opened in unison. The lighting made it impossible to take in the details of the newcomers right away. They were shadows, one broader, while the one on Roger's right was shorter and slimmer. For a second, an irrational hope flared that the one on the right must be Zack. But the figure was taller than Zack, and, though narrow in the shoulders, not quite narrow enough.

The bigger shadow stepped into the light.

Callum Wright had a gun in his hand, the weapon up and pointed at Roger. While he shared Zack's gray eyes and delicate nose, the similarities ended there. Where Zack was the wind, Cal was the unforgiving rocks, relentless and punishing to any wave that dared brush against him. He was thick with muscle and taut with anger. He sneered with a malice that matched the worst of Roger's nightmares.

"Put the weapon away," the figure on the right said.

That voice rent Roger's heart into pieces. *Zack never said that he sounds just like his father.*

Thomas Wright walked into the light. He was lithe for someone who had to be near fifty, clearly making an effort to remain physically fit for his line of work. His light brown hair was the same shade as Zack's, only he had streaks of gray starting from his temples. And though Zack had his mother's eyes, he had his father's jawline and squared his shoulders in the same fashion. Everything about him was a glimpse of what age would bring to Zack.

There was so much familial familiarity between Zack and Thomas that Roger was glad the Wrights were dealing with a spat between them. If he'd had to speak, his cracked heart would've shattered, and he couldn't afford weakness around these predators.

"I said put the gun down," Thomas ordered.

"I see a fucking bloodsucker and no Zack, so no, Dad, I'm not putting the gun down," Cal replied sharply.

"Oh my God, you are the fucking worst!" a higher-pitched voice declared.

Both men jumped and turned toward their truck. Roger had the advantage of seeing someone crawling out from the back seat while both men shielded their eyes in the headlight in an attempt to spot the interloper.

But from the way they frowned, they clearly knew the voice. Thomas called out, "*Amber*? What the hell do you think you're doing?"

Amber joined them outside the vehicle. Though she was the shortest of the three by at least six inches, she had the same defiance in her posture. The dark gave her longer shadows, but Roger was accustomed to picking out details. She had a few acne blemishes, but the softness of her features gave away her youth. She was practically a child, and yet she had an enchanted dagger in a sheath on her belt. Roger couldn't remember if Zack had ever said her age. Sixteen was too generous of an estimate. Was she fifteen? Fourteen?

She had the sort of determination that Zack had had when Roger first met him. The confidence of a freshly minted hunter suited her. Roger only hoped that she wasn't so entrenched in her family's beliefs that she was a crusader like Cal.

"Maybe if you two hadn't been arguing since this morning, you would've seen me sneak into the truck," Amber declared.

"Get back in the truck," Thomas said.

"Zack is my brother." Amber stamped her foot as she came to stand between them. "I'm not letting him down more than we already have."

A flicker of a deeper emotion crossed Thomas's face, but he quickly schooled his features into the firm countenance he'd first displayed.

Cal didn't bother hiding his disagreement. "You've got it wrong, little sis. Zack's the fucking disappointment."

"He is not!" Amber whirled on her brother. "I can't do a third of the research he pulled off at my age!"

"Because you actually get to do the *job*," Cal said.

"When are you going to get that research is part of the job? You can't just shoot everything until it stops moving!"

"I find cutting heads off works pretty damn well, too."

"Enough," Thomas snapped with parental authority.

Watching the three of them only strangled Roger's heart. No wonder Zack had been so hurt when they had disowned him. Family was something Roger had never really had, not like the Wrights did. He had seen plenty of them to know that the Wrights were tight-knit. He'd assumed Zack had never fit into their weave, but was he wrong? What was he like with his sister, his father?

Roger prayed he'd find out one night soon.

"We're not unaware that something happened at Chateau de Vampire last night," Thomas said. "We have our resources, and the community has been lit up with rumors about the ball. You texted on Zack's phone that you needed our help. What's happened to my son?"

"I'll tell you what happened," Cal growled. His finger half squeezed the trigger of his gun. "This bastard seduced him and then got him killed. Let's put him down."

"I am not a starved nest vampire eager for my next blood fix," Roger said, matching Cal's tone. "I have been contending with greater threats than you could dream to be for centuries. Put the weapon away so we can have a civil conversation, or go pout in the truck like the small child you are. Zack needs us to cooperate."

Cal took a step forward.

Thomas moved at the same time, reaching out to catch Cal by the wrist and force the point of his gun toward the ground. He was face-to-face with him. "Callum, I came to learn what we can do. Wrap your head around the mission, or do what the vampire says."

"We know what happened. He turned Zack into his blood bitch. He's probably luring the rest of us into a trap," Cal replied. "Let's end him and join Mom in Indiana before we wind up in the ground. Or worse, enchanted into mindless blood bags like Zack was."

This was the brother that Zack had once idolized. This was the man the family had chosen over Zack. Kind, courageous, compassionate Zack had been cast out, and his monster of a brother was the one loved and adored.

Roger embraced how anger petrified his heart and allowed that stillness to creep over his limbs. All the rage and self-disappointment that he'd been putting off compounded inside him, and he turned that into fuel for his cold and distant attitude. Every second bickering was a waste.

"I have seen a thousand petty pieces of shit like you, Callum Wright," Roger said, the snarl and hiss working into his voice. He curved his lips into a cruel smile. "At their rotten core is the fervent wish to drag everyone into the mire with them because they can't figure out how to rise above their heartless, loveless selves."

Cal paled. He wrestled free of his father and quickly raised the gun. "You son of a—"

By the time the bullet cleared the chamber, Roger had blurred into action. The world seemed to stand still as he rushed forward. He gripped Cal around the throat. Humans had such soft and destructible bodies. He wouldn't need to apply much of his strength to break bones or crush Cal's windpipe.

But he held back. Instead of ripping Cal's head from his spine, he forced Cal against the truck's hood and applied pressure to pin him in place. "Your brother is twice the hunter and four times the man you will ever be. If you were in danger, I would have to beg him not to go to your side. *I. Do. Not. Like. You.* You are alive because *Zack* wills it. But he is not here. So give me a reason to snap your neck. *Please.*"

Cal scrambled against Roger, but he didn't have the strength or leverage to move Roger's hand.

The tip of a blade poked Roger in the back. Amber

wouldn't be fast enough to stop Roger from killing Cal, but she was in a good position. One solid push and she'd send her silver dagger into Roger's heart. He might be able to avoid it—he could attempt to drop into shadows for a flash of a moment like he had on Halloween in order to escape Seamus's grip—but the fact that he hadn't felt her move until it was too late either spoke to her expertise, or his rage was blinding him worse than he'd thought.

"Point's made," Thomas said. The eldest Wright had his enchanted dagger in hand. The shape of it was closer to a dirk, with a wider blade at the hilt. The runes carved into it glowed with bright white light. "Now, take your hand off of him before we have a bigger problem."

Roger released Cal and then blurred with movement to where he'd stood before. Impressively, Amber spun toward his direction with little lagging. Thomas was slower, and Cal had to recover from the sudden lack of force holding him up.

Sliding his hands into his coat pockets, Roger pulled on his colder demeanor again. Zack had called it his Master Vampire face. *God, I miss him.*

"Your text said you needed to meet with the family to discuss a mission for Zack's sake," Thomas said. "We're what you've got. I'm guessing Zack isn't here because no force on Earth could've convinced him to sit by while all this bullshit went on. What has happened to my son?"

"After the ball, we were ambushed," Roger said hollowly. His rage at Cal drained back to the hold it'd flooded from. As infuriating as he was, he wasn't the true target of Roger's anger. "Anton and Seamus surprised us, and though we fought valiantly, they won. They took Zack and Takashi. I *need* to get them back."

"Who the fuck is Takashi?" Cal demanded.

"Takashi Sato?" Amber asked.

Cal scowled at her, and Thomas frowned in confusion.

Amber lifted her chin, just like Zack might have. "We

almost failed to stop a cult from raising a demon this last Halloween because no one was picking up the research slack. So when Zack mentioned he had another boyfriend, I did what he would do. I went looking."

"Mentioned?" Cal repeated. "When did he *mention* another boyfriend?"

"Not the time, Cal," Thomas said warily.

"No, no, no. See, he didn't have any boyfriends in Taliville. He had a bloodsucker he might've called one, but only the *one*. So when did he tell you about this other boyfriend, Amber?"

"Oh, grow up!" Amber threw her hands up and turned to glare at her brother.

"Mom said—"

"I don't care." Ignoring her brother, Amber slid her blade back into its sheath and addressed Roger. "Did you mean Takashi Sato or not?"

"I did," Roger replied.

"Why take them but leave you?" Amber asked.

"Seamus knows that I'll agonize over what could be happening to them." Roger straightened his shoulders. "But I refuse to stand by while it happens. I know his mansion and where he keeps his prisoners within it. I've drawn up plans for it and had someone who knows it assist me in fleshing out any changes."

"He may suspect you'll come for them," Thomas said. "That makes the job tricky."

"Are we talking about a rescue op? Seriously?" Cal scoffed. "We should burn the place down."

Roger kept his gaze on Thomas. "Seamus has long preyed on the unfortunate. Most of the humans he seduces into his collection of pets are hardly older than your daughter. He has a skill at picking out weaknesses and exploiting them."

"Any way to get them out while we're at this?" Thomas asked.

"Not likely. He terrifies them into obedience and slaughters those who attempt to leave. I only managed to take one at the ball because an Unseelie noble stepped in," Roger replied. "The boy was left alive because Seamus wanted him to deliver a message to me."

"Why don't you go in yourself and get them?" Cal demanded. "Why do you need us if you're such a badass?"

"Because if they're not able to move under their own power, he'll need help carrying them," Thomas said, a haunting, knowing quality changing his voice. There was a distance to his gaze and an emptiness to his expression.

Cal had an echo of that emptiness on his face suddenly.

In the quiet, Amber strode forward until she was a foot from Roger. She met his gaze with her brown eyes and held it. Staring contests were a frequent occurrence in Roger's life. And often, he had backed down in them, given way so that he could convince the other party he believed they were in the right. Sometimes, those others had been; sometimes, he had been conning them. With Amber, he held her gaze and remained motionless.

"Zack said you had some mission for him, but he wouldn't tell us what," Amber said.

"I was hoping he could help me kill Seamus so I could become the master of the coven," Roger replied.

"What happens once you get him back?" Amber demanded. "You go back to making him wear a collar and making a power play?"

"Once I have them back," Roger whispered, "I will dismantle everything Seamus has ever held dear. I will burn his clubs. I will decimate his mansion. I will pull apart his coven until every vampire that holds him in esteem is a corpse. But I cannot risk Zack and Takashi. I cannot let him use their safety to keep me in check."

"Okay. I'm in," Amber said. She turned to face her brother and father.

Thomas ran his hand through his hair. Light and shadow played across his features, making him harder to read. After a moment, he nodded. "We'll save Takashi if we can, but Zack is the priority. Deal?"

Roger nodded in agreement. *Because if I have Zack, we'll be able to save Takashi together.*

"With you involved, we're limited to a nighttime strike," Thomas said. "That'll put us humans at a disadvantage, especially if the master of the house is in."

"He won't be," Roger said.

"How can you guarantee that?"

"Because Seamus will have to make an appearance when a high-ranking member of another coven stops in for a spontaneous visit," Josefina said loudly from her hiding place in the house. She stepped out into the night and dropped down to the ground. Despite the hunters' slight scramble at the sight of her, she approached Roger's side calmly. "I assume that's the real reason you asked me here."

"I was hoping you'd assist," Roger said.

"Eh, I suppose," she replied with an air of nonchalance. She had a hint of worry in her eyes, though. Takashi had been part of her coven longer than she had and was one of Nell's closest sirelings, likely making them close as well. And though she had a tough shell, she'd gone to great lengths to help Zack prepare for his role at Roger's side. She wouldn't have put in the hours if she didn't care for him.

"Excuse me, but who are you?" Thomas asked.

"Josefina, captain and beloved of Nell."

"Nell as in *the* Nell? Taliville matron Nell?"

"That would be the one."

Thomas looked from Roger to Josefina and back to Roger. In a hoarse whisper, he said, "What the hell has my son gotten into?"

"The middle of his favorite sick fantasy," Cal grumbled.

Amber stepped on her brother's foot hard enough to make Cal jump. He shoved her in return.

"Knock it off," Thomas warned. He crossed his arms over his chest. "It's nearing the middle of the night. We need to make a plan to strike. You have anything written out, or do I need to break out the pen and paper?"

Slowly, Roger reached into his inner coat pocket and took out a set of folded papers. He'd written down everything he knew about the mansion and had had Vincent help him where he could. He offered the papers over to Thomas.

"Cal, grab the lantern," Thomas said as he walked around to the back of the truck. "And turn the engine off."

"I've got it," Amber replied as she hurried to the cab.

"Since the threat of murdering each other appears to be over, I'll be going," Josefina said. "Roger, a word?"

While the hunters spread the floorplans and Roger's notes across the tailgate, Roger accompanied Josefina over to her car. She lowered her voice to the barest whisper. "Have you thought about Dmitri?"

"It's possible that he's still alive," Roger admitted. "Anton said the gamble wasn't settled after all just before breaking my neck. Seamus could have come up with some new condition. Some other comparison to start. I don't know. But if I try to win back everything I've lost in a single move, I'll be crushed under the weight of my goals."

Josefina put her hand on Roger's arm. When Roger had seen her as a mortal, she'd been demure with a caring soul. After she'd been turned, the softness in her brown eyes had died. A hint of that old warmth came back now. "My love put her faith in Zack and Takashi, but mine has been in you. Ever since you told me what you did for me, I've had a new filter to view the past. I can see you clearer now. You have a strength in you, Roger."

"All a show," Roger murmured.

"It's not." Josefina squeezed his arm. He bent his head

down, and she touched her forehead to his. No romantic love had ever existed between them, but their quiet kinship was its own loving bond. "Save our lost dear ones and watch your back. I want many more decades hearing your voice."

"I'll try." Roger smiled, but it felt hollow.

Once she was driving away, Roger returned to the Wrights. They were already deep in the discussion of the best approach to the mansion, and Amber began to pepper Roger with questions he hadn't thought of.

But a plan was forming. Roger had experienced allies, even if he couldn't trust Cal not to stake him in the back. *Hold on one more night, loves. I'm coming.*

CHAPTER 6

The bedroom lacked a doorknob. Takashi had noted that before he'd fallen asleep, but he could do nothing about it.

Otherwise, the bedroom had a lovely bed, no windows, a wardrobe and dresser, a matching desk, and a small bathroom. The subtlety didn't elude him. Of course, Seamus would say that the lack of windows meant no fear of sunlight penetrating the space, but that also meant Takashi couldn't escape through them. A wardrobe could store clothing as well as a closet, so there was no need for that extra space. And the bathroom didn't have a lock because why would he need one? The space was only for him.

It was a prisoner's cell disguised as a guest's lodging. Takashi had seen its like before, though the lack of a doorknob was new.

Effectively locked in, he had showered, slept the best he could, and then woke. The clothes in the wardrobe fit him but weren't any of his personal, tailored pieces. They were store-bought and a fraction too wrong for him.

Hours had passed.

How long would he be forced to remain in the room? In the mansion? What had happened to Roger and Zack? Were they being tortured while he walked back and forth? Were they waiting in some similar room and worrying over him?

Breaking walls was a noisy prospect, and there was no telling what might be hiding *in* the walls. Takashi paced slowly, his hunger growing, and watched the door. Seamus couldn't hope to continue his charade if he didn't give Takashi an opportunity to feed. Did Seamus know that Takashi knew that this was one massive lie? Had he given away too much information the night before and Seamus decided he no longer needed anything from him?

No. If that was the case, he'd be dead.

Takashi started counting his steps. Then the number climbed too high, and he stopped before it drove him into paranoia. His bloodlust was clawing at his insides. He had gone nights without feeding before, but each one had been a test of his patience.

Surely all the walls couldn't be booby-trapped. Maybe there was even a secret exit. Older vampires loved hidden passageways.

A knock on the door interrupted his thoughts. Takashi started for it, remembered there was no handle, and called out eagerly, "Yes?"

A teenage boy swung open the door. He kept his head bowed, gaze never lifting from the floor. He had stark moonlight-white skin and wore a dark-colored vest and shorts that accentuated his angular frame. His collar was a deep red.

He smelled delicious, but Takashi kept his fangs to himself.

The boy motioned for Takashi to follow him out of the room.

Perhaps leaving the bedroom wasn't what Takashi wanted at all. But he couldn't remain behind. He followed the boy. They wound their way to a staircase and to the first floor. All the doors were closed, leaving Takashi with the impression of long halls with only art pieces and vases of flowers for reference. Such things could be easily moved about.

Even a labyrinth has a way out. Takashi kept track of the number of doors he passed. He was fairly certain he hadn't been this way the previous night.

The boy led him to a sitting room with a crackling fireplace. Several bookcases lined the walls, and they were filled with hardback novels. The collection spanned the last couple of centuries and seemed to run in chronological order of publication from a cursory glance. Across the dark wood floor was a rug that smelled of deep woods and brought forth an image of moonlight. The swirling, interlocking design also spoke to its Unseelie make. The chairs were leather, with bright brass finishings outlining the seams, and a low cream-colored sofa was against the right wall.

Three humans stood in front of the sofa. They were naked except for the gray band on each of their left arms.

Anton sat in one of the leather chairs. He had pulled his platinum-blond hair into a high ponytail and dressed in jeans and a hoodie. He had on *sneakers*. All of which seemed painstakingly new.

The vampire had always seemed so impressively old that Takashi had assumed he'd been somewhere in his thirties when he'd been made. But as he sat reading a leather journal, he looked young. In his current outfit, he'd have fit in on a college campus without raising any suspicions.

The curiosity almost eased Takashi's mind into a sense of calm. Then he noticed that Anton was reading Zack's journal.

First Seamus had his notes and the journal. Now Anton's reading it.

His attire suddenly made a sick sort of sense. Anton was dressed like Zack preferred whenever he wasn't dressed up for an evening out.

"There we go," Anton said with a sigh of pleasure. He lifted his head and grinned, a wicked spread of his lips that only chilled Takashi. Whatever merriment he'd found grew, and his ruby eyes sparkled with glee. "I would've thought you'd hide your fears better, but they are right there for the plucking. You're easier than a piano."

Anton had set up a little test and apparently liked the results so far.

Does immortality become so dull that everything has to be a jest with a razor's edge? Takashi managed a small smile of his own. "I'm glad I've brought you some amusement, master."

"Don't call me that tonight. I'm trying to understand the common mortal mind."

"Zack's mind is anything but common," Takashi replied, keeping his tone light despite how badly he wanted to rip Anton a new one for underestimating his boyfriend.

Anton's smile grew. "True."

Cautiously, Takashi stepped into the room. The rug had magic in it, but other than adding a freshening scent, it didn't seem to hold an enchantment. He walked over to the fireplace and watched a few of its embers. The humans were close. The gray bands on their arms dulled out their emotions and kept them in a state primed for accepting orders. The bands broke the Pact of Chicago, yet they were still in use.

"Are you hungry?" Anton asked.

Reflexively, Takashi glanced toward the gray-banded humans. He hated how he hungered for their blood, but they were there. They were a kind of food.

"Not them. At least, not yet." Anton pulled up the arm of his sweatshirt and held out his bare wrist. "I want to feel your fangs first."

Blood was a powerful conduit. The night before, Anton had ripped through Takashi's mental shields. Who knew what he might be capable of if they had a more direct connection?

Takashi put his hand on the mantle, adopting a neutral expression. Anton had already displayed that he had no trouble reading Takashi's emotions, but he hoped to disguise his growing anxieties behind a mask of growing bloodlust.

He reached for that tiny core of power left within himself and extended his reach out to sense what he could of Anton.

For a creature who only seemed to do as he pleased, Anton had a fierce mental shield, but he wasn't projecting any sort of desire. He was playing everything closer to his chest. Cracking it would take more energy than Takashi dared to expend if he wasn't going to feed that night. *Then I'll have to rely on observation.*

"Do you play these games because you're bored or because you have more fun learning what you want to know?" Takashi asked.

Anton lowered his wrist to his lap. "Game?"

Takashi motioned at Anton's attire. "How long have the tags been off those clothes? Or did you craft them into existence with your arcane abilities?"

Anton tensed and closed the journal. He narrowed his ruby eyes. "Perhaps you should leave the man behind the curtain alone."

"You're much more powerful than some charlatan leading with illusions." Slowly, Takashi approached the other chair and sat down across from Anton. Stroking egos was a more delicate process than keeping his fangs from nicking a lover's tender member. He relaxed into the seat and ran his gaze over Anton. "Why did you try to dress like Zack? Is this a ruse for my benefit? His? Seamus's?"

A *flicker* went across Anton's face when Takashi said Seamus. Just a fraction of a scowl.

We can't help who we love. And he's loved Seamus for so long. And Seamus was the definition of a manipulative bastard.

The way to survive this is to convince them I have value beyond being useful. Takashi slid to the edge of his seat and dipped his voice low. "Are you trying to understand him? Or be him?"

Anton set the journal aside and mirrored Takashi's movement. "Why does it matter to you?"

"I won't help you torture him," Takashi replied. "But if you're attempting to understand Seamus's fascination with him, well, that I might be interested in myself."

"I know what my lover wants of him," Anton said with a low growl.

The laughter was gone. No hint of a jest in sight. Takashi let the slightest grin tug the corner of his lips. A false ego might push Anton into revealing his hand. "You don't know *why* he wants what he wants, though, and that's bothering you."

"Are you arrogant enough to believe that I don't know every inch of my lover?"

"I have traveled the world and known many of our kind. I've seen ancient lovers have difficulties."

"You think I'm having relationship trouble?" Anton spat out. "We've been together for eight hundred and forty-nine years."

Carefully, Takashi said, "I think that life would be far too dull if everything worked perfectly. You don't seem one for tedium, not even with your lover."

Anton rose from his seat and crossed over to the fireplace, taking the place where Takashi had stood. He watched the flames for a long moment without letting his psychic guard slip. The silence carried on so long that Takashi became aware of the hunger burning in his stomach again. The burn was turning into a soul-deep ache.

"He loves me," Anton said.

"He said as much last night," Takashi replied.

The temperature in the room dropped. One of the gray-banded humans shivered. When Anton glanced over his shoulder at Takashi, his eyes were glowing deep red. His frown had the intensity of a snapped support beam. "I do not need you to tell me what I already know."

"But you are trying to understand Seamus, aren't you? For some reason, he's obsessed with Zack. He doesn't want what he normally wants from a mortal with him, does he?"

With a blur of speed that Takashi didn't catch, Anton went from standing beside the fire to holding Takashi by the throat. He shoved him against the chair hard enough that Takashi and the chair went backward with a clatter of sound. In his other hand, he had a burning piece of firewood, and he brought the flame close to Takashi's eye.

"You are *very* clever," Anton said with an impassively cold voice, "but invasive. Many have tried to expand the cracks between us, and we only become stronger for the effort. I love Seamus deeper than you could possibly understand, let alone feel."

Rather than struggle, Takashi stilled, fighting with his muscles for a sense of calm. Every word was a roll of the dice, but he had to keep rolling. He had to try. "I love Roger. I am falling in love with Zack night by night. They are as different as the moon and the tide, but they are mine, and I am theirs. Do not tell me I know nothing of love."

Takashi gripped Anton's wrist. Touch heightened a vampire's ability to read. He unwound his mental shields and let himself feel the terror for his loved ones that he had been resisting since Seamus stepped through the hotel door.

Slowly, Anton withdrew. He tossed the firewood back into the hearth and started for the door. He paused and said, "Drink what you want of the gray bands. Then the boy here will take you back to your room. Go anywhere else, and I will put embers in worse places than your eye."

Then he walked away. The room wasn't any warmer for his absence.

Takashi took a long moment, then rose. He set the chair upright. *Did I win that round? Or am I completely fucked?*

CHAPTER 7

The planning session had gone well, but the Wrights and Josefina needed until dusk the next night to enact their portions of preparations. The impending time felt like Roger would have to wait for eternity, but he couldn't rush into the raid. Getting stuck in the same trap that Zack and Takashi were currently held in wouldn't help any of them.

Kit and Vincent would need something more than greasy bar food and takeout to keep them fed, so Roger made a stop at a grocery store on his way back. Dawn was less than an hour away, and his arms were full of bags when he knocked on the back door of the Last Deal. He tapped out a rhythm from a 1960s punk song, one both he and Nathaniel thought was ridiculous.

"About damn time," Nathaniel grumbled as he opened the door. He started taking the bags from him.

"I've got it," Roger said.

"Just give them over." Nathaniel continued grabbing the bags. "The she-devil kept pounding on the front door until I let her in. Was about to text you, but they haven't been talking long."

"They?"

"Better see for yourself."

Before Roger could ask for answers, Nathaniel was halfway up the stairs the stairs toward his apartment. Roger locked the back door and then made his way into the bar.

Somehow, without the patrons, the bar remained cozy. The faux fireplace still had a crackling blaze, but the digital flames provided little illumination. The sconce lighting would have been considered dim for mortals, but it was bright enough for Roger to see plainly. All but one of the tables had their chairs on top.

Candide sat at a table in the center of the room. She had her hair down, something she never did, and it had a deep honey glow. Typically, she prided herself on her immaculate fashion, but she'd dressed in jeans and a T-shirt. A *T-shirt*.

In doing so, she reminded him of the nights centuries ago when she was newly immortal and lonely and hoping he would be more than a friend. He had disappointed her on those nights. Women held no romantic or sexual attraction for him. But he and Candide had formed a friendship rather than give way to animosity, an enduring relationship they both treasured.

Across from her was Kit. They were in better shape, though they held a hand to their stomach and were still pale from blood loss. The softness of their youthful features had melted a fraction. In their other hand, they had a red collar with a crest tag. The round steel piece had Candide's crest on it, a stag with a magnificent set of antlers.

Roger lacked the energy to bring any of his social masks to the forefront. The multitude of tiny psychic cuts he'd lived with for so long were unbearable. He'd played his part for so long. Now that he was free, he couldn't stomach slipping into an old habit with her.

"What's happening here?" Roger asked.

Candide put her hand on top of Kit's knee and squeezed. In a gentle voice, she said, "I can handle this if you want."

"I've got it," Kit whispered. They stood slowly and approached Roger.

Watching them move between the tables, every movement ginger and careful, ripped open Roger's heart further. They were in pain because he had put them in harm's way. Had they remained in Taliville, they would've been safe. Unhappy, but safe.

Roger had once prided himself on being a terrific master, but he'd never given Kit or Carver the attention he had his pets in the past. He'd paid them, flirted with them, and did more than flirt with Carver on occasion. But he hadn't been their master.

Kit stared at the collar in their hands before drawing in a deep breath, exhaling, and then speaking in a clear voice. "I've always wanted more from you, and I've known that you didn't really want to give it to me, but I thought maybe with time, you would. But you don't, so I started looking for a real master. And I know the timing is shitty, and we only talked about this last night, but I've been feeling this way for a few weeks now."

"You've already been searching for a real master," Roger murmured. He put his hand to his lips, then shook his head.

"Yeah." A serious weight landed on Roger's shoulders as Kit met his gaze. "Roger ... you've been planning this dangerous stuff since Taliville, and you didn't share that with Carver or me. But Zack was in on it. And now Carver's dead. And I almost died. And you ran off tonight without a freaking word."

Pushing away the disappointment in himself, Roger gently put his hands on Kit's shoulders. "I don't blame you for wanting to leave, and I release you without condition. I'm sorry that I failed you, Kit. If you ever need sanctuary and I can provide it, I will. I promise you that."

"I appreciate that," Kit said quietly.

Roger smiled at them with every ounce of genuine

warmth he could muster. "One of the bags upstairs is still yours. If you need help bringing it down, ask Vincent."

"Thanks."

Candide coaxed Kit toward her with her finger. "Come here, petit renard."

Kit went back to her, and she took the collar from their hands. Instead of making Kit kneel, she stood and smoothly buckled the collar onto their neck. A flush brightened Kit's cheeks, and a warm desire rolled out from them. That warmth grew when Candide kissed their cheek.

Roger had never brought that emotion out of them. *Never tried to either. I'm an ass for risking their life without being what they needed.*

"I'll be back in a minute, mistress," Kit said.

"Don't rush. A wound like yours is still healing, and I need a moment to speak with your old master."

Kit nodded.

Candide became as motionless as a statue while Kit to walked out of the room. Cold and professional was her default nature, but there was a glint of anger in her eyes.

Roger mimicked her stillness and waited until he heard the click of the door at the top of the stairs. Exhausted, he dropped all pretense of holding himself apart from his emotions and crossed the room to the bar. He found a bottle of rum and two glasses and began to pour. "I swear to God, if you're going to throw a shit fit about what happened at the party, I will drive a semitruck through the Chateau."

Candide strode over, each step purposeful and silent. "Oh, you will?"

When she went to take one of the glasses, Roger caught her gaze and said warningly, "Don't start."

"It has taken me seven years to host the Winter's Grand Ball. Do you know how many times I hosted it before that? Three times in over a hundred years. How often were you hosting it before you disappeared?"

"Every five," Roger muttered.

"Every five years. And how much work did you really put into the event?" Candide asked sharply.

Roger put both hands on the bar. "You used my name to get what you wanted because the asshole misogynistic mages wouldn't respect you. You benefited. After all, you took my money and built your glorious donor house in my absence."

"That isn't the point, Roger." Candide swiped one of the glasses of rum and clutched it tightly. "One night, you're promising to become a leader, and weeks later, you're jeopardizing my long-standing relationship with the fey courts by causing not one but two scenes with our wretched sire. In addition to appeasing the Chicago Court of Shadows, I have Seamus watching my every move!"

She threw the glass at him.

Roger caught it. The force and speed of her throw had sloshed the rum, but most remained in the glass. As a point of pride for catching the damn thing, he drank the remnants. "Finished? Or are we going to have a proper fight?"

"Nathaniel has built a darling, if rustic, establishment." Candide crossed her arms. "I would rather not ruin such a wonderful place by kicking your ass."

"I wasn't going to let Seamus ruin your party by infecting it with his mystical manipulation. I believed showing off that I could inspire more lust than he could exude fear would serve me in the long run," Roger replied.

"That one, I understood. But you stole his head pet."

"Vincent relinquished Seamus's collar of his own free will," Roger said.

Candide scoffed. "We both know that Seamus's pets never think to give those things up."

The rumble of anger surged upward. Roger wasn't the only one who had been at Seamus's side for centuries. Candide had been there, too. The realization unlocked all kinds of chests at the bottom of his mental sea, and the emotional contents of each were rushing toward the surface. He couldn't slam the lot of it back down where it belonged.

And he didn't want to.

"You're right," he rasped. As he spoke, his voice grew louder. "We have stood by and witnessed what he has done to mortals over and over. I don't mean the ones that he murders in a night or a week. We know about those, too. But we have watched him tear beauty from one after another of his 'pets.' They aren't cared for, Candide. They aren't submissives with a quirky name. Not his. His are *victims*."

"We have had to safeguard our own survival," Candide countered.

"We have," Roger said. "But when is his villainy too much to bear? When is our survival nothing but a coward's excuse to do nothing and pretend we don't mind what's happening?"

"Look at what has happened to you! Your name in ruin, your position revoked, your lovers kidnapped, and your pets murdered or nearly so!"

"And I will pull him into the ashes with me," Roger growled. "I will *bury* Seamus if it is the last thing I do on this Earth."

Bloody tears welled in Candide's eyes, but she spun away from him before a single one could fall. She held her arms tight, a hand going to her face, and smothered her tears.

"I can't continue like it was," Roger said as he approached her. Gently, he put his hands on her shoulders. "Something has to change. You agreed with that."

"It was easier to pretend without you here. You have always made me wonder what joy might feel like." Candide tilted her head back. "I wish you hadn't woken."

Roger froze colder than blood in an arctic wind. In the months since he'd woken from his enchanted coma, he had told very few about what had truly happened to him. Anton had known on his own, but he had made it clear that he hadn't told anyone either.

Candide was not someone that Roger had told. "You know about the curse?"

"I do."

The shock clouded the rage. Numb, he spun her to face him. "Was it you?"

"That put you to sleep? No." Candide slipped out of his grasp and walked over to the table with its chairs down. She put her hands on the back of one as if to steady herself. For once, all her masks dropped away. The innermost version of Candide was a tough core made from a long-conditioned endurance, but he spotted a weariness in her expression. "But I did ensure that Seamus could not find you."

"*What*?" Roger demanded.

"Do you remember what June 1989 was like? Truly? Or do you remember it the way you like to remember everything else? With a million filters and only the pleasant bits of reality?"

"Candide, I am struggling to control my temper. Don't test me."

Candide narrowed her eyes at him. "Heaven forbid I call you out on your own bullshit. Up until recently, you might have believed you were only playing the part of a vapid playboy, but we both know that con came from a place of truth. You *wanted* that ignorant life to numb your own pain. I always enabled it because your attitude allowed me to ignore my own agony."

Roger stalked over to the other chair and put his hands on the back of it to mirror hers. "That version of me is dead."

"That remains to be seen," Candide replied.

She didn't have confidence that he would stick to his guns this time. He wasn't sure he could blame her. From her perspective, he had been this way and that, thrown about like a kite without a string.

He needed to remain grounded. To gather information instead of dismissing it.

"What did you do?" Roger said.

"I was expecting you the night of June nineteenth, do you remember that? You had asked me to put you in contact with someone who sold enchanted weapons. It didn't take a clever person to put together that you, Ezra, and Dmitri had had enough. After Anton's little farce of killing Ezra's love onstage—I know that he and Seamus had killed the poor boy long before their public display—the whole coven was on edge. Ezra was furious, and Dmitri was grumbling about how our kind are the worst devils. And you were changing, mon cher. You were different. You were secretive, and then you asked for weapons.

"Then you were simply gone. I feared that Anton had finally devoured your soul. Don't give me that look. I have known since before I was made. I thought the vampires they ate were the ones that disappointed them, so I made it my mission to remain eternally useful. And I have, but we both know that they eat who they want. I was terrified you had been one.

"I looked everywhere for you. I finally heard rumor of you leaving a blood club with a beautiful fey boy. I tracked the boy down, who was no mere boy but a fucking *lord*. I couldn't convince him to tell me more than that you were safe in slumber." Candide pulled the chair farther out and then plopped into it. She buried her face in her hands. After a long moment, she composed herself. "He was willing to tell me what the 'scheme' was if I could strike the right deal, which made him a threat. Anton and Seamus would have never bargained for you to disappear like that, but they were already tearing the world apart looking for you. I saw opportunities opening for me, and you were safer than any of us. If they were distracted, I could cement my own power out of sight of their inspection."

"Is that why you were eager to help me? Place me on the throne, and you would rule from behind the seat?" Roger said.

"As much as Seamus acts like he is the sole authority of the coven, operations on this scale require more than one leader," Candide said firmly.

She wasn't wrong, but Roger hadn't seen that her support had been self-motivated. He should have noticed it. Should have known that nothing she ever did came without its price.

Everyone plays me. Uses me. Wants something from me. The anger was rising too quickly. It was bringing a storm with it. He would be caught in a thunderous downpour with a cyclone on the waves if he could not manage his emotions.

Part of him wanted to release it all. To finally unload this stored treasure.

But Candide was a friend. He loved her, and at the very least, she cared for him. Though she had used his absence for her own gain, his long years away had been spent peacefully. Had he woken earlier, he wouldn't have met Zack. Or their meeting would have been dramatically different. Without him and without Takashi, Roger would have caved and abandoned his plan to overthrow Seamus. He would have come back to Chicago and fooled himself into believing that he was too weak or that no one wanted him.

No, the only pieces of fate he wanted to change were Carver's death and that Zack and Takashi were taken from him.

"You failed to strike a deal for the information? Or was my disappearance a greater asset than having me back?" Roger asked.

Candide glared at him and stood. "The former. I wanted you home, but the prick's price was too high. Since he seemed willing to bargain that secret away, I figured it would only be a matter of time before he offered it to Seamus. I had a mage curse him into another form. Then I killed the mage. No one knows where that fey lord is." She half grinned. "The Seelie and Unseelie have been on edge with each other since that happened."

"You could've started a war," Roger said.

"They won't war without proof, and there is none but my word to find."

And mine. I could let loose this fragment of a secret. But that wouldn't start a war between the fey courts, but one between the vampires and the Unseelie. That was a nuclear option if Roger was willing to risk innocents in Seamus's destruction.

With long, careful strides, Roger approached her. "I do not want anger or misconception between us. I intend to rescue my loves and then ruin him. When I am done, there may not *be* a Great Lakes Coven."

Candide met him in a staring contest. Her youth had long ago become a stone façade. She was old inside her soul, and with that strength, she did not waver. "There will be something. There always is. Spare me and mine and we have no quarrel."

"He may suspect you'd aid me," Roger replied.

"He won't want to cross me, not if you become a thorn in his side," Candide said. She tilted her head to the side. "I hear my new pet coming. You're honestly all right with my taking them, mon cher?"

"I have always said that my pets truly belong to themselves. And I have failed Kit miserably." Roger kissed her cheek. "Pamper them."

Candide laughed lightly. "I always spoil the good ones."

Kit came into the room with Vincent behind them. They sheepishly gave Roger a hug, which he returned.

"Be safe," Roger whispered in their ear. "Be happy."

"Get them back," Kit murmured. They squeezed tighter, then released him.

Surprisingly, Candide stole a quick, sincere hug from Roger. "You better not die."

"I don't plan to."

"Perhaps not, but you are *terrible* at planning." She kissed his cheek, took Kit's bag from Vincent, and left the bar with Kit a half step behind her.

Roger locked the door behind them. By the time he turned around, Vincent was putting the chairs on top of the table. After that, he headed for the bar and put away the bottle of rum Roger had grabbed.

"You don't have to clean up after me," Roger said. "That's not something I expect from you."

"You don't expect anything from me," Vincent muttered. He motioned to the glass with rum in it. "Can I?"

"You don't need my permission either," Roger replied.

Vincent nabbed the glass and tossed back the rum in one swallow. He took the other glass and began to wash them.

Clearly, telling the boy that he didn't need to do anything wasn't the way to release the tension between them. Was he expecting a relationship like the one he'd had with Seamus? Did he crave that sort of contact in a healthy way rather than the abusive situation he'd been in? Roger made his way over to the bar, keeping the wooden structure between them in order to give him space.

I'm already failing him. "You don't have to stay with me if you don't want to."

"I don't have anywhere to go."

"What about your parents?"

Vincent scowled, and his face twisted in disgust. "You mean the woman who was so caught up with her vampire boyfriend that she didn't give a shit what he did to me? Or the man who took me in after she got herself killed, only to kick me around whenever he got pissed—and he was always pissed. At least I could make Seamus happy."

The anger in Vincent's voice left behind an ache that reverberated through Roger. Slowly, Roger walked around the bar and found a clean dish towel. He took one of the freshly cleaned glasses and began to dry it.

Perhaps he had already opened too many of the chests at the bottom of his sea. Perhaps the agony had already been floating to the surface, and now that the storm was settled, he could more easily spot the detritus of old terrors. Either way, the pains weren't forgotten. They were scraping his hull, threatening to tear it.

"I know your pain," Roger said quietly.

"Sure you do."

We cannot heal wounds we do not tend. I've let this one fester too long. Not wanting to see Vincent's reaction, he focused on drying every drop from the two glasses. "Father and mother are words I've never understood. I ran away when I was twelve. I did anything I could to find a warm bed to sleep in. Anything."

Vincent remained quiet.

That silent respect and patience helped Roger continue. "I made my way to the coast and found work on a ship. There is nothing in the world like sailing across the sea. I learned how to be part of a crew. Found a ship where my worth wasn't based on the shape of me. I worked. I drank, I fought, I fucked, I loved. It was pure freedom.

"A storm struck, as they do, and our ship was damaged. We found the nearest port and thanked God it had a settlement large enough to do the repairs." Roger put the glasses back where they belonged. "The island was called Devil's Cove. By the end of the first night, I was dead. Three nights later, I rose as Seamus's sireling."

"Did he give you a choice?" Vincent asked.

"No." Roger leaned against the counter. "I woke with incredibly powerful senses and a bloodlust, but other than that, I felt the same. Only I had a master. I kept him happy because it kept me alive, and I'd wager you've done the same. I lived in terror of him for three hundred years, at times convincing myself that my life wasn't a wretched waste because you have to in order to keep from going mad.

"I know you tormented Zack with that online video, but I doubt that you were trying to bully him into submission. You were trying to make him unappealing because you were afraid to lose Seamus's admiration."

Vincent's lip quivered. "Did … did Zack talk to you?"

"Not about you."

"Then how did you know?"

"Because I've done the same," Roger replied. "I was young, and I made another pirate a sireling. Seamus liked him, seemed to like him more than me. I was only ten years a vampire, but I'd seen his habits. I convinced my sireling to do something that humiliated Seamus in front of the crew. When he disappeared, I told myself that he ran away and joined another ship."

"But he didn't."

"I have no proof, but I doubt he did." Roger drew his shoulders straight. He had to face his past and refuse to allow it to drag him under its riptide. "His death was my fault, and it's a sin I don't feel guilt for. I can't stop to think of all the wrong I've done to survive. The guilt would grind me into dust. Whatever you've done, I won't judge you. I don't have the right, and I too keenly understand the need."

A bubble of a sob was lodged in Vincent, and he held it in. He had his clenched fists on the counter in front of him and bit his lip. Tears began to fall. Once started, they became rivers, and the sob broke out of him. "You're not supposed to get it. You're supposed to be a bastard and use me like the rest of them."

Roger put a hand on Vincent's shoulder. At first, the boy moved to shake him off, and Roger planned on allowing that, but then Vincent plunged toward him and locked his arms around him. As tenderly as he could, Roger returned the hug.

Each of Vincent's sobs rocked through Roger, shaking something loose deep in his soul.

The boy he'd been had never had a hug like this. Had never spoken once of what he'd endured. The man—the vampire he was—had barely mentioned the surface of his wounds from Seamus to his loved ones.

And because he couldn't hug that long-lost boy, he hugged Vincent with everything he wished he could have had himself.

CHAPTER 8

Another sunset. Every minute past dark added another pound to the weight on Roger's shoulders. Endless possible failures paraded through his imagination, each worse than the last. Would he be too late? Had Seamus broken Takashi's sanity? Was Zack still alive?

Roger could very well be leading Cal, Amber, and Thomas to their deaths. Even if they succeeded, Roger would have to watch out for treachery. Amber and Thomas seemed to hold him as an ally, but Cal never would.

Their meeting place was at a park a quarter mile from the edge of Seamus's property. Roger parked the car he'd borrowed from Nathaniel again farther away than that and used a burst of vampiric speed to bring him to the location well before the arranged time.

He'd outfitted a belt with his own version of a hunter's kit. He had a UV flashlight, a silver-plated dagger he'd found in a magic shop down the street from the Last Deal, and three stakes that Vincent had carved for him that day. In addition to those supplies, he had a small backpack with a few blood bags in case Takashi was starved.

The Wrights arrived on schedule. However, only Amber

hopped out of the truck. Cal and Thomas remained within while she approached. "They're just taking a second to go over the plan again."

Glass vibrated with their voices, transmitting far better than walls did. A human might not have made much sense of the muffled sounds, but Roger could pick out words. Cal wanted to stab him in the back before they ever left for the mansion. Thomas was scolding him.

Roger folded his arms over his chest and leaned against the tree. *Knew he would be the problem.* The rage he'd found last night churned again.

Instead of giving in to it, he focused on the exterior. He said dryly, "Honestly, I was hoping that they'd leave you at home."

"Because I'm a girl?" Amber demanded, voice full of teenage vitriol.

"Because you're a *child*."

She glared up at him. "I have more field experience than Zack does."

"Considering the hours he's put in on my mission, that's debatable," Roger replied. "Do you know why your parents deemed him 'unfit'?"

Amber's gaze darted to the side. She didn't squirm, didn't give in to the tiny burst of fear that expanded inside her. The fear was too vague and transient for Roger to discern what sort it was. She said, "I know. Up until this summer, I thought ... I thought Zack was the fuckup. But he values life. He spared someone who needed a chance."

"What changed over the summer?" Roger asked.

"We're not friends, okay?" Amber snapped. She gestured between them. "This is not some amazing bonding moment. You're on my shit list."

"Because the family dictates me an enemy?"

Amber stepped closer despite having to crane her head

farther back to glare up at him. "Because you got my brother kidnapped by psycho, torture-happy, ancient freaks."

She was her own person, but the pieces of her that mirrored Zack clawed at Roger's heart. *God, I hope he's alive.*

The truck doors opened. Amber whispered, "Hey, you should know—"

"Cal plans on putting a stake in my heart at the earliest convenience," Roger finished.

"Yeah ... guess that's pretty obvious."

Cal and Thomas stepped out of the truck. They were armed for combat in entirely different styles. Cal had gun holsters, multiple weapons in sight against his black clothing. His hunter's belt had a section of shotgun ammunition. He had an ammo belt that ran across his torso and a shotgun in his hands. A wealth of silver bullets glinted in the dim streetlight.

Thomas had a sword on his hip, a quiver on his back, and a bow over his shoulder. On his belt, he had a wooden stake, two flashlights—likely at least one of them was UV—and his sheathed enchanted blade. Amber was outfitted like her father, with a crossbow instead of a bow and a backpack.

"Let's get this fucking over with," Cal said as he stomped off in the direction of Seamus's mansion. Amber was quick to follow him.

Roger and Thomas brought up the rear. Roger said quietly, "I thought the plan was discretion. Why does he have firearms?"

"He's convinced we'll have to blast our way out. Might not be wrong."

"And he might be planning to kill innocents like he did in Texas," Roger snarled. He motioned at Cal. "I struggle to reconcile that *that* is the brother of a man I love. *That* would have left Vincent to rot. Zack does not condone my every action, but he makes an effort to understand. He calculates with compassion. He escaped the mold you pushed him into, and for that, you disowned him."

Thomas was quiet for long enough that Roger was certain their conversation was over. Then, in a soft whisper, he said, "He's always been brave. I didn't understand how brave until recently."

The thinnest touch of the desire to do things differently—regret—radiated from Thomas despite the shield of his hunter's tattoo. Roger allowed the silence between them to grow.

Cal must have sensed how close they were because he stopped creating unnecessary noise and began to slip through the darkness. The group's footfalls became as soft as predawn whispers between lovers.

When they reached the iron-wrought fence surrounding the property, Thomas held out a hand and took out his enchanted blade. He murmured a spell, and the blade's runes shifted in color to a dull orange. Carefully, he neared the fence, and the runes grew slightly brighter. "Basic intruder spell. Nothing lethal. Amber."

Amber pulled her backpack off and took out two iron hooks with a cord of silver between them. She knelt beside the fence and murmured a soft incantation as she put the hooks onto the fence. They were spaced two feet apart.

Once she'd nodded and backed away, Thomas used his blade and incantation to check that the spell was gone between the hooks. He nodded for Cal to go first.

"If I get cursed, I'm burning shit," Cal muttered. He grasped the iron fence. When nothing happened, he climbed over it.

Amber's spell and equipment had nullified a spot of Anton's magical defenses. The idea was simplistic and brilliant. Roger wouldn't have believed it could be done. Had Zack thought of such a scenario? Did he know the spell? Would they have been successful in defeating Seamus if

Roger had stopped to listen to any of Zack's ideas? *I will beg him to go through every possible plan. Every thought. I never want to give either of them up.*

Roger jumped over the fence, and then Thomas climbed over it, and finally Amber. The process took only seconds.

While light streamed out from various windows, Seamus's mansion loomed across the lawn. Roger had witnessed the construction of this mansion, visited it time and time again when Seamus wanted to check on the progress. Built in the 1920s, it imitated the structure of a French palace, yet it lacked any of the polished charm. Its edges felt cold and severe rather than graceful.

A pair of guards making their rounds pricked Roger's hearing before he saw them. He motioned for his group to fall in behind a tree. Tapping into his shadow abilities, he gathered darkness around them and deepened the shadow on top of them, obscuring them. The patrol passed on without hesitating.

Roger made a signal to wait and stretched out his senses to check the area. No one else was close. He gestured for the Wrights to move.

Thomas led the way to a window. He repeated his quick ritual to test for a magical barrier, but nothing came up. Quickly, he used his knife to slide open the window lock. After sheathing his blade, he hauled himself through the window first. Then Cal helped Amber in.

That left Cal and Roger outside, waiting for the other to go first. The next patrol wouldn't be forever. One of them would have to surrender and put their back to the other. *Am I the scorpion or the frog? Feel like the frog.*

With a huff, Thomas leaned out and offered his hand to Cal. Cal grimaced, handed his shotgun over to his father, and climbed through the window. Roger followed him.

As they moved down the hallway, Roger continued pushing the extent of his senses. The mansion was still, almost too still. Other than the Wrights' pulses, the occasional beating heart sounded far away. No distant conversations, no heavy breathing. Seamus must have taken most of the household with him to meet with Josefina.

But there was something ... else that Roger was feeling. It reminded him of Halloween—of when he'd felt the siren cast a spell on the mortals. There had been a snap in his mind, and suddenly, he had simply known more. This time, it was like running his fingers across a floorboard and finding the grooves left behind from use. Nothing discernable, nothing active.

Magic had been in this place.

How did he know that? Some aftereffect of his coma?

The path to the basement door was clear. Roger slipped on a pair of leather gloves and reached for the silver door handle. Standing so close to the door, a wave of ingrained fear rumbled through him. Not much of it was new fear. So much had happened around and beyond the door that it was stained with the remnants of terror.

The damn thing was locked.

Amber took out her lockpick kit while Cal, Roger, and Thomas kept an eye on their surroundings. Her movements with the lock were smooth, near silent.

"I don't like the feel of this," Cal whispered. "Too fucking easy."

Must be a cold day in Hell. I agree with him. Roger continued focusing on his senses rather than responding.

A moment later, Amber unlocked the door.

Roger took point as they headed down the basement stairs. If some surprise was waiting for them, he wanted the Wrights to have a chance to run or prepare. He wouldn't be able to buy them much time, especially considering the speed that supernaturals could move as opposed to humans, but they were trained for that sort of limited opening.

Cal followed, then Amber, and Thomas brought up the

rear. The weight that came with Cal's presence was almost enough for Roger to ignore the increasing sense of compounding dread bearing down on his soul. *No. I have to stop hiding from the pain.* He refocused on what was happening around him and the sensations his extra senses were telling him.

The basement was made of concrete and heavy stone so that the sound of the individual rooms was entirely blocked out from one another. Anyone in the hall might have heard echoing screams slipping through doors—and Roger was startled that there were none.

But that strange sensation of magic interrupted his chain of thoughts. It was less of a groove and more of a deep, empty river bed. *What has Anton been doing to my loves?*

Roger tried each door as he went past. The first four revealed identical, empty rooms. Ten feet by ten feet, they were clearly designed to be cells for captives. Though decades had passed, Roger had thrown others into these places before. Always at Seamus's bidding, but that didn't lessen his growing guilt. He could've said no. What would Seamus have done? How far could Roger have pushed him before he decided that the bet wasn't worth winning and killed him?

His spiral into what-ifs ended when he reached a fifth door and found it locked. Roger stepped out of the way and nodded to Amber, who set to work with her tools. Hope flared as soon as he heard the tumblers click open. He gripped the handle and pushed the door open.

Spanning from wall to wall and floor to ceiling, silver wires crisscrossed the room. The low light glinted off the wires. They had been stretched in a pattern that brushed against the man in the center of the room, threatening more damage if he moved.

The man hung from the ceiling by his wrists, toes barely touching the floor, without a stitch of clothing on his pale body. With his head fallen forward, his dark hair hid his face.

The silver touching him left angry red lines on his skin. Thin blood trails had danced down his arms, his cheeks, and his chest but were dried.

Roger knew him. He'd seen this man naked countless times.

Dmitri.

Old wounds were torn open and salted. Dmitri had believed Roger couldn't follow through with killing Anton and enacted a reckless plan that had ended with Roger killing a hunter in front of a crowd. During their last conversation, Dmitri had spoken oddly, displaying symptoms that he was giving in to his worse, self-destructive impulses. He'd wanted his agony to stop.

And Roger had been too willfully ignorant to realize that Dmitri's depression hadn't ended in his mortal days but continued into his long nights as a vampire. For three hundred years, Roger had been too caught up in his own shit to see that the man he'd tried to love time and time again was drowning in despair.

Roger had thought he was dead. Had thought that was what Anton meant when he said the gamble was settled.

I never know what's going on.

This wasn't the time to brood on his inadequacies as a lover and a friend. He glanced around at where the silver wires connected to the walls, searching for some way to dismantle them.

"Oh my God," Amber whispered, horror plain in her voice.

"We have to get him down." Roger stepped into the room. He tugged on a wire, and it pulled taut against Dmitri. The sizzle of skin started immediately, and Dmitri cried out, jostling into other strands. Instantly, Roger let go. In order to break it from the wall, he'd have to use more force, which would increase its tension against Dmitri. "Tell me one of you thought to bring wire cutters."

Amber slipped her backpack off her shoulders and dug into it.

Thomas had his enchanted blade in one hand and a stake in the other. He examined the room. "Is this Takashi?"

"No," Roger said.

"Then we need to move. Amber—"

The rage inside Roger whipped into a violent storm, and he grabbed Thomas roughly and shoved him against the wall. A note of thunder rolled into his voice. *"We are not leaving him."*

Sternness filled Thomas's eyes, the kind that came from having to make life and death calculations too many times. "We don't have the resources to rescue inconsequential—"

"That is Dmitri, he who has been by my side longer than anyone else on this Earth. That is the man who has kept me sane, though I have never been able to do the same for him," Roger snarled. "If you need a *tactical* reason, he has been in charge of Seamus's finances for over a hundred years. He has a wealth of knowledge that I am sure he would *love* to share with hunters."

During Roger's speech, the soft sound of snips of metal began. Amber continued cutting away the silver as she said, "Also, this is too fucked-up to not do something, Dad. And we don't have time to argue."

Concern entered Thomas's expression before Roger mentioned Dmitri's knowledge. Upon his daughter's words, Thomas made a gesture. That tiny flick of movement brought Roger's attention to what was going on beyond them. Cal had the shotgun aimed at them, likely not taking any shot so he wouldn't wind up shooting his own father, but clearly prepared to blast them both if he had to. He glared intently at Roger before nodding to his father and carrying on down the hall.

"We'll keep searching," Thomas said. "Work fast."

Roger nodded and released Thomas. He stepped back into

the room. Amber had dismantled enough of the wires that he could approach Dmitri. Using an abundance of caution, he did so. Gently, he cupped his face. "Dmitri, it's me."

Dmitri lifted his head. His dark eyes were layered with rings of exhaustion and dried bloody tears. His voice broke with pain as he asked, "Roger?"

"Yes, sweetheart." Roger looked for a mechanism to lower him from the ceiling, but it was through more wire. He pointed it out to Amber.

"I know," she murmured under her breath and kept cutting. Roger was about to tell her to hurry, but he noticed that she wasn't dawdling in how she cut the silver. She was taking a few extra seconds between snips because she was ensuring that whatever she cut next wouldn't whiplash across the room and hurt Dmitri.

"I'm going to get you out of here," Roger whispered.

Dmitri began to cry. Fresh, bloody tears coated the old ones.

"I love it when I'm right," Anton said with a joyful sigh.

Roger spun. The shadows in the corner of the room thickened, and Anton walked out of them as if he were walking through a door. He was pale as white marble, his eyes were deep red, and his platinum hair was tied back for a change. He dropped the jacket of his pinstripe black three-piece suit and began to roll the sleeves of his white dress shirt.

"I told Seamus that Josefina's visit was terribly convenient, but he insisted that we both go meet her. Luckily, I had alarms set on my favorite toy." Anton grinned wickedly.

Dmitri whimpered, and the overwhelming anxiety pouring from him sparked a chain of lightning into the impending storm of Roger's rage.

Relying on every ounce of speed he had, Roger grasped one of the silver threads hanging loose in the room and weaved through the remaining strands in his way. Anton started to extend shadowy tendrils to catch him, but he countered by using his own shadow as a blade against them. He wrapped the thread around Anton's throat.

Anton managed to get his hand between his throat and the wire. The bastard was laughing.

Cutting off his hand would work. Roger pulled as tight as he could, even as Anton attempted to yank the wire free. With effort, Roger managed to wrap the wire around a second time. He shoved Anton against the wall and hissed in his face.

Desire oozed from Anton, a sickeningly thick sensation against Roger's mental shields. He murmured, "You've always been pretty, but now you're fucking hot."

"Fucking die," Roger snapped.

"We have the wrong energy going here." Anton's dark red eyes flared a brighter red.

That thick, invisible, mucus-like desire crept over Roger, but he had long known where his own wants lay. He had manipulated other's emotions with the same power Anton was wielding.

And he had a burning wish for vengeance. He pulled that into a mental wall so thick that Anton's attempt to control him slithered off.

Anton's smile turned slyer, and he rolled up against Roger. He purred, "Honestly, this way is hotter. It's been a while since I've wanted a spanking, but you have me yearning for all kinds of nasty punishments."

"I'm not playing a fucking game," Roger snarled.

"Oh, but games are wonderful *distractions.*"

Damn it, I've been focusing on the wrong thing. Roger had missed when the snips of wire had stopped. Sounds of scuffle in the hallway told him that combat was going on there as well. The blast of a shotgun roared from farther away.

That fractional slide of his attention gave Anton the opportunity to rear back and headbutt him. The blow stunned Roger for less than a second, but between creatures who could move quickly, it was too long. Anton slammed his free hand against the center of Roger's chest and knocked him against the opposing wall, snapping wires as he went.

Dmitri wailed like an animal in pain, and his bloody tears now coursed down from his cheeks to his chest.

Roger landed beside Amber. She had drawn her dagger, but it had slipped her grasp and fallen to the floor. Tendrils of shadow held her pinned to the wall despite her attempts to yank herself free. One of them was locked around her neck, and another was over her mouth. As Roger watched, the one on her mouth thickened to block her nose. Her cheeks flushed pink from exertion, and terror filled her eyes.

With a growl, Roger snatched her dagger from the floor and pulled his silver-plated one from his belt. "Let her go."

"Oh, but she is marvelous," Anton said smoothly. He made a small hand motion with his right hand, but his left continued to move as if orchestrating strings. "You can feel it, can't you? That first primal terror. She's never been overpowered like this before. Her blood would be rich, Roger."

"If she dies," Roger said, "no corner on this Earth will be able to hide you from the suffering I will bring you before sending your soul to rot in Hell where it belongs."

And, unsurprisingly to Roger, Anton's smile only grew. "I must say, once again, how absolutely fucking *hot* you are right now."

"Anton!"

"I would have thought that you cared more about Zack's well-being than hers. Or his." As Anton threaded his way to Dmitri through the remaining wires, he plucked them. He put a hand on Dmitri's chest, and the sound that came out of Dmitri was unnaturally high. "I heard your little threat to the older hunter. I know you still care about our poor, sad Dmitri."

Anton mimicked a pout. His eyes still sparkled with a joke.

"If you're going to talk, let her breathe," Roger demanded.

"Fine," Anton said with a roll of his eyes. He gestured with his right hand, and the tendril blocking Amber's nose thinned to cover only her mouth, and the one on her throat eased. His left had stopped moving, but sounds of combat were still going on in the hall.

What else was Anton doing? Was he bringing Seamus here? Stalling for his arrival? Torturing someone else? Roger hated not knowing, but asking would lead him nowhere. Everyone else's lives were games to Anton.

And though the games changed, some of the basics remained the same. Roger had played through other versions of this. If he used that knowledge, he might be able to maneuver out of this. Roger asked lightly, "Did Seamus drag you out of the mansion so you couldn't play while he was gone?"

Anton narrowed his eyes.

"He considers Zack and Takashi treasures, and he's warned you not to spoil them," Roger replied. "Let me walk out of here with them, and you'll have his full attention again."

"This attempt at being clever is making you quite dull," Anton said with a sigh. He stroked Dmitri's chest. "However, I am prepared to make you a deal."

Roger's heart dropped like a stone. Anton always kept his deals, but he'd once seen him offer a man that he wouldn't harm a hair on his head and then promptly use a spell that made the man lose all his hair. Then the torture had started.

But he had to do something. Sooner or later, Seamus would come home.

"I'm listening," Roger said.

"I can let you leave with your little band of hunters, and I'll even give you Dmitri. Or—" Anton's eyes glittered, and his smile returned. "—I can keep everyone but you, and I'll tell you where Zack and Takashi are."

Callum Wright was worth nothing. Thomas would be a loss, but Zack would survive it.

But Amber? No. Roger couldn't let her suffer. He had sworn no more innocents would come to harm because of him, and she was only in danger because he'd failed to prepare for this. He couldn't abandon the others, not if he wanted to be able to meet his lovers' gazes again.

And then there was Dmitri, for whom his heart would always ache.

Without hesitation, he said, "I'll take the hunters and Dmitri."

"What an interesting choice!" Anton declared. "I must say, I *love* this new side of you, Roger. You're finally something close to fascinating."

Anton snapped his fingers, and the shadowy tendrils gripping Amber melted away. She started to fall, but Roger caught her. Still fighting for air, her first instinct was to snatch her blade back from him, and he let her have it. The runes glowed with bright white light, and she fought for her balance to face Anton.

Anton's attention was on Dmitri. He stroked his cheek and murmured, "I'll see you again, my sweet."

Roger held on to Amber because if he let her go, he would try to kill Anton again, and they would all lose.

"You have ten minutes until I call the mansion's security," Anton said without taking his gaze off Dmitri. He grinned broadly as he backed away into the shadows. "Maybe less."

Anton vanished the way he'd arrived. Knowing that the trick was going to happen, Roger could use that extra sense to feel the shape of where Anton had been. Could he have followed him? *But where is he going?*

He had to deal with what was before him. Though he'd stopped her from hitting the floor, Amber was unsteady on her feet. They didn't have time to waste. With a note of authority in his voice, he said, "On your feet, hunter. We need to get him down."

Amber had a hand on her throat. But his tone and words gave her focus, and she nodded, pushing down the fear until it was a minor pulse against Roger's senses.

By the time she had undone the mechanism, Roger was prepared to catch Dmitri. He broke the handcuffs off him. Then he swept him up into his arms and murmured words of comfort to him.

Dmitri clung to him like he hadn't done for centuries. His cries might have been sobs if he'd had more energy. The emotions that Roger could read from him were incoherent. *Can he even hear me?*

Thomas came to the door of the room, though he kept his true attention on the hallway. "Got it handled out here for the moment. You two all right?"

"Alive," Amber croaked.

Stronger than his tattoo could hide for him, fear for one's child emanated from Thomas. He glanced at Amber, and a righteous fury was clear in the clench of his jaw.

"We have to go," Roger said.

"We haven't found Zack."

The truth stabbed Roger in the heart. He'd known they hadn't, or Anton wouldn't have bargained with the information. *We're in the wrong place. We won't find either of them down here.* "If we stay, we're dead."

Thomas puffed up.

"Dad, the op is blown." Amber stashed the wire cutters in her backpack and put it on with professional quickness. She kept her blade in her hand, and it continued to flare with white light.

Amber's words cut Thomas's resistance to shreds. Needing a hand free, Roger gently put Dmitri over his shoulder, and the four of them made their way out of the building and escaped into the night.

CHAPTER 9

Without a clock or a window, Takashi had to rely on his internal sense of time. Sleeping had thrown off his estimates, but he could feel in his bones that the sun was down. Considering his hunger, he figured that the hour was probably in the neighborhood of ten o'clock.

Pacing wasn't an effective use of energy, but he wasn't content to sit still and wait for someone to fetch him. He needed patience to see him through this terrible turn of events, but he needed movement to settle his mind. Summoning calm wasn't easy on an empty stomach. The gray bands the night before hadn't been satisfying. Disconnected from their emotions, they were as fulfilling as a glass of ice water—gratifying for the moment he was swallowing, but not for long after.

Midstep, his shadow reached up from the floor and wrapped around his ankle. It yanked him toward the floor. He avoided faceplanting on the wooden boards, landing on his hands and knees. Tendrils roiled out of his shadow and latched around his wrists, forearms, and thighs. No amount of pushing freed him from the inky-black pseudopods. When he growled, a tendril snaked up and wrapped around his mouth.

This sort of magic had to be Anton's doing. But why pin him to the floor of a room no one else was in?

Agonizing minutes later, the door swung open. Anton was dressed for an evening out, though he'd left behind his suit jacket and rolled up his sleeves. He regarded Takashi with the same impassively cold demeanor he'd had at the end of their last conversation.

A twinge twisted Takashi's heart because Anton was *breathtaking*. He knew what he was, what he wanted, and the only opinion that mattered was his lover's. People spoke of greatness as if it was something achieved, but it was grown. Nurtured and cultivated. Where other older vampires faded into pettiness, Anton was a mystery. An undead force of magic and persistence.

He was a blazing star.

You're falling for the same bullshit that's broken your spirit too many times. Sergei. Kuwat. Nobu. Faustino. Roger. Charismatic, gorgeous men had always lulled Takashi's sensibilities. He was drawn to their orbit, unwilling to deny their gravitational pull, even when he knew better. *I cannot afford to drop my guard around this monster. He will devour me. Perhaps literally.*

"Come along," Anton said, crooking his finger for Takashi to follow him. He turned on his heel and walked out of the room. His bootheels clicked, each sound echoing with confidence.

Takashi was about to make a noise despite the gag in his mouth to point out that he couldn't do as commanded. Then the shadows rose up underneath him and carried him into the hall. The touch of them became colder, firmer, almost as if they were solid creatures. Riding them was like being carried in a blanket by several others. One side would jostle him, the other dipped. It was unnerving.

Anton stopped beside a window and leaned against the

wall, gazing outward. Languidly, he waved his hand, and the shadows receded into the floor, depositing Takashi. In a musing tone, Anton said, "I have been thinking about you a great deal."

Slowly, Takashi stood and joined Anton. The view beyond was of the darkened yard. The mansion's grounds went on for a little way, and a tall fence marked the edge of the property. Other than a few large trees and the occasional set of bushes, the field of grass was unremarkable. Due to the light in the hallway, the details were harder to pick out, but as far as Takashi could tell, there was nothing interesting to see.

"I'm flattered," Takashi said smoothly.

"You don't know what sort of thoughts I've been having," Anton replied.

A ghost of a grin graced Takashi's lips, and he leaned against the opposite side of the window from Anton. "Well, I'm not screaming in agony nor confined to a box at the bottom of a ravine, so I'd like to believe they aren't all that negative."

"Always clever. Always careful." Anton rested his head against the window frame, and a wistful smile creased his lips. "I remember the first time you came to the city. You were hiding in Nell's shadow. You sought the edge of the room, watching us with wide eyes."

"I was less than thirty years a vampire surrounded by beings more than ten times my age in a city run by gangsters. A little trepidation was in order."

"I suppose." Anton's gaze sharpened as he met Takashi's, and his smile grew sly. "How much of it was a front?"

"Excuse me?" Takashi asked. But his voice threatened to catch in his throat. Only experience kept his tone even. "I don't know what you mean."

Anton stepped closer and put his hand on Takashi's chest. "I raked my claws through you, Takashi. I may not know your thoughts, but I know the shape of your desires."

The deflection was quick to his lips, but Takashi paused. Bluffs were the easiest way to survive the various covens of vampires that he dealt with.

But eventually, there had to be a time when the bullshit was dropped. Anton had been in his mind and pillaged for those deeper feelings. The walls between his outer self and inner self had a gap, and Anton was pressing his eye to it, peering through to him.

Takashi lightly pushed Anton's hand away and turned toward the window. "And you must know that I love Roger. That I want to see him and Zack safe and happy."

"They are easy to love, aren't they?" Anton asked. "Handsome, sensual Roger, who constantly pleases everyone around him. Beautiful, brilliant Zack, who can pierce through the thickest shield. They were plotting my lover's death, but I don't hate them."

Anton was speaking of them as if they were still alive. That might be a ruse, but Takashi allowed the detail to raise his spirits. He slid his hands into his pants pockets and stared out into the darkness. Somewhere, his lovers were alive. *How can I play my cards to convince Anton to tell me what I want to know? Can I trust anything he says?*

"Watching the wheels of your mind turn is marvelous," Anton said cheerfully. He brushed his fingers through Takashi's black hair. "I am especially amazed at how you suppress your truest self."

Takashi dipped his head out of Anton's touch, shot him a quick glare, and then returned his gaze to the dark yard. Creatures as old as Anton always wanted entertainment. Giving in easily never thrilled them. Walking the line between teasing them, denying them, and flattering them was a tough, high-wire act, but he'd had decades of practice. Every vampire court had someone like Anton, though he usually didn't wind up with so much alone time with them.

"This time I'm certain that I'm lost to your meaning," Takashi replied.

"I was in your mind," Anton said, his voice slithering. "You play the part of gentleman well, but I know what lies beneath."

Once more, Anton put his hand on Takashi's chest. He slid his touch upward, reaching to caress Takashi's throat.

Takashi caught his wrist and tugged his hand off. "I wouldn't want to upset your lover nor either of mine."

"If he knew what I knew, you'd be *dead*," Anton whispered into Takashi's ear. Then he moved behind him to continue speaking in his other ear. "You paint a pretty picture with the way you carry yourself. The way you smile and speak. You are a very clever boy. Of course you were not content to be Nell's errand fledgling, flitting about the globe at her whims. You certainly won't be happy as my lover's captive—*sorry*, 'guest.'"

Anton was attempting to elicit a reaction. Takashi had played this sort of game with dozens of others over the years. Even Nell pushed him like this from time to time. He chose to say nothing.

"Perhaps this will help." Anton lifted a hand, and the lights in the hallway snapped out. He purred, "Now, it's you, me, and the darkness. You can admit it to me."

"Admit what?"

"What your heart desires." The movement of Anton's jaw lightly brushed his skin against Takashi's. "You knew Roger was weak, yet you threw your lot in with him anyway. Because you seek what she was never willing to give you. Power."

"Who of our kind doesn't?" Takashi countered.

"Perhaps," Anton murmured. "But not like you. You don't seek the glory or the fame. You don't want a throne. Your greed won't be satisfied with that."

Takashi fortified every gap in his mental walls. He sought

to seek any interference, but Anton wasn't pressing into his mind again. That one deep glimpse the other night must have given him everything. *Or have I been obvious but surrounded by fools?*

"You hoped that Roger was strong enough to claim the mantle," Anton continued. He stepped back from Takashi. "One can hardly blame you. He has always been a charmer, but he is too weak to become a master of a coven. He is no leader, and part of you knows that. Wanted to take advantage of that."

No, part of him declared loudly. But it was part of the lie he had been telling himself. Roger had always looked outside himself, and Takashi had seen that as an opening. When Nell had pushed them together in Taliville, Takashi was overjoyed that his chance at real freedom, and the power it would take to keep it would come with Roger. Because Roger would treat him like an equal and would *need* him to manage responsibilities. Roger would seek his guidance.

A spark of love had always existed between them, but Takashi had been willing to snuff it out if he had to, especially when Roger declared that Zack's happiness came first.

Instead of shoving him away, Zack had pulled him in and kissed him. With Roger's charm, Zack's brilliance, and Takashi's networking, they could become a force the world would have to reckon with. All that stood in their way was Seamus.

No. What stood in our way was Roger's indecisiveness. He cost us everything. The thought was bitter, and Takashi hated it. He had glimpsed beneath the veneer of Roger's bright smiles. Roger had the deepest wounds of anyone Takashi had ever known, yet he continued to live. To love. To hope.

"You are strangling the fiercest part of yourself. All for a man who isn't worth the effort, Takashi." Anton leaned against the window frame and looked out.

A two-person patrol was striding along their path, the

slow creep of their progress speaking to the sheer size of the property. Was it supposed to be some metaphor?

But then Takashi spied a group of figures moving away from the mansion and toward the fence. Four individuals were running, with a fifth over the tallest one's shoulder. There wasn't enough light in the yard to perceive color, only dim grays and blacks of shadows. The tallest figure was one Takashi had seen too intimately, even in shadows, not to recognize.

"Roger?" he whispered.

"He came for you and Zack," Anton crooned, "but he found tortured, damaged Dmitri."

Experience enabled Takashi to keep his expression neutral rather than give in to the sad frown threatening to wash over him. Dmitri was Roger's love-that-never-worked-out. In the 1920s, they'd been recently broken up, and Takashi had seen how the two looked at each other when they thought the other wasn't. A hundred years later, that longing remained, though hidden further below the surface. But to choose him over Takashi? Over Zack?

Anton is at my ear, and he is running. Something must have happened between them. At least Roger had made an attempt. After two months of hardly making waves in the GLC, he hadn't taken that long to seek them out. *But this also means Roger believed that Zack was here. Seamus and Anton must have abducted him as well.*

But Anton wasn't forcing Roger to stay behind. Despite plotting against them, Seamus and Anton didn't think of either Roger or Dmitri as a threat. *Considering how quickly they kicked our asses at the hotel, they might not fear us at all.* Then why keep Takashi? Why try the tact of polite hostage keepers rather than resort to the torture they were known for? Of course, torture didn't come in one shape, and pain could be rendered to the soul as easily as the flesh, but if that was the case, they were taking a slow approach with him. What were they doing to Zack?

In theory, Takashi could leap through the window in front of him and try to reach Roger. That might be why Anton was showing his escape. This whole act was a setup to see how Takashi would react. Perhaps it wasn't even real but rather an illusion.

Everything between vampires was a game. Analyzing strategy was how Takashi had stayed alive through the various courts he'd visited. Right now, Anton was feeling him out and applying pressure where he thought it'd have impact. He'd fallen onto the subjects of love and power. He'd called Takashi out on not being true to himself. And Takashi couldn't. Bits of mortal morality still clung to him at the worst times. Seeking power for power's sake, that was the mindset of a vampire.

Yet if I'd been doing that, perhaps Zack and I wouldn't be fucked. Roger would be the coven master already, or we'd be dead and not having to run this gambit. Takashi lowered his gaze at that thought. Ambition was a fine thing in theory, but to follow it purely with intent over centuries was what led to the heartless vampires Takashi had seen across the globe.

Anton opened the window. Cool night air rushed in and enveloped Takashi as Anton stepped off to the side. "You can flee with Roger if you like. My love will be angry. He'll probably put a price on your head. You'd have to keep a low profile, even if you left our territory. You could return to Roger's side, continue scheming against my lover and I.

"Of course, you'd also sacrifice the opportunity sitting in front of you. After all, my lover hasn't killed you yet. He's sought your advice about international vampires. He values your expertise. You and Zack could have places in my lover's court and in our home. With us, you could rise to become something more than a weak vampire's idea man. What do you want more? A little bit of passion or to manipulate strings for centuries?"

Takashi put his hands on the windowsill. Everything Anton was saying was technically true. If he left with Roger, he would find himself in the same hole. Certainly, Seamus would have stripped Roger of his position in the coven. That he was still alive probably had more to do with the bet he and Anton had. But why let him run free unless it was either torture for him or they believed him so weak he was inconsequential? *Likely both.*

If Takashi stayed, he might be able to help Zack. Additionally, he'd be in a better position to study Anton and Seamus. Opportunities to shove wedges into the cracks between the two were far more possible inside the mansion rather than out in the world. *What is so wrong about wanting power? About longing to be heard and appreciated by one's peers and not just one's lovers? Why should I fear it?*

The only thing he knew Roger could offer was his love, and that would be tainted with sadness of their separation from Zack.

The fleeing figures were nearing the fence at the edge of the property. Takashi could still drop from the window and join them in seconds. A good man would run. *That's what Roger is. He needs me to be a good* vampire. *I am far more useful here.*

Takashi reached up and closed the window.

"I do love when I'm right," Anton said with a smile. He put his hand on Takashi's shoulder. "Let's find you someone to eat."

CHAPTER 10

Few runs in Roger's life had been filled with the growing dread and guilt that currently filled his veins. The last few feet to the Gladwell Manor door. The night he'd fled Paris, constantly looking over his shoulder for the hunters on their tails. And this one. Anton had let them go, but his bargain was also fulfilled. Would he sweep in and demand another? Take Dmitri back?

Dmitri was practically a dead weight over Roger's shoulder. After being lifted into place, he hadn't moved. Hadn't made a sound. Roger had never seen a vampire die without losing their heart or their head. Yet his stillness was troubling. *Dmitri has to be alive. He just has to be.*

They reached the parking lot where the Wrights' truck waited. Roger was about to zip off into the night, but Thomas grabbed his arm and made him turn around.

"What happened in there?" Thomas demanded.

"Who gives a shit?" Cal snapped. And he aimed the shotgun at Roger's head.

As Cal began to squeeze the trigger, Roger pivoted to the left. He used a burst of speed to move to the far side of the parking lot and deposit Dmitri. Then he rushed back toward

Cal. The first blast had fired; Cal was sweeping around to aim at him a second time.

Roger pounced, knocking Cal to the ground. If Cal wanted a fight to the death, so be it. Roger needed the blood anyway. He lunged for Cal's throat.

But Cal managed to get the shotgun barrel between them. He used it as a bar against Roger's chest to keep him back.

Another denial. Another failure. Roger was so sick of failure. With a growl, he grabbed the shotgun and pressed it downward. A mortal's strength was no match for his, and he didn't have to have this fucker's blood. It would've been a bonus. But all he truly wanted was this monster before him to stop moving. He forced the barrel under Cal's chin and began to choke him with it.

"Roger, stop!"

Zack?

The thought, the blink, the moment was enough to snap him out of his survivalist anger. He eased his grip only a fraction.

Which was likely the only way he didn't knock Cal's head off when Thomas tackled him. Roger disentangled himself from the scramble and rose to his feet.

Thomas held out his hand in a stop gesture. Zack hadn't spontaneously arrived; Thomas had called his name. His voice had sounded too much like Zack's and unintentionally tricked Roger. He continued holding his right hand toward Roger while he made the same signal to Cal with his left. "We have enough going on without you two trying to kill each other!"

"He started it," Roger snarled. "I am tired of his fucking bullshit!"

"And I'm tired of yours! I bet you handed Zack over to him, you freak!" Cal shouted, his words breaking from the effort on his damaged throat. He reached for his shotgun.

Amber slid it out of the way and pulled it into her hands.

When Cal motioned for her to hand it over, she took three steps back and raised it to aim at him. Her hands trembled. The red mark around her throat had lessened to a fine line that was bound to become a bruise. She was hurt. Terrified. Her jittery finger was on the trigger.

She was a fatal accident waiting to happen.

As much as Roger longed for Callum Wright's death, he couldn't let Amber be at fault. Not when she was clearly trying to help by keeping the weapon away from her brother. He reached out with his power and fed her desire for calm, for peace.

She blinked, and the light shaking throughout her body began to steady.

"Amber," Roger said softly. "Do everyone a favor and unload the weapon."

"Got it." Quickly, Amber emptied the shotgun shells to the pavement. There had been another three rounds.

"Did you see *that*?" Cal demanded as he leapt to his feet. He gestured at Amber while addressing his father. "You're not going to ignore that, are you? Stake the son of a bitch!"

"Shut up," Thomas said with the tone of a man who'd been waiting too long to utter the words. "Just shut the fuck up, Cal."

"Dad—"

Thomas whirled on his son. "Roger just saved your life."

"After he—"

"Enough, Cal!" Thomas snapped. "Roger could have convinced her to pull the trigger. Instead, he spared you. I don't know that I'd have the strength in his place. So right now, I don't want to hear another goddamn word out of you. I don't want you to move a goddamn muscle. Because I just might let him snap your neck."

Cal hadn't shown a second of remorse after accidentally staking Zack in the shoulder, and he showed no regret now.

He looked at his father with the anger of the betrayed, but he shut his mouth.

Thomas stepped to the side rather than turn his back to his son. Speaking to Roger and Amber, he asked again, "What happened back there?"

"Anton," Amber croaked. "Came out of nowhere."

"He said that Dmitri had some sort of alarm spell on him," Roger said.

"So we might have found Zack if we hadn't stopped." Thomas clenched his fist.

"I don't think so," Roger replied. "Anton offered a bargain for the information. I don't think he would have done that if I was close. He would want their location to be a taunt. Three doors down isn't as painful as being in the entirely wrong place to him."

"But you don't know for certain," Thomas said.

"Dad, he was going to kill us," Amber said. "And you saw how Dmitri was tied up. Zack wouldn't have wanted us to leave him."

"What if your brother's in that condition? Or worse?" Thomas demanded. When Amber dipped her head, Thomas let out a frustrated groan and wiped a hand down his face. "I'm sorry. I'm not angry at you. You saw pain, and you wanted to help stop it. You're right. Zack would want to do the same."

"If he was really a Wright, he'd already be *dead*," Cal complained. When Thomas glared at him, Cal shrugged. "What? We're not supposed to be taken alive. Who knows what kind of family secrets he's already given up to his fang master over there."

"God, why did I ever waste time thinking you were the cool brother?" Amber said.

"I *am* the cool brother," Cal replied. "If you're thinking otherwise, it's because that bloodsucker is messing with your head. When we get home—"

"I'm not going home," Thomas said quietly. The words were so soft that Roger almost didn't hear them in the commotion, but the look in his eyes as he met Roger's gaze was one of conviction. "Not until my son is safe."

Roger nodded.

"Same," Amber said. "Though I mean brother, not son. Obviously."

"Amber, you need to go—" Thomas started to say.

"Do you honestly believe she would be safer with them?" Roger asked softly.

The question startled Thomas. He first stared at Roger like he was an alien for the suggestion, but a moment passed, and a glimpse of understanding hardened his expression into one of deep regret. The Wrights and the Gladwells were toxic, and Thomas must have finally seen that in how they treated Zack. *Hell, his other son is proving the point for me.*

"You switched me to homeschooling. I can do my home-work literally anywhere," Amber said. Then she winced and rubbed at her throat.

Thomas wiped his hand down his face. The bags under his eyes were darker than they had been a minute ago. "All right."

"You can't go with him!" Cal thrust his hand out toward Roger.

Thomas slapped a set of keys into Cal's hand. "Tell your mother that the passwords are taped to the underside of the drawer in Zack's room. She probably won't think to look for them there."

"Dad, I heard what Mom said tonight. If you don't come home—"

"Your mother has to realize she doesn't decide what's right and wrong for everyone else," Thomas said.

"She is going to flip if Amber doesn't come back with me."

Amber stepped closer to her father, and Thomas put an

arm around her shoulders. "I guess we'll have to see how that plays out. Go home, Cal."

"But in a moment." Roger rushed forward, grabbed the keys from Cal's hand, and tossed them so they slid under the truck. Then he hurried to grab Dmitri again and rejoin Amber and Thomas. "We should get moving."

"Goddamn son of a bitch." Cal ran over to the truck, but he had to crawl under it for the keys.

"Why'd you do that?" Amber asked.

"Didn't need him to attempt to run us over." Roger nodded in the direction of Nathaniel's car. "I'll lead the way."

With Amber and Thomas following and Dmitri over his shoulder, Roger crossed the parking lot and threaded his way through the trees of the park toward the car on the far side. *Takashi. Zack. I'm so sorry. I will not give up on you.*

CHAPTER 11

Darkness.

Utter, complete, world-encompassing lack-of-light darkness.

When Zack first opened his eyes, he wasn't sure he had. The seamless black didn't change no matter how many times he rapidly batted his eyelids. He couldn't see. With a shout, he reached for his face to feel for the damage.

But his face was smooth, not a blemish or a bruise. He wasn't in pain either.

That doesn't make sense. Does it? Why would I be in pain? What happened?

His memories came in a confusing blur. Certain things he knew as true: his name was Zackery Benedict Wright. He'd been born October 31, 2001. He had an older brother and a younger sister. But he'd been living with Roger since his parents disowned him a few months ago.

There. A recent memory snapped into place. He'd fought Cal because Cal was trying to kill Roger. And he'd pushed Roger out of the way and taken a stake to his shoulder. A day later, he'd moved into Nell's mansion with Roger for extra security, and he'd discovered that his family had locked him out of his social media accounts and changed the passwords on the family accounts that he'd monitored.

Was that what he was supposed to be recovering from?

No, no. Life had gone on after that. Zack raced down the road of memories leading from that first signpost. He'd moved to Chicago with Kit and Carver and Roger and Takashi. *Takashi*. Roger and Takashi were his boyfriends. Takashi had given him a beautiful necklace for his birthday. Reflexively, Zack went to touch his neck and discovered it was missing. When Takashi had given him the tiny white-gold dagger, he'd kissed him.

He and Takashi had shared a dance at the ball. That was where he'd worn the necklace. And Zack had danced with Roger. That dance, *God*, that dance had changed the world, hadn't it? Because not only had Roger stood up to Seamus, but he had nullified Seamus's attempt to cause fear among the partygoers. Roger had started to pull Zack to his side as an equal instead of upholding the vampire bullshit of calling him a pet.

But Zack hadn't been able to relish what Roger had done because he'd noticed Vincent was missing. Vincent ... confusion threatened to sweep in, but Zack held to the road. Vincent had been in the bathroom. He'd been beaten, and Zack had insisted on helping him.

The group of them had left the party. Carver, Kit, Vincent, Takashi, Roger, and him. Not left, fled. Because Seamus was pissed. And Roger had learned ... something that was eluding Zack. That something was important.

But not as important as the way Seamus broke into the hotel suite and tore into Carver's neck. Zack had come out of the master bedroom, dagger in hand, and he'd thrown it straight for Seamus's head. The fucker had dodged, but Zack had felt the movement of his cold aura and met him in battle.

Battle.

Fuck me, I lost. Zack ran his hands down his cheeks.

Thinking of the blows Seamus had landed caused phantom aches, so he refocused on the present.

The room was too dark. The bed too stiff. Hospital beds shouldn't be so goddamn stiff. Only, Zack didn't have any wires or machines attached to him. They'd need to monitor his heart rate, right? Were hospital rooms ever pitch-black?

How long was I out? Zack groaned and started reaching for the edge of the bed. He touched a wall on his right and then another on his left. The firmness had to be some sort of trick. They must have boxed him in out of caution. *I guess they didn't want me to accidentally roll out of bed and hurt myself.*

He moved to sit up, but his head bumped into the ceiling within a few inches. Something stiff was at his back.

Ceiling? What was he doing close to the ceiling? As he lay back down, he realized his enchanted dagger was tucked into the back of his belt. What was that doing on him? Weird to put that in bed with a patient. And weird that he'd have it and be up against the ceiling. He ran his hand along it, the slick satin cool to the touch.

Satin.

He wasn't in a bed.

He was in a *coffin*.

They buried me alive! Zack put both hands on the lid and pushed, but it didn't budge. "No. No, no no no no no no."

With a scream, he pushed with all his might. Adrenaline surged, making him stronger than he'd ever felt, but even that wasn't enough. He teetered toward panic and gave in to repetitively pounding on the lid.

He was going to die because no one had noticed that he was still alive! Screams tore out of him. His panic grew. *Stop it! You'll run out of air!*

A calmer, more detached version of his own voice answered, *Why haven't you already?*

The singular thought shunted his panic to the back of his mind. He held his hand to the satin lining. If he had been in a coffin long enough to heal his injuries, he should have run out of oxygen. And Roger and Takashi would have been able to hear the slightest sign of life.

So, to test his forming hypothesis, Zack held his breath and waited for his lungs to burn.

And waited.

And waited.

And *waited*.

No burn came.

That shouldn't be possible. Zack thrust his hand through his hair, holding on near his roots to ground himself from the new wave of mounting anxiety.

Another memory sprang forward. For a fraction of time during the fight, Seamus had grabbed his hair like this while raining blows down on him. Each slam of his fist or foot had brought such pain that Zack had struggled to stay conscious.

Zack had clung to one desperate desire: the urge to kill Seamus. Beyond the need for survival, the hot liquid pull of revenge had filled him. Because Seamus had killed Carver. Had forced Zack's hand into cutting Kit. Was planning to hurt his lovers. Seamus was trying to kill his family; not his blood family, but his *actual* family.

I promised myself vengeance. And then … And then Seamus had cradled Zack and told him he could slip away into death, or he could drink Seamus's blood and become a vampire. Seamus had said, "All you have to do is open your mouth, and it's yours."

There had been other words, ones that Zack couldn't recall with perfect clarity because he'd been caught in the moment of that choice.

Go out in a valiant effort.

Or become everything his parents and grandparents and ancestors had always hated.

A corpse couldn't have revenge.

A vampire could.

He'd opened his mouth, and Seamus had put his wrist against it. His blood had been honey-sweet, and it brought a strange tingling zip to Zack's tongue that coursed down to his fingers and toes. He'd swallowed once, twice, and then he latched onto Seamus and drank as fast as he could. He'd ... oh, God, he'd chewed into Seamus's arm when his blood had begun to slow and reopened his vein.

"Go on." Seamus had stroked his hand through Zack's hair like he was trying to comfort and encourage him. "Drink your fill, my precious boy."

Each drop brought more of that electric feeling, and a distant part of his mind knew what it meant. Vampiric magic was infusing his veins. He couldn't get enough of it. The taste —the sheer *power* in it was everything he'd ever wanted in the world. When he came back from the dead, he would be stronger than he'd ever been. He would survive.

If he couldn't save his loved ones, then his enemies would feel his wrath.

The past and present blurred as Zack tumbled down a pothole in memory road that left him stuck in a vivid play-back loop.

The tingling in his fingers and toes crawled up his limbs to his chest and formed a molten core. That heat was intoxicating, nearly as orgasmic as sex, and Zack kept drinking in hope that it would flood through him and make him whole.

But that liquid heat wrapped around his heart and froze in place. The cold worked outward and sliced through every nerve as his injuries began to knit together.

In this moment, in the coffin, those injuries were gone. Healed. But he continued reliving the agony before his death. He screamed and broke away from Seamus, writhing on the balcony. He couldn't curl into a ball now like he did then. The world had been—was again—ice and fire and tiny stars blackening into oblivion.

Seamus had pulled him back into his arms. "Shh, child. Shh. Embrace the night. You will be well when you wake."

Well? *Well?* Zack was a freaking vampire stuck in his coffin reliving his death. He had fucking *died.* And he had become everything his family had said he'd be. A monster. *You know you don't have to be that. Roger. Takashi. Josefina, Nell. They've shown you that being a vampire doesn't mean becoming the worst version of yourself.*

Are Roger and Takashi still alive?

What would he do if they weren't? What if he was now trapped in this immortal body, and the only ones waiting for him on the outside of the coffin were Seamus and Anton and his birth family, who would likely start hunting him the second they discovered what he'd become? Zack could practically hear his brother convincing other family members—grandparents, cousins, aunts—that hunting Zack to oblivion was the "right thing." Even his father wouldn't be able to resist turning against him.

What if the world was only pain?

He slammed his hand against the coffin lid. A burning sensation started in Zack's chest. The lack of air was finally suffocating him. *That doesn't make sense.* Maybe his immortal body didn't totally remember he was dead.

You are remade, a voice that sounded far too much like Seamus said in his head.

Seamus.

His killer.

His *sire.* He'd turned Zack into this ... this *creature.*

Zack was going to tear him apart.

With what little leverage he had, he punched upward. He rocketed his fist upward again. And again. The wood started to crack, so he continued pummeling it. When it finally splintered, dirt skittered down onto him.

No wonder he couldn't open the damn thing. Seamus had fucking buried him. How many feet was he in the ground?

Three? Six? He only knew that the more he broke the lid, the more dirt rained down on him. Icy fear seized his lungs, and the burning in his chest grew, but he kept going. He didn't need anything except an escape.

His knuckles broke and healed and broke and healed. Over and over. He punished the wood with every ounce of fury in his soul. Finally, the hole grew large enough, and he pulled himself upward into the dirt. Clawing and fighting, he searched for the surface.

The burning ache in his core clenched his stomach. *Hunger* was too mundane a word for the growling emptiness inside him. Thirst didn't encompass the roughness of his throat. His whole being *needed* a source. As he stretched, reached, and pulled, the crackling ache spread from his core through the rest of his body. Dirt filled his mouth, and it wasn't what he needed.

His fingertips brushed frigid air. He choked on dirt as he cried out in surprise. But there was *air*. He yanked upward, and the next thrust plunged his hand into that bitter void. With one hand free, he fought to break the other one out. Desperately, he scrambled. He managed to push out his entire arm and used that to heave himself upward.

The crisp air was welcoming to his lungs, but it couldn't cool his throat. It did nothing to alleviate the burning heat in his body.

But he smelled something *good*. He needed that good thing. Twisting his head, he caught sight of a woman sitting at the end of the dirt patch holding him down. She trembled like a leaf on a blustering wind and fell over. Her heart thundered in his ears. Relentless and fast-paced, it called to the void inside him, and that void screamed its need to consume her.

He crawled, quick handfuls over loosely packed dirt, toward her. The dirt tried to keep him pinned. He growled as he worked himself free.

Suddenly, she was on her feet, and a man stood beside her. A man he should know, but he didn't give a shit. The man didn't have a heartbeat and smelled like rain and dirt. The man said ... something. Something that didn't matter.

Then the woman ran.

In a desperate, hungry surge, he pulled himself out of the patch. She was what he needed. She was a *source*. That was all that mattered. He chased, and exhilaration joined his hunger.

As she fled, she stumbled over smooth stones as if she couldn't see them, but they were in plain sight. He vaulted over a large rock and cut her off. Her hands were bound, which made grabbing her easier. He didn't care that she had something in her mouth. Her blood was in her veins, her neck. She wriggled in his grasp, fighting like a fish already drawn into the air.

With a snarl, he took hold of her hair and wrenched her head to the side. Her pulse jumped in her throat. He sank his fangs into her soft flesh.

Delicious, mind-bending liquid filled his mouth. He was made of stardust and darkness, and the blood fueled his journey. He clutched her close and moaned as he swallowed each wondrous spurt of warmth. It dripped into that burning, aching void inside him. Finally, his throat was soothed.

If you keep going, you'll kill her, a rational voice whispered. His voice. Zack frowned and drank more. Who would he kill? *The woman*.

But he still had an ache in him, and the blood was so *perfect*. And coming so fast.

Stop!

He growled, angry at that voice. He drank. Her heartbeat was quick and loud, and he raced against it. Then it skipped. And the skip became longer.

She's dying.

Startling clarity struck Zack as if someone had activated a

breaker in a darkened house. He broke away from the woman and released her. She sagged to the ground.

She was near dead. Technically alive, but not for long. *Wasted blood.*

No. No, he couldn't have possibly thought that. Zack backed away, smacking his ass into a nearby headstone. Headstone? *Fuck, I'm in a cemetery.* He held on to the granite while his mind caught up to the world. The plethora of sensations that came with reality threatened to overwhelm him.

His hunger wasn't fully satisfied. It lingered like a ghost teasing the corners of his sight—present and unwilling to leave him alone or step into focus.

He had her blood all over his chin, on his shirt. And this suit he was wearing felt awful and wasn't anything he'd ever owned. Every fragment of dirt on him was a grain of sand rubbing against tender flesh. Too much of it coated him; he couldn't easily knock it off.

Her heartbeat was slowing further.

"No," Zack cried. He rushed forward.

Seamus stepped in front of him. Zack could track his movement and tried to step around him, but Seamus remained that fraction faster and caught him by the arms. "Ah, ah. Let's not have any accidents."

"*Accidents?*" Zack demanded. "She needs help!"

"The last thing we want is for you to try to feed her your blood to 'help' her," Seamus replied sharply.

"We need to put pressure on the wound."

"She's *gone*, Zackery. The way she should be."

"What the fuck is that supposed to mean?" Zack yanked backward.

Seamus let him go. "It has been a thousand years since I was a father. Don't make me ruin this joyous occasion by punishing you, son."

Son? Zack ran through the information that he'd gathered on Seamus over the last few months. Though he would have had more details with his notebooks in front of him, he realized he could recall his notes faster and with better clarity than he ever had—and his Grandma Bonnie had always called him one of the brightest hunters of his generation. *Wait, do vampires* think *faster than mortals? What the fuck?* He stashed that question for later research.

He narrowed his eyes. "You don't refer to any of your sirelings as your children. What's your game?"

"Souls as special as yours are rare, Zackery," Seamus replied.

Meaning that Seamus saw a killer in Zack. *Just like me, little bro,* Cal's voice said. *But he's got you switching sides.*

I'm not the same as him. Zack slid his hand behind his back and under his suit jacket.

You're a freaking murderer, little bro, the Cal voice continued.

The two vampires Zack had killed had been out of self-defense. One had been actively trying to kill him, and Anton had demanded Zack kill the other. And they were hardly innocents.

But he had a new tally to that list. The woman on the ground. She was dead.

Zack shook his head. "You're wrong about me."

"You were dying, clearly defeated, and yet your bloodlust overwhelmed that. I could feel it despite your tattoo." Seamus smiled warmly at him. "You kept fighting. You wanted to kill."

Seamus was roughly Zack's height, though slightly broader. In a fair fight, Zack should have stood a chance, but vampirism and a thousand years of experience had given Seamus unnatural advantages.

A bit of vampire lore threaded into Zack's calculations. The way that vampires created sirelings was to seed a bit of their own power into their sireling. Just after making another, a vampire was weaker.

Zack was stronger than he'd been. He'd taken that power

from Seamus. *We're as close to level on the battlefield as we're going to get.*

"I wanted to kill *you*," Zack snarled. For the first time, he felt his fangs and the strange, reflexive way his lips curled back to keep from piercing on his sharpened teeth. A full-blown hiss was in the back of his throat. As he pulled his dagger, he indulged that primal urge.

"Tantrums are expected in the young," Seamus said seriously. "But see reason, son. You took my blood eagerly. None of my sirelings have ever drawn from me like you did. Part of you wanted to become like me. To belong to me."

Zack pulled his dagger and slid into a fighting stance. The runes of his blade were glowing with red light. That light should have been white, but it, too, had changed. Did it have new powers? He did. Seamus was quicker than him, but not by much. *This could work.*

"Son," Seamus said, his demeanor growing colder, "stop your foolishness and put away the blade."

"You're not my fucking father!" Zack shouted.

"Our bond is eternal, Zackery," Seamus said as he stepped forward. "I will never throw you away like he did."

Zack flinched. How had Seamus known about his father disowning him? Who'd told him? When? Had he known since Zack had arrived in Chicago? Since before that?

His eyes closed only for the briefest flicker, but a rush of cool air came at him. Instincts clicked into place, and he reacted, rolling away from the rush and slicing at it in the same motion. Seamus grunted, and Zack grinned. As he readjusted his stance, he watched the wound across Seamus's forearm heal.

"I'm impressed," Seamus said quietly.

"You can stop this fucking nice-guy act," Zack replied. "I know what you are."

"I understand why you are upset. No doubt Roger has been filling your head with all kinds of stories, and I can't fault you for believing them. I didn't understand until recently what his interpretation of events was."

"You're seriously playing the 'two sides to every story' card?" Zack shouted.

"You are so very young, Zackery. You don't yet know what the world is truly like. But given time, I believe you'll come to understand what I have done and who I am," Seamus said, his tone one of a patient teacher. "I gave you my blood because you are capable of so much more than mortal limitations, including their basic moralities. I see in you the weak man I once was, and I know you can evolve beyond that."

He means you're a monster like him, the Cal voice snickered.

With a furious scream, Zack lunged at Seamus. Seamus dodged his first strike and his second. But Zack wouldn't let up, and he drove him backward through the graveyard. He had his target, and he would fucking kill him.

Seamus was that fraction of a second faster. The only strikes he made were to counter Zack's attempts to hit him. And Zack began to predict them. Began to feint and strike true. He plunged his dagger into Seamus's shoulder and laughed.

And Seamus laughed *with* him. He put his hand around the hilt and kept it in place.

"Shut up!" Zack snapped in his face. "Fucking shut up!"

When Zack tried to pull away, Seamus grabbed him by the collar and kept him close. "A fire as bright as yours happens once in a century. You are *everything* I could want for a son."

"Take that *back*!"

"I won't," Seamus replied. "I told you. I will never throw you away."

Thick tears crawled down Zack's face. The monster who had torn apart his lovers and friends wanted him close? Wanted to be his immortal *father*? It was fucked up. It was *too* fucked up.

He hated how Seamus's words soothed something deep in him. How he wanted someone to approve of him. Roger, Takashi, and his friends all did, but at the same time, they always looked down upon his hunter's training. At the violent side of him.

Zack still had his silver dagger burning in Seamus's shoulder, and the fucking bastard was *praising* him.

Zack sagged against Seamus and sobbed.

Seamus wrapped his arms around him and held him. After the worst of the sobs eased, he pulled the dagger from his shoulder and put it into his coat pocket. "Shh, son. It's all right. Let's get you home."

CHAPTER 12

The broken-down house seemed more forlorn than the last time Roger had crossed its threshold. Clouds covered the moon, leaving little light to filter into this place. The boards creaked under his weight as he drifted between the long shadows. Their dry, rotted sounds were nothing like the way a ship would moan its aches on the open ocean. This complaining was a soul-weary deepness within the house. Age and decay had worn away the place. No one had taken the time to care for it. Likely, no one ever would, and it would tumble into dust.

Roger laid his hand upon the wall beside the second-story window. A kindred exhaustion was in him since leaving the mansion with Dmitri in his arms. He rested his other hand on Zack's pendant. A shop down the street from the Last Deal had fixed the chain's clasp for him.

Dmitri was lying on Nathaniel's bed and, the last Roger had checked, hadn't moved in the two nights since Roger had put him there. In his boredom—or anxiety—Vincent had cleaned Nathaniel's shabby apartment, filing off the layer of crud of a hardworking bachelor living alone. The Wrights were safely housed in a hotel not terribly far from the Last

Deal, but Roger couldn't bring them directly into the building. That would be rude, considering Thomas's grandfather had tortured Nathaniel for years.

He had promised Thomas and Amber that he was working on another plan, but he was unsure of what direction to push. He was breaking another promise. Failing yet again.

How many storms had the abandoned farmhouse weathered? How many more could it withstand before falling entirely?

How much more could he take on his own?

Headlights drew his attention out to the gravel road leading up to the decrepit house. The car was quieter and a sleeker, more expensive model than it had been before. He waited until it pulled in alongside his own before he dropped from the window to the ground below.

Josefina stepped out of her car and slammed the door shut. The crunch of her boots—first on the gravel and then on the dry grass—was thunder rolling toward him. Her voice carried, no hint of it lost to the wind or darkness. "I risked my life and my lover's domain for you, and you didn't have the decency to text me when your mission was done!"

"I had my hands full." His voice was hollow, reverberating through the nothingness growing inside him.

"Anton departed in the middle of my evening at the Chateau. I had to sit there and pretend I had no notion of why he might suddenly have to leave. I had to smile and make nice with that bastard Seamus, who I hate above all others, and then you leave me to wonder what occurred for two nights! And make me drive back out here to the middle of nowhere!"

"I couldn't say the words where anyone else might hear me," Roger said hoarsely. "I owed you more than a text."

Josefina paused. Her anger had always been a liquid steel, cold and brutal, but one that she controlled with finite precision. She continued to glare at him, but her hardness was no longer one of pure rage. "What happened?"

"I went into the basement and found Dmitri." Roger had let his numbness shield him, but speaking that fragment fractured his self-control. Bloody tears slid down his cheeks, neither hot nor cold. They simply were. "I and the girl were freeing him while the other two continued to search. But before we could release him, Anton arrived. I had to make a choice, Josefina. I could take Dmitri and the others and leave, or he would tell me where Zack and Takashi were. The girl's life would have been forfeit. All of them would have been. Anton's bargain didn't guarantee I would be able to reach Zack or Takashi either. You should have seen that room. I couldn't leave Dmitri. Nor could I sacrifice Zack's blood family."

Josefina moved in a blur, and Roger prepared himself for the blow. Instead of striking, she wrapped her arms around him in a tight embrace. He slowly returned her hug. He had never stopped to consider he needed to save his former lover. And now, Zack and Takashi might be facing the same or worse, and Roger had left them to it. They might not even be alive. He may never see them again.

Something unfurled inside him, and his strength left. His knees gave out. If not for Josefina, he would have fallen to the ground, but she held him upright.

He had never stood a chance at all, had he? His mortal family had been a nightmare, his life at sea mired with violence and that life stolen from him. All for the sake of two bastards' game. He was no prize, no vampire worthy of becoming a captain in a coven, let alone its leader. He was nothing but failure through and through.

When he closed his eyes, he could picture the five of them together—Carver, Kit, Takashi, Zack, and himself. They had had a few nights in, a few times where they relished each other's company and forgot about the outside world. In those moments, Roger had wished that might be their ever after. That in some way, they would be able to hold on to that sanctuary, no matter what.

But Carver was dead. Kit had left. Roger had been fooling himself then and longing for that fake peace now only hurt all the more.

"All right," Josefina said with sympathy but an element of firmness. "Pull yourself together."

He was a million pieces of dust floating into the wind, tiny fragments scattered along three centuries of living. His last hope of holding himself together had faded. He was broken. *No. No, I won't let Seamus win. If I can't have them, then I will destroy him. Even if I die in the attempt. What else is my shoddy life good for?*

He withdrew from Josefina's hug and found the will to stand on his own two feet.

But suddenly, she latched onto his forearms and kept him close. Worry filled her brown eyes, and she shook her head. "Whatever you're thinking, don't."

Roger traced his mental focus along the edges of his usual walls. At some point, he had slipped and let them fall. Josefina wasn't pressing into his mind, but she'd be able to read whatever he was emanating. Which meant she likely picked up on his desire to burn the world in his desperation.

"He has taken *everything* from me," Roger growled. He yanked his arms away from Josefina and began to pace toward the house.

The old rotting wood whispered secrets in its darkness. Its shadows were deep, never-ending, and reached toward someplace cold. A place beyond fury, beyond light. He sensed a lurking power, not in the house, but in that strange connection. A fragment within himself screamed, and the scream became a howl.

"I played his games. I smiled. I seduced. I killed. I fucked. I sat at his side and let him do whatever he wanted and prayed he would not see me," Roger said. Each word was a liberation born from the chests at the bottom of his mental sea flinging themselves upward. "When I was at my strongest, I balked. I was still afraid of him. Of what he might do to me. To them."

Slowly, Josefina came into his eyeline, but she was twenty feet away. She crept as if she was keeping alert for danger, and yet her expression did not waver from sternness. The traces of her worry were gone. A pulse of curiosity slid out from her. "Was I wrong? Was that not self-destruction I felt in you?"

"Forgive me if I don't give a damn for this." Roger put his hand on the center of his chest. "This is still here. I endure. Not because of any strength. But because he is a prideful bastard, and my life is a toy to him. I cannot live that way anymore. I will not bend and disappear into exile. He has made it so that I am worthless, so no, I no longer care what happens to me *so long as he burns*."

The more he thought of what had happened in his long life, the more rage bubbled and boiled to the surface. Mortals died; that was the way of the world. But so many of them hadn't needed to die the way they had. The horrific massacre at Gladwell Manor—children and adults tortured until they lost their minds. Roger hadn't done the worst of it, but he had stopped none of it either. Letting Mary Gladwell run wasn't near enough penance, not when he had failed her descendent, too.

Josefina was a beacon of red light in the shadows that roiled around them. The moving grays had shapes, some like ropes on a runaway ship. He could grab hold of them and tie them in place. Direct them.

A strange sensation coursed through him. He felt a rush as if he'd drunk blood, but he'd only had a blood bag at dusk. Molten heat burst underneath his mental sea, a wealth of power bubbling up. Something in the house cracked, and a beam fell. *Was that me? How?*

"Roger—"

"I will not be a coward anymore," he rasped. "I will not be weak. He will pay for what he has done. He and everything he loves will burn. You cannot stop me."

"I wouldn't dream of that," Josefina replied. She took careful steps forward. "But if you die in the undertaking, even if you succeed first, he will achieve his greatest victory. You need to live through this, Roger."

"If they're gone, I can't promise that I'll want to," Roger murmured.

"Roger—"

"If he had taken Nell from you? Reed?" Roger snapped.

Josefina pursed her lips. She rested her hand on his shoulder. A shallower version of the longing to rip and shred came from her, but it lacked the flame of need and the heat of desperation that currently fueled Roger. "Roger, I will stand at your side and see you through this. For the sake of Zack and the sake of Takashi, both who I love, too, I will *not* see you destroy yourself."

Roger laughed, the sound bitter and mean. "You'll be able to do that safely watching from a thousand miles away?"

"I'm staying."

"What about dragging a war to your lover's doorstep?"

"I'll worry about Nell and ramifications."

He loved her desperately, needed her friendship, but he couldn't let her remain with him. "Josefina, this isn't your fight."

"The fuck it isn't," she said angrily. "He hasn't taken them from just you. I have claim to my anger and grief as well. I will see that he pays for it."

"You have been adamant that you cannot be caught helping me," Roger said.

"You have been skirting around your anger rather than

embracing your wrath for as long as I have known you. But if you are finally ready to bring a war to him, then I won't leave you to face it alone. Especially if you believe this is worthless." She put her hand on his chest. "You have held on to your heart, Roger. I owe at least Takashi enough to ensure you live long enough for that chance to reunite with him."

"If they're dead—"

"We have no confirmation. Until we do, we carry hope," Josefina said. "If you can't, then I will hold on to it for you."

"I wouldn't have thought you the type," Roger said wryly.

"You introduced me to the love of my life. You got me out of this fucking hell, and I have been in paradise for almost a hundred years," Josefina whispered gently. "I owe you more than I can ever repay, Roger, so much so that I am terrified to speak of its debt in case you would hold it over me."

Though the rage was still churning inside him, the worst of it settled after listening to Josefina. She had been a beautiful human girl and an angry young vampire. Since then, she had become the stunning, powerful creature before him. She'd had the opportunity because of him. Because he had managed at least one good thing in his life. *Not everything I've attempted has failed.*

He put his forehead against hers. "You will never owe me a debt, Josefina. To know that you love and are loved heals a wound in my heart."

"There you are, asshole," Josefina said. Her laugh was tinged with a soft cry. "I was worried your first casualty would be your true self."

"Carver was the first." Roger stepped away. "I haven't told his family. I don't know if he had any, to be honest. Worse, I don't know what's happened to his body. I had to leave him."

"I've already put Reed on it," Josefina replied.

Roger put an arm around her shoulders and tugged her

close. "If you keep looking out for me, perhaps I will survive this."

Lightly, Josefina pushed him away rather than letting him drag her in. "You still have to do something. I won't let you sit idle either. Do you have a plan?"

"No, but I think I have a brilliant idea." Roger grinned at her. "Why don't we see what we can do about emptying the coven's coffers?"

CHAPTER 13

The body remained in the graveyard. Zack had been too numb when they first walked away from the corpse, but when he tried to go back, Seamus caught his arm. He murmured something about ghouls and whisked Zack away from the cemetery.

Seamus didn't force a conversation during their ride to the mansion. In fact, he spent his time on his phone, periodically typing. Since words had fled Zack, he tried to study Seamus's minute reactions to whatever he was doing, but Seamus had a schooled, calm expression. He was unreadable.

But not entirely unknowable. Even when Zack wasn't looking at him, he could *feel* Seamus. It was like knowing where his dagger was, but more like having a rope tied around his waist and the other end being tied to Seamus with no slack in the middle. They were connected. Bonded.

I will never throw you away. Zack hated that there was an ounce of comfort in those words. Hated more how some emotion was tickling at the edges of his mind. It wasn't his. It was like a pop-up ad that just kept showing up in front of his thoughts. This calm nugget of peace was an emotion from Seamus. Zack wasn't sure what that desire was supposed to mean, only that it wasn't sexual. He'd thought vampires could only feel and manipulate fear and lust, but desires could run to other stuff. Academically, he'd known that but figured vampires trained themselves to feel and manipulate the other stuff.

Instead, he was just sitting there, on the other side of the limo's back bench seat from Seamus, and that weird desire for calm kept springing to mind.

Zack's gaze drifted toward the window. Old memories joined the confusing mix of his concentration. In vivid clarity, he remembered Cousin Denny's tenth birthday party. He'd been allowed to play with the big kids for the first time, only to wind up as the "damsel" and tied up in the tree house for an hour. Then he relived prom his sophomore year of high school; atypical for teens that grade, but an older girl had asked him. Turned out she was hoping to meet and hook up with his older brother—which Cal had been into—and the night had been a disaster for Zack. Then there was the time during his first and only semester of college where he'd handed in a persuasive paper for an English course. The professor had praised his creativity but given him a D. All those preventable pains if only he'd been that bit smarter, that bit cleverer—just that bit *more*.

The external desire for calm pushed into him as if someone was attempting to steal his phone from his hand and shove a book into it instead. With a quick glance, he saw that Seamus wasn't typing on his phone, only looking at it.

"Do you want a son or a puppet?" Zack asked, his voice rasping from a renewed thirst and dryness. *Now I want more blood. Awesome.* "If the answer is 'son,' stay the fuck out of my emotions."

Seamus lifted an eyebrow and slid his phone into his coat pocket. "I was attempting to steady you."

"Then fucking talk to me."

"Please stop swearing, Zack. It's unbecoming."

"So is raping your way through the centuries, you fucking shithead asshole."

A *flicker* passed over Seamus's features, and a sudden violent desire popped into Zack's mental screen with an almost audible chime. But that window closed on its own, and Seamus managed to retain his calm demeanor.

But Zack had seen the thin gap in Seamus's mental wall, and the tiny victory buoyed his spirits.

"Did that feel good?" Seamus said smoothly.

A little *too* smoothly. Zack narrowed his eyes and waited for the other shoe to drop.

"I asked if intentionally upsetting me made you feel good, Zack," Seamus said.

"You're not going to try to make some parallel between pissing you off and raping someone, are you?" Zack replied. "Because they are nowhere near the same ballpark."

"You pushed to find power, and you reveled in it." Seamus continued to hold Zack's gaze. "And what confirmation have you had that I raped anyone?"

"Roger—"

"Who talked you into sparing his life because he wanted to kill me," Seamus said. He motioned at Zack's neck. "He nearly tore out your throat. You managed to turn the tables on him, and he needed some way to convince you to stay your hand. He spun a story about his evil sire."

"I've seen with my own eyes what kind of asshole you are," Zack growled.

"Nice vampires do not live a decade, Zackery. I am what I need to be in order to survive," Seamus said with a sigh in his voice. "I do hope that you'll realize this petty mentality is standing in the way of your greatness sooner rather than later."

There was no point in trying to hold a conversation with him because Seamus kept spinning everything. Zack didn't believe a word of it, but clearly, Seamus wasn't going to be swayed either. With a huff, Zack folded his arms and slumped against the corner. *Bound by blood to another fuckhead with an explanation for everything. Fan-fucking-tastic.*

Every angry thought slipped to the back of his mind as Seamus's mansion came into view. Zack researched what he could on the building, but he hadn't found much.

And holy fuck, was it a flex. The building was massive, stretching out hundreds of feet on either side of a central entrance. The damn thing would barely fit onto a football field. Built in the 1920s, it had the sharp, elegant beauty of an art deco palace. Sporadic lights were on and providing some illumination out into the darkness, but that didn't take away from the impressive, foreboding feeling the mansion exuded. Statues decorated the long circular drive; each one was a figure seductively offering themselves up for a dramatic bite —their wrist, their neck, their inner thigh, anywhere that could bring intense pleasure.

Zack was suddenly too aware of his new fangs and the thirst drying out his throat. Despite the stone nature of the artwork, he was straining to hear a heartbeat. But there wasn't one; even their driver was a vampire. *I'm getting blood-horny because of freaking statues. Greaaaaaat.*

Seamus smirked. "Don't worry. I had a few meals brought for you tonight. You won't go hungry."

"I'm not killing anyone else," Zack said. "You can't make me."

"I didn't make you kill the last one."

"You turned me into this!" Zack gestured at himself and glared at Seamus.

The limo came to a stop underneath the central entrance's overhang. Seamus leaned toward Zack and lowered his voice. "I gave you a choice, and you took full advantage of it."

"Because—"

"Because you were on death's door," Seamus said. "If you don't like the deal, then walk out into the dawn. But before you consider that, I would like to know one thing, Zackery. What, in your entire existence, have you chosen *for yourself*?"

"What the fuck is that supposed to mean?" Zack snapped. "I've made plenty of choices."

"In the pursuit of others' approval. First your family's, then Roger's, then Nell's." Seamus leaned in farther, and the world seemed to narrow to his blue and red mottled eyes. A bubble of some desire touched the edge of Zack's mind, but Seamus didn't push it into him. As they remained locked in their staring contest, Seamus continued. "You drank from me, and you knew exactly what you would become. I felt the way you drew my power into you. You were eager for it. *You wanted it.*"

The last words were a whisper that Zack wanted to deny, but those final moments of his mortal life flickered into view.

And Seamus wasn't wrong.

But he couldn't be right. Zack blinked, bloody tears pricking the corners of his eyes. "I didn't want to die. That's all."

"The longer you lie to yourself, the longer you hurt yourself," Seamus said sadly. "There is no shame in what we are. You can cast aside that pain, son. You have the power to become whatever you want."

"Not an eighty-year-old grandfather," Zack replied. "I can't become *that*."

"Not in the mortal fashion you're talking about, but why have such a limited idea of how to create an experience? A life?" Seamus licked his thumb and then brushed away a piece of dirt stuck to Zack's cheek. "Explore your potential, and you'll discover a world full of depth and wonder that you've never dreamed of."

By that point, the limo driver had gotten out and opened the door. Seamus stepped out into the night, shoulders back, head held high.

Talking to an archvillain wasn't supposed to make Zack

want to be like him. He hated Seamus. Hated everything he'd ever done. Ever. Well, except for turning Roger into a vampire. But he hadn't given Roger a choice, and he hadn't given Zack a real one either. Death or vampirism? No one was going to pick death.

But you didn't even hesitate, little bro, the Cal voice said.

Shut the fuck up.

You've been reading those fucking books and fantasizing about this night for fucking years. You've always wanted to be this. Monster.

Zack ground his teeth, and his fangs pricked his gums. He forced himself to climb out of the limo as his mental war continued. *I didn't have a choice. I was dying.*

A few thousand more times, and maybe you'll believe it.

I do.

Some part of you clearly doesn't.

The double doors to the mansion swung open and revealed a grand foyer. White veins stretched across the deep red marble floor and matched the color of the walls. A sweeping, elegant double staircase curved on either side of the hall up to the second floor. Since the ceiling went all the way up to that floor, a few of the paintings took advantage of the huge space. They depicted a wide array of scenes: a snowy landscape, a busy street, an artistic rendition of a vampire orgy. The overwhelming scent of roses greeted Zack, and there were a half dozen vases on the ground floor alone. They were in shades of soft yellow, subtly blending in with the décor.

A tall, spindly man stood to the left of the foyer's center. His white skin was the shade of bleached paper, lending him an unreal quality. Everything about him fell into that same category. His limbs were too thin to have any substantial musculature. He was eight feet tall. His hair was black and gray, though one streak of gray seemed to be changing to a stark white right before Zack's eyes. The strangest part was his smile, which seemed to literally stretch from ear to ear.

Zack made the mistake of meeting his gaze.

The shade of the man's eyes was somewhere between a howling abyss waiting to devour the entire planet and the darkness that came from closing one's eyes and praying that the monster under the bed was just a series of sounds one hadn't figured out yet.

Fuck this guy. I just crawled out of my own grave. Zack squared his shoulders.

The man continued to smile and held his gaze for a moment longer, then chuckled to himself as he dipped his head in a respectful semi-bow. He had a voice like dried leaves rustling along concrete in a fall wind. "Ah, Master Zackery, a pleasure to formally meet you."

"You've informally met me?" Zack said.

The man lifted an eyebrow and ran his gaze down the length of Zack.

The clothes. Someone would have had to change him out of the ruined tuxedo and into the black funeral suit. An odd incongruity happened in Zack's head because he was embarrassed, but no heat was coming to his cheeks. *Guess it's harder to blush now. Yay?*

"Oh." Zack threw his next question to Seamus. "You have a fey butler?"

"Grimsby is the estate manager," Seamus replied.

"What's that?"

"A fancier title for a butler with a few more responsibilities, young master," Grimsby said. He turned toward Seamus and slightly bowed as he spoke. "Master Seamus, your inferiors have arrived. I've shown them to your conference room."

"Fantastic. Take Zack to his rooms—"

"*Rooms?*" Zack echoed.

"—and ensure that he has anything he might need. Zack, freshen up and then join me for the meeting," Seamus said without stopping for Zack's interruption.

"I'm freshly dead, and you want me to go to a meeting?" Zack asked.

"You were planning to help Roger take my coven. I thought you would want to see what it takes to actually run the thing so you could understand how ill-equipped Roger was for the position. However, if you'd prefer to pout in your room all night about the best thing that ever happened to you, be my guest."

Seamus's tone alone drove needles under Zack's skin. The fact that another little pop-up was crawling toward Zack's conscious thoughts drove the needles in further. Seamus wanted him to understand something, but picking up on exactly what he was feeling from someone else wasn't obvious. *Screw him. He's had a thousand years to get used to his power. I haven't had a thousand minutes to understand mine.* Zack puffed up, a growl in his throat.

"Perhaps the young master would benefit from your newest guest," Grimsby said.

Seamus narrowed his eyes. "Fine. But I expect both of you down at the meeting in no more than two hours' time. Do you understand, Zackery?"

"Do I understand that you're a maniacal bastard who thinks that he can somehow manipulate me into believing my boyfriend wasn't monster enough to run the coven? Yeah, I get that," Zack replied snidely.

Seamus grabbed him by the chin, fingers wrapping up around his jaw, and held him painfully tight. "You are wearing my patience thin."

Zack couldn't help a grin. "What about 'I'll never throw you away?'"

The gap in Seamus's mental armor was widening. The outline of his desire for violence was growing brighter. But then it vanished. He released Zack with a small shove and stalked away. "Grow the fuck up, Zackery, before our world grinds you into ash."

Zack wanted to claim that as a win, but he was scraped out and hollow inside. The biting remark hadn't filled him with any real sense of glee. At least when he used to push Cal's buttons, Cal would actually pop off and say something awful, and Zack could double down on his anger at his big brother. Seamus was taking the higher road. He wasn't supposed to do that. He was supposed to be all evil and asshole and give Zack a fight for his life. Not tell him he needed to grow up and then just walk away like he was too busy.

And oh, fuck, Zack was never going to physically change. *I'm going to be scrawny, baby-faced, and five foot six* forever. He tried to run his hand through his hair, but his fingers caught on dirt. Suddenly, every speck of filth covering him was worse than a million spiders crawling along his skin.

"If you'll follow me, young master," Grimsby said. With his hands clasped behind his back, he started toward the left staircase.

Since his only other viable option was to run out into the night without a clue of where to find Roger or Takashi, Zack hurried after Grimsby. They went up the grand staircase and then down a long hall. Every once in a while, bouquets in ornate vases decorated the space while providing a pleasant floral scent. There was something underneath of it that smelled, well, a lot like Zack currently did. Dirt and dust and musty oldness. Zack took a sniff of his clothes. The oldness wasn't clinging to him.

Paintings hung on the walls along their path. Zack had never seen this many. Visiting Chicago, even for a school trip, had been out of the question. Mom had been too paranoid to let him go to "the heart of the enemy." And since coming to Chicago, he hadn't made any time to do anything besides train and research. *I have the time now.*

Fuck, he could learn how to paint if he wanted, and he could spend centuries perfecting his art. Takashi had learned ten more languages after becoming a vampire and was on his eleventh, bringing the grand total up to fourteen with what he'd known as a mortal. Zack could do that, too. Or he could learn how to code. Or he could tackle his giant to-be-read pile. *What have you chosen for yourself?* Not a whole lot, but he had the time to do everything he'd ever dreamed of.

Seamus wasn't supposed to make sense. He was the fucking bad guy.

Zack cleared his throat. "Why is a fey working for Seamus? Does he pay you, or did Anton bind you?"

Grimsby glanced over his shoulder, and in his gaze was the scream of a terrified child. "As you are, ahem, *newer* to this side of interactions with the supernatural, young master, I will do you this one favor. One small lesson. Do not ask fey such impertinent questions. Rudeness finds swift consequence among my kind."

"Crap, you just called it a favor," Zack muttered. "So I owe you."

Grimsby chuckled as he turned his attention forward. "At least your parents didn't fail you completely. Don't worry, young master. I won't ask for anything outside of your capabilities when the time comes."

That time could be in a minute or centuries from now. A cold stone dropped into Zack's stomach. Forever seemed like fun, but it also stretched ahead into an infinity of consequences.

"Here we are." Grimsby opened a door. "I can bring your guest now, or I can give you the chance to clean up first."

Were all questions rude to the fey? Zack suddenly wasn't sure. But if the "guest" was someone he would wind up killing, he wasn't ready for that. His hunger was a growing ache, but the woman's limp body came to mind. He had panicked in the moment. Would he have given her his blood to try to save her? If he bled someone else without supervision, would he wind up making an accidental vampire? He didn't think so, but he hadn't felt like himself when he fed. What if every time was like that?

Grimsby was a servant and treating Zack like he had some control over what happened in the house. So if he followed along those rules, then some questions shouldn't be in the realm of disrespectful. In fact, Grimsby might be the one to break etiquette if he didn't answer.

"Who is this 'guest?'" Zack asked.

"I can't say, young master." Grimsby's smile became strained.

That was an odd reaction and specific wording. Zack tilted his head. Was there some magical condition on Grimsby? He'd have to find out. "Okay. Do you think I want to see this guest?"

"I imagine you'll be pleased and distraught."

Seamus kidnapped me. Something must have happened to Kit, Vincent, Roger, and Takashi. The guest could be one of them. Zack steeled his nerves. "Then go ahead and bring the guest here, please."

Grimsby gave a nod-bow and then headed back down the hall from the direction they'd come, though he made a turn they hadn't taken.

Preparing for the next level of mindfuck, Zack walked through the open door of his suite.

The first room was a living room, complete with couch and multimedia setup. A large flat-screen was mounted to the wall, and the cabinet underneath it housed every latest-gen gaming console *and* a VR headset. Along with a Blu-Ray player, there was a bona fide VHS machine. Tall cabinets on either side of the big screen held dozens of 4ks, Blu-Rays, a couple VHS tapes, and two whole shelves of one cabinet were dedicated to hard copies of popular video games.

On the other side of the room was a record player and a slew of cellophaned vinyl records. In addition to the long, dark brown leather couch in the center of the room, there were a few deep chairs. Each of the *Twilight* movie posters was framed on the walls, one in each corner of the room, and there was a basket of orange-scented potpourri sitting on an end table beside a chair.

What captured Zack's attention were the three bookcases on the wall next to the door leading into the bedroom. A good percentage of the spines didn't have titles on them; their bindings led Zack to believe they were older texts. He did spot Sun Tzu's *Art of War* and Machiavelli's *The Prince* and other titles from mortal war strategists.

There were also books that had been written by supernaturals for supernaturals. One was written by *the* Dracula—or supposedly written by him—detailing methods for blending into modern society and taking it over for vampire kind. Hunters had always assumed it was a myth. *Mom claimed it was the vampire equivalent of* Mein Kompf. Was it? Or had everything his family ever told him a lie?

Holy crap, the bedroom was just as awesome as the living room had been. The bed was a four-poster king bed with curtains and was made of a beautiful dark wood. The dresser and desk were made of the same material with elaborate, decorative woodworking. On the desk was an onyx leather journal. He explored the room further to discover a closet filled with fine, handsome clothing in his size. Most of it was black.

The dresser had boxes of accessories on top and more clothing inside. Again, black was a predominant color. One black hoodie was soft and had a graphic of a pair of fangs and the words "I Bite" written in the shape of teeth between the fangs. Two little illustrated blood drops were dripping from the fangs. It was funny, and a little too on the nose, and he wasn't sure if he wanted to laugh, cry, or ruin everything in the elegant bedroom.

He had just a little more left to explore. Besides the closet door and the living room door, there were two more doors in the bedroom. One led to his own bathroom, fully stocked with high-end products. The shower was big enough for three or four people, and the claw-foot tub was deep and could easily fit two.

The other door led to a small closet with a coffin in it. The black wood gleamed in the low light coming from the bedroom.

Had the one he'd been buried in looked like this? It was sleek and stylish for being something to hold the dead. Slowly, Zack lifted the lid and felt the satin inside it. The touch of it was the same. It had to be a duplicate; he'd ruined the one he'd actually been buried in.

When he closed the lid again, he caught the subtle glimmer of paint near the head. He let his fingertips drift along the smooth wood as he moved to take a closer look.

Vampires had a heraldry system, though not all vampires had a crest. Having one seemed to go in and out of fashion, and only old, arrogant vampires made their own. They had to be given, though some vampires eventually updated theirs as they went, adding little symbols of accomplishments in the image.

The crest on Zack's coffin was a stylized dagger, tip pointed downward. A snake was wrapped around the hilt and the blade, its head near the hilt with the mouth open wide in a hiss. It had long fangs. Above the dagger was Seamus's crest, a snake eating its own tail with a crown over its head. It had one red band near its head, marking Zack's connection to him as a first generation.

Zack had been obsessed with vampire heraldry when he was a preteen. Blades were an uncommon image—the hunter theory was that since vampires had fangs, any sign of weaponry was a weakness—and he wondered what it meant among vampires. Snakes were commonly interpreted as traitors or as very clever vampires. The dagger snake's tail was just starting to curl up, as if it, too, might eventually grow and twist around and up to form an ouroboros.

The design was beautiful. The whole fucking suite was what he'd dreamed of. *What, in your entire existence, have you chosen for yourself?*

I shouldn't want this, a small voice whispered.

Why not? Zack lightly touched the edge of his crest. *What's wrong with wanting to be young and immortal and powerful?*

You know, the Cal voice said.

There were footsteps in the living room. Whoever his guest was had shown up.

The Cal voice kept going. *Fucking little monster.*

Hey, asshole voice in my head? You can suck it. Zack slid his hand down the length of his coffin as he headed back toward the living room. *I didn't take the blood to beat myself up. I took it to live. And I'm going to do that.*

He was a vampire. He was going to use these fine gifts Seamus had given him, soak up every bit of knowledge that he could, and then murder the bastard. *I am going to be the greatest vampire to ever vampire. So choke on that, Cal voice.*

CHAPTER 14

To avoid obsessing over being trapped in a bedroom, Takashi mentally translated Shakespeare's famous "St. Crispin's Day" soliloquy into Modern English, Japanese, and French. Currently, he was working on his Farsi version. Unfortunately, he couldn't quite remember all the words of the original speech. He was ninety percent sure he had somehow mixed the entirety of "Tomorrow and Tomorrow and Tomorrow" into the poem, but since it was doing the important task of occupying his mind, he didn't give a damn.

The previous night, the silent boy who had led him around his first night in the mansion had dropped off four blood bags and then left. Takashi had been abandoned, waiting for either Seamus or Anton to summon him. Would another night pass the same way? *More* than one?

When a knock finally came, he jolted out of his thoughts and stopped pacing. "Yes?"

Slowly, the door opened. The boy was back, head bent so that he was staring at the floor, and he motioned out to the hallway.

Takashi took a second to steady himself and followed the boy out. He still had little reference for the path they traveled.

All Takashi was certain of was that the mansion must be large, even by vampire coven master standards.

The boy led him down a staircase and back along the hall. He stopped beside an open door and motioned for Takashi to go inside.

One must always dazzle the audience, Takashi. An audience will forgive anything so long as one is delightful, Geoff Pierro, the ringmaster of the circus, had said when Takashi had first begun his performances. The words had carried him far in his mortal and immortal life.

He found an easy smile, lifted his chin, and walked through the door.

The room was a sleek, modern living room. Everything had a new-quality sheen to it, and he couldn't help wondering how long it had actually been put together like this. The *Twilight* movie posters were an odd touch. There was another open door that led to a bedroom. *What was the purpose of bringing me here?*

The soft click of the door made Takashi glance over his shoulder. The boy had shut the door, remaining on the outside. This side of the door had a handle, which was a small relief. But Takashi didn't relax. He had a sense that he wasn't alone before he heard the soft footfalls of someone coming out of the other room.

Takashi believed he was prepared for the worst that Seamus or Anton might throw at him.

Then Zack stepped into the doorway.

The dirt caked into his hair altered its color to a darker brown. His black suit was ripped and had streaks of dirt. His hands were filthy.

That clue would be obvious enough, but the change vampirism had brought to Zack was astonishing. His skin was white as porcelain and seemed to give him a soft glow. His youth was no longer mutable, no longer aging in the minor ways a night could bring. The scar that Roger had given him on his neck was still there, barely visible under the collar of his shirt. It was fainter than it had ever been, but it would remain.

His eyes had lost their gray and were a shade of deep ruby. Was it his hunger that had changed the color? Or was this a permanent change? Only older, powerful vampires had eyes that remained consistently red, but something was different about Zack than the typical fledgling. Vampires had auras that grew with age, and yet Zack already had a stronger presence to him.

In addition to that, Zack's gait had changed. He held his head high and his shoulders straight. Though he'd done that as a mortal, the effort had been noticeable. In this moment, he had a natural confidence. He was graceful. Elegant.

This was exactly who Takashi had suspected Zack might become if only he stopped standing in his own way.

Another reaction quickly chased Takashi's awe. A seed of anger sprouted into a full tree because Seamus had stolen something precious from them. Though Zack's mortality wasn't what Takashi had valued about him, he, Roger, and Takashi should have been together when Zack rose as a vampire. Roger and Takashi should have been the ones to usher him through his changes when the time was right, when he had chosen it. The act should have been done with love, not with violence or force.

Zack's confidence wavered, and he emanated a growing fear of rejection.

Feeling Zack's emotion so freely was another change. His tattoo must have died when he did. *And now he can feel me.* Takashi remembered how difficult interpreting others' desires and fears was his first few years. Likely, Zack didn't understand that Takashi's violent wishes weren't aimed at him and was growing wary from misunderstanding.

No words would suffice. Takashi threw up a mental wall to shield Zack from his desire for revenge and focused on his budding want to bring Zack close. He opened his arms wide, offering an embrace.

Zack smiled softly, the joy brightening his eyes, and hurried into Takashi's arms. He smelled of fresh dirt and a touch of wintery night. The undercurrent of mortal copper was gone from him. His embrace was stronger and firmer in a way that swayed Takashi's heart.

A weight lifted from his shoulders because Zack was *here*, and he was relatively safe, and he hadn't been suffering these past few nights. He'd been transforming into this marvelous being that Takashi was holding tight in his arms. Though their present situation was far from ideal, they would have *forever*. The three of them could weather the centuries together.

Takashi's desire was a stone dropped into the smooth lake that was Zack's wants, and he felt the way his emotion moved through Zack, rippling and building momentum rather than fading away. Zack nuzzled him and then moved so that their lips brushed when he spoke. "How are you all right?"

"I'm a well-kept hostage," Takashi murmured. "'All right' is a very loose term for how I am."

"What's happened to Roger? Carver? Kit? Vincent?" Zack's voice had an ethereal quality that Takashi had only ever heard from much older vampires. Roger had a bit of it, which lent him a sexier purr that Takashi loved, but Zack's dripped with otherworldliness and a hint of a fathomless strength.

Takashi put his hand on Zack's neck and caressed the edge of his jaw. He missed the feel of Zack's pulse, but oh, the touch of him was something divine. Wishing for happier news would not make it so, and he couldn't ignore the information Zack needed in favor of seeking comfort. Though the longer he stood beside him, the more he craved crawling into bed and keeping him close. *If only Roger were here …*

"Carver's gone," Takashi whispered, hoping that by keeping his voice soft, he might not break the gentle air between them. "The wound he took was grave, and I don't believe he survived it. I don't know what's happened to Kit or Vincent. Roger's alive. He's not here. He's out there."

"You're sure?"

"I saw him running from the mansion two nights ago," Takashi said. "Anton said that he had come looking for us."

"But he left without you."

"He had others with him, and he was carrying Dmitri." Takashi rested his forehead against Zack's. Many of his lovers had been taller than him, but Zack was shorter. Or he had been, at least by a smidge. Zack must have been standing straighter because they were equal height. "You know Roger has a good and cautious heart."

"Yeah," Zack said softly. His voice hitched as he continued. "I don't think mine's that good."

And Takashi could feel what he meant. Zack was radiating with a brimming desire to reach for more. The touch of that want was addictive. Takashi longed to strip him and discover what else might have changed about his lover. There would be no need to be as gentle with him anymore, not unless the moment called for it, and Zack ... oh, Zack had been fun in bed before. Takashi wondered what his cock would feel like inside him. If he was as cold everywhere as he was in his hands and face.

Those longings weren't entirely like Takashi, though. Well, wanting sex wasn't out of the ordinary for him. He had those cravings. But his lust was building when he should have remained focused on the present.

"Zack, what are you thinking right now?" Takashi murmured.

"I should be thinking about how we kill Seamus and escape," Zack replied hoarsely.

"Wasn't the question."

"The answer goes back to my heart's not good."

"Good is entirely relative."

"I don't think 'good' would be thinking about ripping off your clothes and fucking you senseless on the couch. Or the bed. Or in the shower because I'm fucking filthy," Zack whispered.

With those words, Takashi could finally source the desire rising in him. Some of it was his own—that was how it had slipped past his notice—but Zack's power was mingling with Takashi's lust. He wasn't forcing his way in. It was more like Takashi had turned on a bath faucet and Zack had cranked up the flow of the water. Takashi could turn it off. He should.

But he had spent three and a half nights isolated and longing for both of his lovers. Now one was with him. And they weren't in immediate danger. And they were different and the same, and they both wanted more.

"Then I'm not very good either," Takashi said. "Because that's all I can think about, too."

"Am I picking that up from you? I have this, like, pop-up on my mental screen, and it makes this feel *right*." Zack slid his arm around Takashi's waist, and their groins brushed more firmly against each other. Zack was half-hard.

Takashi was thickening in response. "We're in a feedback loop."

"One of us got a little bit horny, the other's picking up on it and giving it back, and it's more and more?" Zack murmured.

"Mmhmm."

"That doesn't sound different than normal lust."

"In many ways, it's not. But it can be more … intense." Takashi leaned his head back. Touching was only increasing the loop. He put his hands on Zack's shoulders. He should push him away, put distance between them. "You're new to your abilities. Saying no might become difficult."

Zack pulled Takashi tighter against him. Light sparkled in his ruby-red eyes. "I don't want to say no."

"Zack …"

"You're worried about me. That's sweet." Zack leaned in and brushed his lips against Takashi's. His touch was brief and featherlight and refreshingly chilly.

All Takashi wanted was more. *Forget good and bad. I deserve him.*

So he kissed him in a slow, gentle slide of their lips. Zack had the faint remnant of blood on him, a little old but tangy. Whoever Zack had drunk from was dead, but that was common on a first night. Takashi grabbed onto his suit jacket tightly, the shirt underneath losing a button as it was pulled too taut in his grip, and traced the seam of Zack's lips with his tongue. A bit of dirt mixed with the blood and the taste of Zack.

"How are you warm?" Zack pressed a kiss to Takashi's cheek, then his neck. He started undoing the buttons of his shirt and slid his hand inside to caress Takashi's chest.

"I'm as cold as I've always been." Takashi untucked his shirt and dropped it to the floor. "You're colder than you should be."

"I am?" Zack kissed behind Takashi's ear. He swept his hand up Takashi's torso until he found his nipple. He rolled his thumb over his tender flesh.

Takashi gasped into Zack's touch. He tipped his head back and to the side so Zack had more area to kiss. "You should be lukewarm, practically room temperature. You're like ice."

"Weird," Zack muttered against Takashi's skin. His lust was growing into a nearly tangible thing. "Maybe I just need more blood. You and Roger are always freezing before you eat."

"Didn't Seamus have someone for you at your grave?" Takashi said. "It's tradition."

Suddenly, the building feedback loop of desire was a cut

cord, and Takashi was left holding his end. The break gave him a clearer mind. There was nothing inherently wrong with what they had been doing, but Zack was fresh from his grave. To him, the fight in the hotel had been earlier in the night. *I should be more careful with him. For his sake.*

"I killed her," Zack whispered. His emotions were sliding into his screaming fear of rejection. He took a step back and lowered his gaze to the floor.

Takashi put his arm around Zack and kept him close. Embracing his continuing desire for him so that Zack might feel it, he said gently, "We all kill the one at the grave."

"Am I going to keep killing?" Zack asked.

"Humans live on death as well," Takashi replied tenderly. "That's what animals do. They gain energy in the destruction and continue on. We vampires are just another kind of animal."

Zack scowled. "You're not comparing drinking blood to eating a hamburger, are you?"

"I'm saying that even eating a salad has taken apart some piece of the world in order to propel life forward. That we don't call the coyote or the hawk evil for eating the rabbit. We vampires have the unique opportunity of not killing our food, but that takes practice."

"This is all messed up." Zack pushed Takashi away. Despite Takashi's attempt to hold on, Zack's strength was greater, and Takashi stumbled backward a few steps before catching his balance. But Zack seemed caught up in his own mind, as if he hadn't put much effort into the shove, and he strode across the room to a cabinet holding Blu-Rays and the like. "Seamus is fucked up. He keeps calling me his *son* and acting like I should appreciate that he gave me his blood as if my choice wasn't death or this."

Some vampires fell into the conceit that their sirelings were a type of offspring; some turned their lovers so they could be with them forever; some found a mortal so special they wanted to preserve them; some chose to make underlings to serve them. Takashi had sired three vampires that fell into the special mortal category. He'd done his duty to them and ushered them into their new lives, teaching them what he could, but they quickly carved their own paths away from him. He didn't resent them for it, but he never felt the bond with them that he did with his own sire.

"Nell treated me like a son," Takashi said. "She never said the word, but she was fond of me, more than some of her other sirelings, and spent time teaching me what being a vampire means."

"Yeah, but that's *Nell*. That's not surprising," Zack said. He gestured around the room. "Look at this shit! He put up *Twilight* posters. Did you tell him about this?"

"No." Takashi went to the bookcase. Volumes upon volumes about war. Zack had been part of a plot to kill Seamus. Why on earth would they give him tactical ideas?

"Takashi—"

Takashi held up his hand to silence Zack. "You're right. This is strange. He should want us dead. We should *be* dead. Instead, he's kept me, and he studied you. I think he's been observing you for a while. Money can move things along, but rooms like this take time to set up."

Zack paused and folded his arms over his chest. "Studied me?"

"He's read your journal and notebooks."

"*Fuck*." Zack started to reach for his hair, then rested his hand back where it had been. "He's got my dagger. Once I get it back, we should go."

"Why?" Takashi asked as he continued examining the various book spines in front of him. Zack was radiating fear, but he shut it out. Fear was an ambition killer, and opportunities were multiplying in front of them.

"Look, I'll admit for a hot second, I was really tempted to stick around and find some way to kill him from the inside."

Zack neared Takashi. "But something really weird is going on here, and it's not sitting right with me. These rooms are filled with stuff I've always wanted, he keeps insisting he's my father, and he wants us at a meeting downstairs. I think it's some kind of coven leadership session. He shouldn't be inviting me into that."

"But he is. There has to be a reason."

"The reason is he's playing mind games to torture us," Zack replied.

"This isn't torture. It's seduction," Takashi said. A few of the puzzle pieces made sense for their shape, but Takashi couldn't grasp the full picture. "We have some value to him. Aren't you the least bit curious why that is?"

Zack shifted uncomfortably where he stood—a very human habit that he'd eventually stop doing. Maybe Zack would never school his body to stop fidgeting like other vampires did, but he likely would. Takashi captured the moment and tucked it away in his heart for another time. Eventually, his drop of grief would expand and demand attention. The bits that made Zack mortal were gone or dying and deserved the noticing of their passing, but the core of who Zack was remained, and Takashi was too relieved and excited for any sadness.

"He's a monster," Zack said.

"I'm not suggesting that we become his friends," Takashi replied. "But he wants something of us, and that gives us leverage."

Zack joined Takashi beside the bookcase. His desires were a roiling mess. New ones brewed quick and hot, then morphed into another before Takashi could interpret what Zack was feeling. There was a steady undercurrent of fear—likely, Zack feared that remaining in the mansion would turn him into a version of Seamus.

"We have each other." Takashi gently put his hand on Zack's elbow.

"Roger spent three hundred years with him," Zack murmured. "I can't do that."

"I couldn't either."

Zack unfolded his arms and lightly took Takashi's hand in his. "What do you think Roger would think of all this?"

"That it's very confusing." Takashi squeezed Zack's hand. "I hope we find a way to ask him sooner rather than later."

Zack returned his grip, though his was stronger, nearly bone-crushing. "Yeah. I mean, if he hasn't left Chicago, then there's got to be a way."

"Exactly." Takashi leaned against Zack. They were side by side and, fates willing, could be until the sun turned the planet to ash. Longer, if they found some way to escape that destruction.

However, in the short term, they didn't have much time. He nudged Zack. "You should get cleaned up."

Slowly, Zack nodded. He gave Takashi a tight smile. "Help me? I'm sure I've got dirt in places I can't reach."

"Of course." Takashi kissed Zack's cheek.

As Zack led the way to the bathroom, Takashi put tighter locks around his growing fears. What was the game? Most coven masters struggled to maintain their status quo from forces inside and out. If Seamus was keeping Zack so close to him, was there a source of danger?

Too many whats and what-ifs. I need to be here for Zack, for both our sakes. So Takashi centered himself and kept his thoughts on the new swagger in Zack's gait. He, Zack, and Roger now had forever with which to build a lasting relationship. Three powerful vampires. *We could conquer the world if we wanted.*

CHAPTER 15

Each new step in this night was a mass of confusion and bizarre changes. Zack had hoped that the people who loved him would still accept him, and yet Takashi's blatant yearning for him was surprising. As Zack held on to his hand, he felt the pop-up growing larger and larger in his mind. He didn't receive a direct image, but Takashi's lust inspired a vivid desire to pin Takashi up against a wall and kiss him until they were both panting.

Only neither of us breathes. So that'd be a while. A longing for more than a kiss grew into a fiercer urge.

He'd died. He could admit what he wanted, at least to himself.

He wanted to fuck Takashi until they were both hoarse from screaming. He wanted to shred his clothes and bend him over. He wanted to do the same to Roger, too—to take him by the hair and yank his head back while he fucked him hard from behind. To feel the way either of them would clench around his cock. To overwhelm them until they were begging for release. To fucking *own* their bodies like he hoped he owned their hearts.

The feedback loop that had died for a moment flared to brilliant life. Zack pushed Takashi up against the bathroom wall. Takashi moaned with a soft, desperate sound that Zack had only heard Roger make him do before.

The fact that he hadn't elicited that specific moan as a mortal but had as a vampire threatened to flip a switch in Zack's mind. Anger attempted to infect his thoughts, but he channeled it into a fierce shield. *What do I want? I want to be in fucking charge.* He grinned at Takashi, showing his fangs.

The pop-up *grew*. Takashi liked him like this. That little thought threatened to resummon the self-doubt that Zack had given an interior voice to for far too long. It wanted to cut through Zack's bond with Takashi and grind his hopes for their relationship into dust.

I've turned him on before. He just hadn't had the inside track to his lover's desires. Now he knew which motions, which caresses were exciting without having to exchange a word or wait for a moan. The emotional reaction came first, the body illustrating it soon after. Slowly, Zack put his hand on Takashi's shoulder, his thumb on the base of his throat, and confidently held him up against the wall while he grinned wider. His smile felt as wicked as his fangs were sharp.

Takashi tried for a kiss.

But Zack leaned just out of his range. The loop was building, and Zack was determined to stay in control. He could keep his head above this. Doing so was surprisingly fun.

"No wonder you chaffed under those rules," Takashi said. "You're a Dom."

"Aren't all vampires?" Zack asked.

"We all play the dominant in public, but some of us find no happiness within that spectrum." Takashi relaxed against the wall, spreading his legs just a little and generally opening his body language. "And some of us like variety."

"I take it that means you're a switch." Zack nipped at

Takashi's lips, accidentally catching one between his fangs. Takashi gasped, and a drop of his blood struck Zack's lip. Reflexively, he licked it. Takashi's blood was ... appealing. He ran his tongue over where the drop had been, but no taste remained.

"Careful," Takashi said. "Blood sharing is a powerful bond, and you won't find my blood as satisfying as a mortal's."

"Does vampire blood always taste weird?"

"Think of it like cola. A bubble, a fizz, but really nothing gained."

"Okay, but I practically lived on that shit."

"You enjoyed the sugar." Takashi chuckled. "You didn't *live* because of it."

"I don't know. Life gets pretty boring without sugar." Zack pulled Takashi's bottom lip between his teeth. He intended to lightly graze a fang against his tender flesh, but he went deeper. A small trickle of blood welled upward. An apology rose to Zack's tongue as he began to pull away, but the scent of blood fanned the burning hunger in his core. He licked Takashi's lip. The bit of blood wasn't enough. Didn't ease the hunger. *I need more.*

Takashi put his hand on Zack's chest and shoved him. Zack stumbled backward three steps.

How dare he, a new voice in Zack's mind declared. It sounded like Seamus.

That voice couldn't be trusted, and yet, there was something right about it. Zack *needed* blood, and Takashi had it. He narrowed his eyes and rushed toward him, even as the rational part of his mind cried out for him to stop. Logic was a burden when the thirst was carving itself through his soul.

He rushed toward his prey. Takashi started to move, started to use that vampire speed to match what Zack had done. But he was too slow. Zack closed the distance and wrapped his hand around Takashi's throat. He slammed Takashi up against the wall, and the surface cracked. Bones snapped, too, and some distant part of Zack screamed. He growled to shove it further away and opened his mouth, readying to sink his fangs into flesh.

The screaming part of his mind grew louder and louder still, as if someone had shoved a microphone into its hands and continued cranking the volume. *I can't lose him. I can't hurt him. I need him. He's going to leave me. He's going to hate me. Everyone's going to hate me.* The strength of that voice wasn't natural, not anymore, but Zack couldn't purge it. He staggered away and put a hand to his head. The climbing fear broke through, and logic put itself back in the forefront.

"I'm sorry," Takashi said softly. "You were going into a frenzy. I had to break it."

"Oh." With his mind precariously balancing, the impact of what Zack had done finally hit him. "Shit. Fuck. Are you okay? I'm sorry. I didn't mean to—"

"It's all right." Takashi stepped away from the wall and smoothed his hair.

But there was a small pop-up coming from him. Zack hovered over it and could see the shape of Takashi's new fear. His voice broke as he said, "You're scared of me?"

"That's reflexive." Takashi raised his gaze to meet Zack's, and the pop-up window shrank. "I should have been faster than you."

Was Takashi scared of him because there was something wrong with him? Or because of the near miss on the blood frenzy? Zack couldn't have killed Takashi by drinking his blood, but it wouldn't have been pleasant. *And what if I hadn't just drunk his blood? Feeding frenzy vamps are dangerous and unpredictable. I've got to keep control.* Especially if he was strong. He'd been nearly as quick as Seamus at the graveyard, and now he had outpaced Takashi without trying.

No, nothing was wrong with him. "Maybe it's the blood they've been feeding you. Maybe it's made you weaker."

"It's the nature of *you*. Do you understand how a vampire is made?"

Zack rolled his eyes. "Seriously?"

"You know the mechanics, of course. But what about the metaphysics?" Takashi asked.

Zack started to bite his lower lip but felt his fangs and stopped. No wonder vampires practiced stilling their motions. The wrong one was too freaking destructive. "A vampire drains their victim, then offers their blood. It forms a connection between the sire and sireling because essentially, the vampire plants like a runner vine in the new vampire. The bond between sire and sireling fades when the magic in the new vamp finally has its own roots."

"That is a more practical understanding. We are talking of magic. The reality is a little more … well, come here." Takashi sat on the lip of the tub and turned on the water until it was pouring in. "Imagine the tub already full of hot water. It's all the way to the rim, slipping over the edges now and then. That's the spirit of a mortal creature. We vampires feed on blood, but we also—"

"Use the blood to drink from the spirit," Zack said. "It's why you and Roger never had to have much of my blood once we really got together. Our connections were deeper, so while you still needed the blood for access, you didn't need as much of it."

"It's also why overfeeding from any source tends to make them lifeless, not just bloodless," Takashi said. "You can steal what brings a person joy by draining away their passions until the very essence of it is gone from their soul. It's what we feed on."

"So much for not feeling like a monster," Zack grumbled.

Lightning-quick, Takashi took his hand. A flash of wanting to soothe popped into Zack's mind. "The more aware you are, the more control you can exhibit. Passion has its own well-spring in a healthy spirit. And you can take care of your pets and nurture their passions, help them grow."

"Passion's like a jet in a hot tub, and I got to make sure it doesn't break," Zack said.

"Exactly." Takashi turned off the tub. About six inches of water were in it. "If I were being thorough, I'd fill this whole thing to make my point. But think of when we feed like reaching in and unplugging the tub. We drain what we need, and if we're not careful, let the whole tub loose. When we make another vampire, we go as close to empty as we dare. The sire then offers their blood, giving that connection to their spirit and putting their magic in place of the drained spirit. You have to be willing to *give*, and the sireling has to be willing to *take*. In most cases, the relation winds up about this much of the tub—pretend it's cold water instead of hot here. This burst of cold brings down the 'temperature' of the remaining spirit, making the person a vampire, and over time, death and the growth of the vampiric magic continues cooling the spirit out and finishes refilling the tub."

Zack shifted his weight from one foot to the other. He had a bad feeling he knew where this was going. *None of my sirelings have ever drawn from me like you did*, Seamus had said. "You think Seamus offered me more than usual?"

"He offered, and you took—and I find no fault in that, Zack." Takashi turned on the water. "You had the opportunity to know what was happening to you, which helped you."

Slowly, Zack joined Takashi and sat on the lip of the tub. Takashi was staring down at the water. "How'd you become a vampire?"

Takashi managed a weak smile, no joy reaching his eyes. "I ran away from home to become a trapeze artist with a traveling circus. My childhood wasn't terrible, not in the least, but my parents were struggling, and I didn't want the future I saw with them. The trapeze was exciting. Almost as exciting as the feelings I had for the boy performer. So I hid in the circus's wagons. When the performers eventually discovered me, they were furious, but I refused to tell them where I came from, and the ringleader had too much of a heart to drive an immigrant boy away. I practiced with an untampered passion, even when my first two years were nothing but endless chores between those late-night practices. Eventually, I became what I wanted. I was even performing with the boy I'd fallen in love with.

"Some performers of our merry band were shifters. It's a lot easier to 'tame the lion' if the lion's a natural-born were-lion who has full control of his senses. We'd heard tale of Taliville, and the management believed it would be the perfect place to winter. I knew of vampires, was told not to venture out into the night on my own, and knew that the town didn't have a mayor but a vampire mistress, Nell.

"We were set to perform for New Year's in order to keep our skills sharp and garner some of that sweet applause we all lived on. The boy I'd secretly loved found out. He … he wasn't happy about it." Takashi paused.

Zack reached out and put his hand on top of Takashi's. When Takashi glanced his way, Zack tried to smile. "He was an idiot?"

"A bigot as it turned out," Takashi murmured, his smile still broken. He was trying, though, and he held on to Zack's hand. "I don't know if he let me fall on purpose during that performance or if it was an accident. Nell certainly blamed him. He was the one she'd brought to my grave for my first kill, so I never had a chance to ask him."

Zack winced. "Brutal."

"We are not kind creatures by nature," Takashi replied. "But my making was a mercy. Nell thought me a light too beautiful to leave the world, so when I fell forty feet to the hard ground, she rushed to my side. If I hadn't taken her blood, I would have had an eternity of painful minutes left on this earth."

"You didn't die instantly on hitting the ground?" Zack scoffed at himself. "I mean, of course you didn't, because you had time to drink her blood. But was there any chance you would've lived?"

"No." Takashi waited a long beat before continuing. "I wanted so badly to live, and Nell gave me her magic. I had a bit more than the average sireling, and the metaphorical water was far colder than what most sirelings receive." He turned off the tub. "I think you had the same cold but something more like this volume."

The tub was half-full. With the size and depth of the tub, it was enough water for Zack to submerge himself. And it was far, far more than the amount it had been before. He stared at the depths. "But he'd have to offer this much."

"He would."

Zack reached for the water. The memory of his last mortal moments began, but he focused on the present rather than letting it sweep away his mind. "I wanted the strength to destroy him. I wanted to avenge us. Why would he give me this much? What's the point in setting all this up? What's his angle?"

"I'm not sure, but figuring it out is my priority." Takashi linked his fingers with Zack's and squeezed. "I am grateful I won't have to do it alone."

"Roger's out there," Zack said. "We could break out of here. Steal my dagger back and run."

"Close your eyes," Takashi said.

"Why?"

"Just do it."

Zack sighed and did so.

"Raise your right hand."

Zack did.

"Now your left."

"What is the—"

"Just listen to me for a moment and do what I say."

"Fine." Zack raised his left hand.

"Drop them both to your lap. Head down, head up. Turn left." Takashi kept the instructions quick. "Where's Seamus?"

"Down a floor and one hundred and eighty feet to the north," Zack said without thinking. Startled, he opened his eyes. "How the fuck did I know that?"

"You're a brand-new sireling. You're connected that deeply." Takashi's gaze was on the water for a long, long moment. Then he seemed to come back to himself. "You need to get cleaned up."

"Will you help me?" Zack asked. "Feels like the dirt is everywhere."

Takashi grinned, and this time, there was a bit of happiness in his eyes. "I'd be happy to, so long as we can keep ourselves from a lust spiral."

"Eh, no promises." Zack stripped off his filthy suit jacket. "It's better to think about that than everything else going on in my head."

"I'm sure we can put our focus elsewhere." Takashi helped Zack pull his shirt off.

Zack kicked off his shoes and unbuckled his belt. "What do you think Roger's doing right now?"

"I like to pretend he's holed up in a cozy house a million miles away from here," Takashi replied.

"That would drive him nuts. He hates being alone." Zack shucked his pants and stepped into the water. It was impossibly hot, but rather than feeling like it was scalding him, the heat sank into his bones and was delightful. "Fuck, that's good. I've never really been a bath person, but—"

"It has a way of warming us," Takashi said. "Maybe Roger's taking a bath."

"Maybe you should join me," Zack said with a grin.

Takashi shook his head. "Don't start."

"Fine." Zack sank into the bath. "But first chance we get, we're buying a hot tub and doing whatever the fuck we want in it. Including fucking."

Takashi laughed, and there was a soft note in it that Zack had never heard when he was a mortal. Was it new? Or was it some trick of his voice that Zack's enhanced hearing could now detect? Either way, Zack had brought it out of him, and that warmed him as much as the water.

CHAPTER 16

The hot bath was like drinking the richest cocoa and having a heated blanket wrapped around him. With Takashi's help, Zack was able to scrub off the last of the dirt. By the time he climbed out of the tub, he swore he had a slight blush of pink in his skin tone. However, that faded from one blink to the next, and he was porcelain white once more.

As he dressed in a black suit, he catalogued some of the other changes to his body. Though he'd always been dexterous, he navigated changing into clothes with a bit more ease. Somewhere along the line, he'd lost a trace of his weight—Zack was willing to bet it'd been water—and his abs weren't super defined, but his muscles were a fraction more obvious. His tattoo was gone from his hip as if it'd never been there.

The wounds and light scars he'd gained during his time with Roger and Takashi were healed to nothing, except for the first one that Roger had given him. Takashi had stroked it during the course of the bath, and Zack touched his skin to feel the ever-so-slight scar tissue. Somehow, still having it was reassuring. That mark belonged to *him*. That moment was his first real step toward becoming *this*, and this? Maybe this wasn't so bad.

"For studying me so much, Seamus put way too much black into my wardrobe." Zack buttoned his cuffs.

Takashi was going through the cases on the top of the dresser. Then he brandished one, holding out a box of cufflinks for display. "It's custom among young vampires, especially ones with sires of means."

"Is the goal to make us more badass?" Zack asked.

"To hide the blood. Drinking without getting it everywhere is an art."

"Oh." Zack swallowed the guilt about feeding on the girl in the graveyard. Her blood had gotten on his mouth, but had he been sprayed with it? He'd been too caught up in his own shit to notice. Just like he was letting that void come for him now. *Focus.* Some of the cufflinks had gems; some were made of gold or platinum. One set was like the crest on his coffin. He picked one up and showed it to Takashi. "You ever know of a newborn vamp with a crest before?"

"Some of the old ones still do that for their young," Takashi said. He raised an eyebrow. "Is that yours?"

"It's on a coffin in that room over there." Zack motioned to the coffin's closet. "Weapons are a sign of weakness, aren't they? Among vampires, I mean."

"Ah, no." Takashi took the matching one out and set the case down. He slid it into Zack's cuff and fastened it. "This means you were a hunter in life."

"Not a lot of hunters become vampires, I guess," Zack said quietly.

"Not really."

"Should I be wearing these?" Zack put the other one in his right cuff.

"We are stuck in Seamus's game. What we need right now is influence and knowledge," Takashi said. "If he's giving you tools and prestige, use them."

"And the more I suck up the attention, the better off you'll be?" Zack asked.

Takashi shook his head. "I doubt we'll get much reprieve, particularly in public. They'll be watching us, but that doesn't mean we can't find advantages."

Zack pulled Takashi close to him and rested his forehead against his. The habit was one of Roger's, he realized, but he gained a sense of calm from sensing the little pop-ups from Takashi's emotions. Just a small fear, just a tiny desire. Nothing that Zack wanted to investigate, but knowing they were there settled his own fears. Whatever happened next, he wasn't alone.

"Guess we should get down there," Zack muttered.

Takashi took his hand and squeezed him tight. "If we're useful—"

"Then he won't get rid of us." Zack groaned. "I don't like the idea of making myself useful to a monster."

"We're biding time to make a plan."

"That's what we *were* doing."

Takashi cupped Zack's cheek. "We were waiting for Roger before. You're not a piece needing instruction anymore, Zack. You're a player at the board."

I have power. Zack nodded. "Right. Okay then. Let's go see what my 'father' wants."

Grimsby was waiting out in the hall for them, and without a word, he led them through the mansion to the first floor. The interior of the mansion was a labyrinth with room upon room of stuff. Zack was pretty sure they passed at least two libraries, some kind of art gallery, three different sitting rooms, and a multimedia room with the biggest screen he'd seen short of a movie theater.

Zack could pick out a multitude of tiny sounds—a distant heartbeat here, a soft footfall down that corridor—but the quiet was oppressive. Each sound felt like it was breaking an unspoken sanctity. *No, it's like prey not wanting to be noticed.*

Voices drifted from farther down the hall, and they lacked the trepidation of the mansion's other sounds. The knowing in the back of Zack's mind easily found Seamus's voice when they were still too far for him to make out words. He was walking ever closer toward the magnet pulling on his soul. The hunger churning in his gut settled into an annoying itch rather than a burning heat. Without it clouding his focus, data was clicking into place. He was picking up more details with his heightened senses—from the brushstrokes in various paintings to the exact stench a group of vampires made.

Somehow, being near my sire makes me stronger? My vampiric magic must be missing its source. Two halves of a whole until we heal.

I knew you were clever, the Seamus voice said.

Zack frowned and put a hand to his temple. That had been a little ... eerie. But imagining the other half of conversations was something he often did, especially with people he hated. *I don't hate Cal.*

Yes. You do, his rational voice replied.

Whatever. I'm about to walk into a hunter's worst nightmare, so this will wait. Zack lowered his hand and continued walking. Takashi was a half step behind him, but when Zack tried to match him, he fell back again. Zack glanced over his shoulder, a question on his lips. Takashi shook his head and mouthed, "Trust me."

Grimsby stopped beside an archway. He bowed his head and motioned into the room.

"Thank you," Zack said softly.

Grimsby dipped his head a touch farther, which Zack guessed was supposed to be some sort of "you're welcome."

Then Zack took a big, unnecessary breath and strode into the room.

One of Zack's favorite rooms at his grandparents' house had been the War Room, where the Wrights, and to some extent the Gladwells and other hunters, organized bigger hunts and operations. When the room wasn't hosting a meeting, Grandpa used it to track hunters and their targets on maps. Even though a lot of things went digital, he persisted in using physical maps. He claimed he'd seen enough of those CSI shows to know that some sort of digital thing could be dug out fifty different ways, but a destroyed paper map was always unintelligible. *If they haven't burned the most recent set of maps and reorganized the hunters, they will when they find out about me.*

Seamus's War Room had a long dark wood table down the center. The ten vampires sitting at it were all on one side, and across from them on the wall was a bank of monitors. There were twenty screens in total, and only two of them were blank. A different person was projected onto each of the remaining eighteen. One vampire was complaining, "If my peer in Champaign would keep her werewolves from terrorizing my campus—"

"I hardly call Eastern a *campus*," another vampire on-screen said, snorting in derision.

The first straightened. "This disrespect is exactly what I mean! My alliance with the Whetstone Creek Panthers is contingent upon keeping werewolves from the university. She's letting them infect students in my territory!"

The second rolled her eyes. "The number of canyons you had to jump in order to reach that conclusion is *staggering* and, honestly, a bit insulting. The pack in Decatur could just as easily be infecting your precious students."

"No, they couldn't," Zack said automatically.

All attention turned toward him. The vampires on the screens were suddenly looking down at their keyboards and fussing—they had to be adjusting their views on the room.

The sheer amount of power in the room became abundantly clear. Not only was Seamus sitting at the center of the table, but he had Anton on his right and Candide on his left. The other seven vampires in the room were ones that Zack recognized from his research on the coven leadership. The remaining captains—Lucille and Dempsey—were also present. The other vampires were lieutenants, among them Marcus and Xenofon, and were more directly in charge of sets of vampire or territory than the captains were. Which meant the ones on the screens were lieutenants in the rest of Seamus's huge domain.

And I just corrected someone. Panic started to set in. With that, the realization that everyone in the room would be able to feel his fear. His spiral started to spin and descend faster. Little pop-ups of others' emotions began to crowd his mental real estate. Malicious desires left vague impressions, but he got the sense that several people in the room wanted him to fail.

Then Takashi put his hand gently on his back, and Zack could pick out his pop-up from the rest. He longed for something good to happen, for Zack to shine.

I can do this. Zack continued. "The Decatur Pack are natural-born shifters, and there's never been a case of contracted lycanthropy associated with their pack. In fact, they see their wolf form as an aspect of their true selves and reject 'infected' wolves on the assumption that everyone who gains lycanthropy winds up seeing it as a separate beast rather than accepting it into themselves. They're kind of dogmatic assholes. They wouldn't work on spreading their strain of werewolf except through having more kids."

The silence in the room suddenly matched the rest of the mansion. Zack was standing in the heart of the damn predator's nest with over two dozen monsters staring at him. *Not monsters,* the Seamus voice said. *Peers. They're your peers now.*

"Who the hell is that?" the Champaign lieutenant demanded.

Seamus smiled with a subtle little pride. "That would be my new sireling and son, Zackery, the Blade in the Night."

An epithet? Already? Though Zack could think at a quicker speed, the idea of it caught him off guard, and he failed to hide his surprise from the others. He loved the sound of the Blade in the Night. He felt dangerous with the moniker. But crests and epithets had to be earned, didn't they? Yet Seamus was just dumping prestige onto him. *Because if he's going to claim me as his son, then I have to be special. Otherwise, he looks weak.*

While the others were older, not all of them had perfectly schooled reactions. Zack saw flickers of surprise and anger flash across their faces.

A glint of pride shimmered in Seamus's mottled red and blue eyes before he turned his attention back to the monitors before him. Xenofon schooled his features into an unreadable mask. Except for Marcus, no one else seemed to care that Zack was now in the room.

Marcus was a pasty vampire who was clearly trying too hard to look like a badass since he was dressed in black leathers. Everyone else at the meeting was dressed in more casual business fashion, including Anton. Marcus's shoulder-length brown hair was styled a lot like Roger's, though the color wasn't nearly as interesting, and while his hazel eyes had a range of color, they seemed the most boring shade of green Zack had ever seen.

Focusing on him made finding his pop-ups in the mess recurring in Zack's mind a little easier, but figuring out *what* he was reading from the other vampire was still a struggle. But then Marcus locked eyes with him, and it became clear.

He wants me dead. Zack lifted an eyebrow. Marcus was the vampire who ran Steward's Garden, where he placed mind-controlling gray bands onto innocent mortals' arms. Zack slid his hands into his pockets and imagined using his new abilities to rip Marcus into tiny pieces. And the reassuring thing was that he possessed that kind of power. Winning a fight wasn't as theoretical as it had been. *Blade in the Night. I can live up to that.*

"Zackery is correct," Seamus said with an authoritative note. "The Decatur Pack does not spread its lycanthropy.

Furthermore, I'm inclined to believe that you've suggested to the Champaign wolves that they invade the territory."

"Master, I haven't—"

"Dempsey?" Seamus said.

Dempsey, a vampire with deep brown skin and who looked absolutely bored in the proceedings, lifted a folder. His suit was a pale purple that reminded Zack of the fading sunlight just before twilight claimed the sky. "The Ardent Circle of Southern Illinois performed a divination for us on one of the newly turned wolves. A member of the Champaign Pack of the Woods was responsible."

"That doesn't mean that *I*—" Penelope began.

"You either have control of your wolves, or you're letting them run wild. If they are wild, rein them in," Seamus snapped. "We cannot afford for them to jeopardize other allegiances. Is that understood, Penelope?"

"Yes, master."

"We have confirmation of four new wolves. You will pay Mathias four million dollars."

"Master!"

Seamus slammed his hand on the table. "Complain again and I will grant Jordan's request for consolidation and absolve you of your responsibilities. Potentially relieve you of more than that."

Penelope looked down.

"Penelope will pay four million to Mathias. Mathias, you are to use that money to make amends with the Whetstone Pride. If I discover you've built another donor house with it, I will have it burnt to the ground."

"I understand, master," Mathias said.

"Let's take a ten-minute break," Seamus said. "At that point, we'll begin with Benedict and Leopold. If the two of you are bickering over whether or not Indiana 39 is a terrible boundary again, I will take those beautiful twins from you."

"I assure you, master, that's not our concern," one of the vamps on a monitor said.

"Good." Seamus hit a button, and the screens went dark. He gestured at the archway. "Refreshments are across the hall, as usual."

The others rose and bowed their head toward Seamus before moving toward the exit. Zack took a step out of their way, then realized that Seamus probably meant him to leave, too, and started to go after Candide.

"Not you, Zackery. We need to have a word," Seamus said.

A sinking feeling dropped Zack's confidence into his toes. Too many times in the past, he'd thought he'd given a right answer only for one of his elders to get upset that he'd interrupted them. Cal had been extremely dismissive of Zack's knowledge. *You don't know what you're doing, Zack. You haven't been out in the field.*

Takashi flashed Zack a quick, warm smile before leaving with the others.

Alone with his sire once more, Zack fought to keep his expression neutral. *I have every right to be pissed at him. He fucking murdered me.* He put his hands behind his back and clasped one with the other so he didn't make a fist in plain sight.

"Was he a pleasant surprise?" Seamus asked without looking at Zack. Instead, he seemed more interested in his tablet.

Zack glanced at the archway. Voices carried in this tomb of a home, and he didn't need anyone else learning his secrets and manipulating him. He closed the distance and sat in Anton's seat so that he could drop his voice to its softest volume. "Fuck. You."

Seamus raised an eyebrow. "You should be thanking me. I could have killed him."

"I doubt you kept him around just for me," Zack replied quickly. "I don't know what your game is yet—"

"I am not playing a game." Seamus sighed heavily and set his tablet down. "Takashi is clever and handsome and makes a decent partner for you. You at least don't mind his manipulations."

Zack stiffened and was about to lash out, but Seamus wasn't *technically* wrong. Takashi had exerted influence over his mind, and Zack had accepted it. "He was helping me."

"You've come down before I anticipated. I thought you and Takashi would spend time reuniting."

"I got distracted by the fact that you've been studying me," Zack replied. "How long did that room take to set up? A month? Two?"

"A few of the better details weren't in place after I obtained your journal and notes earlier this week," Seamus said as he stood. "But I've been preparing for the last seven weeks."

"You've been *planning* on turning me into a vampire?" Zack snarled.

Seamus caught him by the chin and held him tight, forcing their gazes to lock. The first time they'd met, he'd done something similar. Unlike then, Zack refused to feel anything other than rage for the monster in front of him. He was ready for whatever punishment that would bring.

Instead, Seamus broadened his smile and let his touch turn tender. "Do you know how many pets piss themselves when they meet me for the first time? Especially Roger's pets? Though I could feel the brush of terror in your heart, you did not cave." Seamus laughed. "You told me I might be disappointed in you! You were pouring your heart into killing me even then. While I admit that is a nuisance, I've overcome worse."

Seamus released him and picked up his tablet. "I had hoped you'd wake last night so that your rising wouldn't conflict with my meeting. I thought about postponing, but several of these matters have been piling up."

"And you wanted me here to see what the leadership is like?" Zack asked carefully.

"You have a mind that connects details." Seamus renewed his smile. "That fact about the Decatur Pack, for example. I'm not surprised that Roger didn't know how to take advantage of your talent. He's never had a head for making the tough calls."

"Is that why he's still alive?" Zack said. "You're not scared of him?"

"He may yet be of use." Seamus held up a hand when Zack opened his mouth to ask another question. "We only have a few minutes before the others return." He raised his voice. "Grimsby, do bring her in."

Zack frowned and was about to question Seamus anyway.

Then Grimsby strode into the room with a bound woman struggling in his arms. She was on her feet, but he was dragging her along. Her heart was pounding, and as Zack zeroed in on the sound, it thundered in his ears. She smelled ... the closest Zack could pin it to was warm apple pie, cinnamon and apple and so fucking good. He wanted to dig his fangs into her throat and take that warmth from her. Wanted to know if she tasted as good as she smelled.

No. He clenched his fists. Biting would likely lead to killing. Especially around Seamus. The bastard wanted him to be a killer. To be just like him.

"You have to eat, Zackery," Seamus said. "Denying your hunger instead of embracing it will only hurt you in the end."

"I'm fine." Zack couldn't tear his eyes away from the woman's neck. Her pulse wasn't jumping in her neck until she planted her feet and tried to yank herself free of Grimsby. In doing so, she turned her head far enough that her neck was taut and her jugular rose in rhythm to her heart.

Seamus snapped his fingers in front of Zack's nose.

Zack blinked and glared at Seamus.

"You're proving my point." Seamus stood. "Did you taste Takashi's blood earlier?"

If Zack had had any color to his face, he was sure it would have drained away. "How did you know?"

"I felt your bloodlust." Seamus approached the woman. He stepped around behind her and grabbed her by the hair. Using that grip and his other arm, he held her tight against him. "The blood drives us in our first nights. Don't fault yourself for that. By indulging, you will figure out how to sate your needs and discover balance."

"I don't want to kill her," Zack whispered. His voice was a hollow, distant thing, and he wished he could take those words back. Seamus would only use them against him.

Instead of any anger, Seamus remained patient, his tone and manner not changing from the calm, fatherly demeanor. "You were always meant to be a killer, Zackery. This isn't a sacrifice of your nobility. If it helps ease your mind, she is despicable. What do they call them? TERDs?"

"TERFs," Zack replied. "You're lying. You don't care about my conscience."

"I don't want you to suffer for the next several decades lamenting because you did what nature demanded in order to survive." Seamus held the woman tighter when she suddenly bucked. He pressed his cheek against hers, and a wave of terror slipped out from her. She froze in place.

Zack could see the change and thought he smelled the difference in her fear. She wasn't cinnamon anymore but salty. Salty, salty fries had been a delicious treat.

"Letting you run around biting everyone in sight worsens my reputation as well, you know," Seamus said. "I didn't parade you in front of the leadership only for you to embarrass me. I want you to learn control, but the only way to do that is to feed and accept that you may struggle to spare them at first."

"Why are you so chill about this?" Zack asked.

"You mean, why aren't I an asshole right now?" Seamus stepped back from the woman, and she remained where she was. "I told you, I understand why your impression of me is so abominable. I forgive you for that, but you should open your eyes and come to your own conclusions. You did about Roger."

The situation couldn't have been more different. Roger had bit him out of hunger and then broke off the fight in order to save Zack's life. Everything that tumbled out afterward between them was two people growing closer. Seamus was trying to manufacture love and trust.

Zack longed for his dagger. He felt for its presence, but it wasn't in the room. Seamus must have tucked it away in the mansion somewhere. Zack could only gain a general feel for the direction it was in.

And he was hungry. And Seamus had a point. Zack hadn't learned how to stake a vampire in one go. It'd taken practice. *Even babies have to learn how to eat.*

"When I had a drop of Takashi's blood, I started to go into a frenzy," Zack admitted. "If I do that with her, you could stop me, couldn't you?"

"Now you're asking me to manipulate your emotions?" Seamus asked neutrally.

"Wouldn't want to be an embarrassment."

"I won't let you attack anyone else. Now." Seamus nodded at the woman. "Come take hold of her. You want to control her upper torso as much as her head. Our fangs are sharp. If she bucks or twists too much, you'll cause more damage than you intend."

Woodenly, Zack approached the woman. The part of him that had taken on a Cal voice was threatening to speak up, but Zack shoved it down. *I'm a vampire. I'm hungry. All I can do is learn.* She wasn't fighting—whatever Seamus had done to her fear was still in place—so Zack had no trouble taking hold of her. He bared his fangs.

"Ah, ah," Seamus said. "Not yet."

Zack scowled at him.

Seamus shook his head and laughed gently. "You wanted to learn control. Across the room, control is easy. Don't look so disappointed. We don't have much time before the others are back, so I won't make you wait long. You never want to bite the front of the neck. The angle is atrocious, but if you're trying to spare them, then you don't want to pierce their windpipe. You'll be tempted to clamp onto the pulse throbbing in her neck. What throbs has blood pressure, and in the neck area, one wrong nick and your dinner is bleeding out in seconds. You want to consume from your bite, not lose it down the front of your shirt."

Somehow, Seamus's teaching tone helped settle the nerves climbing inside Zack. *Just because he's the bad guy doesn't mean he's wrong about everything. I mean, I haven't met a more prolific killer. Except maybe Cal.* Zack minutely nodded along to Seamus's speech while waiting for his opportunity. Blood was right there for the taking, and he *needed* it.

"All right," Seamus said. "Now you can bite her."

Zack took an extra second to map out the different things Seamus had said to avoid. Then he sank his fangs into her. Blood welled as he closed his mouth around the wound. He swallowed the first mouthful. More was waiting for him. Each swallow brought the soothing liquid into him and smothered the burning hunger in him. The taste was too novel to put into words. Zack slipped from himself to that place between consciousness and bliss, just a half step from forgetting reality entirely.

You'll kill her, the voice in his head said.

I'm. HUNGRY.

So he drank.

The taste of the blood changed, becoming bitter. Startled, Zack released her, and the woman crumbled to the floor.

She didn't have a heartbeat anymore.

"Shit," Zack said. He started to bend down toward her.

Seamus put his hand on Zack's shoulder. With his other hand, he tipped Zack's chin back up. When Zack started to move, Seamus put more weight into his grip. "Never apologize for doing what you need in order to thrive, Zackery. You are worthy of this life."

The sentiment had to be a lie. Another manipulation. Seamus didn't care about anyone other than himself. That was what Zack had heard over and over, and he'd seen it for himself. A few nice words and a room full of expensive shit didn't change the fact that Seamus had beaten him to death's doorway. He'd only offered Zack the chance to become a vampire because it suited him. Zack just had to figure out *why*.

And he had to ignore the seed in his heart that threatened to sprout. Seamus couldn't be sincere. He was evil. Everything he was doing had to be an act. Zack had to match him and keep pace, or he'd drown.

But Zack wasn't sure he was acting when he managed a smile at Seamus and murmured a warm "Thank you."

CHAPTER 17

The other vampires led the way across the hall and three doors down. Takashi fell into step at the back of the group. Anton separated from the pack and carried on farther into the mansion while Xenofon, who had taken the front, opened the door. The smell of mortals drew Takashi's attention, but he pushed his hunger back into its place. These were the other powerful elites of the GLC, and he had spent weeks attempting to know them. Without Seamus or Anton or even Roger, this was his chance to make an impression on them. He followed them into the room.

The space was barren of features except for eight wooden posts. Each side had a metal hoop attached to it. The same kind of heavy metal hoops were attached to the walls at regular intervals. Sixteen mortals—all human, Takashi realized from the smell—were gagged and tied to these hoops. Each was a fair distance from the next. All were naked. Some were weeping, while others seemed too checked out to realize what was happening to them.

Takashi had been in rooms like this before. Ancient vampires rarely had any caring for a mortal's sanity, let alone their well-being, unless they belonged to their collection.

Selections like this were like grapes on a vine, a ripe grouping meant for the plucking and pleasure of a fresh bite.

Before Takashi had taken his third step into the room, Marcus whirled on him. He squared his shoulders, using his few inches of height superiority to puff up and loom over him. While he was nearly two hundred years old, Marcus barely had a scent of the grave. He flared his eyes red, but it was a pale, muddy color. His anger was an obvious and superficial thing. He put his hands on his hips and demanded, "What did Roger do?"

"Pardon me?" Takashi said.

Jong-Su, one of the other lieutenants, stepped up beside Marcus and narrowed his eyes. "One minute, Roger seems like he's ready to suck Seamus off for the umpteenth time, and the next, Seamus is casting him out."

"Oh, good lord," Aileen, another lieutenant, said with a roll of her eyes as she strode to the far side of the room. "Roger declared that human boy his boyfriend at the gala. He's clearly gone soft. Seamus can't stand a weak captain, and none of us should tolerate one."

"I'd buy that if the same human wasn't now Seamus's 'son,'" Xenofon said. He stood beside a boy who might have been eighteen. As he spoke, he was casually using his power on the boy, toying with the boy's fears and desires in a way that made his body react. The behavior was vulgar and cruel.

And one I've seen too often. Interrupting another vampire with their food was a faux pas. Takashi dropped another mental wall into place. Who was to say the boy was an innocent? Takashi had fed on many "good people" who had used their privilege and wealth to intentionally harm others. The boy could have easily been one of them. Takashi didn't owe some random boy his own life, and wasn't about to jump up and down on a wire he was struggling to balance on.

"So," Xenofon was saying, "what did our illustrious Roger do?"

"He was plotting to take the throne," Dempsey said simply.

Decades of living as a diplomat among dangerous creatures kept Takashi from a knee-jerk reaction. Dempsey had been among the group Roger had trusted. He was one of Candide's oldest sirelings, one *she* trusted and treasured.

"A real laugh that he thought it'd work," Lucille added. She, too, was of Candide. Every ounce of her teenage good looks was morphed by the sadistic glee in her grin into a reflection of the worst Takashi had seen from their species. She gestured at Marcus. "He hates those gray bands of yours, Marcus."

"They serve a practical function!" Marcus announced defensively.

Lucille shrugged.

As subtly as he could, Takashi kept Candide in the corner of his eye. She had been at the same meeting where Roger had brought Lucille and Dempsey into his confidence. Dmitri and Takashi had been there as well, though Dmitri had left upon hearing Roger's intentions for their gathering. Dempsey had been advocating for a coven support system for artists like himself, especially for ones that could be turned and join the fold. Lucille had seemed relieved that anyone was willing to overthrow Seamus.

And they were both Candide's sirelings.

Roger had been confident that Candide was on his side. Was she a traitor?

In public, Candide tended toward smiles and exuded a charismatic warmth. She had a charm that was impossible to deny, but Roger had told Takashi that that was a false face. She used her guiles to lure people into believing her good moods were for them. *She's warm, then cold, then genuine*, Roger had said about her. Recently, Seamus had nearly broken through her outermost façade when he'd threatened Ezra.

At the moment, her gentle smile had a strain to it, one nearly imperceptible to anyone who wasn't looking for such a thing. She tsked at her sirelings as she circled the room to find a victim. She settled on one near the back of the room. Takashi had a clear line of sight to her, but few others would, especially since they were focused on him. "Now, now, mes petits, it's rude to insult those who aren't in a position to defend themselves."

"Give it *up*, Candide," Xenofon complained. He said toward Takashi more than the others, "You'd think after almost three hundred years, she'd figure out she has the wrong equipment to please him."

"And you'd think after two hundred, you'd learn how to enjoy a meal without torturing it first. I suppose that's why Seamus likes having me around. He's lacking in sophisticated subordinates," Takashi replied with a light tone.

The gamble had been a big risk, but the die was cast. Takashi couldn't take back the quip that had come out of his lips.

Xenofon abandoned the boy in front of him and moved with a liquid speed at Takashi. Though he was quick, Takashi saw him in motion. A few nights without good blood weren't enough to dismantle Takashi's powers. He could move out of the way with only a little effort.

Instead, he let Xenofon grab him by the throat and shove him up against the wall. Xenofon's incredibly emotional response was something that the young were supposed to indulge in, not someone this old. *These fuckers love to think they're so powerful and they're so easy to play.* Xenofon was snarling in his face. The intimidation attempt would have worked—if Takashi had been two nights old and not an experienced vampire who'd had multiple private conversations with Anton that week.

Inspiration struck. Unpredictability had its uses. Takashi leaned back against the wall and laughed in Xenofon's face.

He watched for the reactions across the room. Marcus's shock was as clear as the trumpet of an elephant. Jong-Su and the final vampire in the room, Kazik, narrowed their eyes at him while doing their best to school their features into expressionless masks. Lucille raised an eyebrow; Aileen and Dempsey continued to slurp blood from their victims.

Candide shot Takashi the glimmer of a brief smile, but it brightened her eyes. Then she bit her prey and ignored him.

Having gathered the information, Takashi slapped his hand over Xenofon's wrist and held on tight. Then he pumped every inch of fear that had driven him across the tightrope of life for the last few nights into Xenofon. Xenofon's grip began to slip, so Takashi took greater hold and twisted his arm hard enough that bones snapped.

Xenofon screamed and went to his knees.

The sound was pleasing. A hypnotic rush was swung through Takashi. The centrifugal force was drawing violent desires outward.

Cruelty was part of being a vampire. Takashi tempered his for moments like this, ones where he could punish the fucking worst—their kind, humanity, the fey, it didn't matter. Justification added a narcotic carte blanche to his actions and absolved him of his guilt.

The right application of pressure and strength would rend Xenofon's arm from his body, and he wouldn't fondle any more boys with that hand. At least, he wouldn't if Takashi managed to destroy the limb before Xenofon could stick it back to himself and heal it.

But that might be the step too far. Seamus would likely blame Xenofon for being weak enough to fall into this position, but how would Takashi ever explain this to Zack? Would he approve? After all, Zack had no problem killing vampires. He'd done so twice without any remorse. Was maiming worse than murder to him? *He's one of us now. His mind might have changed.*

Only so far, Zack seemed roughly the same, apart from his newfound abilities and traumas.

Roger, on the other hand, might struggle with the morality of it. In all their conversations about what the coven would look like, he had shied away from any discussion of punishment. Taking someone's arm probably appeared on his list of don'ts.

Without knowing, Takashi decided to uphold his reputation as a stately professional in complete control and released Xenofon. He kicked him over in order to put Xenofon onto his back and make any move of retaliation more obvious. However, the psychic and violent display seemed to have worked. Xenofon cradled his arm and made muted noises of pain, but he didn't seem in the mood to strike.

Takashi bent down. He let the ice in his soul crisp his voice. "Put an unwelcome hand on me again and lose it."

"I am twice your age," Xenofon snarled as he stood. "You will show me the respect I deserve."

Takashi rose as Xenofon did. He kept half his attention on his peripheral vision. He stood alone in a room of predators. But he was one of them, and he would show his fangs rather than cower. Nell had had a muzzle and harness on him; Roger had had his leash of hesitation. Now he and Zack were in the midst of dangerous glory-seekers, and his strength would help shield his lover. *I've been looking for an excuse to let go.*

"I do not respect that which is not worth a drop of spoiled blood," he said calmly.

Xenofon snarled and stretched his hands out like claws, his nails filed to dagger points. He started to rear back for a strike.

Takashi shifted his weight, one shoulder slightly forward, his other foot back. Narrowing his body would limit Xenofon's easiest target zones. *If he goes for strength, then a little maneuvering should work. I could counter a strike, use his momentum to flip him ...*

"He has a valid point," Anton said. The elder vampire was suddenly leaning against the doorframe as if he'd been watching the whole interaction from there. He pushed off with the same sort of bored attitude he'd spoken with and strolled into the room. "I *begged* my love to round you up and allow me to turn you to ashes. I mean, honestly, Xenofon. You might be twice Takashi's age, but you've never been half as talented.

"But do you know what we need from you in this new millennia? What we have not seen?" Anton demanded. He finished half a circle and strode into the center of the room. He made eye contact with each of the vampires in the room except for Takashi. Every single subordinate lowered their gaze. Candide took the longest, but even she bent her head. "*Loyalty.* For the rare one among you, it is misplaced, but at least you have it. The rest of you prefer to spend your time guzzling blood, playing with your toys, and shoving each other out of the spotlight in petty displays of what you perceive as strength.

"We have no use for pathetic subordinates. My love will take our coven into a new era, and if you are not ready to devote yourselves to him, then I have a room in the basement for you. At least until I have the fires ready." On the last word, Anton finally swept his attention to Takashi.

His point was clear. A misstep would lead Takashi to that fate. *Likely sooner than it would any of the others.* Keeping his gaze locked on Anton, Takashi slid his focus to the edges of his vision. Any mirth in the room had evaporated, and the resulting chill was a familiar one. The others had fallen into an icy stillness common to the long dead.

Anton grabbed the boy that Xenofon had tormented by the back of his head and yanked him forward. Doing so strained the boy against his bonds, and he let out a cry of pain. Over that, Anton said, "Now, I suggest you all stop fucking around and eat."

Anton sank his fangs into the boy. The smell of fresh, vibrant blood awoke the hunger churning in Takashi. As others began to feed from their victims, that scent compounded and became a hypnotic call. The mortals' pounding heartbeats were a race, with some already finishing their last run.

Takashi went to the mortal closest to him. Details blurred into the realm of inconsequential information. This was food, nothing more. He threaded his hand through their hair and forced their head to the side, revealing more of their neck. They were whimpering, but that was a flavor that Takashi hadn't indulged in a few weeks.

He bit his prey, and blood quickly pooled in his mouth. Each swallow was calming the fire twisting through him, and he eagerly drank down every drop. All too soon, the mortal's heart tripped, skipped, and began to fail.

He could rationalize his action—after all, in circumstances like this, killing the mortal was to be expected. Leaving this one alive in a room where others were dying was liable to break the mortal's sanity. The excuse was an easy one to make.

But the sweetest blood from a victim came from the moment before death, and Takashi hadn't indulged in that taste in months. He drank down his prey's last moments, and something inside him finally *relaxed*.

His joy lasted the breadth of a singular fractional eternity; while he was in it, it stretched on forever, yet the glory quickly dissipated, and he was left with the reality of a corpse in his arms. Tenderly, he released the body, and it went slack against the bonds still holding it in place.

Anton placed a hand on his shoulder, squeezed, and whispered into his ear, "Come with me."

The others were still finishing their victims. Xenofon was

going for a second as Anton steered Takashi out of the room. Not all of the mortals were on death's door yet. Jong-Su had left his very much alive, but Takashi was certain that even if the mortals survived this particular night, they wouldn't leave the mansion.

As he stepped into the hall with Anton, he spied four black-clad security guards at the far end. They would dispose of the bodies, likely taking them to whatever pack of ghouls the GLC worked with. Mortals were just part of the ecosystem. Vampires devoured their blood, and ghouls feasted on their corpses.

Anton paused outside the conference room with Takashi. When he turned toward him, the demeanor of the professional leader was gone, and an inquisitive spark in his ruby eyes gave his smile an impish gleam. He pushed Takashi up against the wall, crowding up against him. "You were marvelous in there. Do you have any idea how hot you are when you're threatening someone?"

"I've an idea." Takashi attempted to slide down the wall, away from Anton.

"I would love to see more." Anton put his hand on the wall to block him. As his smile grew, he showed off a hint of his fangs. "Perhaps we should skip the rest of the meeting." He skimmed his finger along Takashi's waistband before gripping a handful of his shirt and tugging upward. "I have a wonderful boy I've been looking to share with someone *fun*."

This was just another of Anton's masks, though. Another role he was stepping into. He was like Roger, shifting from persona to persona. First, the demanding leader. Now, the horny vampire. Unlike Roger, every word and sexual twist from Anton had a hollow reverberation, like the slam of a metal tube against the ground. A note rang, but it didn't evoke anything in Takashi's heart or loins.

Except a small, cautious question poised itself at the edge of Takashi's mind. He wasn't ready to dive into it yet, wasn't sure what to do if the answer he suspected was true, yet it only continued to twist as it waited for its chance to drag him under. *Is Anton lonely?*

"We are expected," Takashi said firmly.

"The meeting can carry on without us. It's petty assholes with insignificant problems," Anton purred.

Takashi grabbed Anton's wrist before Anton tried to put his hand down his pants. At any second, others could be joining them in the hall. There were security personnel just down the way. The thought of getting caught in a public act didn't bother Takashi, but who he was with did. While Kazik and Xenofon would likely make crass remarks if they spotted Anton and Takashi like this, no one in the leadership would likely care. Upper elites in covens screwed all the time. *Hell, I might earn more points as a scary asshole if they did see me making out with him. They'd think I had his ear, at least for now.*

What Zack and Roger thought did matter. Though they hadn't minded Takashi's occasional physical moments with Carver, Anton certainly was *not* in the remote possibilities of acceptable hookups. Not that Takashi was interested in him either.

And yet, the real reason Takashi continued to hold on to Anton's wrist and held off from acting on any urges was the shadow of loneliness he glimpsed deep in Anton's eyes. He caught a faint echo of an off-tune note, a hint at the broken spirit. Anton had laid layer upon layer over his mental wounds. He had grown around them.

He was the deadlier for it. The more untouchable immortal.

What would Roger have been like without Zack? Without me? Another hundred years, two hundred—could he have morphed into something like this?

"You won't win my loyalty with a quick fuck and a nice drink," Takashi said softly.

Anton pulled his hand away. His grin turned sly, another

behavior slipping into place. He held his shoulders a fraction straighter, shifted his weight so he wasn't pressing up against Takashi so closely. "That's all Roger seemed to need. Zack, too."

Takashi pushed away from the wall and forced Anton to take a step back. "Blindly applying pain takes no skill, Anton. If you want to hurt something, go animate a doll. I doubt anything living will give you the satisfaction you crave."

As Takashi began to move away, Anton roughly grabbed him by the arm. His shell cracked. A boiling anger brewed in his voice. "I could get it out of you."

However, with that contact, Takashi could steep in Anton's desires and fears. He slithered through the less obvious gaps in his mental defenses, reaching past the barrage of surface wants and terrors that Anton kept in place to guard against such intrusion.

Anton wanted someone to depend on him. He was desperately scared of losing the love he had. Reading emotions couldn't give refined thoughts, but Takashi could make an educated guess. Zack was taking what little spare time Seamus had, and he would continue to do so for weeks —possibly years. Raising a sireling was not a one-night endeavor.

"Try all you like," Takashi said in a low, serious voice, "but I will not be your plaything as you wait for your lover to pay attention to you. Find. Someone. Else."

Anton narrowed his eyes. "Perhaps Zack will be more amenable."

A laugh threatened to bubble out of Takashi, but he managed to close his lips in time. The sheer idea of it was so ludicrous, and yet Anton had said it with complete sincerity. Had the arrogance of centuries made Anton believe he was capable of doing anything? Given enough time, perhaps he could—assuming his target wasn't one of the most stubborn beings in all of existence.

"Zack would never bend," Takashi replied.

"Then perhaps he will break," Anton said.

"Your dear true love would be angry with you." The others were filtering into the hall, so Takashi leaned in to whisper, "Besides, if broken toys made you happy, you'd already be drowning in ecstasy."

The words must have struck home because Anton released Takashi's arm, and rather than going back into the conference room, he strode down the hall. Takashi watched him leave far longer than he needed to, allowing the others to return before him.

Candide paused beside him. "I see you are no plucked flower, wilting without its sustenance. Rather, you are the caged lion. Careful how you prowl your confinement, mon cher."

"If spectators poke, I will claw them," Takashi said and gave a slight nod toward the direction Xenofon had gone.

"As you should. But be mindful of the keepers."

"Are you worried about me?" Takashi asked, putting on an air of lightness.

Candide checked the hall for any obvious eavesdroppers and tightened her lips upon spotting the security detail far away. Then she let her shoulders drop and smiled brightly with a small laugh. Her socialite graces came into play as she threaded her arm into Takashi's. "I clearly don't need to be. It's not as if you're a fox whimpering at the door of my den. I need not shelter you."

Fox. Kit was a werefox. Was she trying to give him a message? Takashi allowed her to link arms with him and kept his best smile in place. "Hopefully, you wouldn't turn me away if I was."

"I might arrange a bed if the circumstance demanded," Candide replied. "One should always be allowed to lick one's wounds in peace."

Kit is with her, and they're safe. Takashi put his hand over

Candide's on his arm and squeezed. Saying anything else on the subject might become too clear a giveaway.

She apparently thought so, too, because she switched topics. "You know, I saw you perform once in that charming circus. 'The Gravity-Defying Acts of the Astonishing Sato!' The way you spun and flipped through the air—I hadn't seen anything mortal like it. I haven't since." She tightened her grip on his arm. "It is amazing how one can twist when one has the need."

Is she wondering if I'd betray Roger? Or is she warning me not to trust her? "Agreed. But I think you've forgotten something about that act. I may have done a few tricks on my own, but I performed with partners. My most complicated tricks couldn't be done alone."

"Oh, isn't that just the way of it?" Candide said warmly, a bubbling laugh in her voice but not in her eyes.

Though they had taken their time, they inevitably had to reenter the conference room. The scent of fresh death warned Takashi of the body before they turned the corner, and the soft murmur of conversation should have told him that something was happening. Yet he was too caught in his own back-and-forth to analyze these things before. So he walked into the room one mental step behind and watched Candide's smile tighten. When he glanced over, he was equally rocked.

Seamus had his hand on Zack's shoulder, and the two of them stood amidst the group of lieutenants and captains. He had a proud, fatherly smile on his lips as he continued introducing Zack to the others.

Matching Seamus's tone, Zack was also smiling. His red eyes sparkled with the brightness common to one who had just fed, and he shook Dempsey's hand with a smooth, easy gesture. A smidge of hesitation creased his grin a bit too wide and made him dip his head when he might have held his chin up. Takashi had been watching him for months; Zack had a habit of looking away when he wanted out of a conversation.

So, he knew the angle Zack would eventually pick to look up. Takashi released Candide as she drifted toward the group while he subtly rounded the circle so that he might catch Zack's gaze. A second later, he did. Zack relaxed just a fraction, and his grin had a hint of fang and warmth. Then he turned that charm on Kazik, who was next in the introduction cycle.

Takashi slid his hands into his pants pockets and continued to keep at the edge of the room. The small lag in Zack's confidence seemed gone. He was spreading his wings, and though rough winds were bound to lay ahead, he was riding the currents for now.

He doesn't want it, Roger had said one night in bed, when Zack was fast asleep. Roger had been in the middle that night, and Takashi had cuddled up against him. Zack had been snoring on the far side. *He doesn't have any interest in being a vampire.*

Bullshit, Takashi had thought then.

This moment was vindication. Zack wasn't wallowing in guilt or grief. Likely those emotions were held at bay, but Zack was maintaining his balance. He was already stronger and faster than Takashi. That wouldn't have been possible unless Zack had willfully taken every drop of power that he could. Someone who, at their core, didn't want to be a vampire simply couldn't take that strength. Zack wanted to be immortal, and Takashi had a feeling that was the part he had glimpsed while reading his journal, drinking his blood, and in those rare moments in bed when Zack truly let himself go. *He was never going to be satisfied on the sidelines.*

Seamus saw this possibility in him, even from a distance. Takashi stalked closer to the edge of the circle for a place among his peers. The pendulum of his rage swung, threatening to crash into his fine mental balance and ruin his control. The choice to turn should have been Zack's. Not as some farce in a bid to keep living but with his true consent. *But would he have been as strong if Roger or I had turned him?*

The what-ifs and anger over past choices didn't matter. Letting himself get riled up over events he couldn't change served no one, least of all himself or Zack.

Takashi slipped in between Jong-Su and Lucille and joined Zack on his other side. He wrapped an arm around Zack's waist and gently kissed his cheek.

Zack leaned into Takashi. The brush of his growing grin made Takashi smile. As they were standing so close, Takashi swept his psychic awareness across Zack's mind, not prodding but scanning. Zack had a flimsy mental wall built from a desire to make someone else happy, but it was enough that he'd know if someone crashed through it.

Seamus slid his hand from Zack's shoulder to Takashi's arm, which drew Takashi's attention. Subtly as he could, Takashi shifted his stance so that he could peer just past Zack to the ancient vampire. A sharp glint filled Seamus's mottled red and blue eyes, and he flashed a hint of fang before looking at Zack out of the corner of his eyes. Then he met Takashi's gaze again.

I never hid that I care for him. But now he knows. Instinctively, Takashi tightened his hold around Zack before he could stop himself. The gesture was minute, but in this crowd, every whisper was a klaxon. *They'll try to find a way to use our connection against each other. To use Roger against us and us against him.*

Zack squeezed Takashi once and then drew in a dramatic breath and sighed. "As *fascinating* as meeting all of you has been, I'm fairly certain there is still coven business to conduct."

"Too true. Enough fooling around," Seamus said. He grabbed an empty legal pad and a pen from the table and handed them out toward Takashi. "Takashi, Anton seems to have grown bored with us. Do grab a seat at the end and take the minutes."

"My pleasure, master," Takashi said with a slight head bow. He began to make his way toward one of the two empty seats at the end of the table.

Zack started to follow, but Seamus quickly put his hand back on his shoulder and steered him toward Anton's vacated seat.

Once upon a time, Nell had kept Takashi that close at hand, involving him in confidential affairs of the coven when he was fresh from the grave. She'd had a far kinder hand, but she had given him rank and status far faster than other subordinates. *You don't adopt a right hand, Takashi. You groom one.*

But why Zack? Takashi scrawled the date across the top of the paper in three languages, fully writing it rather than relying on numbers just because the meeting had yet to restart. What was the deeper game? Upsetting the hunters? Putting Anton on alert that he could be replaced in some fashion? Giving Anton more space to work by taking a few responsibilities off his shoulders? Hell, putting the *rest* of the coven on alert that a new boogeyman was at Seamus's side? After all, Zack had killed a vampire in public not long ago and had challenged Seamus at a ball before everyone.

The screens flicked on, and the other lieutenants rejoined the meeting by their digital means. Takashi slipped into a mindset that would allow him to take adequate notes while still holding back the details he truly gathered for himself. Power lay in information, and he and Zack needed every scrap they could muster.

CHAPTER 18

Nathaniel set the scissors down on the kitchen table. "Done my best."

"I don't think it looks that bad," Vincent said as he wandered over to where Nathaniel kept his cleaning supplies. He grabbed the broom and began to sweep the floor around Roger.

Josefina had a hand over her mouth. She sat on the kitchen counter, an empty blood bag beside her. Changing their hair had been her idea, and she had allowed Nathaniel to lop off her long braid in favor of a much shorter cut. Her hair still reached her shoulders, though.

Roger took up his phone and turned on the selfie mode. His hair hadn't been so short since 1857, the one and only time he'd considered keeping to a mortal fashion and trimming his hair up from his shoulders.

But now, his hair was up above his ears. Vincent had helped him bleach his ebony locks to a light brown. He'd also started cutting Roger's hair, but Nathaniel had caught sight of what he was doing to Roger and what had happened to Josefina, and he declared that he was taking over.

No wonder Josefina was ready to laugh. He looked

horrible. Nathaniel wasn't bad with scissors, but he was far from a professional.

Roger played with the strands and made a face at the screen. A real-time "reflection" was still a novelty and one he typically enjoyed. This was like watching a stranger.

"Stop fussing. It'll grow back. Eventually." Nathaniel reached into the fridge and took out a blood bag. "Has he drank yet?"

"I left him another bag, but he hasn't touched it."

"I don't have the blood to keep wasting like this."

"I'll pay you back," Roger promised.

"It's not that," Nathaniel grumbled. "I can't go out and buy another dozen blood bags every couple of nights. Someone's going to wonder why I keep getting more. It's going to raise flags."

"Something we can't afford," Josefina said.

"I can feed you," Vincent offered.

"No one's drinking from you for at least another two weeks," Roger said.

Vincent puffed up. "I have blood, and you need it."

Roger gave him a stern look. The boy had been wearing Zack's clothes for the past few nights, which was a special pain. While he smelled a little like Zack—the washing of clothes hadn't entirely removed Zack's scent from some of his older garments—he didn't carry himself at all the way Zack did. And despite Roger's effort to keep from being Vincent's master, Vincent kept offering to become his pet in little ways if not completely.

"Your health has been suffering for too long. You need your blood, Vincent."

Vincent met Roger's gaze but swiftly broke off from the impromptu staring contest. "Fine. But if you get me money, I can buy more blood. I used to do it for Seamus all the time."

"People will know you're connected to me, and I am in

exile. That means if anyone suspects you are acting on my behalf, you will bring trouble on yourself."

"Then find *something* for me to do. I'm going stir-crazy!" Vincent snapped.

"I might have something," Nathaniel drawled. "My apartment's never been so clean. If you're that bored, I've got a storeroom that needs cleaned and inventoried."

"You'll pay him?" Roger said.

Nathaniel glared at him. "I'm going to pretend you didn't insult me by suggesting I'd take advantage of your lot's current situation and start using slave labor. Yes, I would pay him. Jesus wept, Roger. You have got to get away from the elite vampires more often."

"How much would you pay?" Vincent asked cautiously.

Roger left the kitchen as Vincent and Nathaniel talked over the specifics of the task. Josefina began to trail after him, but he made a motion for her to remain behind. Quietly, he went into Nathaniel's bedroom.

The windows had been bricked over long ago so that the sun couldn't penetrate the sleeping space. Roger had turned on a soft-glowing lamp on the nightstand the first night that he had brought Dmitri in here. The lamp had remained on.

Roger had taken care to wash the blood off Dmitri before putting him in the bed. Once placed, Dmitri had curled into a ball, and Roger had put a blanket over him. Dmitri hadn't moved, at least not as far as Roger could tell. The blood bag he'd left in the room sat on the night table. The blanket was eerily smooth, suggesting that he hadn't thrown it off and pulled it back over himself.

Time could provide healing, but Roger couldn't keep pacing in hopes that Dmitri might come back to himself. He shut the bedroom door and moved to the end of the bed. "Can I sit?"

No response.

"Dmitri, please," Roger murmured, "I need to know that

you're conscious. If you don't want to speak, move your hand or something at the least."

Still, no response.

Moving slowly, Roger rounded the bed. He lifted the blankets and carefully folded them back enough to see Dmitri's face.

Dried blood trails created paths down Dmitri's cheeks. A bloodstain colored the sheet under his face. Several different shades of dried red mottled the puddle. He'd cried more than once.

As the light reached him, fear clouded his eyes until he focused on Roger. Then he frowned. His voice was dry as bone as he whispered, "I thought I was hallucinating again, but I would never picture *that*."

"That?"

Dmitri pointed at Roger's head.

Self-consciously, Roger touched his hair. "Ah."

"Anton wouldn't give you a blond streak."

"I thought Vincent knew what he was doing, but he was reading instructions from the internet. Josefina claims she didn't know any better either." Roger motioned at the empty space on the bed. "May I sit?"

"Not like I could stop you," Dmitri muttered.

Raw, terrible pain filled Dmitri's voice, and Roger hated how it echoed through him and struck a familiar note. For three hundred years, they had suffered side by side and yet never spoken a word of what haunted their waking hours.

Because Roger had laughed and drank and pretended that his life was not so miserable. He had never told anyone of the nights he had crawled into bed and cried like this. To the best of his ability, he'd made himself forget them, too. If the pain wasn't felt, it couldn't be real. Yet that only left him with gaping wounds that had only recently begun to heal. His lovers had done that for him.

Dmitri had been his lover. They'd tried to make a relationship work again and again, only to break each other's hearts over and over. *Or perhaps we were already too broken and our jagged edges cut one another too deeply.*

Roger remained at the edge of the bed, but he knelt so Dmitri would not have to raise his gaze so high. "I won't crowd you. I want to care for you. That's all."

Slowly, Dmitri slid his hand along the bed, reaching for him. "You came for me. That's enough."

Guilt made Roger hesitate.

Some facet of his anguish must have crossed his features because Dmitri frowned. "You didn't?"

The pressure of centuries of failure threatened to drag Roger down. With a careful, light touch, he put his hand in Dmitri's and let him feel the depth of his regret. "I thought you were dead and beyond reach. Had I known … I won't lie to you, Dmitri. I don't know what I might have done. But once I saw you, I couldn't leave you behind."

"How long did they have me?" Dmitri asked.

"A few weeks. Much has happened." Roger quickly sketched out the details of what had occurred, lingering on how Anton had told him at the ball about the wager. "He claimed the bet was settled, then took that back during the attack on the hotel suite. Do you have any idea what he meant?"

Dmitri closed his eyes, then tightened them further. "He … he kept bringing in these tools. I thought he was preparing me for the draining ritual, but if he's let me go, then he must have been doing something else."

Trying to remember was clearly distressing Dmitri. Roger brushed his fingers through Dmitri's dark hair. "Let's not worry about that now."

Anger twisted Dmitri's frown into a scowl as he opened his eyes. He sat up, pulling away from Roger, and the blanket puddled over his lap. Though Nathaniel had set out clothes for him, Dmitri hadn't put them on. He was still naked. The red marks from the silver wires had healed. His skin was smooth and perfect again. Outwardly, he seemed better.

Inwardly, Dmitri had always struggled. Depression created a vicious cycle he had never broken in life, let alone in his immortality. "That is your specialty, isn't it? Ignore the pain. *Running.*"

The accusation was one of the oldest between them. Roger had never faced the truth of the stinging word.

Because when Seamus and Anton had descended on Dmitri and Roger behind the tavern, Roger had slipped Seamus's grasp. At least, he'd believed he had. Seamus had been playing a fatal game and allowed him those ten steps. Ten awful footfalls where Roger had abandoned the man he had claimed to love with all his heart and ran.

He had left Dmitri.

He had abandoned him yet again on that horrible stage in the modern Devil's Cove.

That didn't feel like something he would do now, but he wouldn't have believed himself such a coward before those pivotal moments. Had he changed at all? Had he grown more craven through the years? Less? Could he manage any bravery?

Old pain would not deliver a new future. Roger cleared his throat. "Dmitri—"

"He did something to me," Dmitri hissed. "Besides his usual 'fun.' And you would ignore it."

Roger moved to the far side of the room from him. It wasn't much space, but the distance was enough to clear his mind of Dmitri's swirling fears. He had always been a tempest, and Roger had always sought calm seas. His own anger bubbled, but Dmitri hadn't truly hurt him. Not in a way that deserved his rage. Oh, how his lungs wanted to vent all his vitriol upon Dmitri and shred open old wounds from their past love.

But he would be a better man. He would not cause harm upon someone who did not deserve it.

Roger took one step forward, then stopped himself and remained in the corner. In one of their more recent arguments, Dmitri had called him the same as Seamus. Another cruel and violent creature. Roger wouldn't be that. Not toward those he cared about. "Just because I choose to smile instead of howl does not mean I am without injuries. You are not the only one they have tortured."

"You had another set of toys taken away from you? How terrible," Dmitri replied.

"I love them."

"You claim it's that, but I've heard you utter such pretty words before." Dmitri slid to the edge of the bed, the blanket covering his lap. "You don't know how to love, Roger. No vampire does."

"No, no. No. You will not disregard my emotions and hide behind that lie," Roger snapped. "I love Zack. I love Takashi. They are my stars and wind. Without them, I am listless, hoping for a tide to carry me onward until, through some chance of luck, I may yet find my way back to them.

"But luck will not bring back Takashi and the beauty of his smile in the first moments he wakes. It won't preserve the starlight in Zack's eyes. I do not know where they are. I had the choice to learn, and instead, I chose to save you. To save those Zack once called family. Because that was what my love would have wanted. And so I am left with a shattered heart that was of my own making twice over. You will *not* belittle my pain, Dmitri."

For a long, agonizing moment, they held each other's gazes. Roger would not blink, would not budge from what he had said. His mind felt scrubbed clean and, though raw, might heal anew.

Dmitri broke his stare and looked away to the floor, blinking rapidly. "I had thought the poet in you had died."

"I don't have to pretend to be a vapid fuckboy any longer," Roger said. "There is a freedom in being exposed to have my own mind. And terror."

Dmitri made a noncommittal grunt.

With a languid ease, Roger sat on the corner of the bed near him. "I do not wish for you to forget your wounds. That wasn't what I meant. I wanted to draw your attention to the present because I need you."

"Do you love them that deeply?" Dmitri murmured.

Roger stared at his hands. The walls of his defenses were remnants, and he struggled to put any of them in place around Dmitri. Too many years of suffering had driven them to this weird place when they might have found strength in one another. Strength like he found with Zack and Takashi.

"From the moment Zack woke me, he has challenged me. He has made me realize that there are things I have not healed and damage I could stop inflicting," Roger whispered. "Takashi has pointed to those same injuries and given me the space to air them. He has faith in what I could be. And they are both so clever and handsome. They knew when to push me and when to hold me."

Silence stretched between them. Eventually, Roger let his gaze drift to Dmitri and discovered that Dmitri was watching him closely. His expression was closed off, but when Roger started to speak, Dmitri cut him off. "Once upon a time, you were that for me."

And that was an arrow through the heart, laced not with Cupid's love but tipped with silver. Roger ached to love Dmitri, to have their tender moments renewed, but that way had poison barbs waiting for him. And he could not—would not—enter into anything without his lovers' approval.

But Dmitri needed hope.

Roger needed a shred of it.

"If you can ever reconcile what you are and stop believing that you are a monster, then there might be time for us. But we can't be like we were before." Roger put his hand on top of Dmitri's. "I can't love your self-hate."

Dmitri's blue eyes went wide. The dried, bloody tears on his cheeks lent his reaction a painful beauty. Longing to feel some bit of comfort, to give what he could to Dmitri, Roger moved forward and pressed his forehead against Dmitri's. He lightly put his hand on Dmitri's cheek and jaw, his fingers more against his neck than anywhere else.

Dmitri shuddered with fresh tears. "I'd forgotten how insightful you can be."

"How do you think I manage to get laid?" Roger leaned back and tried for a smile, but no joy crested his lips. "I'm sorry, but I did have a purpose in disturbing you. I've had a wild idea, and you might be able to help me."

"I doubt it," Dmitri said. He grabbed the sweatpants Nathaniel had put out and slid his legs into them. "What idea?"

"I want to empty Seamus's bank accounts. Drain him and the coven of everything."

Dmitri twisted and, in his haste, started to topple over. With liquid grace and speed, Roger caught him and helped him steady. Dmitri finished tugging up the borrowed pants and gaped at Roger. "You want to *what*?"

"Honestly, I want to burn the entire coven to the ground," Roger replied smoothly. "I want Seamus to feel every ounce of pain that I have tenfold. Since what he cares for is status and money, obviously, the money has to go. You were his financial advisor. Could it be done?"

"I ... I could. I've dreamed of it enough times." Dmitri grabbed the T-shirt set aside for him and pulled it on. "I built an administrator back door for myself. Provided no one's found that, I could wipe clean what is in my—at least what was my—firm."

"What would you need?" Roger asked.

"Ten minutes in the firm's server room."

"That long?"

"Accessing the money wouldn't be the difficult part. It's the sending of it." Dmitri folded his arms over his chest and pondered for a long moment. "It won't be everything. He has a little with an Unseelie firm, and there are his general bank accounts. I have access to them, but the bank would likely shut down large withdrawals until they had his approval, which we clearly won't have."

"But we're talking a significant amount," Roger said, trying not to let his giddiness get to him.

Dmitri smiled. "Eighty percent of his. Seventy-five percent of the coven's, should we empty those as well."

"That will definitely hurt him."

"You're not hoping I will dump all this wealth on you, are you?" Dmitri asked.

"I want it to disappear," Roger replied. "Though, if we could slide five million to Nell so she won't come after me for a debt, I'd appreciate it."

"I could arrange that if I had an account number for her."

Roger grinned broadly. "Oh, I might know someone who could help us with that."

"We'll have to deal with security. The place runs all hours anymore."

"If you can sketch out the details, I'm certain Thomas will aid us in figuring out how to combat it."

Dmitri narrowed his eyes. "Who is Thomas?"

"Zack's father."

"You've managed to get another Wright to help you?" Dmitri put a hand to his head. "Perhaps I am still hallucinating."

"You aren't," Roger said gently.

"If you say so." Dmitri sighed and leaned against Roger's shoulder. "But should I open my eyes and find myself still tied in silver, I won't be surprised."

Instinct begged Roger to slide an arm around Dmitri, and

so he did, giving Dmitri every opportunity to move away from him. Instead, Dmitri leaned into him all the harder. No one in the world might understand what the other had endured so much as they could understand each other. Roger yearned to haul him close, to let him deeper into his heart. But he couldn't betray Zack and Takashi like that, couldn't risk hurting Dmitri's heart or his own.

He ought to prod for answers, descriptions—anything to make his plan move forward. But he hoped they wouldn't want him to deny Dmitri this moment of solace and comfort as he sank against Roger and relaxed.

"You're anxious for action," Dmitri murmured.

"I am," Roger said. "I've waited too long to strike like this."

Dmitri laughed, wiping away a tear as he sat straight again. "You have no idea how good it is to hear you admit that. Come. Nathaniel must have paper and pen. Call your Wrights. Perhaps together, we can rob the monsters blind."

CHAPTER 19

Waking was a languid thing; Zack was in an incredibly soft bed with a perfectly divine comforter and was up against a pleasantly warmer person. Takashi, he was sure of it. He had his arm over his chest and knew the feel of him. So he scooted his butt back to search for Roger.

But that side of the bed was empty.

Realization brought back memory, and that drew aside the heavy curtain obscuring consciousness. Zack was a vampire. He was in Seamus's mansion. The previous night's meeting had ended close to sunrise, and he had barely had his eyes open while he shucked off his suit and changed into pajamas. He'd fallen asleep nearly as soon as his head hit the pillow. Takashi must have crawled into bed with him.

It is Takashi, *right?* Zack opened his eyes.

And was met with pure, seamless darkness.

He hadn't climbed out of his grave. He was caught in his coffin. He'd been hallucinating.

A terrified scream ripped from him as he sat up. He flung his arms out, trying to find the lid and failing. If he couldn't find the lid, then he couldn't break free. There was movement beside him. Scrambling. Oh God, was it maggots? Beetles? *Worms*?

"Whoa there," Takashi said. His voice pierced through the panic but didn't calm him.

A bedside lamp flicked on and illuminated the massive bedroom in a soft, gentle glow. Zack's mind flailed, reason refusing to speak up on reality's behalf, and he scanned the room over and over. Bed. Bedside table. Desk. Door. Dresser. Door. Door. Bookshelf. Painting. Beside table. Bed. None of these were his coffin lid. None of them were the way out.

"You aren't trapped," Takashi said. "Zack, look at me."

Zack snapped his head to the side, a snarl on his lips, but it died in his throat. Takashi was sitting beside him, and there was a lamp behind him. A world around him. Not a hint of a coffin.

The intensity of the fear broke, but the aftershocks tumbled through Zack. He drew his knees to his chest and put his forehead on them. He couldn't have curled up like this in the coffin. He hadn't had Takashi with him. Everything that had happened was real, not a hallucination. He wasn't trapped. He wasn't. "Fuuuuuuuuuuuuuuuuuuuuuuuuuck."

Gently, Takashi wrapped an arm around his shoulders, and Zack leaned into him without moving much. "I wasn't thinking. I should have left the light on."

Bloody tears were pricking the corners of Zack's eyes, and they began to tumble despite his vain attempt to stop. "I shouldn't be a fucking mess."

"Hey." Takashi nudged Zack.

But Zack didn't want comfort. Becoming a vampire should have made him strong, not prone to more bullshit panic attacks. He pulled his knees in tighter.

Takashi bumped him again. When Zack didn't budge, he circled around to Zack's front and roughly pushed on both shoulders. Zack rocked back, running into the headboard, and accidentally pierced his bottom lip with his fangs as he bit down on it. If Takashi had an ounce of pity for him, Zack was going to shatter, and his last shred of dignity would be as dead as his humanity.

"*Zackery,*" Takashi said sharply.

A thousand words were on his lips; a hundred thousand screams were ready to sound. Zack drew in a breath so that he might let any one of them loose and find a sliver of solitude for his anguish by driving Takashi away. He steeled himself for the sad way that Takashi was bound to look at him. After all, he was a broken thing, sobbing for no reason yet again. As always.

Instead, Takashi met his gaze and held it with a level of patient sympathy that Zack had never known before. His dark blue eyes weren't watering with bloody tears for him. He didn't show a flicker of discomfort at seeing Zack in such an awful state. He wasn't trying to make things better.

"Everything you knew was ripped away from you," Takashi said firmly.

And though of course Zack had known that, hearing Takashi put it into solid words made it *fact*. Tears continued to slip down Zack's cheeks.

Takashi made no move to wipe them away. "And not just once."

Zack started to bite his lip again but managed to stop himself. When he'd left his parents' house, he hadn't known it'd be for the last time. Taliville had become a comfortable place, if not a home, and he'd left that for Chicago. Then he had been ripped from the hotel suite, from Carver and Kit and Roger, and he had Takashi, but Takashi wasn't exactly the same either, was he? He was sharper and stronger in the best ways, and yet ... yet there was a distance. *Maybe he doesn't like me anymore.*

Maybe he's been through his own shit the last few nights, his rational mind replied.

"You were *murdered*," Takashi said.

I was murdered. It wasn't some nebulous thing that had happened to Zack. It was a *fact*. It was truth that another being saw. Not just any being but his lover. *His.* Yes, he shared him with Roger, like he shared himself with Roger, but here, in this moment, he knew that there was a part of him that was for Takashi alone and a part of Takashi just for him.

His rational mind wanted to remain responsible. Wanted to look after Takashi. Wanted to hold fast. Be strong.

But then Takashi continued in his fact-speaking way. "You *should* be a mess."

The words shone moonlight on Zack's soul. The sobs broke free. He lunged forward and wrapped his arms around Takashi tightly, and with accelerated speed, Takashi hugged him back. They held each other tightly.

Zack continued to cry, letting the pain out with each sob. Bloody tears poured down his cheeks. Yet, with each one out in the world, the broken layer of himself peeled away. It was like cleaning the rust off an ill-kept blade. Underneath the tarnish, he was steel. He had survived all the crap thrown at him. He was stronger than ever.

And he wasn't alone.

Screw the rest of the world. He'd cry as long as he needed to.

CHAPTER 20

When Zack finally let himself go and unspooled, Takashi maneuvered them so he was sitting against the headboard, and Zack leaned into him. Each sob reverberated through Takashi, and a distant part echoed that pain. He was a few nights shy of his own rebirth anniversary.

A hundred and twenty-six years was not enough to completely smooth away the scars of his death. If he closed his eyes, he could vividly picture the ground beneath him and the way it rushed toward him. He had dared to climb to the trapeze after his death, but once there, he had shaken and remained until Nell scooped him up and brought him safely down. Ever since, he hadn't stepped on a ladder. Heights weren't the problem—so long as the surface was solid. Planes were fine. A hotel suite on the forty-second floor? Wonderful view. A ladder? *Fuck no*.

The twist of thoughts was slipping away from him, threatening to spin him downward into a tumble of his grief. He stroked Zack's hair and began to compile his schemes. Seamus had been in a good mood during the meeting, which was strange enough. Stranger still was the fact that he'd

allowed Zack and Takashi to see so much of the higher operations of the coven. *Clearly, he doesn't plan on letting us go
anywhere anytime soon.* And that was troubling, too. Would he
keep them cooped up in the mansion? Zack's doors had door
handles on them, so in theory, they could leave.

But Zack and Seamus were bound together. Since Zack
could detect Seamus's location, Seamus would have the same
capability. So unless Takashi was willing to leave Zack to his
fate, he couldn't escape.

He wouldn't do that to him. Not now. Not when he was
young and needed someone who honestly cared for him.

Besides, escaping would forfeit the small ground Takashi
had been making into the coven hierarchy. There was a gap
between Anton and Seamus. If Takashi could just figure out a
way to pry the two of them apart, then they might stand a
chance at killing Seamus and taking the coven. *To do what?
Put Roger on the throne? That will never work.*

It wasn't the first time he'd had the thought. When Nell
had summoned him to Taliville and told him she was
supporting Roger's plan to take the GLC, Takashi had nearly
laughed. Roger? A leader? The toughest call Roger had ever
made was which vein to bite.

Takashi had smothered those thoughts and buried them in
a twelve-foot grave. Out of all the lovers he'd been with in his
long life, Roger was the one that had brought out a new life in
him. He'd been Takashi's first lover. While Nell had taught
Takashi how to be a vampire, Roger had shown him how to
thrive in the night. He'd been tender and thrilling, and
Takashi had always yearned for more time with him. Their
brief moments had never felt like enough.

When Roger had strode into Nell's office with Zack
behind him, Takashi had thrown himself into the belief that
he'd misjudged Roger. After all, Nell was backing Roger's
coup, and she never made such moves willy-nilly. She must
have seen the makings of a master in him.

But Roger had never shown real command. Though Zack and Takashi had nudged and pressured, Roger had hemmed and hawed on a decision.

That wasn't leadership material. Not in a world of vampires and certainly not when the intricacies of inter-coven and inter-species politics came into play. A coven the size of the GLC needed someone who could lay out a plan, who could correlate data, who wasn't afraid to call out people's bullshit, who demanded answers, who didn't hesitate when one of their favorite humans was getting his neck torn open.

A wild, insane, impossible, beautiful solution tickled the edges of Takashi's mind. He batted the notion away. Such a thing wasn't done. No one had *ever* pulled that off. And yet it crept up. It took root and bloomed and begged for water.

Coven Master Zackery Wright, the Blade of the Night.

Oh, it was ludicrous. It had to be! This was only Zack's second night as a vampire!

But on his first night, he'd proven to be faster and stronger than Takashi. He had the martial training. He had the knowledge. The intelligence. The ruthless drive to shove a stake into a vampire who threatened him. He would have Roger and Takashi, who were capable of charming just about anyone they met.

Nell would support him, especially if Takashi made the case. All she really wanted was someone who was "weaker" to the north of her. Zack would appear weak, possibly *too* weak for Nell's liking, but Takashi could talk her into it. She liked Zack and had respected him as a human.

A little support from her would make the other North American covens hesitate. The right phone calls to a few friends overseas would keep the international covens from descending en masse.

The real problem would be holding the coven together. Anton was right; the group of vipers that made up the leadership were petty dilettantes. Getting them to turn on each other wouldn't be hard, but that might lead the coven into a civil war.

Candide would be key. She had the respect of other supernaturals in the city and ran the largest donor house in the country. That was blood *and* revenue. *If she's not on board, Roger might be able to convince her. Or at least convince Ezra, and he can bend Candide's ear. If that doesn't work …*

Zack had quieted from sobbing to gently crying a few minutes before, but Takashi missed the moment he stopped entirely. With tender grace, Zack sat up, still leaning into Takashi. He kept his hand on the center of Takashi's chest. His brows pinched together, and confusion clouded his red eyes.

They don't turn gray. They're always red, like an ancient's. How much power did Seamus share? Takashi put his hand on Zack's shoulder, then touched his cheek instead. "What is it?"

Zack's scowl deepened. "I'm trying to figure out what that feeling is."

That was when Takashi felt the pressure of Zack in his psyche. Takashi had put up a firm wall, but somehow, Zack had slipped past his natural defenses. An instinctive, self-preserving fear kicked in, and Takashi used that to push Zack to the outer edges of his desires.

Zack blinked and pulled back. "What the hell?"

"Peeking that far into my mind isn't polite."

Zack's soft scowl hardened into a stern glare. Vampires tended to make the young. In fact, Seamus had likely been thirty at most when he'd been turned. Nell younger than that. Takashi was used to seeing youth gain the sharpness of experience's edge. But Zack had never seemed so mature before. The bloody tear trails helped. "I was not 'peeking.' I was vibing. You let me glimpse whatever that was."

"You couldn't tell?" Takashi asked.

"I haven't had even a crash course in desire-reading." Zack motioned at his face. "And I thought it was pretty obvious I'm still struggling to understand my own fucking emotions."

"I don't know when Seamus will interrupt us, but if you're feeling up to it, we could practice a few things." Takashi started to sit up.

Zack put his hand on Takashi's chest and pushed him back against the headboard with a *thud*. He shoved away the comforter and straddled Takashi's legs. "Great. Let's start with definitions. What was that desire?"

"Why don't you tell me what you think it was, and I'll tell you if you're right or wrong?" Takashi countered.

Zack narrowed his eyes.

A simmering want seeped from Zack's cool touch into Takashi. He wasn't pushing it out, but his broadcast was so clear that Takashi couldn't help tuning in.

Zack wanted answers, and he longed for some measure of control.

The urge to flirt, to be just enough of a pest that Zack might be compelled to lightly punish him, swept upward through Takashi. His cock had the indecency of starting to thicken, which wasn't helped with the way Zack clenched his jaw.

"This is making you horny? Seriously?" Zack said, his voice dripping with a new note. Something deeper, something that resonated in Takashi and made his cock harder.

Authority. That was what it was. Despite his knowledge, Zack had never displayed such innate command before. He had always balked or lowered his gaze until confronted, and then he was a burst of impatience. Roger had said that the Wrights had done a number on Zack's confidence. Takashi had thought he'd seen some measure of it before, but now, Zack was in full bloom.

Then, for a moment, he began to wilt.

"I'm not using my powers on you, am I?" Zack asked with a hint of hesitation.

Takashi checked for any sign of external influence in his desires but found no sign of intrusion. Zack's cooler energy wasn't diving behind his walls anymore. "You're not."

An unpracticed haughtiness overcame Zack as he went up on his knees so he could look down at Takashi. All the while, he slid his hand up between Takashi's thighs until he cupped his balls. "My face has dried blood all over it. I'm annoyed you're holding out on me. Somehow, that's making you hard?"

Zack was radiating lust of his own. *He likes being in control like this.* Takashi kept his gaze locked on him, watching every little change settle and become this new wondrous side of his lover. *He could do it. He could lead a coven.* "You've never been more handsome."

"What if I won't fuck you until you tell me what you were feeling before?"

Takashi grinned slyly. "What if that's not what I want? What if I'm thinking about risking your fangs and fucking that luscious mouth of yours?"

"I don't think that's it." Zack mirrored Takashi's smile. "I felt the way your lust jumped when I suggested fucking you."

"The prospect is enticing," Takashi replied.

"Well, tell me what I want to know, and we can turn it from prospect to reality."

The night Zack had killed a vampire at Devil's Cove, Roger had been forced into killing a hunter. Zack had been upset about the loss of mortal lives but not the vampire's. For all the adjusting he'd done to their world, that backslide left Takashi questioning whether or not Zack had conquered the prejudices his family had ingrained in him. He'd asked him what sort of future Zack pictured for the three of them.

Instead of answering, Zack had shut down.

His confidence had wavered in this intimate moment between them. *He isn't ready to hear my vision for us.* Takashi needed to assure him that he would stand by him, and he needed Zack to be as strong and fierce as when he sent his dagger sailing toward Seamus.

So Takashi leaned up and said sweetly, "Why don't you see if you can fuck it out of me?"

CHAPTER 21

The greatest challenge in the bedroom that Zack had ever faced was trying to figure out how to get his dick in Takashi while Roger was already in him. Usually by the time Zack was in the mood to go for what he wanted, he was in the middle of sex.

No one had ever shot him such a cocky, mind-blowingly hot smile as Takashi was currently giving him. No one had ever been mischief incarnate, daring *him* to be bossy and commanding. He'd daydreamed about getting people on their knees before—especially a jock from senior year who'd been giving him a hard time—but this wasn't fantasy.

This was Takashi. Looking up at him. His desire wasn't a pop-up in Zack's mind anymore but billboard signs. No, a full-screen vid with noisy, sexy-groan-filled visuals. No, no, no, reading Takashi wasn't that intangible. It was like Zack had opened a journal and could run his hand across the hand-written words. His lust had a weight, a touch to it, and not just the heaviness of Takashi's hard-on.

Then the unsexiest of sensations crawled along Zack's cheeks. The drying blood was starting to itch and flake. *Don't let it shake you*, the Seamus voice whispered. *Seize the night.*

In his favorite book series, *From the Grave*, characters never had to worry about such bullshit things like dirty faces. But now that Zack had felt the dried blood, he longed to scratch it off his face. And because he'd been crying so long, there was a streak of blood on Takashi's chest. *Keep. Your. Cool. Zackery. You can be a sexy mastermind. Just don't do what you normally do.* He took a deep breath, then stroked Takashi's jaw slowly. "I am going to wash my face. You are going to see if this weirdly lush prison cell happens to have lube."

Takashi laughed lightly. "All right."

Zack nipped at Takashi's bottom lip and then dashed away to the bathroom. Habit had him shutting the door for privacy. Finding a washcloth and using the sink for hot water was no problem.

His actions were giving him distance from the moment on the bed with Takashi. Roger had always made confidence look easy, even when he was shaken to his core. Zack wasn't anything like him. He couldn't saunter across a room and make people weak in the knees. He had no idea how to saunter. *I am the least sexy thing alive.*

Dead, technically, his rational mind provided.

Zack buried his face in the washcloth he'd been using to clean his face and let out a frustrated groan. *Fine. I am the least sexy dead thing.*

Ehhhh …

Least sexy vampire. All right?

Why must you be so hard on yourself? the Seamus voice asked. *Relax before you cause yourself a migraine.*

Great. Now the evil voice in my head is coming up with reasonable suggestions. Zack groaned again. Then he shook his head and finished cleaning up his face.

Maybe he should call off the whole sex thing. There was no way he could do this.

Except …

Ah …

Holy fuck, did he want to try. Takashi was interested in Zack—not Roger, then Zack or Zack on the way to Roger. He hadn't withdrawn or scrunched up his face when he saw Zack naked in the past. Just now, he'd comforted him and been there for him because they were boyfriends. And Zack could fuck his boyfriend. Especially since his boyfriend had dared him to.

Yeah. Yeah. I got this.

He'd donned a pair of black flannel pajamas for bed, and his tears had soaked into the collar of it. That was unattractive. He pulled the shirt off and dropped it into the hamper. Then he wiped up the bloody tear trail that had crept down and dried on his chest. After a second's hesitation, he shucked off his pajama pants, leaving just his black briefs on.

The only thing Zack wished he had was the necklace Takashi had given him for his birthday. He'd been wearing the white-gold dagger necklace in his last mortal fight. Did Seamus have it? It hadn't snapped off in the fight, had it?

A matter Zack would solve later. He grabbed a fresh washcloth, soaked it in warm water, wrung out a bulk of the moisture, and then opened the door to the bedroom.

Takashi sat on the end of the bed, completely naked. The sheer cockiness of his smile was turning Zack on as much as his lean gymnast's muscular tone. He'd raked his fingers through his black hair to resettle it, and he was propping himself up with his arms as he leaned backward.

He was putting on a show, trying for sexy. He *was* sexy, but that silent insecurity Zack had noticed in him at other times was written on the page Zack could read in his mind. The older, gorgeous, world-traveled ambassador was still nervous that Zack might not like what he saw.

I am going to blow his mind. Zack straightened his shoulders, lifted his chin just a little, and strode across the room toward him.

"I did find a cabinet in your closet." Takashi glanced down

at the array of items on the bed beside him. "I pulled out a few things."

The wide butt plug caught Zack's attention first. A flicker of self-doubt crossed his mind. Wasn't his own body enough to make Takashi come? *Well, duh. But this stuff could be fun.* Alongside it was a roll of bondage tape, a set of leather cuffs, an adjustable chest harness, a blindfold, two different lubes, and a studded paddle. Zack thought the studs were stainless steel, but he ran his finger across one and hissed as it burned him. Silver.

Zack had had long summer days waiting for something to research and a whole empty house he was trying to forget about, so he'd spent an inordinate amount of time on porn. It helped him explore some of his cravings. His urges weren't always vanilla. He'd gone down more than a few rabbit holes of BDSM sites, particularly featuring vampires and other supernaturals. He'd seen all these toys in action but never used them.

The Cal voice started to speak up. It was forming some kind of insult.

But Takashi wouldn't have brought any of this out if he thought Zack couldn't handle using them.

Takashi slid forward, and his leg brushed against Zack's. "If it's too much—"

"Wrapping my head around it," Zack murmured. He ran his finger between the studs on the paddle. "You want me to dominate you."

"Only if you'd like to," Takashi said softly.

Takashi's tiny flicker of the fear of rejection grew. *I wonder how deep it goes. Did that mortal boy who broke his heart cause it?* Zack met Takashi's gaze and brushed his thumb over his lips. He could fall into the grooves of that fear and chase it downward. He could find its source. Find out how much it really did shake and shape Takashi.

Takashi closed his eyes. "I can feel you pushing."

"I'm exploring my new ability. Sorry if I went too deep. I'm trying not to." A vampire's abilities were a kind of magic. The principles had to be the same. Belief and willpower were the crux of using them, and they'd be the cornerstone of controlling them. So he pulled back his mental image of delving into a groove until he was tracing the shape of a word on paper again. "Is that better?"

"Much," Takashi sighed. He nodded at the toys on the bed. "You could experiment with that power while using these."

"How?"

"Here." Takashi took Zack's hand and pressed it to his chest, over his heart.

Reading the page became easier. Some of his desires were written in large block letters but in marker, so they had no real depth to them. The writing wasn't exactly words or images, at least not yet.

"Many emotions come down to a twist of fear or desire. Understanding the intricacies of how they interact takes practice," Takashi said.

"All magic does," Zack whispered.

"Yes."

The ink and writing were living things, moving and slithering. They had an impression to them, and that gave them substance. *Like grains of sand becoming a river.* Zack frowned. "But I hardly know what any of these mean."

"Because you're young. Your mind will have an easier time correlating what it's sensing with emotions you're familiar with."

"So if you had the desire to crawl into a hole and never see anyone ever again, I'd be able to grasp that," Zack joked.

"Don't stress on figuring out the specifics. Start with the basics." Takashi laid his hand over Zack's. "Call me the most humiliating thing you could think of."

Uh, me? Zack's mind unhelpfully supplied. But he didn't voice that, not even as a joke. Takashi had such a serene, peaceful patience about him. Zack had to respect that and take him seriously. "You are a filthy, cock-hungry, little fang-humping twink."

The mental ink swirled and settled into a large *NO*.

Zack tilted his head to the side. "We can feel the opposite of desire?"

"Disgust is the desire for something to end," Takashi said. "We should probably unpack why that was your go-to insult."

"Not right now." Zack slid forward. If Takashi disliked that kind of talk that fiercely, maybe praise was what he enjoyed. Zack lowered his voice, trying for a husky quality. "I am so grateful to have such a deliciously hot teacher like you. I only hope you're this patient when I'm sliding my dick into your amazing ass because I am going to draw this out until you are *begging* me to come."

A longing rolled upward from Takashi as he leaned his head back. "Feel that?"

"Yeah."

"Know what that is?"

The shapes had a complexity to them that slid past his grasp like a camera backing out of focus, but Zack saw the gist of its meaning. "You want more."

"I do." Takashi grinned at him. "Don't worry about the specifics. Master 'stop' and 'more' first."

"All right," Zack said. "Promise you'll vocalize if I'm pushing too far or too hard."

"Of course." Takashi put his finger on Zack's lips. "Promise these are the only parts of your mouth I'll feel. Losing you to a blood frenzy would ruin the mood."

"Good point." Zack nuzzled Takashi but refrained from kissing him. "No mouth would be better. Now, I really want to see how that harness looks on you."

Takashi picked up the harness and began to slide it on. "That can be arranged."

But he still had the smear of bloody tears on his chest from where Zack had cried up against him. Zack blurted out, "Wait."

And Takashi paused.

Having someone listen to him shouldn't have felt like a novel concept. Zack had asked others to do stuff for him before. When he'd been recovering, his days had been a series of requesting help or having people fetch stuff for him.

This was different. Zack let the weight of Takashi's trust in him settle the nerves threatening to climb. *What have I ever chosen for myself? Him. This.* For once in his life, he had both feet on the ground, and his head wasn't clouded with a thousand worries that were going to drive him insane. Slowly, he brought the warm washcloth to Takashi's chest and methodically cleaned the dried tears off.

Then he stepped back and threw the washcloth toward the bathroom. It sailed across the room, through the open door, and splatted against the far wall. *Uh. Right. Vampire strength. I really got to watch that.* He cleared his throat. Immediately, a wave of embarrassment flooded his system, but he drew in a deep breath and quashed it. He was in charge. The tiny slipups weren't major fuckups. Takashi was still radiating want. That was all that mattered.

"Put it on," Zack ordered. His voice had an oomph to it that resonated deeper in his chest.

For a fraction of a wild second, he was certain Takashi was going to laugh and call the whole thing off.

Instead, the swirling mental inks that filtered through Zack's mind scored the journal page he was reading. The force of the word practically opened a canyon, and Zack had to hold to the edge out of respect. *BELONG.*

That was a desire Zack knew inside and out, both sexually and not. Takashi's want went deeper than sex, even though at the moment, it was charged with an energy that was far from platonic. And feeling it woke a rumbling predator in Zack's soul. Craving blood was a necessity—a need that had to be obeyed in order to survive. What crept forward was a yearning that made something beyond mere existence possible. Following this impulse felt like *thriving*.

Power settled over him, coursed through him. There was nothing magical about it, at least not in the arcane fashion. Zack was shedding an ill-fitted persona. He could feel the bits of the gasping, scared boy who'd let Cal torment him, who'd let his cousins tie him up as part of a game, who'd tried to please his mother over and over and over, who had waited and waited and waited for his boyfriends to make a fucking plan—that scared boy didn't deserve to be in this new chapter of his life.

Takashi finished putting on the harness. It went around his shoulders and had straps across his back and front. At the center of his chest was a metal ring, and there was another at the center of his back. When he was done, he shot Zack a sly grin, yet his desire to belong pulsed stronger. A lock of his dark hair hung over one of his eyes, lending him a rebellious look.

"I am going to get that answer out of you," Zack said firmly. "You better make me work for it."

Zack didn't need his psychic ability to tell him that Takashi liked his new tone of voice. Takashi was sliding his hand to his dick, preparing to take himself in hand and stroke.

"None of that. In fact—" Zack stepped forward and grabbed Takashi by his wrist and the center of the harness. Using that hold, he pulled Takashi to his feet. Then he spun him around and pushed him down so that his ass hung off the end of the bed. The inky connection streamed *more more more* to him.

Knowing that what he was doing was right was an elixir

he hadn't realized he'd been missing. He roughly pulled Takashi's arms behind his back and used the leather cuffs to secure his wrists. A stifled moan slipped out from between Takashi's lips.

"Already vocal for me?" Zack asked. He stroked Takashi's spine just above where his hands were bound up to the chest harness and back down. With his other hand, he grabbed the butt plug and teased the cleft of Takashi's ass. "I haven't done anything yet."

Takashi snorted softly, which turned into a moan when Zack used his free hand to slowly spread his ass cheeks.

"Come on," Zack murmured, "be a good boy and tell me why you're so fucking hard for me already."

But Takashi buried his face in the comforter. Zack's attunement to that mental journal page had too many flittering emotions, yet he spotted that thin fear growing larger. Rejection.

Zack eased his hand away from Takashi's ass and trailed his fingertips over and down to his legs instead. "I know you want to be good for me."

The inks were settling into patterns of *MORE* and *don't reject me*.

Still no words, though. Zack sighed softly in disappointment and took the paddle up. One side was free of the silver studs, which was useful. First, he grazed Takashi's lower back and then his right cheek with the silver studs, barely letting them touch him.

"Why?" Zack asked lightly.

Takashi mumbled something against the comforter.

Zack's voice threatened to stick in his throat. Was he doing something wrong? According to what he was picking up, he wasn't. He let out a deep breath, the action calming, if unnecessary for living. Carefully, he ran the paddle up Takashi's other cheek. The silver was leaving thin red track marks that healed almost as instantly as they were made.

Takashi turned his head to the side and said breathily, "Because you're hot."

The answer shouldn't have surprised Zack. Shouldn't have split open another layer of his heart. Of course his boyfriends thought he was hot. Roger had spent plenty of time telling him he was handsome. This wasn't the first time Takashi had been horny around him.

But he wasn't the same as he'd been. He'd been mutated into this *thing*—a vampire. Takashi had witnessed a panic attack overcome him, held him while he sobbed, and he was still offering himself up and professing his attraction.

I won't disappoint him. Or me. Zack wasn't sure he'd ever gotten so hard in his entire existence. He stroked his hand through Takashi's hair and rested his hand at the base of his neck. As he let his thumb draw idle circles there, he drifted the paddle in the same slow circle around his ass. "That's my good boy. Now, let's see if I can get that other answer out of you."

CHAPTER 22

Zack began with slow, light taps of the paddle. The silver was never against Takashi's skin long enough to really burn him, but each brush of it brought a deep sting that soaked into Takashi's bones. Not every stroke brought the silver either. Zack varied which side of the paddle he used.

Takashi bit into the comforter hard enough that his fangs sliced through fabric. He deserved this. Wanted this. While Zack had been in the bathroom, doubt had crept into Takashi's heart. Thinking that he could push Zack into becoming a coven leader when he was freshly turned was a malicious ambition. An old fight with Sergei about over-reaching had clouded Takashi's resolve. Finding the toys in the closet had provided a solution. A little light punishment would take the guilt away. *And prove if Zack has an ounce of what it will take to lead hundreds of vampires.* He'd adopted a bratty persona in hopes of forgetting what he was: an ambitious bastard with no heart.

If you care about how he feels, then you have a heart, dumbass, his mind had tried to tell him.

Takashi hadn't been sure Zack would step into the role of

a dominant, much less use any of what was laid out on the bed.

But here he was, domming Takashi like he was born to it.

Takashi had his legs stretched wide, the plug in his ass. Only his tiptoes bracing him on the floor, the rest of his weight was held up by the bed. His poor cock was trapped under him, leaking from the slight friction he got with every spank. He lost track of how many smacks went across his ass. With his healing, physical pain was a fleeting thing.

Zack had found a way to make it last. Not in the strength of a hit—not even in using only the silver. His timing, the variance, the little ways he seemed to wait for the right moment. Takashi was losing too much focus to be able to check the strength of his mental walls. Was Zack using his power on him? Not directly. But he could be using it to gauge his actions.

Meaning he was purposefully practicing how to take Takashi apart.

Takashi moaned, the blanket in his mouth getting caught up in his fangs and tongue. He gagged on it.

Zack crawled onto the bed beside Takashi. He remained on his knees, so from Takashi's angle, all he could see was a hint of his lean, powerful leg. When Takashi tried to tilt his head upward, Zack put a hand on the back of his neck. He rubbed a soothing circle. His voice held a gentle, commanding assurance when he spoke. "Takashi, open your mouth."

Takashi's eyes pricked with tears. Zack's voice was so beautiful.

"I don't know what happens when we swallow something we shouldn't," Zack continued. "Open your mouth."

Takashi did.

"That's my good boy." Zack stroked his cheek while pulling the bits of comforter out of his mouth. "I'll have to find a ball gag if you keep that up. Which would be a shame. I love hearing you moan."

Eager for any touch, Takashi licked Zack's fingers. Nimbly, Zack plucked the last of the comforter pieces from his mouth. Takashi was soaring, and the little bits of contact synced their minds. They weren't tumbling into a lust feedback loop, not yet, but he could sense Zack's growing wants. But because Zack probably didn't know what those specifically were, all Takashi could read from him was the urge to claim and *devour* in that unique way a dominant could take a submissive's control and hold it.

"You're such a gorgeous mess," Zack whispered. "I'd be worried about those tears, but they're good ones, aren't they?" He stroked down from the top of his spine, skipping over where his hands were bound, down over his ass to rest between his thighs. "I can feel you calling for more, more, more. I'm so fucking thrilled you're trusting me like this, Takashi. This is so fucking cool."

Cool was such a weird and funny word. It brought a tumble of a laugh out of Takashi, and that morphed into a hiccupping sob.

With a quick tenderness, Zack rolled Takashi over and wiped his tears. He stared at the bloody water on his fingers. A bubble of primal fear expanded in Takashi, but it was cased in a dense layer that made it feel far, far away. Zack must have noticed it, though, because he jumped a little and then rubbed his hand on the comforter to get rid of the tears.

"Maybe we should stop," Zack muttered.

Takashi whined, and the note was high and demanding and a pitch foreign to his ears. He hadn't made a sound like that in *ages*. And in case his whining wasn't obvious enough, he raised his knees up and parted his legs wide for him. "*Please*."

"You still haven't told me what I wanted to know," Zack replied.

Wait? What? Oh, that. Somehow, Zack had held on to that? Takashi was twisted into a thousand knots, ready to burst if he didn't find release *soon*, and Zack wasn't drowning in the same sea of lust? With a groan, Takashi arched back against the bed. His ass was sensitive, throbbing almost as much as his dick was.

"Takashi," Zack chided.

On his back, Takashi couldn't even rub against the bed and find some relief. Wriggling around, he managed to twist so he was on his hip, but that brought little friction to his cock. He met Zack's ruby-red gaze. "Please."

A stony expression slid across Zack's features. He pushed Takashi onto his back again, grabbed the bondage tape, and used it to tie Takashi's ankles to his legs, keeping them bent. Though Takashi had the strength to snap through all of these bonds, there was an electric intensity in staying as he was told.

"I want you to keep being good for me," Zack said, never raising his voice, though the authority in it compounded. "Because this has been amazing. But I can feel you holding back. There's that little desire to hide something from me. I'm picking up on that one. And it seems connected to that fear I probed."

Takashi slid his gaze to the side and then pressed his cheek against the comforter. He couldn't hide anymore. All of this had been his stupid idea. *A part of you hoped he'd take you this far. That he'd lay you bare and see you.*

Zack leaned in and grabbed Takashi by the chin. With minimal nudging, he coaxed Takashi to look at him again. "I know that fear. I'm having to strangle my version of it right now."

Tears were leaking out, and Takashi blinked them away. "I don't want you to hate me."

"Just be honest with me," Zack said.

Zack wasn't a centuries-old, skilled liar, but Takashi had

had mortals rip out his heart before. Zack wasn't that either, and he wasn't shielding his longings. He was bare, too. And Takashi found a soothing relief in finding that same fear in him. His surface desires yearned for sex, but almost as loudly, he was crying out for connection.

Takashi knew that shape intimately.

Zack put his forehead to Takashi's. "Please?"

"Ambition," Takashi whispered hoarsely.

"You were having fantasies about the future?" Zack murmured. "Figuring out our next move?"

A plastic click happened, but Takashi was caught up in Zack's proximity. "Figuring out our forever."

"Our forever." Zack smiled. He pressed lube-covered fingers against Takashi's hole and began to work them in. "What happens in our forever?"

Takashi moaned. Suddenly, Zack stopped. Takashi choked on a sob, but dim realization dawned. He'd stopped talking, so Zack had stopped. With a whine, he said, "We take the coven."

"Mmm, we've had that planned for a while." Zack hummed a few notes. His fingers delved farther into Takashi, ruthlessly working to spread him wider. He still had his underwear on, and his cock pressed up against Takashi's leg while he leaned back and dripped more lube onto his fingers. "We kill Seamus, and Roger sits on the throne."

"Roger is no king," Takashi whispered.

The moment stretched as Zack looked up from what he was doing to meet Takashi's gaze. The weight of it dragged on the tightrope Takashi had been walking and threatened to buckle every ounce of trust they had placed in each other.

"You?" Zack asked, though the look in his eye said he knew that was the wrong answer.

Takashi shook his head.

"Me?"

Takashi nodded once and braced for Zack to wrench away in disgust.

Zack had one hand flat on Takashi's stomach. The dominant persona he'd inhabited slipped away to reveal a cautious young man. He frowned in gentle confusion. "Roger's in our forever, right?"

"If he wants to be," Takashi said.

"Me on the throne with the two of you at my side?"

Takashi nodded once.

Slowly, Zack inched his fingers in farther. "That is one hell of an idea."

Takashi was glad he didn't need to breathe. He wasn't sure he could have held his breath during the long moment Zack was taking to say more. The rejection hadn't come, but he couldn't relax just yet. With Sergei ... he'd trusted Sergei, and that had ruined him. *A hundred and twenty-six years hasn't been enough to heal that? I'm hopeless.*

"Wait," Zack said, and the rumbly, growly deepness was back in his voice, "were you getting hard because you like the idea of me being a badass vampire?"

"Yes." Takashi arched when Zack touched just right inside him, but the movement was too quick and too shallow to bring satisfaction.

"But ambition isn't making your cock leak, is it?" Zack asked.

A tiny, icy fear—the twin of Takashi's—was crawling through those words. So Takashi laid his mind open, praying Zack wouldn't delve through him and tear him apart. He embraced honesty. "No."

Zack stroked that special place inside a few times. Takashi moaned and fought to keep his eyes open. He shuddered, nearing the brink.

"There are drops all over your abs," Zack continued. A possessive rumble surged upward, wiping away the fear. He stepped off the end of the bed, dropped his underwear off to the side, and then crawled up between Takashi's legs. Slowly, he spread one of the cum drops across Takashi's stomach. A deliciously hot and haughty expression filled his red eyes, and Takashi nearly came from that. "What has you ready to come?"

"You," Takashi said.

"That's right. *Me*." Zack withdrew his fingers from Takashi's hole and probed him with his tip. "And *you* have me ready to fuck 'til we're senseless."

Zack pushed into him. Takashi tried to relax into the stretch and pull on his body, but without being able to move his legs much, he couldn't adjust his position. He had to take what Zack offered. The constriction was getting in his way, but he wanted to be good for Zack. Good for his lovers. He needed that.

With a blur of speed, Zack undid the bondage tape on Takashi's legs. He took Takashi's left leg and pushed it up while keeping his other hand on Takashi's right thigh. Pinned open, exposed—Takashi had less movement than before, but this position was better. He wasn't being used; he was being held. Not fucked but pleasured. Filled and stroked inside and out with every flex of Zack's hips, every caress of his fingers. Touched. Wanted.

When he came, he clenched and relished the way Zack gasped and bucked into him. Soon, Zack orgasmed, and that toppled him further into wonderful oblivion.

They were a mess, the pair of them, and yet Takashi didn't want to move a muscle when Zack finished unbinding him afterward. He was a puddle on the bed, and he let Zack scoop him up and spoon around him. *He is worth every risk.*

CHAPTER 23

Orgasm typically turned Zack into a metaphorical goo that slowly solidified back into a thinking being. However, once the initial blast of pleasure had shot through him—and it was an intense fucking blast—he dropped into a sense of absolute clarity. In the middle of the act, he'd finally gotten Takashi to fess up to what he'd been thinking about before. *He thinks I could take over the GLC?*

That had to be the craziest idea he'd ever heard. Well, apart from the time that Cal thought running through a forest screaming, "Can't catch me, I'm the gingerbread man!" would actually attract the pack of vicious redcaps that were killing hikers. Actually, Cal's dumbest idea had been wrapping Mom's car in the last roll of plastic wrap on April Fool's Day.

Okay, Zack had been privy to crazy plans before, not all of which were Cal's. One could argue that Roger's intent to take the position of master had been more insane than naïve. All of their talk had revolved around how to take the coven and why they couldn't do it yet. Roger claimed he'd spoken with a few leadership members like Candide about what changes he'd make as leader, but he'd never really gotten into the subject with Zack. He'd never really made a plan. He'd barely set a date for Seamus's execution and had rejected all of Zack's ideas on how to make it work.

The coven meeting the previous night had given Zack access to a whole slew of information that Roger had never even mentioned. The coven ran like a massive business, not entirely unlike how the hunter network worked on the higher levels. As the de facto stay-at-home caretaker for his familial pod of hunters, Zack had been the one to coordinate missions and ensure the financials were paid. Those skills would be far more applicable to running a coven than he'd known. Vampires didn't just have gobs of money and underlings and expect it to just run itself. They had to manage things. *And apart from the drinking blood until I kill people, I really don't mind being a vampire.*

Zack tightened his arm around Takashi, pulling him a fraction closer. They were still a mess of lube and cum that was quickly drying. Normally, he or Roger would have been rushing them off to the bathroom to clean up, but he lacked the urge to move, and Roger wasn't here.

Thinking of their missing lover created a sore spot, but Zack had done something entirely new. He'd flirted with topping with a bit of dominance before, but he'd found a place inside himself. And rather than confining and restricting him, he felt like he'd stretched a muscle that had been clenched too long. His limbs didn't actually ache— vampire healing for the win—but he was comfortable in his body in a way he wasn't sure he'd ever felt before.

Takashi was comfortable, too. He had linked his fingers with Zack's and held Zack's hand to the center of his chest. But if he was thinking bigger thoughts and burning with brighter desires, he was keeping them behind a very contended mindset.

But this couldn't last. Had Takashi meant what he said?

Would he ever talk about his idea? Zack almost bit his bottom lip, remembered his fangs, and sighed instead.

"You're tensing," Takashi murmured. "Careful how you squeeze me. You might crack a bone."

"Sorry," Zack muttered. Somehow, quiet voices were his standard go-to. Speaking at a louder volume felt like shouting anymore. He eased his grip. "Guess I don't know my own strength."

"We all have to adjust." Slowly, Takashi loosened his hold on Zack's hand and then turned toward him.

Zack kept his arm over him and did his best not to stare at Takashi's perfectly kissable lips. A growling burn deep in his gut was starting, and tender skin was beginning to look edible in a not-good way. He cleared his throat, hoping to distract himself from his building thirst.

That didn't work. Conversation might. "Why me?"

Takashi gently ran his hand up the length of Zack's arm and settled his touch on the crook of his neck. "You are my boyfriend. Why shouldn't we fuck?"

Zack narrowed his eyes. "Roger dodges important conversations the same way."

"What way?" Takashi asked with a fake innocence that was all at once darling and utterly needles-under-skin annoying.

"Sex talk." Zack nudged Takashi. "Why do you think I should be on the throne and not him?"

Takashi lowered his voice to the barest of whispers. "We both know that Roger doesn't have the conviction it takes. We wouldn't be in this position if he did."

"Why not you?"

"I do better in the shadows," Takashi replied. "I can move with a freedom there and make deals and alliances that would garner your position better strength. Besides, if I took it, everyone would assume I was doing it for Nell."

Zack sat up. "You think I can do better in the spotlight? Vampire society is all about sex shit, and I *freeze*."

"You can overcome that." When Zack shot him an incredulous look, Takashi sighed and rolled onto his back. He stretched, and Zack was more than a little distracted by watching him. "Your family ruined your confidence. You don't have to shove yourself down in hopes of pleasing them. You were never going to make them happy. They made that very clear."

"Amber—"

"I'm not talking about individual members. I'm talking about the Wrights and the Gladwells as a whole," Takashi said. "Am I wrong about them?"

Zack scowled because he couldn't immediately say no. While Amber and his father had started coming around, *everyone* had agreed with his mother that he had done the wrong thing in Detroit. Everyone had acted like taking research from him should be verified by a second source, not from due diligence but because they weren't sure he could be entirely trusted. Cousin Denny had called him a "someday blood bitch" during the last time they ever played rescue the damsel, and no one had ever made him apologize.

With a tender slide, Takashi rubbed Zack's arm and drew his attention back to him. His expression was softer. "You can be great. You just have to stop getting in your own damn way. My current desire to never move again is proof of that."

Somehow, that was funny. Zack laughed once. "Is it?"

"You need a confidence boost? I have not been spanked and fucked that well in ages." Takashi grinned up at him. "Dom!Zack suits you very well."

"Did you just use a fanfic convention on my name?"

Vampires didn't really blush, but Takashi exhibited all the features of doing so without the color in his cheeks. "Well, I … maybe."

Having people make fun of him was how Zack had gotten

such a shit view of himself. Stepping outside himself, he could see how everything Takashi had just done—opening himself up, offering for Zack to be in full control, even this conversation—was support for him. So the last thing Zack wanted to do was make Takashi feel like he couldn't be trusted with all aspects of him.

He flopped back down on the bed beside Takashi. "Do you have an AO3 profile?"

"I may have heard of the site," Takashi said.

Zack could feel a flicker of a desire to hide. *He's shared enough. If he's actually got an account, he'll show me in time. We have Our Forever, after all.* "I have one to make comments on stuff. I think I've read like everything in the *Twilight* tag. Or at least, everything written up until August. Okay, maybe not every *everything*, but I've spent a ton of time there."

"Somehow, that does not surprise me." Takashi's smile brightened again. "Honestly, I've been reading in the *From the Grave* tag lately."

"Oh, I've been there, too. There's this one where—" Zack stopped as he realized the ice-cold magnet that was Seamus's presence was nearing. He sat up. "Fuck. Seamus is on the way."

CHAPTER 24

A wave of panic was on its way to demolish all the joy and budding determination that Zack had been building. His mortal parents had never caught him fucking, though one time in college, they'd come incredibly close to showing up at his dorm room as he was finished going down on his then-girlfriend. Cal had liked to mock him about overhearing him masturbate since he was thirteen. Sex was just not a subject brought up in the Wright household. His dad had given him *the speech* twice—once to explain the birds and the bees, and again after Zack came out as pansexual to him in order to explain how anal sex wasn't really anything like the other things he'd explained—and that had been the end of the discussions.

Now, Seamus was marching down the hall, and Zack had no doubt the bastard was coming straight to his suite.

Any remnant of postorgasm glory was gone. Was Seamus going to be upset that Takashi was in his room? Was he going to lose it when he saw the very nice comforter now had a hole in it where Takashi had chomped on it? Was Zack supposed to be dressed? *Oh shit, he's not bringing someone in here, is he?* Zack raked his hand through his hair.

The last thing Zack wanted Seamus to see was the sex toys. The next to last things he wanted on display were his and Takashi's naked bodies. Using a burst of speed, Zack grabbed the toys and lube, threw them into the closet, and zipped through his wardrobe until he found two robes.

"Zack—" Takashi called out.

"Here!" Zack raced over to him and thrust one of the black silk robes to him.

With his patented patience, Takashi took one and slipped into it as he stood. "He's not likely to care that we had sex. If he didn't want us spending time together, he would have ordered me back to my room."

Zack already had his arms through his robe and finished tying the sash around his waist. The freaking thing felt like wearing nothing, but at least it looked like clothing. "Oh."

"Also, he'll be able to smell our spunk."

"*Shiiiit.*" Zack slapped his forehead. "Ugh, I don't think we have time for a shower. Vamp speed doesn't make water happen faster."

Takashi took both of Zack's hands in his. "Settle down."

But Zack could feel the thinnest fear in the inky mental swirl of Takashi's mind. *He's managing a brave face. I can find mine.* While holding Takashi's gaze, Zack took a deep breath and nodded. He didn't feel any calmer, but at least his thoughts stopped zooming at a rate of 10G.

A light, polite knock sounded on the outer door. When Zack didn't move, Takashi raised an eyebrow. The knock came a second time.

"Right! I need to get that." Zack let Takashi's hands go and started to hurry for the door.

"Zack," Takashi said.

Zack stopped at the door from the bedroom to the living room. "Yeah?"

"We're vampires. We don't rush." And then Takashi lay back on the bed like he didn't have a care in the world.

All of that was a front. Zack could still sense the swirl of fears and desires from him. *Everything is a test,* Josefina had said. *Always be prepared.*

Every vampire Zack knew had wildly different personas they'd spent centuries developing. Hell, he'd been different with different people before, too. He'd been crafting the nonchalant pet identity to specifically deal with the vampire world. Last night, he'd started trying on a mask of a socialite like Candide often used.

However, Seamus was bound to be suspicious if Zack started oozing pleasantries all the time when they weren't in public. Besides, Zack wasn't sure he could erase his rage at the bastard. He could shove it down, but Seamus was his killer.

So Zack adopted an attitude he wished he could've used with his mom and Cal. As he padded over to the door, he raked his hand through his hair a few more times and let his anger out in a deep scowl. He swung the door open with a large huff and glared at Seamus. "What?"

"Good evening to you, too, son," Seamus replied. He was smirking.

However, for the first time, Zack really noticed how he and Seamus were of a very similar height. Somehow, the asshole had always seemed larger, though Zack had intellectually known they were nearly equal.

Seamus was wearing sneakers, dark jeans, and a lightweight black long-sleeved T-shirt. He had a black coat over his shoulder. He also had Cal's Bowie knife in a sheath on his hip and Zack's dagger hidden somewhere on his person. Seamus's magnetic bond had hidden the presence of the dagger, but once he was within a few feet of Zack, he could sense its similar pull.

With that same selfish smirk, Seamus pushed on the door so that it slid out of Zack's grasp and opened far enough for him to stride into the room. "Hopefully, I'm not interrupting anything. You seemed done."

"Done?" Zack asked with a frown.

Seamus sighed like he was disappointed that Zack didn't understand exactly what he meant with the first sentence. "You sensed my nearing presence. Noticed a few of my emotions last night, correct?"

"Yeah …" Then realization struck.

Since *he* could feel *Seamus's* desires, *Seamus* could feel *his*. And since he'd had experience, he could probably feel them through their bond at a distance.

Which meant that Seamus knew that Zack had been having sex. Had probably known the second he had come.

That's so much worse than smelling or seeing the toys. Zack struggled against the freshest wave of panic.

"Settle," Seamus said, and his voice had a resounding note in it that quelled the fears climbing inside Zack's mind.

Clarity arrived again like breaking clean from an ocean and realizing he had reached a sandy shore. Zack didn't need to breathe, but he had been doing so and yet freezing out of habit. After Seamus's command, he could relax again.

At least, he could until he realized he felt Seamus putting pressure on his mind. It was like finding out a comfortable blanket was covered in ants. His skin was starting to crawl.

"You can fight me and go back to having a panic attack," Seamus said, "or you can accept my gift for a brief moment and calm yourself."

I shouldn't accept any gifts from him, his angry side said.

Not even your immortality? the Seamus voice replied. *You seem to be enjoying your vampirism so far.*

"Panic attacks do suck." Zack pointed his finger at Seamus as he continued. "But I swear on Mary Gladwell's grave, I will fucking *murder you* if you mess with my desires. Or with my fears in other ways than this."

Seamus glanced at the open door and gestured for Zack to

close it. Zack did while Seamus took a seat on the couch. "I understand the impulse to doubt my intentions, but you have to give me some credit. You are far more … present in my mind than I thought would happen. Our bond is stronger than I anticipated."

"Really? Because you had to offer up the power." Zack folded his arms over his chest.

Seamus met his glare with an impatient frown of his own. "And you had to take it. I knew in the moment that you were grabbing for it, but that didn't mean it would take root. I see that it has."

"Wouldn't you want your *son* to be strong?" Zack demanded.

"I would. Hence the offering." Seamus relaxed, putting his arm along the back of the couch. "Look, I'm not going to talk in circles about this. We both got what we wanted with your transformation. I have an errand for us to run, and you must be getting hungry. So, go shower and dress in similar attire to me and come back. Oh, and send Takashi out here. I'd like to speak to him."

Zack hated the idea of following Seamus's orders, but short of throwing a fit and stomping his feet like a toddler, there wasn't anything else he could do. He continued to glare at Seamus on his way across the living room and strode into the bedroom.

Takashi was already standing and heading for the door. He paused beside Zack long enough to kiss his cheek and squeeze his arm.

Since Zack was beginning to feel gross, he headed for the bathroom.

The conversation from the living room was in quiet voices, but Zack could hear them as if he were sitting next to Seamus.

"He seems to be acclimating faster than I feared he would," Seamus said. "Your influence?"

"Some," Takashi said lightly.

"Thank you. He wasn't listening to me."

Zack puffed up, preparing to storm out there and shout at Seamus. Of *course* he wasn't going to listen to the bastard. Why on earth would he? Taking a shower because he suggested it felt like betraying some piece of his soul. But he started the shower and stepped into it. Just like with the bath, all of the soaps and shampoos were orange-scented.

The rush of water didn't block his hearing.

"You can hardly expect him to be complacent and thrilled with you," Takashi said. Zack recognized that dry tone. He'd used it right after the incident at Devil's Cove when Zack had been flipping out about Roger killing a hunter. "All things considered."

"I expect that he would kick and scream around me for a while. Hopefully, not too painfully for either of us. I would like to remain proud of him."

"You're proud?"

"So far, very. He rose on Christmas, one of the hardest nights for our kind to rise. Also, I saw the way he was eating up information last night. The Wrights have been letting him waste away. I'm quite glad to have stepped in. He may yet reach his true potential." A moment passed. "Now, Takashi, are you going to remain in these rooms with Zack, or are you interested in the new ones I'm preparing for you?"

"That depends," Takashi said. "Do the new ones have a door handle on the inside? Do they have silver in the walls?"

Takashi had said his "all right" state was relative. He hadn't shared what he had been going through, not really. Zack had been so caught up in his own crap that he hadn't dived into the topic with him.

The urge to protect Takashi swelled, and Zack snapped off the water, though he was only half done in getting clean. What good was newfound confidence if he didn't yell at the bastard making his lover's life a living hell?

"Drop the attitude, Zackery," Seamus said sharply. "I will

remind you that the two of you were conspiring to kill me and that locking Takashi in a comfortable room was the kindest thing I could have done to him."

Zack paused with his hand on the shower door. In the softest whisper he could manage, "Did you hear the shower turn off, or was this a bond-sense thing?"

"Bond-sense," Seamus replied. "Then I heard the shower stop. And now I know how good your hearing is."

"I was merely asking for clarification," Takashi said. "Because if I have the choice of staying with you or returning to a prison cell, I obviously choose you."

But the fact that he was thinking about having his own rooms at all pulled Zack's heart toward a cliff. *Hey, it's not a bad thing for him to have his own space. You might need it from him, too. What you just shared should be proof he's not really going anywhere.*

"Zack, finish showering. You and I have somewhere to be," Seamus said.

Grumbling to himself without any real words or meaning, Zack spun the shower faucet back on and continued washing up.

"The rooms are a mirror to Zack's and are just across the hall," Seamus said conversationally. "You'll have to forgive them for being a bit bare in comparison, but as time goes on, we can change that. Naturally, you can come and go as you please, though I would advise you to remain within the mansion unless we take a group trip."

"A generous upgrade to my situation. I'll have to consider it," Takashi replied.

"You needn't make the decision tonight. You'll find the clothes in here tailored for Zack, but you two are of a similar size. You'll make something work, assuming you plan to dress at all."

From there, Takashi guided the conversation into fashion, of all the weird-ass things to discuss. Zack concentrated on what he was doing, which meant he didn't catch every word from the other room, but they seemed to be discussing who among the local tailors had the best sense of style.

At least Zack didn't have to pick out some fancy suit for the evening. *Worst part of vampirism has got to be an eternity of keeping up with the latest looks.*

Eh, maybe you'll learn to like it, the Seamus voice replied.

Great, I've replaced one asshole voice for another. Zack scrubbed a little too hard and winced. *Just what I need in my life.*

Rather than take a limo, Seamus led Zack to the mansion's garage. The limo was there, parked out toward the front for convenient use, along with fifteen high-end sports cars. Zack tried not to be impressed by them. Cleary, Seamus was just trying to show off his wealth with all of the amazing vehicles.

That wealth had likely come from theft—he had been a pirate—and some robber baron shit that had managed to build over the centuries rather than crumble away.

Seamus opened a cabinet and plucked a key from it before strolling between the cars as if he were walking in some everyday garden of reasonably maintained plants. Zack trailed after him with his arms across his chest and did not stop to gawk more than twice. Only he was so caught up in looking around that he did nearly run into Seamus when he stopped beside a beautiful black Lamborghini roadster. "What do you think of this one?"

"It's, uh, nice," Zack said.

"'Nice.' Hm. You'll have to let me know what you would prefer, then." Seamus continued walking to a different black car just beside the Lamborghini. Out of all the cars in the garage, it was the most discreet, almost average-looking. He unlocked it and then slid into the driver's seat.

Zack hurried into the passenger seat. "You're planning on giving me one of these?"

"No!" Seamus said with a laugh as he turned on the engine. "These are all very much *mine*. But I will buy you one of your own."

"You'd buy me a hundred-thousand-dollar sports car?" Zack asked.

"I'd never be that cheap. It'll have to cost at least a quarter of a million." Seamus put the car into gear and began to drive out of the garage and into the night. The engine was nearly silent, only the slightest purr serving as an undercurrent to their conversation.

Instinctively, Zack rushed to buckle his seat belt. Seamus didn't and snorted a chuckle softly, but he didn't say anything about the seat belt.

Five minutes of being somewhat nice doesn't erase a millennium of being a dick. Zack relaxed into his seat, and the damn ride was almost too comfortable to stay actively pissed at Seamus. "Why would you buy me an expensive car?"

"I have openly declared you are my son to the most important vampires in our coven," Seamus said. "If you go out on the town looking like a pauper, it reflects poorly on me."

Zack let several long minutes slide by. "You're going to let me out on my own?"

"Eventually," Seamus replied.

"You'd trust me not to bolt?"

"I know exactly where you are at all times, Zackery."

So if I run, I have to figure out how to sever our bond. Zack folded his arms over his chest and stared out the window. Rather than taking the interstate toward the city or toward the Chateau, they were heading southeast, which would eventually take them into Indiana. "Where are we going?"

"To take care of a problem."

A boulder dropped into Zack's stomach. Each minute of

dragging silence only compounded that weight. He blurted out, "I won't kill Roger."

"This isn't about Roger," Seamus said with an annoyed sigh. "Do you believe this is the first time he's upset me?"

"He wants you dead," Zack replied.

"If I killed absolutely everyone who wanted me dead, the world would be a much emptier place." Seamus kept his focus on the road out in front of them.

Zack tried to use their bond to figure out what Seamus was feeling, but all he could pick up on was a bland desire for quiet. It was like a pop-up window again rather than a written page. There was nothing for Zack to dive into. With a frustrated grunt, he went back to staring out the window.

"I was distraught when he disappeared," Seamus said.

Another few miles slipped by before Zack controlled his anger enough to speak. "Must have sucked to lose one of your favorite victims."

"I have read your notes. You don't have enough data to say that definitively."

"*Bullshit.*"

After twenty minutes of silence, Seamus finally spoke. "I may not have understood Roger as well as I thought I did, but I know for a fact that he is not some innocent in need of saving. You were very thorough on my history and Anton's— you even delved into a bit of Takashi's past. But your notes are sorely lacking on the subject of Roger's adventures."

Zack really hoped Seamus was going to shut the hell up because this was not a conversation he wanted to have. What was a good way to get out of it? Flirting was *not* going to happen, so Roger's example was no good. Thomas Wright wouldn't have been stuck in this situation in the first place. Candide or Reed would smile and find some bullshit thing to talk about instead.

Screw it. With a hiss, Zack said, "You paid Quinn to seduce Roger into loving him and turning him into a vampire."

"No, I paid Quinn to offer Roger his blood and to sleep with him if he was amenable."

"You showed up at Quinn's grave while Roger was waiting for him and boasted about how much you paid him."

Seamus rolled his eyes. "That wasn't what happened at all. This was, I forget the exact year, but I know it was not long after the American Revolution. Did Roger happen to mention Malcolm? At least I think the boy's name was Malcolm. At any rate, one of Roger's beloved pets had died in a duel. Roger had been grieving for *years*, and he and Dmitri were close to reconnecting again. So when Roger showed a fraction of interest in Quinn, I realized that he was the perfect one to bring Roger out of his depression and keep him from going back to Dmitri. Ah, ah, I feel that little impulse to tell me I should have let Roger and Dmitri rekindle their flame. *You* weren't there to see them in 1734 or 1772. Or 1837. Or 1918. Dmitri does nothing but make him miserable. I was doing him a favor."

Zack glared out the window because grabbing his dagger from Seamus and slamming it into the bastard's heart wasn't a good option with the car going eighty miles an hour down the interstate.

"Finding out that Roger's been stretching the truth shouldn't upset you. We grow old, we have a habit of twisting what happened, and we particularly spend time retelling the story in a way that makes us seem the most favorable," Seamus said. "I've read your journal, Zackery. I know that you were distrustful of all supernaturals until you met him. Of course the only version of his life he was going to share with you was the one that appeals to your morality."

"*You raped him*," Zack snarled. "And you *murdered* me. You going to find some 'version' of those stories where you're somehow the 'good guy'?"

"We are vampires, Zackery," Seamus said coldly. "Good and evil are words for mortals to give meaning to their shallow, fleeting existences. I have seen them twisted and turned about countless times. Do you know how much damage they have done in the name of 'good'? How much is still done? By your own brother, no less? And, for the last time, *you* were trying to kill *me*. I could have left you dead."

Seamus had a counterargument for everything. Zack fumed and kept his mouth shut because what was the point? Anything he said, Seamus was going to find some clever new thing that would keep any of the fault from him. *Must be nice to be so confident that you're always in the fucking right.*

You could learn something from that, the Seamus voice in his head said.

It sounded too much like Seamus. Zack scowled at him. *Can you hear me?*

Nothing happened.

Each silent mile grated on his nerves, and eventually, his hunger began to burn in his stomach. Zack huffed. "How long until we eat?"

"How quickly you've come around on that subject," Seamus teased.

"Oh, you know, if you're going to be a fucking—"

"I have told you. Stop. Swearing."

"I thought I was supposed to do whatever the *fuck* I wanted," Zack taunted. "Wasn't *that* what you wanted for me?"

"Do not paint manners and rules as if they are some confines from which you need to escape," Seamus replied. "Etiquette is what separates us from the ferals and the nest vampires."

"Are we really that different from them?" Zack demanded. "Guzzling blood. Torturing people."

"Enough arguing," Seamus snapped.

Zack shut his mouth. *I got a rise out of him. And he didn't call me out on it. I'm going to call that a win.* With a smug smile, Zack relaxed into his seat.

CHAPTER 25

After showering, Takashi donned a pair of slacks and a hoodie from the collection in Zack's drawers. The sweatshirt had an ironic graphic—a pair of cartoon fangs dripping with blood and the words "I Bite" written underneath—which did seem like something Zack would eventually enjoy. Takashi thought it was amusing.

He also opened the cases on top of Zack's dresser. Along with rings, watches, cufflinks, and tiepins, Seamus had very helpfully provided Zack with an array of sunglasses. Artificial light could be intense for newborn vampires. Fledglings also frequently wore sunglasses in order to hide their inability to control the redness of their eyes.

But they also had other uses. Takashi examined a few pairs before settling on one. He snapped the earpieces off. The long, thin pieces of stable wire would come in handy if he discovered any locks. In the closet, he found a drawer of gloves. Luckily, a leather pair fit, and he stashed them in his hoodie pocket, along with his makeshift lockpicks.

He slipped out into the hall. He took a cursory glance at his suite across the way from Zack's. The rooms were a standard affair meant for a long-term guest. The color scheme was black and red, and the coffin closet had a bland wooden box in it, but it was functional. *I'd rather not sleep away from him, though.*

Quietly, Takashi backed out of the suite and began exploring the mansion.

Zack's suite turned out to be on the second floor of the building, and there were four to which Takashi found easy access. Retracing the few paths that Takashi had taken, he went down to the first floor and to the study where he'd first woken in the mansion. Along the way, he scanned a few rooms. Other than the occasional security guard or staff member caring for the house, Takashi was alone.

The study door wasn't locked, and Takashi slipped inside without issue. Anton's blood had been cleaned off the Victorian desk's massive corner. Zack's notebooks, their laptops, and the ropes that had bound Takashi to the chair before the desk were gone. Besides that, the room was the same.

Takashi tugged on the pair of leather gloves. *Time to get to work.*

Many vampires had been suspicious of an ambassador from another coven in their midst, and they'd have every right to be. Takashi's job was to facilitate Nell's relations with other powerful supernaturals. Sometimes, that was to attend parties and bring lavish gifts to celebrate new masters.

Sometimes, his job was digging for the dirt. Spy was almost as accurate a job description as ambassador.

He skimmed the top of the desk, running his fingers along the underside edge to see if there were grooves or telltale marks of a hidden compartment. The walls behind the three paintings in the room were also blank, as were the back of the canvases.

He swept back around to the desk and began to carefully comb through the drawers. Each side had three, and there was one in the center. The side drawers contained various papers and envelopes. One drawer had nothing but discarded invitations from other covens. Another was just loose blank printer paper pages. Takashi took one out and held it up to the light. No secret messages appeared. He wished he had one of his rings that he'd left behind in the hotel suite. It was charmed to detect invisible magics.

Since the rest of the room was more staged office than actual working space, he folded a few blank pages and put them in his hoodie pocket. The center desk drawer was a mess of pens, many of a far cheaper variety than Takashi anticipated finding. He began to slide the drawer shut.

Hold on a second. He tilted his head as he reexamined the center drawer. The difference was subtle, but the drawer wasn't as deep as it should be. He pulled it out farther and discovered that one of the pens in the center didn't move. After taking a moment to memorize the pens' placements, he took hold of the glued pen and lifted out the false bottom to reveal a slim secret compartment.

The only thing in the hiding spot was a switch, connected to a wire that ran into the back of the desk. It disappeared into the depths of the Victorian monstrosity.

What do you lead to? Are you friend or foe? Takashi got onto his hands and knees under the desk. The plush Persian rug didn't show any disturbances of a wire running anywhere underneath. If it didn't go anywhere, then it was probably a trap. Just to make sure, Takashi carefully lifted the corner of the desk. When it came up easily from the floor without the tension of a wire dragging it down, he discarded the idea of pressing the switch. He put the false bottom and pens back where they belonged and gently shut the drawer.

As he headed for the door, he took a closer look at the vases of roses. The round black-and-gold porcelain was shaped in such a way that the very bases of the vases wouldn't actually touch the pedestals they sat on.

Takashi arched an eyebrow. He'd come across far more inventive hiding places, but double-checking couldn't hurt. Gently, he lifted a vase off a pedestal.

There was a circular button about four inches in diameter. Takashi set the vase off to the side and nudged the pedestal. The wood was bolted to the floor. He went to the other and discovered the same thing.

Now, *this* could lead to something interesting. He removed the other vase so he had access to both switches. They were spaced just far enough apart that he had to stand in front of the door in order to touch both at the same time. Was one a trap? Would it alert Seamus or the mansion's security?

Who knows if I'll get another chance at this. Takashi pressed the switch to his left. Nothing happened. He pressed the right. Minutes crawled by, but he heard no running approach. *All right then.* He pushed them at the same time.

An audible click sounded, and then a section of the far wall swung inward, revealing another room beyond.

The Amazing Sato does it again, folks. The memory of applause was not as great as living it, but an echo of that thunder was in his ears as he strode into the secret room. There were two switches just inside the door. One activated the lights in the room, so he doubled back to the light switch by the door and turned off the main room. *In case anyone is passing by in the hallway. Don't need them suddenly noticing that fraction of light under the door, not with the secret room open.*

Where the rest of the mansion had overt signs of wealth, the hidden office was pure functionality. Takashi didn't doubt that Seamus dropped more than a few pretty pennies on the private space, but there was a sleekness to the lines of the desk that he hadn't seen elsewhere in the building.

The desk sat against the far wall, nearly as large as the Victorian desk in the other room, and a bank of monitors was attached to the wall above it. A set of metal shelves beside it held a home server and a desktop computer tower. At the bottom was a LaserJet printer. All fairly standard from what Takashi had seen in recent years from tech savvy immortals.

His own laptop, along with Zack's journal, notebooks, and laptop, was sitting neatly in one corner of the desk. He resisted the urge to wipe the data from the laptops. Computers had the nasty habit of logging everything done on them, and if Seamus was as paranoid as Roger claimed, then he might have uploaded software that would keep a record even if Takashi cleared everything else. The damn things might even send an alert to Seamus's phone, so the computers were low on Takashi's interest list.

The rolling metal bookcases on either side, though, were *very* interesting.

Each side of the room was about four feet deep. The bookshelves were on tracks, with one end facing Takashi. There wasn't enough space between them to navigate, but each one had a large handle. An individual created more room at the desired bookcase by nudging the others along the track.

The bookcases to his right contained a multitude of books that ranged in size and condition. Some were quite old, the smell of their ancient pages that of parchment rather than paper. None of the bindings had a title on them. However, as Takashi continued toward the back of the room, he noticed that the books were newer and newer. At the far end, they were modern, leather-bound volumes. Luckily, the books and shelves were dust-free, so he plucked one off the last bookcase and opened it.

March 31st, 1976

I swear, if Anton does not stop his mewling about how poorly his research has been going, I may finally drive a silver stake through his heart. You would think that after funding his quest for magic for more than seven hundred years, he would have discovered the magic he promised me, but no. He is as much a failure as the rest of them. And he thinks I'm unaware that he kept more of the power from our last ritual. Oh, he claims I got the most, but I feel no change and it has been two months. The bitch is holding out on me.

Takashi gently closed the journal and returned it to the shelf. Whispering to himself, he said, "Well, that shatters the illusion of the happy couple."

The other shelves were full of slim, black binders, and they had names neatly written in little cards on their spines. At first, Takashi thought they were members of the coven, but then he spotted a whole section of Wrights, including Callum, Amber, and Zack. Takashi took a moment to note whether there was dust on anything—there wasn't—and pulled Callum's from the shelf.

The binder had labeled tabs: Summary, Recent, Early, Psych, Accomplishments.

Takashi sat cross-legged on the floor and opened the Summary tab. Each page was plastic with printed paper inserts. The first had a picture of Cal Wright. Takashi had only seen him in research materials. Josefina had sent him a dossier on the hunter after he'd invaded Taliville looking for Zack, but Takashi had been aware of the Butcher for a while. American hunters were the topic of conversation among bored vampires. They tended to point at the "plethora of rampaging barbarians" as a uniquely American issue when they had hunters in their own territories as well.

Cal was a handsome man, in a rough-and-tumble man's man way. Beautiful people turning out to be complete assholes had long been one of the injustices of the universe.

The section went on to list Cal's attributes, including his birthday and education. He'd dropped out of high school, which made Takashi wonder if Zack had finished. His occupation was filled out as hunter. Takashi flipped to the next page. At the bottom was the category "Potential." Cal's was a 6.

Underneath that was written: *The challenge would be keeping him from hunting his own kind upon first transitioning. Best approach would be extended manipulation of desires in order to prepare him for the change. But is he worth that much effort? Not likely.*

Quickly, Takashi skimmed through the rest of the binder. The contents went into detail from what was in the summary. Cal's "Accomplishments" was a list four pages long of murders.

It was a recruitment evaluation.

Takashi closed the binder and put it back. He drew out Zack's and immediately went to the "Potential" section of his Summary.

10. He makes me miss Bran in all the best ways. Willful. Smart. With the Wrights disowning him, he must long for family. Best approach would be welcoming him with open arms, which won't be hard. I'm beginning to love him as a son already.

"How long ago did you write this?" Takashi murmured. He closed the binder and put it back on the shelf.

Was every binder on these shelves about a hunter? Takashi rose to his feet and picked a binder at random. Samantha Warren's occupation was listed as a professor. He slid it back in place and chose another. Kevin Williams was a scientist, and his potential was rated at an 8. Hyacinth Vale was a college student; her rating was a 9.

The bookshelves had to hold hundreds of binders. Seamus must have been considering all of these people as possible sirelings, but why? If he didn't take the time to regain his strength, he simply wouldn't have it to give to another. There was no way he could turn all of these people within their lifetimes. Even if Anton helped him, he'd still weaken himself too much.

Unless they're stronger than they let on. Roger had said they'd been absorbing power from sirelings for centuries, but Seamus hadn't shown any talents beyond what was common of a vampire a quarter his age. Takashi had assumed he'd given a large portion of his vampiric strength to Zack in order to turn him, but what if that wasn't the case? What if the bath of Seamus's power was running over, and he had been able to fill up Zack's soul with just the excess?

Had the fight in the hotel suite been cats playing with mice, or had Roger and the others presented the slightest challenge? *Considering how quickly we were defeated, I think the answer is the first.*

Takashi wasn't playing one game of four-dimensional chess against Seamus and Anton; he was playing fifty. At the same time. And pieces were going to fly off the board any minute.

There were more answers in this room, he was certain of it, but he'd already spent a long time in it. In all likelihood, Anton or the boy who'd been bringing him blood would start looking for him, and he couldn't afford to be caught here. He ensured that he left both the secret office and front study exactly as he'd found them and slipped out into the hall.

Still alone, he took a moment to lean against the door and conquer the fear welling up. He bricked it up behind three layers of worry about Roger. After all, there was nothing to be done about the fact that Seamus was likely holding out how powerful he was. It was just Takashi's hypothesis. Perhaps he was wrong. *You know you're not. You know you've barely seen what he's truly capable of.*

Perhaps the answer wasn't to wrestle the coven from Seamus in the way Roger had originally intended at all. A stealth assassination would put the leadership into a freefall, but they were never going to win a fair fight in public. Something else would have to be done. A revolution? Preposterous. Vampires had tried to rise against their elders before, and it never went well without time, money, effort, devotion, and a smile from the fates. Roger, Zack, and Takashi were lacking in a few areas, especially the favor of the fates.

Maybe not. We are still here. Takashi pushed away from the door and headed off into the mansion. He had a lot more of it to discover, though he was going to keep the rest of his exploration to the more public areas for the evening. He'd already pressed his luck spending any time in Seamus's hidden office. Trying again would be asking for trouble. *And we clearly have enough of that in our cards.*

CHAPTER 26

Seamus parked the car in the middle of a dark field. They'd crossed the border to Indiana some time ago, but Zack wasn't sure exactly where they were. The farthest he'd ever been from his parents' house had been Taliville, but that was farther south in Tennessee. This random field was, in theory, as close as some of his relatives in Wisconsin were, but he'd never traveled this way. He wasn't sure he'd be able to recognize some isolated barn far off the interstate anyway.

"What errand could you possibly have out here?" Zack demanded.

"The kind you'll enjoy." Seamus opened the car door and stepped out. "We need to clean out a poachers' lair."

Zack scrambled out of the car and started to swing the door shut.

Seamus zipped over and caught the door. He eased it shut rather than allowing it to thud. In a whisper, he said, "Stealth, Zackery."

"What do you mean 'poachers' lair?'" Zack said under his breath.

"You were paying attention in the meeting last night,

weren't you?" Seamus pulled Zack's sheathed dagger out from his jacket and offered it out.

"Of course," Zack snapped. He took the dagger from Seamus. Without a belt, he couldn't slide it into place, but he could slip it free from the sheath and attempt to stab Seamus. *What if he has something set up where if he doesn't call, Takashi dies?* "But nobody said anything about poachers. Why would we give a shit about people killing animals? Unless—wait, you mean *vampires*."

"Precisely." Seamus nodded toward a barn down the field from them. "Now, do you remember what Leopold and Benedict's complaint was?"

"A vamp nest situated almost perfectly between their territory. Leopold was complaining that Benedict should take care of it because its location, Benedict claimed Leopold should handle it because they were stealing the humans from his territory," Zack said quietly. They were a distance away from the barn. How good was vampire hearing?

How good is mine? Zack stretched his senses. The interstate was pretty far, but he swore he still heard the rumble of a semi going past. From the barn's direction, he heard … talking. Music. Slurping. Some other noises that made him decide to close off his hearing after all.

"But they didn't know where it was," Zack said. "How did you find it so fast?"

"I didn't. At least, not on my own," Seamus replied. "You've been tracking this nest's activity for weeks in one of your notebooks. You nearly had them pinpointed."

The urge to call bullshit died on Zack's lips because he could feel a weird pressure building in the magnetic pull in his core. During the drive, Seamus had blocked him, but he was letting Zack glimpse at some of his fears and desires. No doubt this was still some trick, some modified response to make him look good, but Seamus was oozing the desire for connection. He wanted to guide Zack and seemed scared that Zack would never like him.

Like he honestly gives a shit whether or not I approve of him. Zack clenched his free hand.

What if he does? the strange, echoey Seamus voice responded.

What does it say about me if the monster wants me to like him?

Maybe he's not the monster you think he is, the echo-Seamus said.

That didn't sound like one of his thoughts at all. Zack glared at Seamus. *Note to self, prioritize research on whether vampires can have telepathy.*

"You are, without a doubt, the cleverest sireling I've made since Anton," Seamus said. "However, everyone has always relied on that side of you and ignored the side I know exists."

"What side is that?" Zack tightened his jaw afterward. He was getting too loud.

Seamus turned toward him. "The ruthless killer."

"I am *not*—"

"I *felt* you last night." Seamus stepped closer so that he and Zack would share breath if either of them had needed air and lowered his voice to a sterner pitch. "I saw how you took after that girl last night and how you drank from the one at the mansion. More than that, I know how the urge to kill me burned through you the night I gave you my blood. I can feel you stamping down upon that desire tonight.

"Your problem is with killing mortals? Fine. You aren't the first sireling I've taught that needed to abandon that peculiarity. I can't make you accept that you have moved higher up the food chain. But—" He motioned at the barn. "—that nest is doing damage. They are killing humans and risking the existence of our kind."

"Our kind is all over social media," Zack replied.

"Few mortals outside of our community believe it real," Seamus said. "Nests like this one could ruin that for us. Then we won't have just hunters to contend with but governments. Chaos would ensue. People would die. Your loved ones might be first. So, you can pout like a little boy, or you can use your new gifts to do what you've always longed to do and take care of a batch of blood-thirsty bastards."

Seamus had a point. The argument about whether or not the rest of humanity needed to recognize the existence of the supernatural was a hot debate in the hunter community as well. Sure, if governments knew, there could be the opportunity to do their work with better funding. On the other hand, there was a conflicting belief that vampires and other supernaturals would sway public opinion and governments to their side and protect them. Zack's mom was passionately against that.

Zack hadn't really formed an opinion on the matter, but as a vampire, he didn't like the idea of police raiding vampire homes and putting them down. He had killed humans, but he couldn't really stop himself from doing it. Did he deserve to go to jail for that?

I'm going to give myself a migraine if I keep thinking about that. Zack slipped his dagger out of its sheath and placed the sheath on the hood of the car behind him. The runes down the length of his silver dagger glowed with the faintest red light. *Great, even my soul doesn't think he's that much of a danger to me anymore.*

He took three steps toward the barn and realized Seamus was staying behind. He glanced over his shoulder. "You're not coming?"

"You're my progeny. They are nest rats weaker than the average new fledgling. I'm certain you'll be fine." Seamus relaxed against the hood of his car and motioned for Zack to go on. "I'll be listening. Say my name if you need me."

I'd rather fucking die.

Would you really, though? the echo-Seamus asked.

Well … it's not going to matter. I've got this.

Zack set off across the dark field. If the nest was smart, they'd have some sort of lookout. Rather than relying on his speed, he ducked lower and made his way forward with a delicate swiftness instead of rushing ahead like a bull. He searched for any sign of movement and started tracking the different sounds coming from around and inside the barn. The music was loud—which would work for him—and he picked out multiple voices. Someone shrieked, and that was met with laughter from at least five voices.

His dagger glowed a little brighter. Zack hid it behind his back as he approached the barn. As far as he could tell, there was no sentry. While still at a short distance, he circled the building. A few lights illuminated the interior, and that spilled light out into the night, particularly the very open barn doors on the north side. He stayed out of that brightness and went around the other way to complete his evaluation. Scents of old wood, fresh blood, cold dirt, and a reek of sex wafted out.

The vamps had been holed up in this place for a little while. They'd grown comfortable.

Easy. Speed and surprise would be the best method. Zack spotted a place higher up the barn, where a few boards had fallen away and left a gap. Quick and quiet, he scaled the side of the building and lifted himself up onto the gap.

Just below him was a loft that overlooked the rest of the barn. A dead man was staring off to the side. Less than three feet away from him, two vampires were fucking as if they were the only creatures left on the planet. Their moans and slaps of flesh meeting were growing louder. One was shouting about how close an orgasm was.

Zack dropped onto the loft beside them as soft as a cat stalking a mouse. Swiftly, he moved forward and buried his dagger into the heart of the vamp on top. The other one noticed him, started to sputter, but Zack yanked his dagger free of the first, then slit the second's throat before shoving his dagger deep in his chest. The silver burned the vampire's heart out, and his skin grayed.

The first vampire was starting to recover, the wound healing, so Zack pinned her to the floor and stabbed her again. He snarled and twisted the blade deeper into her chest, ensuring that the silver burned out her heart. Her color drained faster, but something *clicked* inside Zack when she was truly dead. Both of the vampires had had bursts of the desire to live. Somehow, he felt when they died creeping through his hand from the dagger.

"Hey, you two finished up there?" someone called out. "Gail brought us some prime fresh meat!"

Introspect later. Zack pulled his dagger free and slunk off to a shadow. The blood on his blade seeped into the runes and turned the light to a deeper red. *Nope. Not analyzing that either. Let's see where the next one is.*

He crept to the shadowy side of the loft and slipped forward to the edge to gain a better view of the party below. Three vampires were feeding on a single victim whose eyes were growing glassier by the second. Another two were standing beside the open back doors of a black panel van. Inside it were four bound and blindfolded humans. Their fear was a beacon, a bright distraction in the mess of the party. Zack put them out of mind and focused on the vampires. They were the priority. Once he killed them, he'd care about the humans.

Another vampire—mouth, chin, and clothes covered in blood—was dancing by himself beside a phone blaring out music. And a final one was roaming out from underneath the loft, shouting upward again. "Hey! We're not going to save any for you!"

The final vampire spotted Zack. Her eyes went wide in surprise, and she opened her mouth to shout.

Zack dropped to the ground and sank his blade into her chest before she had the chance to speak. He snarled as he slammed her down and held the blade in place. Her skin began to gray. When he pulled his blade out, a thin red mist of energy followed upward and sank into the runes. *That's new.*

The remaining six vampires stopped what they were doing and hissed at him. They spread their hands like each finger was tipped with a claw, but nails weren't a threatening weapon to him. The boldest of them launched herself toward Zack.

But she was clumsy, slow, and telegraphing her strike. Zack slipped inside her attack, knocked her arm farther off target, and sank his blade into her heart. Instantly, the magic in her faded and abandoned her body. *Four down, five to go.*

He had been waiting for this fight for his whole life. Training. Preparing.

The five still standing rushed toward him.

He grinned.

His new strength made snapping bones and crushing flesh easy. As he relied upon his supernatural speed, they seemed to move like a video on buffer, fits and bursts but nothing that caught up to where he was. Another dropped; another heart burned out by his silver. *Five down.*

Everything he had ever practiced had never felt so simple. He became living ice, cold and sharp and brutal. He broke one vampire's head clean off its body. Six down.

Then seven.

Eight.

The last vampire finally grasped how badly the fight was going and ran for the open barn doors while Zack was twisting his blade into the heart of his eighth kill. Before he could escape, Seamus sauntered into the light and plunged Cal's dagger into the would-be escapee's chest.

This was supposed to be *his* hunt. Zack shouted, "He was *mine*!"

Seamus smiled at him with a warm pride Zack hadn't seen from Thomas in years.

The rational part of Zack's mind had gone silent during the fight. Every part of him had thrown himself into that moment. Adrenaline didn't course through him, but the come down from action still lightly shook him. He waited for some rogue thought to ruin his moment.

The only ones that circled were demands that Seamus would pay for taking what was his.

Seamus took a handkerchief out of his back pocket and cleaned Cal's blade. "Forgive me. I've had a few grueling nights myself. I wanted in on the fun."

"Fun," Zack repeated. The word had never felt completely wrong and right at the same time. His heart was racing in his ears.

Not my heartbeat. Zack swallowed and slowly spun toward the van. Now that he was aware of the mortals again, he could hear their breathing, pick out the individual rhythms. Could taste their fear on his tongue like a rim of salt on glass.

The burning hunger inside him dried his throat and his eyes. His trembling grew, and his knees buckled. He started to plummet toward the ground.

Seamus caught him by the arm and held him up. In a soothing voice, he said, "Our strength comes at a price."

With his arm around Zack, Seamus guided him over to the van, where the four mortals were tied up. The effort to struggle would take too much precious energy that he didn't have. The lore he'd learned from his family joined the growing need for blood. Vampires needed several pints of blood a night, enough that feeding from one mortal meant killing them. Younger vampires tended to need more, but Zack had always suspected that was from a lack of knowing how to drain a victim rather than the need.

The facts helped stabilize his control so that he didn't launch himself at the helpless people in front of him. But they were breathing. They had heartbeats. They had *blood*. He was thirsty.

"Take your pick." Seamus nudged Zack closer to the open van doors.

Zack braced himself on the edge of the van, arms spread wide like he was holding himself over an infinite abyss. "I … I can't."

"Why not?" Seamus said patiently. He was at Zack's ear.

Zack tightened his grip. Metal crunched under his fingertips. "These are … innocent people … We should let them go."

"How do you know they're innocent?" Seamus put his hand on Zack's shoulder. "And why does that matter at all? They're *food*. You need to eat."

"I don't want to be a monster," Zack said desperately.

"Monsters only exist in fairy tales." Seamus squeezed his shoulder. "If it helps, know that whoever survives us will go to Steward's Garden."

"We should let them *go*."

"Why?" Seamus asked.

Logic felt like a singular sticky note inside a pile of loose paper pages four feet deep. Zack had to push and fight to find it. The reason. There had to be a reason not to do this. One came to him, and he looked over his shoulder at Seamus. His voice was weak even in his own ears. "Because it's the right thing to do."

"Says who? Your human parents that abandoned you? The hunters who would plunge their weapons through us simply for what we are? Humans who would claw and kill each other to survive if they have to?" Seamus asked. His voice was calm, and that held a soothing appeal.

He's tricking me.

Tricking you into surviving? How dastardly, his practical voice replied.

"No matter what I do, they're dead?" Zack whispered.

"Yes. You may as well take what you need."

One of the humans whimpered, and that drew Zack's attention. The tang of his own fear was on the back of his tongue, but he was thirsty and before him was exactly what he needed. *I can have control over my feeding or go into a blood frenzy. And this way, they won't suffer.* He grabbed the feet of the nearest man, hauled him out of the van, and sank his teeth into his neck.

Seamus stroked his hair as he fed and murmured, "That's my boy."

CHAPTER 27

Gathering the resources for the heist took a few nights, but as Roger finished strapping a third silver dagger to his belt, he couldn't deny the comfort in being well armed and prepared. Josefina had used her connections to discreetly purchase an old brick building roughly three miles from their target, which made it an ideal staging ground. Once upon a time, the building had housed a dance studio. One wall had the remains of broken mirrors, and through them, bits of movement were reflected. Roger had to suppress his urge to alert to each tiny bit of activity in his peripheral vision.

Ready for the mission, he checked on the others.

Like him, everyone was dressed all in black, complete with black gloves and ski masks. Josefina already had her mask on her head, though it was rolled up for the moment. Seeing her with short hair instead of her long braid was still an adjustment for Roger. Along with a short sword, she had a collapsible truncheon and a heavy UV flashlight.

Roger had invited Nathaniel, but he had pointed out that he had a business to run, and it'd be suspicious if the attack happened on the one night he wasn't tending bar. Nathaniel had recommended Janiyah to the job in his stead. She maintained an icy glare whenever she glanced Roger's way, and her coldness seemed to extend to Thomas, Amber, and Vincent but not Dmitri or Josefina.

Thomas was a natural choice for inclusion, even if his mere presence continued to remind Roger of his failure to save Zack. After a few nights working together, Thomas was beginning to stand out as his own man, but there remained an aspect to him that slid under Roger's skin and festered. Something about the way he stood was too much an echo of his son.

Against Roger's better judgment, Thomas had insisted on adding Amber to their team. He pointed out that his daughter had tactical experience that they needed. When Dmitri had seconded bringing another trained hunter, Roger had conceded. Dmitri was the one who knew the building and security.

Since much of the planning had happened within Vincent's earshot, he'd invited himself. Roger didn't have the heart to deny the boy a measure of revenge against Seamus. No one was particularly happy about an untrained compatriot, but Vincent knew how to drive. Making him the wheelman meant a trained fighter was free to join them inside the building, and no one had disagreed with that idea.

Still, Roger found himself lingering near Vincent as the group finished their preparations. Vincent leaned against a wall and spun a set of keys around his finger. His color was better than it'd been, and his movements had a quickness to them he hadn't had.

Softly, Roger said, "Remember—"

"Stay in the van," Vincent recited. "Keep the engine running. If anyone launches an attack on the van, blare the horn as long and loud as I can."

"If the vehicle's compromised?"

"Make my way back here on foot if I'm able. If I think I'm

being followed, do my best to slip into a mortal bar or restaurant and blend in."

Roger put his hand on Vincent's shoulder and squeezed. A tiny thrum radiated from Vincent, not like an emotion at all but like a burst of static electricity. Pushing aside the strange sensation, Roger focused on the moment. "Stay safe, all right?"

Vincent almost smiled. "You too."

A few other muted conversations were happening, and Roger eavesdropped to check on the moods of his companions. Josefina was stressing the importance that Dmitri filter a sliver of the funds to Nell in order to compensate for Roger's debt, and he was reassuring her that was part of the plan. Whether Dmitri would live up to that, Roger wasn't sure. But he had hope.

Amber was attempting to engage Janiyah in conversation, but while Janiyah wasn't unfriendly, she treated Amber with a cool distance. She'd said during one of the planning sessions that she was doing this because Nathaniel stressed it would change things for the coven as a whole. In general, she didn't give a shit about the elite vampires in leadership positions. Roger couldn't help agreeing with her. The only one left in power that he cared about was Candide, and she would continue playing her cards to her advantage.

Thomas was checking his quiver for the third time. When Roger drifted toward him, Thomas said, "Wish we'd had a practice run."

"They could discover Dmitri's back door at any point," Roger replied. "We can't afford to lose any more time."

"Hopefully, they haven't already," Dmitri added.

"You mean this could all be for nothing?" Amber said as she joined in their conversation.

Now, everyone was paying attention to them. Roger said, "Either we'll be able to drain Seamus's accounts, or we won't. At the very least, we will send a message that he is not as invulnerable as he believes. Shaking even a fraction of his confidence loose is worth this risk."

"Let's hope," Thomas said under his breath.

Roger scanned each of their faces. The grim note in Thomas's voice had lowered the mood of the group.

Decades had passed since the last time he'd truly led anyone into a battle, and even then, he had been a captain for Seamus and moving on his orders. Coordinating the rescue mission had been Roger's first true attempt to lead, and that had failed. If they failed again, he wasn't sure what would be left of himself, let alone the others. In the best-case scenario, they all survived, and Seamus was robbed of nearly four billion dollars.

But there was the possibility of a horrific outcome. Not death—death would be terrible, but it would be a finality. If they were captured, that would lead to war between Nell's coven and the GLC, which would result in too many innocents' deaths. And there was no telling what sort of torment Seamus, Anton, and other sadistic vampires of the GLC would do to this brave group if given the chance. Roger didn't have to think hard to envision a dozen different miserable, torturous scenarios.

All of them knew that there was a chance this mission would lead to worse than disaster. He might be leading them to their worst hells. But they were willing to try.

He couldn't ignore that. Couldn't let them think for an instant that their willingness to risk themselves meant nothing to him.

"We can do more than hope," Roger said. "No one has made an attempt like this. Win or lose, we will make a difference. No doubt about that. Let's do this."

The attitudes of the others didn't magically lift. In fact, Roger wasn't sure he'd had much of an impact on them at all. Yet no one balked. No one rolled their eyes or stormed away. They were ready to follow him.

So he led the way out the door to the back alley, where their white rental cargo van waited. Vincent claimed the driver's seat while Amber took the front passenger seat. Everyone else climbed into the cargo van's open back.

Roger was the last to step up into the van. Closing the doors brought a thud that he tried not to compare to the slam of a coffin lid. *Once we do this, there's no turning back.*

"Is the great pirate Roger is nervous about a robbery?" Josefina teased.

"Been a while since I've done one," Roger said quietly. He glanced to Dmitri. "Must have been the 1920s."

"The O'Malley twins' place." Dmitri leaned his head back against the side of the van, letting it bounce as the vehicle did. "I was thinking it must have been in Connecticut."

"I was quite the terror on the roads in England." Roger tried to grin. He resisted the urge to run his fingers across each of his silver daggers' hilts to ensure they were still there. Instead, he rested his hand on the stakes in the wrist launcher that Thomas had given him. "That time, I was sent to bring Ezra home. But this is more like being on the ship."

"Is it bad if I do miss those nights?" Dmitri said softly. "The rare ones."

The ones where Dmitri and Roger had been new vampires who relished the moments of freedom they gained whenever the chaos of battle and plunder had taken over their ship. They'd been able to drink their fill, glutting themselves on blood. Ripping through the enemy and satisfying their hunger had always settled Dmitri for a few nights, provided their target hadn't been a passenger vessel. For a short, glorious time, they'd been newly dead and never more alive.

But there was a gleeful wildness to those nights that Roger no longer trusted his memory to paint accurately. He had spent so long ignoring the pains inflicted on himself and others that holding on to the bleached notions of passionate, thrilling nights was a different sort of pain. How much of his pleasure had come from the blood of innocents? From those too much like himself, unable to trod another path in life?

Denying the shred of fondness that he had for those nights would only hurt Dmitri. There was no point in shattering him when he was barely holding himself together.

"I know which ones you mean," Roger said gently.

"I don't," Janiyah said brusquely.

"I assume they're talking about their pirate days," Thomas replied with an edge of judgmental tone.

"We had to make money somehow," Roger said. "Cobbling didn't pay like stealing the goods from rich pricks."

"Cobbling?" Janiyah asked.

"It's an old word for shoemaker," Vincent answered.

"Enough discussion," Josefina declared. "We're close, yes?"

"Three blocks," Vincent said.

Roger slid his black ski mask on, and the others followed suit. The final few seconds were an eternity of anxiety.

The instant Roger felt the van come to a complete stop, he shoved open the back doors and stepped out onto the pavement. Everyone behind him fell into step and followed him toward the double doors. Amber left the passenger seat and took up the rear position as they swept into the lobby.

The security guards behind the desk were already reaching for phones and alarms. Roger rushed one, and Josefina zipped at the other. Not taking a chance, he had a silver dagger in hand and plunged it into the heart of the guard he'd caught. Only as he held on to the man did he catch his scent of the grave. A vampire. *Someone just doing his job.*

This was no time for guilt. Josefina dropped her guard to the ground, another victim motionless, and cleared the way for Dmitri. Keeping with the plan, Dmitri disabled what security he could at the front computer. If the guards had triggered any alarms, he would know.

After a few seconds of typing, he gave a thumbs-up. Then

he ripped the computer off the desk and smashed it against the floor.

One step done, many more to go. Roger took a set of keys off one of the dead guards and led the way to the staircase. Amber and Janiyah remained behind in the lobby to protect their exit while the remaining four of them began a stealth march up to the sixth floor. As the only mortal, Thomas made the most noise, but even he was a whisper of a professional.

The keys gave them access to the floor, but Dmitri had been confident that they wouldn't work on the door they needed. Roger handed them off to Thomas. With a nod, Thomas slipped them into his back pocket and pulled an arrow from his quiver. The hallway they were in extended in long sections either way, and he stayed to guard the stairway door.

Dmitri took point and headed down the left hall. When it joined at an intersection, he turned left again and halted.

A guard was walking the hall. As his hand went for his gun, Roger flung a dagger at him. It struck the guard in the shoulder rather than the heart. The scent of mortal blood filled the air, and hesitation stalled Roger's plan.

Josefina surged forward and snapped the man's neck. She took the walkie from his belt and held it out toward Roger.

The guard would have done his job and stood in their way, complicated everything. There was no reason to let him live, especially since he would have endangered the ones Roger cared about in this place. His death had been a necessity, and yet Roger had paused. *I am so tired of collateral damage.* Grimly, he took the walkie from Josefina. *But there will be more before we're done. And every drop of blood has to mean our freedom. I have to make it all count.*

Silently, Dmitri strode forward, and Roger followed him. With Josefina bringing up the rear, they navigated their way to the server room door. A biometric lock barred their path.

Dmitri put his hand on the pad, but it flashed red. He tried a second time. Same result.

Josefina took one of the smaller detonation charges out of her bag. Explosives had been the backup plan, but the floor was silent. The noise of a bomb, however small and targeted, was certain to drag attention. And attention meant more guards.

Securing their exits had seemed like the smart strategy, but their group was spread thin. A sudden image of an over-whelming number of vampires swarming the ground floor and Thomas came to Roger. The security wasn't endless. If Roger and the others fought well enough, they might even win.

But so much could go wrong.

The door wasn't seamless in the wall. The thinnest gaps existed—they had to—and in those gaps were places the light didn't touch. Anton managed to use shadows to travel whole miles in an instant. He could call on them to do his bidding.

Roger had managed a facet of that. On instinct, he'd once slipped Seamus's grasp through some form of shadow manipulation. *I didn't turn my arm into shadow. I pushed my arm into the shadow space.* If he could do that, he could manage a few inches to the other side of the door, couldn't he?

He motioned for Josefina to stay back and then put his hand on the crack of the door. The strange, otherworldliness awareness was at the edge of his mind, like a friend waiting for him to answer his phone. He picked up, letting it speak to him.

Something beyond his mundane senses opened. Reality became a web of stimuli, sticky with concrete details and gossamer with that weird elseness. The shadow under his fingertips had a cold, liquid feel to it. Despite its thinness, he sensed that the surface went deeper and the shadows extended into the room beyond.

He had dived into crystal-clear waters where the depth

had been so much more than the waters seemed at first sight. Perhaps the shadows were the same. All he had to do was step to the edge of reality and take the plunge. He pushed into that thin space.

Moving into the shadow was like dropping into an icy ocean, though these ethereal seas were colder than any wave had ever been. While he didn't need air in the real world, in this moment, his lungs screamed for oxygen. He opened his mouth to suck some in but found only murky otherness. The world was shapes in darkness with ill-defined edges except where the light touched. The shadows roiled away from the light, and yet some of them were biting at it. They seemed to have some level of consciousness or at least a feral instinct. They had to be the kind of shadow that Anton commanded into tendrils.

He realized that even in the act of turning around to look at the light, he had stepped past the door. The shifting blacks and grays defined the borders of the server room. All he had to do was find his way back to the normal realm.

When diving, his greatest challenge had been reaching deeper. The surface had always called him upward. Physics, Zack would have said. And he didn't belong to this other-place. Closing his eyes, Roger felt a tug toward the surface. He leaned into it, and the cold fell away. Air brushed against the thin strip of skin left exposed by his ski mask.

He opened his eyes to darkness, but a familiar empty-feeling shadow rather than the inky living gray matter of that other realm. Gently, he reached out and touched the door. The handle turned easily, and he pulled the door open.

Dmitri and Josefina stared at him with wide eyes for an instant, but they recovered and moved into the room as soon as he stepped out of their way. Moving swiftly, Dmitri went to the back and took a laptop from his sling bag. He hooked up to one of the machines.

Josefina took a position by the door with Roger. She whispered, "You didn't tell me you were gaining ancient powers."

"This didn't feel like a vampire ability," Roger murmured. "Something weird is going on."

"Whatever it is, you make good use of it," Josefina replied.

"Hm." Roger glanced around for any sign of a camera but didn't see one. That didn't mean the room was free of them. Zack had taught him that cameras could be smaller than a button and still capture quite a bit of area.

The long minutes waiting for Dmitri to finish with the servers were eternities unto themselves. Each one brought a new hellish imagining of what hell they would endure if they were discovered. Seven painful ideas were far too many, and yet an eighth added its weight. A ninth.

"How much longer?" Roger asked.

"A couple more minutes," Dmitri replied.

"Anyone notice you?"

Dmitri didn't answer aloud, but he had an intense desire to keep going and a thin want to suppress information. That was an emotion Roger was all too familiar in feeling from him. Back in the early 1700s, he would get the same way when they were robbing carriages and the job was turning against them.

"Damn it," Roger swore under his breath. "Set the charges."

"Are you sure?" Josefina asked.

"Ten minutes. Do it."

Josefina nodded and set to work.

Roger poked his head out of the door. The stillness of the floor was disturbed, though he didn't hear a distinct sound at first. Then there was a running footfall, and another. He stepped out into the hall and pulled two of his daggers.

But the guards weren't running toward the server room door. They were rushing elsewhere.

Thomas. With a burst of speed, Roger hurried back to

where they'd left him. As he did, the sounds of a fight broke out. A body thumped to the floor, and Roger turned the corner in time to see a vampire fall with a wooden arrow in their heart. He stepped over them and grabbed a different guard attempting to blur past him. He snapped the guard's neck and moved on to the next opponent.

Between Thomas and Roger, the other three fell quickly. Before Roger could relax, the elevator doors dinged in the distance. A faint red light pulsed at the far corners of the room. Perhaps subtle for a human, but Roger noticed it.

"We're discovered," Roger said to Thomas. "Go."

"What about—"

"I have this door. *Go.*"

Thomas nodded sharply and then hurried into the stairwell. Once the door shut, his footsteps were muffled, but they continued growing more and more distant as he made his way down.

The more concerning footsteps were the ones rushing from the elevators toward Roger. He spun his daggers in his hands, wished he'd thought to have a silver cutlass made, and turned to face the oncoming attackers. Four guards rounded the corner; all were vampires.

Hoping to disguise his voice a fraction, Roger roughly told them, "Last chance to walk away."

One guard did pause but then fell into step with his coworkers.

A bulk of the vampires in the GLC were under a hundred and fifty years old, most being turned after Seamus had claimed Chicago the heart of his territory. These four were no exception, and even outnumbering him didn't give them an advantage. Roger's training with Nell had sharpened his reflexes, and he tore through them in an instant. His silver daggers burned out their hearts. Small puffs of red mist dissipated in the air.

Two more sets of running footsteps headed toward him,

but Roger recognized one. Dmitri. In a fraction of a second, he and Josefina hurried around the corner and toward the stairwell. Roger stepped out of their way and motioned for them to go ahead of him. They didn't hesitate, and the three of them sped down the stairs, catching up to Thomas as he reached the bottom.

They poured out of the stairwell and into the lobby. The sounds of the fight upstairs had masked the noise of the one happening on the lower level. Amber let a shotgun blast loose at two vampires that were closing in on her. Janiyah was trading blows with another security guard up against a wall.

The elevator doors dinged open. The vampires who ran out weren't dressed as guards but like office workers. The glare of their red eyes and the variety of weapons in their hands gave away their intent. One raised a pistol, aiming for Thomas.

Roger dashed forward and sliced his daggers through the flesh of the one aiming for Thomas, and plunged a dagger into the vampire's heart. The vampire howled, screaming in agony as the silver burned him, and he slid off Roger's dagger with a sickening, dead thud to the floor.

The other three vampires emerging from the elevators had been concerned with Amber and Janiyah, but now they saw Roger, Dmitri, Thomas, and Josefina coming out of the stairwell.

Chaos erupted. Dmitri bolted for the exit, throwing one of the vampires Amber had shot out of the way. The other latched onto him and dragged him to a halt.

Josefina engaged with a vampire leaving the elevator and cracked bone with her truncheon, while Thomas fought with his short sword and enchanted dagger beside her.

A vampire almost slipped past Roger, but he buried one of his silver daggers into her heart and held her in place until her heart burned away. The grunts, snarls, and strikes of the others in the lobby were a constant noise. Underneath them, he heard the pounding of footsteps. More were coming down the staircase. Roger glanced over his shoulder to his companions.

Amber missed with her next shotgun blast, and the vampire who Dmitri had tossed closed the distance with her. The vampire Janiyah was fighting dodged her strike but also failed to hit her. Dmitri continued to struggle to throw off the vampire hanging on to him.

The mission was done. Staying and fighting would only mean they'd become overwhelmed.

"Run!" Roger ordered.

His companions started to make for the doorway as the next wave of security and office workers reached the lobby floor. Amber and Janiyah made it out into the night, and Josefina blurred across the lobby to rush out with them. Thomas and Dmitri were caught up in fights with vampires who crowded them.

With a snarl, Roger punched one of the vampires harassing Thomas and stabbed through the throat of the other. Freed, Thomas started for the door.

A dozen vampires poured out from the stairwell. And still, the thundering of feet told Roger that more were on the way. He snapped necks and sliced and stabbed as fast as he could, but three still caught up to Thomas, and more reached Dmitri. One office worker near Roger swung a stapler at him and caught him in the forehead with it. His skin healed and pushed the bit of metal out within an instant, but it wasn't the only wound he had to heal. Roger could push off from them, outrun them. He might be able to slip into the shadows and escape that way.

But that would mean leaving Thomas and Dmitri to their fates.

No. Roger roared and punched through a vampire's chest, taking its heart clean from its body. He threw the organ against the far wall and pushed another with all his might.

Three vampires flew from the one shove, and he seized the opportunity to head for Thomas.

Before he could reach him, a vampire sank its fangs into Thomas's neck.

Another was poised to plunge a broken chair leg through Dmitri's heart.

I will not lose. A desperate storm struck lightning in Roger's soul. The world tilted, the colors changing. A halo of color surrounded each person in the lobby, becoming a sea of dim red. Thomas had an orange aura, and though Dmitri's was red like the other vampires, he had a rainbow sigil on his chest.

The light was not what Roger sought. With so many people in the lobby, the number of shadows had quadrupled and lengthened. He reached out into those cold spaces like he'd reached for his own shadow. They roiled and twisted, not answering with voice as much as a distant touch.

He could bring them forth.

As he'd seen Anton do so many times, Roger pictured those shadows wrapping around the attackers. He commanded them to form into ropes and bind his enemies to the floor. Then he gave them the tide in his soul to power them, to coax them further into his reality and obey.

For a heart-wrenching split second, he'd thought they were going to ignore him. He screamed in the terror of his doubt and redoubled the mental wave he felt.

Ten voices echoed his scream as the shadows tore up from the floor in ropey tendrils and wrapped around the ten vampires fighting in the lobby. All ten went to the floor, caught and bound by the shadow tendrils.

Thomas and Dmitri were spared and stumbled away from the vampires who had been hurting them. Both of their expressions were blank with shock.

Dmitri recovered quicker, motioning for Roger to follow them.

Elation tore through Roger. He ran for the van, feet barely touching the ground, and flung himself into the back of the vehicle behind Dmitri and Thomas. Vincent was taking off down the road before Josefina finished shutting the doors, but she managed to swing them shut. Everyone was ripping off their ski masks, except Amber and Vincent, who were in the front.

The back of the van was washed in a multitude of colored auras. Dmitri, Janiyah, and Josefina had faint red, while Thomas remained orange. Amber's was a golden shade. White light poured out from Vincent, though shimmers of rainbow colors pulsed inside that light. The rainbow sigil on Dmitri's chest was brighter than it had been in the lobby.

Roger had a fraction of a moment to admire it before Thomas grabbed him roughly by the shirt and hauled him up so they were face-to-face. The strangely colored vision faded away into his regular sight.

"What the hell was that?" Thomas demanded.

"How long have you been able to command the dark?" Dmitri asked.

"What the what?" Janiyah said.

"There was this shadow thing," Amber replied. "Did you see it?"

"How could I see it back here?" Janiyah snapped.

"I was talking to Vincent."

"All I saw was you guys jumping into the van," Vincent said.

The lightness in Roger dropped off into an aching tiredness that he didn't usually feel unless he'd stayed up well past dawn. It wasn't quite as bad as when he'd first woken from his coma, but he was growing hungry. The blood he'd had earlier that night was a diminished reservoir.

"Oh my God, Dmitri! Don't lean back." Josefina shoved Dmitri's shoulders forward.

A piece of the chair leg was protruding from the center of

the Dmitri's back. With a quick and careful pull, Josefina freed it from his back.

From the angle of the injury and the length and width of the piece of wood, it should have struck Dmitri's heart. He should have died. Josefina met Roger's gaze, her eyes wide, so he wasn't the only one who'd thought that. *Why does Dmitri have a sigil and other vampires don't? What did Anton do to him?*

"Hey!" Thomas shouted. His fear radiated, a dim flicker despite the tension in his voice. "Answer me!"

"It's a new thing. A very new thing," Roger managed weakly. He locked his gaze with Dmitri's. "I couldn't let anything else happen to you."

Dmitri dipped his head and looked away, but he glanced back through his dark lashes after a second.

I shouldn't let that unfetter my heart. Roger pushed away from Thomas and slumped against the side of the van. The plan was to head out of the city, swap to a different van, and drive back in later on. Roger hadn't counted on needing blood, and he wasn't about to ask the mortals with him for any.

The crashing boom from the bombs Josefina had set was just at the edge of Roger's hearing. There was a chance someone might have been hurt, and Roger swallowed that guilt.

Amber tore off her ski mask as she turned around in her seat. "Did we do it? Is the money gone?"

Slowly, Dmitri smiled. "I did it. He has lost *billions*."

We fucking won, and none of us died. A laugh bubbled out of Roger, and soon, the entire van was celebrating so rowdily that Vincent shouted at them to knock it off as he was driving. Their glee was quieted but not stifled. *Sweet victory, I have missed the taste of you.*

CHAPTER 28

In life, Zack had been a cuddler, but the way he held on to Takashi, even in his sleep, melted a piece of Takashi's heart. Over the last few nights, an odd routine had developed that began with Takashi waking in what was technically Zack's bed. The only painful part of their rest was the absence of Roger.

Inevitably, Seamus interrupted them. By the third night, Zack climbed out of bed well before the knock came on the door. Seamus and Takashi would make bland conversation while waiting for Zack to finish preparing for the evening out. Then Zack and Seamus would leave.

Takashi roamed the mansion, quickly exploring everywhere that wasn't behind a locked door. He hadn't investigated Seamus's secret room a second time just yet, but he had discovered a locked door on the first floor that was steeped in residual fear. Every time he'd gotten close to using his makeshift lockpicks on it, a pair of security guards would patrol the hall.

And that was a strangeness as well. For all the staff, security, and mortal pets that Seamus kept, the mansion lacked the flicker of warmth that came from mortals. Other than the security guards, anyone that Takashi came across would bow and then excuse themselves as fast as they could from being in the same room as him.

At some point in his evenings, he would happen upon Anton or the red-collared pale boy, or one of the two would find him, and a cursory offering of blood was made. Then Anton would excuse himself on the grounds of "research," or the boy would disappear into the depths of the mansion, and Takashi was alone again.

Takashi wasn't sure if his listlessness was developing because of the lonely way his nights were passing or from the lack of decent blood. One might have begun to feed the other.

But there wasn't much he could do. His search for a phone had turned up nothing, not even the hint of a landline. Seamus was keeping them isolated. The closest he had come to communications with the outside world were the computers in Seamus's secret office, and those were likely to be trapped.

Takashi was growing almost desperate enough to find out. One email, one small word to someone beyond the mansion, might be what made him feel more like himself.

And if Seamus was watching, then that same email would paint a target on whoever Takashi reached out to.

Takashi had been in tense positions before; attending any foreign vampire court was like playing chess with skilled masterminds. Every gesture and word was another glide of a piece across the board. Some courts feigned their manners better, but all were filled with vampires that would ruin him in an instant if doing so suited their plans. He had accepted that and relished surviving in those places. The right word in the right place typically turned the situation around. Other covens respected him, even if they weren't overly fond of him.

Nothing had prepared him for the grind of stress that was living in the mansion. Roger hadn't wanted to speak about what life with Seamus and Anton was like. Though Roger's experience had been harsher and he hadn't always lived with the pair, Takashi was beginning to understand his scars more fully. There were no words for his current situation, except, perhaps, he was on the road to madness.

Still, Takashi waited until Seamus and Zack left for the evening. Then he dressed and explored the halls. When he reached the front hall, the scent of fearful mortals drew his attention. He followed his nose to a lavish sitting room.

Anton relaxed on one of the couches, one arm along the back and one leg crossed over the other. He was wearing a fine, dark gray suit, and his long blond hair was pulled back with a matching gray band. Despite his general carefree display, his brow was pinched in concentration until he noticed Takashi at the doorway. "Ah! Just in time. Come in!"

Across from Anton were three teenage girls in matching black school uniforms. One had a copper and red tie, another deep blue, and the last had a black tie with threads of green. Their blazers had the school crest for Versinal Academy. They were bound to wooden chairs by wrist, waist, and ankle. Each had a white cloth gag tied around their mouths.

"You've kidnapped mage students?" Takashi said, affecting a note of boredom. Decades of practice made his outrage easier to hide.

"I did no such thing. They came to meet me," Anton said impishly. His grin said otherwise. He held out a phone toward Takashi. "Technically, they thought they were meeting *you*."

Takashi entered the room, took the phone, and skimmed the open messenger, rushing through nights upon nights of back and forth with the girls. The oldest conversations started weeks ago around Halloween. "You catfished them. Using me. Why?"

Anton took the phone back. "I could hardly use my own picture. They wouldn't have spoken to the diabolical vampire warlock who was the subject of cautionary tales of their youth."

"You don't know that," Takashi replied shortly. "You could've held a unique allure. Without dragging my name into it."

"Oh, be *fun*, Takashi." Anton playfully swatted Takashi's arm. "These three have kept our little secret. They thought they were the special chosen of a world-traveled ambassador. I believe Katie there was quite moved that you picked her."

"They are children of Enduring Circle mages," Takashi replied. "You should release them before you start a war."

"If the mages truly had power anymore, then one of these young darlings would have already gotten out of her bonds," Anton replied. "None of them are skilled enough—and they've already turned eighteen! By their age, I was setting fire to whole houses with a snap of my fingers."

Anton raised one hand, fingers ready to snap.

Fearful he might set one of the girls on fire as an example, Takashi clamped his hand over Anton's and pushed it back down to rest on the couch as he sat beside him.

Anton rolled his eyes and sighed. "The point is, the Enduring Circle is toothless. It's only a matter of time until it crumbles. They wouldn't dare start a war with our kind. Now stop fussing and feel honored. They want to become your vampire brides."

Takashi had to refrain from clenching his fists. Exactly what had Anton promised these girls? "Oh, do they?"

Anton's grin would have been devilishly handsome if he wasn't discussing such a malicious scheme. "They sent me—well, *you*—a lovely little video last week showing how well they'd get along. You should see it."

"No, thank you," Takashi said sharply.

"You're getting worked up." Anton put a hand on Takashi's elbow. "I thought you would be more fun."

"Luring innocent girls into a kidnapping isn't my version of fun," Takashi replied.

"Right, you prefer to stalk bigots and catfish them into their graves," Anton said seriously, all hints of teasing gone for a second.

Takashi glared at Anton. That was the truth of one of his hobbies, one that he had keenly avoided sharing with Zack. Roger knew, but then Roger had been asking how he handled his urge to bring death upon mortals. *Anton must have discovered that secret while rooting around in my desires. Or he somehow broke my passwords on my laptop.*

"The prim, proper, and mortal-palatable Takashi Sato has a dark side." Anton leaned in closer, their faces only inches apart. His smile was back, slick and mocking, and he smelled faintly of fresh blood and old dirt. "Whatever will happen when the world discovers just how thick your mask is?"

But Anton wasn't the only one who could see beneath a well-crafted mask. Takashi said softly, "You started courting them after Halloween. Was that when Seamus told you he planned on turning Zack into his son?"

Anton flinched, a micro-expression that vanished back into his smooth persona. He leaned back against the couch and considered the girls before him. "At what time my love was planning on bringing a new addition into the family isn't what we should be discussing. We have three beautiful young women, and we should decide what to do with them."

"Bizarre thinking, but you could simply let them go," Takashi said.

Anton snorted. "Gods below, don't tell me you're going to keep clinging to that boring façade. I was in your mind, Takashi. I know you like the blood and death as much as I do."

I doubt that. Takashi settled into the corner of the couch. "You clearly had a plan before I wandered in. Don't pretend you need my ideas."

"That's true." Glee sparkled in Anton's ruby eyes. "I thought of gifting one to Zack as a pet."

"He's too young to keep from killing her, and he would hate how you found her," Takashi said. "He won't have a slave for a pet."

"Ugh, fair. And I can't stand to watch him brood more than he already does." Anton stroked his chin while he mused, "I am certain that you should turn at least one of them."

"I'm sorry, what?" Takashi asked.

"Oh, come on." Anton gestured at the girls. "They aren't that much younger than you were, or Zack was. I wager you could share enough power for the three of them to be fine young fledglings. And they did come to meet 'you' because they wanted to become beautiful immortals."

"You've had me on a crap blood diet for a week," Takashi replied.

"As if one week is enough to diminish a powerful sireling of Nell, the Pirate Queen and Master of the Smoky Woodlands Domain."

"You are many times older than me. I'd think you would be capable of turning all three."

"I have to conserve my strength for the time being," Anton replied. He nudged Takashi's leg with his foot. "Turn at least one? I'd love a foster daughter."

"You want me to turn one of them and let you raise her," Takashi said.

"We could do the raising." Anton put his hand on Takashi's shoulder. "Think of how darling she could become under our mutual tutelage."

The girl could grow into a terrible, brilliant nightmare. A true mastermind against mankind, with the perfect fuel for revenge upon them. How Anton missed that the girl would likely hate them for all eternity, Takashi wasn't sure.

Perhaps he could divert Anton's attention. Tactfully,

Takashi frowned and asked, "What about Zack? Aren't you raising him? He is your love's offspring."

"Yet I'm given no time to mold him!" Anton sighed. "I'm surprised my lover allows you anywhere near his precious prodigy. Now, please, Takashi. Let's do this."

The proposition had a million red flags. Versinal Academy was one of the premiere magic schools in North America and was run by the Enduring Circle, a very powerful group of magic practitioners based in Chicago. Even if their arcane prowess wasn't a challenge, their wealth and connections would be. In addition to that, Zack and Roger would never approve of these circumstances for making a sireling. These girls had been tricked.

But they also weren't long for this world. Anton had them and had already declared that he had no intention of letting them go. Their fates were sealed. Death, new life, or something worse awaited them.

Three vampires were impossible for Takashi unless he wanted to give away nearly all his strength or give them so little that they were practically human. However, if he made one into a vampire ... *she'd be bound to me. I wouldn't have this loneliness aching in my bones because I would be connected to her.* She would be stuck in the mansion with him, and becoming Anton's foster daughter wasn't likely to be entirely pleasant. But she might have access to the mansion in a way that Takashi didn't. She would be a piece on the board that could work for him. An asset.

Takashi was in need of assets.

"You'd have to treat her like a daughter," Takashi said slowly.

"Of course!"

"Not a doll or a toy or a role in some drama in your head, a daughter," Takashi reiterated.

Anton mellowed, his cheerfulness becoming more subtle.

He dropped his charade and became serious. "She will be a treasured being."

"I want a phone. A brand-new one, sealed in the box, with no manipulations on it," Takashi said.

Anton raised an eyebrow. "You want me to trust you with a phone?"

"I'm trusting you with my offspring." Takashi held Anton's gaze, unblinking. "At the moment, I could disappear into the night if I was willing to forsake Zack. If you have my sireling, you'd be able to easily track me. Even if I were to take her with me, the blood trail we'd have to leave would hinder us. This is no light feat you ask of me. You want my blood, my *power*, and you want to shape her growth. You are asking for a piece of my soul. You can give me a goddamn phone."

"You won't be absent from her life," Anton murmured. He put his hand on Takashi's as he continued holding his gaze. There was something almost gentle in his smile. "I know that Zack has settled faster because you have been at his side. You are a fantastic teacher."

"I wasn't starting on the wrong foot with Zack," Takashi replied. "What will you do if she's stubborn like him?"

"We'll deal with that." Anton squeezed Takashi's hand.

"That wasn't an answer," Takashi said quietly. "And you haven't promised me what I asked for."

"Such a stingy negotiator."

Takashi pulled his hand away from Anton's. "You could ask a dozen of your sirelings. You could find a new vampire to adopt within a fortnight, I'm certain. Instead, you want to raise what should be mine, and a flowery saying of 'ours' isn't enough when I am a prisoner within these walls."

"You chose to remain," Anton replied sternly.

"Because you said I would gain power here," Takashi returned. "However, all you and your love have done is take, and all I have been is patient. I am not a fool. You look to bind me more firmly to this place, and I am willing, but I have named my price. Tell me what you would do if she disobeyed. Promise me a phone."

Slowly, Anton stood and moved over to a lamp on an end table. He drifted his hand along the lampshade.

At the same time, Takashi felt a push into his mind. He buried his desires under a cold bank of insecurities. He was scared of what Seamus was doing to Zack the long nights they were out of the mansion; he was afraid that if he chose one of these girls, her life would become hell; he was terrified that something had happened to Roger; he had a small, thin fear that he'd picked the wrong slacks to go with his shirt. One desire remained outside his wall, and he focused his thoughts on it. *I want someone close. I don't want to feel alone.*

"I believe the mortals call it 'gentle parenting,'" Anton said, an ancient power resonating in his voice. All jokes and levity were absent. "You aren't the only one hoping for a little more joy in their evenings. I can arrange a phone, but know that if you conspire against my love, your Zack will be the first to die. Roger the second. The girl you make will scream for years before I break her. And you will be present for every second she is in agony. Do we have an understanding?"

Takashi wasn't going to get a better deal. He nodded once.

"Fantastic. Now. If you would." Anton motioned at the girls.

In the last one hundred and twenty-five years, Takashi had only made seven vampires. The first had been his mortal niece. She had found him, discovered the secret of Taliville, and begged him for eternal life. His second had been a nurse who had grown sick with the Spanish Flu. The third and fourth had been lovers who he'd foolishly believed he might have a forever with. They were still on decent terms, but their love had faded. His fifth had been an artist who still toiled away at his craft in the mountain forests around Taliville. His sixth, a young lover dying of AIDS in the 1970s who was now an ambassador in Seattle, and his seventh, a darling musician who was certain that with enough time, he could create the perfect symphony.

Unlike him, they had all known their choice. They had understood what being a vampire meant before he turned them. Mortals were for feeding, and transcending one to the existence of a vampire was no easy decision.

Takashi centered himself and stretched out his ability to sense the girls' fears and desires. A screaming panic formed a strong wall, but each had cracks, and Takashi slipped into them.

The girl with a copper and red tie was in denial. She wanted to wake up from the nightmare with nothing changed. The girl with the black-and-green tie was seething with a desire to burn both Anton and Takashi to ashes. Her hatred was in her eyes.

The third one, with her blue tie, had an emotion that Takashi recognized from the night he fell from the trapeze. The spark of yearning for immortality. Finding it was like discovering a note in perfect harmony to a song almost forgotten. Mortals as young as her didn't often understand what forever might truly involve. But as Takashi met her gaze, she took a deep breath. She had cried at some point, but she'd also stopped long enough that her tears were dry. She gripped the armrests of the chair she was bound to and continued watching him.

She looked young, but Takashi had seen younger vampires. Her brown hair was a mess of curls that had likely been mussed further during her kidnapping. She had a layer of makeup that her tears hadn't completely smudged. But underneath her pale olive foundation, he noticed a smattering of freckles.

Mage students were often taught ballroom dancing as part of their instruction, but she had an athlete's physique. A gymnast, Takashi was guessing. Or perhaps he was hoping he might have something more in common with his soon-to-be fledgling other than being stuck in the same hellish prison.

"Her," Takashi whispered.

"I knew you'd choose Katie." Smoothly, Anton moved back to the couch.

While Takashi had made other vampires, he'd never had an audience for the act. He pushed his awareness of Anton out of his mind and focused on the girl, Katie, in front of him. Slowly, he undid the gag around her mouth and then the ropes binding her to the chair.

"Will I lose my magic?" she asked in a rough whisper.

"I don't know," Takashi replied gently. "There are vampires capable of wielding arcane magic. Anton is one of them. But not every practitioner who becomes one of us keeps their craft."

Takashi stood and held his hand out to her. After a brief hesitation, she put her hand in his and let him guide her up to her feet. She was about his height, less than two inches shorter than he.

Just as Takashi was steeling his nerves, she tilted her head to the side and swept her hair off her neck. Of all the things the girl could do, she was inviting him. Takashi put one hand on her shoulder and the other on her cheek. But he sensed no outside influence on her emotions. Her fears had cooled and fallen away behind a jumping hope of getting something wonderful.

She has ambition. He couldn't fault her for that, not when his own was pulsing behind his tongue and molding this moment into opportunity.

He soothed her fears further and drew her into his arms. He bit into her neck, and she gasped, leaning in toward him. Cinching his arm around her, he held her close and drank deeply. Warm, wonderful, chaotic blood spilled over his tongue and into him. After a week of paltry offerings, Katie's blood was astounding. He groaned as he swallowed yet another delicious mouthful.

Even with a slow bleed, her heart eventually pounded fast and fiercely. Her emotions funneled downward into one blazing desire: *live*. The taste of her blood sweetened, but Takashi pulled himself away before claiming her final moments. She swayed on her feet, and her eyelids drooped. Without intervention, she was as good as dead.

Takashi bit his wrist and held it up to Katie's lips. She roused from her growing stupor and licked the blood from his wrist. She gasped. Then she latched onto his wrist and drank. Each sucking pull drew more of the liquid coolness that kept Takashi moving. He offered that strength up to her, let the numbness in his limbs grow. She'd need every bit he could afford to spare in order to keep up with them.

Takashi's legs were threatening to give out. He started to collapse to the floor only to find Anton steadying the two of them. Warm, gooey happiness filled Anton's red eyes, and he pressed a kiss to Takashi's temple. "More than enough."

The confirmation hadn't been necessary. Still, Takashi waited for Katie to take one more long draw before he yanked his wrist clean of her mouth. She began to whine and reach for his wrist.

Then the magic took root.

She buckled, and Takashi held on to her tightly so she wouldn't drop to the floor immediately. With a scream from her and a shout from him, they started to sink, and Anton eased them down. What he'd given her spun and settled inside her. Her heart stopped, but he felt the thread binding them together. She'd rise in a few nights' time.

"Beautiful," Anton murmured in Takashi's ear.

Some part of him believed Anton right. Another part warred within him to claim that this was too much to take. But that thread binding him to Katie was a connection he hadn't felt in decades. The nature of his work had kept him from bringing his other sirelings with him, and they'd been able to move on from him within a few short years. The thread to the others had always thinned so quickly. *Will it be the same with her? Or will she need me longer?*

Gently, Takashi laid her on the floor. "I want to be there when she wakes."

"Of course," Anton replied softly.

"She'll have her own suite?"

"I'll have one set aside tonight." Anton nudged Takashi. "There is one that isn't far from yours and Zack's."

"If she decides she wants to be away from me—"

"Nonsense. You're her father now."

It was a conceit Takashi had never fallen into with his other sirelings. Nell had never called him son either. He wasn't about to force it on Katie. He stood, his head swimming, and reluctantly let Anton steady him. "Only if she calls me that. Don't be harsh with her if she takes time to like you."

"I will be on my best behavior." Anton rested his forehead against Takashi's temple.

Takashi was too tired to push him away. He should. He needed to. Anton was not someone he wanted close to his heart. But the exhaustion continued to seep into his veins. He'd given too much of himself, and he just wanted a touch of comfort. He leaned into him.

After a long moment, Anton started to slip from Takashi's side and let him stand on his own. "Now, we have two delightful meals to regain that waning strength of yo—"

The front doors of the mansion burst open with a volume of sound that echoed down the hall to the sitting room they were in. Seamus's voice followed, loud and full of rage, "*Anton!*"

"That sounds like a problem," Anton said on his way out of the room.

Takashi made it as far as the doorway before he stopped and leaned against the frame. Whatever the problem was, it would have to come to him.

CHAPTER 29

This chapter contains depictions of domestic abuse. My intent in the telling of these events was not gratuitous, but neither is it vague. You are the best keeper of your mind and deserve the opportunity to avoid content that may disrupt your health and enjoyment.

Errand time with Seamus alternated between killing pockets of "poachers" and taking notes in the back of the room while he did business with other leaders around town. The end of the year was apparently a big time for supernaturals. Seelie fey were at their weakest, while Unseelie fey were at their strongest—leading both to ask the master vampire to meet with them. There were assurances and gifts and discussions of the schedule for lavish social parties and who was going to be responsible for what when it came to dealing with the mundane authorities.

The most surprising meeting was the one with a ghoul patriarch. Zack's family had always taught him that ghouls were the vulture version of humans and just as wild. But the family had gotten that wrong, too. Mr. Bander had a waxy skin tone, but he could've passed for human. A creepy human, but he was polite and seemed decent enough. The ghouls were how the coven disposed of bodies. Zack wasn't sure if he was more disturbed about that or the fact that his first realization was how that was practical ecology. No part of a human went to waste, apparently, and there was less lingering evidence for police or hunters. It wasn't the *worst* idea Zack had ever heard of. *Yup. I'm definitely a vampire now.*

They had just finished with a gathering of the Chicago-based lieutenants at a private club downtown. On the outside, it looked almost like a town house, but the inside was lush furnishings, fey and shifter servants, and willing humans. It was an exclusive donor house, only open to the elites that Seamus named. While everyone else at the meeting had had their pick of donors, two of the staff had brought Zack bound captives. He'd tried to keep from killing them, but he hadn't pulled back in time.

Eating had been the last bit of the meeting, and Zack wiped at the corner of his mouth with his thumb as he followed Seamus down the steps to the street level. There was a spot of blood, and he felt more of it on his lips.

Seamus held out his hand for the key from the valet and handed Zack his handkerchief with the other. "I know you have these in a drawer at home."

"I've never used them." Zack took it and wiped at his mouth. He was almost sorry to let the blood dirty the cloth rather than find some way to consume it. A part of him tried to flinch at the thought, but he quelled it. "So I forget they exist."

Seamus sighed. "Time was, a man didn't go anywhere without them."

"Wasn't there a time before that where a man didn't bother with them at all?" Zack asked. "You're frigging ancient. You can't tell me you've always had a handkerchief."

"All right, I haven't," Seamus admitted. "However, I have gotten into the habit."

"I'm sure you find them *handy*," Zack said.

Seamus grinned at him. "Did you just make a joke, Zackery?"

"I, uh, guess I did." Zack finished cleaning off the blood and offered the handkerchief back to Seamus, but Seamus shook his head. Zack tucked it into his pocket instead.

The valet returned with their car, quickly stepping out of their way to hand it off to them. Zack slid into the passenger seat while Seamus rounded the front and took the driver's seat.

As Seamus began to pull away from the curb, his phone vibrated. When he answered, the car's Bluetooth took over and fed it through the speakers. A tight soprano voice said, "Master, I have troubling news to report."

"Troubling news is never good from my financial advisor, Ingrid," Seamus said. He told Zack, "Ingrid has stepped into the acting managerial role at XV Investments."

That had been Dmitri's firm. Zack nodded once since Seamus was acting like he was teaching him new information.

"Master, I … you have to know that I have been doing all I can here tonight," Ingrid said.

"What happened?" Seamus demanded.

"Master, there was a break-in. We have some limited footage of who the intruders are, and we have greater evidence to their identity based on what was done, but honestly, we don't know who all of the intruders were. We think it may have been a mix of humans and vampires, but we're fairly certain who two of them were."

"What did these intruders do?"

"Master, please, you have to remember that he was in charge here for a very long time, and we thought—"

"Ingrid!"

Ingrid spoke in a soft whisper, but the words were brilliantly loud inside the sports car. "The servers were destroyed, and as far as we can tell, your investment accounts and the coven's are now at a balance of six dollars and sixty-six cents. Combined."

Seamus slammed on the brakes, and Zack was glad for his seat belt and supernatural healing. He would've had a massive bruise for days otherwise.

The temperature in the car dropped. Ice formed along the dashboard and inner side of the windshield. The desire to scream and punch flooded Zack's mental mind frame so hard and fast that he went numb. *That's not my emotion. It's his.*

"What?" Seamus said slowly, drawing it out to two dagger-like syllables.

"Master, please understand, I have been going through the systems with a fine-tooth comb. I have been searching and repairing and seeking to block any such exploits. I have hired the bes—"

"How. Did. This. Happen?" Seamus demanded.

"Dmitri was one of the intruders. He established these systems, master. He spent more time with them than anyone. I've been working to create an entirely new system rather than rely on his, but such development takes time and—" Ingrid paused. "Forgive me, master. Dmitri broke into our server room, used an exploit I had not yet uncovered, and sent your funds in a thousand different directions. He must have had this programmed from the beginning to have it happen so fast. And the destruction of our servers means we will have to rebuild our hardware as well as our software. We won't be able to do business reliably until we have our digital security restored."

"And the other vampire?" Seamus tightened his hands on the steering wheel.

"One of the attackers was able to walk through shadows and manipulate them. He bound several security guards in shadows to allow his team to escape," Ingrid replied.

Seamus snarled and moved his foot from the break to the

gas pedal. When Ingrid continued to sputter, he punched a button that ended the call. His rage poured through his bond to Zack, and Zack struggled to push it down. He didn't care about the money. Didn't care about the disrespect. His heart hurt with betrayal and a desire for vengeance. *Not my heart. His.*

Seamus gave no regard for stoplights or speed limits and swore in an ancient tongue at every car that was minutely in his way. Soon they were hurtling on the interstate and headed for the suburb where the mansion was.

A strange pitch was rising and falling in Zack's ears. *That's not my heart racing in my ears. That's ... that's language.* The realization helped him break apart the sounds, though he had to reach for his vampiric power in order to understand the speed at which the words were moving. He struggled to figure out the individual words until he noticed that they weren't in English. Zack only knew a little German and Latin from studying his family's texts, and his understanding was of the written form, not the spoken. But he was pretty sure this didn't sound like either of them.

Vampires didn't suddenly learn new languages upon their rebirth. Zack put a hand to his temple. The rage and the sounds were threatening to overwhelm him, and fighting them began to give him a headache. He glanced at Seamus, but as far as he could tell, his lips weren't moving. He wasn't speaking the words. *What the fuck?*

The drive should have taken them almost an hour, even in the dead of night's slower traffic, but Seamus made it to the mansion in less than twenty minutes. He screeched to a halt in front of the mansion's front doors, threw the car into park, and then stormed out of the vehicle, leaving the car on and the door open.

An electric tang was on Zack's tongue, and he staggered out of the car and up the stairs to the front door behind

Seamus. Already, his sire was inside and screaming at the top of his voice, "*Anton!*"

"That sounds like a problem," Anton said in the distance.

Zack stopped just inside the door and held on to a side table with a vase of roses. The compounding pressure was building. He ached with the need to smash. To break. To rend. With a snarl, he shoved the vase off the side table. The crack of glass against the ground was satisfying but not nearly enough to sate the foreign desire.

"The traitorous piece of shit," Seamus snarled under his breath, in an almost quiet echo in Zack's ear. Then he raised his voice, "You traitorous piece of shit!"

"Love, I don't know what you're talking about." Anton arrived in the front foyer with a zip of speed. His eyes glowed faintly red with his power.

Seamus stalked forward, grabbed Anton by the throat, and threw him through a door with enough force to break the wood and send him into the room beyond. He said with echoey softness, "How long have you been planning it?"

But then he repeated himself again. "How long have you been planning it?"

Zack scowled and started to take a step behind Seamus, but then he caught the scent of spilled mortal blood, and his stomach yearned for it. Sinking his fangs into tender flesh would be fantastic and might further satisfy the burning need in his bones that came from the rage. He followed the scent to a sitting room not terribly far down the north hallway.

Takashi leaned against a doorframe. His tawny skin was paler than usual, and his worried blue eyes had deep bags under them.

Beyond him, in the room, were two teenagers bound to chairs. One girl was crying; one was frantically attempting to yank her wrists upward. A third girl was on the floor and wasn't breathing. There was blood on her mouth. All three were dressed in school uniforms for Versinal Academy.

Zack frowned.

I can't believe he would betray me like this, the echoey Seamus voice in his head said.

Zack put a hand to his temple. *He hasn't. I ... I don't think anyway.*

And there was that strange language again. In his ears. In his head.

"Zack?" Takashi asked.

"What the fuck have I come home to?" Zack demanded, his tone sharper than he meant it, but it vented a tiny fraction of the pressure in his skull. He started to push past Takashi.

Takashi put his arm across the doorway and blocked the entrance. Zack could have forced his way through, but there was a surface tension in his mind. The desire in him wanted to shred and rip. Giving in to it would be like slipping into that place he'd found when he'd dominated Takashi.

But this wasn't the same at all. This didn't feel like the calm he'd found when topping his lover. This was violent. Angry. Not something he would be in command of, but impulses that would ruin everything around him.

So he stayed outside in the hallway.

The pressure had to ease, though. He had to find a way to release more before it exploded and forced him into that malicious place. He shouted at the girl, "For fuck's sake, you're a fucking mage. Stop making the knots tighter, and use a thread of kinetic energy to undo them. If you can't manage that, try burning or freezing the damn thing. Fucking idiot!"

Takashi glared at him. "What is wrong with you?"

"*Nothing*," Zack snarled. He hissed.

Takashi straightened, and a pulse of cold anger came from him.

The coolness doused a minute fraction of the burning rage within him. Zack took a few steps backward and put his palms to his eyes. "Seamus. It's Seamus. I can hear ..."

"The fucking, no good, useless piece of shit! Eight

hundred years! Eight hundred fucking years and he does this to me!" Seamus shouted with that echo quality.

But at the exact same time, Zack heard him snarling and growling. Seamus snapped, "I have loved you eight hundred years, and you do this to me? *To us*?"

Confusion was better than the rage, and Zack clung to it because it was a life buoy of his own emotions in a tidal wave of desire that had nothing to do with him. He tried to focus on what he was hearing, but Seamus continued to have two voices at once.

Doesn't make sense. Zack frowned and blinked, bringing his hands away.

"I will figure out his fucking game," Seamus said while also saying, "How long have the two of you been planning to stab me in the back?"

"What did you just hear Seamus say?" Zack asked Takashi.

The pinch in Takashi's brow shifted, anger morphing into concern. "He's accusing Anton of betraying him."

"My love, I don't know what you're talking about," Anton said, the plea in his voice obvious even at a distance.

"He's always been good at playing a part," Seamus said in echo, and more loudly, at the same instant, "You have always sought greater immortality, and now that you've found it, you don't need me anymore. Is that it?"

"What did Seamus *exactly* say?" Zack demanded of Takashi.

"'You have always sought greater immortality, and now that you've found it, you don't need me anymore. Is that it?'" Takashi repeated.

"And that's all you heard?"

Takashi frowned more and stepped, reaching for Zack's shoulder. "What's wrong?"

"Love, please, explain what I've done. I've many skills, but I'm not a mind reader," Anton said.

Mind reader. *Am I one?* Zack thought. *Not possible.*

"Zackery, this is not the *time*," the echoey Seamus voice said. But he was also diving into his argument with Anton, accusing him without explaining anything.

Zack glanced down the hall. Cold dread tempered the rage more. "Takashi, did you hear Seamus say my name?"

"No," Takashi said.

Zack clenched his fist. *Am I hearing your fucking thoughts?*

I've been talking to you since you rose, you stupid little shit, Seamus replied.

"The bastard's in my head," Zack whispered.

Takashi's eyes went wide, and Zack didn't need his vampiric ability to understand the fear in his eyes. There was no safety, no place to hide, if Seamus could slip into his mind and read whatever he liked.

With Seamus's rage filling him, Zack was filled with a burning fire of desire for violence. Seamus was providing the fuel and the flame already, but Zack's anger was a burst of fresh oxygen, bringing even more life to the emotion roiling inside. He clenched his fists so hard that his fingernails cut into his palms, and blood dripped.

The scent of his blood was so different than the mortal girl's. His smelled of earth, of a tang of ozone, like his scent of the grave did.

And suddenly aware of what he could smell, he picked out two other blood scents nearby. The mortal girl's coppery blood. And Takashi's grave scent. His blood was exposed nearby.

His blood is on the girl's lips. Zack whirled his attention to Takashi. "Did you fucking *turn her*?"

"We can talk about that later. What do you mean, Seamus is in your head?" Takashi asked.

"I can fucking hear his thoughts." Zack shoved Takashi into the room.

The mortal teenage girl who had been yanking on her

bonds had finally figured out how to use her magic and undone the rope on her right wrist. She was hurriedly trying to untie her other wrist. When Zack stalked through the door after Takashi, she fumbled with the knot, scrambling to get free.

She reeked of fear, less so than the girl who was still sobbing, but she was full of juicy blood and tangy fear, and she would taste so fucking good. But he'd killed already that night. And he didn't want to keep killing. He didn't want to hurt the world the way he was hurting inside. Carver had held up a mirror to him and told him to stop being a shithead like that. He was better than this.

Kill. Feed. I don't fucking care, the Seamus voice—no, Seamus, said in his head.

I can hear you. You can hear me. You can feel my rage. My desires. Just as much as I feel yours. Zack ripped a painting from the wall and threw it at the corner. The frame shattered, and the canvas tore. And the destruction felt good. He hoped the damn thing cost a small fortune because he was going to find some measure of control in this. He was not going to be like Seamus. Not this part of him. *Never this part.*

"Get them free," Zack growled.

Takashi said, "Zack—"

"I don't give a shit what was going on earlier. We'll talk. But those two, they're fucking leaving, and they're doing it before Seamus gets done with whatever the fuck he's doing."

"The guards—"

"I would *love* an excuse to break bones into pieces, and the guards are at least supernatural enough to heal," Zack said. "There's a car, right outside the front door. All they have to do is get in it. Help them get free. I can't do it. I'll ... fuck, it's taking everything I have, Takashi. All I want to do is break the world around me. Break anything."

Takashi started to move toward him, but Zack used his superior agility to zip back out into the hall. He took another vase off another side table. All the fucking endless roses in the house would never cover up the rot that was Seamus's soul. And yet he kept trying. *Bastard*. Zack threw the vase as hard as he could. Hardly a flicker of satisfaction passed through him as it sailed down the long hall and smashed into the wall at the end. What was that distance, a hundred and fifty feet? Two hundred?

Movement caught his attention, but the smell and press of the girls' fear was too much like an echo of his own that he'd once seen before. It'd been forever ago. That first mission he'd been on, in Detroit. The girl he'd saved.

I wish strangling him would do something, Seamus thought.

Who?

Him.

Zack ran his hand through his hair, dimly aware of the smattering of his own blood going across his cheek. The girls were running down the hall, feet and hearts racing as they made their way toward the front door. The predatorial urge in Zack longed to catch one. To rip open a throat and drink deeply.

He started to stalk down the hallway. One of the girls saw him, and she let out a terrified yelp before turning forward and rushing to get ahead of her friend.

But as he followed them, as he sought to shove his mind to a place of control rather than the endless screaming rage that Seamus pumped into him, he brushed across a new psychic disturbance. Something deeper. Something just as primal as the killer in his skin and yet completely different.

It held a fear he recognized. One he'd felt long, long ago.

Rescue the damsel had been a stupid game. Children pretending to be their parents, pretending to hunt the monsters. But in order to hunt, there had to be the villains and the heroes, and for the heroes to have any meaning, they had to rescue someone. That was the point of the game. Save the helpless victim. Cal and Cousin Denny had always campaigned that the gender of the damsel shouldn't matter. Damsel was just more fun to say than victim. Made it more of a game, they claimed. And if Cal or Denny got to pick, or were just loud enough to annoy their other cousins into agreeing, they'd choose Zack.

Zack had wanted so desperately to be one of the big kids, be like everyone else, to play with them, that he'd go along with it. He'd complain about getting tied up. Complain about getting chosen for the role of victim again. They'd still choose him when they could, and he'd still go along with it.

So he'd gotten good at sliding out of ropes.

So the "monsters" started leaving a "guard" with him.

The last time the game had been played, Denny had been the "guard." Zack had been thirteen. And he had recently realized that he had a crush on a boy in his class, recently figured out that the reason he really liked *Twilight* so much was that he liked looking at *everyone* in the movie. That if they were all his age, the butterflies in his stomach would make more sense. In trying to understand, he'd talked to his family. Even to Cal. And Cal had told Denny.

And Denny. Well. Roger wasn't wrong in thinking there were bigots in Zack's family. Denny's bigotry wasn't limited to human versus supernaturals. While Zack was tied up, Denny started to hit him.

The way Seamus had killed him hadn't been as terrifying as that afternoon. Zack had shoved that memory into the furthest corner of his mind so he didn't have to think about it the next time he saw Denny at his grandparents' house. When he saw him posting on the HIN. When he had to deal with him being always at the edge of his fucking life.

But he still knew the curve and taste of that fear he'd felt from the inside. The worst was that it wasn't pure fear. In his mind's eye, with fears and desires existing like ink on pages, the shape of the words was terror, but the color and touch of the ink was desire. Terror at what was happening, and yet, deep down, the longing for another's faith. To be loved. To be forgiven.

Zack had been there. Had lived with his older cousins and brother mocking him and being upset with him because he'd "ruined" the game. Had them feel justified when he'd "screwed up" in Detroit and let a teenage vampire girl run. They had called him weak and a monster lover. And through all that pain, he had only wished his family to see him. To be accepted by them in the way he was accepting them.

Roger had once said that he hated what Zack's family had done to him.

And here, in the last place he'd ever thought he'd be, Zack traced Anton's mental page and felt the familiar shapes and inks, and *God, no wonder Roger hates the Wrights and Gladwells for my sake.* They weren't this level of wrong, his fears of them not nearly so sharp, but fuck, it was too close. Too real. They had fucked him up in so many ways beyond teaching him to hate supernaturals.

And Seamus had fucked up Anton.

Rather than letting it break his heart, touching Anton's fear pushed the fires of Seamus's rage from Zack's mind. His own fierce impulse to protect became a wall, then a fortress with an abyssal moat. The firestorm could rage outside. He would not cave to it.

The sound of flesh striking flesh, of a low grunt before a devastating kick, of the snap of bones and the sharp, stifled moan of pain was a song too familiar. As Zack drew closer to the room where Seamus and Anton were, he had to find the strength in his walls to keep from tumbling into the memory of his death. He teetered on the edge, and his panic was on the tip of his tongue.

Then he reached the broken door, and the world outside his mind took his full attention.

Seamus was bent over Anton, and he drove his fist downward into him. Over and over. Each strike was followed by a crunch. The smell of Anton's blood overpowered the roses in the room and the hallway. Though he had supernatural healing, the seriousness and consistency of his wounds was hard for his body to heal. Zack had never seen a vampire bruise, but Anton had two black eyes. A broken nose. Worse.

Zack eased his way through the broken door and strode into the room.

"Do you have any idea what you've done to the plans I've been making?" Seamus demanded. "Answer me!"

"What plans?" Anton asked desperately. "You haven't shared in so long. My love—"

"Don't call me that when you've betrayed everything we've been!" Seamus screamed as he hoisted Anton up and then tossed him like a rag doll across the room.

In that split second when they were separated, Zack filtered through data at an inhuman speed. Anton was known for being capricious. Out of all the vampires Zack had met, he had perhaps the most masks. He was violent and bloodthirsty, and he could wield the power of shadows and arcane forces. Yet there he remained crumpled on the floor without a hint that he was going to raise any of that formidable power against Seamus.

Memory combined with the information he'd gathered. Roger had killed a hunter on the stage at Devil's Cove because violence was the only way to convince Seamus that he was a loyal vampire. He'd let Seamus kiss him there. He'd repeatedly said that he'd adopted the carefree persona because it was how he survived.

Roger had only been with Seamus for three hundred years.

Anton had been surviving him for *eight hundred*.

That didn't excuse his evil. Zack was certain Anton had harmed Dmitri in worse ways than Seamus was visiting upon Anton now, and he definitely had something to do with the teenage girls in the other room.

But Anton suddenly made sense.

No wonder Roger had focused on his want to kill Seamus. He truly was the rot at the center of everything. Anton was likely past any point—or desire—for redemption, but Zack couldn't help wondering what he would be without Seamus in his life.

Those thoughts passed in quick succession in a fraction of a second. As Seamus began to stalk toward Anton, Zack raced ahead of him, turned to face him, and stood directly in his path. Seamus snarled at him. His face was twisted with so much anger that he finally looked like the monster he was. He swung at Zack.

Seamus had been burning through the energy he'd taken that night.

Zack hadn't. He saw the punch coming in almost slow motion and easily slid out of the way. The next was simple to dodge as well. On Seamus's third attempt, Zack grabbed his wrist tightly and then slammed his hand against his chest. Seamus groaned as Zack dislocated his arm. But the monster's pain didn't matter. Zack spun him by his injured arm and then threw him to the opposite of the room.

The desire to rend was turning toward him.

I don't know why you're suddenly pissed off, Carver had said after Zack had been cruel to him, *but I know it's not because I tried to help you get up from a fall. And if it is,* you're *the one who can fuck off.* Had Seamus seen Zack's desire to lash out at others when he was pissed? Had he assumed that was the same as what he did to others? Was that why he thought Zack would make a good son? *I wish Carver was alive so I could thank him for stopping me from turning into a bigger asshole.*

Seamus stood and shoved his arm back into place. "You have one opportunity to step out of my way, Zackery."

"Oh, grow the fuck up," Zack snapped. He gestured at Anton on the floor behind him. "I'm a newbie, and I can tell that the only desire he's feeling right now is one to please you. He wasn't the one who stole your money."

"Money?" Anton asked. He was dazed, slowly sitting up while holding on to the wall behind him.

"The vampire who helped Dmitri walked through shadows." Seamus pointed at Anton. "That is the only bastard in North America who can do it."

"Not the only one, technically," Takashi said dryly. He was standing on the other side of the ruined door, remaining in the hallway. "I can think of a half dozen others. A charming five-hundred-year-old vampire in Mexico City can cross a hundred miles in minutes."

Seamus hissed at him.

Zack watched Seamus for any hint he might move toward Takashi. "He has a point. Others are capable."

"*Others* didn't release Dmitri from his cell."

"It was a bargain, my love," Anton said. "Roger had come for Zack and Takashi, but I wanted to see what he would choose. He chose Dmitri. And my love, remember, he has manipulated shadows before."

"So you want me to believe that *Roger*, of all the pathetic fledglings in the world, has somehow gained this power?" Seamus snapped.

Takashi straightened, all of his concern going too quickly to an expressionless mask.

"What was that?" Seamus took one step toward him.

Zack darted to stand in front of Takashi.

With a growl, Seamus demanded around Zack to Takashi, "What did you think of?"

"Halloween," Takashi murmured. "For a split second, I could have sworn Roger wasn't on the balcony with you. But I took it for a flicker of movement. Something minute that I couldn't see from across the room."

"I thought that I had blinked," Seamus muttered. He was stunned, the desire for violent vengeance fading to a dull blaze rather than an inferno. "He slipped my grasp through calling on darkness."

So Roger could have been the one helping Dmitri. Zack bit his bottom lip as soon as the thought came to mind.

Seamus nodded once, though he seemed lost in distraction. "Dmitri and Roger. Three hundred years, and now they choose to defy me. Why *now*?"

"Maybe they finally got tired of your abusive bullshit," Zack replied hotly.

"Do not test me, boy." Seamus pointed his finger at Zack. "I can end you as easily as I brought you into your new life."

"So much for never throwing me away," Zack said.

Seamus took an angry step toward Zack.

Zack shifted his weight, subtly sliding into a better stance and narrowing the area Seamus could attack.

"My love," Anton called. Though he was only across the room, he seemed to be miles away from the tension growing between Zack and Seamus. A sweet brush of calming desire took over the page in Zack's mind. Judging from how Seamus startled, he felt it, too. Gingerly, Anton moved toward them, his eyes glowing brighter from the use of his power. "I know they took our money, but so what if they ruined a few short-term plans?"

With a groan, Seamus closed his eyes and rolled his shoulders. Zack could feel the way the desire was coating Seamus's anger, like a blanket over a flame. Was that how Anton had survived? He'd become a master at taming Seamus's desires for violence?

While Anton was focusing on manipulating Seamus's emotions, Zack had an easier time reading his connection to his sire. Seamus was resisting. But through their bond, Zack soaked the soothing desire Anton emanated and then redoubled it back toward Seamus.

Seamus opened his eyes and glared at Zack, but he had only a flicker of heat. The burning inferno was snuffed out.

"Clever, but if the two of you don't stop, I will introduce your hearts to silver blades."

The glow in Anton's gaze dimmed to his normal red irises. He folded his emotions out of Zack's easy view, effectively closing the book of his mind. But Zack glanced one last fear in huge letters. *Will he kill me?*

That might become useful information, but Zack couldn't linger on any thought or scheme. If he did, Seamus could hear him. *There has to be some way to block him.* Zack winced.

"Yes, I heard that," Seamus replied. "I spend most of my time blocking you, Zackery. I would appreciate it if you put in a little effort on your side."

"You're that closely bonded?" Anton asked.

"Yes." Seamus picked up a chair that had been overturned during his rampage. Apparently, it had taken too much damage because one of the legs fell off as he attempted to return it to its place. He sighed with disappointment. "I had high hopes for what Zackery and I might accomplish, but all of that will burn."

"I don't understand why you're filled with such dread, my love," Anton said.

Zack could feel the zing of Seamus's fear, though he didn't understand the specifics of it. But the general understanding he could pick up on. "You're afraid of something big. Powerful. Who have you pissed off?"

"No one. Recently." Seamus moved over to a high-back chair and sat down. He ran his hand through his light brown hair, but he didn't speak until he dropped his hand back into his lap. "Zackery has the correct idea in his notes. I do want to declare a kingdom, but not out of greed. A war is on the horizon, and our kind must unite. We need one leader. One cause. All of this bickering over territory is merely a distraction to keep us from our real enemy. I will put an end to the divisive squabbles for our species' protection."

"You were planning on bankrolling a war," Zack said. "Humanity will never—"

"Humanity is food and hardly a challenge. Do you think their petty concerns and inability to perceive the threat we are to them is an accident? Myself and other elder supernaturals have spent centuries guiding them to the state they're in now. It wasn't even hard to use mankind's greed against itself," Seamus said. He met Zack's gaze. "Our true enemies are the dragons."

CHAPTER 30

A terrible dread settled into Takashi's bones. Being sent away from Seamus wasn't easing the creeping inside his veins or the urge to look over his shoulder. Zack's beautifully decorated living room didn't soothe the inkling of foreboding that was growing in Takashi. The puzzle pieces didn't make sense, but he had the bigger picture they belonged to. He was missing the fine details and more than a few elements to the puzzle. However, knowing where they were meant to go answered questions and raised others.

"Dragons are the true enemy? He's got to be making that shit up, right?" Zack asked as he paced.

Takashi leaned his head against the back of the couch and stretched his legs out ahead of him. On one hand, he was glad that Zack was distracted with what Seamus had said. On the other hand, the absolute last scheme he wanted to think about was Seamus going to war with *dragons*.

And on yet another hand, he was exhausted from turning Katie into a vampire. His own intelligence was cursing him as he'd rather ignore the way the pieces were clicking into place.

Seamus had bookshelves filled with binders of potential

soldiers. But to turn more than two in a five-year time span was rare, more than three unheard of. *Does he mean to turn them all into vampires? Create some sort of brood? That shouldn't be possible.*

"I mean, if we're going off what myths everybody talks about, then first of all, dragons are massive creatures. People would notice if Godzillas were running around the planet smashing shit," Zack continued. "They'd certainly notice fire-breathing giant lizards."

Watching Zack was draining what little energy Takashi had left. *No, what's draining me is trying to keep from thinking about that long-ago night.* The dragon in his memory was a looming shadow, a voice that had cackled, and a snuffing breath that had made Takashi shiver. *Not this one.* He'd never been so glad to be rejected.

Zack had been lost in his thoughts, even if he had been sharing them aloud, but he paused and frowned at Takashi. "You haven't said anything."

"I don't know what you expect me to say," Takashi replied carefully.

Zack narrowed his eyes, scrutinizing him. "You've got your quiet, reserved face on. That means you're trying very hard to say the right thing. What aren't you saying?"

"Quite a bit." Takashi crossed one ankle over the other and stared at his shoes.

"The evasive act isn't funny." Zack knelt in front of him and put his hand on Takashi's leg.

It wasn't skin contact, but Takashi didn't want him anywhere near his mind. Gently, he nudged Zack's hand off his leg. Zack took that as a sign to hold his hand instead. When Takashi pulled away, Zack opened his mouth to speak, his concern obvious.

"I've had a long night," Takashi said, cutting him off. He sat up. "Unlike you, I haven't been feeding right."

"Which considering that you did something incredibly stupid tonight, which I'll get to, but first, dragons. Seamus is crazy, right? Dragons don't exist," Zack said firmly.

The gray of Zack's eyes had been banished by his transformation, leaving only the deep red. After Seamus's revelation that the two shared a telepathic bond, Takashi doubted he'd ever see Zack's beautiful steely gray again. Seamus couldn't have the power to make another vampire like Zack anytime soon.

Could he?

Something wasn't adding up, and that bothered Takashi, increasing the dread in his stomach. It became a silver gag against his tongue.

"Takashi," Zack complained. "Don't hold out on me."

"Dragons are real," Takashi said quietly.

"Bullshit," Zack said as he sprang to his feet. He had said the same word to Seamus just before they were sent away. Nervous energy poured off him as he renewed his pacing. "I've studied more lore than anyone else in my family. If dragons were real, I'd know."

"They have spent the last seven hundred years hiding themselves," Takashi replied. "They are real, Zack. A school of them have an island in Lake Michigan."

"Dragons have *schools*?" Zack asked.

"No, that's the name for a group of them." Takashi leaned forward, putting his elbows on his knees. "Dragons are one of the purest forms of shapeshifters. They don't just use magic, they *are* magic. As humanity grew and other supernatural creatures either found their way to our reality or increased their influence, dragons were hunted close to extinction. They migrated to the fey realms. Over time, they have regained their numbers and began influencing this world again. The fact that less than one percent of the population controls half the wealth of the world is not an accident, nor only mortals' designs."

"Dragons are running the world," Zack said incredulously.

"Have you ever heard that the most fantastical feat the Devil ever accomplished was convincing humanity not to believe in him?"

"Something close to that. But, I mean, the conspiracies it would take to keep them a secret—"

Takashi wiped a hand down his face and stood. "Says the trained vampire hunter now turned vampire who waltzed with a fey lady at a donor house that routinely engages in murder and yet has never been suspected of a crime."

"Wait, Candide allows murder at the Chateau?"

Takashi headed for the bedroom, and he wasn't surprised that Zack came with him. "Accidental deaths, at the very least. Vampires drink and play out their fantasies there. Not everyone walks away from that."

"Yeah. Duh. I ... I haven't been able to stop myself from killing. Clearly not the only vampire that would ever have that issue, and some vamps don't care," Zack muttered. Then he cleared his throat and asked, "Wait, that massive dragon statue in Taliville, is that really a statue?"

"It's a petrified dragon." Takashi kicked off his shoes and headed for the bathroom. Some of Katie's blood had dried to his cheek, and his own wrist was covered in saliva and blood. "That would be Trisoldelf. One of the local witches had stolen her egg. She came to level the town, and the witches petrified her instead."

"Where was Nell in all this?" Zack asked.

Takashi soaked a washcloth and then began to clean up. "With me in Nashville. She was teaching Eulolia how to be a vampire, and I was teaching Yukio."

Zack took the washcloth from him, wet it again, put some soap onto it, and then wiped at the mess on Takashi's face. He pursed his lips for a long moment before releasing a long breath. "Who's Yukio?"

"My first sireling. I turned her in 1919."

"Partner?"

"Mortal niece."

Zack's eyebrows shot up.

Takashi smirked. "You've never thought about whether I might have relatives."

"I ... no." Zack turned his attention to Takashi's wrist. "I guess I assumed every vampire lost contact with their mortal family."

"Far from it." Takashi took the cloth from him and finished cleaning his wrist. Instead of watching Zack, he kept his gaze on the sink. If Zack wasn't going to broach the subject, then he should. Waiting for him to do so was murdering his nerves. "Go on. Ask."

"About the girl tonight?" Zack crossed his arms over his chest and leaned against the counter. "I imagine a mage girl from an academy might have a family. A big, wealthy, probably capable of hurling fireballs at us family. What the fuck were you thinking?"

"Anton lured the girls into a trap by pretending to be me," Takashi said.

"That's not an 'I decided to make a vampire' explanation," Zack replied.

Takashi turned around so he could hold on to the edge of the sink. The press of it against his palms grounded him. "Anton was set to kill them. If you hadn't come home, then the other two would be dead."

"Again, that's—"

"I made a bargain," Takashi said. He finally met Zack's gaze. "Anton is lonely. He asked me to make a vampire that he could raise, and I made him promise to give me a new phone."

"You traded a girl's life for a *phone*?" Zack demanded hotly.

"You may have not noticed, but we are stuck." Takashi

pushed away from the counter and stepped into Zack's space. "The phone won't be tapped. We'll be able to reach out beyond these walls."

"If the phone is on their plan, they'll be able to see the numbers," Zack replied.

"We can work around that," Takashi said. "Besides, the phone will have another asset. I'll be able to take pictures of what I've been finding in the mansion and analyze them in greater detail."

"You thought a girl's life was worth some information and a few unmonitored phone calls?"

"She was dead anyway, and this way, we will be able to seek support. And we'll have another ally in this household," Takashi replied shortly.

"Another newbie vampire isn't much of an ally. What if she hates you?"

"She understood what was happening."

Zack rolled his eyes. "You had a long conversation of 'hey, I know you're a teenager, but here's your ticket to immortality'?"

"She goes to a magic school, Zack! She likely knows as much about the supernatural as you do!" Takashi took a moment and collected himself. "I read her desires. If her choices were death or vampirism, she wanted to become a vampire."

Zack narrowed his eyes as he scrutinized Takashi. "What else are you holding back?"

Was Zack being perceptive? Or was he relying on his powers? Takashi traced his defenses and found no intrusion past them, but Zack's power was brushing up against them. Keeping his guard up constantly was exhausting, yet he didn't want Zack to read him. He was still so mortal where his morals were concerned.

If Zack lost his faith in him, then Takashi would be stripped of what little aid he had left. Roger would likely follow Zack's opinion as well. He hadn't wanted to enter into a relationship with Takashi without Zack's approval. To lose one would mean to lose both, and they were his anchor to sanity. Without Zack and the hope of reuniting with Roger, he would continue tumbling toward rock bottom. He never wanted to learn how far down that place was. He could never afford to fall again.

"That I am drained, that's all," Takashi said softly.

After a long moment, Zack replied firmly, "Bullshit."

"We are in too precarious of a place for you to question me like this." Takashi slipped past Zack, navigating around him without touching him.

Zack remained still. In his clear, confident voice that resonated with a novel power, he said, "Our situation is too dangerous for you to hide anything from me. You need to tell me what you're thinking."

Takashi stopped in the doorway to the bedroom. Few vampires he had met had the sort of echo in their voice that Zack already had. *What was it they called it in Paris? Voix d'au-delà?* It had a quality to it that demanded obedience, slipping toward a subconscious pull. If Takashi hadn't been aware of it, he might have fallen into the trap of meekly obeying Zack.

Did Seamus have that power? He must have some form of it for Zack to have acquired it already. But then, how vampirism manifested was different for everyone. Some older vampires never gained new powers, while some younger ones displayed rare gifts. Takashi longed to speak with a few of his friends overseas. They might know more about what was happening here. Nell would know.

And he could no longer ignore a new danger that had shown itself earlier. Takashi turned toward Zack. "I can't tell you."

"Why not?"

"You are telepathically connected to him."

"Now that I'm aware of that, I can protect myself."

"Can you?" Takashi asked.

As Zack drifted toward him, Takashi stayed where he was. In the last few nights, Zack's perfect prison cell had become the closest place they had to a safe haven inside the mansion. Except that was a lie as well. Did Seamus know about Takashi's scheme to make Zack the coven leader? Was he talking to Zack now? How much influence did Seamus have on Zack?

Every move that Takashi had mapped out had been done with tarnished pieces.

"Look, if he knows about our ambition, he either thinks I'm too weak to kill him, or he's a million steps ahead of us and still has use for us in his ludicrous plan to go to war against dragons," Zack said gently.

"Are you suddenly a mind reader?" Takashi asked.

"If I was, I wouldn't have to ask you the same question fifty times." Zack frowned. "What could be so awful that you're working this hard to hide it from me?"

Zack wasn't going to stop. His dogged stubbornness was a trait that Takashi couldn't help admiring, even as he was attempting to dodge him.

"You'll think me a selfish monster," Takashi murmured as he took a few steps away.

"Yeah, I got that you're scared I'm going to suddenly turn on you. Unless your goal is to abuse that girl every night for the next eight hundred years—which I sincerely doubt—I'll get over myself."

"Promise?" Takashi said.

"Promise," Zack replied.

Takashi walked the length of the dresser and let his fingers coast along the smooth wood. When he reached the corner, he faced Zack. Allowing his exhaustion to rise to the surface, he said, "I am so tired of being alone."

"Alone?" Zack's frown faded into a greater sadness. "I've

made you feel alone? I thought we're in this together. You, me, and Roger, when we can get back to him."

"I don't even know what Roger's goals are anymore," Takashi said. "Bankrupting Seamus and the coven was a stupid idea if he's planning on taking the reins. All Dmitri has ever wanted was to burn everything Seamus built to the ground, and Roger is working with him. He may not believe in what we want to accomplish."

"Okay, but that's because we haven't had a chance to talk to him," Zack said. "He probably thinks we're dead or something. Once he knows we're alive—well, relatively alive—and a version of all right, he'll change course again. We can convince him of that. But if I've done something to make you feel like you're alone, then tell me what I can do to fix it."

Takashi sighed heavily. "Some things are beyond your power, Zack."

"Takashi—"

"I am, at best, your fourth or fifth priority," Takashi snapped. He hated that he'd lost his temper for even a fraction of a second, but Zack's constant pressure had worn down his reserve of patience. His hand was trembling as he brought it up to his face.

"That's not true," Zack replied sharply.

"You don't mean for me to be that low," Takashi said in a calmer voice. He made his way over to the bed and sat on the edge. "You care for Roger, you're tied to Seamus in a way that demands your attention, and you have yourself and morals. I know I won't be a priority for Katie, but we have a connection that I can already feel growing. I've had to let go of that bond with my other sirelings almost as soon as they were made for their own benefit. I have never been able to grow roots." He held on to the edge of the bed. "She is one of my first steps to building some sort of family of my own."

"What about me?" Zack said.

"I am in awe of you, Zack, and I want you with me, but

I'm not fool enough to think that you'd ever sacrifice anything for me," Takashi replied.

Zack stalked toward him, towering over him with the scantest of height advantage from their positions. "I have been swallowing a bunch of bullshit tonight, but this has got to be the worst of it. My blood family is a bag of dicks, but I do know what family is. They're the people who will back you up without fucking question, and if you don't think I'd do that for you—"

"I know you would. I just also know that if you had to choose, I wouldn't be first pick," Takashi murmured.

"Tell me you're not stupid enough to sit there wondering what I would do if some random force declared that I could only have one boyfriend."

Takashi hadn't thought exactly that, but only because he'd known what the answer would be. If forced to answer it, he wasn't sure what he would say either. He couldn't choose between Zack or Roger any more than he could decide which fang should be pulled from his head. But that didn't mean his lovers felt the same. He shrugged.

Zack stilled rather than fidgeted. Despite his quiet, his energy was loud, screaming his discontent. Finally, he bit out, "Maybe the problem of your loneliness isn't me. Maybe it's you."

"What?"

"I felt your need to belong that night I dominated you. But this is the closest you've ever gotten to being vulnerable with me."

"You had me tied up and fucked out of my mind," Takashi said. "I was incredibly vulnerable."

"With your body, maybe. But you keep hiding this." Zack put his hand on Takashi's chest, right over his heart. "You're never going to feel less lonely if you keep throwing this beneath a thousand gilded layers."

Takashi put his hand over Zack's. Belonging meant

allowing others to see his weaknesses. Sergei, that beautiful mortal boy Takashi had loved with all his heart, hadn't been where he should be. Takashi had reached, literally and metaphorically, and Sergei had withdrawn his hand. His memory tried to play tricks on him, tried to tell him that Sergei had reached for him, but the dreadful truth haunted Takashi's worst dreams. At the last second, Sergei had closed his hand and let himself drift just out of reach. In the middle of the circus tent, Takashi had fallen.

He would be bones in a grave if not for Nell. All because he had trusted someone unworthy of his faith. She had claimed she had a sanctuary for their kind, but she was willing to sacrifice anything to keep that peaceful place. *Sometimes one must pay for the safety of others*, she had said. He didn't matter enough to her to warrant unending protection. He wasn't even sure that Josefina did.

So he had done everything he could to escape that seemingly idyllic place. He had joined Roger's desperate cause. He had let himself hope that Roger might be the one he'd been wishing to find since he'd been a boy and dreamed of love.

And as much as Roger tried, he was a man drowning in the seas of his own pain. Roger was charming and caring and gentle in a world that sanded away all kindness until only the emotionless survived. Takashi could continue throwing lifelines to him. He longed to know what Roger was like if he could truly become his own man.

Zack was … undefinable. Zack had taken his hand and pulled him into his relationship with Roger. He had accepted Takashi's birthday gift with a warm smile and called him boyfriend. Though Seamus had tried to scorch away what made Zack wonderful and forge him into a better weapon, Zack was only becoming stronger. More confident. More handsome and powerful. He was a force of nature.

Takashi had ignored the deeper calls of his heart because he hadn't wanted to hear its song. He didn't want to hurt.

Even hoping that Zack might be someone who would catch him rather than watch him plummet would bring pain in the end. Because Takashi was bound to be wrong. He was always wrong. His heart was his worst traitor.

But he was also fucking tired.

Carefully and ever so slowly, he leaned against Zack. Zack sat on the bed beside him and wrapped his other arm around him.

Takashi sank into him and murmured, "I am doing everything I can to better our position on the board."

"I know," Zack said softly. "But you're not making these moves alone. We're together."

"Mm." Takashi nuzzled Zack. He was warm for a change, almost reminding Takashi of his mortal heat.

Zack stroked his cheek, then nudged him to sit up straight. His frown returned tenfold. "You're ice-cold."

"I'm fine," Takashi murmured.

"You're not." Zack cupped Takashi's cheeks and made him look him in the eye. "How much did you give the girl?"

"If she's going to survive, she needs to be strong." Takashi put his hands on Zack's elbows. Keeping his eyes open was a struggle.

"Fuck. Takashi, you didn't have that kind of energy to spare." Zack started to stand. "I'll go find one of Seamus's pets."

Takashi held on to him. "Don't."

"You need blood."

"I don't have permission to drink from them," Takashi said.

"Then I'll get permission from him."

"If you start asking for favors, he'll use that to manipulate you."

"Shit." Zack sat down beside Takashi again. "Drink from me."

That Zack had offered his blood freely, without restraint or second-guessing himself, threatened to kindle the ember of hope in Takashi's heart more than his blunt observation had. He whispered hoarsely, "You don't understand what this means."

"Look, I remember what you said," Zack said. "This can be dangerous and not very filling. But you're drained, and that's a problem. And I can fix this one at least a little. Please, let me help you."

"It's not only giving away power that makes this hazardous." Takashi forced himself to hold Zack's red-eyed gaze. Looking away would have been easier. Then he might pretend that whatever Zack's reaction was whatever he wished to believe. But he had to watch him. Had to know if he understood and accepted what he heard. "If you're too open, I will be able to sense all of you. I'll know you in ways no one else ever has."

"You've had my blood before," Zack said.

"Not like this. I'll know you on an instinctual level if you don't guard against me, and you don't have the experience to effectively block your psyche."

Zack grinned. "Maybe then you'll finally figure out how much I care about you."

"Zack—"

"I got it. You're Mr. Walls Are My Lifestyle, and it would freak you out to do this. But I can't watch you suffer when I can help."

Nothing changed in the way Zack met Takashi's gaze. His concern remained, and his smile was half parts consoling and caring. Zack was a clever boy—man, Takashi corrected for himself. As young as Zack was compared to him, the last week had matured him. Death and rebirth had changed so much and yet hadn't robbed him of his ability to care for others.

How could anyone resist falling in love with him? How could anyone turn him away?

"Has anyone ever told you that you are incredibly charming when you're playing the hero?" Takashi murmured.

"Naw. People are usually too annoyed at me for having morals." Zack brought his wrist up to his mouth and tore into his tender skin with his fangs.

Dark red blood welled in the small cuts Zack had made on his wrist. The smell alone roused Takashi, though the blood was a magnet for his focus. Nothing else mattered. Why had he resisted this? He dipped forward and licked the wound.

Takashi's mortal mother had made a soul-warming miso soup whenever he'd been sick as a child. Zack's blood had that strange quality, not only tasting savory but reaching past the physical ails to soothe what Takashi kept behind the mental walls even he'd forgotten existed. His exhaustion melted away, and renewed energy brought more to his sense of taste, hearing—his everything.

When the blood stopped and the next flick of Takashi's tongue across Zack's skin revealed freshly healed flesh, Takashi whimpered. He had had a sip and only just begun to feel like himself. Already, the buzz in him was settling into a low, *low* simmer.

"You can have more," Zack said gently.

Takashi glanced up, accidentally catching Zack's gaze. Zack had always been easier to read than most, but there was a subtlety to him that Takashi had missed. The seed of who he would become had taken root. Yet for all the trauma he had been through recently, he still had a genuine heart, one that was reaching out toward Takashi.

Zack leaned his head to the side, inviting Takashi to his neck.

Dignity didn't matter as much as his delicious blood did. Takashi scrambled onto Zack's lap, straddling him, and threaded his hand through Zack's hair. He tilted Zack's head farther and sank his teeth into his neck. Blood pooled into his mouth, and he slurped it down. Where the first sip had been comfort, this was electric. This was like a perfect kiss, one long and torturously slow, and stroked previously unfathomable places.

Every nerve lit up like a purr just before Zack moaned, his pleasure coming through his blood before his throat had a chance to voice it. And Takashi knew—he knew so many tiny little things now. Zack got a thrill from his superior speed, was terrified he was putting the wrong outfits together, hated some of the GLC's upper echelons just from the way they scowled.

There were the big things, too. Zack did want him, not in the surface way Takashi had feared but all the way through. He trusted him. Wanted to protect him. To be the king that he and Takashi both needed in their lives. Though he longed to have Roger back, this moment wasn't about him. It was about them. Takashi was what mattered.

He was growing hard. They both were. Zack had always mingled blood drinking and sex when he was a mortal. The only times Takashi had drunk from him before had been in the middle of the act. No surprise, then, that this would make him horny.

Feeling what he'd felt, walls in Takashi's heart were crumbling. Hesitation, restraint, all of it was bullshit keeping him from truly enjoying what he and Zack were building despite their terrible situation.

When his bite healed, Takashi groaned with need. But blood wasn't what he wanted. He pressed a kiss to Zack's lips, then another and another until they were tangling lips and tongues, and oh, he nicked himself on Zack's fang, and his blood spilled into Zack's mouth. Zack's blood and his mingled into their kiss, and fuck, he was so fucking hard now.

"I need more," Takashi moaned against Zack.

"I could spare a little more," Zack whispered.

"Not that." Takashi rocked his hips down, grinding against Zack's erection.

"Oh, that. Yeah. Yeah, we can do that."

Takashi laughed softly into their next kiss. How was it that Zack always brought a smile to him? This had to be love, and he dared to let it fill his heart. Perhaps, for once, it wouldn't drop him.

CHAPTER 31

Takashi's kisses were the wildest, most feverish they'd ever been. Somewhere in the midst of the feed, Takashi had lowered his defenses entirely. Reading emotions or minds or souls or whatever Zack currently had access to of Takashi's wasn't easy. He wasn't sensing the journal page or the mental screen with pop-ups. Takashi was like another presence inside his body, sort of like Seamus's voice but entirely different. He knew Takashi was horny for him. That was the easiest to figure out, as his own libido was skyrocketing.

But there was something else. Something deep and beyond definition, and yet it longed to have a label.

Love? Is that what he's feeling for me?

For a brief flicker of a moment, Zack had worried he'd misjudged Takashi. Roger had been too scared to engage in the horrific ways vampires manipulated each other, while Takashi seemed to have thrown himself into what roles he could gain power with inside the mansion. Zack had thought that maybe Takashi was too cold and jaded. Then he'd spotted that crack in his armor, the same one he'd seen on his birthday.

The aloofness and stoic persona made a kind of sense.

Takashi reminded Zack of a character from his favorite book series. He hadn't seen it in real life. Hadn't known what it might actually look like until he realized that Takashi was terrified of being truly alone.

And as soon as he'd pointed that out—well, here they were, making out in the hottest way Zack had ever been a part of. They kept nicking each other's tongues on fangs, bringing bits of blood into the action and making every kiss more intense than the last. There had been times in his life he'd come earlier than he wanted and was embarrassed, but he'd never been this close to coming in his pants before.

"Wait," he said, having to dart his lips out of the way of Takashi's next eager kiss. He cupped Takashi's cheeks and held him close but also kept him from kissing him. "You are ... *wow*. This ... I ... *holy shit*."

"Yet you stopped," Takashi whispered. Moonlight on a clear night had a quarter the magnificence of his smile. He writhed against Zack. "Why?"

"Because I want to be in you before either of us comes," Zack replied.

Takashi reached for the buttons on his shirt. "*Yes*."

Stripping was a delicate twist of limbs and cloth that took far too long. They were shredding their clothes. Buttons flew —mostly Takashi's as Zack took hold of his shirt and tugged. He'd meant for the gesture to be light, but his new strength had won. The ruined garment was worth the moan Takashi let out when Zack stroked his chest, thumb brushing over his nipple.

They rolled onto the bed together. One of them reached for the lube. Zack lost track of who exactly. He had been going for it but had gotten distracted running his hand along Takashi's arm and tracing out places that made him shiver. Little touches led to flares of want that continued to fuel the desire pouring from him.

More kissing. Caresses that traced firm lines into tender

places. Zack nipped Takashi's shoulder and drew a few drops of blood that danced on his tongue. The blood lust didn't dry his throat. His hunger was still sated, but he was with Takashi. He needed *more*.

The kissing and nipping and touching became a roll and slide of movement until Zack was on his back, and Takashi put a hand on his chest to keep him there. Takashi sat up, straddling Zack's lap once more.

Zack reached for him and intended to bring him down for another kiss but was struck with the sudden clarity of just how handsome Takashi was. His short black hair was mussed, completely broken free from style for a change. Tiny drops of blood dotted his fawny skin here and there from where Zack had nipped him and somehow missed a drop. Some were gaining the momentum to move and slid down his lean muscles. His wicked grin and the sparkle in his red eyes were all for him.

Zack rested his hands on Takashi's hips. Fuck, he seemed made of solid muscle.

"I don't know if I've ever felt anyone want me this badly," Takashi murmured. His voice was a velvet purr that brought a moan to Zack's lips. He stroked down Zack's chest in slow, gentle spirals.

Takashi's words couldn't be true, but Zack didn't detect a lie from him. And he knew, in his soul or gut or whatever, Takashi meant what he was saying. An instinct deeper than observation kicked in. *He wasn't blocking himself off from me when I took sips from him. I know him like no one else does.*

"I know we're immortal," Zack said, a grin shaping his lips and feeling wondrous and strange all at once, "but my dick really wants attention *now*."

With a soft laugh, Takashi wrapped his hand around Zack's cock. "What happened to taking it slower?"

"I didn't say anything about slower." Zack tried to sit up, to go for a kiss, but Takashi pushed at him to lie back down.

He did with a groan. "What I said was I wanted to be inside you before either of us came."

"So you did." Takashi dragged himself across Zack's tip until his hole met Zack's cock. He sank slowly, steadily.

Zack watched with growing fascination. He'd never been in this position before. He'd seen Takashi ride Roger a few times, but that wasn't the same. Takashi's eyelids fluttered and then closed. His mouth dropped open just a little, and Zack had a full view of his fangs and the blood lingering on his teeth. Bit by bit, Zack disappeared up inside him. The tightness and friction around his cock was too fucking fantastic.

When Takashi was fully seated, he opened his eyes again. His smile turned sly, and he reached for his own cock. As he stroked himself, he said, "You should see your face. Fucking concentrating so hard. I can feel you holding back. Wanting to make this good for me."

Zack clenched his teeth to keep himself from coming. With slow caresses, he touched Takashi's inner thighs, eventually bringing his hands up to rest on his hips.

"So fucking patient," Takashi said. Then he pushed upward with his knees, sliding up Zack's cock, and slowly lowered himself again. He continued at that languid pace.

Gently, Zack guided Takashi up just a fraction farther, and then he pumped upward into him. He tried a few times, and though Takashi moaned, he wasn't lit up with pleasure. So Zack experimented with other movements until he found the rhythm that made Takashi gasp. Takashi began to move his hand furiously up and down his shaft while Zack dragged him down his cock over and over, occasionally bucking into him as he did.

Words tumbled out of Takashi, and they verbally didn't make any sense to him, but he could feel their meaning. *Fuck yes. There. Harder.*

Zack gave him everything he could, holding out his own

orgasm. Then Takashi spurted long lines that decorated Zack's chest and came with the sort of shout that transcended souls without a need for magic. He tightened around Zack, but more than that, his overwhelming ecstasy flooded over him.

He toppled over the edge, too. He came with a long, satisfying groan and pulled Takashi down to cuddle him.

They settled together, first with Zack's cock still in Takashi and then Zack's chest to Takashi's back while they were on their sides. The covers were a mess, again, and they somehow found their way beneath them.

Before long, Takashi settled into sleep. Zack sensed the moment it happened from a complete calming of his desires, though something stirred deep within. A dream in his subconscious, maybe. He hoped it was a good one.

But Zack had a sizzling zip of energy in him. Unable to rest, he extracted himself from Takashi as carefully as he could. Zack slid out of bed, took a moment to clean up in the bathroom, and then grabbed one of his silk robes.

Dragons. They couldn't be possible.

There was a laptop in his desk drawer that he hadn't attempted to use. If Seamus and Anton were thorough, everything he did with it would be tracked.

Still, Zack had to learn more. He found a notebook—far higher-quality paper than he was used to using and a freaking fountain pen rather than the cheap ones his parents could afford—and began his research. A huge-ass conspiracy couldn't exist without some sort of evidence. Could a race of mythical creatures really rule the world with no one noticing?

The Hunters' Information Network had been his online home, but he'd been kicked out months ago. Since then, he'd started his investigations with social media, particularly Night Deets. He hadn't looked at any of his social accounts since his transformation. Before had been bad enough. What kind of crap would people say when they found out he was a vampire?

He set up a dummy email and created a college student persona. He'd made several of these before. They were a good way to get in contact with professors and academics who were more tuned in to the local history. Sometimes, he claimed to be working on a paper or article. Other times, all he had to do was ask a few passing questions, and he got loads of information. Not all of it was useful for hunting whatever supernatural the family was after at the time, but he'd learned a lot.

He started with people based in Tennessee, though he didn't contact Taliville directly. A giant, petrified dragon in the middle of town was likely to have made a few local stories, especially if it'd just shown up one night. The Taliville librarian would probably be a better source, but she might have to report such questions to Nell. Better to avoid her for the moment.

His next batch of emails were off to professors of the occult in Chicagoland. Takashi hadn't been lying—or at least hadn't believed he'd been lying—about a school of dragons having an island home in Lake Michigan. As he was sending off his tenth email, the magnetic pull connecting him to Seamus tugged his heart, gently rocking him back in his seat.

Come to me, Seamus said in his head.

Zack nearly clenched his teeth before remembering how his fangs would slice his gums if he did that wrong. *Why?*

Come here.

I'm not dressed.

Then do so and come here.

Great. He wasn't going to get any peace unless he listened to the prick. Sighing, Zack shed his robe and tossed on a pair of jeans and a sweatshirt. He didn't bother with shoes, and he padded down to the first floor. The pull guided him toward Seamus.

On the way there, he caught the scents of sex and spilled blood. He caught a hint of movement through an archway ahead. Some voices were making sounds but not really talking. Slowly, he approached the archway since it was on his way toward Seamus.

Blood splattered the walls, most of the furniture, and the floor, soaking into the rug in the center. The acrid smell of fear, or piss, or both, hung just underneath the coppery tang. Five of Seamus's collection of pets were in the room, each mortal wearing a varying shade of red collar with a steel tag that bore Seamus's ouroboros crest.

The three that were still living were recovering. One was passed out on the floor beside an overturned sofa. The other two were in a corner, resting against each other. All three had bite marks from two different sets of fangs.

Zack was intimately aware of the difference between forceful, greedy bites and gentle, erotic nibbles. He'd experienced both from Roger, though his vicious bite had been because Zack had woken him from a decades-long coma and not intentional.

Vampires keeping mortals as pets made sense in an economical way to Zack more and more lately. Nell, Josefina, Candide, and Roger all treated the mortals in their collections as special to them. There were ways of pleasing everyone.

Seamus didn't. Zack had figured that out from Vincent's health and behavior. Hell, everything about Seamus screamed that he was a piece of shit in all ways.

But to see Grimsby picking up the body of one poor girl who was still wearing Seamus's crest and lay her next to a dead boy on a tarp just hit a switch in Zack's mind. These teenagers were around his age—*maybe*. They were young. Full of life. And Seamus had ripped their vitality away.

Had he been mortal, he might have thrown up.

Instead, a cold rage embraced him. Screaming, flying off the handle, or yelling at Seamus wouldn't change what happened here. Nothing could bring them back or erase their suffering. The best Zack could do was grow stronger and overcome Seamus.

The thought was little solace, and then near panic bubbled in him. What if Seamus heard that? How much could he hear?

Zack would not panic. Not anymore. Time to do what the other vampires he knew did. Pretend he was a badass hard enough that everyone else believed him. Emotional responses were the enemy. He had to keep a clear mind, a disaffected scowl, and a level chin.

Seamus was sitting in a chair on a patio just outside the mansion. He was sprawled, legs akimbo out in front of him, and had a wineglass in one hand. The bottle and a second glass sat on a small table beside him. From a distance, Zack's heightened sense of smell picked up an earthy note to the wine and the buzz of magic against his nose.

Darkness hadn't yet given way to the softer light of dawn, but a weariness was beginning in Zack's bones. Rather than taking the chair on the other side of the small table, he leaned against the railing and faced Seamus. "Well, I'm here."

"You are getting better at that," Seamus said with a grin.

"At what?"

"Pretending the bloodshed doesn't bother you."

Of course, Seamus had set him up to walk past the room where he'd abused his pets. He'd known that as soon as he smelled the blood. *Everything is a test.* Josefina's words were still accurate. Nonchalantly, Zack said, "Is there something you wanted? Or did you expect me to be impressed with how you and Anton carelessly chewed up your collection?"

Seamus laughed. "You have been growing your fangs, son."

Zack longed to smack him for saying that. He didn't bother trying to hide the disgust.

"Sit. Have a drink. We should talk." Seamus poured him a glass of wine.

"About?"

"I suspect we could talk for ages on many things, but for now, I mean about the birds and bees."

Slowly, Zack took the seat. "You're not going to tell me the birds and the bees are in a conspiracy with dragons, are you?"

"Don't be an ass, Zackery. Did Takashi tell you?"

"Tell me what?"

Seamus sipped his wine. "That he's met a dragon. About Taliville's 'statue.' Or did he feign ignorance? I wouldn't put it past him. He's a magnificent liar."

Everyone is. Zack picked up the wineglass and sniffed at the liquid. It was definitely fey wine. Not in the mood for whatever the latent magic might bring out in him, Zack set the glass down. "He told me enough."

"You're very loyal to each other. That's wonderful."

"You mean, 'that's a fantastic thing for me to exploit.'" Zack slouched in his chair. His dagger was somewhere deeper in the mansion. The exact location was hard to pinpoint, but he'd be able to seek it out like he did Seamus. *I wonder where he sleeps.*

"I grow tired of hearing you plan to kill me," Seamus said with a sigh. "I thought we were past that."

"You nearly killed Anton tonight because you thought he betrayed you. Forgive me if I'm a little short on trust."

"So you openly admit to thinking of betraying me?"

Zack folded his arms over his chest. "I'm prepared to safe-guard my ass. Something I'd thought you'd appreciate, *Father.*"

"You mock the word, but I am doing my best with you," Seamus replied. "That you continuously reject everything I have to teach only means you won't be prepared for the world you are now walking in."

"For the record, I was doing research into this dragon

conspiracy when you called me down here," Zack said. "Why would you want to go to war with them?"

"I have been subject to their abject tyranny for too long," Seamus said.

Zack laughed before he could stop himself.

"I know you do not appreciate how I run the coven, but I have built the largest in North America and the second largest in the world. And yet, there are limits to what I am able to accomplish."

"Fuck that. What about what you just did in there? You killed two of what should be precious to you. For what? A little fun? As some sick apology to your partner for beating the shit out of him?"

"You kill, Zackery. I watched you do so earlier tonight."

"But I didn't torture them first, and I can't control my thirst yet." Zack sank into his chair. "You can keep telling me how much it's in a vampire's nature, and I can continue hating you for it, or you can just stop rubbing my nose in how much you like to screw with people."

"All right," Seamus said, raising his hand in some sort of surrender. "I will do better to keep my feeding out of your sight."

Somehow, that didn't feel like a win. Zack shot Seamus a suspicious glare and tried to read his emotions, but they were a bland sort of "I'm enjoying this nice evening air" vibe.

"We need to discuss what you and Takashi just did," Seamus said.

"I had the sex talk from my real father when I was eleven," Zack replied.

"I assume he didn't cover what can happen when vampires feed from each other," Seamus said casually.

"I'm sure they do it all the time," Zack said. *You do not need to know about what happened with Takashi.*

Seamus raised an eyebrow. "If I weren't privy to your

inner workings, I would have bought that as ignorance. You let Takashi feed and gain strength from you."

"Did Anton tell you? He begged Takashi to make a foster sireling for him. Since you've been keeping Takashi on a terrible diet, he wasn't well. I wasn't going to let him suffer."

"I was not suggesting that you should, only that you should apply a little more care in what you're doing. Did he warn you about what might happen?"

Zack clamped his mouth shut. *What we talked about isn't your fucking business.*

"I heard that. Listen, if he didn't tell you that by offering yourself up like that, you might bind yourself to him, then you should be wary of him."

Zack stared off into the darkness. Takashi had said something to basically that effect. *I'll know you intimately.* As soon as the thought crossed his mind, he snarled softly at himself. *Fuck. But how do you stop thinking?*

"I don't spend all my time listening to your thoughts," Seamus said. "I have a coven to run, and now, thanks to Roger, finances to rebuild. Though your growth is important to me, I do have my own life."

Wish I had mine, motherfucker.

"Honestly, Zackery, there's no need for that type of language," Seamus said patiently. "For what it's worth, Takashi told you the truth in a romantic fashion. If you let him draw from you like that, you give him access to the deepest parts of yourself. He will have an easier time swaying your emotions, especially if you don't watch your mind for intrusions. However, there is no permanent harm in sharing blood. With time and distance, any bond can be broken. But I would be an irresponsible sire if I didn't point out the potential danger to you."

"You're telling me this because you care about me," Zack drawled.

"You should believe that I do." Seamus put his hand on

Zack's shoulder. The wall Zack had instinctually constructed turned transparent—he was more aware of its absence than its creation—and he glimpsed at what Seamus was transmitting to him. There was a caring and fondness.

The closest Zack could relate it to was when he used to help his sister learn to read. Amber had always pouted and cried until Zack figured out she liked really spooky fairy tales, and then they'd spent hours upon hours together reading every edition they could get their hands on. It was a kind of love.

Seamus wasn't allowed to feel that for him. He was a monster. And him caring about Zack would only make Zack a monster. He was sure of it.

But fighting every second of every night with him was exhausting. Zack grabbed the wineglass and took a huge gulp. It tasted like mud and blood and the bite of a winter storm up his nose. He choked on it and spat half of it back into the glass.

"We'll have to work on your appreciation for fine things," Seamus said smugly.

Zack set the wineglass down.

"Obstinate about everything still?" Seamus asked.

"About the wine." Zack stood. "If you'll excuse me, I'd like to get back to what I was doing."

Seamus smiled, and this time, the expression seemed genuine. "It has been a long time since I felt a passion for information like that. We have a little time before dawn. If you sit down, I'll tell you about dragons."

The information was likely to be biased, but it *was* a starting point. Zack dropped into his seat.

Seamus poured himself more wine and took a sip before beginning. "The dragons have been plotting their return to our realm for the last two hundred years ..."

CHAPTER 32

The moon provided little light in the graveyard. The stars glimmered in their distance, with the rare cloud passing silently to obscure them. Only the general light pollution of the city kept them from true darkness. Takashi stood beside the granite headstone with his hands inside his coat pockets. The coat was as new as the grave before him and as bespoke as the calligraphy for Katie's name was beautiful. Anton had gifted it and the tailored black suit he was wearing to him. He hadn't asked how Anton knew his measurements. Perhaps he was observant; maybe he simply hired the same tailors that Takashi had already used during his stay in Chicago.

Midnight was swiftly approaching. Katie had been in the ground for three nights. This cold, beautiful evening would be her first opportunity to rise.

The mortal man at the other end of her grave had finally given up shouting into his gag. Takashi wouldn't have had sympathy for him—a fledgling had to feed—but Anton had allowed him to assist in finding the offering. They'd dug up a pissant who had messaged Katie inappropriately on a semi-frequent basis. He'd thought he was meeting her to "show her what being a grown-up was like." The world needed fewer of his kind, and Katie would be rid of one potential stalker.

Anton sat atop Katie's gravestone like he was a statue of a gentleman. He was dressed in black as well, and his gaze was fixed on the dirt. "Can you feel her yet?"

"I promised you that I would mention when she stirred," Takashi replied. The silence, both within the grave and around them, was excruciating. The night might prove fruitless. Though Takashi was finally out of the mansion, waiting in a graveyard wasn't much of a change of venue. "Will we have any problems with the mages?"

"Zack did us no favors by releasing the other two girls," Anton said. "Luckily, Magus Coldwell is an old prick who doesn't care for much besides prestige. Should Katie show that she has kept even an ounce of her arcane powers, then he may actually be ecstatic. She's on an 'errant' branch of the family tree, apparently. Not a Coldwell in name, her mother and grandmother both having married mundane men."

"He cares more about reputation than her well-being?" Takashi asked.

"That was the impression I received. His son has a soul bond to a warlock. He seemed more upset that another scandal was about to drop on him after finally managing to mitigate the last." Anton tapped his fingers on Katie's headstone. "How did Zack take the news?"

The slightest hint of mist formed close to the ground. A spark lighted below, but it caught and bloomed in the ground. The spark twisted and grew into an invisible rope, tugging Takashi toward his new fledgling. "She's awake."

"Fantastic!" After a long moment of quiet, Anton said, "Convenient escape from my question, however."

Takashi could feel Katie's fear as she realized she was trapped in the coffin. Swallowing that and allowing her to continue without interference was the tricky part. He could reach through their bond and settle her fears, but she needed to emerge on her own strength, mental and physical.

"We came to an understanding," Takashi said.

"I have been attempting to figure out what she will be to him. Do you think sister or cousin would fit better?" Anton said.

"You could let them figure it out."

"Oh, don't be dull. We'll be a family, the five of us, and I want them to get along." Anton nudged Takashi's shoulder. "What do you think would work best?"

The last few nights had been odd, even compared to what had been going on in the mansion beforehand. Zack was more pensive than ever before, rarely speaking. He didn't withhold touch; in fact, he often dragged Takashi close to cuddle. But unless Seamus whisked him away, he was always reading, always thinking, always writing notes in his notebook.

Seamus had spent much of the evenings out of the mansion without any of them. "A war chest to rebuild," he had said.

And Anton, for his part, had been caught up in preparations for Katie. He'd consulted with Takashi, asked his opinion far more than Takashi had thought he would, and had seemed to settle from his manic games into the genuine role of vampire-father-to-be.

At a glance, Takashi would have to admit that Anton had a point. They were a vampire family. Seamus's pets should have been considered a part of the household, but they were shadows rarely seen. Zack had mentioned that two of them were dead, bringing down the number in Seamus's collection. Yet in all of Takashi's wanderings around the mansion, he hadn't discovered where the mortals actually lived. Nell's mansion hummed with life; Seamus's remained a freezing tomb.

It wasn't the home Takashi wanted. Walking on a

tightrope was easier than a conversation with Seamus or Anton, but something close to kinship was forming. *I'm merely making the best of the situation.* Or perhaps that was simply the effect of growing closer to Zack. Maybe he wasn't comfortable with the house or Anton or Seamus at all, only with him.

Except talking with Anton was becoming almost pleasant.

Could they be a family with a monster at the head of the table? *How long until Zack is strong enough to chop that head off?*

"I think you should give them time to bond," Takashi said.

The crack of wood was distinct despite the heavy earth on top of Katie's casket.

"That's what we've been missing. Bonding activities," Anton said brightly as he took out his phone. "What a fantastic idea. She's not close to the surface yet, is she? I don't want to miss her emergence."

"A few feet down still," Takashi replied. He honed into his sense of her. "She's fallen into a rhythm. Shouldn't be long."

Anton slipped his phone back into his pocket. "I'll research later."

About ten minutes passed, and then Katie broke through the layer of dirt, her fingertips squirming as she groped the air. Her next movement brought her other hand up.

The bound man at the end of her grave began to scream again. His muffled cries didn't matter.

Katie emerged bit by bit, yanking herself forward along the cold ground, and her wandering gaze quickly focused on the nearby human. Anton had insisted on braiding her hair, a small claim that he didn't want the dirt to mess with her curls too drastically. Her olive skin was paler, looking a lot like Roger's skin tone in that way, and her face had the fierce quality of marble. She was a gemstone of youth without any of the polish she'd gain in the years to come.

Takashi hadn't known what he'd feel when he saw her again. He had never thought of his sirelings as children before. But as Katie pulled herself free, something within him stirred. Zack had a point. Unless he opened himself, the loneliness would never end. Katie could be a daughter, a companion to him and those he loved, and he could draw her into his trust.

I don't know her. But then, what parent ever truly knew their child before their birth?

But she wasn't to be his daughter, was she? Not entirely. Anton wanted her. *Will he keep his promise to let me be part of her life?*

"You should have the honor," Anton said quietly and seriously.

"Thank you," Takashi replied. He walked around her grave, careful not to step on the dirt, and knelt beside the man. After ripping the rope off the man's ankles, he hauled him upward, making him stand.

Katie growled and snapped as he drew the man two steps away. She started to push herself up to standing. Her white dress was streaked with dirt. Eyes blazing red, she hissed at him and bared her fangs.

"Run," Takashi whispered into the man's ear. Then he released him.

The mortal man remained frozen in place, and the awful scent of piss tainted the air. Katie reached for him all the same.

Takashi could let her have him this easily, but the first chase was part of the tradition for Great Lakes Coven risings. When the man stayed locked in his fear, Takashi reached into his desires and found his flight response. He yanked that need to the forefront.

The man took off like a shot. With his hands bound behind his back, his running was clumsy.

Katie ran after him, and Anton and Takashi followed her at a respectable distance. At first, her steps were jagged, lurching movements. Then she caught her balance. The man was still ahead of her. She picked up speed, not quite to the point where mortals would only see a blur.

Suddenly, the man tripped. He began to plummet head-first toward a headstone.

If he died before Katie drank from him, then his blood wouldn't finish her transformation. She might run for her next victim, but that would be someone randomly on the streets in the middle of a winter night.

Takashi started to move to catch the man, but Anton grabbed his wrist and halted him.

The fractions of a second were sliding away. The man was going to cave his head in. There wasn't time. Takashi snarled and tugged on his arm. Only Anton hung on tightly. His ruby eyes brightened, and his grin was wide.

Just before the man made impact, a jolt pierced Takashi's chest. Never had anything run through him like the burst of energy, and he put a hand over his heart.

The man was flung backward into the air and slammed into Katie's open arms. She wrapped him into her embrace and sank her fangs into his neck.

The jolt was gone. An echo of the tingling buzz remained long enough for Takashi to locate his bond to Katie as the source. Her arcane power had touched him when she called on it. Had she siphoned strength from him? Takashi had heard of practitioners who could channel other creatures in that fashion, but he was fine. Not an ounce changed. *I felt it like I can her emotions, that's all.*

Anton clapped his hands together and then shook Takashi by the shoulders. "She's marvelous!"

"Hold off on your awe until we learn if she's feral," Takashi replied quietly.

"Oh, poo on that. Even a feral arcanist would be *amazing*," Anton said cheerily.

"You can't raise a feral."

"Well, not with that attitude."

Katie dropped the corpse. She stumbled back from him until she brushed up against a statue of a young girl. With a trembling hand, she touched her own mouth and drew away blood-covered fingers. After staring at them for a long moment, she stuck them in her mouth.

Takashi looked to Anton. Was he to have this moment? Or would he be robbed of it with this sireling like he and Roger had lost the chance to turn Zack? He tried to remain his stoic self. Cool professionalism had served him for decades upon decades.

Anton put his hand on his shoulder and murmured, "Together?"

"All right." Takashi waited, but Anton nodded for him to go first. He approached Katie cautiously, and Anton mimicked him, slipping away from him to approach her from her other side. "Hello, there."

Katie jumped as though he'd broken a trance. She took her fingers from her mouth and wiped her hand on her dress. Then she became distracted by the stained white cloth. Frowning at it, she said, "What the fuck?"

"Stunning first words," Anton said with a chuckle in his breath.

Katie snapped her attention up to him. "You!" She started to step away but stopped when she noticed Takashi. "And you!"

"You remember us?" Takashi asked.

"I—I do." She put a hand to her forehead. "You're my ... technically not my anything, are you? He—" She pointed at Anton. "—he tricked me."

"I did," Anton said unapologetically. Rather than continuing to move toward her, he sat on another gravestone. "What about yourself, girl? Do you know your name?"

"Kathleen. My friends call me Katie." She glared at Anton. Her glowing red eyes settled to a shade of dark brown. "Friends you killed."

"He didn't," Takashi said. "They were freed."

"I'm supposed to believe that?" Katie snapped.

"I wouldn't if I were you," Anton replied happily. "I would have killed them. Actually, I probably would have let you kill them."

"You—I … oh shit, I killed someone." Katie turned toward the corpse. "Wait, I know him. He's been trolling me for weeks. He's a total perv."

"Now he's nothing," Takashi said.

Katie tilted her head as she regarded Takashi. With her hand, she gestured at Anton. "I'd think you were some sort of vigilante vampire, but you're working with that evil spawn of the night."

Were Zack and Roger with him instead, Takashi would have let her remark slide. But Anton wanted a daughter, and Takashi had promised to deliver. Eventually, he hoped to have a chance to sit down and explain everything to her, but he had no opportunity for that at the moment.

Besides, not everything Anton did was wrong, and the care he'd put into Katie's first night gave Takashi an odd hope. It would likely all blow back in his face, but he had to keep pushing his pieces further across the board if he was ever going to succeed. To trust Anton, though? *He would be a powerful ally, if he could be brought to our side.*

"Morality is an ever-shifting philosophical argument," Takashi said slowly. "There are those that would call any murder wrong. There are those who would have seen this man suffer far worse fates. Evil is a judgment that we need not overthink."

"Okay, but *he* straight up catfished me, kidnapped me and my friends, and talked you into turning me into a vampire," Katie replied. "That's *evil*."

"Do you hate it?" Anton asked lightly.

"Excuse you?" Katie demanded.

Anton slipped off the gravestone and slowly strode

toward her. "Has the confusion of death made you forget how you begged to become something greater than you were? Did you not notice that you cast magic without effort when you have struggled in your studies for years?"

"How do you ..." Katie closed her eyes and shook her head. "Duh. I wasn't talking to Takashi. I was oversharing with you."

"I treasure what you revealed to me," Anton said. "Out of the three of you, I was most interested in meeting you."

"Me?" Katie widened her eyes. "Seriously?"

"I know you believed my interest was romantic, but that wasn't my true intent." Anton lowered his voice to a gentle whisper as he reached out to touch her cheek. "Over a century has passed since I've found anyone who might make a worthy apprentice to my arcane studies. Longer since I discovered a kindred spirit like yours."

"So you kidnapped me."

"To offer you everything you've ever wanted. Eternal youth. Immense wealth. Arcane knowledge beyond your wildest dreams. The opportunity to become what everyone at your school will forever envy," Anton replied. He circled around Katie, lightly placing his hands on either of her shoulders. While speaking to her, he caught and held Takashi's gaze. "Imagine what possibilities lie ahead of you. Power. Respect. Anything and everything. All you have to do is learn how to grasp it and make it yours."

Anton's ruby-red eyes had a simmering, molten heat to them. His smile had a coaxing twist, like he was preparing to ask Takashi for a kiss.

Those words weren't just for her. He sees something in me that he likes. Were Anton anyone else, Takashi might consider bringing him close. But he couldn't. Anton played games and ruined lives and— *And how much of that is to survive Seamus?* Roger had shown a few of the traits Anton displayed regularly. He flirted too often, smiled and teased when he was hurt to bluff his way through difficult situations. He distracted anyone growing close to him with whatever version of himself he thought the other person wanted.

Was this some role for Anton? Had the abuse Seamus put him through twisted Anton so that he was a creature who enacted his hurt on others to retain some semblance of sanity after eight hundred years? Or was the torture he inflicted on others part of who he'd always been?

Was he truly a monster?

Takashi couldn't say for certain, at least not to himself. *I need more time to gather information.*

"Shall we go home?" Takashi asked.

Anton grinned wider. He squeezed Katie's shoulders. "Yes. Our daughter should change before I take her hunting."

Our. That was becoming a heavier and heavier word. Takashi had never thought to include Anton in the vision of the future he hoped to build.

He couldn't help wondering if he should.

CHAPTER 33

Video games and television had never held less allure. For a couple hours, Zack tried to make use of the massive entertainment system set up in his suite's living room, but the screen was too bright, the shows too slow, and the games too easy.

Reading was something he occasionally enjoyed but hadn't made time for since he'd finished Blake's copy of HT Moss's latest *From the Grave* book. He combed through the books on his bookshelf to get a better look at what was there. Surely something would catch his interest.

The Cal voice tried to resurface and tell him what a horrible person he was for thinking about reading anything on the shelves. *I'm a fucking vampire, not a human. So nothing you say matters anymore.* When no Seamus voice added its opinion, Zack relaxed a little bit more.

But that did mean he was totally, utterly alone for the first time in weeks. Since before his transformation even. Sure, there was still the staff in the building, but they tended to be ghosts. *Actually not sure that they're not ghosts.*

They are not ghosts, Seamus said in his head.

Knew you were listening, Zack replied.

At some point, I hope you have a sireling who is just as loud as you are. Then you'll understand my predicament.

Zack snorted as he continued skimming the books. There were two that were supposedly by *the* Dracula. One was supposed the "true" account of "what happened in England." *You feel really far away. When are you going to interrupt my chill evening?*

Unfortunately, business is occupying my time. You can blame Roger for this interruption in your lessons. Don't worry, you have plenty of food. I know you are opposed to gray bands, so I've made other arrangements. All you need do is call for Grimsby, and he will assist you, Seamus said.

What even is Grimsby? Zack thought before he stopped himself.

Always curious, Zackery. Perhaps you should spend your evening in the library.

Of course there was a library in the mansion. The place was huge. Zack put the Dracula book back on its shelf. *You trust me to roam about the mansion unsupervised?*

It's your home. Do as you like.

Zack tapped his finger along the edge of the shelf and scowled out at the wall. Seamus's permission had to be some kind of trick, didn't it? The evil mastermind wasn't just supposed to let the good guy wander the castle.

However, exploring the mansion sure beat staying in his room waiting for Takashi to come home or for his hunger to get unbearable. He headed for the hallway, poking his head out first just to make two black-clad security guards weren't waiting to shove him back inside. Seamus's security for his mansion always seemed to move in twos.

No one was out there. No sounds drifted through the still-ness either.

Being home alone had lost its thrill when Zack was sixteen and he'd convinced his parents he could stay at the house while Amber stayed with their grandparents. He'd been able to jack off in peace, which was nice, but that'd gotten old quickly. Well, fairly quickly. He and Cal shared a wall, so Cal being out on a hunt with their parents meant no one was on the other side of the wall to possibly overhear him. And he'd been able to dive into the porn he liked without worrying that someone was going to interrupt him. *Great. Now I'm having all the horny thoughts.*

As much as Cal had mocked him for his interest in vampire porn, Zack could experiment with bringing his fantasies to life a little bit more. Takashi seemed to share a few of his kinks. If they could find a mortal …

Thinking of owning people? the Cal voice said derisively.

Not owning. *Forming a mutually beneficial symbiotic relationship*, his rational voice provided.

Parasite.

Zack sighed and rolled his eyes at himself. He was in the beginning of a new interesting chapter in his life, and yeah, some shit sucked, but his inner doubt needed to fuck off. Instead of engaging with it further, he focused on the hall he traversed.

Seamus had a lot of art and a fondness for vases full of flowers. The whole mansion had a rosy, floral scent that bothered Zack's strengthened sense of smell. Flowers had been a rare commodity in his mortal parents' house. They were an expense when his family spent its spare money on weapons and research. If a new computer hadn't been useful for keeping up with his duties as a researcher, Zack was pretty sure he'd have to deal with Cal's old busted machine for another few years.

Zack drifted down the hall to the grand staircase in the foyer. He could go up to the third floor from this staircase, but he chose to go down to the main floor.

The low, growling hunger in his stomach had been with him since he woke. He'd ignored it because he'd thought Seamus would show up. Now that he knew that wasn't going to happen, he had to figure out when he should eat on his own. Should he wait?

Naw. He glanced around, seeing no one. Supposedly, all he had to do was call for Grimsby, but Seamus hadn't said if he'd needed to use a phone or something to do so. Of course, Zack hadn't seen a phone, so that wasn't likely.

"He is a magical butler," Zack muttered to himself. Louder, he said, "Grimsby, I'd like your presence, please."

Within a minute, the tall, skin-and-bones fey was walking down the hall toward Zack. Grimsby had his hands clasped behind his back. His black hair was grayer, and it was waving counter to his movement. He grinned broadly at Zack, his smile wider than a mortal could've pulled off, and dipped his head when he came close. "Young master, I appreciate your politeness in summoning me. What might I assist you with?"

Zack straightened. He wasn't better than Grimsby, but getting called master was sort of ... cool. The way Grimsby acted was slightly deferential, which wasn't a surprise, but there was an element of respect to his voice, too.

People in Zack's life respected him—okay, Cal definitely hadn't—but plenty had. Blake, Kit, Roger, Takashi, Josefina, and Nell all did. But except for that time he dominated Takashi in the bedroom, no one had shown him respect like this. Like he was someone with some power. And this was oddly nice.

"Seamus mentioned that he made arrangements for my feeding tonight and that you could help me," Zack said primly. "I'm thirsty and would appreciate something to drink."

Grimsby nodded once. "If you'll follow me, young master, I would be happy to show you to your selection."

"Excellent."

Grimsby headed down the hallway from the direction he'd come, and Zack followed. They made their way through the massive first floor to a room not far from where Seamus had had his annual summit with the GLC's leadership. With a sweeping bow, Grimsby opened the door.

Inside the room were several wooden posts, each with metal loops fastened onto them. Additional loops were secured on the walls. It was a bare, ancient-timesy, prison-like room.

Three men were bound at different places in the room. They had gags in their mouths. When they spied Zack and Grimsby, their heart rates raced. The cacophony of their beating hearts thundered through Zack. Those thuds were life. Were blood pumping through veins. Were filled with the fear of those who didn't want to die.

But they were kidnapped mortals. They didn't deserve death.

A freezing cold spread through Zack, its touch so frozen it scorched him. He needed warmth. The mortals had it.

Just enough. I don't have to kill. Zack moved toward one man. His legs trudged forward like he was caught in deep water, but when he pushed forward through the pressure, he moved with lightning speed. Suddenly, he was on top of the man, and he didn't know what to do.

No, he did. But he didn't want to think that he did.

Every time he'd fed before this, Seamus had been there to guide him through it. To practically shove him into doing what his body needed. But Seamus wasn't around.

The aching cold wouldn't end on its own. Zack took hold of the man's chin and forced his head to the side. A pulse jumped, extending the flesh. That wasn't where he was supposed to bite, not if he wanted the feed to last. *I can stop myself. I can. All I need is a little blood, and I'll be fine.*

Zack sank his fangs into the man's neck. Hot blood poured into his mouth. He swallowed, and the cold thawed. The strength in his limbs was greater. Mouthful after mouthful brought more and more of the warmth into him. He moaned and pressed up against the man, pinning him against the post and drinking deeply. No drop would be wasted. Nothing would slip past his lips. He would take it all.

I'm killing him. But how could he stop when the cold was still there, scratching in his throat?

The blood gained a sharp, pungent flavor. With a gasp, Zack stepped away.

There were only two heartbeats in the room.

He hadn't meant to, hadn't been forced to, and yet he'd been too hungry to stop himself. He backed away and ran into one of the walls. A metal hoop dug into his shoulder, and he put a hand on the wall to push away from it. Something invisible but slimy touched his hand, and a jolt made his throat clench. The walls of the room were soaked in fear. *And I've added to it.*

"Young master?" Grimsby called.

Getting called that didn't sound so fun anymore.

Doesn't it? his rational voice replied. *If you want to lead a coven, you'll have to be used to a little death. Get a hold on yourself. You can do this.*

Zack ran his hand through his hair and took a breath to steady himself. He was still thirsty but not like he'd been before he fed. The last few nights, he'd been able to go most of the night before killing again. Maybe he could get through this one with just the one death. That meant leaving two living men in the room, but he had no idea if they were good men. Did it matter? They knew about vampires, had seen him kill. The practical thing would be to ensure they died anyway.

But he didn't have to solve it now. Didn't have to come up with the answer.

"I'm all right, Grimsby," Zack said, surprising himself with how smooth his voice was. He almost sounded like an immortal badass in his own ears. He pulled a handkerchief from his pocket and wiped his mouth as he left the room. Only a little blood came away on it. He was getting neater.

Getting out of the room helped steady him. He could let

what he'd done haunt him later. Instead of wallowing, he'd find a way to be productive. He had to make his time count. "I heard there was a library in this huge-ass mansion. I hope this is not a rude question. Does it fall within your duties to show me where it is?"

"We actually have four libraries in the building, but I believe I know the one that would please you best, young master," Grimsby replied. "If you'll follow me?"

"Lead the way."

CHAPTER 34

"This is where you live?" Katie asked as she stepped out of the limo.

"Where we live," Anton corrected.

Takashi was the last to step out of the vehicle. The driver closed the door for him and then went around to the driver's seat. However, the limo didn't pull away but continued to idle in the front circle driveway in front of the mansion.

For the first time, Takashi was able to admire the splendor of the large structure. He had seen vampires who lived in actual palaces, and Seamus's grand building clearly aspired to that level of wealth. Light poured from large windows, highlighting details along window casings in the dark. Spotted here and there in the front gardens were more statues. Like the ones along the driveway, they depicted humans in a variety of states of ecstasy, all offering themselves up to be bitten in erogenous zones.

Katie stopped at the bottom of the steps leading up to the main door. "Hold on, do you mean 'we' as in *I* live here now, too?"

"That would be what I was implying," Anton replied. "Is there a problem with that?"

The bond Takashi shared with her tightened. Then she shook her head.

"Remaining with us would be wise, especially until you learn to control your bloodlust," Takashi said.

"Not only that," Anton said as he headed up the stairs ahead of her. "You should see your suite! It has everything a blossoming young practitioner like yourself could possibly desire!"

"Are either of you hearing music?" Katie grabbed her skirt and lifted it just enough that the white material didn't drag on the steps as she rushed after Anton. "I keep hearing these odd notes."

"Are the melodies speaking any moods to you?" Takashi asked quietly. He was the last one up the stairs and into the mansion.

"Sort of. Oh! This must be how my mind's interpreting my new psychic abilities! Neat!" Katie grinned. "I feel my magic like the way a breeze moves. These notes sound almost like wind chimes. I didn't think they'd combine like that. But what are you so worried about?"

"Many things, none of which you should let disturb you," Takashi said.

Anton had his arms spread wide as he twirled in the foyer to face them. "Welcome home, daughter!"

"It beats the dormitory at Versinal." Katie's eyes widened as she took in the painting of a vampire orgy on the foyer's wall. "Though we certainly didn't have anything like hanging up in the entrance. Hey, do I have to go back to school? I mean, it's not going to work out, right? Because of the whole daylight thing?"

"You'll be sluggish after dawn, and daylight would fry your pretty skin," Anton replied. He held his hands out toward her, and she took them. He spun with her in another circle. "I'll be a far better teacher than your former professors."

"Will I be able to take the Circle tests?" Katie asked. She let go of Anton's hands and continued making circles on her own. Graveyard dirt skittered off her long skirt as it flowed out around her. The tail end of her braid was undone, and her hair was beginning to loosen. "I don't really care. It's just a stupid title. Magus Coldwell made it sound *so* important, but really, it just gets you a discount in their stupid clubs and with their 'approved' component sellers. You have enough money that that doesn't really matter, does it?" Katie stopped spinning, her equilibrium not compromised at all. "It doesn't, right? Because I don't have to worry about money anymore? That's part of the package here, isn't it? I'm your daughter, and you're both insanely rich, and you're going to teach me magic and how to be an amazing vampire, and I'll become *awesome*."

She was dazzling with vibrancy, not with mortal lust for life but a longing to plunge into the world full and new and complete in every way. Takashi slid his hands into his slacks' pockets and continued to watch her dance. None of his previous sirelings had taken to their transition with such a zeal for the unknown. They'd been resigned or in love, never so brilliantly hopeful.

A brush of arctic cold swept into the foyer before Zack made his entrance. He had a book in hand. In the last few nights, he had begun sliding a disaffected attitude into place in order to hide his emotions. The effect wasn't perfect—Takashi knew from the way he held his shoulders that he was tense—but he was more the vampiric for it.

"You are our treasure," Anton promised gleefully. He kissed Katie's cheek. "You will never have to worry about anything."

"That's a bit of a lie," Zack declared.

Startled, Katie let out a soft short as she spun to face him. "Who are—wait, I know you. I've seen you on the Fang app. You're the frigi—"

"Katie, darling," Anton said, overly sweet, "you needn't bring up what that horrid pest said about your cousin."

"Cousin?" Katie tilted her head.

"He is part of your new family."

Zack started to draw in a breath to speak.

And Takashi saw the potential that he would spoil what was otherwise a wonderful moment. Strange, perhaps, but astonishing in the way it swelled in his heart. He stepped forward, drawing Katie's attention, and continued on to stand by Zack, speaking as he went. "As far as blood is concerned, he is a cousin in that respect. My sire and his sire were created from the same demon long ago. The mansion actually belongs to Seamus, who is the beloved of your foster father, Anton. But even if we weren't bound by blood, we could find our way to family with our hearts."

"There's also trauma-sharing," Zack drawled. "After all, you were kidnapped and then murdered while I was murdered, then kidnapped."

The hollowness in his words lacked the anger Takashi had expected, but their impact drained the joy from Katie's face. Anton stilled, and his eyes hardened.

"Look, a car ride isn't long enough to forget that, yeah, *he* —" Katie pointed at Anton. "—messed with my friends and I. But he also wasn't wrong. I mean, I *thought* I was meeting my vampire boyfriend who wanted to turn my friends and I into his immortal brides, so I was prepared to become a vampire. My fathers still have a lot to make up for, but I've decided to give them a chance. Plus? I can do this."

A twinge of electric shock went through Takashi for a fraction of an instant before a wind knocked Zack off his feet. The arcane blow was quick, but Zack caught himself before he fell on his face and stood.

"You're still a caster," Zack said as he regained his composure.

"I am," Katie replied.

"Awesome." Zack sounded completely unimpressed.

"*Zackery*," Anton said with a snarl.

Zack flicked a flat glare in Anton's direction and then stalked toward Katie. Anton stepped between them, putting his arm to block Zack from simply walking around him to get to her. The heat in Anton's red-eyed glare would have melted a glacier in a tundra.

Just when Takashi thought Anton might set Zack on fire, Zack smiled broadly and laughed under his breath. "Okay. You pass."

Anton blinked. "Excuse you?"

Zack's smile turned smug, and he stepped back to Takashi's side, putting an arm around his waist. "Everything's a test, Anton. Katie is bound in blood and power to one of my beloveds, so yeah, I wanted to see if you actually give a shit about her." Zack leaned so he was looking around Anton to more directly speak to Katie. "Your adopted father's been in love with my sire for hundreds of years, and he was about to fry my ass if I did anything to you. Congratulations, your new vamp dad and adopted vamp dad really do care about you."

This time when Katie's eyes went wide, Takashi sensed her longing to belong settle deeper into her psyche. She took hold of Anton's hand. "You're really serious about calling me your daughter?"

"Of course," Anton said as he turned to face her. He cupped her cheek gently. "I am sorry that I led you on otherwise. Teenage mortal girls seem more caught up in boys than anything else."

"Boys are all right," Katie said. She started to reach up to brush a tear from her eye, but Anton wiped it away for her. "I'm not sure how into them I really am."

"They are good for eating, if nothing else, but you have eternity to become whoever you are truly meant to be, darling." Anton pressed a kiss to her forehead. "Now, you must be getting hungry. You have a whole suite with some fresh clothes waiting for you. Zack, are you and Takashi joining us?"

Zack hugged Takashi, holding him close. "Seamus left some dinner behind."

"Dinner! That gives me a brilliant idea." Anton grinned. "We'll see you two later. Come along, Katie. Wouldn't want you to get lost in the house."

After Katie and Anton were gone long enough that even their footfalls were bare whispers in the distance to Takashi's hearing, he murmured in Zack's ear, "What the hell was that?"

"That is what we call a double win," Zack whispered. He nudged Takashi and then started walking down the first floor's hallway.

"What were you double winning?" Takashi asked as he followed.

"Mm, Anton really does consider Katie his, which means he's going to be extremely protective of her. Since she's got a magical umbilical cord attached to you, I wanted to make sure of that," Zack replied. "And added surprise upside, we will have the house to ourselves soon."

"You are in a remarkably good mood."

"Is that a bad thing?" Zack asked.

"No. Merely surprising, given how you were acting with Katie."

Zack shrugged one shoulder. "I was practicing being an immortal badass. Now, as for why I'm in a good mood, Grimsby showed me this."

With a dramatic flair, Zack pushed open a set of double doors and revealed a gleaming library. The east, west, and south walls were bookcases from end to end, while the bookcases on the northern wall were broken up by either a large window or a massive painting. The room didn't smell floral or musty, but rather the heavy odor of countless paper pages and rich leather. In addition to the bookshelves along the walls, there were rows of them as well. Sporadically throughout the library were rolling ladders so that one could reach the upper shelves nearer to the room's high ceiling.

"People in my family would sell their souls to have a night in this place," Zack said. He carried on through the room. "I haven't figured out the system, but what I have stumbled across are books on fey and shifters. This has to be one of the greatest collections of supernatural lore on the planet."

"I can certainly understand your attraction to it." Takashi drifted among the shelves. There were old tomes neatly sat beside much newer books. Every binding was pristine; every book appeared perfectly maintained, even though some of the older books should have seen different treatment in their upkeeping than standing on a shelf. *Unless they're treated with magic.*

"You seem a little out of it," Zack remarked.

"A rough night, in some ways," Takashi replied. In the center of the room was a small seating area with lush leather chairs. On either side of that setup was a long, polished table with a wooden chair on each side. "I've been exploring the mansion in my free time. I hadn't come across this."

"That's because this place is huge." Zack plucked a book off a shelf, opened it a few pages, and then closed it and put it back. "More shifter lore. Did you find anything interesting in the rest of the house?"

A few nights ago, Takashi would have told him without hesitation, but that was before he knew that Seamus could read Zack's mind. Was the danger less now that Zack knew of it? Or more? Was he able to keep dangerous thoughts away from Seamus? Or unable to stop himself from thinking them constantly?

He had Katie's safety to consider as well. Anton might attempt to protect her, but as powerful as Anton was, he hadn't raised a hand in defense when Seamus attacked him. *I should get all of us out of here.* Takashi put his hand on one of the polished tables. Wood this smooth was still a pleasure to touch, and the sensation grounded him.

No one ever advanced across any board without taking risks. He couldn't keep this from him.

"A few things, actually," Takashi said. "I've been meaning to share them with you, but we haven't had time."

Zack raised an eyebrow. "We go to bed together every night—er, every morning. Well, dawn. Whatever. We share a fricking bed."

"And these are the sorts of things that would be hard to keep yourself from thinking about obsessively, especially when you have nothing else to preoccupy yourself before sleep."

Abandoning the bookshelf he'd been investigating, Zack crossed the space to Takashi. "We've got the time now."

"Almost." Takashi glanced up at the ceiling. Katie's suite wasn't directly overhead, but it was close. "Once they leave for the night."

"We don't know how long Seamus will be gone," Zack whispered.

"But you'll be able to sense when he's coming back to the mansion, and I will be able to tell when Katie is returning. Anton should be with her."

"That is … that'll work." Zack leaned against the table. "But you won't tell me anything?"

"I'd rather show you. Now, if you'll excuse me a moment, I want to put this coat away and slip into something a little more comfortable."

"I thought suits were your thing," Zack replied.

"Not always." Takashi started to head for the door.

"Hey." Zack took hold of Takashi's hand and lightly dragged him close again. He pressed a soft kiss to Takashi's lips.

The casual confidence of the act, of a lover simply wanting to give him a parting kiss, was a novelty. Roger was always like that, full of touches and kisses and cuddles. Zack had always been more distant, but like so many things about him, that was changing.

"I can feel how much you want me," Zack murmured, his voice dipping low and gaining its ethereal note.

Takashi nuzzled Zack's nose with his own, then teased his jaw with a light nip. "Yes, but we can screw, or we can seek secrets."

"Can't we do both?" Zack whined.

"Not at the same time," Takashi laughed. "I'll be back." He pressed another quick kiss to his lips and then left the library.

True to his word, Anton had settled Katie into a suite not far from Zack's, and technically Takashi's since his was across the hall. Takashi passed by her suite, noting the distance he was from her, and went into Zack's.

Anton was sitting on the couch, one leg over another and a small box in his hand. He smiled broadly at Takashi, but there was a slight tension in the careful way he held himself. "Brought you what I promised."

After shutting the door, Takashi joined Anton on the couch and took the box from him. "Thank you."

"Do you think she'll be long?" Anton said. "Women are notorious for taking forever to get ready, aren't they? And now she'll have to do it without a mirror. Hmph."

"You could buy her a tablet, something with a screen and camera," Takashi replied. "The newer cameras are capable of capturing our likeness."

"I'm aware of that, Takashi," Anton said shortly.

"My mistake." Takashi shed his coat and laid it over the armrest. "Is there something bothering you?"

"What could possibly bother me on such a wonderful night?" Anton said smoothly.

Takashi relaxed against the couch. He sought Anton's psychic impression but found a blank wall. If he couldn't cheat his way to more information, perhaps he could poke some out of him. "You're guarding your emotions extremely well for someone who acts like he has no care in the world."

"I have cares." Anton stood, and his platinum blond hair fell in a perfect curtain to obscure his features.

"I am certain you do."

"I know what you're attempting to do."

"What would that be?" Takashi asked lightly.

Suddenly, Anton whirled toward him. He moved with a greater speed, but Takashi didn't try to move. Instead, he let Anton grab him by the throat and push him back against the couch, his head at a painful angle. Anton's red eyes flared brighter, and he snarled, baring his fangs, as he loomed over Takashi. He had one knee between Takashi's legs, and he was dangerously close to grinding Takashi's balls. His hair became a halo with a touch of light illuminating it.

He was stunning. And deadly.

"You should be terrified of me," Anton growled.

"I am," Takashi said.

"Doesn't feel like it." Anton tightened his grip on Takashi's throat.

Air was needed for speaking. Takashi could only drag in enough for whispers. "Doesn't seem as if nothing is bothering you either."

"Why do you care?" Anton demanded. "You have no interest in being, as you said, the plaything while I wait for my lover to pay attention to me."

"It is remarkable how little we comment upon as *yours*," Takashi replied. "The mansion, the collection, the coven—it's all *his*."

Anton squeezed tighter, and Takashi felt bones break. He would heal, but not while Anton had a hand on him like this. "I am not insignificant."

"Never said you were," Takashi managed with his last breath.

For a long, terrible moment, Anton continued to apply pressure, and Takashi thought he might lose his head. Then he huffed and walked away, heading for the door to the hallway. "You and Zack should stop attempting to point out my lover's faults."

"What faults?" Takashi dared to croak. "We have only spoken truths. Why is that so terrifying to an immortal as powerful as you?"

Anton paused, a fraction of a half step of a moment that would have been missed by mortals and by most supernaturals less keenly observant than Takashi, but the hesitation was there. The moment where the gears in Anton's mind must have halted, reversed direction, before they ground back into forward motion and continued onward.

Anton opened the door.

"You know what a monster he is," Takashi whispered gently. "We all do. But what would you be without him?"

With a cold glare over his shoulder, Anton declared, "I never want to know."

Then he snapped the door shut behind him.

Takashi collapsed back against the couch and carefully probed his neck. The bones were healing; he would be fine in a matter of seconds, perhaps a minute. *Maybe I rattled him enough to shake him loose from his agony.* He doubted that hope, though. Love was the universe's greatest creation, and too many lies donned a facsimile of its allure.

CHAPTER 35

The only reason waiting around for Takashi didn't suck was because Zack was truly in a slice of heaven. This library must have taken centuries to curate, and yet, as far as Zack could tell, there wasn't any system to its organization. Had Anton put it together? Seamus? Grimsby? Knowing who might give him some inkling as to why books on the history of European witches sat beside volumes that questioned the nature of reality itself.

Were there books about his kind? Demons? Dragons? He couldn't wait to find out.

He'd discovered a fascinating book from the late eighteen hundreds about the difference between cursed werewolves and spelled werewolves, which were entirely different from those who had been born with lycanthropy. The theories in the book weren't unfamiliar to him, but this was like reading the seed of what his family taught. Of course, the Wrights taught that "spelled" meant cursed. That wasn't what this author proposed at all.

"Perhaps I shouldn't disturb you," Takashi said quietly.

Zack jumped and spun to face him. An excited bubble of information was on his lips, but then he noticed the slight nervousness in Takashi's eyes. Despite saying he was going to change, Takashi was wearing the same clothing.

Zack set aside the book and joined him at the end of the bookcase. "Are you okay?"

"The world will one day tremble at your power of observation," Takashi teased.

"Don't avoid the subject."

"I had a conversation with Anton. Speaking with him is always challenging."

"Because you're not sure if he's going to use shadows to rip your body apart or because he doesn't seem to know that he's another one of Seamus's victims?" Zack asked.

"You've noticed?"

Zack leaned against the bookcase. "Hard not to. I can't help thinking that we got to Roger in time, you know?"

"I've had those thoughts as well."

"You know there's no 'saving' him, right?" Zack whispered. The topic felt like a forbidden thing, even though they were alone. He hoped that Seamus was too preoccupied to listen to his thoughts. *Maybe I should start singing in my head all the time.*

When Seamus didn't respond to that, Zack relaxed a little.

"Anton might—"

"Don't go for 'not be so terrible without him,'" Zack said. "We have a very limited knowledge of what he's done, and every bit of it is terrible. Roger's been going through some of the same shit. He's not a villain like him."

"He's not the hero of every story either," Takashi replied.

"Yeah, but Roger didn't just kidnap three girls and make you turn one of them into a vampire!" Zack snapped.

"Anton could be an asset."

"Wait, are you developing feelings for Anton?" Zack demanded. "You know I'm a Gladwell, right? Do you have any idea what he did to my ancestors? For the fun of it? And that's just *one* of his horrible deeds."

"And who was at his side?" Takashi tched and pulled out two pairs of gloves. He handed one pair to Zack. "I don't want to argue about this. It's not like I'm professing love for him. He may be useful, that's all I'm saying."

"Right," Zack said slowly.

"Observing and coming to the wrong conclusions is worse than not noticing something in the first place," Takashi replied.

"You're getting defensive. Should I be observing something about *that*? Or will that be a wrong conclusion?"

"Do you want to waste time having a nonconsequential argument, or do you want to see if we can discover something of value?"

A smart answer was on Zack's tongue, but rather than jump for it, he relied on his vampiric abilities and sought the touch of Takashi's mental page. There were big letters attempting to disguise smaller emotions. Zack brushed his mind against them, seeking the shape of them without plunging into the depths. Takashi didn't want to fight—and didn't want to examine something he was feeling. He wanted to ignore a part of his mind.

But it wasn't the same as wanting to hide something, and he wasn't harboring a passion for Anton.

"I want to see what you've found," Zack replied.

"Excellent. This way."

Takashi led the way out into the hall and then into the maze that was the first floor. They cut through one of the galleries, and every painting in it was of Seamus or Anton where different artists had had their take on the two in a variety of styles. The love they professed to have for one another was on full display whenever they were in a portrait together. But the gallery was one big, massive edited selfie, curated to a specific story.

What would the story be for Zack, Roger, and Takashi in a hundred years? Would they look fondly back at the beginning of the twenty-first century? Would the time Zack and Takashi were separated from Roger feel like a blip rather than a drawn-out nightmare? Would they tell everyone they were happy constantly, even if they were miserable with each other? *Maybe forever is too long to be together.*

I'll deal with that if we live that long. Zack picked up his pace and fell back in step behind Takashi.

The room Takashi led him to was a boring office with a big desk. Takashi lifted a vase off a pedestal next to the door and nodded for Zack to move the other one. Removing the vases revealed buttons underneath. After Takashi set down his vase, he pressed the two buttons together.

A section of the far wall opened into a whole other room. Zack set his vase down and headed for the inner room. There were more bookcases in here, and along the back wall was a sleek, modern desk and a massive computer setup. "How did you even find this?"

"Seamus interrogated me in the outer office on my first night. When I had the chance, I did some investigating." Takashi went straight for a bookshelf closer to the desk. "You spend enough time doing what I do, you learn how people hide things."

"I thought you were an ambassador," Zack said.

"Ambassador is another name for spy in our world." Takashi knelt down and took a binder off the shelf. "You should see this."

Zack took the binder and flipped it open. The first page had a picture he'd uploaded to social media when he was still in high school, and the summary section had details about his life stretching back years. Each sentence added a drop of anxiety until he had trouble keeping his hands still as he continued to read. "He stalked me. He's *been* stalking me."

"Not just you," Takashi said solemnly.

As Zack began to ask who else, he realized that the rows of in front of him were full of black binders like the one in his hands. Each shelf held over a dozen, and each bookcase could easily hold a hundred on one side alone. And there were eight other bookcases on this side of the room alone.

"Are they all … 'potentials'?" Zack asked.

"They seem to be."

"There must be thousands of names in here." Zack wandered over to the other row of shelves. "These are different."

"Journals stretching back centuries."

Zack handed his binder off to Takashi and yanked one of the journals from the end of the bookcase. The entries were dated in 2018. He put it back, went to the lowest shelf, and pulled the last journal out. It ended in June of 2021. *Six months ago. Where is the current one? Shit, don't think too hard.* Hurriedly, he put the journal back and went to the desk.

"We have to be careful not to leave a trace," Takashi said.

"Yeah, yeah," Zack replied noncommittally. The desk had a center drawer, and he opened it. Inside was his own journal and a smooth onyx leather journal identical to the one he'd just been reading. He pulled it out of the drawer and flipped to the back.

"You may not want to read that."

"Oh, I fucking do." Zack danced out of Takashi's attempt to grab the journal from him. The benefit of being quicker than him meant he could keep one step ahead of Takashi while reading the page.

December 26th

As predicted, Zack is not thrilled that I am his sire, though I sense he may come around and realize what a blessing I have given him. He is strong-willed, stubborn in a way that I can't help admiring when he's not being contrary to me. Last night, he walked into the meeting and immediately pointed out the flaw in Penelope's argument! Clearly when it comes to matters of himself, he is inse-cure, but when it comes to information or relying upon instinct, he is a marvel. I can feel his mind at this very minute, working to dismiss that self-doubt which must have ruined his mortal life. He is thriving. I don't believe I could have made a better choice for the launch of my new generation. It seems my fear that mortals these days were incapable of taking the true essence of what I could offer them was unfounded.

Anton's choice for a distraction has proved ineffectual in capturing his interest. At least the boy is appetizing to look at. His dark hair is not quite the shade of Roger's, but if I wished a proxy to take out my current frustrations, he would do. I shall have to see if my beloved has decided another purpose for this seed or if I might make use of him until the time comes to steal more from Grandmother.

The entry went on to complain about the meeting's tedium and Seamus's excitement at the prospect of taking Zack out for a night of slaughtering "the worst of the descendants," but Zack barely absorbed those words.

He couldn't let himself think too hard. He couldn't risk letting Seamus hear what he had learned.

"You look as if you've seen a ghost," Takashi said as he took the journal from his hands. Quickly, he put it back in the drawer and shut it. "What did he have to say?"

"There's a lot to unpack." Zack shoved his hand through his hair. His gaze fell on the bookshelves of binders. He was the beginning of a new generation? What was that supposed to mean? Who the fuck would Seamus call "Grandmother"? "You told Katie that Seamus and Nell were sired from the same *demon*. That was the word you used. Not vampire, *demon*."

"That was what Nell referred to him as," Takashi said.

"Makes sense," Zack muttered. "Vampire is a relatively new word compared to Nell or Seamus. Hunters have a theory that the reason vampiric powers are so hard to predict is that the word is a shallow classification to lump creatures that only seem similar. It stands to reason that there might be one progenitor for vampires that had all their powers, but it'd be from beyond our reality. From a hell or maybe even something corrupted out of a heaven. Just, something not from here. Or maybe some force that is older than the Earth. Or maybe there are multiple vampire-like ancient beings that mixed with mortals and created the undead menaces we know. That we're part of."

"Zack, you're speaking too quickly for me to understand most of those words," Takashi said slowly.

No, he was saying them at his normal speed. Zack was panicking, and that was causing him to rely on his superior capability. *Oh, fuck. How do I slow down?*

If he could sense Takashi's desire for calm, or if Takashi had a better understanding of how intensely his fear was spiraling out of his control, maybe he could help. Zack peeled the glove from his right and touched Takashi's cheek.

Warmth spread from Takashi and coasted into Zack. It rolled upward, through his arm, and across his chest.

Takashi took a step back and blinked at him. "What was that?"

"I ... I was trying to feel your desire for calm," Zack replied. He was steadier, but the fear was still clawing at the back of his throat. His thirst was returning with an eager need. "Sorry if I pushed into your head too much."

"You didn't." Takashi touched his cheek where Zack had touched him. "I'm not sure what you did, though."

"Are you all right?"

"Yes. You?"

"Except for being the pride and joy of a master manipulator—the answer's still no." Zack examined the shelves of journals. Moving a collection like this around the globe must have taken some effort. How much had Seamus committed to paper? "Fuck, the information lurking in just this room is astounding, but we can't spend all night in here. I was reading Seamus's entry from the other night. I think there's another vampire in the mansion. Not a guard or anything. Someone Anton recently sired."

Takashi stilled. "I haven't seen anyone. It wouldn't be hard to hide someone in this place, though I think I have an idea of where to start looking."

They covered their tracks as they left the secret office and then the outer study. After going out into the hallway, Takashi led the way to an ordinary locked door with a silver handle in one of the plainer hallways on the first floor. It reeked of an acrid scent, and a shiver went down Zack's spine.

Takashi pulled out two thin pieces of metal that looked like they'd belonged on a pair of sunglasses once upon a time and then set to work on the door's lock. While he did, Zack took a moment to double-check that there were no magical runes on the doorframe and found none. In a moment, Takashi managed to open the door.

It led to a bland stone-and-concrete staircase and a basement, which was more of the aggressively simplistic same. Steel doors with plain silver handles dotted the hallway. Zack was glad for the gloves as he tried the first handle. The door swung open to reveal a ten-by-ten room with no windows and no hint of comfort. "A prison cell?"

"Some might call this a dungeon," Takashi said quietly. He continued down the hall, lightly testing door handles. "Not uncommon. Nell has one."

"She does?" Zack followed. Along the way, he spotted a shotgun shell on the floor. He picked it up. Panic threatened to swell again as he recognized the shade of green plastic. "This is Cal's."

"Are you sure?"

"Yeah. Silver shot's a custom thing. This is what we use to make them. What the hell is this doing here?"

"While you were in your grave, Roger infiltrated the

mansion to find us, remember?" Takashi said. "Cal must have been one of the people I saw him flee with."

Zack closed his hand around the empty shell. "What if he didn't leave? What if he's ..."

"Then we will deal with that outcome." Takashi put his hand on Zack's shoulder and squeezed. "But we won't know what's down here unless we continue."

Zack nodded. When Takashi turned to head down the hall toward the intersection, Zack tucked the shell into his pants pocket. The feel of it was as reassuring as it was nerve-racking. Roger had somehow convinced *Cal*, of all people, to come for him? Of course, Cal had believed he was still human at the time—no way would Cal rescue a vampire ever—but he'd come along. Had he been the only one? Had Zack's mom or dad been part of the failed rescue?

And what the fuck was Roger planning? First, working with hunters, then ripping off Seamus? What was the endgame? *He knows that his life's been one big game for Seamus and Anton. He doesn't know what's happening to me or Takashi. Maybe he's out for revenge.*

At the intersection, they chose the left hallway. Several more of the same steel doors were on either side, and another one was at the end. The further they progressed, the greater a strange odor bothered Zack's nose. It was heavily metallic and like blood, but not appetizing the way a freshly bit mortal was. "What is that?"

"The smell?"

"Yeah."

Takashi tried the door handle at the end of the hall and discovered it was locked. He took his makeshift lockpicks and began to work on the lock. "That's what it smells like when fear and desperation have soaked into a place."

"It doesn't smell like mortals' fear. Or what I thought stale mortal fear would," Zack replied.

"I've never run into it this pungently."

With all the steel doors and silver handles, the dungeon wasn't designed to hold mortals. "Maybe it's vampiric fear?"

"Hadn't thought of that." Takashi twisted the lockpicks, and the door sprang open.

The smell worsened beyond the door, but the sight before Zack drove the ability to concentrate straight out of his mind.

In the center of the chamber was a wooden rack that had a dark stain underneath it. The rack had sigils running along the edges, especially around the cuffs that would bind a person to it. Sections of wall between the doors held a variety of torture instruments, most gleaming with silver in the dim light.

Unlike the rest of the dungeon, the doors in this large room were bars instead of solid steel. Each led to a tiny cell, no more than three feet across and six feet in depth. The occupant of the one nearest to the door leapt at Zack and shoved his hand out between the bars to attempt to grab him. He might have been more like a man at some point, but his skin was pale enough that his veins were plain to see. He snapped and growled at Zack. His teeth were nothing but fangs, and his fingers had long, curling nails. His eyes were black voids.

The prisoner in the next cell was sitting at the back of his chamber, curled up and rocking back and forth. At some point, he'd scratched a word into the wall. *Cursed*. The one in the cell after that was a corpse just standing and staring at the wall. Another cell contained a half-man, half-bat creature that was drawing on the floor with a long clawed finger.

"Don't pay them any attention, sweethearts," Roger said.

Stirring at his voice, Zack finally turned his attention toward a cell on the other side of the chamber. Roger stood behind one of the cell doors. His long black hair brushed his shoulders, and his smile was warm, though exhaustion was obvious in his brown eyes. He was as muscular as he'd ever been, but he leaned against the wall as if it took everything to stand. He had no shirt, and his pants were bordering on too torn to hold together.

Zack's libido attempted to rally. *Not the time*. He rushed to the door, realized he didn't have any tools to unlock it, and motioned to Takashi. "Quick, we have to get him out."

Takashi crossed the room and knelt down to begin working on the lock. "I don't understand. Anton said he let you go. I saw you run."

"He caught me later on. Fuck, is it good to see you two." Roger reached out between the bars, carefully not touching them.

Zack stepped forward to feel him. His touch was warmer than Takashi's at first, but then suddenly, it wasn't. "Wait, something's not right."

"Because he's fucking with you," a voice said, the clarity and pitch echoing off the stone walls.

Not him. Zack spun to his right.

A young man a few years older than Zack was in the near corner cell. He was fairly tall, just shy of six feet in height, with dark brown hair that always got redder in the summer sun. His skin was the gray of a tombstone, and his once dark brown eyes were a faint shade of red. He had broad shoulders and a strong jawline with a dimple in the center of his chin. And Zack had never noticed that he had such long eyelashes before, but they were there.

"*Dennis*," Zack snarled. "What the fuck are you doing here?"

"Great to see you, too, coz," Denny drawled. He pushed himself up to his feet. He touched the bars as he did and hissed as they burned him. "That over there is an incubus."

"Succubus, technically." The fake Roger smiled wickedly. "Since I prefer to be on the receiving side."

"Shit," Takashi muttered. He slid back from the lock and shoved his makeshift picks into his pocket as he stood.

Denny grumbled, "Point is, that isn't who you think it is, Zack. It's a demon."

"I know what succubae are, thanks," Zack snapped.

"This is little Zacky?" the fake Roger asked delightedly. He shimmered with a red light. Between one blink and the next, he changed into a skinny boy with light brown hair and steel-gray eyes. His appearance was identical to Zack's younger self. With glee, he pointed at his face. "You're him?"

Hearing his own younger voice speaking to him pushed Zack further to numbness. "Wait, hold on, succubae are sex demons. I knew you were a prick, Denny, but seriously? A pedophile?"

"Gross. No," Denny said.

"A sex demon knows what I look like!" Zack gestured at the succubus.

"To be fair to our poor Denny, this isn't about sex. I would *love* to feed on nothing but that desire, but pickings are a little scarce down here, so I'll take as much regret as possible. And this? Mmmmmmmmmm." The now-fake-Zack licked his fingers. "Delicious!"

"Regret?" Zack asked.

Denny crossed his arms over his chest and stared at the floor of his cell. "Don't overthink it. He's starving, and I'm the only semi-sane thing left in here."

"I don't need to 'overthink it,'" Zack growled and clenched his fists. "I was a child that you helped tie up, and then when we were alone, you beat me. I was *defenseless*."

"All I wanted was to play with you guys," young-fake-Zack said, pitching his voice high and tight like he was about to cry. "What did I do wrong, Denny? Why did you call me those names? Why do you hate them so much? Why do you hate me?"

Big, wet tears started to roll down fake-Zack's cheeks, and he sniffled.

Denny was crying, too. His tears were drops of blood that made tracks down his cheeks.

"Zack," Takashi whispered. "Perhaps we should leave."

That would be the smart move. Zack could forget about this horror show and whatever was happening in this torture chamber. Out of all the people in his life, Denny was certainly one of the prime candidate assholes for abandoning to actual Hell, not just hell on Earth.

But he could sense the deep chasm of regret in Denny. He refused to dive into it, didn't want to know whether the source was some desire that he wished he'd done more or not. But villains didn't cry about the pain they caused.

Once he touched Denny's regret, he could taste it on the air. And it was zipping across the chamber to the demon in the cell.

I am so not ready to forgive him. I don't care how bad he feels. But he also wasn't about to give up on his and Takashi's exploratory mission. They'd come to learn secrets the mansion held. *We were always going to find something fucked-up like this.*

Time to be the badass vampire I'm supposed to be. Zack squared his shoulders and unclenched his fists. "Not just yet. Denny, what happens in here?"

"Oo, I know the answer to that one!" fake-Zack said, raising his hand and jumping a little.

"Would you fucking *stop*?" Denny screamed.

Fake-Zack cackled with laughter. "So fucking good!"

Denny launched himself at the bars, shoving his arm through. Smoke drifted up from his skin, but he continued attempting to scramble through the metal that was hurting him.

He'd called himself semi-sane.

How long had he been down here? A realization burst across Zack's consciousness. He couldn't free Denny because then it would be obvious that someone had been down in this room. Though Seamus might read his thoughts and discover it, there was a difference between curiosity and screwing with Anton's things.

But he couldn't stand still and have the two of them waste his time. Takashi was right; they needed more assets. Their cell was less literal, but Zack and Takashi were just as trapped in the mansion. They needed more people on their side.

Zack pulled off his leather glove and grabbed Denny's bare wrist. He wasn't so much a journal page but a stone tablet with engraved lettering that went miles deep.

Magic was about working with metaphors. He'd learned that from the same person Denny had. So he imagined taking a large marker and writing *Peace* across the tablet of Denny's mind.

It wasn't changing anything.

The times where he and Takashi had created a feedback loop, he'd felt the desire in Takashi link with his own lust. If he wanted Denny to feel calm, then he had to figure out calm. *Cuddled between Roger and Takashi, laughing with them on the couch as we watched an old movie. Being with Kit and Blake and watching the pillow sail over the edge. Joy. Peace.*

Denny gasped and tumbled back into his cell. He sank to the floor, holding the hand Zack had touched as if he'd come in contact with snow for the first time.

"That was mine!" fake-Zack wailed as he shimmered with a red glow. When the light faded, he was roughly Zack's height. His skin was a vibrant maroon, and his eyes were solid black. He had jet-black hair with hints of burgundy and a long tail that ended in a spade shape. Short horns on either side of his forehead jutted up like elegant spikes, sloping slightly backward. They came to sharp tips.

Though they weren't as sharp as the glare in his eyes. His voice wasn't much deeper than it'd been as fake-Zack, and he whined, "Not fair! I'm hungry!"

Doing his best master vampire impression, Zack said, "You can get back to torturing my cousin in a minute—"

"Wait, you're not going to let me out?" Denny asked, crestfallen.

For a second, the hurt in Denny's voice made Zack itch to help him. But if he did that, he'd be putting Takashi and himself at risk, and he couldn't help anybody if they were all in cells. "I can't. Yet. I'll work on it, okay? What is Anton doing in here? This isn't just some fucked-up way for him to pass the time, is it?"

"I don't know. I haven't been here long," Denny replied.

"How did you even get here?"

"Doesn't matter." Denny pulled his knees up to his chest.

"I know the answers to both," the demon said sweetly.

"Well?" Zack asked as he turned toward him.

The demon leaned against the wall of his cell and examined his pointed nails as if they were far more interesting than anything in the whole wide existence. "Well, what? *Oh*. You want me to just tell you? After you cut off the meal I've been cooking up for a week?"

"We should go," Takashi murmured.

"Ah, yes, go without learning anything valuable at all so you can sit and fester upstairs like we do down here," the demon replied. "You'll probably join us once I tell Anton you were in here, scheming to let Dennis go."

Shit. Zack ran his hand through his hair, then internally kicked himself for his nervous habit. Badass vampires were supposed to be cold as statues. He lifted his chin and approached the demon's cell door. "My soul's not any good to you."

"Aw, precious boy, you think a vampire's soul is worthless to my kind? You're so very wrong," the demon replied. "However, the delivery takes far too much investment. Besides, souls are good for currency, but they're not the only thing worth gaining in the world."

"What do you want?"

"I want to visit your dreams." The demon gazed at Zack with half-closed eyes. "You are all kinds of my favorite things."

"This is a bad deal," Takashi said and began to offer his hand out to Zack.

Zack held up a hand to stop Takashi from reaching for him. "That's too open-ended. How about you can visit while you're trapped in this cell?"

"How about while I'm in this cell and a year to the night after I'm out?" the demon replied.

"And what I want is information. You answer anything I ask, and you reveal none of my conversations to Anton, Seamus, or anyone working for them," Zack replied. "This visit counts as one of those conversations, so you don't mention that we came down here. And that year is an Earthen calendar year. No bullshit on using some other realm or another planet's cycle."

The demon laughed and spun a quick circle. "Shrewd! Demanding! I love it! You are fucking hot, did you know that? Unf, tell me to bend over already, daddy."

"Don't call me that," Zack said.

"Ooo, got enough daddy issues going on already? Okay," the demon purred. He came up to the bars and wiggled excitedly, his tail swaying. "Deal suits me fine. Kiss makes it real!" He puckered up, carefully sliding his face as far forward through the bars as he could.

"You don't have to do this," Takashi said.

Zack glanced over his shoulder to him. "You said I'm capable of making tough calls. This is one of them. Could be good to have a succubus on our side."

Just as Zack started to slide forward to kiss the demon, Takashi caught his arm and tugged him back. "Letting him into your dreams is a powerful thing, Zack. This creature relishes in torture."

"You're the one who doesn't care where our assets come from," Zack whispered fiercely. He yanked his arm free of Takashi and pressed his lips to the demon's.

A cool jolt went through his lips down to his toes. When he backed away from the demon, the tingle remained until it dulled into a buzz throughout him.

"To keep our deal, I need you to invite me into your dreams, Zackery," the demon said smoothly. "Call me Phyrull."

"You're welcome in my dreams, Phyrull," Zack said. The words had a deep echo in him, and he could feel a hook in his heart tugging him toward the demon. It wasn't as strong as the magnetic draw pulling him toward Seamus or his dagger but present within him. *Probably what Takashi was worried about.*

"Ah," Phyrull sighed. He put his fingertips against his bottom lip and twirled until he rested his backside against a wall in his cell. "Fucking hell, I think you're my new favorite drug."

That sentiment unnerved Zack in a way that he did his best to suppress. His previous research into demons had been on the basics—different ways to identify them and rituals to exorcise them—and there hadn't been much on succubae in the family's lore. At least there was a massive occult library upstairs that might have more answers for him.

"Deal was for answers," Zack said sternly. "What is Anton's purpose for this room?"

The fishhook feeling in his heart wriggled as he made his demand.

Phyrull trembled, a brief, slight movement that would have slipped the notice of Zack's eyes when he was mortal. His voice came out like silk. "He continues his experiments into true immortality, your excellency."

"He's a vampire. Why is he exploring that?" Zack demanded.

A shiver again. Phyrull gasped softly. He turned his head to look at Zack, his black hair falling over one eye.

Imagining Phyrull on his knees and opening his pretty mouth to suck Zack's cock wasn't hard. And there were a million other things that Phyrull could do on his knees. He didn't even need to suck on Zack. If he just opened his mouth while Zack jerked off, Zack could shoot his load and decorate Phyrull's forked tongue …

"I invited you into my dreams, not my waking thoughts," Zack growled.

"Forgive the impertinence, your excellency. I couldn't resist," Phyrull murmured. His words slurred together.

"Answer my question."

"Even the undead can be forced to leave this world," Phyrull said. "You should know that with your knowledge, your excellency."

True immortality's got to be impossible, right? Zack backed away from the cell. Legend said there were mages who had figured out a magical way to expand their lifespans, but the ones that could pull off that sort of spell were extremely rare. Zack's family didn't know of any, and the Hunters' Information Network had only speculated. Vampires were as close as a mortal being could get to living forever.

But of course, Phyrull was right. Vampires were still extremely killable. True immortality for a vampire would have to come with invincibility.

His magnetic connection to Seamus was strengthening bit by bit. "Shit, Seamus is on his way home."

"Then we need to go." Takashi headed for the door.

Zack took two steps after him.

Denny called out, "You're really going to leave me here, with him? You have no idea what I've been through in here! Come on! We're family!"

His tone was too much like Cal's, too much like his family's constant needling that resulted in nothing but getting disowned. A part of Zack had been shattered, something that hadn't begun to heal until he was fully dead.

Now, the bastard who had caused the first of Zack's worst nightmares, who had pitted his peers against him, who had kicked off the slide into the bad graces while remaining in everyone's fucking favor, was making a demand of *him*.

Seamus had chosen him. Had given him more power than he'd given anyone else in possibly *ever*. Believed him to be the start of a new generation and a potential dragon slayer. He was not a child begging for his family's approval anymore.

With a hiss, Zack moved with liquid speed. He reached between the bars, took hold of Denny's shirt, and yanked Denny up against the bars, all without touching them himself. Denny screamed, but his attempts to push away meant putting his hands on the silver and hurting himself more.

"Aw, have you been suffering?" Zack said with every ounce of biting sarcasm he'd been holding on to since he'd risen. "How terrible! Must fucking suck to be the damsel caught in the dungeon."

"We were kids!" Denny shouted.

But Zack sensed how badly he wanted to hide from the truth. "I *trusted* you, and you *beat* me. Not just with your fists, but your fucking words. So I don't owe you anything."

"Zack, please, you don't understand!" Denny wailed.

"*I don't want to!*" Zack roared. He shoved Denny hard enough that he sent him into the other wall. A resounding crack of bone echoed.

"I was fucked-up," Denny sobbed. Instead of trying to get up, he curled into a ball on the floor. "I ... I'm still fucked-up. I'm a vampire. The family's going to kill me. The only one ... I don't have anyone ... and Anton. He's ... he's done stuff to me. He puts me on that rack and ... and cuts me open. Does spells."

"How long has he been here?" Zack demanded of Phyrull.

"Time is hard to gauge in here, your excellency, but I think a couple weeks," Phyrull replied.

He hasn't suffered long enough, a slick, angry, masterful voice inside of Zack decided. But he couldn't leave him without any hope or leave him to Anton's tortures forever.

"I will do what I can *when* I can to get you out of this cell." Zack turned his back on Denny and started heading for the exit. "If you're lucky, I'll get around to it before you spend a decade cutting yourself to pieces on the inside."

He tried not to let Denny's sobs soothe a part of him. A good guy wasn't supposed to like anyone in pain. *Guess I'm only decent.*

The doors locked behind them as he and Takashi made their way up to the first floor of the mansion. As cold as it had seemed, the stillness was welcoming after the blunt stone and horrific torture chamber. Zack rolled his shoulders, but the tension in them was more psychological than physical. Weird vampire physiology at work again.

Cautiously, he ran his gaze over Takashi and checked in on his mental page. Though he could feel the shape of words, he couldn't grasp their meaning. "Did you, um, hear? What happened at the end?"

"I did," Takashi said softly.

"You thinking about breaking up with me?"

"What?" Lightly, Takashi put his hand on Zack's shoulder and turned so they faced each other. "Why would you think that?"

"Because I just left someone to rot in a dungeon, and I don't feel guilty about it," Zack replied. "Plus, I made a deal with a demon that you didn't agree with."

Takashi linked his hand with Zack's and then kissed his knuckles. "You had a point in making that deal. I worried about what you would think of yourself after the fact and that you were making a steep bargain."

"Trust me, I'm going to spend all my free time in that

massive library trying to figure out the intricacies of succubae deals, dragon lore, and how to jump-start disconnecting myself from Seamus," Zack said. "Not exactly in a great position on the board, are we?"

"We're not."

Zack stepped closer to Takashi so that they were chest to chest. "But we've got this, right?"

"Right," Takashi replied.

Zack kissed him, quick and gentle. Then he squeezed his hand and headed down the hall. "Seamus left three guys. I only need to drink one more, which means there's one more for you to eat."

"And you're all right with that?" Takashi asked lightly.

The fear that Zack was masking his pain was there, written in big, bold letters that Takashi was quickly covering up with hope that he'd be okay. A few nights ago, killing would have bothered him. It should have, still, but they needed the blood to survive. Zack couldn't control his hunger, and Takashi hadn't been allowed to properly feed in over a week.

He wasn't going to drag his feet through however long he had to live. Would the people he fed on have done any different? Probably not. *Why should I feel guilt for what I am?*

"I'll manage," Zack replied. "They're this way. Come on."

CHAPTER 36

The world did not collapse in the nights following the robbery. In fact, as far as Roger could determine, the world did not even notice that they had done anything at all. He hadn't expected the mortal news to make a comment, but Vincent found no remarks on the supernaturals' social media platforms. Nathaniel heard nothing in his bar. Had anyone other than Dmitri been in charge of breaking into the finances, Roger might have doubted their success.

The new year came without fanfare or celebration. Roger spent that evening and the ones following by writing every down everything he knew about the Great Lakes Coven. With Vincent's and Dmitri's help, he added better details about the security and importance of various targets. Soon, he would strike again.

Ideas were plenty, but his resources were less. Six fighters weren't enough to launch an attack on most of their targets, especially if they aimed to make a splash rather than discreet strikes. The formerly abandoned dance studio that had been their staging ground for their heist was now their loose command center and training ground. Nathaniel had sent a few trusted vampires their way. Every vampire was woefully underexperienced because Seamus had never encouraged expertise, always relying on overwhelming numbers for a fight. Thomas had grumbled about "training the enemy." His complaints ended when Roger suggested he bring in trusted hunters. Their numbers were growing.

But he still wasn't sure *where* to strike.

After two weeks without the slightest tremor in the GLC, Roger needed more information from someone in leadership. He contemplated kidnapping Xenofon, but that vamp had never paid attention to much outside himself. And though torturing Xenofon would have been justice for his many victims, Roger couldn't use that as justification. He wasn't innocent either.

Instead, Roger texted Candide. When three more nights passed without an answer, he decided that a visit was in order.

Chateau de Vampire was Candide's jewel, a donor house with a private section for herself. But it wasn't her only lair. Dmitri assured Roger that she hadn't abandoned her penthouse in the Gold Coast neighborhood.

Roger made the journey on foot, crossing the miles of Chicago after dark. Once he was within a block, he used his supernatural speed to close the distance. Modern cameras weren't quite capable of capturing him moving that fast.

He entered the building behind a tenant, encouraging their desire to have someone near so they didn't mind having him close. Two security guards were in the lobby. One man began to scrutinize him, so Roger reached out with his power and heightened a desire to check for messages on his phone. He deepened the shadows of his face so that any cameras in the lobby wouldn't have a clear image of him. That little trick had been a suggestion of Vincent's in order to fool facial recognition software.

The top two floors of the buildings belonged to Candide. Once upon a time, the second to the top had been Roger's, but he'd moved out in the 1970s and sold it to Candide. The place had become tainted for him after Seamus visited one night. *He has soured too much of my life.*

A short hallway connected the elevator door to the penthouse door. Roger could have sworn he felt spider silk strands breaking as he walked forward, but he found no hint of webs. The hallway was bright and clean. Pushing the weirdness from his mind, he knocked on the penthouse door.

After a moment, he heard two voices just on the other side.

"I think it's Roger." The first voice belonged to Kit.

"Think?" a second voice asked.

"He looks different."

"Doesn't matter who it is," a third voice said. "Mistress didn't tell us to expect anyone, so we don't open the door. He has one minute before we call security."

"Mistress didn't tell us to do that. Are you sure we can?" Kit replied a little too sweetly. They weren't a fan of whoever the third voice was.

"Look, you're the new toy of the month, okay? Don't think you know Mistress better than we do just because you're getting all the attention."

"It isn't my fault you're a boring brat. Maybe if you behaved more, you'd get ignored less."

"Darlings," Roger called out, "let me in."

"No!" the second voice said.

"Then I'll wait out here until your mistress comes home. But I will see her."

"Not if security hauls you from the building!" the third voice said.

"Security didn't even look at me on my way through the door. They don't have a hope of stopping me, and your mistress wouldn't want to sacrifice their lives if violence erupted in an effort to remove me," Roger replied. "Now, let me in."

There was muttering, and then the second voice whispered, "I'm calling, okay?"

Kit opened the door. They were wearing plush sweatpants and a T-shirt along with their light red collar. The girl beside them had a collar the same shade of red and was equally dressed in comfortable clothing. She reached forward to shut the door, but she was on the phone. Kit won the tug-of-war.

The third was Candide's fey boy, Dryden. He wore sleeker leisure clothes, accentuating his lithe frame. His long auburn hair was loosely braided, and there was a sharpness in his indigo eyes. The last time Roger had seen him, he was wearing a light pink collar. Now, he had one almost the same shade of red as Kit's. He folded his arms over his chest.

"Come in, master," Kit said politely as they opened the door a little farther.

"Thank you," Roger said with sincerity. He stepped into the home, the shiver of a threshold letting him through. Where mortals called a place home, a threshold could bar him from entry. Candide's pets had been known to cause a threshold barrier within a night of moving in. She made them feel safe. Loved.

The fact that Kit had the power to invite Roger over the doorframe was a testament to her care as well. Three weeks with their new mistress, and Kit already called the penthouse home. Roger might have been heartsick if he hadn't been so overwhelmed with relief that they looked healthy and happy. He'd been wrong for them; Candide was a good fit.

"If you'll come this way, master," Kit said and gestured to a parlor to their left.

Roger followed them, not giving a damn that the other two pets were watching him closely.

Candide's home was as extravagant as the Chateau de Vampire, though her style here was a slight touch more comfortable. When Roger had "disappeared" from the coven, his condo on Lake Shore Drive and its contents had been sold. Candide must have been part of the process—or at least keenly aware it was happening. Several of Roger's art pieces were on display at the Chateau, and more were here in her parlor. The most prominently placed was one he'd commissioned around the turn of the twentieth century by an artist who'd never gained fame, but Roger had loved his skill with lighting and emotions.

For the painting, Roger had modeled for the role of Lord Wotton, and he was whispering into the ear of James, a handsome, gorgeous man who Roger had been hopelessly in love with. James was playing the part of Dorian Gray in it and had still been mortal at the time. He had been a warlock worthy of earning the title mage, but the mage society circles of Chicago wouldn't accept him because of the color of his skin. The fictional version of themselves were talking in a nighttime garden, Roger leaning in with a smile promising devious behavior. James was examining the flowers, but the artist had perfectly captured the way he tilted his head when he was listening.

Wherever you are, James, I hope you'll be happy to learn that you were right about me. I was a coward. With a dry tone, Roger said, "Candide should have no problem with me in her home." He pointed at the painting. The damn thing had been a treasured possession, even after James left him, and Candide, of all people, knew that. She hadn't mentioned that she had it. "I am here all the time, technically."

The girl's jaw dropped open, but she recovered as someone finally answered her call. She turned away, and Roger politely ignored her conversation as if he couldn't hear every syllable on both sides.

An easy task, considering he had a parlor to explore for more of his former belongings. Like the Tiffany lamp he'd bought in 1899 and his favorite end table. He wasn't sure if the collection of books on a delicate bookcase was truly his, but many of the titles came from the secret artistic society he and Candide had nourished until the early 1970s.

And then there was his favorite chair that used to sit in one of his playrooms. He'd sat in it and watched his pets have all sorts of fun with each other before joining them. He'd administered punishments and given rewards from that chair. It was the closest thing to a seat of power he'd ever had.

Gently, he traced a long line up the wooden arm. The wood was still sturdy, and there was no mistaking it as a similar piece. He found the scratch in the exact place he'd left one on accident. The stain of the polish made it nearly invisible, but it was there.

Candide had said that she had aided in obscuring his location because she wanted to protect him. Had she collected so many of his things in order to remember him? Or had she been jealous for centuries? Had their friendship been a lie? Their closeness a ruse? What if she had lied to him? What if she was the one to work with an Unseelie to lock him in a coma?

He didn't want to believe that of her. They'd understood each other for centuries. She was his dearest friend.

The chair was for a dominant master. He considered sitting in it, trying to reclaim that piece of himself. But that felt like giving whiskey to a ghost. Whoever he was becoming, he wasn't the vampire he'd been.

Roger drew in a deep breath and roused from his long thoughts. He took a seat on the leather sofa and discovered it was far more comfortable than it appeared to be at first glance.

"Would you like any refreshments, master?" Kit asked.

"I'm fine, thank you." Roger crossed one leg over the other and rested his arm along the back of the couch. Holding himself still helped calm the storm of emotions building in him. He wasn't sure if he was scared, angry, sad, or all of it at once.

Knowing how Candide trained her pets, he gave a dismissive wave to the three hovering near the parlor door. "You likely have chores or something to do, yes? Don't worry. I'll inform her of how I forced my way in here. She won't mind if you leave me alone. I promise not to ruin anything while I wait."

Kit, the girl, and Dryden bowed their heads and then went farther into the penthouse. Roger could track their movements if he wanted, but he closed down his senses rather than rely on them. The painting on the wall in front of him dragged him into memories of James and those nights posing for the artist. They had been a wonderful time in an era surrounded by the constant stress of Seamus gaining new ground in his territory.

"I have done it!" Ezra's English-accented voice rang down the hallway, and his quick footfalls echoed out as he hurried down a flight of steps. "Candide, are you home? I thought I heard—blast it all, fox, you can do more than shake your head and point."

"Master Roger is here, sir," Kit said quietly. They were some distance away.

"Roger? Excellent! He'll do," Ezra replied. "Fetch me a pair of pants, please? Nothing jean. Anything else will do."

A moment later, Ezra strode into the parlor. His red hair was standing as if he'd been raking his hands through it constantly. His steel-gray eyes burned with joy. Despite wearing nothing more than a pair of tight bicycle shorts, he walked with a commanding presence. That might have been his two hundred and seventy years of immortality or the fact that he'd been an English nobleman before Roger turned him into a vampire.

Though he was paler, with a few more delicate features, he looked more like Zack's brother than Cal did, which was a painful reminder that Ezra's twin sister had spawned a line of hunters, and thus, Zack was one of her descendants.

He had in his hands a thick stack of papers, and he proudly set the pile on the end table beside Roger's old chair. "I am finally done with the fucker. Which means I'm done with that fucking room! What glorious timing you have, Roger. Why do you look like I've punched you in the heart with silver?"

Watching Ezra light up with passion was like watching a mirror of Zack, and Roger was glad he didn't need to breathe. "It's been a hard few weeks."

"I imagine." Ezra took a seat on the other end of the couch. "How have you been holding up? Do you need blood? Rum? Tea? Is something wrong? You're brooding more than I would have expected."

Roger kept his gaze on the manuscript Ezra had placed on the end table. He couldn't pretend to be angry that Ezra had found a new way to lash out. Ever since Seamus and Anton had butchered Ezra's family in 1755, Ezra had clung to a shield of rage. Usually, when his anger became too great to ignore, Roger would arrange for him to return to England and to take up his role as a nobleman and continue to reap the benefits of position.

But in the last thirty years, Ezra had finally abandoned aristocracy and used his time away from the coven to launch a career writing erotica based on his fellow vampires.

"I take it HT Moss strikes again?" Roger asked. "Do I get a happily ever after?"

"This is a brand-new series," Ezra said. "I need to write another *From the Grave*, and I will! But this was a mystery I'd been brewing for a while, and I decided to go for it. Seriously, Roger, I would have thought you would be over the moon."

Roger frowned at him. "Why on earth would I be happy?"

"Because of the debut party next week," Ezra replied. "That's why you're here, isn't it? To talk over the details with her? Where are Zack and Takashi? I would've assumed they would want to be part of the preparations."

Roger slid to the edge of his seat and held on to the rage in his heart with white knuckles. Ezra's tone was completely blithe like his words weren't laced with holy water. "What the *fuck* are you on about?"

Confusion clouded Ezra, and he frowned. "I know I saw the invitation. 'An intimate debut for two wonderful new fledglings of the Great Lakes Coven. Zackery and Kathleen.'"

Roger stood. Somehow, in doing so, he knocked Ezra's manuscript over, and the pages fluttered. Swearing, he knelt and started to collect them, but his hands were shaking. No, the pages were shaking. *What the hell?*

Ezra gasped and hurried over to gather his book. They worked together, though Roger could hardly see his hands from the red starting to swarm his vision. *Fledgling. Zackery. Intimate debut.* That meant … that meant he'd been a vampire for a little while. That meant … *I'll tell you where Zack and Takashi are,* Anton had offered smugly. Roger had sensed the trap in those words, had assumed that it meant Zack and Takashi were someplace hard to reach. *Nowhere is farther than the grave.* Was Takashi in a grave? Had he been killed? And Zack. Zack. Zack had sworn he'd never want to become a vampire. But he was a sireling. He had to be *Seamus's* sireling.

It had to be a move of desperation, hadn't it? A last moment's choice. What sick game was Seamus playing to have some sort of debut party like Zack was any other vampire? Who the fuck was Kathleen?

Why the hell was Ezra acting like he should be glad?

Ezra stopped picking up his pages. He set them aside and started to reach for Roger but hesitated. Softly, he said, "I … I feel as though I may have missed some events of the past few weeks."

"Weeks?"

"It's been part of the process. Candide locks me up in a room with a typewriter—don't worry about these pages, I've had a laptop without internet to work on this draft—

and I focus. I don't spend *all* my time in there, but she leaves the outside world very outside while I work. I only know about the invitation because I saw it on her desk when I went looking for her just now." Ezra retreated a bit. "The last bit of news I have was the closing of the Winter's Grand Ball."

"She's told you *nothing*?" Roger demanded. He slammed his fist against the floor. Once wasn't enough, but twice would only break his bones, and he didn't need that pain. It wasn't conducive. He needed to rip and shove and tear something apart.

No. No, he wouldn't be like Seamus. He would release this rage some other way. When the time was right. Not at Ezra, who was proud of himself for good reason and only trying to be a good friend.

"Kit hasn't mentioned anything?" Roger continued.

"What would they have to mention?" Ezra asked.

Roger clenched his fists tighter, but he held them to the floor. The invitation that Ezra saw must have been opened by Candide's hand, mustn't it? She knew Zack was a vampire, that he belonged to *Seamus*, and she had said *nothing*.

The sound of a heartbeat, a breath, and light footsteps drew Roger's attention. Kit had arrived with a pair of Ezra's pants, and they remained at the doorway. Their shoulders were tight, their lips a thin line, and they clutched Ezra's pants tightly between their hands.

"You haven't told him?" Roger rasped. A rustling noise began.

"Do not become cross at Kit!" Ezra dashed in front of Roger, blocking off view of Kit. "You know that Candide turns her homes into sanctuaries."

"Heaven forbid reality set in," Roger growled.

"Kit, leave the pants, and take the others to the bedroom," Ezra said. A slight thump of fabric and then the running of feet marked Kit's departure. He locked his gaze with Roger. "I can't believe I, of all people, need to say this to you. You have to calm down."

"Calm. Down." Roger stood, and Ezra mirrored him. But Ezra was short like Zack. *And Zack is a vampire like him. Only I didn't make him.* Roger towered over Ezra and kept their staring contest going. "You have no right to say that to me. Anton murdered your lover, and you nearly staked me for my cowardice. Seamus has changed my beautiful Zack into one of us. He has bound Zack to him, and our 'beloved' Candide has known without saying a damn word to me."

There was a whip of movement in the corners of Roger's eyes. A breeze was moving through him. The waves of his mind were rolling, but he was sailing those waves. The wind, the water, it was *his*, and it was angry with him.

Ezra grabbed Roger's wrists tightly. Roger had ignored his vampiric abilities since sitting on the couch. With bare skin contact, Ezra's compassion was clear. That desire to help was painful to behold.

Roger didn't want help. He wanted to hurt the world as he was hurting. Wanted to scream. Wanted to let it out.

"Roger!" Ezra shouted. Fear for himself, for Roger, and for the penthouse tarnished his compassionate desire. "Please! You have to stop!"

"Stop? Stop caring? Is that what you've done?" Roger yelled back. He'd needed to yell. Why ... why was he having a hard time hearing? What was the clattering going on?

"Look around!" Ezra broke their locked gaze and stared out at the room beyond them.

An acidic response on his tongue, Roger followed Ezra's gaze.

Ezra's manuscript, the furniture, the books—all of it was rotating around them as if they were the center of a tornado. A brief flare of wonder broke the anger in Roger's heart. Everything fell to the floor in an uneremonious mess.

The sensation of a breeze in his soul, of the waves and

ship, stilled. The building rage was no longer a pressured heat needing release, but his heart ached with the pain of his anger and life's betrayals. Silver would have been easier to bear.

"I … How was I doing that?" Roger murmured.

"Clearly, you have magic," Ezra replied.

"That's not—I have never had magic beyond our abilities as vampire. I have never seen a vampire with telekinesis." Roger waved at the overturned sofa that was beside the now cracked Tiffany lamp.

"I have. This is what manifesting arcane powers looks like." Carefully, Ezra pulled his pants out of the mess and slipped into them.

"How do you know that?" Roger asked, shock making him numb. No sense of clarity came to him, but at least the rage was far, far below the surface where it belonged.

Ezra began to clean up the mess as he spoke. "Look, I know you loved James. I know that's why he became your sireling. I also know that he grew resentful when he lost his magic after his transformation. Yes, I was jealous of your relationship with him and convinced him to run away to Alaska, but he hardly needed a nudge."

"Why does that matter?" Roger said.

"Because once he was gone and you turned your attention to Dmitri and then whatever pretty boy you found next, I thought maybe you somehow knew I was responsible for James leaving. You were happiest with him, and I encouraged that to end. So, my logic went, perhaps if James could regain his arcane abilities, he might return. Then you wouldn't have cause to be upset with me." Ezra lifted the couch, rolled it right side up, and gently put it back down in its rightful place. "I had money. Time. Why not spend both with mages and warlocks like you and Candide did with artists? After all, isn't magic another kind of art?

"In doing so, I learned a lot about the onset of powers,

often called manifestations. You see it in children the most. Telekinetic quakes. Seeing the world differently than others." Ezra gave up on collecting his manuscript and returned Roger's chair to its place.

That did sound like some of the strange occurrences that had been happening around Roger. "I'm no child."

"True. But this is a manifestation."

"Could it be some aftereffect of the coma?" Roger said.

"Coma?" Ezra asked.

"She really has told you nothing," Roger replied. "Let's begin at the beginning, shall we? The last time we saw each other, prior to our run-in at the Chateau, was in 1989. A few nights after our last chat, I was cursed ..."

CHAPTER 37

"Family mealtime" was what Anton called the ritual he initiated the night after Katie moved into the mansion. He insisted that the five of them should have their "breakfast" together every night, no matter what. Often, Seamus excused himself after a brief appearance, but they were together each night for a short time.

They would gather in what Anton had dubbed the "dining room." Instead of the usual setup, it was an irregular living room with couches and chairs. The high-end couches were covered in plastic, and the floor had a wall-to-wall plastic layer. Though there were a couple of normal chairs, there were a half dozen chairs that Zack had only seen in his family literature about "twisted" vampire practices. They were designed to restrain a victim while leaving plenty of the mortal's arms, torso, and legs accessible. No way would it be comfortable; the person trapped in it would have to feel incredibly vulnerable.

On the first evening, Anton had clapped his hands to begin the meal. Servants had brought out the first "course" of humans, and he had declared that it was time to teach the "babies" how to eat.

Over the next two weeks, mealtime became lessons in how to use vampiric abilities to "season" a mortal's blood, how to drain victims, and practice on personal restraint from killing a mortal. Anton, Seamus, and Takashi had different tips and techniques, often related to the same concept but different in their execution.

"Breakfast" wasn't the worst of Anton's ideas. He and Seamus seemed to have no idea that Zack and Takashi had explored the basement. If Phyrull had made a visit in Zack's dreams, he didn't remember it.

Zack bit the mortal bound to the chair in the tender part of his upper arm. The wound bled slowly, which let him savor the coppery taste before swallowing. Flickers pressed against Zack's consciousness, and he threaded together letters of longing, trying to keep them on the mortal's mind. His prey relaxed, and he moaned as he drew another deep drink in.

Blood just tasted so freaking good.

"Zack's going to kill again," Katie said in the singsong voice she had a habit of using whenever she thought she was doing better than him. Her pleated black plaid skirt, black knee-high socks, and red dress shirt made for a very vampire-meets-private-schoolgirl look. He wasn't sure if she'd chosen the attire herself or if Anton had stocked her wardrobe full of things just like this. She'd been wearing similar attire ever since she'd risen from her grave.

"I am not." Zack pulled back from feeding. But as soon as he did, he realized she was right. The mortal's heartbeat was too weak. "Shit."

"Zackery," Seamus chided. He was sitting in the high-backed chair that Anton had labeled the head of the table, though there was no table in the room. "Language."

"Sorry," Zack said reflexively.

Seamus made a noise of acceptance, then bit his victim again. The fact that he killed most of his prey wasn't seen as a fault of control. But when he was drinking like this, Zack could taste the dry burn of his hunger through their bond. Was he in control of his need to feed? Or was he faking it?

Anton and Takashi murmured to each other while they went over their planning materials for the upcoming party. According to the invitations, Katie was being presented as Anton's sireling. Anton had included Takashi in the preparations, especially when Seamus brushed him off as too busy to do menial work.

Zack was glad his opinion wasn't needed. Party planning was awful. However, his gut twisted when Anton and Takashi sat too close to each other. He wasn't fond of the wrenching in his stomach or the way Takashi relaxed around Anton. They had to act like they hadn't learned about Anton's experiments, but that didn't mean cozying up so close to Anton, did it? *I don't like how Anton looks at him.*

"Do you need to finish mine, too?" Katie motioned at the human in front of her. She must have perfected being a mean girl in life because she was too damn good at it.

"I'm fine, thanks," Zack drawled.

"Are you sure? I wouldn't want you to go hungry." Katie picked up the bloody wrist of her human and waved it at him.

Honing his senses to pick up the heartbeat of her mortal, Zack listened to the waning rhythm. He leaned forward. "Looks like I'm not the only one who overdid it."

"What?" Katie lifted the head of her human. The mortal wasn't opening her eyes. "Shi—oot."

Anton rubbed his brow. "Perhaps we shouldn't accept any pet in their debuts."

"But you promised, Papa!" Katie whined.

"If you're able to go three nights in a row without killing. You've only gone one, and Zack hasn't been able to manage that," Anton said. "I don't want you to offend our guests by immediately killing their gifts. We're still a week out. No one's arrived. We can easily tell everyone that it's too soon for pets."

"We're not even sure anyone's planning on presenting you with any," Takashi added. "You might be getting your hopes up for nothing."

"But Papa said he'd get me someone if that happened," Katie said.

"I will find you a pet when the time is right. Not a moment before," Anton declared.

Katie pouted.

"I think waiting's a great idea," Zack said smugly.

"Way to be a jerk," Katie replied.

Zack shrugged one shoulder.

She stuck her tongue out at him.

"Children, if you're finished, go elsewhere so I can eat in peace," Seamus growled.

"Yes, master," Zack and Katie said in unison.

On the nights when Zack didn't wind up going with Seamus on his errands, he would spend as much time as he could in the occult library. Katie joined him whenever Anton was too busy for her magic lessons. They headed down the long hall together.

Katie got a mischievous look in her eye. "Bet I'll get there first."

Then she took off at vamp superspeed.

Zack ran after her. The first time they'd had a race, he outdid her by a margin big enough that she accused him of using secret passages to get there. He was just outright faster than her, so he'd started challenging himself to arrive a fraction ahead of her during their impromptu races.

Because Katie had made one thing abundantly clear.

Zack wasn't *normal*. Takashi had told him so his first night upon rising, but Katie had a level of control that Zack still lacked. Her eyes often faded back to their mortal color. She didn't always kill her prey. She wasn't overwhelming anyone with her ability to read them.

It wasn't like she was a weak spawn either. Both Seamus and Anton seemed impressed with her bursts of speed, her casual strength, and, of course, her magic. Her arcane power was the only thing that set her apart from a typical fledgling of a powerful vampire, though.

New generation. The words became stuck in Zack's mind anytime a difference between them came up. What was that supposed to mean?

Hopefully, a hint was in the library somewhere.

Zack reached the library doors just before Katie, zipped in, and opened the left one wide. She had a habit of zooming too fast to stop herself from hitting it.

"Shoot! Not fair!" Katie declared as she came to a halt.

"How is it not fair?" Zack asked.

"I had a head start. I know your sire's a gajillion years older than mine, but come on!"

"You've got to stop saying shit like that, or you're going to slip up in public next week," Zack told her.

Katie rolled her eyes. "And you have to stop saying 'shit.'"

Fuck, I miss Amber. Zack waited for Seamus to make a remark. Nothing came.

They'd set up working at the two tables in the middle of the library a few nights back. Hers was strewn with books while he kept his work in orderly stacks. The books deserved respect. Some went back to the Middle Ages, and Zack suspected a few might be older than that.

"I didn't find *Richmond's Guide* very illuminating," Katie said as she neared her seat. Growing up in schools run by the Enduring Circle of Chicago Mages, she had the benefits of a magic-based education. Where Zack's focus had been monsters and how to kill, her studies had focused on how to craft spells and brew potions alongside the typical mundane studies for private schools of wealthy elitists.

Hunters tended to drop out of high school—Zack had graduated, but Cal had dropped out at sixteen—but mages went on to prestigious colleges, some going so far as to get doctorates. From what Zack understood, getting a degree in advanced magical theory was usually attributed to either physics, chemistry, or philosophy, depending on the student's area of focus in order to keep mundanes from asking too many questions.

Which meant Katie was pretty great at doing the math for how much salt was needed for a binding circle of whatever size, but she didn't have specialized knowledge of how shifters worked. She'd been curious, so Zack had suggested his default since she hadn't read it.

"Shifters are as different as vampires are." Zack flipped open the notebook where he was compiling his dragon research. "What were you hoping to learn?"

"I don't know. Something new." Katie sat in her seat with a humph. "I didn't think being a vampire was going to be boring."

Zack waved his arms around at the massive number of books around them. "I'm sure you don't know everything in the library."

She sighed as she dragged the nearest book closer and opened it. "But some of us don't get off on reading musty old pages."

"I don't—"

"Just an expression, Zack. Lighten up." She disregarded him to stare at the page in front of her.

He settled into his own stack of books. Treating the books with care meant not reading things at incredible vamp speed. If he relied on that power, he had a habit of accidentally moving a page with too much strength. He'd ripped more than one page. Whoever was keeping the collection had laid some basic enchantments, and the books had repaired themselves, but he didn't want to tear up books and hope that'd keep happening. Plus, if he overdid his vamp ability, he wound up extra hungry.

However, he didn't take long to work through his current stack of dragon lore. Most of the books kept repeating the same information. The dragons had left the world after making enemies of just about everyone on the planet and spent their time in the fey realms. Mages had a tendency to blame the lack of magical prowess in the world as a fault of the dragons' departure. In their theory, dragons were literal magic made flesh. A shifter philosopher was pretty sure that the Age of Reason had dampened abilities, positing that the increasing population of humans who began to reject the supernatural as part of their reality was creating a psychic field that suppressed all magic.

The theories were great, and he was thinking of starting up a paper, only he wasn't sure where he'd try to get it published or if Seamus would even let him. *One, he'd probably love it if I built a reputation as a scholar. And two, why the fuck should I let him stop me?*

Once again, no Seamus remark.

He took the stack of dragon books and put them back in their original locations the best he could. Then he went into the section he'd discovered the night before.

Turned out that the library did have books on vampires.

Using his mind's eye, he moved through fighting maneuvers. Seamus probably hadn't lied when he said he didn't constantly watch Zack's mind, but Takashi had said that building a mental shield of other thoughts would be good practice. Keeping up the buffer also helped Zack remember his training.

Unfortunately, the book he'd been reading didn't have any answers. He reached for the next, discovered it was in French, and went for the one after that. Flipping open to the title page revealed a stark, serious font that declared, *A Translation and*

Continued Examination of the Theories Proposed by Beatrice the Profane Sorcerer by Edmund Weldrick.

The text was overdramatic, and the author was clearly trying to show off his language skills and vocabulary. Apparently, Beatrice the Profane Sorcerer believed vampires inherently had a connection to the Shadow Realms. Weldrick was adding on that the fey realms were tied to the shadows, which was what made all vampires abominations.

The book was theory without evidence, but Beatrice hypothesized that all vampires should be capable of moving within shadows along with a myriad of other powers. She agreed that the mundane world's attempts to quash magic were working and that even supernatural species were not immune to having their magical abilities clipped. Weldrick claimed that was utterly preposterous—and from there, he began to argue with everything Beatrice had to say.

True power will not return to the world until true dragons return, Beatrice claimed. Weldrick took affront to that and spent three pages describing how his grandfather Ross Weldrick had performed some of the greatest feats of magic in written history.

The flaw in that point was that there was no way Edmund could consult all of written history, and he didn't address the idea that such things could have been written and then lost or that powerful magic could have happened outside of written history. The Wrights and the Gladwells had lost many homes in their fights with supernaturals. Valuable tomes and even personal journals were destroyed nearly every time. That was information about magic lost, and Edmund probably hadn't considered his hunter contemporaries as a source of knowledge. He seemed to put all his respect into mages, and he was making disdainful remarks about warlocks.

"Forgive my intrusion, Master Zackery," Grimsby said smoothly. He was only a few inches away.

Zack jumped. Somehow, he'd missed Grimsby walking up

to him. He scowled upward into Grimsby's thin, bony face. The guy had a habit of popping up. In fact, Grimsby had likely snuck up to him just to test his senses.

"Ah, hello, Grimsby," Zack said, doing his best impression of a chill, powerful vampire. Giving an attitude of no fucks to give took practice, and Zack was pretty sure Grimsby was holding in a laugh. But that might not have been about him. He had that kind of smile a lot.

"Master Anton has requested that I see to your needs this evening, should you have any," Grimsby replied.

"Then I'll call for you if I need anything," Zack replied.

Grimsby clasped his hands behind his back and then admired a nearby shelf.

"Odd that you're hanging around." Zack slowly shut his book. Hopefully, Grimsby didn't know which book he'd been reading. Would he report it to Seamus if he had seen? Zack still wasn't sure where Grimsby's loyalties lay. "I wonder what might make you linger."

"You have discovered an interesting section of the library. One might conclude that you're investigating your own kind, which would be strange considering your upbringing and nature," Grimsby said.

So they were playing the skirt-any-questions dialogue game again. Zack leaned against the bookshelf behind him. Faeries were living creatures, so Grimsby had a heartbeat. It was slower than the average human's and subtler. He couldn't be certain if all of them hid their emotions as well as Grimsby could or if Grimsby was skilled at protecting his feelings from prying minds.

Either way, he had no cheat code for figuring out what Grimsby was up to.

"You could conclude that my education was poorer than people believe," Zack said. "Or that I'm eager to have access to books I've only heard referenced."

"I could." Grimsby trailed his finger along one dust-free

shelf and discovered no evidence that housekeeping had skipped a spot and then grinned at Zack. "I think I would be wrong to assume those answers."

"Yet you're free to do so."

"You're better at concealing your interest, young master," Grimsby said.

"I couldn't possibly know what you mean," Zack said, lifting his chin.

The toothy smile Grimsby gave him told Zack he hadn't thrown him off any. Grimsby drew a book off the shelf. It had a deep blue cover, and he nonchalantly opened the book and drifted his fingers down a page. "Mortals have such limitations in their histories. Their short lifespans make the passing of information from one generation to the next so very vital. If no one repeats an event, it becomes utterly lost within a few years. I believe that to be quite tragic."

"Admittedly, I am sort of looking forward to being a repository for knowledge," Zack said.

Grimsby's smile took on a wistful, sad twist. "Ah, but even your kind may not last forever. You are not impervious to death, only extremely resistant."

Zack tried not to think about Anton's torture room. Denny was still down there. What if Anton managed to make him invulnerable? *Why the fuck am I getting jealous he might gain more power than me instead of upset that my cousin's suffering?* "The same could be said of the fey, Grimsby."

"A keen observation, young master. However, also like yours, pieces may yet remain." Grimsby closed the book and held it out to Zack. "You may find this account enlightening, should you be able to read it."

Slowly, Zack took the book from him. Like the one in his lap, it had no title on the outside. He turned the page to the front. *The Fal of the Undede-Kynge by Thei Who Loved Him*. The words were printed in a stark font. There was a quick note that the text had been copied and printed to the best of the

publisher's ability with a lament that the beautiful illumina-
tions hadn't been able to be transfered. Then the book
launched into a poem that looked like English but had
misspellings and confusing words.

Because it's not Modern English. It's Middle English. Zack
raised his gaze from the book. He was formulating his next
not-question question, but Grimsby was gone.

Okay. For some reason, this book might hold something of
value. He scooped up the Edmund Weldrick book. Part of
him screamed to hide the book. He started to follow the
impulse and then caught himself. His mother had been the
one to insist that books about vampires, particularly fictions,
were a corrupting influence.

But he was already undead. She'd already disowned him.

So what's the point in trying to hide it? Zack pulled the
Weldrick book back from the shelf, slipped it into the same
hand as *The Fal of the Undede-Kynge,* and perused the shelves
for a couple more reads. Takashi might be curious about
these, too. The idea that one of his partners might love
reading as much as him buoyed his spirits, and he indulged
the greatest of whims: book shopping.

CHAPTER 38

By the time Candide returned to the penthouse, Roger and Ezra had cleaned up the living room and had a long, detailed conversation filling each other in on the details of their lives. From the start of the conversation, Candide's penchant for control had been obvious.

But she had been manipulating both of them.

Roger was currently struggling to contain his anger as he combed through two hundred and fifty years of memories of an individual he'd long considered one of his best friends. No, not one of. The only one outside of his own bed and mind he'd ever trusted. And she had hidden truths from him. She had intentionally left Ezra clueless about the events going on around him.

He'd let her take Kit. Thought that was what was best for them.

As much as he longed to, he couldn't throw Kit over one shoulder and Ezra over the other and carry them out. Violating their choices would only tear what little good he might do for them to pieces. And in the case of Kit, he had no grounds. He had kept information from them, too.

If they were within listening distance, they had learned quite a bit about Roger and Ezra. Roger had held back nothing, telling Ezra everything that had happened since their meeting with Dmitri in 1989 through his decision to come to the penthouse that night.

Ezra had shared plenty in return. He'd turned one of Roger's unintentionally abandoned donors and helped her transition both to life as a vampire and life as a woman. Savanna was currently in London, keeping an eye on Ezra's house while she continued a romance with what Ezra asserted was a lovely young mortal who was madly in love with her. Though HT Moss had earned the coven's ire, Savanna's own literary career was growing completely unnoticed by Seamus and the other leadership.

They'd been sitting in companionable silence for about five minutes when Candide strode through the front door with two pets and four of her personal security with her.

Anger stirred in Roger, but it didn't have the power that had built in him before. A cool tide in his mind would grant him the magic he'd done before, but further wrecking her home wasn't on his agenda.

Besides, Ezra had finally put the pages of his manuscript back in order. It'd be rude to throw them around again.

"You'll want to dismiss your security," Roger said hoarsely. He dared to lock his gaze with Candide's. She was colder than ever. That had always been her way, and he usually didn't care. But now he wondered if she had built a wall between them long ago, that he had never seen the true her.

Don't grow paranoid. Don't be like him. Don't hurt those you love. Roger dropped the invitation to the debut party on top of Ezra's manuscript. "I don't think you want them to hear what I might say."

"It seems my abundance of caution is unnecessary. You are

dismissed." Candide turned to her nearest pet, kissed her cheek, and motioned forward. "The two of you as well."

The six mortals departed. The four security guards left the penthouse while the two pets went farther in.

Candide's heels clicked against the hardwood as she otherwise silently walked across the room. With an effortless grace, she sank into the wingback chair that Roger had once owned. She folded her hands together, her elbows on either armrest, and held her head high.

Did she feel the same sense of power he had from it? Or was she, like him, putting on airs in a vain hope to convince herself that she had any control over her own life?

"Well?" She lifted an eyebrow. "How shall we proceed? Shall you drive a stake through me for my supposed misdeeds?"

"God, no," Ezra muttered. "And people think I'm the dramatic one."

Candide tilted her head. "I'm being *dramatic*? Roger practically declares war on the coven, robs Seamus, and then forces his way into my private sanctuary. Then I find the two of you sitting side by side like a pair of judges ready to determine my fate."

"I don't want to hurt you, Candide," Roger said.

She remained perfectly still.

"I don't."

"You bade me to send away my security so that you could speak. What would you have to say?" she demanded.

Ezra leapt to his feet. "My God, this is *Roger*. What's gotten into you?"

Candide looked away.

Her mind was a fortress, but Roger spied telltale signs of where she was covering her emotions the hardest. He knew the touch of that exact mental shield. She was more than obscuring the truth. She was actively hiding something.

His stomach dropped to the ground floor. The Arctic wasn't as cold as his heart was now. "How long have you known what happened to him?"

She dragged in a ragged breath. Small beads of tears formed at the corner of her eyes, but Roger didn't trust her display of emotion. Her mental walls were still formidable. Everything she was doing could be an act. "Since the annual meeting."

Christmas. Three weeks ago. She'd known that long. She'd known that he was ready to tear the world apart to find his love, and she'd said *nothing*.

"*Candide!*" Ezra shoved his hand through his fiery red hair. "How could you keep this from him? From *me*?"

"You and I had an arrangement," Candide replied. She swept her gaze to Roger. "I didn't know what it might do to you, mon cher."

"Don't call me that right now," Roger growled. "What's become of Takashi? Have you seen either of them?"

An agonizing eternity passed, but Candide finally spoke. "I've seen them both. Zack multiple times."

"You knew they'd been kidnapped, and you've seen them, and you didn't say anything to Roger?" Ezra put his hands on his hips. "Love, that is just cruel."

"Cruel would have been telling him what I have seen," Candide snapped. She glared at Ezra rather than look Roger's way. "They were there for the annual meeting. Seamus introduced Zack as his *son*. When, in all our years, has he ever called a fledgling his offspring?"

Roger wiped his hand down his face. Words failed him.

Cold emanated from Candide, and her eyes shifted to a shade of bloodred. Her rage was palpable, and the air around her began to shimmer with a soft red as well. Her aura was visible—to Roger, at least. When he glanced at Ezra, he didn't seem to notice anything different. Though anger colored her, there was a shadowy presence up against her skin. The mystery of what he was beholding was nearly enough to distract Roger.

Her voice drew him back. Her tone was sharp, like a wind-honed icicle. "You have forced your way into my home and assumed I have misled you. I was protecting you both and would have told you everything in time. Because I was not immediately forthright, you want to accuse me of ill motives. Fine. I have weathered worse."

"I came to ask for your help," Roger said, his voice rough. He had been dragged over jagged rocks and left to dry in a blazing sun. The wounds in his soul were gaping, ugly things, and he could sense they would only grow wider. *I must hold myself together.* "I tried to be polite about it."

"You could have called."

"I texted you."

Without breaking her glare, Candide snapped her fingers. A moment later, Dryden stepped into the archway. She issued a command for her phone, and he brought it. She raised her eyebrow as she examined it. "I apologize for missing that."

"You were too busy planning a party for Seamus's captives," Roger said tightly.

"You say they were kidnapped, but I have seen no evidence," Candide declared. "Zack is Seamus's sireling, and he is a formidable one at that. The second name on that invitation, Kathleen, is Takashi's freshly risen fledgling. Anton is toting the girl as his own, but I know the difference in their scents. She smells like Takashi, not Anton. You grow suspicious of me, who has been your friend for centuries, without stopping to think that your dear lovers may be the traitors."

Roger had seen the gut punch comment coming, and yet he sucked in a deep, hurt-filled breath at the words being said aloud. Even after centuries, some mortal habits remained.

"We also know what Seamus is like," Roger said hollowly. A thin hope was keeping him tethered to reality rather than losing himself to the abyss of heartbreak. "He forces others to bend to his will and appear to enjoy being with him. We have behaved that way ourselves many times."

Candide softened, a gentleness crossing her features as she unclenched her jaw. "I know, mon cher. They may be in that Hell, but you should harden yourself in case they are not what you've built of them."

Zack. Takashi. Liars? Roger didn't want to believe that of them. He had been with them for weeks. Had shared a bed and hopes and dreams and scars and wounds. He had held Zack through his pain and turned to Takashi with his own. The best nights of his life were ones with them.

Reflexively, Roger's gaze turned toward the painting hanging on the wall ahead of him. He had believed he'd known James more intimately than Zack and Takashi. They had shared so much, too. And they'd believed themselves deeply in love. Yet Roger had never fully opened himself to James. When James asked him to stand by him, Roger had caved, and James had shown a side of himself that Roger hadn't seen. Their love had withered, and Roger had blamed himself.

But had it been entirely his doing? How well had he known James or any of his lovers? Just as Roger never shared himself, he never dug deeply into them. *Because if I didn't know them, their leaving couldn't hurt as much.*

That hadn't been his approach with Zack and Takashi … had it? Could they have been fooling him?

"I have to see them," Roger whispered. Brokenly, he spun toward Candide. "Will you help me?"

"No," Candide said sternly.

"Bollocks." Ezra held up the invitation. "This debut party is at the Chateau. You can sneak Roger in and out, and no one will be the wiser."

Candide hardened further. "'An intimate gathering' is a lie. Seamus has ordered the Chateau closed to all but the invitees that evening, and he has representatives from other covens on the guest list. This will be a gathering of the most important vampires and their representatives in North America with a slew of international vampires as well. I will not risk your safety or the safety of the others that I love to play friar in Roger's Romeo and Romeo and Romeo production."

She's trying to protect me, too. Roger held his hand to his lips and pushed his renewing anger back to its depths. Though she was as stone-faced as ever, she wasn't being cruel. Candide had relied on her practicality the way he had used his charm. They were survivors, all of them.

Ezra puffed up.

Roger motioned for him to wait. Then he slipped out of his seat and went on one knee before Candide. "Not that long ago, you hoped I had a greater plan than just killing Seamus and Anton. I came here tonight to ask for your help in my war against the coven. I robbed Seamus of every cent I could, and yet, the whole of our coven doesn't seem to know anything has changed. But you mentioned it."

Warily, Candide met his gaze. "I know. You bankrupted the coven's main fund as well. I receive a stipend from them for my operating costs, which did not come. You've made this year much harder, mon cher."

"A wise woman like you will have the resources necessary to keep her establishment afloat," Roger replied.

"True."

Roger held his hand out toward her.

She frowned but placed her hand on his.

Rather than attempting to read her, he released his own tense mental walls. He allowed his fears and anger to swell, not like a raging storm but the inevitable tide within. His desires were there, too, on display for her to take in. "Even if I cannot see them, I will continue my war."

She leaned forward. With her free hand, she pushed one of Roger's short strands of hair away from his face. Then she pressed her forehead to his. "Oh, you love them so, mon cher."

"I do." He tightened his hold. "Now, you have always been the most driven of us. I want my next blow to him to hurt. Guide my blade, Candide. Tell me where to strike."

In silence, they stayed where they were. Roger danced through a plethora of memories, each of her and their friendship. She was right. She was someone he'd trusted for so long. Yet part of him did worry that her ambition would ruin him.

"If you are looking to break his heart, you won't. He doesn't have one." Candide clutched Roger's hand. "If you are looking to break his pride, you know what he loves."

"His mansion," Roger murmured. "Candide, if I am to strike there—"

"Then speaking to your men may be of help." Candide leaned back. "You have a point. And a need. I'll arrange a meeting for you."

"Thank you."

"Thank me if your heart remains whole afterwards. Zack has changed."

No doubt he had. Roger kissed Candide's fingertips and then rose. He kissed her and Ezra on their cheeks before leaving the penthouse.

In the elevator, he collapsed against the wall, his strength leaving for the moment. Zack. A vampire. The consequence of Roger's actions had led to Seamus hurting more people. Always more and more and more. And some new power was within Roger's reach, something he had never considered before.

Burning down Seamus's house would certainly be a statement. If he could do it with his own arcane abilities? Seamus wouldn't be able to hide that. People would talk about the castaway fledgling who dared to ruin his "master's" home.

With international vampires in town, word would quickly spread across the world.

As the elevator reached the ground floor, Roger recovered and smoothed out his jacket. His ragged psyche would heal. He would see Zack and Takashi again in a week's time.

Until then, he had an attack to plan.

CHAPTER 39

The phone lay on the center of the coffee table in Zack's living room, where Takashi had placed it ten minutes before. It was charged. He'd made sure of that these last two weeks. However, he hadn't dared to call anyone from it yet. While his new phone lacked his old one's stored contacts, he had memorized a vital set of numbers.

One was Nell's.

Anton had sent out actual invitations to Zack and Katie's debut party. Either this night or the next, Nell would receive one. If she somehow hadn't heard about what had happened the night of the Winter's Grand Ball, she'd definitely know that something was amiss after that.

Though Takashi had called her a few times before being brought to the mansion, their last in-depth conversation had been months ago in Tennessee. *Of all my sirelings, you have always had a clear vision of the bigger picture,* she had told him. *Keep Roger on track.*

He had failed miserably at that. Would Nell blame him for his lack of foresight? For taking things slow? For falling in love rather than pursuing the objective? She had Josefina, who she was devoted to, but Takashi knew that if Nell had to sacrifice her in order to protect herself, she would. She'd given Eulolia over to a dragon and never looked back.

Despite a vampire's long life, stalling was still a bullshit move. Takashi sighed at himself, then grabbed the phone and headed into the closet where Zack's coffin lay. He dialed. As he pressed the phone against his ear, he leaned back against the door.

"Hello?" Reed, Nell and Josefina's favorite pet, said. Takashi had met him a handful of times, but he never forgot a voice.

"Hello, Reed. It's Takashi. Is our master about?" Takashi tried to keep his tone light.

There was a slight shuffle of noise on the other end, but within seconds, Nell said, "Are you all right?"

Takashi blinked. Nell sounded genuinely concerned for his well-being. "I am ... safe is an overstatement, I'll admit. What do you know?"

"Roger has brought Josefina into his mess," Nell replied. "I hope that he has told her everything."

"He trusts her. I imagine he has." Takashi closed his eyes. He had to focus to listen both to his conversation and for any indication that someone was entering Zack's suite or passing too close. "You've heard what happened at the hotel?"

"Seamus took you and the hunter," Nell said.

"We're at his mansion. The situation has become complicated. Very complicated."

"I appreciate your concern for propriety, but I have been waiting weeks to hear from you. Unless you have ages to speak, forget your trepidations and talk."

Bluntness was one of her better traits. Takashi let the words unspool from him. "The night we were brought to the mansion, Seamus made it clear that if I cooperated, he would be lenient. He doesn't seem to care much about what Roger does, considers him nothing more than a toy. But we had a long conversation about international affairs. I betrayed nothing of your deals or your domain."

"I know you wouldn't," Nell said gently.

"I've been a valued hostage. Better than what happened in London, not quite as nice as what happened in Tokyo in '75." Takashi continued scanning the background for any sign someone was nearby, but so far, no interruption. He decided to skip over remaining to stay in the mansion during Roger's rescue of Dmitri. Nell might not understand his reasons. "What you need to know is that I've created a new sireling, Kathleen. She's shown arcane prowess already. In time, I think she'll be quite strong."

"You are dancing around another point." Nell's voice was sharper. "I can feel it."

"Seamus turned Zack into a vampire. I think—"

"Kill him," Nell commanded.

"We plan to, but Seamus—"

"Not Seamus. Zack."

Words were a scrambled mess in his mind. He hadn't had a chance to explain how strong Zack already was or that Zack would make an excellent leader for the coven. He'd believed that Nell would accept Zack as a vampire without issue.

Instead, she was ordering his death.

"When you put a stake in Zack's heart, whatever portion of Seamus's power is within him follows him into his true grave," Nell continued.

If she learned just how much power resided within Zack, she might dare to send actual assassins.

"Roger's in no position to claim the territory," Takashi said.

"Let the GLC fall to rubble," Nell replied without missing a beat.

She had sunk time and resources into aiding Roger and training Zack. However, she had also pushed Roger to have a timetable, to hurry. If Roger had come back to the city and quickly killed Seamus, his position inside the GLC would have been tenuous. Challengers always rose when one vampire claimed another's position, but Roger would have been swarmed with those who doubted he had any strength since he had been gone for decades.

Civil war was inevitable. The only question was how much of the GLC and its territory would remain when the smoke cleared.

A brilliant, terrible epiphany struck.

Nell hadn't cared about the money she loaned to Roger. What were a few million dollars to an empire of billions? When Zack and Roger moved into her mansion, she must have noticed their attraction for each other. She'd likely known that Zack was never going to turn his blade on Roger. She had noticed that Roger was reluctant to take a stand.

So she had called Takashi, her loyal fledgling, and he had dropped everything to come home to obey her orders. She had told him to be mindful of Zack's temper and intelligence, to be wary that Roger's smiles were false, and that the GLC was full of the worst sort of tricksters. She'd told him to be on his guard, not to allow Roger to come too close to his heart. After the meeting with her, Zack, and Roger, she'd promised that she would gladly bring him back into her coven when the time was right.

If the GLC no longer existed, she would be able to sweep anyone who wanted to join her into her ranks without issue. In fact, she could offer her protection to the willing, and they would likely run into her arms. She would be able to leverage her laws upon newcomers rather than attempt to enforce them upon the unwilling.

Why become a conqueror when she could be a savior?

She had never been satisfied with the size of her domain.

She had never wanted Roger to succeed.

And if all that were true—and it must be; Takashi's gut

and heart were in sync with the horrible realization—then something that had bothered him made terrible sense.

After all, Roger had been in a coma in the heart of her sanctuary for over thirty years. She'd known about the coffin and done nothing? Just allowed an unknown vampire to sleep in the basement of one of her citizens? No. No, that wasn't like her.

The whole world had known that Seamus was looking for Roger. It had been one of the hottest pieces of gossip in every coven Takashi had visited. Seamus's international reputation had suffered, and speculation had run rampant. Everyone —*everyone*—had considered it an inside job, that most likely Roger had finally run away. Until Takashi saw him again, he was certain of the same. Very few knew the truth about the magical coma.

But how better to destabilize a powerful neighbor than to make one of his favorite playthings disappear into thin air? To wait out the years, knowing that the perfect pawn was slumbering well within arm's reach? And when the time was right, release that pawn to create absolute chaos in order to finally bring down that enemy.

Nell had sent him with Roger, counting on Takashi to be who he was and Roger to be himself and for their connection to never run deeper than a few good rolls in the bed. If not for Zack, Takashi would have kept his heart sealed away. They both would have.

"What was his name?" Takashi asked, his voice dry.

"Whose name?" Nell said carefully.

"The pretty fey you convinced to put Roger to sleep," Takashi replied.

"I don't know what you mean."

Takashi knew that tone of voice. He'd heard it many times over the last hundred years. She was lying. "How long have you been planning to kill Zack for interfering with your schemes?"

Nell said nothing, which spoke volumes.

Being right should have felt pleasant, but Takashi only had a coldness growing in his gut. "He completely ruined your timetable by waking Roger early, didn't he?"

"What do they know?" Nell asked icily.

"Nothing. I only just figured it out myself," Takashi replied. He heard footsteps in the hallway, so he lowered his voice. "I thought you cared for humans, at the very least for our kind."

"I *do*," Nell snapped. "That is the reason the GLC must be destroyed. There is no purging the rot when everything has been infected. Zack will be an unfortunate casualty, but the lives saved in the end will be in the thousands. Hundreds of the thousands.

"Stake him. Grab your sireling. Come home. I can hide you until Seamus is finally ashes. We can work together to establish control over the GLC's territory the right way."

Which would put Takashi right back where he started, under her thumb, never to hold true power. Never to be the one who made the decisions that mattered.

Never again to hold the two men he loved.

The outer door to the suite was opening.

"I have to go."

"Takashi—"

He ended the call and placed the cell phone into Zack's unused coffin, gently opening and closing the lid. Then he strode out into the bedroom and headed for the living room.

Zack interrupted him by walking through the bedroom door. He was making a beeline for his desk, and he was practically glowing with a chipper energy. In his hands was a stack of eight books that he balanced effortlessly. He danced around Takashi and continued on. New vampires had a habit of moving too quickly when they were excited. Zack had never shown that habit, but he was doing so now.

"I thought you'd be stuck in party planner mode until

dawn." Zack sat the stack on his desk and dug in the drawers to pull out a pen and a fresh notebook.

"We've settled on everything important," Takashi remarked as he casually walked over to Zack. "Anton is talking of having another party here at the mansion in a few weeks."

"Let me guess, he wants to throw a 'bloody Valentine's Day' party with like actual hearts in jars."

"I reminded him that dismembered body parts were gauche these days. Where did you find these?" Takashi laid his hand on the top book.

"The massive library that younger me would have sold his soul to find." Zack paused. "Okay, maybe that's not that funny since I let a demon in my dreams. I'm still not sure who's curating it. Maybe Grimsby."

"The infamous fey butler I have yet to meet?"

Zack scowled at him. "You've seen him."

Takashi raised an eyebrow.

"He's eight feet tall, sort of looks like a skeleton with skin, extremely thin. I've seen you and him in the same room," Zack replied petulantly.

Kill him, Nell had ordered.

Perhaps because she'd issued the command, or perhaps because he had already tumbled off the tightrope of keeping a level head, Takashi was certain that he had never loved Zack harder than he did in that moment. His excitement, his energy, his everything called to Takashi in a way that was deeper than his soul. Zack was a missing piece of him.

"He must be using an illusion on himself," Takashi said softly.

"Then why do I get to see him but you don't?"

Takashi shrugged with one shoulder. "You're the son of the master of the house, and I'm, at best, a guest?"

Zack scrunched his nose in such a perfect, utterly him way that Takashi hoped he would see him continue to do so for the next five hundred years or more. The movement was brief, reflexive, and gone by the time Zack turned his gaze toward Takashi. Zack narrowed his eyes and tilted his head. "What's up?"

"Hm?"

"You're doing a lot of intense staring."

Takashi wrapped his arms around Zack and tugged him closer. "It's been a while since I've seen you excited and happy like this."

Just as Takashi was about to kiss him, Zack put a finger on Takashi's lips and pushed him back an inch. Intelligence sharpened Zack's ruby-red eyes. "You're hiding something. You have that whole 'keeping a secret' vibe."

"Don't worry about it," Takashi murmured.

Zack's gaze hardened to a glare. "I thought we agreed not to hide shit from each other."

The last thing Takashi wanted to do was declare that Nell was not someone they could trust. The revelation would have to be shared, but Seamus might read Zack's mind. If Seamus learned, he might launch an all-out war on Nell, and that would cause far more death than Takashi wanted.

Of course, not telling Zack was a risk as well. Takashi didn't doubt that Nell was figuring out how to put assassins in place to destroy Zack.

They won't reach him tonight.

"I learned something upsetting," Takashi whispered, "but I don't want to ruin this mood of yours. I want to cherish it and you. Please?"

"You promise to tell me?"

"Yes. In a while." Takashi rested his hand on the stack. "What did you find in the library, lover?"

"I've been digging into dragons for the most part. No luck on demon deals yet, but I've also been reading up on our kind. Everything Seamus put in my room is all 'vampires are the supreme predators.' The library has whole shelves on what vampires can be like." Zack twisted around, remaining in Takashi's loose hold but facing his books. "Mom would've called this propaganda. There's this one book by Edmund Weldrick that's a translation of another—do you know Italian?"

"No." Takashi stepped behind him and slid his arms around Zack from behind into a more complete embrace. "Weldrick, as in the mage who began mage circles?"

"His grandson. He spends most of this book arguing against the theories of Beatrice the Profane Sorcerer," Zack rattled on. "She's confident that when the dragons left our world, real magic started to fade."

Takashi kissed behind Zack's ear, then his neck, while Zack continued to speak. Hearing him so excited, so thrilled at the prospect of learning, was invigorating. "A theory she's still teaching."

"Still?" Zack straightened, which neatly lowered Takashi's right hand to be over his cock. "She's still alive?"

"A few practitioners have figured out how to slow their age. She's one of a dozen, perhaps." Takashi nibbled on Zack's ear, careful not to touch his fangs to his tender skin. "She lives in Southern France these days."

"I would *love* to talk to her. Do you know her? Like, well enough to call her up?" Zack asked. He gasped when Takashi stroked his thumb down the length of his clothing-covered dick and squirmed as Takashi slid his other hand under his shirt. "And what are you up to?"

"Do you have any idea how incredibly hot you are when you're a bubbling fount of knowledge?" Takashi murmured in his ear. He pressed a kiss to his jaw and another right beside the first.

"All right," Zack said slowly, his natural skepticism turning into a slow squirming in Takashi's arms. He leaned his head farther to the side, and Takashi continued kissing and nipping him. "I read this whole book that theorized that nest vampires aren't actually related to ancient vampires like Nell or Seamus at all. And I found this other theory that all born shifters are actually descended from dragons, which I don't think makes a lot of sense, considering there are born shifters who can spread their ability to regular people through infection. And—*ah*."

Takashi grinned against Zack's neck. He'd unbuttoned Zack's fly and was pulling his zipper down slowly. As he eased Zack's underwear down enough to release his hardening cock, he nudged his own still-covered member against his backside. Zack gave a longer groan and laid his head back against Takashi's shoulder.

"What have you found out about dragons?" Takashi asked.

"Hard to think that they're still real and the family journals never mentioned them," Zack murmured. He drifted his hand down Takashi's arms until his hands rested over his. His fingertips brushed against the between places of Takashi's knuckles and remained there. "But then our records only go back about two hundred years. At least my family's. Dragons have been gone since the 1300s, though there are some—ah, yes, do that again—sightings and lore later on that get written off as folklore and fiction. I guess—*mmm*—I guess—hey ..."

Takashi took his hand off Zack's cock and used both hands to undo the buttons of Zack's shirt. He nibbled on him. "Keep going."

"Fine," Zack pouted. He perked up when Takashi turned him around and pressed him up against the desk. Then he swore, twisted enough so he could scoot the books out of proximity of his ass, and braced himself against the desk.

Takashi chuckled against his neck, then kissed his way down as he went to his knees in front of him. As he planted one kiss against Zack's hip, he murmured, "You were saying? About the dragons being gone?"

"Me rambling is really doing it for you?"

"Yes." Takashi placed a kiss close to the base of Zack's shaft. His own cock was hard, pressing against his pants and straining the material, but he was content to leave himself waiting. Slowly, he licked a line up the underside of Zack's dick. "You're not talking."

"Sorry," Zack breathed out. "Kinda distracted."

Takashi risked a glance up, and the heat in Zack's eyes was a blaze that warmed Takashi's heart. He had dulled his psychic sense to protect Zack from his own fears and, in turn, had lessened his ability to feel Zack's lust. He dared to open himself a fraction, and the flood of Zack's desire rocked him backward.

Zack reached down and gently threaded his fingers through Takashi's hair. His smile turned smug. "Now you're distracted."

"Can't blame me. I like looking at my very attractive, smart boyfriend," Takashi replied.

"I'll start talking when your mouth starts working," Zack teased.

"All right, then." Takashi smiled up at him, and the joy in Zack's face made his heart swell.

And Nell would rob him of Zack. Would have him ruin everything he had spent his whole life wishing for and the last three months actively working to build so that she could destroy the Great Lakes Coven and add more to her own empire.

Takashi had been a fool to think she was satisfied ruling from her sanctuary without ambition. He had traveled the world, had spoken with countless vampires. None of them were ever sated. Why had he believed she was different? Because she claimed it?

If not for Zack tugging him into bed with Roger, Takashi might have remained Nell's loyal lieutenant. She was the best of the masters he knew.

But she never saw him as more than an assistant.

Roger and Zack had seen more in him. He had known Roger was his chance at freedom. But Zack?

Zack was always the surprise.

Zack tapped one finger against the end of Takashi's nose. "When I get older, am I going to get lost in my own head all the time?"

Wanting to seize the moment he was living, Takashi pushed aside his worries. He had meant his words when he declared he intended to cherish Zack. His grin returned. "Perhaps not. But you'll likely learn patience."

"I can be patient, if it's worth the time," Zack replied.

"Mm. I'll make sure it is." Takashi leaned forward again, sighing happily as Zack threaded his hand into his hair once more, and began to kiss near the root of Zack's cock. With one hand, he kept him pinned against the desk. The other he used to slowly stroke Zack. Between kisses, he added, "You're supposed to be telling me about what you learned."

"There are seven kinds of dragon," Zack said quickly. A moan underscored his words, as if ready to erupt with the right pressure. "Earth, air, water, fire—those are the obvious ones. Then there's radiant, umbral, and spirit. I swear spirit's just a catch-all term for 'we built everything around elements.' They like their hoards—material, people, land, anything that can be stockpiled."

Takashi hummed as he began to lick Zack's member in long slides. Whenever he reached his tip, he brushed it against his lips, teasing that he might draw it into his mouth, but he didn't.

Zack groaned throatily and nudged forward. Takashi put a little more pressure into his hold on him. Zack could've overpowered him, but he didn't, choosing to remain against the desk.

"There's this guy who thought all the gods might be dragons," Zack said. Soft moans interrupted his speech. "Because of their magic and their shapeshifting. It'd be a good scam.

Just convincing people you're so powerful you deserve the best of their stuff? And some people think that they're from another dimension entirely. That they brought life with them —and Takashi, *please*, I need to feel more of your mouth than that."

With a little laugh and a devious idea, Takashi spun Zack around. He spread his cheeks and licked close to his hole. Zack held on to the desk with both hands and whined loudly. His pleas turned into a loud, grateful moan when Takashi pushed his tongue into his hole. But Zack had stopped talking, so Takashi slipped his tongue out and rested his cheek against Zack's butt cheek, nose brushing along his sensitive skin.

"Oh, come *on*," Zack complained.

"I like the sound of your voice," Takashi murmured. He kissed Zack tenderly.

"It's taking all my fucking control not to spin around and pin you to the fucking floor and fuck you," Zack said, his voice going low and rough.

A sliver of ethereal quality echoed in his words, bringing out a deeper resonance that went straight to Takashi's already hard cock. He started to reach for his own cock but stopped. *Not yet.* "You still have that control, though," he whispered. "So, talk."

Zack moaned in frustration and dipped his head. His body was tense, long, beautiful lines of muscle. The desk cracked, just a little, and he spat out, "The world got populated."

Takashi continued probing him, pushing his cheeks wider apart so he could spear him further.

"*Ah.* Fuck, yes. I'm talking, I'm talking, don't you dare fucking stop!" Zack growled. He pushed his ass back toward Takashi, which Takashi took and used to his advantage. Zack's interspersed moans were hungrier, more demanding. "Mortals got smarter. Other supernaturals got jealous. And dragons are living magic. Every part of them can channel great power. So they were hunted, their own magic used against them. When their numbers got too low, dragons made a pact with the fey and disappeared to their realms. Mostly. Some stayed, apparently. And I am so fucking done with talking."

Zack's words were warning enough, but his desire went from a liquid pressure to a solid force. He whirled and caught Takashi off guard with his speed and strength. Effortlessly, he trapped Takashi against the floor, body over his, and kissed him with a needy, demanding tongue. He was overwhelming in every way.

Takashi let go of his control. He was in Zack's hands.

Zack was quick to strip him bare. Somehow, losing his clothes felt like baring his soul, though that could have been from the way Zack raked his gaze over him. A feral light was in his ruby-red eyes, and he was possessive in his kiss. Takashi opened to him, spreading his legs when Zack spat on his hand and then spread his spit on his own cock. It wasn't nearly enough to ease the push of his cock into Takashi, but Takashi liked the burn. He arched and relished how Zack tugged his hair to pull his head even farther back.

Zack nipped his neck, his ear, his shoulders—everything within easy reach of his mouth. His fangs bruised and pierced, but the wounds healed nearly as soon as they were made.

Their rhythm was slow at first. Zack was having to push, thick and full and stretching Takashi. Takashi wrapped his legs around Zack's waist.

"Yes," Takashi whimpered, leaning into Zack's hand still in his hair. Every little movement of Zack's brushed against some part of him, inside or out, and tears formed at the corners of his eyes. It was too much and not enough.

Then he was stretched enough that Zack slammed into him, deeper and deeper.

Zack tapped into his supernatural strength and speed, and all Takashi could do was hold on and ride every fucking wave of pleasure that pounded him. He spent across his chest, splashing Zack as well, and yet Zack wasn't done.

Taken apart, put back together, apart, and finally, the bliss-filled void with only one thought. *I never want to lose him.*

Eventually, time and space had meaning. Zack was curled over him, an arm slung over his chest despite the mess, and he rested his head against Takashi's shoulder. Lazily, he grinned at him. "There you are."

"You fucked my brains out," Takashi replied. He was a mess inside as well as out. Zack had come at some point after he'd lost connection with reality. "They take a while to come back."

"I should start timing." Zack had a devious note in his voice. "See how long I can make it last. I've got eternity to perfect it."

The sentence rubbed the raw place in Takashi's mind. *Kill him*, Nell had said. As if destroying him should be easy. As if Takashi should simply obey her, no questions asked.

"You're pulling back." Zack scowled at him. He propped himself up enough to look down at Takashi. Worry filled his red eyes. "What's wrong?"

Slowly, Takashi reached up and pushed a strand of Zack's hair back. Hiding the truth would leave him exposed. He offered Zack his wrist. "Drink."

Zack's scowl tightened. "Takashi—"

"I don't want you to doubt what I feel for you when I tell you what I've learned," Takashi replied seriously.

Carefully, Zack turned Takashi's wrist so the angle was better for his mouth. He planted a kiss on his skin, then bit. His fangs sliced with only a hint of pain, and blood quickly welled. He sucked on the wound.

After only two swallows, Zack pulled away. Dark blood was on his lip, and he licked it quickly. A fresh uncertainty was in his eyes, but not the worry of someone who feared for their relationship. No, this was what Takashi felt. The fear that someone might be truly a piece of him.

When Zack met Takashi's gaze, his ruby-red eyes softened. He stroked Takashi's hair. "You love me. I love you, too. Now, what has you freaked-out?"

"Nell wants me to kill you," Takashi said quickly.

Zack stilled, no breath, nothing, and a long moment passed before he said, "You aren't hers to command. You belong to the GLC."

"I belong *with you*," Takashi whispered. "With Roger and whomever else we declare as ours."

"You do." Zack kissed his temple, then his lips gently. "Was that all Nell wants? Not that my death's a small thing to demand."

"No." And Takashi told Zack everything about what Nell had done to Roger.

CHAPTER 40

Memories of James and of the early nights with Zack continued to haunt Roger as he made his way west to the old dance studio. In the weeks since their takeover of the brick building, they had neatened the exterior. The large windows at the front of the building revealed a room that they hadn't used yet, preferring instead to use the secondary dance studio room for their practice and planning. The location was supposed to be a secret, and with everything happening, no one had made cleaning the bigger front studio room a priority. Anyone peering closely would see the traces of light in the back of the building, but obscuring the windows more than the dust, dirt, and ragged curtains did would also be a sign of use.

Roger saw a figure moving through the deep shadows of the front room. Josefina was slipping through to the side door, so Roger went around the building and met her at it. She had her phone against her ear, but she paused to scrutinize him. She asked, "What's happened?"

"Plenty." Roger nodded at her phone. "Who's that?"

"Nell."

"Talk to her. I'll fill you in later."

Josefina nodded and continued down the alleyway until she was nearly at the end of the block.

Steeling his nerves, Roger went into the building.

The melody of conversation mingled with the tempo of the thuds and clinks of exercise. Roughly a dozen different voices, the largest number of people in their makeshift head-quarters, had gathered. His allies had brought in others to aid in their fight. They needed fellow fighters if their revolution was to succeed, so their building had turned into a training ground as well as a war room.

Roger put his hand to Zack's necklace and let the touch of metal reconnect him to his body. Each gem was a polished, edged bump. Sliding into his demeanor that Zack had once called Aloof Vampire, he strode into the training room.

Amber was sparing with Janiyah on a set of mats. One of the hunters Thomas had called in, Lacey, was observing them. Lacey was a woman in her early thirties who had light brown skin and a cheerful and detail-oriented disposition. She had one of the infamous Wright blades tucked into its sheath on her hip and tended to dress in black. Three of the revolution's vampire recruits were sitting on the floor between the practice mats and the mirrors. All were closely watching the fight.

In a corner of the room, they had set up a few tables and chairs. Sometimes, Roger brought his information there to lay out and discuss with the others. For the last few nights, Roger and Thomas had been laboring over their lists of potential targets.

Tonight, Dmitri sat in one of the chairs, and he bore a pensive expression as he watched the three men before him. Two were men that Roger didn't recognize. One was a shorter man with light brown hair and a wand sticking out of his back jeans pocket. The other was a taller man who had full tattoo sleeves on both arms. A gray tabby cat was twisting around his ankles.

The third was Thomas. His black backpack was resting on

one table, the zipper open, and he was writing quickly in his leather-bound journal as the three men continued speaking. The pinch of his brow as he focused was nearly identical to Zack's.

Zack will never grow old. Weeks ago, when the realization had struck Roger that Zack was truly mortal and would age, he had hated the idea of a world where Zack was no longer with him because he had lived the course of his mortal life. Roger had offered to turn Zack into a vampire, but Zack had soundly refused him. Spending time with Thomas had led him to regard Zack's mortal future wistfully. It had been a thread of hope he'd clung to.

But Zack had died in the hotel, and now in his undead, immortal life, he would never grow into an old man. He'd be twenty forever. No gray hair, no laugh lines, no possibility for mortal children. Until meeting Thomas, these things had seemed like the portents of death.

Now, that far-off day would never be. A sliver of grief was a splinter in Roger's heart, and the mere act of standing and beholding Thomas was like pressing his finger squarely on the wound.

Dmitri spotted Roger first. Roger's attempt to remain distant must have cracked—or perhaps Dmitri knew him too well—because Dmitri slightly frowned at him, and an unspoken question filled his eyes.

Roger pulled himself from the brink of his grief and smoothed his expression once more. He crossed the room to Thomas and his two companions. Despite Dmitri's closeness, the three didn't seem to be in conversation with him.

"Ah, there you are," Thomas said as Roger neared. He gestured to the two men beside him. "Roger, let me introduce you to Bastian Stone and Noah Clarke-Coldwell. Bastian's an exorcist and technically in the Greater Circle of the Unyielding. Noah is a warlock from Artie Pendragon's Burrow. Do you know Artie?"

Basic conversation wasn't what Roger had prepared for. He mentally fumbled, gathered himself, and pushed away his shock. "I think I've come across something about the Burrow in my recent research. Artie is Arthur Warren?"

"Yeah," Noah replied.

"It's been some time, but I've met him," Roger said. "Thomas, could I have a word?"

"Sure." Thomas set down his pen.

Josefina was still out in the alleyway, so Roger led Thomas farther into the building. The studio had once boasted three different dance classrooms. The last one was significantly smaller than the other two and was beside the short hallway that led to a storage room, an office, and two bathrooms. What had been the office had two cots set up in it, and recently, Amber and Thomas had stayed there. Thomas was still looking for an apartment.

He'd need to be able to sleep in that room. Roger couldn't bear the idea of making Thomas's life harder than he had already. So, he led him into the third classroom. The only light was what came from the hallway.

As soon as they were alone, Roger's mind blanked of words entirely. What series of sounds would be the correct ones to tell Thomas that his son, and one of the men holding a piece of Roger's heart, was now one of the creatures Thomas spent his life killing? Would he even accept his boy? Would telling Thomas destroy the fragile alliance Roger was attempting to build with willing hunters?

"Candide knew something about what's happening to Zack, didn't she? That's why you've got your Serious Vamp face on," Thomas said quietly. His voice was rough, a raw emotion filling the gaps between his words. A hint of his terror for Zack's well-being hung in the air like the faint reminder of sun on pavement just after dark.

For once, Roger was glad that hunters had invented a

tattoo that blocked vampiric abilities. He wasn't sure he could have taken the full weight of Thomas's fear.

"She did," Roger murmured. He didn't want his words to carry any farther than Thomas's ears. "Zack's a vampire. Seamus turned him."

Thomas began to collapse, and only Roger's supernatural speed allowed him to grab him before he fell. Clutching on painfully, Thomas choked out, "When?"

"He rose by Christmas. He likely died in the initial attack," Roger said quickly.

"We never had a chance to save him," Thomas whispered hoarsely.

Roger tightened his grip on Thomas's arms and forced him to stand a little straighter so that he had an easier time glaring into the man's eyes. "He still exists, and he still needs us to free him from that tyrant."

Thomas regained his balance and shoved Roger away. "Do you have any idea what his mother will do when she finds out? What Cal will do?"

"We can deal with that after we've freed him and Takashi," Roger said.

"So you can live your vampire happily ever after?" Thomas demanded, his voice growing in volume. He thrust a hand out toward the second classroom where the others were. "We're training *vampires* to be more deadly. How long until you turn that on the rest of us?"

The grief that had walled away Roger's rage cracked and became a torrent in the downpour, washing him clean of pain. Anger took its place, but he would not let it break him. He clenched his fist, held his ground, and glared at Thomas. "You are in shock. I do not blame you for that. But do not use this as an excuse to backslide to your bullshit beliefs."

"My 'bullshit beliefs'?" Thomas snapped. He took a step closer to Roger. "I have had my time to investigate you. You are no fucking saint. The Gladwell Massacre. The slaughter of my grandfather and his people in Indiana. Your reputation as a seducer, drawing in the naïve to become pawns in your master's coven."

"I had no choice in any of that," Roger replied.

"Oh? None? You could have walked into the fucking sun. You could have run—"

"I tried!" Roger screamed. "I ran from him. I skirted his law. I ignored his wishes until I pushed him to his limit and he reminded me of what I was. *His*. Not some treasured sireling, but his fucking toy. A *thing*. And I thought I could stand. Zack and Takashi gave me the courage. Without them, I would have caved when I returned to the city. I know that now."

"Boo hoo," Thomas spat out. "You would've partied and had your fill of sex and blood. How pitiful for you."

"My choices were stripped from the moment he sank his fangs into me. You have no idea what it took to *survive*."

"I know I'd rather die than suffer under some fucking brute for hundreds of years," Thomas declared.

"You know *nothing* about what you would do in my position." The floorboards shook out from Roger. His inner tides were roaring in his ears, stronger than Thomas's heartbeat by a thousandfold. The pain and anger were too much. He had been holding it so tight to his chest.

Roger straightened to his full height, gladly glaring down at Thomas. A coldness overcame his voice. "Seamus never calls his sirelings his children, but he's done so with Zack. He must have read Zack's journal and believed he needed a father."

The words had the vicious, sharp edge he'd sought, and Thomas stepped back as if he'd been physically struck. His eyes went wide, and he paled.

And except for his eyes, he looked just as Zack had after the party where he killed Quinn. Zack had been in deep pain, and Roger had dared to be vulnerable with him because he was certain Zack was sweet and kind and wonderful. Seeing Thomas brought that back to mind, and it was a dagger to Roger's heart.

Too caught up in their wounds, neither said a word. They stared at each other, horror and agony digging new trenches into their souls.

There was a shuffle of sound, the lightest scrape of shoes against wood floor, and a caught breath. Roger shook himself once and slid his attention to the doorway.

Vincent was watching them. He had one hand on the fraying doorframe and one in a tight fist against his chest. His eyes were wide as saucers, and his mouth hung open. Time slowed. The world whirled on, and yet the three of them were frozen for a fraction of a moment that was its own eternity.

Then tears rolled from Vincent's eyes. An intense burst of the want for revenge struck Roger like lightning to a mast. Vincent spun on his heel and ran.

Thomas was still in shock. Roger wasn't about to apologize for his words, and he knew of nothing to say to him. And Vincent's desire for revenge was odd. It had a different touch than the one he'd been nursing the last few weeks.

Roger took off after him, following him into the lit classroom. "Vincent!"

Vincent was heading for the side door.

With a burst of speed, Roger cut him off. He stood in his way, dodging to keep in front of him when he made to move past him. The room had already fallen into stunned silence before their entry. Everyone's focus was on the two of them.

"Get out of my way!" Vincent shouted.

"I'm not letting you run out into the night like this," Roger replied.

"Like you fucking care! I'm not your precious Zack!"

"You matter to me." Roger held his arms wide when Vincent tried to duck past him again. Thankfully, his vampire speed gave him an advantage over Vincent's wily dexterity. The air began to smell of ozone. "Once you calm down—"

"Fuck calm!" Vincent slammed his palm against his own chest. "I was good! I obeyed. I did awful ... I ... He ... Promised me! He promised over and over that if I was good, he'd turn me!" He choked out a sob and took two steps back. Something cracked in the near distance, but Roger didn't take his eyes off Vincent. "I never stopped him. Never raised my voice. I asked him. I asked *once* for him to do what he said. And he beat me and left me for dead in a fucking bathroom. But he turned Zack? *Zack*? Zack never had to ... Never ... I *let* Seamus do things to me ... Never fought him. Never disobeyed ... I was good!"

The ache in Vincent's unsaid words echoed the abyss that Roger tried to cover in pretty words and sly smiles. But the thin layer of veneer was cracked, and the rot beneath the boards was there, longing to be purged with fire. Roger swallowed a thick cry of his own pain. The seas within him surged, and he felt his mind dragged along with the power.

Others in the room were moving, and their motion distracted Vincent and drew Roger's attention. Lacey began to usher her students toward the front room. The vampires, including Janiyah, quickly ran with liquid speed. Amber hesitated, sending fraught glances between Vincent and Thomas, who was emerging from the back.

Bastian, the tattooed mage, locked gazes with Noah, the warlock. Noah nodded once, a slight jerk of his head, and both pulled out wands.

Dmitri was gaping. Utter surprise was not an expression Dmitri had often.

The lights flickered throughout the room. Vincent was breathing rapidly. His heart was racing. As Noah and Bastian started to raise their wands, he screamed at the top of his voice, "I'm not the problem!"

The mirrors cracked, spiderweb fractures crawling across

their surfaces. Roger could feel the tides of his mind swelling and roiling within him. He had no clue what the mage and warlock were planning. Worse, he had no idea what to do with the surge of power in him. As soon as he'd noticed his power in Candide's penthouse, it had died away. This time, it wasn't doing that.

"He's right. It's me," Roger said. "Don't hurt him."

Bastian cast a sideways glance at Roger that became a full look as he pivoted. "*Shit.*"

"We're not going to hurt anyone," Noah promised. "But Vincent, buddy, you have got to breathe. Do it with me now, come on. One …"

"Fuck you!" Vincent howled. Every mirror in the room shattered to the floor.

Roger's vision swam, and the world changed color. Bastian's tattoo sleeves burst into vibrant color while a bright white aura emanated from him. A similar aura sprang to life around Noah, while soft, yellowy-orange auras encircled Amber, Thomas, and Lacey. Bastian's cat shimmered as if it had pearlescent strands in its fur.

Dmitri was bathed in a red aura, but the rainbow symbol glowed faintly against his chest. The glimmer of the shifting colors caught Roger's eye for a fraction of a second.

Then his attention returned to Vincent. A neon rainbow aura pulsed from him, each color striping out from him at a faster and faster pace, nearly becoming a white light.

"Fuck all of you!" Vincent slammed his foot on the floor. The building groaned as a shock wave went through it.

Bastian cast a glance up toward the ceiling. "Mundanes need to get out of here. Now!"

"Because God forbid anyone ever know anything painful!" Vincent continued. "He hurt me over and over and over, and *he's calling Zack his son.* I thought he was joking. He was putting together this whole room, and I thought … I thought maybe … It should have been *mine!*"

A wind was kicking up, dust and debris rising into the air. Mirror shards whipped around the room. Amber screamed as Lacey yanked her backward. Thomas reached out for his daughter, and a shard sliced into his arm.

Dmitri blurred, grabbing Amber and Lacey, and hurried the three into the back of the building. There was an exit back there, covered in debris of what had been a storage room, and crashes happened as things were tossed to the side and out of the way.

"Vincent, I know your pain," Roger said, calling out through the rising storm. "I know what he's done. I know about his broken promises. You aren't alone."

"Yes I am! No one wants me!" Vincent returned.

"Screw this," Noah muttered. He began to move, the tip of his wand glowed with a dull blue light. "Dor—"

A flash of seeing Takashi fall to the floor in the hotel room struck him. Takashi's neck had been snapped. He would have been fine, but to see him crash to the floor was still the visual of his lover collapsing dead in the moment.

Roger had failed too many times. He wouldn't again.

Instinct kicked in, and with a cry, a blast poured out from him, like the pressure of steam screaming through a kettle. A burst of white light jumped out of him, heading for Noah.

"Defluito!" Bastian called out.

An invisible dart flew into the ball of white light, and it popped harmlessly in the air, never reaching Noah.

"—mi nunc!" Noah finished. A bolt of blue flashed from the end of his wand and struck Vincent in the temple.

Vincent's eyes rolled upward, into the back of his head, before his eyelids fluttered shut. The radiating neon rainbow faded to a dull gray, and he sank toward the floor.

Roger rushed over to him and caught him. Vincent didn't rouse as Roger hoisted him into his arms.

The rolling, tossing waves were growing higher, and Roger had no desire to do anything other than ride the current. Logic was a distant call, an echo of reasonability that his rage drowned before it could truly reach him.

Thomas had called these strangers. And these strangers had hurt Vincent, who had trusted him.

The cold of the shadows seeped up through him.

"What. Did. You. Do?" Roger roared. Tendrils of shadow answered his call and began to rise from the floor.

"Shit," Noah said, eyes going wide. He danced backward with a grace Roger might have admired if his anger wasn't overwhelming every thought. He aimed his wand at Roger.

Bastian knocked Noah's wand downward and kept the tip of his own pointed at the corner of the room. "He's fine. He just needs to grab control."

Control. What had control gotten him? What had patience won him? A murdered lover who was bound to the monster who had made his nights living hells and another lover who might have been a traitor in his bed.

Roger snarled. The shadows coiled at his thought. They only needed direction.

"Roger!" Dmitri called. "Listen to him! Vincent is asleep! That's all!"

With a feral growl, Roger pivoted toward Dmitri. The rainbow sigil on his chest shone in gentle, shifting colors, and the sight of it brought to mind the rainbows of his mortal days. A long-distant memory flickered through his mind, and he saw Dmitri standing on the edge of the ship with a breathless laugh on his lips. He hadn't seen a rainbow in ages. He loved their light. "*A promise that the rain will leave us new*," Dmitri had declared in his thick Russian accent. The wind had tossed his hair, and Roger had known love.

"You are better than this," Dmitri said in the present.

I am. I have to be. The shadows of centuries clung to him, but Roger pushed them away like he had that first brush of love. He was not his rage. His anger was a vent upon the ocean floor, spewing heat, but the pocket was not endless, nor did it have to dictate the motion of the waves. He eased the way he gripped that sharp piece of his soul, and the shadowy tendrils melted into the floor.

Josefina stepped through the doorway leading from the side entrance. Her eyes had the remnants of tears. She took in the room and demanded, "What is going on?"

"Oh, nothing," Bastian drawled, "just two practitioners coming into their powers."

CHAPTER 41

Roger set Vincent on Thomas's cot in the small room and moved to stand in the doorway. He leaned his back against the frame and crossed his arms over his chest. His inner sea continued to churn. There was something agitating it, but so far as he could tell, his anger wasn't the source.

Thomas had disappeared with Lacey and Amber, though since valuable belongings remained, Roger assumed they would be back at some point. Likely, Thomas wanted privacy as he discussed with his daughter and cousin what had happened to Zack.

Josefina had seen that the building wasn't crashing down and declared she was taking the other vampires back to their residences with an attitude so cold Roger knew something was wrong with her.

That left Noah, Bastian, and Dmitri.

And Bastian's gray tabby cat, who strode underneath Roger's legs and entered the room as if they owned the place. They sat at the end of the cot and watched Vincent with feline intensity.

A familiar scent drifted on the air. Roger took a deeper

sniff, but it fell apart underneath the overpowering aromas of dust, wood, sweat, and cat.

Dmitri stepped into the hall. At a soft, gentle volume, he said, "Bastian would like a word."

Roger could hear the end of the conversation happening in the second classroom, though it was muffled to near silence. In the relative silence of the building, Roger shouldn't have had a problem eavesdropping. They must have used a spell, but his hearing was sharp enough to pierce it.

"I have to take this back to Pendragon," Noah said fiercely. "It's one thing allying ourselves with a vampire who wants to fuck up the status quo. It's an entirely different thing to throw our lot in with a vampire warlock who could be using us to stage a coup."

"I don't think he's like that," Bastian replied. "You saw how he didn't have control over his magic. He's new at this."

Noah sighed, his frustration clear. "Look, I think backing Roger is the right move, but I can't speak for the whole community. Pendragon has to weigh in."

"*You* could still work with him, even if Pendragon won't ally the Burrow."

"And that is a whole other conversation I have to have. With my husband," Noah replied. "Which, knowing him, he'll say yes, but I still have to talk to him. Plus, I'm fucking tired. Do you have this?"

"How long will the sleep spell last?" Bastian asked.

"I infused it to run a natural course. Kid looked exhausted, so at least a few hours. You shouldn't have any problem lifting it if you have to. If you do, call me," Noah said.

"Will do. Be careful."

Noah snorted. "You're the one sticking around with two ticking time bombs and a bunch of killers."

A door opened and shut, and then there were only three heartbeats in the building. Roger pushed off from the doorway and took a step toward the lit classroom, but the steady heartbeats pulled him to a pause. Something was off. Quickly, he isolated each. Bastian's was the steady of thrum of someone who'd been in conversation and was now moving toward rest. Vincent had settled into a deep sleep, and his heartbeat reflected that.

The cat was weird. Roger moved back to the doorway and frowned at the creature. Their heart moved at a pace similar to Bastian's. For such a small beast, that was *wrong*. It should have been at least twice what Bastian's heart was doing.

Not wanting to leave Vincent alone with a potential shapeshifter—or some other mysterious creature—Roger zipped into the room and grabbed the cat. Predictably, the cat was not a fan of that course of action, but Roger was faster. He managed to grab the cat by the scruff and hold it out in front of him so they couldn't scratch him.

The cat meowed pitifully, then began to snarl as Roger carried them into the lit classroom.

Dmitri silently stepped out of his way and moved to lean against the wall beside the door inside the classroom.

Bastian lifted an eyebrow. "Is there a reason you're carrying Lee like he's a snot-filled handkerchief?"

"This is not a cat," Roger replied. "Can you keep him from going back to Vincent?"

"He's curious about the boy. Nothing foul involved," Bastian said.

"Vincent is under my protection. I will decide what motives are foul, and since I don't know what this beast has in mind, I would prefer he remain away from the boy. And I notice that you didn't deny he's not actually a cat."

"He's not, but he won't be changing into anything else for a while." Bastian gently took Lee from Roger and cradled the cat in his arms, scratching his belly. He strode across the room to the turned-over chairs, righted two of them, and sat in one. "Think you can keep a level head about you?"

"Despite what you saw, I'm not known to give in to impulses of violence," Roger replied. Slowly, he took the chair that Bastian had set up for him. "What happened earlier ... Vincent and I have some shared pains. I—"

"Hey, I don't need you to divulge your traumas." Bastian deposited his cat onto his shoulder, and the creature remained there, casting his silver-eyed gaze on Roger. "I take it your magic is something new to you."

"I would say I don't have magic," Roger said. "At least, before tonight, I didn't think I had anything in common with arcane practitioners. Vampires my age are known to gain new abilities, but this doesn't have the touch of them, except for the shadows."

"There are some arcanists that can manipulate shadows, but I have seen it more with vamps."

"I am over three hundred years old," Roger said, allowing his shock into his voice. The night had been full of long plunges up and down high waves. "I should have shown some sort of power like this before, correct?"

Bastian took a very long moment before he said, "I wager Thomas hasn't told you much about me, so let me tell you a little more about what I do. The Greater Circle of the Unyielding concerns itself with bigger matters than the day-to-day politics of mages, which is a fancy way of saying I spend my time going from one magical disaster to another. I'm familiar with power manifestation.

"Vincent gave us a clear picture of some of the trauma he's been dealing with. And you told me just now that you can relate." Bastian looked up from the floor to meet Roger's gaze. "In my experience, abuse is more likely to suppress the onset of arcane manifestation. Abusers and manipulators excel at making their targets feel not only physically power-less but spiritually weak. Forgive me for having overheard, but you told Thomas you had been surviving for centuries."

"He's saying that because you molded yourself into a

vapid fuckboy, you couldn't be anything more than a vapid fuckboy," Dmitri said. He thumped his head back against the wall and stared up at the ceiling. "I am such an ass."

"You?" Roger asked.

"I haven't helped," Dmitri replied, his voice growing more distant.

"You two seem like you've got a lot of history, but I need you to dissect that later," Bastian said. His cat slipped off his shoulder, landed on the floor quietly, and sat a small distance away, like he was another member of the conversation. "Right now, yeah, it seems like you've had some sort of arcane break-through. You were casting wildly, but you moved with intent. You weren't trying to blow up Noah. That spell was a raw undoing, the same sort of spell I used to disperse it. When you turned on us, it was out of protection. I think you'll do fine in a standard lesson structure, starting tonight if you want."

Bastian pointed toward the back room where Vincent slept. "He's a different story. His manifestation nearly brought the building down. Your power is raw, but you have a better handle on your emotions. He doesn't have that. He could be a danger to himself and to others."

Roger narrowed his eyes. "What do you propose to do about that?"

"For the time being, nothing without consent," Bastian replied.

"For the time being?"

"I'll repeat, he's showing signs that he is dangerous. His magic is incredibly volatile. I'm not blaming him. It's clearly unintentional at the moment." Bastian produced two metal bracelets. "My first suggestion is that he wears these until he learns how to separate his emotional state from his power. They'll dampen his magic so that if he manifests like he just did, it'll come out like a breeze instead of a tornado."

"May I see one of those?" Roger asked.

Bastian tossed him one bracelet.

The metal was lighter than Roger expected, and it wasn't silver like he'd initially suspected. Instead, it was aluminum. A series of runes covered the outside and the inside. As far as Roger could tell, Bastian wasn't lying, but Roger didn't know the man. He pulled his phone from his pocket, snapped a few pictures of the bracelet, and sent Ezra a message with the images. Ezra had said that he'd researched arcane manifestations. Both Ezra and Bastian could lie to him, but Ezra wouldn't have the motive.

And Roger had to trust someone, or he might lose his mind.

Within a minute, Ezra sent back a message confirming what Bastian had said. The bracelets were a common tool among "troubled" cases of manifestations.

Roger ran his thumb along the runes and then tossed the bracelet back to Bastian. "You won't force them on him?"

"These things are designed to work with the willing," Bastian said. "If I were to shove them on him, he could wreck the enchantment the first time he has a fit. For the record, I want these to work for him. I want to find him a mentor that'll give him the time he needs."

The cat let out a loud, meaningful "Mrrreow."

Bastian startled and then frowned at his cat. "Seriously?"

The cat flicked his tail and swiveled his head to face Bastian. His next meow was forceful and insistent.

"All right, but he's got to agree," Bastian said.

"The not-a-cat has an opinion?" Roger asked.

"Lee's full of them." Bastian wiped one hand across his lips and sighed. "He thinks I should take the kid under my wing. Which I hope"—he raised his voice a little and aimed his words at the cat—"he realizes that means we might have to settle down here in Chicago for a while."

Lee strode up to Bastian and rubbed up against his leg. He

wrapped himself around Bastian's ankle and then lay down across his foot.

"You're a pain in the ass," Bastian said to Lee. He cleared his throat. "When Vincent wakes up, I'd like to talk to him. I'm guessing there aren't parents in the picture."

"No. I'm the closest thing he has to a guardian, though he is eighteen," Roger replied.

A distant look filled Bastian eyes. One of his tattoos must have blocked vampiric abilities because Roger couldn't read his fears or desires. However, he'd seen enough mortals to know when someone was thinking through everything they'd learned. Eventually, Bastian nodded once to himself, then dragged both hands down his face as he sighed.

Clapping his hands together, he said, "All right. Give me five minutes to set up, and I'll be ready to guide you through some novice focus practices."

"Just like that, you'd teach me?" Roger asked incredulously.

"Whenever Tommy calls, I know shit's not only hit the fan, a sewer's spewing in a china shop. And there are monkeys who have covered the wares in shit and are trying to outthrow the sewer's sewage. Vampire though you may be, I noticed that boy didn't have a fresh bite mark on him. Neither does Tommy or Amber. Even if you are going out and slaughtering the innocent behind Tommy's back, you're not stupid enough to kill me." Bastian gave a wolfish grin. "And if I'm teaching you, then I'll get to know what your magic feels like. So if you do turn out to be a maniacal undead warlock, I'll have an upper hand on knowing it's you *and* knowing what you're capable of."

Allowing Bastian to help him meant sharing a newly discovered part of himself. Roger had barely wrapped his mind around the notion that he had arcane power, and now he was supposed to trust this stranger? So what if Thomas had called him in—Thomas's allegiance to Roger was clearly thin. *And I likely ruined it.* If Thomas relied on Bastian in disastrous situations, then either he believed he needed stronger people on his own side, or he thought Roger's mission needed bigger players.

You asked him to find talented people. You asked for warriors. Roger put a hand to his forehead to shield his eyes. The world was too much. Zack a vampire. Takashi with a sireling. His own power. Vincent's manifestation. Seamus throwing fucking parties after Roger had crippled him financially.

Quietly, Dmitri moved over to his side. He put his hand on Roger's shoulder and murmured in his ear, "You can do this."

I thought he was preparing me for the draining ritual, Dmitri had said during their first conversation in Nathaniel's apartment. What Roger had been seeing must have been magic, and the rainbow sigil on Dmitri was proof of what Anton had done.

But without learning magic, Roger wouldn't know what it was or how to help him.

Centuries of helplessness, and I could be as powerful as Anton. Roger put his hand over Dmitri's and squeezed him tight as a brittle smile crossed his lips. Standing motionless had aided no one. If he could move forward, he had to.

"Five minutes," Roger agreed. "Then I guess I'm learning magic."

CHAPTER 42

The night was wearing thin, and yet Zack struggled to stay in bed with Takashi. Being with him was great, but Zack couldn't shake what Takashi had told him.

Nell wanted him dead.

Nell had been the one to betray Roger and arranged a deal with a fey to put him to sleep.

How far did Nell's reach extend? Josefina clearly had to be working with her lover, right? Had Kit or Carver been in on her scheme? What about Blake? Fuck, he hadn't spoken to Blake since the night before the Winter's Grand Ball. He had no idea if she knew he was a vampire or not. Had her neighbor's cat given birth yet? Why was that where his mind went?

Because it's easier to want a kitten heist than to think my role models are the enemy. Slowly, Zack slid his hand through Takashi's hair. After getting cleaned up, Takashi had quickly dropped off to sleep. Zack wasn't sure if it was the late hour or that he still wasn't allowed much fresh blood. If Katie was bound to Takashi like Zack was to Seamus, then she could be taxing his system, too.

I can't lose him. Zack curled around Takashi and held him close. No one was going to save them. Except for Takashi, he was utterly alone. Roger was becoming more of a memory. He missed him, especially in the lonely dark, but they'd spent weeks apart. Plus, Roger had thrown away the script. Bankrupting Seamus and the coven had never been in any of the plans they discussed.

But then, he barely knew what to do while stuck in his own shoes. He had no idea what he'd do in Roger's place.

Come downstairs, Seamus said in his head.

Seamus would call for him when he least wanted to move. Zack clung to Takashi. *I don't want to talk.*

I can tell you need to, Zackery. Come here. Please.

The *please* threw him off. Seamus nearly sounded sincere, but the monster wasn't capable of it. He'd almost killed Anton without stopping to consider that he didn't have a motive for the theft. Just because Anton was the only one that he'd known with the power to shadow walk, he'd leapt to a conclusion and resorted to violence. And he supposedly loved Anton.

What would he do if he knew what Zack had been up to? What was he hoping to find in the library? The answer to how to unlink them had to be there, somewhere.

Don't make me make you come down here, Seamus said.

Sadness burst into fury because that was far more useful an emotion. Zack sprang from the bed and, using the magnetic pull to Seamus, rushed through the mansion to find him sitting on that obnoxious patio. He had a bottle of wine and two freaking wineglasses again. Despite the snow on the ground beyond the patio, Seamus was dressed like he expected to go to a Sunday brunch any minute. He had a light blue polo on and gray slacks, none of the material designed for winter weather. Beside his chair was Zack's old backpack.

Zack was only in his sleep pants, but the cold January wind didn't bother him. He clenched his fists. "Here. I showed up. Can I go to bed now?"

"I'm your father, Zackery," Seamus said, empathy flowing in his voice. "I wish you would talk to me."

With a glare, Zack fell back on his abilities and sought what Seamus was actually feeling. Rather than the journal-like visualization he'd stumbled into more and more frequently, all he read from Seamus was like computer pop-ups. The word and flare of wanting to care for Zack was there, but it didn't have the substance that Takashi's wants had.

"I've seen what you are capable of doing to your 'loved' ones," Zack said coldly. "Anton may act like nothing's happened, but I will not forget."

A flicker of regret crossed Seamus's face as he tightened, but then he relaxed. Calmly, he opened the bottle of wine and poured two glasses. "I believed that the love of my life of over eight hundred years had betrayed me. I lost my temper."

Zack folded his arms over his chest. If he couldn't trust Nell, then there was no fucking way he could trust Seamus. *But he sounded so proud of me in that journal entry ...*

The monster wants you to be a monster, the Cal voice said. *Why are you so determined to make that a good thing?*

After taking a sip of wine, Seamus said, "I didn't ask you down here for another three-round fight about right and wrong. I sensed your distress, son. You need someone to talk to."

"I should talk to you?" Zack sneered. "You fucking murdered me, *Father*. You took me away from everyone."

"Did I?" Seamus reached into Zack's backpack and withdrew his journal. "Because the boy in these pages had no one."

Zack snatched his leather journal from Seamus's hand. "I know you only read this to get in my head."

"Takashi read it, and you consider him your lover," Seamus replied. "Anyway, that journal isn't the clearest picture of you. You weren't terribly honest with yourself either."

A tightness spread across Zack's chest. "Yes I was."

Seamus leaned forward. A softness filled his muddled blue and red eyes. "You know you weren't. On the surface, the words you wrote were about your experiences, but I took the time to understand your meaning and the things you were not saying, even to yourself. Your mortal family left you behind because you made one calculation they didn't like. Then they abandoned you again after Cal attacked *you*. You yearned for Roger's love, Josefina's acceptance—you have sought to prove yourself over and over. You have never had to earn my love, Zackery."

Snarling, Zack stepped into Seamus's space. When Seamus leaned back, Zack slapped a hand on either armrest and growled in his face. "You *killed* me."

No flicker of anger overcame Seamus. Not even their mental connection gave Zack anything other than Seamus's want to comfort him. After a beat, Seamus said calmly, "I know you well enough to say you have armed yourself with your anger because you are frightened. You are terrified by what it would mean to trust me."

"You make humans into slaves and hurt people for the fucking fun of it," Zack snapped.

"You believe that if you do the wrong thing, I will hurt you? Your lover?" Seamus asked.

"Isn't that why you've kept him around?"

"You deserve to come into your power with those who will nurture your gifts," Seamus replied, a note of fatherly warmth in his voice. "Takashi is a worldly vampire who has been helping you bloom in your new life. I wager he's even given you ideas."

"Ideas," Zack repeated slowly. *Does he know? Shit. Can't think about it.*

Lightly, Seamus put a hand on the center of Zack's chest

and nudged him back out of his personal space. "Yes, I know you're hoping to kill me and claim the coven. Yet you and Takashi live. I allow Takashi's spawn to live."

"Why?" Zack asked numbly.

"Because you are my son, and I love you." Seamus picked up his glass of wine and gestured to the glass and empty seat beside him. "Besides, life is nothing without a little ambition."

Zack sat down in the seat. "You're not pissed at me?"

"I don't spend this much time on anyone who annoys me, Zackery. Your journal makes it clear how goal oriented you can be. The ambition of taking the coven directs some of your anger at me into fuel rather than festering into depression." Seamus sipped his wine. "I hope, with time, you won't hate me. With the kingdom I am building, I will need reliable vampires alongside me."

"You're counting on me to be part of the foundation of this kingdom, aren't you?" Zack said carefully. *A new generation.*

"You've been in my journals," Seamus replied.

The cold winter wind didn't compare to the ice in Zack's veins. "I don't know what you're talking about."

Seamus withdrew his cell phone from his pocket and flicked open its screen. After a moment, he set it down on the table between them. A string of text notifications was on the screen. Each was just a date and time stamp with the word "Opened."

"Takashi is clever, avoiding the switch in the desk like he did. But he either didn't account for modern technologies or decided to risk exposure for the want of gaining new information." Seamus took the phone back and put it in his pocket. "Suffice it to say, every square inch of the main floor and the dungeon have discreet cameras as well. I know where you went. I know what you saw."

"That was weeks ago. You haven't said anything," Zack said. "Haven't done anything."

"Just as you haven't thrown a single fit about your cousin

being locked in a cell or used what you read as reason to disobey me. You've thrown yourself into research, which I can admire. Your intelligence is worth more than that silver blade of yours, but you are centuries behind your foes." Seamus nudged the glass of wine toward him.

"You've researched all those people. Why choose me?" Zack asked. His voice felt like a ghost in his throat.

"I was honest with you, Zackery. Rare is the soul who not only understands what it means to drink my blood and be reborn but also pulls for that source. You have only just begun to settle into your new powers. I am thrilled to see how you will grow."

"Who is 'Grandmother'? What have you been stealing from her?"

"You are not ready for those secrets."

"Does it have something to do with the rituals you've been using your sirelings for? What exactly do you and Anton do?" Zack asked.

Seamus set his wineglass onto the table between them with a definitive clink. He folded his hands over his lap and held Zack's gaze. The mottled red and blue swirled together and deepened into a maroon while the whites of his eyes became pitch-black. Ice coated the table between them and frosted the surfaces of the glasses and the bottle, soon coating the metal as well. His fangs were longer, his nails sharper.

The bond between them cinched, like a rope that lost all its slack in an instant, burning as it went. The tugs of Zack's dagger and the hook to Phyrull were all the more obvious as they pulled in other directions than Seamus. The air was scorching in Zack's nose, down his throat, and he ached to feed with a desperation he'd only ever felt in bed.

Underneath all of that was Seamus's hunger for Zack's affection, for his loyalty. And the only ease of pressure was the pinprick of Seamus's love for him.

"You are not ready, Zackery," Seamus said firmly.

Then the instant was over. Seamus's eyes were the same as they'd been a moment before. The ice remained on the glasses as the winter air could keep it cold. The suffocating hunger in Zack's belly dimmed.

"You're not ... you're not upset that Takashi and I went snooping," Zack managed.

"I would have been more disappointed if the two of you had wasted your opportunities."

"You've spent centuries crushing your intelligent offspring."

"Candide would beg to differ. Besides, I am finally prepared to change the order of things." Seamus poured more wine into his glass. "I want you to be among the vampires at my side well into the future."

"What about Takashi?"

"I suppose."

"But not Roger?"

"If your heart wants Roger, perhaps we'll be able to arrange something. A house outside the city where you can keep him and he can remain out of the politics he's never had a taste for," Seamus said. "However, dawn is coming, and I didn't drag you down here so you could doubt me all over again. I'd like to ease whatever was burdening your mind."

Zack stared out into the dark. Beyond the iron fence were trees, and past that, the great wide world. He didn't want to run for that fence anymore, and that change had nothing to do with the bond between him and Seamus. Where would he go if he left the mansion? He had no idea where Roger was or what he was planning. His mortal family would want to kill him on sight. Was he supposed to hide out in Blake's house? With her parents? Go on the run with Takashi? Sure, they might be able to get away to some far corner of the globe, but what was he supposed to do then? And would any corner be far enough if Seamus's ambitions went unchecked?

Seamus knew about what he was goals and didn't give a

damn. Of course, the bastard could be hiding his anger. He could turn on Zack in an instant. He'd done it to Anton. This was all manipulation. It had to be.

But Zack was so fucking tired.

He leaned forward, his elbows on his knees, and hung his head. His hair had barely grown in the three weeks since his rebirth. Since his last haircut had been well before his death, he should have been irritated that his hair was getting too long. Instead, he combed his hand through it and found it the perfect length. *Rude that it didn't change with me.*

Slowly, Zack dragged the glass of wine off the table. Staring into its depths didn't bring forth any solution. *I could start a war.*

One's already here, his rational voice declared. According to what Takashi had said, that voice was right.

Zack's mortal days were behind him. He needed to focus on his immortal nights. Straying from Seamus wasn't the answer. He couldn't keep his eyes on someone out of sight.

Finally, Zack brought his head up and relaxed into the seat. "If you want my trust, you won't harm Takashi after I tell you everything."

"I won't promise that until I know what he's done," Seamus said. "If he's been acting against—"

"What he's done has brought to light a conspiracy," Zack replied. "And I don't need your promise, because if you take what I say and use it as an excuse to hurt him, then I will know that every word you have told me was a fucking lie."

Seamus stilled, and then a small smile of pride crossed his lips. He motioned for Zack to speak.

"Roger didn't disappear willingly from your coven," Zack said. "He doesn't know this yet, but Nell worked out a deal with an Unseelie to put him in a coma. I was the one to wake him back in August. Yes, we began to plot your demise from the moment I met him. But he wasn't very … driven."

"Acting on violent impulses has never been Roger's strong suit, until recently perhaps." Seamus sipped his wine.

Zack swirled his in his glass. "Right. So Nell's had it out for your coven for a while. I mean, we're talking a decades-long plan."

"One you foiled," Seamus said.

Zack nodded.

"Mm, and now that you're my sireling, she wants you dead because it would weaken me and therefore make me easier to kill," Seamus continued.

Surprised, Zack sat up a little more and frowned at him. "How did you—"

"It's a common enough conceit. She's not the only one trying. Why do you think we're having the debut party? Everyone who wants my coven for themselves will see who else is thinking of doing the same thing. They'll learn who they need to eliminate for their own plans to succeed, which should keep them preoccupied for a decade or so. At least long enough you're your strengths will grow." Seamus chuckled once under his breath. "Using Roger, though, that was clever of her."

"I thought high school was full of drama," Zack grumbled.

"Throw enough sentient minds together, and there will always be dramatics."

Zack snorted and then took a tiny sip of his wine. It tingled on the tip of his tongue. The taste of rich berries filled his mouth, and the calm of a long winter night washed over him. Voicing the problem plaguing his mind had helped; this particular blend of fey wine soothed him further.

"Why did you think I'd be angry about that?" Seamus said.

"Because of how Takashi found out." Zack focused his inner eye on Seamus, keeping his senses peeled for any sign that he was angry. "He made a deal with Anton when he turned Katie. A brand-new phone for the girl."

"Ooo, he is more diabolical than I gave him credit for," Seamus said with another laugh.

"You sound pleased."

"When Takashi came here in the 1920s, he was cute, but meek. He has grown in the last hundred years." Seamus tapped his wineglass and set it down. Then he leaned on the armrest closer to Zack. "Do you trust that he's as loyal to you as he claims? Or will he conspire with Nell?"

"He was horrified at her command."

"You're certain?"

Zack took a long drink of his wine and sat it down. "He fed me a little of his blood so that I wouldn't doubt him. He loves me."

Seamus touched Zack's shoulder and squeezed him comfortingly. "That's good."

"What are we going to do about Nell?" Zack whispered. "If she has her way ..."

"She's a problem for another night, sweet boy." Seamus stood, taking his glass with him. He squeezed Zack's shoulder and leaned down to kiss the top of his head. "Take your glass and the bottle, go see if your lover's awake enough to enjoy the wine with you."

The weight of the journal on his lap bothered Zack. All of his former hopes and dreams and problems were written out in the leather book his mortal sister had given him. But he had been reborn. He was different, now. Not the scared, angry boy. Confused, out of his depths, but that wasn't the same at all.

He lifted it up for Seamus to take. "Could this belong to the library?"

Seamus took it back. "I think it'd be a fine addition. Now come along inside."

Zack grabbed the bottle of fey wine and his glass. They

parted ways in the long hall. The mansion's stillness was no longer the cool touch of a grave waiting to be filled. The silence was there, and the solitude, but that brought a sort of piece.

But when he reached his suite, the loneliness faded away. The game controllers were out of place from where he and Takashi had left them the other night in the living room. Clothes were strewn about in the bedroom, and a stack of books was on the corner of his desk. Takashi was asleep in the bed, his body utterly relaxed against the bed.

Zack took the bottle and his glass over to the desk. After flipping on the soft-glowing desk lamp, he quietly dug through the drawers until he rediscovered the slick, onyx leather journal he'd discovered on his first night. He took out a pen and began to write about his new life. One that was full of mystery and intrigue and wasn't so awful at all …

CHAPTER 43

Dawn was kissing Chicago's streets. Roger continued to stand in the deeper shadows of the hallway in the old building. Physical fatigue had never been a problem since he'd become a vampire, but after running through a series of exercises with Bastian, his soul-deep tiredness manifested in aches in his limbs.

They'd worked for a few hours until Bastian was exhausted and Vincent had stirred. Bastian and Vincent had their chat, which Roger had done his best to not listen to, and then Bastian had taken off for the day.

Josefina messaged to say that she needed to clear her head and get some rest. Roger bade Dmitri to take Vincent back to Nathaniel's apartment, where they were still staying.

Needing a bit of space to think himself, Roger remained at their makeshift headquarters. Also, given the time to cool down, he wanted to check in with Thomas. As dawn continued to brush along his portion of the world, Roger realized that Thomas was likely avoiding the building as long as possible.

Roger would survive a bit of direct sunlight, but the way to the Last Deal was long, and he didn't have a car. *I wonder if the shadows could take me that far.* He stroked the wall beside him. Traveling through an inch of shadow had been suffocating. Anton was able to travel across long distances, but he also had the experience. *Given enough time, I'll be able to do that, too.*

The side door opened. Thomas said, "Hold on."

"Dad, I'm tired," Amber replied with a huff.

"The lights are still—"

"So, someone's still here." Amber tromped across the classroom toward the hallway, where Roger was waiting.

Roger rounded the corner into the classroom.

Immediately, Amber stopped in her tracks and shoved her hand into her coat pocket. Thomas's hand went toward his dagger on his hip, but he stopped himself from grabbing the hilt. Both hunters had deep bags under their eyes. Thomas grimaced, silently proving to Roger that the older hunter had been hoping he wouldn't still be there.

"Not cool, lurking in the dark," Amber grumbled. "What you said to my dad was super shitty."

Thomas said, "Amber—"

"It was!" Amber stormed up to Roger, craning her head back in order to glare up at him. "And everyone heard you."

"Your father said unkind things to me as well," Roger replied. "Did you defend me to him while you were out?"

Amber looked away swiftly. Zack had done the same thing when Roger initially called him out on so many little things.

Roger stepped back from her. He moved slowly, in part because the hunters were already jumpy and also because doing so gave him time to form his next thoughts. Thomas and Amber seemed to be waiting on what he had to say. *Or perhaps they're too embarrassed.*

"What I said was meant to cause you pain, I'll admit that," Roger said. "I know that grief was strangling you, but what you said—"

"Was extremely terrible of me," Thomas said with a heavy sigh. He rubbed his hand against the back of his neck before finally meeting Roger's gaze. "You'd think after working together a few weeks, I would've gotten to know you a little better. I've got a lifetime of bullcrap to unlearn, but some of my instincts aren't wrong. I'm worried about Zack becoming a vampire."

"Because you've always assumed the worst of his fascination with my kind?" Roger asked coldly.

"Because he has always been a brilliant boy with a big heart, and maybe it won't happen today or tomorrow, but he has the potential to become one of the worst vampires," Thomas said with a strangled plea in his voice. "There has to be a reason Seamus is calling him son, and I doubt it has anything to do with either of us. Not to dredge this up or agree with it, but you called yourself his toy. As petty as he can be, you don't live a thousand years surviving on pettiness, and getting revenge on a plaything is pretty petty."

"What could he possibly want with Zack?" Roger said.

"Uh, besides the insider knowledge on how to take out the rest of the Wrights?" Amber replied.

"Sweetheart, I know you're young enough to think we're invincible, but there's a reason we hunters stay out of Chicago. If the vampires wanted to eradicate us, they could. Probably the idea of the numbers that would be lost is what's kept an all-out war from starting." Thomas scratched behind his ear. The bags under his eyes were deeper than they'd been, with an echo of sadness in his eyes making him appear more exhausted. "Though I can't say one's not on the way with Zack becoming a vampire. Maybe Seamus does want to lure us out, but somehow, I think there's a side of this we don't know. Thing is, his plans could be hundreds of years in the making. Every night Zack spends with him is the chance for Seamus to shape him. And Zack's stubborn, but no one's unimpressionable forever. I can't help worrying that he's part of whatever Seamus has been cooking up."

Thomas's words sank into Roger, the drop of them causing a ripple of understanding to push thoughts into theories. Roger had seen the possibility of turning Zack into a better weapon. He'd fallen in love, but if he'd focused on honing Zack's skills and ridding him of his compassion, would it have been that hard? Zack had been on the edge of believing vampires were an irredeemable enemy. Surely Seamus couldn't morph his beliefs on humans so quickly.

What would Seamus even want a living weapon for? For the last three hundred years, he had cut down anyone who had gained too much power. Yet he was elevating Zack. Either he was posing in order to draw the hunters out, which Roger had to agree was short-sighted, or he had a bigger scheme, one that Roger had never been privy to.

God, do I know anything? Roger put a hand to his forehead to shield his eyes while he gathered himself. *Focus on the next step.* He cleared his throat. "I didn't hang around solely to discuss Zack. Candide was able to help me figure out our next target." He dropped his hand away. "Seamus has been hiding that we've demolished his and the coven's accounts. With vampires flying in from around the world, there would be one thing he couldn't cover up that would weaken him, damage his reputation, may free Zack and Takashi, and be an extremely loud 'fuck you.'"

"What do you propose?" Thomas asked.

"We burn his mansion to the fucking ground," Roger replied. "And we plan the attack near the dawn after the party."

Slowly, a sly grin crossed Thomas's lips and brightened his eyes. "Well, that would be extremely hard to ignore."

Roger nodded, and then he and Thomas launched into a conversation about what they would need to bring a plan to fruition.

CHAPTER 44

For the better part of a week, Anton had kept Takashi busy from sundown to sunrise. Seamus had taken Zack on errands nearly every night, and what time he didn't spend with him, he spent in the library or reading books in their suite. Takashi had read a few that Zack had brought into their bedroom.

Zack had been tight-lipped, and Takashi worried but didn't blame him. Though Zack was growing in his defenses, Takashi could still read his emotions plainly. The greater evidence was in how they went to bed each dawn. Zack cuddled him close, always making sure they were together.

The nights passed. The debut party was the next evening. Takashi's stomach was a pendulum, threatening to sway until he lost his balance and crashed. And Zack was quieter than usual.

"You've been extremely pensive lately," Takashi said as he buttoned up his black dress shirt. As subtle as he could, he watched Zack dress in the corner of his eye. Vampirism had made him slightly leaner than he'd been as a mortal, and his tailored slacks perfectly hugged his delectable ass. Takashi swiftly looked farther away. Since sharing blood with Zack, horniness was easier to come by, and that was opposite of his intentions. "One might say you're developing Brooding Vampire face."

Zack finished fastening his pants and turned to lean his backside against the dresser. He folded his arms over his chest and pursed his lips.

"Now I am worried," Takashi said and raised an eyebrow.

"Promise you're not going to be pissed at me," Zack said seriously.

"Never an auspicious start."

"Takashi, please. I'm trying, okay? But I've got like five hundred pounds on either arm, and I'm having to balance walking a wire over an endless chasm, and I've never walked a wire before." Zack raked his hand through his hair. A hopelessness was in his eyes.

Gently, Takashi took his hands. "I will not be pissed."

"He knows."

"What exactly does he know?" Takashi said slowly, though he could piece together the answer.

Zack looked down at the floor, staring at a spot as if it would suddenly sprout a mouth and speak for him. After a moment, he lifted his chin, and his features smoothed to an expressionless mask only vampires perfected. "I told him that Nell's gunning for me. He's known about our ambition for me to take the coven for weeks. Probably since we came up with it."

Takashi had to quell his instincts to keep from stepping away from Zack. The connection he shared with Zack was muted, but rather than opening it, he kept it closed. *I was a fool to trust him.* "You told him about Nell?"

"Don't pull away from me," Zack said.

"I'm right here."

"I can see it happening." Zack tightened his hold on Takashi's hands. "He claims some bullshit about how having a goal is good for me, and I know we can't trust him in the long term. But telling Seamus about Nell wanting me dead is the right move. If she thinks you won't do it, she'll find someone who will. And this might be a huge shocker, but I don't want to die."

"But you *told* him," Takashi said. "You hate him, and you told him our secret?"

"Nell wanting me dead shouldn't be our secret!" Zack walked away from Takashi and spun to face his desk for a long moment. When he turned back, he was wiping bloody tears from his eyes. "I don't want to trust him. But apart from you, he's the only one that's cared about me this much."

"Zack, he doesn't—"

"You're not part of this bond. You don't fucking know what I've felt." Zack put his hand to his heart. "Everyone in my entire life has been planning to use me or threw me away because they saw no use for me. Even Roger. At least what you wanted for me, you wanted for *us*. So that we could have the power to make the rules. You and me and Roger could take the bent pieces of this coven and form a better picture. I want that future for us.

"But we're also in over our fucking heads here! He knows where I am all the time, and he is stronger than we've given him credit for. You should have seen the way his eyes morphed. I've never seen anything like it." Zack gestured to the books on his desk. "I haven't found anything like it yet either. I know it's insane, but he *wants* me to be his son. I hate what he's done. I hate who he hurts, but until I break this link with him, what choice do I have? The best I can do is make sure he doesn't hurt us, and he won't because he's got this weird need for me to like him. To trust him. And he trusts me, or we'd be dead by now."

"Zack—"

"He knows we broke into his secret office! He knows we saw Anton's torture chamber!" Zack shouted. "He actually admired us for breaking in."

Takashi stilled his body and cleared his mind of the nerves

attempting to overwhelm him. Panicking wouldn't bring him any solutions. He needed to take in the data and process it. He'd been in worse positions. Montreal. Dubai. London.

No, none of them had been this bad. He'd been in love before. Been caught in schemes before. But he'd never been falling for the sireling of a powerful immortal whose end game remained a mystery. Seamus had said he wanted a war with the dragons, but what would be the point in that? How could vampires even take on such creatures?

If more of them were as strong as Zack, if Zack had time to grow, if Seamus—there were ways, but they were decades off from fruition. *We're not caught at the end of preparations. We're in a beginning stage.* That was why Seamus had been incensed about losing his funds. The war chest would have been useful as he built an army. With that kind of money, he would have been able to enact his schemes on an international level. With Zack and Takashi, Seamus might mend his reputation. He'd be able to point at the two of them as examples of the future of his coven. Even Katie was a prodigy.

We're not players at the board. We're pawns. Takashi raced through his possible courses of action. Simply grabbing Katie and running off into the night wouldn't work. Katie cared about Anton. Zack was tied to Seamus, and ... *We have to get out of here before Seamus corrupts him.*

Roger would know what to say. Roger would be able to help us weather this with love.

"You were the one," Takashi said slowly, choosing his words carefully, "that insisted we couldn't count on Anton for anything because of the monster that he is. But you trust Seamus? We saw what he did to Anton. What he did to Vincent. We know what he's done to Roger."

"Fuck, I know. I know!" Zack wiped fresh tears from his eyes. "But the whole fucking world is against me, Takashi. What the fuck am I supposed to do?"

On a long-ago night, Takashi had known that loneliness

when Sergei had discovered his letters and their friendship had mutated to hate. The betrayal had cut him to the bone, and yet they'd had to perform one last time together. And Takashi had fallen. He'd died because the man who should have been there wasn't.

Zack had held on to Takashi in a way no one else ever had.

Takashi longed to do the same for him. He zipped over to him and grabbed him by his shoulders. "We will find our way out of this. We'll be together hundreds of years. *Thousands*."

Zack held on to his hands. "Promise?"

"Yes," Takashi whispered. "We won't have to hold on forever. We'll break free."

"How?"

"Work in progress." Takashi grinned. "Tomorrow night will be a good time to get the lay of the land outside this house."

"Yeah." Zack perked up. "You've been working with Anton for the party. Does that mean you've invited friends from other covens?"

"I've reached out," Takashi replied. "I have no idea if anyone's accepted my invitation. Anton declared that he wanted the final guest list to be a surprise for me."

"But there's a chance."

"Yes."

"Will any of these friends be able to help us?"

Takashi managed a smile. "Their presence certainly can't hurt."

"Come with me," Seamus said after their family meal.

Zack rose from his seat.

Seamus shook his head and pointed at Takashi. "You."

Before Takashi could say anything, Seamus headed out the

door. Takashi followed him. The long stretch of hallway was dotted with fresh bouquets of flowers, yet the scent of old dirt clung to Seamus so profoundly that Takashi still smelled it in his immediate wake. There was a touch of burnt coal dust, the tiniest whiff of it. Nell and other ancient vampires had a similar hint in their scents of the grave.

When they neared the front doors, Seamus stopped, spun on his heel, and raked his gaze over Takashi from head to foot. "You need to change."

"Can I ask the occasion, master?"

"You and my love have invited all these blasted vampires from other covens," Seamus said. "You should help me greet tonight's arrivals."

"As you wish, master." Takashi gave Seamus a slight nod and then hurried off to change. He slipped into a navy blue suit with a clean white dress shirt and forewent a tie altogether. He zipped down to the foyer.

"Much better," Seamus said approvingly.

A limo was waiting outside for them, and the driver sprang out to open the car door for them as they stepped out of the mansion. Seamus motioned for Takashi to slide into the limo first. Once they were both in, the driver shut the door and returned to his seat. The limo soon got underway.

"I'm glad you invited me to come, master," Takashi said.

"I've been so preoccupied these last few weeks that I must apologize for not taking time to get to know you better," Seamus replied. "Between raising my son, my duties, and everything else going on, I've simply been too busy. I hope you don't feel neglected in any way."

"Not at all." Takashi knocked away a piece of imaginary lint from his knee.

Seamus laughed smugly. "So you'll continue to play the part of a well-mannered guest. Takashi, you're part of my household. You can speak your mind."

Such an invitation was bound to be a lie. Yet it couldn't be ignored either. "I worry about Zack. He told you what my sire commanded?"

"He did. He doesn't seem concerned that you'll obey her."

"Why would I?" Takashi said, feigning a light air. "I love him, and I am part of your coven, master."

"Yet you called her." Seamus's grin turned sharp. "One might wonder why."

"I feared she was worrying over me. I called her to let her know I was all right."

"You weren't calling her to scheme about putting Zack in my stead?" Seamus asked.

Silence would be better than outright lying, but Seamus was staring at him like he expected an answer and already knew what it was. "Does it matter? She wishes your territory for herself, master. She'd rather him dead than another competitor."

"I'm surprised you don't want to take my position for yourself," Seamus replied. "But then, you would have to take responsibility, wouldn't you?"

"I don't know what you mean, master."

"You slide from one place to another." Seamus moved to sit beside him and put his arm along the back of the seat, crowding Takashi. "Jumping from one lover to the next. You have been everywhere, and for some reason, you were willing to settle with Roger? I should have doubted that loyalty. No sooner than I bring you into my house do you begin to worm your way toward my Anton."

"Anton and I have never—"

Seamus caught Takashi by the jaw and held him tight to cut him off from speaking. His words were laced with a deep-set anger that trilled every alarm in Takashi's mind. "I have seen the way you and my beloved have been talking. The closeness. You saw his chamber below, and yet that hasn't altered your opinion of him, has it? You find him captivating.

He believes you're fascinating. But you're just another leech, aren't you?"

"I don't—"

Seamus forced Takashi's head up farther, making speech impossible for him. The air in the limo was growing cold, and Seamus's eyes were bloodred, the whites becoming pitch-black. "Zack confides everything in you, doesn't he? And now, my lover is raising your offspring. That wouldn't be a problem, except he considers you a co-parent, of all the fucking absurd things. But do you know what has truly gotten under my skin?"

Takashi put his hand on Seamus's elbow and tried to push his arm down, tried for any sort of leverage, but couldn't find any. He scrambled, and his tormentor wasn't showing the slightest bit of strain in holding him.

The glare in Seamus's eyes was that of a devil's about to slice the wings from an angel. A longing to rip and rend pulsed out from him. "I didn't have a reason to check the mansion's footage until you and Zack invaded my office. Zack took off in such a rush I had to track his movements. The two of you went to the dungeon, and that's *fine*. You should know what's down there so you know what may still become of you.

"I figured that since I had the footage pulled up, I should catch up on the last few weeks. See what my beloved has been up to. I have to keep an eye on him, you understand. His proclivities need monitoring at times. That's why he has that little chamber down there in the first place. But do you know what I discovered?

"That little shapeshifting shithead has been turning into *you*. He's been doing it for weeks now. My beloved has been fucking him while he wore your face. Again, not the problem. We've been together for centuries. We have a love that will last. We've even invited others into our bed before. Roger, for example." Seamus dug his nails into Takashi's jaw, cutting into his flesh. Through clenched teeth, he continued. "But the *way* he fucked that facsimile of you wasn't fucking at all. He was tender. He was caring. He was talking. *Sharing* himself. Succubae feast on all kinds of desires, you know. None so much as budding love."

Takashi clutched onto Seamus's wrist. He still didn't have a prayer in moving his hand. Without being able to speak, he couldn't defend himself. Letting Seamus read his emotions would only result in him pillaging his psyche, and that would do more harm than good.

"I will not share him," Seamus growled in Takashi's ear. "Is that understood?"

Takashi gave the best affirmative grunt he could manage.

"Excellent." Seamus released Takashi and slid to the other end of the bench seat. With a casual dismissiveness, he withdrew a handkerchief from his pocket and tossed it at him.

Slowly, Takashi took the offered cloth and wiped away the blood from his now healed wounds. His hand threatened to shake, but he stilled that nervous energy. He let himself grow cold rather than hot with defensiveness. An overly quick response could lead to the wrong one, and he was in dangerous enough territory. *How did Roger do this for so long?*

The kiss at Devil's Cove came back to him. Roger had been onstage, had killed a hunter at Anton and Seamus's beckoning, and then let Seamus kiss him in front of everyone. Roger had been trading his body for his safety. He must have been doing so the entire time he was a vampire. *I cannot do that. I don't have the stomach.*

"Nothing slick to say, ambassador?" Seamus teased. "No pleasing words you think I want to hear?"

The malicious note in Seamus's voice was a red flag that one would have been able to see from across an ocean. Takashi tucked the handkerchief into his pocket and fussed with his cuffs. "Your point is made, master."

"Do remember it because I won't be repeating myself, no matter how much you make Zack happy."

Takashi had had his leg caught in a bear trap this entire time. Only his lack of struggling had kept him from cutting off his leg in desperation. Every night had been closing the trap further and further despite his efforts. Zack trusting Seamus at all was bad enough, but this torment was the sign of a festering wound. Seamus was worse than rot; he was a disease preparing to graduate from an epidemic to a global pandemic. Takashi had foolishly invited those he thought would help him, but there was no power to be had in the GLC except that which Seamus allowed.

For now, Zack's ambition was seen as a good thing, but one talk from Seamus had quelled Zack's urge, hadn't it? Zack was confused. Isolated.

The party was a step toward fixing everything. Takashi just needed to keep his head level.

By the time they reached the airport, he'd managed to find the calm within and adopt a neutral smile. Supernaturals had their own exclusive airport outside of Chicago, nearer to the Wisconsin border, and the limo driver was able to pull up on the tarmac not far from the private jet.

After parking, the limo driver slipped out of the vehicle and opened the door for them. Seamus stepped out with a wide smile on his lips, no hint of the bastard who had threatened Takashi anywhere in sight.

Takashi joined him outside, grateful for the night air.

Despite the relatively early hour, two planes had already landed. Takashi was very familiar with one of them; he'd been in Nell's airplane more times than he could count. The other boasted the logo of the NAC—the New Amsterdam Coven. Though the city's name had changed from New Amsterdam to New York City centuries ago, the coven refused to update its name. Leadership had changed hands a few times, which had led them to the custom of making a logo for their coven rather than relying on their master's crest.

Takashi had been expecting NAC to send their domestic ambassador to the party. That had been the vampire he'd encouraged Anton to send the invitation to. Instead of a darling young vampire about forty years turned, Faustino sauntered across the tarmac with his entourage behind him.

Faustino was roughly six feet tall with the physique and posture artists had loved to paint and sculpt since the late Renaissance. He never had a problem stripping down to reveal the well-toned planes of his chest and the thick, curly black hair that covered his chest and created a thick line down his abdomen. His skin was a light brown, while his eyes were dark as the shadows of a moonlit forest. As always, his taste in suits was subdued and bespoke, the hue of red bringing out a charmingly rustic note in his attire. Those following him were in equal, understated splendor.

Decades ago, in a Manhattan blood club, Faustino had publicly broken up with him, declaring him too much of an elitist sycophant. Worse, he'd come crawling back to Takashi that night, begging forgiveness. Takashi had given it. Then he'd discovered himself barred from NAC establishments with absolutely no explanation. Faustino refused to answer his calls. Humbled, he'd left the city and been a wreck until stumbling into Roger at the rare meeting for vampire kind in Nashville in 1985.

At least Nell had sent someone he liked. Evander was a vampire twice his age, and while he could be a little cocky and presumptive, he was someone who relished a good book and a great conversation. In his entourage was Collin, a slim vampire who looked frailer than a sheet of ice standing in the sun.

"Master Seamus!" Evander said brightly as he bowed. "I am honored to represent my master, Nell, Keeper of—"

The group from Taliville was still bent in their bow when

Seamus strode up to Evander and ripped his head off his body with one sickening twist.

Everyone on the tarmac froze. Takashi was left to stare as Evander's body dropped to the asphalt. The callousness, the sheer act of it, violated every protocol Takashi had learned. He'd seen vampires die; he'd seen masters kill subordinates. But to kill someone in a greeting?

This was an act of war.

Seamus tossed the head at Collin, who managed to catch it, and said, "Take that back to Nell and tell her that any of her people in my territory will be executed less politely than that was. Remind her that she began this conflict by ordering my son's assassination. If she wants peace negotiations, tell her to send an email."

"Understood," Collin said so quietly that Takashi almost didn't hear him. The group gathered Evander's body and hurried to the plane.

As Takashi watched them leave, Seamus's words sank in past the shock. Seamus had deliberately told Collin about the order. Nell would assume that Takashi had told Seamus or correctly guess that Takashi had told Zack, who had told Seamus. Whatever she came to believe, Takashi's relationship with her was ruined. She would, at best, see this as idiocy and, at worst, believe him to be a traitor.

If she told others that she no longer trusted him—and he had no doubt that she would—then his reputation would collapse. Scheming among vampires was common, but this was a sign of allegiance. His loyalty to his sire was always assumed. To show dedication to another ancient master meant giving himself over to their command or playing the game to his own benefit.

Everyone was always looking out for themselves in his circles, but the proof of it was like flashing his cards to cutthroat gamblers while having a gangster breathing down his neck for a debt. It was clumsy. It was unprofessional.

It was the end of him.

And Takashi had to stand there on the tarmac as if nothing were wrong. He had been infected with the rot that was Seamus, and there was no cure in sight. Zack was the only soul he could trust, and *Zack* had been the one to do this to him. *That isn't fair.* But was it any less the truth? For all Zack's protestations, he would never be able to choose Takashi over Seamus. *Never* was a strong word, but Seamus was already worming his way into Zack's heart and spoiling him from the inside.

Takashi was slipping from the trapeze all over again, and this time, there would be no one to scoop him up from the hard-packed earth. His heart was still in free fall, was still daring to hope that maybe, *maybe* Zack's love was enough. That with enough time, Zack would break from Seamus, that they would reunite with Roger, and all could be well. But the chances of that were diminishing every night. Yet hope—the fucking traitor that it was—persisted.

He was doomed.

Faustino stepped forward, his shoulders tighter, and said, "Master Seamus, I hope I won't have trouble keeping my head where it is."

Seamus clasped his hands behind his back and turned toward him with a fang-baring grin. "Has your master threatened my son?"

"She has only well wishes for the boy," Faustino replied. "Besides, we've been too concerned with our own affairs of late. My mistress is hoping that you will remember her fondly. Ludovicia took the reins at New Year's."

"Ah, Ludovicia! Was she able to make use of the gift I sent her?"

"To great effect. She is most grateful for your assistance and bade me to bring you several presents, some of which are in my luggage, a few of which stand behind me."

"Excellent. You must tell me everything about the regime change." Seamus motioned at the limo.

When Takashi woodenly began to follow him back to it, Seamus put a hand on his chest and stopped him in place. With a flick of his gaze, he gestured at the black SUVs rolling up toward them. In a whisper, he said sharply, "Take your place with the toys, leech."

"Of course, master," Takashi replied under his breath. He bowed his head as he stepped back. He didn't bring his gaze up from the tarmac until he heard the limo doors shut. Never in all his vampiric life had he been happier that he didn't have to breathe or that he'd learned to control the finite tremors that could stem from fear. *I am so utterly fucked.*

CHAPTER 45

The training room had been converted into an armory over the course of the last week. More tables had been brought in, and each was laden with holy water, UV flashlights, wooden stakes, silver chains, and swords. One table was filled with handguns and special ammunition, but only trained fighters —ones like Lacey, Josefina, and Thomas—who had years of experience with firearms and combat training were carrying firearms. In the wrong hands, knives were deadly enough. Roger wasn't willing to risk friendly fire for the sake of maybe taking out an enemy.

Since winter nights were so long, the plan was for teams to filter in, take their weapons, and prepare to rendezvous at their given locations around the mansion. Team leaders had synchronized watches and would launch their attacks at 6:25 a.m. That was almost twenty minutes before the sun would completely clear the horizon, which should be enough time to strike and get their vampire compatriots into hiding places before they burned in sunlight. Seamus might be able to tolerate some light, but the daylight would keep him at bay, too.

All attention went to Roger as he stepped into the middle

of the room. The team leaders were the only ones gathered so far. Among them were Dmitri, Josefina, Nathaniel, Bastian, and Thomas. Like them, he was dressed in black tactical gear. Josefina had managed to get her hands on some, and Ben Clarke-Coldwell, Noah's husband, had managed to buy more.

"I know I don't have to give a big speech," Roger said. "These last few weeks have been intense, and we've been spending a lot of that time together. What we're doing is risky, and I don't know that I'll have a chance to say this later on. Thank you. Thank you for trying, thank you for seeing that this is doable. For believing. I've spent so much of my life not believing, in suppressing any possibility of hope because I was afraid it was going to crush me. We will pull this off, and when we do, we will send a clear message that the Great Lakes Coven will burn. That Seamus's stranglehold is coming to an end. I hope to see all of you on the other side."

Lacey began to clap, and a few of the others joined in the applause.

Roger nodded to the group and ducked back toward the wall. Time was moving in peculiar jumps and drags. Every time he thought an hour had passed, only three minutes had, and when he thought only a minute had gone by, at least half an hour had. The agony of a winter's night was in its length. At barely past seven p.m., Roger both had far too much time before he was due at the servants' entrance to Chateau de Vampire and not enough. He touched Zack's pendant and then slipped it under his black shirt.

Noah, the slight warlock who had spelled Vincent to sleep during his violent magical outburst, joined Roger at the wall and surveyed the room before them. "Inspiring speech."

"Thanks," Roger said. "Do you have it?"

"Already in your left pocket," Noah replied.

Roger frowned but reached into his pocket and pulled out

a gold necklace with a medallion on it. Runes were carved into it. "How do I activate it?"

"Slide it over your head, concentrate however your magic speaks to you, and say 'alius sui.' Medallion's set to do the rest of the work for you. When you want to end it, just slip it off. Should work five times before the charm wears off." Noah cracked a lopsided grin. "Illusions are a specialty of mine. One reason I'm on team Post-Game. My husband's on team Firestarter."

Roger ran his thumb over the runes. In one of the first honest, long conversations Zack and Roger had ever had, Zack had attempted to drop as many news updates on him as possible. Same-sex marriage had come up, and the reality of its existence had made Roger ready to weep. So long in the shadows, pushed down and away, and yet there had been change. There was reason for hope. Life didn't have to stay the same.

But one still had to fight.

"Thank you, for this." Roger held up the necklace before sliding it back into his pocket. "A week isn't enough to master the sort of spell I needed."

"Eh, happy to help. The more involved I get with the Burrow, the more bullshit I realize goes on in this city. I'm looking forward to shaking up the status quo." Noah patted Roger's shoulder and then walked away.

Roger took one last look around at the people gathered. That more would filter in and out and join the mission was mind-boggling. He'd always assumed that no one would dare to take on Seamus because he'd been unable to for centuries. But his people weren't doing this to save Zack and Takashi— several of them were aiming for that to be part of their outcome, but it wasn't the group's primary focus. They were willing to take on one of the biggest powerhouses in Chicago because Roger had finally said enough was enough. How many lives would he have saved if he had acted sooner?

I can't save the past. Only the future.

Silently, Roger slipped away to the alleyway.

Before he'd gone more than a few steps, the building's door swung open, and Thomas stepped out. Darkness filled the narrow alley as he let the door close behind him. The streetlights were farther away, leaving long shadows that made Thomas seem older and haunted. "Not much of a goodbye there."

"I'll see you later," Roger replied.

"I know you will. But here. I was hoping you would take this." Thomas held out an envelope.

"What's this?" Roger took it from him.

"A letter for my son." Thomas cleared his throat. "If everything goes well, I'll have a chance to talk to him after we're done tonight. That letter is for … if you can give it to him at the Chateau, I'd appreciate it. I want to tell him that I'm sorry and I love him. I don't want him to think that I stopped caring."

"Even though he's a vampire?" Roger asked.

"He's my son," Thomas said firmly. "I've failed him for too long. I won't do it again."

The sincerity in his words left an ache in their wake. Thomas was trying to mend what he'd broken. Roger folded the envelope and slid it into his back pocket. "I can't promise a favorable response."

"He'd be within his rights to tell me to go to hell," Thomas replied. "Either way, I want you to know I am part of this fight as long as it takes. If I have to do it far from Zack, I will."

"I'll keep that in mind." Roger held out his hand. "I'm glad you came when I called."

"I'm glad you reached out." Thomas clasped Roger's hand. They shook once, solid and firm, and then Roger departed for his car.

CHAPTER 46

Zack had read until dawn, until the drowsiness daylight brought claimed him and pulled him under to sleep. Takashi hadn't returned to their bed. The first they'd seen of each other had been "breakfast," which had been a quick meal where Zack had failed to not kill his prey. After that, Seamus and Anton had given a lengthy lecture reminding Zack and Katie about the expectations for their behavior during the party.

Takashi had sat silently through the entire thing. He hadn't even looked at Zack.

When Seamus dismissed them to get ready, Zack slipped his hand into Takashi's. Though Takashi held his hand, there was no warmth in his touch, no small smile or sparkle in the corner of his eye.

Halfway back to his suite, Zack let Takashi's hand go. He waited until they were in his suite and the door was shut before he said, "You said you wouldn't be pissed. Promised, in fact."

"I'm aware of what I said." Takashi continued into the bedroom and headed for the closet.

"You were fine when you left last night," Zack said. "What happened with Seamus?"

"I can't talk about it." Takashi opened the closet door.

Zack paced in the bedroom while Takashi brought out their outfits for the night. He'd expected that he'd have to wear some kind of tuxedo or costume, but his attire was a beautiful black suit with a bright white dress shirt. Takashi's suit was a wine red, and his dress shirt was the black of Zack's suit.

With dutiful care, Takashi laid the suits out on the end of their bed and then went to the dresser to pull out accessories from the boxes on top. His motions were economical, the barest of necessary action to complete what needed to be done. The wall around his emotions had never been thicker. Zack couldn't glimpse even a blanked-out pop-up from him.

What did you do? Zack demanded in his mental connection.

Seamus didn't respond.

Zack came to a stop and clenched his fists. *What. The. Fuck. Did. You. Do?*

Still, nothing from Seamus.

Okay, the bastard wanted to be like that? Zack closed his eyes and let out his breath. He began, at the loudest of his thoughts, to scream, *WHAT THE FUCK DID YOU DO?*

Zackery! Seamus snapped.

I can go all fucking night if I have to, prick. Hell, I can go centuries.

A moment of silence passed. Zack restarted his demand.

Fine! Finish preparing and then meet me downstairs.

Zack opened his eyes.

Takashi finished laying out their cufflinks and tiepins for the party with a definitive clink. "What did he say?"

"You suddenly a mind reader?" Zack asked.

"You wanted an answer I wouldn't provide. He's the only other one who knows, and all you have to do is think at him,"

Takashi replied. "One needn't be a genius to figure out what you were doing."

With his chilling precision, Takashi strode back to the suits and began to change into his. Though his grace was still there, he was the least seductive he'd ever been.

The familiarity of his motions finally sprang forth a realization. Zack had suffered years of cold shoulders at family events. Now Takashi was giving him one. *So much for love fixing any problem.* Joining Takashi in silence, Zack quickly changed into his new suit. When he struggled to slide in one of his cufflinks, Takashi started to reach to help him, but Zack dipped away from him.

The micro flinch that passed over Takashi brought low bubbles of guilt in Zack's gut. But he wasn't the one who had begun this distance. If Takashi wanted to hide beneath a thousand layers again, then Zack was going to let him. He could put his own walls up, too.

They descended to the foyer together. Takashi went to Anton and Katie while Zack strode past Seamus's three-pet collection and followed his inner compass to find Seamus in a parlor. It was the room that had been wrecked the night Seamus had attacked Anton, but it'd long been repaired and set to rights. Well, not entirely repaired. The couch was a new one, the smell of the leather almost overpowering Seamus's musty scent of the grave.

Zack's stiletto dagger was in a lovely new sheath that had his crest, the dagger with a snake wrapped around it, and it sat on the end table beside Seamus.

"Look at you! So devilishly handsome!" Seamus smiled at him. "Go on, do a spin. I want to see if the tailor managed perfection or only did the front correctly."

"I'm not in the mood," Zack replied. Though his immature approach had forced Seamus into this conversation, he sought the place of balance and control he'd first discovered in dominating Takashi. That was the part of himself that was powerful and could see him through this, and the part he had to show at the debut party if he was going to display strength. "What happened last night?"

"I greeted several of the vampires you'll be meeting tonight and welcomed them to my domain," Seamus said lightly.

"Yeah, and what else?" Zack motioned back at the foyer. "Takashi slept in his own suite last night and won't look at me."

"Ah. I was afraid that might happen." Seamus stepped closer to Zack and lowered his voice. "I had a small discussion with him."

"Discussion," Zack repeated. "What was the subject of this 'discussion'?"

"I understand that you believe that you have found the true loves of your life, but those two are not worth your time, Zackery. You'll come to see them for what they are, a puppet and a leech."

Calm master vampires do not scream obscenities at the top of their lungs. Zack slid his hands into his pants pockets, where he could hold his fingertips against his leg. That way, he couldn't reflexively form a fist and attempt to punch Seamus through his smug fucking face. "I thought you approved of Takashi."

"I understand you have affection for him, and I won't hurt him as long as you cling to that, but you must know that he isn't partner material, not in the long run," Seamus said smoothly. He leaned in closer to murmur in Zack's ear. "How can you stomach him? He traded a girl's life for a phone. A *phone*, Zackery. One that he used to call his sire. How can you be certain that he won't attempt to follow Nell's order and kill you?"

"He would never."

"I'm certain he said he wouldn't. He is that smart," Seamus continued. "But he is a known liar. I don't blame him for that. We all tell falsehoods when needs must. But you can't expect me to hold regard for someone who conspired against me, bartered with my lover, reached out to one of my enemies in another conspiracy attempt, and convinced my son that he could become a powerful coven leader within a few hours of rising! Either he isn't as smart as we've been led to believe, or he is playing a deeper game than we know."

"You said having a goal was a good thing for me," Zack said under his breath.

"I have a new one for you. Find a worthier partner," Seamus said. "Perhaps you'll meet them at the party tonight."

Words failed Zack. Nothing he said would change Seamus's opinion of Takashi, and he was left wondering if Seamus's constant assurances of support had anything to actually do with him. The errands, the killing of nest vampires—even the fucking debut party—were tests of his abilities. Seamus was only trying to see if Zack had become a monster like him. He'd only ever mold him further into a villain.

He'd been naïve to trust Seamus for even a moment.

"Why is my dagger out?" Zack said hollowly.

"I hope that I've eliminated the potential threat for the evening, but in case I haven't, you should be armed." Seamus handed over the blade.

Would Seamus kill him if he attacked right now?

"Don't do something that would ruin this wonderful evening," Seamus said seriously. Clearly, he had heard Zack's thought.

After the party was a different beast. Zack slid the sheath onto his belt, putting it in place so the dagger was at his back. It wouldn't be a quick draw, but it wouldn't be out in plain sight either. *I will get him out of this.*

Seamus laughed and put his arm around Zack's shoulders. He tugged him along as he headed for the foyer. Telepathically, he said, *In time, you'll forget about the leech.*

The only one Zack hoped to forget was the one who'd promised to never throw him away. It stung that someone who seemed to care so fucking deeply for him was the worst monster he'd ever met. But toxic obsession wasn't love. He'd jeopardized real love because he'd thought he needed Seamus's protection.

He would never make that mistake again.

CHAPTER 47

Ezra met Roger at the Chateau's secret entrance. Nestled away near the staff parking lot, the door melted perfectly into the wall unless one knew which specific stone was a handle. That particular patch of wall was also in deep shadows, providing obscurity.

Ezra wore a gray leather collar with Candide's crest tag and an impeccably tailored dark gray suit. His red hair was tamed in a loose style. "You're not going to blend in looking like that."

"Don't worry, I have a disguise." Roger pulled out the medallion that Noah had given him and put it around his neck.

He hadn't had much time for magic lessons over the last week, but he'd run through many of the basics with Bastian. The internal seas that had been rising and falling were how his arcane abilities spoke to him. He imagined floating along them, not inside of a ship but as if he were on the waves himself. "Alius sui."

The tangy scent of burning ozone itched his nose. When he lightly touched it, his hand gently tingled. The sensation was a faint buzz, but other vampires might be able to sense it. He'd have to be careful not to touch anyone else.

"That is a different look. Different smell, too," Ezra said.

"What do I look like?" Roger asked.

"You appear to be a six-foot blond with decent enough taste in suits but nothing remarkable. In fact, my gaze slides past you."

"Thank the Heavens for talented warlocks."

Ezra grabbed the stone and twisted the handle. The door opened inward to a dark, narrow hallway. The occasional tiny LED light provided ample illumination for a vampire, and navigating the passage was a breeze. It reminded Roger of the back ways into speakeasies and secretive donor houses, only the Chateau's was far neater. There was no hint of fear soaked into the walls, no concern that one might get caught in illicit activities. Instead, a brush of warmth greeted him. Desire.

Oh, how he hoped the evening would end in love rather than terror.

"Did you decide upon a fake name?" Ezra said.

"You're the writer. Choose one for me," Roger replied.

Ezra groaned softly. "Pure torture, making me come up with a name. You're Harry, a friend of mine from England. You do still remember how to speak with an English accent, don't you?"

"That aristocratic London version or my actual dialect?" Roger replied.

"I hate to say it, but aristocratic. If you sound poor, that'll attract attention." Ezra scrunched his nose. "I hate that I just said that. How long until the revolution?"

"Not long," Roger promised.

"See that it isn't."

"You could participate rather than telling me to hurry up."

Ezra paused. He had the benefit of being shorter and slimmer, and he turned around to face Roger. Sneaking around and having him near reminded Roger of how they'd been in their early nights together, when Ezra was still a mortal. No flicker of romantic love sparked, nor did a long habit of falling back on sexual interests renew. Roger didn't want to avoid the troubles ahead—and the realization of that was an unburdening, like finally breaking free of water to breathe fresh air when drowning had been so near.

"You're serious," Ezra murmured. He pushed Roger's shoulder lightly. "Why the bloody hell did you wait so long to ask me?"

"Well, I believe you were a bit preoccupied not answering your phone." Roger flicked the crest tag on Ezra's collar.

With a frown, Ezra put his hand to his collar. Shame darkened his steel-gray eyes, and he lowered his gaze before straightening his shoulders and meeting Roger's gaze. "I only wanted some joy. I never expected it."

"I'm not angry," Roger replied. "But after tonight, sides will be drawn. Candide will choose herself."

"We're standing in the middle of a secret passage on our way to rendezvous with your lovers underneath the nose of an ancient monster who uses any excuse to punish those around him. One might say she's already chosen a side. Yours."

"I had to show up on her door and guilt her into this, Ezra." Roger put his finger under Ezra's chin when Ezra started to look down again. "We know her. She will defend what's hers, but she will never fight for change."

"I hate when you're right." Ezra brushed a forming tear from his eye. "Forgive me for hiding?"

Roger managed a smile. "I've been hiding in plain sight for a few centuries. I suppose I can forgive you for sticking your head in the sand a few months."

Ezra laughed, wiped quickly at his other eye, then began to lead the way again.

They trekked up three flights of stairs, bypassing a few other turns and exits. The first room that they stepped into was empty. It appeared to be a small library or an office with many bookcases. Upon closer inspection, Roger noticed that much of the furniture was discreet kink pieces. The Chateau catered to fantasies, and not every vampire had the urge to invade a bedroom or lock their prey up in a dungeon.

After they had both stepped through, Ezra swung the fake bookcase shut. "The door opens on this side by pulling the copy of *The Three Musketeers*. Every interior room on this floor has one of these secret doors. Try not to get lost in the labyrinth back there. Once the party is in full swing, those passageways will have mortals flitting back and forth."

"Allowing her patrons all the privacy they need and hiding any bodies from sensitive mortals," Roger said. "Just as she did in London."

"Ah, right. I was barely ever in that place. Smelled awful after I became a vampire."

"That was the Thames," Roger replied, putting on his English nobleman's voice as they left the faux library.

"Eh, that's likely." Ezra continued on to the stairs that led downward. His demeanor brightened to avid host. "The party shall be on the second floor, with permissions granted for third-floor usage, of course. Anton has insisted that no expense be spared for this grand party, and the last time I checked, the guest list had two hundred vampires on it. Do you remember Faustino? Oh, and Abhijit?"

Roger knew the names. He and Faustino had tangled a few times when Seamus had first moved their group to New York. Those entanglements had included a very loud breakup in a tavern for gay men. The last Roger had heard of Abhijit, he had moved to Los Angeles. That had been in 1983, and Roger hadn't tried to track him down.

"I think Abhijit's probably one of the few men over two hundred that I haven't slept with," Roger said.

A classical song drifted from the strings of a violin into the hall. Chattering party guests were already in the hallway and in rooms. Mortal pets followed their vampire masters. Donors that worked for the Chateau wore white collars with Candide's crest tag. They were dressed in black vests and shorts and carried trays with drinks between rooms.

A vanilla-and-floral scent enhanced the earthiness that came from vampires congregating while covering any hint of mustiness. Here and there were vases of beautiful bouquets of red and gold. Little tables had black chits laid out on them with piles of red chits at the back.

Roger picked up one of the red to closer inspect it. The chits were meant to be handed off to donors so that they could prove a recent feeding and earn their pay. They were sitting out like party favors for anyone to grab. Red meant a longer drink with some possibilities for play; black meant an intent to be rough on a donor, possibly to death.

These chits had a crest on either side of them. One was a dagger with a snake wrapped around the hilt and the blade, not quite forming an ouroboros. The other was a raven with its wings spread wide and carrying a rose.

Two new fledglings with crests were serious business. Anton and Seamus hadn't presented anyone in society like this. Roger had been given his during a quiet night in Paris, while Anton had never graced Dmitri with one.

"Apparently, Faustino is a big shot these nights. Candide told me that he brought multiple gifts to shower upon the new fledglings," Ezra said, carrying on their conversation. He caught Roger looking at the chit. "Ah, yes. Anton insisted on having those made. A bit darling, but a waste of plastic in the long run, in my opinion. Will you be feeding tonight?"

"I should like to." Roger pocketed the red chit. "Do you know if they plan to abide by tradition?"

"That was what I heard," Ezra said, and only from knowing him did Roger spot the worry in his expression.

The custom was that the new fledgling show off and drink from their prey in front of a crowd at midnight. After that, everyone else was allowed to feed. *Did Seamus prepare Zack for that? Or is he hoping that he'll freeze up and make a fool of himself?* "I wonder if I'll be able to snag a hello before we descend into revelry."

Ezra caught Roger's eye, and the quick nod meant he'd gathered Roger's true meaning. "I'm sure we'll be able to arrange that. For now, though, let me introduce you to a few of my friends. We have so many vampires from out of town that I'm surprised any of my fellow coven mates made the list!"

With the grace and charm of enduring noble manners, Ezra linked his arm with Roger's and began to take him around the party as if he were an old friend and everyone they spoke to were complete strangers to him. Roger had endured worse, and he faked politeness while keeping his eyes peeled for Zack's or Takashi's arrival.

Takashi straightened his sleeves after stepping out of the limo behind Seamus's pet collection. The three mortals shivered in the cold. Their jackets were thin, gauzy material unfitting for an Illinois winter night. But they made no complaint as they hurried along the path to the front doors behind Seamus, Zack, Anton, and Katie.

Anton wanted Katie's debut—and therefore Zack's—to be sophisticated in the eyes of their visitors. That was one reason they'd selected the Chateau to host the celebration rather than Seamus's mansion or the club Devil's Cove. Such affairs were supposed to be classy, and though the mansion was a display of wealth, letting vampires know that Seamus's home lacked the basic protection of a threshold was a massive security flaw. Some elder vampires would consider it a sign that he was a poor master if the mortals he kept never felt safe enough to call their house a home.

Chateau de Vampire had all the elegance of a palace and the exclusive air of a private club. As requested, the donor house was closed to the public that night. Red lights illuminated the outside of the building and the three statues along the walk. The center one, which the sidewalk curved around on both sides, was of Seamus. Between the light and the shadows, his long fangs seemed to drip with blood. The last few times Takashi had been here, he'd thought that the statue had a handsome charm, but he only saw the malice in the stone's form from the way he grinned to the rough hold he had on the nude figure in his arms.

Another of the statues depicted Anton in a billowy shirt. The artist had pulled off the manic quality of his grin, yet Takashi couldn't help feeling that it was a mask even for the marble Anton.

The last of the statues was of Candide in a centuries-old fashion. The full skirts of her dress nearly hid the kneeling figure at her feet, a nod to how she was known to always have a few mortals at hand.

Two other statues had once decorated the walk, but even their pedestals were removed. They'd been of Roger and Dmitri. Apparently, their fall from grace was complete. Seamus was attempting to erase their presence altogether.

Several black-clad and brown-collared security guards were checking guests in at the door. When they spotted Seamus, they bowed and motioned for him to go ahead.

"Master!" Candide said, bubbling with her French accent. Her blonde hair was in a beautiful braid, and she wore a dark purple dress that had the lightest of sparkle in the weave. She held her hands out for Seamus to take them, and then she kissed him on either cheek as he drew close. "I do hope you and your son will be satisfied with the party tonight! Anton and Takashi have worked so very hard to ensure I nailed every detail!" She let go of Seamus and held one hand out to Anton.

Anton swept in and kissed her cheeks. "You look ravishing."

"Thank you." Candide turned her attention to Katie. "Aren't you darling?"

For the party, Katie had donned a carmine satin dress that ended just above her knee. It was modest without over-playing her youth. She had a gold necklace of a raven with its wings spread and holding a rose. Anton had given it to her, had chosen it as her crest but hadn't told her yet.

As she chatted with Candide and twirled to show off her dress and high heels, Takashi felt a distance that an elephant couldn't fill. His tether to her was still there. He could sense her delight in the moment and her growing hunger, but he was hardly standing there inside his own skin. His gaze wandered and landed on Zack.

Zack looked dashing in his black suit. His hair was an artful mess that Takashi wished he'd taken the time to tame a little. In the Chateau's light, he was a perfect porcelain, the pale pink undertones of his skin having gone almost white after his transformation.

"Zackery, wonderful to see you again, mon cher," Candide said as she greeted him. Zack managed a smile for her, even when she insisted that he twirl for her, too.

After that, her attention started to drift toward Takashi.

"I believe people are waiting on us, darling," Seamus said with a grin that was too wide.

"Of course they are. And we are clogging the entryway! Come, come. I have an arm for each of you magnificent new children of the night! Now, I know Zackery was here as a mortal, but did you ever have the chance, Kathleen?" Candide turned to begin leading the way deeper into the Chateau. She held her arms out for Zack and Katie to join her, and they did.

"I never had the pleasure, master," Katie said.

"It's mistress, if you insist on being formal, which I insist that you don't! You're Anton's offspring and a promising young mage, I hear," Candide replied. "I may be a captain, but you, my girl, are royalty. You both are. I hope to see you here all the time. Beautiful young people deserve plenty of time out of the house."

Candide launched into a spiel about how the Chateau ran and what it offered. Seamus had already set up accounts for Zack and Katie so they could feed at the coven's donor houses. At least, he had, in theory. His funds weren't infinite, and something would have to give.

Bitterly, Takashi hoped that Roger had managed to bankrupt Seamus so ruthlessly that the bastard would lose his grand mansion.

The bulk of the party was on the second floor. Many of the rooms had a handful of vampires and their retinues. Faustino had a mortal with a white collar under each arm while he boastfully chatted to the others that, yes, he could be spotted in Manet's "Masked Ball at the Opera." That was a line that had worked on Takashi back in their early relationship. Now, it was a braggart's painful attempt to be influential.

Takashi nearly laughed when a young pale vampire with white-blond hair proclaimed there was nothing amazing about a painting when he had a million views on his most recent film. An argument erupted about whether or not a vampire should engage in creating pornography, but the pale vampire didn't seem to care what the others thought of his profession.

Candide continued wheeling Katie and Zack through the party and pointing out tiny details that were specific for the evening—like the chits with both crests on them.

"Both?" Katie exclaimed delightedly. "Wait, do I have one?"

"I was going to make a show of telling you tonight." Anton nodded to Katie's necklace. "A raven and a rose. Death, magic, and beauty."

"Do you know yours?" Katie picked up a black chit from a nearby table. "Dagger and snake. What does that mean?"

"Killer and survivor," Seamus replied. He plucked the chit from her hand. "You needn't worry about carrying one of these tonight."

"He's right," Candide said. "I would have supplied my own gifts for you to drink from, but many of our guests have brought offerings. I should be introducing you two to some of them, unless you would like to take over that duty, master?"

"I enjoy watching you play hostess, Candide." Seamus kissed her cheek. "You have always impressed me."

"Thank you, master." Candide dipped her head in acknowledgment, then steered Zack and Katie to a room farther in.

For Takashi, keeping in step behind them was an exercise in walking on broken glass and smiling through it. Seamus hadn't glanced his way. With Zack's focus on what was happening to him, would anyone notice if he slipped away?

He held off from a step, then another. When no one, not even one of the pets trailing after Seamus, turned toward him, he slipped into one of the nearby rooms.

Light conversation was happening in this room, but Takashi wasn't immediately sucked into the verbal wordplay. Instead, he stayed up against one of the walls beside the entry. No call of his name nor one of Seamus's people came to fetch him. He was free.

"Ah, Takashi!" Ezra said.

Takashi cursed his luck, then fate, and for good measure, destiny. If any of those entities existed, certainly they believed only the wicked deserved any peace. He plastered on a smile he knew was too weak and faced Ezra.

Ezra was handsome in his gray suit and collar. He had another man on his arm. Something about the dark blond, white vampire was oddly familiar, but Takashi couldn't place his finger on the reason why.

"I didn't expect you to be a wallflower," Ezra said. "I don't know if you've met my good friend Harry. He's from England."

"A pleasure to meet you," the man said, his English accent thick.

And one Takashi had heard before. That was Roger's voice. He rarely fell back on his older accents, but he'd used it shamelessly in bed back in 1921. Takashi scanned the details of the man's face and settled on his brown eyes.

The disguise was fantastic, but those eyes were Roger's eyes.

Roger was alive. He had come into the heart of the beast that wanted him dead.

Takashi could cry, but he couldn't allow himself to do so.

"Yes, a pleasure," Takashi said breathlessly.

"I am hoping that you can keep my good friend entertained while I see to a few things," Ezra said. "Candide is the hostess, but she did beg of me to help her this evening."

"Perhaps we'll be able to meet you upstairs?" Roger asked.

"Mm, yes. In about half an hour?" Ezra replied.

"I'm looking forward to it." Roger slipped from Ezra's side and took up a position against the wall beside Takashi.

"Wonderful." Ezra dashed off.

The relief of having Roger next to him robbed Takashi of his senses. He searched for other minutia of his lover that he'd missed, but Roger was even standing differently. His swagger and posture had been like a cat on the prowl. Now he moved with a stalwart set to his shoulders and a confident control in his step.

Speaking at all would break Takashi's voice, he was certain of it. After the tumbles and pitfalls of the last few evenings, his composure was a fraying rope. Once it broke, the fifty-ton weight of pressure he'd managed to hold off would crash into him, obliterating what little calm he had left.

If only he and Roger were alone, he might be able to find some strength from their reunion rather than feel that it was cutting away at that fraying rope.

They needed privacy, and they wouldn't find it in crowded rooms full of vampires with fantastic hearing. Takashi cleared his throat. "I hear there are all kinds of rooms on the third floor. Any fantasy could be fulfilled."

"A few more minutes," Roger whispered. "I've only just come down the stairs. Might seem odd to turn around and run up them."

Takashi nodded. He let his hand hang down, closer to Roger, and Roger brushed the back of his hand with his. Their light touch tingled, and it took Takashi a second to realize that magic, not love, was causing the sensation. Roger's disguise was so complete because he had arcane help.

"This is, perhaps, the most excruciating night in my entire existence," Takashi murmured. "And I will remind you that I died with my brains spilling out of my skull."

"Careful now," Roger replied. He had his gaze out on the room. "We've only just met."

"I am sick to death of games," Takashi said. "They are a poison for which I have no antidote."

Roger raised an eyebrow. "Perhaps we needn't wait so long."

"My thoughts exactly. To the third floor. Now."

CHAPTER 48

Zack lost interest in keeping track of names after Candide introduced him to a seventh visiting vampire because he noticed that Takashi was nowhere to be seen. He wasn't sure exactly when Takashi had ducked out, and that bothered him more. Were things bad enough that Takashi was going to run away? Flat out leave him and Katie with Seamus and Anton?

He had to find a way to distract himself so he wouldn't think too intently and alert Seamus. His attention wandered to the mortals in the room. There were over two dozen of them, most cozying up to the vampires who'd brought them or the others they knew. Each had a heartbeat, and as he keyed in to that frequency, he heard multiple pulses. Every draw of breath and scratch of fabric was suddenly right in his fucking ears.

The lights had seemed perfectly fine, but as the pain started in his head, they were brighter than a hot summer sun. And the smell was gag worthy. The humans reeked of sweat and copper and bodily fluids, and the vampires stank of dirt, and the flowers were nothing but pollen.

"Pull it together," Seamus said in his ear. He put his hand on Zack's back. "You're fine."

With a glare, Zack tried to send his pain along the bond to Seamus.

Seamus blinked twice and grimaced before recovering.

"Oh, there you are, my mistress!" Ezra said as he approached Candide.

A murmur went across the room about that. Vampires called their superiors master, so it was not completely weird for Ezra to say that to Candide. However, he was wearing a collar, and that was something not really done. Some probably wore them behind closed doors, but in public, collars were for mortals. They were signs of being owned, and that was a weakness. *The rest of us only pretend we don't share that weakness. Seamus owns us.*

Candide lightly kissed Ezra. "How are you finding the evening?"

"It is a lovely party, but I can't help being restless," Ezra replied. "I see our guests of honor have arrived. You must be Kathleen. I'm quite honored to meet you."

"This is Ezra," Candide said.

"Nice to meet you," Katie said.

"Zack! You look astonishing!" Ezra moved to embrace Zack.

The mere thought of being touched compounded the headache shoving its way into Zack. He stepped back, putting a hand to his temple. When Ezra looked wounded, Zack said, "Forgive me. Suddenly, everything's … a lot."

"Sensory overload?" Ezra asked sympathetically.

Zack nodded.

"Uff, I used to get the most dismal headaches," Ezra murmured. "A bit of quiet will set you right. Come along with me."

Escaping from the endless parade of greetings sounded amazing. Zack started to follow Ezra.

Seamus caught his arm. He leaned in close to whisper in

his ear, "Not more than ten minutes. You are meant to be down here meeting people. Understood?"

Narrowing his eyes, Zack focused on the screaming pain ramping up. *I'll take as long as it takes.*

With another wince, Seamus let him go. "Perhaps twenty, if necessary."

Ezra ushered Zack from the room. The noise and light weren't any better in the hallway, but before he could comment on that, Ezra whisked him up the staircase. Though the floor was open to guests, the floor was blessedly empty. Echoes were still chasing them, but Zack was able to ignore that better.

Ezra opened a door, cursed, and then closed it. He opened the next and did the same. And again with the third.

However, Zack hadn't heard anyone in those rooms. No smells of blood or sex lingered on the air either. "What are you looking for?"

"A surprise," Ezra grumbled. "Which I should have designated a better where. Unless we're the first ones up here. Fuck, I'm an idiot."

"What sort of—" Zack's sense of smell was still on overload, but he thought he caught a whiff of Takashi's scent. As far as he knew, Takashi had never been up to the third floor of the Chateau. He followed his nose to a door and opened it.

The room looked like a modern office, complete with filing cabinets. In the center, Takashi was hugging a tall, blond man. The man was holding on to him just as tightly. They were comfortable with each other, familiar in a way that made Zack ache with jealousy.

"Here we go," Ezra said. "Good find."

"Good find?" Zack hissed.

"Well, yes. You found the surprise."

At the sound of the voices, Takashi and the man broke apart. Takashi brushed bloody tears from his cheeks.

"What the hell—"

"Zack," the man said. Only he said it exactly how Roger should. While Zack's brain attempted to come back online after that startling realization, the man took off a necklace.

The illusion vanished, and before him was Roger. His hair was horrible, overall short and in some places brownish, and he was wearing the sort of black tactical gear that hunters tended to wear on bigger missions. But otherwise, he was Roger. Tall, handsome, warm smile, and big-hearted Roger.

He opened his arms wide.

Zack flew into them, and their hug was one of the top three in Zack's entire life. The wash of relief soothed away his headache, and he clutched to Roger. He was barely aware that Ezra stayed out of the room and shut the door for him.

Takashi's crying made sense. A sob was in Zack's throat, too, and he wasn't sure where it was coming from. It didn't feel happy. He should have been nothing but blissful that Roger was here, was with them, and was safe. Instead, sadness overwhelmed him. *I don't deserve this.*

He latched onto Roger's emotions, seeking something happy in him. Trailing his mind along Roger's inner journal page, he ran across shapes that held no meaning and a firm feeling that Roger wanted everything to be good.

"Someone has some natural talents, I see," Roger said gently.

Slowly, the inner journal closed, not leaving behind a pop-up or anything else for Zack to read. Roger just closed his mind off as if it was just that easy.

"You have to teach me how to do that," Zack said.

"I will." Roger kissed his forehead.

His touch was reassuring, and that broke the storming clouds of sadness. With Roger here, everything would be okay. That was what Roger did. Zack researched, Takashi schemed, and Roger made things okay. *I want everything to be okay.*

You are the one that makes things difficult, Seamus said in his mind.

The echo of Seamus's voice startled Zack back from the brink of his joy, and he pushed away from Roger. One stray thought might alert Seamus, and then they'd all be in danger. The three of them might be able to fight him and win, except a couple hundred other powerful vampires were partying downstairs. Killing Seamus would mean claiming the throne of the GLC, but how many others would immediately leap at the chance to kill the new master and take it for themselves? If it became a free-for-all fight, then there was no telling how many threats were downstairs.

"I can't be here," Zack said. "I-I-I just can't."

"Zack, wait," Roger said.

Zack took a step back toward the door. Doing so brought Takashi into view. All the regret he'd swallowed since he spoke to Seamus at the mansion rose, and he wouldn't choke it back down. "I'm sorry, Takashi. I am so fucking sorry."

The coldness that Takashi had had in his blue eyes melted, and that would have to be enough because Zack couldn't stay and risk the two people he loved most. Using his amazing speed, he rushed for the door. He had it open and was about to step through the opening.

With an invisible force, the door started to close. Caught off guard, it was far stronger than him, and he barely danced back from it to keep it from slamming into him. When he tried to open it again, it remained shut. Alarmed, he turned back to tell his lovers about the weird occurrence.

Roger had his hand outstretched like he was holding on to the door handle. Instead of brown or red, his eyes were a blue so pale they were a silvery white.

That wasn't a color that Roger's eyes had ever turned before.

Some supernatural entities could take on the appearances of others. Nell would have no trouble hiring an assassin, and taking Roger's form would be the perfect way to get through their guards. *We've been tricked.* Zack reached for the hilt of his dagger. "Whoever you are, you're going to wish you'd picked a different face to steal."

Roger frowned at him, his brow pinched with confusion.

Takashi ran forward and put his hand on Zack's shoulder. "It's our Roger."

A brief warning flared in Zack's mind, claiming that Takashi could be in on the assassination attempt. But as Zack met his gaze, he knew that was far from the truth. However Takashi was certain that this was Roger, he was right. He had never wavered in his love for either of them. Never betrayed them.

Zack was the traitor.

And he might accidentally be so again.

He sucked in a deep breath and said, "Roger, you have to let me go. You both do."

CHAPTER 49

The mortal steel in Zack's eyes had been replaced with a crimson color that belonged to a much older vampire. As a mortal, he'd slouched a little, let his shoulders dip whenever he wasn't sure of himself. He'd been full of rage and tears, but he had been sweet, too.

Now he stood tall, with his chin level and his shoulders straight. In a voice laden with an ethereal quality, he repeated his demand. "Seriously, you have to let me out of here."

When Zack had initially reached for the door, Roger had reacted on instinct. His arcane power had known the shape of his will before the instant he'd realized what he wanted. This was his one chance to speak to his lovers after a month, and he wasn't about to let it slip away.

Even if something was clearly wrong between them. The turmoil was obvious in the way they were avoiding each other, and seeing that strengthened Roger's resolve that the three of them needed to talk.

"You're worried about the bond with your sire," Roger said, fighting through his numbness. He'd rehearsed different speeches in his head, and though he'd hoped it wouldn't come up, he knew that sires and their sirelings could share each other's strong emotions. He had never expected Zack to flee because of it. "All we need to do is create a believable lie for whatever you're feel—"

"He can read my mind," Zack snapped.

That's new.

Zack hurried for the door again.

Roger closed it with telekinesis.

"Roger!" Zack hissed.

"I have been fighting for a month to see you. I am not about to let you run away," Roger replied.

"He could—"

"Fuck him. This is about us." Roger swept forward and held Zack's cheeks with both hands. "You are not going anywhere until we talk. If I have to unleash an earthquake upon Candide's beautiful palace, I will. I don't care. You are what matters." He reached a hand out to Takashi as he met his gaze. "The two of you are all that matters."

With a wan smile, Takashi took hold of Roger's hand and squeezed.

"I imagine that our time apart has been eventful for you like it's been for me," Roger said. He took Zack by the hand as well and drew both his lovers toward the desk. If Zack tried to zip out again, he wasn't sure he'd be able to pull off the feat of getting the door shut. Zack was faster than any fledgling he'd ever seen, almost as quick as himself.

He rested his backside against the desk and held on to Zack's and Takashi's hands. The two of them drifted off to either of his sides. They had their mental defenses up. Takashi's was fierce as a fortress. Zack's was paper-thin. Roger could slide through both, but he didn't need to. Zack had apologized with a tone of voice Roger knew came from the broken place inside him; Takashi was withdrawn the same way he'd been when he said his goodbyes in 1921.

Additionally, their hurt was the sort that had to come from deep feelings. At the Winter's Grand Ball, they had danced, and they had sparkled together, but they hadn't shone with love. *Somewhere along the line, they fell in love without having to go through me.* He loved that for them. When he had told Zack that he deserved all the love he could handle, this was the sort of thing he'd meant.

What they needed was patience, and Roger found a well of it. Rushing the mending of hearts would only shatter them further. But their time was also limited, and he needed them all on the same page before he left. Or, at the very least, in the same book.

He kissed Zack's fingertips, then Takashi's. They were still as statues.

"I have plenty to say, but first, what's happened between you two?" Roger asked.

Both looked toward the floor in the opposite direction of the other.

His lovers were intent on keeping up their shields, so Roger decided to lower his own. He let the ache he had harbored for both of them since they'd been taken from him out from his heart. Rather than stowing the fear he'd felt for their safety, he untied it from its mooring and let it loose.

They would have to choose to read him.

After a long moment, Zack slumped and put his hand to his face to cover his tears. Takashi tightened his grip on Roger's hand.

They must have peeked at what he'd shown them. They knew how deeply he loved them.

"I fucked up," Zack said. "I ... I massively fucked up."

Takashi looked to the ceiling, batting his eyes so that his tears wouldn't start. "In trying to build something, I have become *nothing*."

Zack frowned at him.

"I know how that feels," Roger said gently. "I have been struggling with that myself. But you are not nothing, Takashi. You could never be."

Takashi laughed, a bitter, brittle sound, and strayed farther to the side. "You don't know what he's done."

"I do, too!" Zack stepped toward the other wall as he turned to face Takashi. He still clutched Roger's hand. "And I am so, so, so fucking sorry."

"Not you," Takashi said, wiping away a tear. "At least, not just you."

"I need more information," Roger said.

Takashi shook his head, his tears running down his cheeks.

"Fine, you want to know? I told Seamus that Nell wants me dead," Zack replied. "He's been *nice* to me. He ... it's weird, and it's fucking twisted, but Seamus loves me like his son. As much as Seamus can love anyone. More than my actual dad does."

"I doubt that."

Zack rolled his eyes, then sighed away his sarcasm. He said sincerely, "Look, I know you're brimming with happiness that you're able to hold us again, but my father—"

Roger released Zack's hand and held up one finger to make him pause. Once Zack clamped his jaws shut, he said, "I have something for you. From him."

"From who? My *dad*?" Zack asked. "How?"

Roger took the envelope from Thomas out of his pocket and handed it over to Zack. "I needed help from someone with your wealth of knowledge and the practical experience I seemed to lack. I reached out to your father, and he answered. I don't know what that letter says, but I do know that he has been trying to right his wrongs. He called you courageous."

"You've been working with my dad?" Zack scowled at Roger. "Seriously?"

"And your sister," Roger said. Takashi's mental shield was

cracking. The desire to scream and howl his pain was growing. Not knowing what was causing the break, Roger held on to his hand firmly. The comfort of his touch was all he had.

"She's just a kid!"

"Seems she shares a family trait. She's stubborn as hell," Roger replied. "Even your father can't convince her to sit on the sidelines."

"What about my mom? Cal?" Zack asked hesitantly.

"Your mother never showed. I did try to break into the mansion to rescue you, but I was only able to save Dmitri, and only then because Anton allowed it. Cal came along on that mission but made it clear he wasn't a trustworthy ally. Thomas sent him away." Roger turned toward Takashi, angling his body in his direction. "Sweetheart, believe me when I say I have been fighting my doubts longer than you've been alive. Until I saw the two of you, I wasn't sure the course I'd picked was the right one. But I am *with* you. Because of the two of you, I am discovering lost pieces of myself. Why did you say you're nothing?"

Takashi started to pull away.

Roger tugged him closer. If kindness wouldn't do it, he'd have to bring out a bit of his own stubbornness. "All right. Then someone needs to tell me what Zack meant about Nell wanting to kill him. Is that true?"

"It is," Takashi whispered. "I called her. Oh God, you don't know. It was Nell."

"What was?" Roger asked.

"She was the one to make a deal with a fey to lock you in a coffin," Takashi continued. Once begun, his pace quickened. "She wanted you to come back to Chicago and cause a civil war so she could pick up the pieces of the GLC. I don't know her exact plans, but Zack waking you wrecked whatever she had in motion. When I told her that Zack was now Seamus's fledgling, she insisted that I kill him."

Epiphanies lit like firecrackers, one after another of bright light, leaving him in a shadow of depression as they passed. Nell had been a friend. An ally. And she'd played him. Roger took a deep breath. His lovers needed him to be their buoy right now, and he would do anything to keep them afloat. "Because if Zack dies, he'll take a measure of Seamus's power to the grave."

"Power I think we've been underestimating," Zack added. "Have either of you ever seen his eyes go completely black and red?"

"I have," Takashi said. "They became like voids with rubies when he was threatening me. Zack, I'm sorry for how I've been treating you tonight, but I didn't know what to do … I still don't. Seamus … he accused me of trying to seduce Anton. Then he ripped off Evander's head and sent it back to Nell, basically declaring open war on her. He made a point of telling the representative that he knew about the threat on your life. The only way he would have known that—"

"Would be if you or I told him," Zack said. "That's not a hard leap to make, especially for a creature as old as Nell."

"And Takashi has built his career on being Nell's loyal ambassador," Roger said. The conclusion spilled out of him as he traced the map of logic he found between Takashi's behavior and his own knowledge of covens. "Siding with one's sire is expected, even after leaving their coven. The fact that you've officially moved, that you've been seen standing beside Seamus, and then that message, everyone will know that you've switched your allegiance. If you're willing to move away from someone so powerful, who has given you so much, then others will assume that what you really care for is your own status and prestige. They will believe you are a false friend at best and an active saboteur at worst."

"I will be welcome nowhere," Takashi said with a nod. "Seamus has made it clear that he will draw out the agony of my life before snuffing it. Everything I've ever done is ash."

Zack launched himself at Takashi and wrapped him in a fierce hug.

Gently, Roger let go of Takashi's hand. With all that he had learned, he needed a moment to adjust to his shifting reality. Nell's betrayal stung, but it wasn't unexpected. Not entirely. She had been forceful about Roger going back to Chicago, and she'd demanded that he come up with a plan to take the leadership as soon as possible. Her claim that Takashi was her assurance that she would be paid back had made sense at the time, but he had never stopped to think about why she cared so much for a few scant million. The whole reason they had settled on that amount was that it wouldn't hurt her to extend the loan for some time.

She'd sent Takashi for exactly the reason Zack had suspected in their first meeting. He was supposed to be willing to kill either of them if he had to.

The night the three of them had first slept together, Roger had delved into Takashi's mind and seen a piece that he kept hidden away. Takashi desired to live his own life as he saw fit. Nell was a decent master—she had far more respect for her subordinates than many—but her underlings were still *under* her. Her fist was not clad in iron, but a hand in a leather glove was able to choke life and happiness, too.

Takashi *had* been out for himself, but that didn't mean he was without love or loyalty. Freedom of choice was the greatest of liberties. That was what Takashi wanted to do. He had grown from a hesitant young vampire into a sophisticated charmer because there was power in saying the right things to the right people. He'd seen what their lives were like and wagered on political capital to grant him some measure of freedom.

It had been a murky decision, but Roger had done far worse to feel an iota of reprieve from Seamus. Takashi had done the best he could.

Zack's fumble was understandable. Though some part of Roger wanted to scream that he naturally should have known better, he knew what Seamus could be like when he wanted to impress someone. Newly dead, bound to Seamus, with only Takashi to provide any counterbalancing logic—Roger had no trouble believing that Seamus could manipulate even someone as stubborn as Zack. And Takashi, for all his strengths, had believed in the social game. He might have known how dangerous Seamus could be, but that didn't mean he'd been prepared. He had been a proponent of working inside the system to change it. He hadn't come to the revelation that Roger had; change from within was impossible. The only path to liberation was with war.

Roger was also certain that Seamus had played a card that was only useful once and that the bastard's hand was fully revealed. Neither Zack nor Takashi would fall for any of his shit again. *Not that I want to give him the opportunity to try.*

His lovers were consoling one another, their distance closing, and the embers of their fight drifting into ash. Roger knew far more must have happened, but his precious minutes alone with them were coming to a close. Though he longed to soothe every stinging pain in all their souls, he needed to keep his head level and his plans moving forward.

"I cannot tell you how much this reunion means to me, but I do have another purpose in being here," Roger said. His voice drew their attention, and they lessened their hug to look at him. Zack had his forehead against Takashi's temple, lightly pressed there. "Actually, stay just like that a moment."

Roger took out his cell phone. Zack started to frown as he had his eyes closed and wouldn't know what Roger was up to, but Takashi shushed him. Roger snapped a picture with his phone.

"Did you just pause whatever doom and gloom you were about to drop to take a *pic*?" Zack asked.

"He did." Takashi kissed Zack's cheek.

"You have got to be kidding me," Zack grumbled. He nipped Takashi's jaw and then turned toward Roger. "You have to let me see."

Roger showed him the photo.

Zack raised his eyebrows. "Uh, why didn't anyone tell me I'm a hot vampire?"

"I believe I did," Takashi replied.

"Okay, no one said I was a smoking hot vampire."

Roger laughed and fought to not get carried away with the lightness it brought to his heart. He put his phone away. As much as he hated for the moment to end, he had to embrace practicality. "Zack, I love you, but if you're scared that you'll unintentionally share thoughts with Seamus, you do have to go."

Zack narrowed his eyes, the same as he always had when he was calculating Roger's intent. "You're up to something?"

"You'll know about it soon enough. I promise. For now, we have to part." Roger brought him in for a kiss.

Zack's touch was cool, his lips soft but chilly. His kiss was surer, his tongue pushing when he'd been pliant. It was a first kiss all over again.

Roger prayed it wouldn't be a last.

It had to end. Zack was the one to pull away first. He gave Roger a tight hug, then gave Takashi a quick hug and lengthy kiss, and then went to the door. Before he opened it, he turned back to meet Roger's gaze.

They'd had so many staring contests, and somehow, this was the first time Roger thought he might be seeing the true Zack.

A soft grin lifted one side of his lips, and Zack gestured at Takashi with a nod. "Our numbskull has a bad habit of thinking he's not important to anyone. Don't let him out of here thinking no one would ever pick him."

Roger raised an eyebrow.

Takashi stiffened, hiding behind his persona of the

consummate professional ambassador. Until Zack's words, Roger wasn't sure he'd noticed how often Takashi threw on that mask.

"I'll do my best to change his mind," Roger assured Zack.

"Good." Then Zack zipped forward, snuck one last kiss from both of them, and then rushed out the door.

CHAPTER 50

Zack's parting words opened the shell of Takashi's heart, and he wasn't prepared to deal with the oyster of pain inside of it. As Roger spun toward him, one eyebrow raised, a welling of shame made Takashi look away. Because Takashi had had a choice, and he hadn't chosen to run away with Roger. He had remained in the mansion. Why should he expect Roger to choose him when he hadn't run after him into the night? When he'd longed for power instead of love?

Not that Roger knew any of that. Nor did Zack know the depth of his sins.

Despite the turn of events in the last few nights, Takashi couldn't say with certainty that he would have run away with Roger after all.

"You shouldn't worry about what Zack said," Takashi said quietly. "I take it you're planning some sort of attack. When?"

"Just before dawn. Tonight." Roger neared Takashi and hooked a finger under his chin. He lightly tugged on him.

Wishing he could resist, Takashi let Roger drag his chin up. "What will you do?"

"I'm going to burn down the mansion and liberate you and Zack from it," Roger purred.

There was a decisiveness to his tone that he had always lacked when talking about taking the coven. This wasn't some mere idea Roger had; he was dressed in the sort of clothing meant for battle. He had risked everything to come see them because he was prepared to gamble everything. Including his life.

I underestimated him. Takashi jerked free of him and rounded the desk to gain distance from him. Having Roger close always made him weak in the knees, and he needed his strength. Besides that, he didn't deserve Roger's care.

"I can tell you're twisting yourself into knots," Roger said. "My plan has its risks, but it has Thomas's and half a dozen others' approval. This will be a coordinated attack."

"You don't know what's going on in my mind," Takashi said.

"Because I refuse to break through your defenses to know exactly what you're feeling." Roger motioned at Takashi. "Your agony is easy to see, if one knows how to look."

"You shouldn't be comforting me. You don't know what I've done." Takashi folded his arms over his chest.

Roger pulled out the chair from the desk and gestured for Takashi to sit in it. Once he had, Roger leaned against the desk right in front of him, slotting one leg between Takashi's. They weren't touching, but doing so wouldn't take much effort on either one's part.

"My absence will eventually be noticed. I should be heading downstairs sooner rather than later," Takashi said. "What do I need to know about your attack?"

"We'll be drawing security to the northwest, west, southwest, and east sides of the property. The intention is to spread security incredibly thin, then launch ourselves through the main doors to capture Seamus's attention. I'll be engaging him, trying to keep him distracted long enough for the others to set the building on fire in several locations. I'll hold out as close to dawn as I can, then make a run for our rendezvous. With any luck, I'll manage to kill Seamus."

"You're counting on luck?" Takashi said.

"He might not fall for the bait, and my team will be our best shot at putting him down. If Zack is right and he has been holding back, surviving is the priority. The coven, this bullshit that we put each other through, it's not worth preserving. Tearing it down means humiliating him first," Roger said seriously. "It's not a perfect plan, but he ripped away those I love and made the two of you suffer. He made *me* suffer.

"Call it petty revenge if you like, but I want him to feel every ounce of shit he has shoved down everyone else's throats. If he's alive, a power vacuum isn't created. He winds up being the one fighting a war within and without, and we'll be able to rid ourselves of his truest believers. We clean house and perhaps find ourselves some allies for whatever we build after the GLC is destroyed."

"I thought you wanted to rule," Takashi said.

Roger offered Takashi his hands.

Slowly, Takashi put his hands in Roger's. His touch was cool, though not as cold as Zack's, and his hands were larger than his. Roger stroked his thumb along the back of Takashi's hand. Reading his emotions was easier. As badly as Roger longed for Zack and Takashi to be at his side, what he truly wanted was a home.

That was something Takashi had never had.

"Our elite society inflicts agony in order to appease its appetites. There are better ways. We can find them. You, me, and Zack. We can build a wonderful new world, together." Roger raised Takashi's hands to his lips and kissed him. He squeezed as he said, "But if we hide parts of ourselves from each other, it'll never work."

"I had the chance to run away when you rescued Dmitri, and I chose to stay behind," Takashi blurted out. He would have risen from his seat, but Roger was right there, trapping him. Caught, with nowhere to hide from Roger's brown eyes, more words spilled from him. "I am not the noble thing I pretend to be. I craved power, believed it could be found within that house instead of with you. So I stayed.

"I stayed, not knowing Zack was going to rise a vampire, and once I knew, I thought that he might make the perfect leader. I pushed him to own that part of himself. To embolden him to make his own choices. And so he left his cousin to suffer, made a deal with a demon, and confided in the worst monster any of us know. Zack wasn't the one to screw up. *I* was. I did it again just now by blaming my situation on Zack and Seamus. My weak yearnings were what dragged me to this place."

Takashi tried to yank his hands free of Roger's, but Roger held on to him. His grip wasn't overly tight, but his presence made Takashi sink forward toward him. Roger slid off the desk and went to his knees so that their hug was easier.

But the comfort was too much. Takashi pushed Roger away and darted out of the chair before he could crowd him again. "I am not worthy. I am a power-seeking leech."

"I thought of the three of us, you were the one who knew themselves best, but I wonder if you've buried your heart too deeply," Roger said.

"You are giving me far too much credit."

"Takashi, why did you run away from home?"

"Nell—"

"Not from Nell." Roger met Takashi's gaze and held it. "Your mortal home."

"I ... my father made it clear that I wasn't ..." Takashi folded his arms over his chest and held on to himself tightly. "The circus was a place where I thought I could be myself. For the most part, it was. The only other time I've felt like that was ..."

"Was with me and Zack?" Roger asked. "Perhaps the

reason you wanted to throw Zack onto a throne was because you believed power was the only way to gain the freedom your heart begs for."

"I don't think I like this much insight into my soul," Takashi murmured.

Roger grinned wryly. "Who does? The important part is that you are loved, Takashi. All of you. By me. By Zack. Nell, Josefina—and so many more hold affection for you."

"Anton," Takashi whispered.

Roger tapped his finger on the edge of the desk. "Has something happened with him?"

"Flirting. Too much of it." Takashi ran his hand through his hair. He could feel Katie growing excited about something. Her bubble of energy brought a spotlight to the softer, more joyful parts of himself. He had been as excited about his new life as she was, once upon a time. But he cleared his mind, throwing up a wall between them so that she would not feel his murky sadness. "Seamus and Anton don't have a seamless relationship. I thought pushing in between them would benefit us in the long run."

"Anton is a monster."

"I'm aware. I've seen his torture chamber." Takashi leaned against the wall. "He has a succubus down there. Apparently, he fucks him while he's shifted to look like me. That was part of what incensed Seamus against me. But I can't help thinking … what would he have been like if someone had intervened? What would you be like if Zack and I hadn't come into your life? When you robbed Seamus, he beat Anton, and Anton never lifted a finger to stop him. He is so … lost."

"He has been raping Dmitri for centuries," Roger said firmly. "Torturing others as well."

"I'm not claiming he's a good man," Takashi said. "I'm not saying we should forgive him either. But wouldn't our fight be easier if Anton were on our side? Betray him later. Punish him for every wrong—we could come up with that after. But if he wasn't lending his strength to Seamus, our odds wouldn't be so stacked against us."

"I'm not delaying my attack," Roger said.

"I didn't ask you to," Takashi sighed. "I'm not even suggesting we spare him if the opportunity rises to kill him."

"I certainly won't hesitate to do so." Roger checked his watch. "I hate to say this, but I am running out of time. Is there anything that you can think of that might help me? I've had Vincent filling in details I didn't know, but has anything changed about the mansion in the last few weeks?"

"Other than Zack rising more powerful than he should be, no."

"What about that demon deal you mentioned? Do you know what Zack's bargain is?"

"Anton's succubus is the one he made the deal with. Once the demon's out of his cell, there's a one-year limit on his ability to invade Zack's dreams."

"Zack let him into his head?"

"He was thinking he needed to buy the demon's silence." Takashi pushed away from the wall. "Anton has made a sireling in recent weeks. Zack's cousin, Dennis. He's also locked away in the same dungeon area as the succubus. Anton's been doing some experiments into immortality. Apparently, he plans to use Dennis as a test subject."

Roger sucked in a deep breath and then ran his hand down his jaw. "Ah."

"What is it?"

"Nothing we can do anything about now. As Zack would say, I need to do some research. Look, when you get back to the mansion, see how many doors and windows you can leave open or unlocked. Try not to get caught." Roger put a hand on each of Takashi's shoulders. "When it starts, and you'll know when, do your best to run. There is a park due west of the mansion. We will have two vans there for those who have to flee the battle. You don't have to fight."

"I shouldn't leave it all to you and your people," Takashi said. "Zack won't want to."

"I know, but there will be other battles. The last thing I could stand is if you two—three with Kathleen. Yes, I know she's yours—were to wind up stuck with the bastard when the smoke clears from the battle."

Takashi slid his hand on top of Roger's left one. "What about Zack's bond? Seamus will be able to sense him."

"I have warlocks that believe they can cover him for a day. After that, we'll figure it out."

"Together?"

"Yes. Everything together from now on."

Takashi wished that could be true. *The only way to turn wishes into reality is to try.* He gave a tight nod. "I need to get back to the party."

"And I have to go." Roger kissed Takashi. "I love you. Be careful."

"You too." Takashi smiled at him.

Roger kissed him once more. Then he slipped the medallion back over his head and murmured two words in Latin. The illusion making him look like a blond man in a suit sprung back to life.

Takashi grabbed one last kiss before they left the room. Just in case the worst were to happen. *Here I thought it already had. Why is there always a worst, worst-case scenario?*

CHAPTER 51

Zack forgot about the envelope still in his hand until he was at the top of the stairs. Reading it might wind up creating thoughts that Seamus overheard. Not reading it was going to drive Zack over a cliff of anxiety.

Thomas was an expert strategist. He wouldn't give away secrets in a letter anyone could get their hands on. However, Seamus might question why Zack was suddenly thinking about his father so much. If he guessed where Zack had gotten a letter, then Roger could be in trouble. Then again, Roger was already an outcast.

"Screw it," Zack muttered to himself and dipped into one of the rooms closer to the top of the stairs. He ripped open the envelope and unfolded the pages, nearly ripping them. His father's handwriting was unmistakable. Zack leaned back against the wall, as even seeing his name in his father's hand brought comfort.

Zack,

I've started this six times and can't think of a smart way to begin so I'm just going to say what it is that I need to say.

I'm sorry.

A father should be a shield, a sword, and a light for his child. He should at the very least try to be those things. I should have been them for you. I thought I was, but my sword's rusted, my light's dim, and I forgot to lift a shield at all. You have always been brave and clever. I saw your courage and I committed the greatest crime, I stayed silent. When the family turned on you, I should have stood up rather than keeping my mouth shut and falling in line. You spared a girl who had been a victim. You let Roger into your life when you could have killed him.

He is a good man. Better than me. He never gave up on you or Takashi. He's launching a war, and I'm going to help him. I know that a few good deeds can't make up for the hurt I've caused you, but I've got to start somewhere.

In case I don't get to say any of this in person, I love you. I know you're a vampire now, and that doesn't change the fact that I love you. I don't want you to think that it ever could. I won't lie and say I'm not worried. You are fucking smart, Zack. You see through people, you saw through the bullshit the family fed you, and you carved your own path. If you abandon your humanity, you could become the greatest of monsters and that fucking scares me because it doesn't matter what you do, I will still love you. You are my son, and despite my and your mother's failures, you're growing up to be a good man. One I will continue to be proud of, no matter what.

I should have said those words to you long ago. Even in our line of work, we take our time for granted. I could have lost you altogether. But you get to keep on living and I get a second chance to make up for my fuck ups.

For the record, after your talk with Amber, she hasn't stopped ranting about how awful the family treated you. Well, she's stopped a little lately. We've been busy.

And this is poor timing and a shitty way to say it, but you should know that I'm divorcing your mother. Our marriage was never built on the kind of love I wanted to have in my life, but staying with her means supporting her and the bullshit she believes in. I can't do that anymore. Not when it hurts you. Not when it could hurt Amber worse than it already has.

You should also know I approve of Roger. He is ... well, I would have hoped you'd pick a mortal partner, but considering you now have forever, I like him for you. If this Takashi I keep hearing about is even a quarter of the man he is, then I approve of him, too. I don't care that you have two boyfriends at the same time. If a million-person polycule worked for you—well, I'd ask that you make sure people stay healthy. All I have ever wanted was for you to be happy and healthy.

I'm sorry that I caused you misery. A father shouldn't do that.

I love you.

Dad

Dots of red landed on the page, and Zack had to hold the papers away before more of his tears fell on them. He didn't have to worry about Seamus reading his thoughts; his mind was blank as comprehension sunk in.

His dad, who had faced more danger than anyone Zack knew, had called him the brave one. There was no condition on it. No expectation to be different than what he was. His dad even knew he was a vampire and wrote him a letter anyway. His dad still loved him, no matter what. He always had.

Roger and Thomas were definitely planning something big. The letter had all the hallmarks of "in case I die" without saying the words explicitly. For all the doubt that had plagued Zack, for all the tears he'd cried thinking his family had completely given up on him, his dad was trying to make it right. Amber was trying to do the right thing.

Suddenly, Zack wanted the one thing he wasn't sure he'd ever have again. He wanted a hug from his dad.

You're distraught. What's wrong? Seamus asked.

Fuck. Zack pulled out his handkerchief and dried his face of tears. Quickly, he folded up the letter and slid it into his back pocket. His hand brushed against his dagger.

Walking downstairs and attacking Seamus in the middle of a party full of people who should protect him was a bad idea. Zack entertained it anyway just to settle himself.

I thought we were past this, Seamus said.

Me wanting to kill you? Zack asked. *We were. Then you threatened my boyfriend like the abusive fucking monster that you are.*

In time, you'll see I am right about him.

Zack rolled his eyes and left the room. He hurried down the stairs to the second floor. The party's atmosphere had shifted from an early-how-do-you-do to the eager energy of a blast in progress. Live music was coming from one room off to his right. Thankfully, nothing was going on in the ballroom. Zack was sick of dancing.

He was also sick to death of Seamus fucking up his life. With a few words and an act of violence, Seamus had also ruined Takashi's life.

As Zack passed a room, an idea occurred. Seamus wasn't the only one who could spew the wrong words to the right people. The crowd was composed of influential vampires. All he had to do was find the right one.

He bypassed the room where he felt Seamus's presence and scanned the others for a group of people who had the right attitude. They needed to be gossiping but not so self-important that they'd be patronizing to a newbie vampire in their midst.

Ah, there. Candide had introduced him to a couple of the vampires in a dimly lit room decorated in dark browns and golds. There were fewer mortals around, too, which was a bonus because the stimuli were threatening to cause another headache.

Dempsey was part of the crowd, and Zack strode over to him. With a raised brow, Dempsey motioned for Zack to sit beside him. A quick round of introductions and acknowledgments of acquittances were made. Then Dempsey said, "Did you get started early?"

Zack frowned.

Dempsey tapped his own collar.

"Oh. No." Zack touched his collar and found a wet spot. His tears must have trailed onto his shirt. He snagged a glass of wine from a passing tray and swirled its contents, putting on his best brooding face and his grandest vampire persona. "Sometimes, having been murdered still bothers me. I was beaten to death, you see. Seamus offered to transform me, and I took it."

The other vampires were practiced enough that no one shifted uncomfortably, but they did begin to still.

Ripping a page from Candide's book, Zack put on a bright smile. "Some of you have to know how that is! Violence has brought many of us into this new life. I'm still adjusting, but I don't regret taking the offer. Dying or living forever, I mean, who wouldn't choose the forever, am I right?"

"That's true," Dempsey said slowly.

"I only wish I'd been smart enough to let my boyfriend Roger do it rather than getting *murdered*. Eh, but then I probably wouldn't be as strong as I am." Zack rushed from the couch he was sitting on, using every bit of speed that he had, and sat between two other vampires across the room. They jumped slightly.

The other chatter in the room died off. He had everyone's attention.

"Was that fast? For a newbie?" Zack said. Shock was crossing more than a couple of faces. "I didn't think I was until Takashi—sorry, *Anton*—made Katie. Ugh, it's hard to keep track of all the pretenses you guys, well, *we* vamps, put on. As much as some of us are vampires. Did you know that that's a fairly new word? I mean, how many of you are over two hundred years old? Only one? Well, then you know that when you were first a sireling, 'vampire' wasn't a common word, huh? Anyway, what I guess I'm saying is 'my father' poured a lot of strength into me. He's hoping to create a new generation of vampire, whatever the fuck that's supposed to mean. Probably more supercharged fledglings like me. He's got a whole fucking room full of profiles of people he wants to turn into his army so he can fight a war against dragons. Because somehow, they're our worst enemies? I don't know. Maybe he's just jealous that they're stronger than him."

Zackery, what are you doing? Seamus asked mentally.

You want to take away what I love? I can ruin you, too. Zack sipped his wine.

Ruining me ruins you, Seamus said.

Hey, I'm a hunter turned vampire whose master just smashed his boyfriend's reputation into rubble. Fucking bring on the drama.

Seamus was drawing closer. *I am the one who should not be tested.*

Says who? Zack finished off his wine and set the glass down. No one had picked up the conversation while Seamus was trying to rip him a new one in his head. "You know, I've got to ask. I spent a couple months as a mortal pet because that was the only way my boyfriends could bring me out in 'polite society,' but is that really the common practice in other covens? Should I be on the lookout for the urge to play out my violent desires on the unwilling? I mean, I haven't managed to keep myself from killing my prey yet. Everybody keeps telling me not to feel guilty about that. Top of the food chain, apex predator bullshit. Oh, sorry, swearing's 'unbecoming.'"

Seamus was standing in the archway to the room, and a cold emanated from him.

"Oops, looks like I've pissed off daddy," Zack said as he grabbed another wineglass. He stood and raised his glass in a toast. "If he should happen to ritualistically murder me and take back the gift of immortality he's given me, it's been real."

Draining his glass again, he sought out the desires of the

others in the room. The other vampires had better mental defenses. However, the mortals didn't. A buzz of wanting to talk came from most of them.

Checkmate, motherfucker, Zack thought on his way out of the room.

Seamus grabbed Zack by the lapel and dragged him along the hallway, clearly seeking some sort of privacy. Zack waved to as many people as he could on his trek, including Katie and Anton.

With a snarl, Seamus shoved Zack into a bathroom and locked the door. He growled, "What the hell do you think you were doing?"

"Sorry, was all of that stuff supposed to be a secret?" Zack asked sarcastically. "Like maybe you shouldn't have blabbed that you knew Nell wants me dead?"

"You ran your mouth because you're upset that I hurt Takashi's feelings?" Seamus scoffed. "I thought you were smarter than that."

"Don't fucking downplay what you did," Zack snapped. "You intentionally ruined his fucking life, and you threatened him for something out of his control."

"Out of—he has been seducing Anton," Seamus replied hotly.

"Maybe if you weren't a fucking tyrant, Anton wouldn't be falling for someone who's been a little bit nice to him," Zack returned.

Seamus's fist struck like a sledgehammer wielded by a world heavyweight champion. The blow cracked Zack's jaw. The pain was sharp. Brief.

And expected. Zack pulled his dagger. Seamus was already in movement for another strike, but Zack slipped past his fist. He shoved Seamus up against the wall and drove his dagger toward his heart. All his excuses for not killing Seamus fell away. He only needed one reason to follow through with it.

To save his lovers.

The runes of his dagger glowed with bright red light. The tip pierced Seamus's chest.

Then Zack stopped. With a grunt, he tried to move his arm, but he was stuck. Words died in his throat because he couldn't move his jaw either. His whole body was frozen. *What the fuck?*

"You are fast," Seamus said smoothly. He had a laugh in the back of his throat as he spoke. Off to the side, he gestured.

Zack's head snapped up so that his gaze was on Seamus.

The whites of Seamus's eyes had been consumed by the black voids, and his pupils were maroon. Seamus's smile had three sets of fangs, all long, and his nails had become claws. His skin stretched across his bones, making him gaunt rather than healthy-looking. The smell that rolled off him was acrid and overpowered the earthy notes of his grave scent.

"You almost had me, son. Almost." Seamus chuckled. He brushed hair back from Zack's forehead. "I wonder if you were intentionally dismissing the idea of killing me just so you could have this opportunity."

Why can't I move? Zack screamed in his mind.

"Because my blood, my power, runs through your veins. I must admit, I wasn't certain this trick would work. You have to absorb quite a bit for me to be able to pull this off. Or am I lying about that?" Seamus patted Zack's cheek. "Take a step back, would you, dear boy?"

Against his will, Zack did.

Seamus fussed over his own shirt, then tched as he examined the blood drops on Zack's. "Crying? On such a joyous night? Why?"

The urge to answer brought words to the tip of Zack's tongue. He tried to swallow them down, but the longer he resisted, the more he was sure he was going to vomit. The best he could do was limit them. "I miss my dad."

"I'm right here," Seamus cooed. "Oh, but you mean your mortal father. The one who disowned you."

"He loves me."

"It pains me that you still believe that." Seamus sighed. "I could erase your desire to see him. I could supplant your entire will, if I wanted to. But I have hope that you will still see reason. Of course, what's happened here can't go unpunished."

Don't you fucking hurt Takashi. Zack felt like he should be crying, but the tears weren't starting like they were supposed to.

"I won't," Seamus said with a malicious smile. "My beloved deserves the chance to redeem himself and to carry on his work. I'm certain Takashi will make a fine addition to his menagerie in our dungeon. Perhaps, if you're good, I'll let Takashi out. In a decade or so, assuming he still has his mind."

I'll tell him to run. Zack clenched his jaw.

"You will do no such thing," Seamus said coldly. "Tonight will carry on exactly how it is supposed to. If you breathe a word of this, I will make you rip out his heart and eat it." He snapped his fingers.

Zack went to his knees. No matter how much he screamed at his muscles to move to his orders, his body stayed put.

Seamus leaned down and murmured in his ear, "Have I made myself clear, *son*?"

"Yes," Zack managed.

"Yes, what?"

"Yes, *Father*."

Seamus patted his shoulder. As he straightened, his more human-looking guise fell back into place. "There's my good boy. Now, take a few minutes to compose yourself before you rejoin the party. And do take care not to spill any more secrets. I can conceive of worse punishments than taking away your favorite toy."

Only after Seamus left the bathroom and shut the door behind himself did the tension forcing Zack to be on his knees cease. Shaking, Zack collapsed against the wall. His dagger was still in his hand, for all the good it had done him.

Takashi's life was in jeopardy because of him *again*. Even if they did try to fight Seamus, Zack would be useless until he broke the bond that connected them. The only way to do that was through time and space, and Seamus wasn't going to give him that.

He had one thin hope that he didn't dare put much thought into for fear of ruining whatever was in the works. The name came anyway.

Roger.

CHAPTER 52

Though Roger hated to leave, he managed to slip out of the Chateau a little ahead of his schedule. Seeing Zack and Takashi continued to grant Roger a sense of peace, even as he had to drive away from them. By the end of the night, he would have them back in his life for good.

But first, he had to make certain there were no traitors in his midst.

Rather than following his plan, he made a quick detour. Josefina was leading her own team, and their initial gathering place was in the parking lot of a mega-chain store.

Roger parked beside her car, hopped out of his, and got into hers.

"What are you doing here?" Josefina asked. "Did something go wrong at the Chateau?"

"Things went as well as they could," Roger replied. "Maybe better than you were hoping."

"I don't—"

"I know Nell wants Zack dead," Roger interrupted.

Josefina went silent.

"You knew," Roger said.

"Of course I knew." Josefina slumped in her seat. "She and I have been fighting about it all week."

That was promising, for Roger at least. But he didn't want to gloat or delight in her problems. Josefina was an old friend. She might value her loyalty to her friends over the love of her immortal life, and doing so was a sacrifice that Roger had to honor.

"She ordered you to kill him?" Roger asked.

"Yes. I told her she's making a mistake, but she doesn't seem to care."

"Takashi thinks that she wants to kill him for revenge in addition to tactics. Seems Zack upset her scheme."

Josefina frowned. "What scheme?"

"The one where I come back to the GLC and cause a civil war that destroys the coven."

"No, you were supposed to become the master, and then we wouldn't have to worry about Seamus's expansions anymore."

"Then why was she pushing a faster timetable on me? Why did she ask Takashi to come along?"

"She released Takashi from her coven," Josefina pointed out.

"And if the GLC splits into pieces or falls apart entirely, she could adopt him right back," Roger countered. "You were in charge of her security. Didn't you ever wonder about the vampire sleeping in a coffin in a basement in the heart of your love's territory?"

"I ..." Josefina straightened in her seat, and her frown turned into a deeper scowl. "I did bring it up. A few times. She always told me not to worry. And so I didn't. She ... God, Roger, do you think she was messing with my desires? Making me want to accept her answers?"

Roger took Josefina's hand in his own. "I hope that she didn't, but I don't know the answer."

After a second, Josefina squeezed Roger's hand. "My problem for another night. Know that Zack has nothing to worry about from me. I care about him. I'm actually looking forward to him being an annoying little know-it-all for centuries to come."

Roger leaned forward, and Josefina met him, resting her forehead against his. He didn't have to probe her emotions to feel the sincerity in her words. "Thank you."

"How were they?"

"Distraught, but nothing time and love can't mend," Roger replied. "I was able to warn Takashi, but Zack says that he can speak telepathically to Seamus, that Seamus reads his mind when he doesn't mean for him to. Have you heard of that?"

"I haven't," Josefina said. "I know you want to liberate him tonight, but if he is that bound to Seamus—"

"We will find a solution. I will not leave him again."

"I like this confident side of you. Optimism is a far better color than despair."

"Don't count despair out yet. We have to make it through the night." Roger backed away, putting his hand on the door handle. "See you on the other side."

"You better be there," Josefina replied.

Roger managed a smile for her and a nod. Then he got back in his car and headed for his meeting place.

The crowd politely clapped as Katie pulled away from her victim. The mortal boy she'd fed from wavered where he stood, but he'd live. Katie curtsied like she was taking the final bow of a theater production.

Since leaving the bathroom, Zack had an urge to vomit. His hunger warred with his nausea, only intensifying the crawling in his stomach. But he had to eat. Everyone was expecting him to before they could claim their blood for the

night, and Seamus clearly wasn't going to permit disappointment.

After Katie was done accepting her congratulations, Zack
took her place in the middle of the room. Dryden, one of
Candide's pets, led a line of five mortals to stand before Zack.
They wore only underwear, but they weren't terrified of him
like all the mortals Seamus had dragged in front of him.
These humans—Zack could tell from their scents there wasn't
a shifter among them—all radiated lust at looking him over.
They were giddy about the possibility of being chosen.

They had no idea he was going to kill one of them. That he
couldn't control himself. That he was a monster.

You're not being fair to yourself, his rational voice declared.
With a furtive glance, he checked to see if Seamus was clued
in to his inner dialogue. No words came, but that didn't mean
he couldn't hear him.

Choosing no one wasn't an option, so Zack started to read
each of the mortals as closely as he could. Maybe he could
figure out which one was the worst human among the group,
and that way, he wouldn't have to feel guilty about not being
able to control himself.

*Or maybe the reason you can't stop killing them is because you
can't let go of the fear that your loved ones will despise you,* his
rational voice continued.

The letter in his pocket said his real father didn't hate him
at all. Thomas was begging for forgiveness, not demanding it
of Zack. He knew he was a vampire, and the only thing he
was worried about was Zack giving up his humanity.

Becoming a monster was a choice.

And no matter what Seamus did, he couldn't force Zack to
be like him.

Instead of picking the human who seemed like the worst
person, Zack scanned their desires until he found the one
most excited about getting bitten. When he held his hand out
to the young man, the guy gleefully put his hand in Zack's.

"This might hurt. I'm still new at this," Zack told the young man, not giving a shit about the audience around them. "I can try to raise your desire, but I might overdo it."

"I'm game for anything, master," the guy said with a wink.

"All right." Zack put his hand on the guy's cheek and let out his breath. The man was an open book, the words written in big letters. Zack trailed his awareness across them until he found his lust. The guy was really wishing to get fucked, to be overpowered and pleasured. Instead of plunging into that want, Zack pictured that he was pouring paint into the crevices, to fill every aspect of the word.

The young man gasped, and his heart picked up speed.

Zack took a moment to study where his pulse was fiercest so he didn't rip open a vital artery. Then he pulled him in and bit his neck.

Every feeding on mortal blood before had been like drinking pure water on a parched throat. It worked. It sated his hunger long enough to forget about it for a while.

The first drops of this young man's blood were sweet as sugar. Zack swallowed, and the hollow place in his stomach quieted. With a groan, he drank another mouthful, and another. There was no elixir like it. Nothing compared to the satisfying warmth—except being in bed, safe with his lovers.

The sweetness became overbearing as the thirst in his throat and the pit in his stomach eased to a muffled whisper. Zack tried to pull away from the young man, but the guy held him tightly. That was when Zack noticed the guy was grinding against his leg, panting and moaning.

Before Zack could do more than blink at what was happening, the guy let out a long sigh of relief, and a wetness darkened his underwear. The smell of spunk was thick. The guy shot Zack a lazy smile; the bliss from coming was heavy in his gaze. He slurred, "Sorry, master. Too good to stop."

Applause burst out in the room while Zack struggled to

keep his panic under control. He'd just made a guy come in a crowded room. He … well, he hadn't really done anything sexual. *I wasn't the one moaning. He was.* And people weren't being rude with their praise. The applause for Katie had sounded polite. The one for him sounded genuine. Felt real.

Zack backed away from the young man and glanced off to the side, not sure what to do with a living donor. Thankfully, Dryden stepped forward and escorted the guy out of the room. Still stunned, Zack managed a tight smile and a bow to the other vampires.

As he stepped out from the center of the room, Candide walked into the focal point. She started talking about how pleased she was that the two young vampires were so promising. She was doing some kind of speech to introduce Seamus.

Zack made a beeline for Takashi, who was practically hiding in a corner. "I did it. I fucking did it."

"You did," Takashi said with a smile. "You still have a little of him on your mouth."

"Want to lick it off?"

"You are in a good mood."

The carefulness in Takashi's tone reminded Zack of all the reasons he shouldn't be. Seamus's threat hung in his mind. Telling Takashi to run wouldn't work if Katie remained in the mansion. She'd be able to lead Anton or Seamus right to him. And Zack wouldn't be able to stop them.

There was nothing he could do except stay in this moment. The monsters couldn't win if he found even a second of happiness. They couldn't taint his love.

"I don't have to be a killer," Zack whispered to Takashi while Seamus droned on. "I did mean it. Do you want a taste?"

Takashi kissed him. Their kiss lengthened, and for once, Zack didn't give a damn if anyone saw them. He was a hot vampire kissing his sexy boyfriend. Anyone who thought otherwise didn't fucking matter.

"No wonder that boy came," Takashi said with a gentle chuckle. "You're basically glowing."

"The glowing happened after. Shit, you don't mind that I made that guy come, do you?"

"Sex and our bite can go hand in hand. I don't care. Roger won't either. After all, we did have our fun with Carver."

Carver. The memory of seeing him at the open door, throat torn out, and the fight that had claimed Zack's life flooded through Zack. He held on to Takashi. Something just as terrible was on the way after the party.

Zack couldn't say nothing. But maybe if he felt his fears hard enough, Takashi would understand him.

Takashi murmured, "You don't need worry so much."

"You don't know what I know."

"I know something you don't as well," Takashi whispered. He squeezed Zack's shoulders. "Everything is going to be okay in the end."

Thomas's letter had been filled with signals that he was prepping for something dangerous. Now Takashi was saying everything would be fine. Whatever the plan was, it was going off tonight. He could imagine—no. He had to trust Roger and Takashi. The best way for Zack to help them was to mentally sing annoying songs to keep himself from thinking something that would put them in danger.

Let's see how many times I can sing "Row, Row, Row Your Boat" in a row.

CHAPTER 53

Takashi abandoned his smile as soon as the limo door was shut. He was in a seat beside the divider to the driver's cabin. Thanks to the general chaos of being at a crowded party, he'd been able to drink enough blood that he felt far more like himself. The situation he was in wasn't immensely improved, but a general cloud had been obscuring his senses. He only noted it for its absence. There had been moments where the fog was lighter—the times Zack had shared blood with him—but even that didn't compare to energy that came from mortal blood.

Seamus's pets sat across from Takashi. The three mortals looked exhausted, bags under their eyes, and the girl leaned against one of the boys. Did Roger have a plan for them? Takashi didn't want to leave them behind, but at the same time, he wasn't sure they'd want to go. As much as they might fear their lives, they might prefer the pain they knew than face the unknown.

Zack, Katie, Anton, and Seamus were at the other end. When Zack tried to slide down toward Takashi, Seamus glared at him. A bright panic—loud as an elephant trumpeting—poured out from Zack and knocked through Takashi.

Zack was worried for him. Likely, Seamus was planning retribution. Over the course of the party, Takashi had heard a few rumors about Seamus's intentions for the future. Murmurings of abuse and lunacy concerning dragons had been almost as common a theme as fawning over the new fledglings making their debut. Only four people could have started that sort of talk. Anton and Seamus never would, and Takashi knew he hadn't. That left Zack.

Whatever patience Seamus had for Zack was rapidly thinning. Takashi would likely be the first target of his wrath, but he wouldn't be the last. *Please, please let Roger come before anything irreversible happens.*

"When do we get to go back there?" Katie said as she stretched out. "I haven't had that much fun ever."

"We'll go soon," Anton said.

"We'll take you to a few other places, too," Seamus said. He had his arm around Anton's shoulders. If one didn't know better, they looked like a perfectly contented couple. "If you thought the Chateau was fun, wait until you have a night at Devil's Cove."

Katie scrunched her nose. "Isn't that a blood club? I heard those places were gross."

Seamus's smile tightened, and his tone cooled. "Just when I believe you're a young lady, you demonstrate that your tastes remain that of a child."

"She's very young, love," Anton said. "You know mortals these days are not like the ones of former decades."

"Perhaps. Or perhaps it is you and Takashi have made a poor choice," Seamus replied, his words as sharp as his fangs. "As I recall, there were three girls, two of whom made off with my sports car? One of them would have been a better vampire. It may not be too late to start over on this little experiment of yours."

Zack stared at his knees, not saying a word. His fists were

clenched, and Takashi could see the tension in his lover that meant an inner war was waging. However, he was staying still. Quiet. Was he biding his time? Or trying to keep from making something worse?

"Maybe Anton could do a lot better than a megalomanic sociopathic prick for an eternal partner," Katie returned.

Seamus narrowed his eyes. "You will treat me with respect, *child*."

Katie clutched the edge of her seat and leaned forward toward Seamus. "I don't respect anyone who doesn't respect me."

A glimmer of intense rage boiled out from Seamus.

Katie had only responded to what had been done to her. She had merely tried to be herself. For that, the turning wheels of Seamus's mind were fueled with anger. No doubt, he was preparing to punish Katie. He was making a fist.

Master vampires often used violence against their subordinates. With supernatural healing, physical wounds seemed like nothing. The violence carried psychological damage, though. Takashi could already see the ripples changing Zack, turning him fearful in a way he hadn't been before.

We can build a wonderful new world. Together, Roger had said.

Takashi wanted to see what that world would be like. He longed to know what a home was. And he couldn't bear the thought of seeing a sliver of Katie cut away because Seamus willed it so. She was part of him, though they still knew so little of each other. Allowing her emotions past his walls, he sensed her bubbling longing for unending life and fun. She was a drop of youth in amber. Seamus wanted to melt away the protection keeping her from fearing him and the world around her.

Takashi's own youth had been cut away in pieces, the first large chunk sliced off when a stranger spat at him. The last of it had been ripped away on a cold shore of an island in Lake Michigan. As young as Zack was, he didn't have the spark that Katie did, and whatever was left of his youth was already falling away.

She deserved safety, love, happiness—everything that was the antithesis of Seamus's household.

Takashi locked gazes with Anton. He willed his own desire to protect Katie toward him.

Anton matched his stare, then pursed his lips and nudged Seamus. "You're being too hard on her."

"Don't you dare begin," Seamus snapped. "I have had enough of the children acting up tonight. I do not need your bullshit."

"My love—"

"Don't."

Anton nestled into Seamus's side and put his hand over Seamus's fist. Seamus yanked his hand free. When Anton tried again, Seamus pushed him away, sending him up against the car door.

"For all the talk of immaturity," Takashi said, "you are the only one behaving like a child. How many tantrums can be thrown in a millennium, I wonder?"

"You will close your mouth if you know what's good for you," Seamus replied.

"Perhaps I will." Takashi turned his attention to Anton, speaking his words to him over anyone else. "Because the result will always be the same, won't it? Life attempts to grow in a garden whose caretaker only sees weeds, no matter the shape or color of the leaves. To him, the earth is not to be tended but salted. Then he wonders why he commands a coven of dust and blames the rain for the muddy, useless ground."

Anton's eyes widened a fraction. Just a minute, tiny difference.

"I have had enough of you," Seamus growled. He blurred, rushing across the limo's cabin.

Though Takashi tried to dodge him, he wasn't quick enough. Seamus grabbed him by the jaw and twisted. Unconsciousness came with a snap.

~

The rest of the ride back to the mansion was silent after Seamus knocked Takashi out. Seamus had continued to sit by Takashi and break his neck whenever he began to rouse. Zack knew intellectually that Takashi's wound would heal, but every time it happened, he flinched and held his breath until Takashi began to move again. He struggled to continue singing repetitive songs in his mind, hesitating more and more before starting the next round.

When they reached the mansion, Seamus dragged Takashi out of the limo and dumped him onto the pavement of the circle drive. Sneering, he said, "I have half a mind to leave him in the greenhouse for the day. However, letting him off the hook that easily won't do. Zack, take him to my love's special room."

"I'll do it," Anton said lightly. But there was a wariness in his eyes.

"I said—"

"I would rather he didn't interfere with my current experiments. Besides, I have keys, and he doesn't." Anton hoisted Takashi over one shoulder and carried him into the mansion.

"Very well," Seamus said. "There's still a little time before dawn, pets. Shall we?"

Seamus strode up and into his mansion, expecting the three mortals to follow him. They did without hesitation.

Zack wondered if a limo drove as easily as his compact car had. It probably didn't. And he couldn't leave Takashi behind. Shaking his head at himself, he went with Katie into the house and up to their suites. She had her arms crossed over her chest, her gaze focused on the floor.

"Why does Takashi care about me?" Katie asked as they neared their doors.

"Because he made you," Zack replied.

"Yeah, but we've barely talked. My ability to read emotions comes out like songs to me, and I always have this sweet, sad song in the back of my head. It makes me want to run outdoors or dance in the rain. Be free." Katie hugged her arms tighter. "When we're apart, the song is for him, and I overhear it, but when we're together, it changes key, and I know that's what he wants for me. Anton has this terrible reputation, but he's been great to me, too."

Zack slowed his pace and stopped beside Katie's door. "Even if Anton is only a monster because Seamus made him that way, that doesn't make him less of a monster. My other boyfriend, Roger, has had to do some pretty terrible stuff, but he feels guilty for it. He wants to be better than that."

"Anton's hard to read," Katie said. "Sometimes, when we're practicing magic, he seems like a completely different person. He's ... a brutal practitioner. Don't frown like that about it. He hasn't hurt me, but the spells and potions he's been teaching me aren't the kind of thing I'd learn at Versinal. Of course, all Versinal professors really cared about was anti-aging creams, tiny glamours, and the theory of bigger spells."

"What has he been teaching you?" Zack asked.

"Shielding, lightning blasts. Maybe we raised a dead squirrel or two," Katie replied.

"You didn't learn anything about that at the academy?"

Katie groaned. "They're not that deficient. But I didn't get to have so much hands-on experience. Everyone said there wasn't a point in wasting effort on that kind of stuff, which I thought was stupid. What I said before, I'm not really that upset about how I became a vampire anymore. I *like* this. Don't you?"

"I ... okay, being a vampire isn't the worst," Zack said. "But ..."

"But Seamus *is* the worst." Katie bit the corner of her bottom lip, one fang lightly touching. "Anton said he'd protect me from everything, but I'm not sure he can."

"I don't think he can either."

Katie nodded. "Okay. That settles it."

"Settles what?" Zack asked as she went into her suite.

She pulled off her heels and tossed them off to the side of her living room. "I'm finding a bag and filling it with as much jewelry and other expensive shit I can take and getting the fuck out of here. You should get out of here, too."

"There's no point."

"Look, I get the whole sire thing means Seamus knows where you are, but it's not GPS. The farther you get from him, the more general it is, right?" Katie continued into her bedroom and into her closet.

"Yeah, but he can still track me down."

"Have you thought about this amazing solution?" Katie rooted through her closet. She frowned, then shrugged and started pulling out the biggest purses in her collection. "You don't stop running until the bond fades."

"That takes money."

"I know." Katie held out one of her bags. "But I bet you've got all kinds of nifty expensive things, too."

If Zack took off for the ends of the Earth, how badly would that distract Seamus? Could he unsettle his sire for a year? Ruin his concentration for a decade?

Would Roger and Takashi come with him? Would it be dangerous to have them at his side? Thomas had said that Roger was looking to start a war. All Takashi had ever wanted was to belong.

Zack couldn't make them give up their dreams of creating a home and flee with him.

I can ask them later. After the thought, he began to mentally sing again. He took the bag from Katie and headed to his suite. The purse wouldn't hold a lot, but luckily, jeweled cufflinks were small. He might even be able to fit in a book or two.

CHAPTER 54

Seconds ticked by and struggled to become minutes until, finally, they raced forward, and the time to launch the attack approached. Roger sat behind the wheel of the large truck. The front had been reinforced with steel. Still, as he put his foot on the gas and picked up speed, he held his breath that this would work. The mansion had a wrought iron fence all the way around. If the calculations were off, the truck wouldn't make it through the gate.

Roger should have no trouble surviving such a crash. His team was in the vehicles behind him. They might stand a chance of breaking in time if he didn't get through, but he was really hoping they wouldn't have to find out.

The mansion loomed in the near distance.

Roger gripped the wheel and pushed on the gas a little more. Thankfully, Seamus's ego demanded he be at the end of a long street. Without having to turn, Roger didn't have to sacrifice any speed.

The gate was right ahead of him.

The truck wasn't going to be able to do this. What was he thinking?

No turning back. Roger slammed his foot down as he

cleared the last of the driveways. With no potential civilians in the way, there was no reason to hold back. The crunch of metal on metal broadcasted that he'd made contact with the gate. At any moment, the front end of the trunk was going to crumple and trap him in the truck. He was sure of it.

The gates bent, then flew back on their hinges, falling off the bottom ones and remaining stuck open. Roger continued to barrel up the driveway toward the mansion.

A cackle of laughter broke free from him. He was in. *Let the bastard try and stop us.*

~

The pain in Takashi's neck wasn't a shock, but it still was unpleasant. He rubbed the back of his neck as he sat up. The room he was in was terribly small and had a silver cell door. Beyond was the room with the wooden rack and torture instruments.

He was in Anton's secret chamber.

"Damn it." Takashi pushed himself up to his feet and neared the door. His view of the other cells was limited.

"He's awake!" Phyrull called out in delight. "Welcome to the dungeon!"

"Don't talk to the demon shithead," Dennis said. "The more you talk to him, the more he gets in your head."

"You should be thrilled, Denny. This means there's someone else for me to play with!" Phyrull announced. Out of the two, Phyrull was the one Takashi had a view of. The demon was in his natural form, tail swinging happily behind him. "I'm glad I finally get time with you. Apparently, I've been slipping in my role lately. Getting to study you will be an honor."

"You assume he won't try to fuck the real thing," Dennis said. "You were just a fucking stand-in."

"You will quickly discover that ramming a nail through your hand is more fun than Denny," Phyrull said.

"Hmm," Takashi said noncommittally. Looking for a little bit of comfort, he took off his suit jacket. It swung heavier than it should as he folded it. He investigated the pocket and found a long key. *Anton gave me an escape.* Would walking out of the basement be so simple? Was it a test? Remain and the punishment would be called off, leave and face worse? *If I time this to Roger's attack, I'll be able to use the chaos to escape.*

But Takashi didn't know exactly when Roger would arrive, just that it would have to be before dawn. "Dennis, are you sluggish yet?"

"Great, you're already crazy enough to ask weird questions," Dennis grumbled.

"You've only been a vampire for a matter of weeks. You should be able to feel the dawn before I will," Takashi replied.

"Oh, he won't know the difference since he's barely been fed," Phyrull said. "However, I could tell you easily."

"Or you'll tell me what you think I want to hear," Takashi countered.

"If what you want to hear is whether or not dawn is approaching, then I would tell you the truth," Phyrull replied. "But I would have a condition."

"A demon deal is not a condition," Takashi said.

"Not even if all I want is for you to unlock my door?"

"What's to keep you from latching onto me and making me your thrall?" Takashi asked.

"Ouch!" Phyrull pouted. "I get plenty of bewitching done outside these walls. I don't need to charm you into being my puppet."

"Need and will are two different things," Takashi replied.

"Fine, *fine*. What if I promise none shall feel my charms until noon in this blasted time zone?" Phyrull offered. "Will that condition work for you?"

"Yes."

"The first crest of light is soon, but dawn will not banish the grays of night for another forty minutes," Phyrull said.

With a retreat planned and vampires as part of the attack, then Roger would have to arrive soon. If Takashi moved quietly enough through the house, he might be able to leave without anyone the wiser. *Except for Katie. Except if this is a trap. And I can't leave Zack.*

Roger wasn't going to leave without Zack, and if Takashi connected with any of the teams, then he might be able to persuade them to aid him. He'd be able to get Zack and Katie and lead them out himself.

Carefully, Takashi reached through his bars and slid the key into the lock. One twist and the lock was undone. Using his sleeved arm, he pushed the door open. He immediately went to Phyrull's cell and unlocked it as well, stepping wide from the door.

"Thank you, my good sir," Phyrull said cheerfully. He saluted quickly, then took the form of a werewolf in its hybrid form, bulky, hairy, and with claws and a snout, but still on two legs. He bounded off for the next door, and there was a crash as he opened it. Soon, he was running down the hall, turning the corner toward the exit.

"Don't draw attention," Takashi called after him, no idea if Phyrull could hear him at that distance or over the noise of the other, less human prisoners.

Takashi turned toward Dennis. The young man bore little resemblance to Zack, but this was his cousin. From what had happened the last time Takashi was down in this basement, he knew Dennis had been cruel to Zack in the past. Zack had been content to leave him down here, suffering as Phyrull made him relive his sins.

Conditions were already terrible, and should Anton or Seamus survive, whoever was remained would have to endure more. Roger had intimated that he was going to burn the house down. Dennis might very well die in the rubble if left behind.

But he might deserve it. Zack had promised to help Dennis when he was able to, but that didn't mean Takashi owed this man a thing.

"When you spoke to Zack, you said you fucked up," Takashi said as he slowly approached the door. "What did you mean?"

"Seriously? You want to stand around talking when we could be running?" Dennis tried to grab the key from Takashi's hand, but the silver bars stopped him. He hissed and backed away from the door, only to come right back up to it.

"When I have the opportunity to fully drink a life, I often choose one of a bigot," Takashi said coldly. "They aren't hard to find, and they are often damaging their families."

"Zack told you what I said to him when we were kids?"

"I deciphered it from context," Takashi replied. He took a step toward the exit. When Dennis remained silent, he took another three.

"My dad was the one who kept saying that kind of crap to me," Dennis shouted with a groan of frustration. "I took it out on Zack. I took it out on a lot of people. But do you want to know how I landed in here? I went looking for my boyfriend. Only I never called him that to his face because I was a fucking coward. The last conversation we had was a fight about how if I wasn't brave enough to tell our team that we were an item, then he didn't want me watching his back. He died and maybe he wouldn't be gone if I'd been braver. But I can't take any of it back. Please, please don't let me die down here."

Takashi zipped back and unlocked the door. He was prepared to abandon Dennis and hurry toward his freedom, only Dennis could hardly stagger from his cell.

Neither Zack nor Roger would leave the young vampire,

especially after hearing his abbreviated tale. Their compassion would have begged them to help. And Roger had a point that vampires were too cruel to each other.

Lending a hand would slow him, but Takashi was capable. It was what Roger and Zack would do.

Cursing under his breath, Takashi went to Dennis's side and coaxed him into putting an arm across his shoulders. "Hold on."

Together, they rushed through the open door, down the hallway, and up the staircase to the main floor. Sounds of crashing distracted Takashi. Windows were breaking in rooms near and farther away, the patter of shattered glass echoing through the halls.

When he turned toward the staircase that would take him up to Zack's suite, he came face-to-face with an incredibly tall, spindly fey. The fey's eyes reminded Takashi of an endless pit that one could never crawl out of.

"What the fuck is that?" Dennis said, trying to slip Takashi's grasp and run in the other direction.

Decorum still had its place, especially with the fey. Takashi said, "You must be Grimsby."

"I am," Grimsby replied. "A pleasure to finally allow you to see this form."

"Because I've seen you before," Takashi said. He realized that Grimsby's complexion was that of the collared boy who'd led him around in his early nights in the mansion. When the boy had vanished, Takashi had assumed Seamus killed him. "I suppose that the reason I can see you now is that the rules of hospitality no longer apply to me or my friend here."

"Your supposition proves correct." Grimsby leaned down toward him. His smile was toothy. "I have no cause to be polite to trespassers."

"But, perhaps, you have cause to escort one from the property. That might fall within your duties."

Grimsby tilted his head, then partly bowed. "I should see a trespasser off, especially on a tumultuous night like this one. The house seems to be falling out of order."

Yet Grimsby wasn't rushing off to join the fray in any way. *Why is he working here?* Takashi unwound Dennis's arm from his shoulders and nudged him toward Grimsby. "He's having some trouble walking."

"Ah, well, that won't do." Grimsby swept Dennis off his feet and began to stride down the hall, going past one of the staircases to the second floor and carrying on.

Okay, one win. Takashi hurried for the stairs, taking them up two at a time. With any luck, he'd find Zack before the battle did.

CHAPTER 55

Zack should have put *The Fal of the Undede-Kynge* into the overly large purse before he swept the rings, tiepins, and cuff-links into the bag, but he hadn't been thinking. He was about to panic, then remembered that he could just use a burst of superspeed. Quickly, he undid, then redid the packing, including the journal he'd begun to write in. *Wish I knew where the other one was. Stupid of me to put it in the fucker's library.*

"Excuse you, take your hands off me," Katie said loudly.

Zack took his dagger out from its sheath and stalked toward the open door to the hallway. Silent as a grave, he made his way over and poked his head out.

"Miss, you have to come with us," one of the security personnel was saying. Four guards were out in the hallway. Two were preoccupied with Katie and, due to her struggling, were blocking the entire path.

One of the other two caught sight of Zack. "Master, we are supposed to take you and her to the panic room."

"Why?" Zack demanded as he stepped out into the hall.

"There's an attack. You'll be safer in the panic room," the guard responded.

An attack. On the mansion. *Roger*. It had to be. Zack slung the purse over his shoulder, the strap running across his chest. He let the guards see his dagger and its faint red glow. With all the command he could muster, he said, "We won't be going to the panic room."

"Our orders—"

Zack spun his dagger once. "You will have to force us. Well, try. I don't believe the odds are in your favor."

Katie yanked her arm free from one of her guards and pulled her wand from her purse. A blue spark gathered at the tip.

"We should work on securing the perimeter with the others," one of the others said.

"Wise choice," Zack replied.

They rushed from the hallway, leaving Katie and Zack behind. Distant sounds of shouting and fighting echoed through the mansion. That was what Roger was planning, why he'd shown up at the Chateau. He'd wanted to clue them in to his big rescue attack. Why he hadn't whisked them away from the Chateau, Zack wasn't sure. But he'd have the chance to ask Roger before he left Chicago as fast as he could.

Come to me, Seamus ordered.

Eh, fuck you. Zack grabbed Katie's hand and began to run for the stairs. Motion coming down the hallway made him stop until he realized it was Takashi. With a laugh, he caught him in a hug and held him tight. "How did you get out?"

"Key in the pocket," Takashi replied. "Roger's launched an attack on the house. He means to humiliate Seamus by taking down the mansion."

Zack's first thought was about the library and the loss of knowledge that would happen if it was turned to rubble.

What was that? Seamus demanded.

Row, row, row your boat, right up your fucking ass, Zack replied.

This is not the time for childish games.

"We need to get moving." Zack nodded down the hall and started to sprint. *Oh, it's exactly the time for them.*

Enough of this.

A weight dropped onto Zack's mind, and he staggered as it felt like something was crawling inside his head. Snakes, slithering, seeking, pressing down his joy, his relief at seeing Takashi, his want for Roger in his arms, his longing to see his dad. All of it being crushed until there was one want remaining.

The urge to kill.

Without anything else, not even fears, to use his energy, the urge plumped and grew into a consuming cloud over his mind. He held on to the wall and tried to force Seamus from his mind, but the slithering snakes were too many and too heavy.

Sliding his dagger into the girl's chest would be simple. Refreshing, even. Blood belonged on his hands, in his mouth.

No. No, that was Katie. Zack put a hand to his temple and screamed.

"Zack?" Takashi said.

Takashi blurred from a familiar lover to a stranger whose only merit would be death. Groaning, Zack pushed away the thought of murdering even a stranger who wasn't a stranger. He knew Takashi. Loved him.

Do as you're told. Kill everyone, a voice in his head commanded.

A pulse went through him, starting at his heart and reaching his fingers and toes. Everything else was falling away.

One fear remained, strangled as it was. He cared about … about someone near him. The girl? The man?

Didn't matter. All he had strength for was one word. "Run!"

CHAPTER 56

The third kick to the front doors finally broke them open.
Roger strode through the mansion doors with a level of confidence he had never dared show in this place before. Behind
him, Bastian, the not-cat Lee, Lacey, another two hunters, and
five vampires poured in, quickly spreading out in the foyer. A
team of guards swept in and were immediately riddled with
arrows from Lacey and two of the vampires.

"Seamus!" Roger shouted at the top of his voice. He sent a
silver dagger toward the heart of a guard who came from a
different hallway and then pulled another so he still had one
in each hand. "I'd like a word!"

"A *word*," Seamus said, the word dripping with hate and
annoyance so thick that the other vampires took a step back
toward the door. Seamus walked out onto the landing at the
top of the sweeping staircase and gripped the handrail as he
glared down at them.

His eyes were pitch-black with red stars burning in their
centers. As Roger watched, his fingers stretched and grew
talon-like nails, his torso—already covered in blood—became
emaciated, and his ears lengthened into long points. Several

pairs of fangs sharpened his smile. That grin promised the end of Roger in a long, excruciating death.

Roger's knees began to buckle. He ought to beg mercy. To fall down and prostrate himself. Perhaps he would be welcome back. He wanted that. He wanted to know the sweet embrace of the vampire who had made him, who he had known for centuries, who he had been with in so many ways.

No. There were snakes in his mind, teasing out his desires and fears and thickening them in unwanted ways. Seamus was trying to twist him.

"What word would you like?" Seamus said with his smug, toothy smile.

"Die," Roger snapped. Then he flung a blade at Seamus's heart.

Seamus vaulted over the railing and plucked Roger's dagger from the air. Before he hit the first floor, he sent it back out, nailing one of the vampires in the heart. The vampire cried out, but before she could yank the dagger out, a puff of red mist exploded out from her. She collapsed to the floor.

"Join. Me," Seamus declared, and he stretched out his hand to the remaining vampires.

The four vampires clutched at their heads or their hearts, but quickly, their eyes were turning glassy.

Seamus had to be manipulating their emotions like he'd attempted to screw with Roger's head. Back in the ballroom, Roger had managed to counter him, but he was realizing that Seamus hadn't used his true strength in that moment.

Or perhaps there was a flaw in his power. Mentally, Roger raced to reach the other vampires with him. Seamus was flooding their minds with fear of what would happen to them and forcing a desire to obey upon them. The fear was founded in each of them, but that desire was too small a sail to move the ships in the direction Seamus intended. Seamus was having to pour energy into them.

Roger sought their instincts, their desires to survive and

thrive, their longing to be rid of the creature before them. His inner tides swayed to his call, rising as he begged for more to save the ones with him. A molten bubble of warmth flowed into the tides, aiding his strength, bringing on a wind that helped him guide the vampires away from what Seamus wanted.

"What?" Seamus snapped as the vampires stood straight, the glossiness leaving their eyes. Lacey was unleashing arrow after arrow; the other hunters were unloading silver bullets. Seamus caught most of the arrows and angled his body so the bullets didn't strike his heart or head. He turned his focus to Roger, and his eyes widened. "What are you?"

"Better than you," Roger growled. He strode forward.

And the distraction served its purpose for this stage of the battle. While Seamus had been preoccupied with the vampires and Roger, the not-cat Lee had slunk around to the other side of the foyer so that he was opposite Bastian. As Roger stepped closer, Bastian released the spell he'd been preparing. A roaring wall of flames wrapped around one side, met Lee, who stamped a paw, and then finished out the circle by racing back to Bastian. The top of the flames met in a dome.

"Shall we dance, *master*?" Roger asked with a sharp grin.

"It will be your last," Seamus promised.

Roger surged forward with a shout.

"Why aren't we going down the stairs?" Katie asked. "That's where all the doors to the outside are."

"We're vampires, we don't need doors. We just need an exit and to not land on stakes or silver," Takashi muttered. He was trying not to shake. Something—no, Seamus—had overcome Zack, and Zack's eyes had mutated colors to become endless pits and ruby red. Seamus had taken control of him in some way without being in the same room. That was not good. Not at all good. *He had enough presence to send us away. He is lost, not gone.*

Finally, at the end of one long hall, Takashi saw a window. Holding Katie's hand, he ran for it as fast as he could. Each step was a mile crossed, and yet the hall seemed to stretch forever.

Anton stepped out around a corner. The shadows beneath him thickened, and the ones in the hall near him grew. Darkness clouded the way, but Anton's eyes glowed red in the dimness. The smell of burnt ozone and dead roses overwhelmed everything else.

Takashi stumbled, and then his foot caught on a tendril of shadow creeping out from underneath a console table, the vase rattling as the shadow disturbed the table's balance. He danced backward a step only for another tendril to wrap around his leg. It cinched painfully, breaking bone, and he held in his scream the best he could.

"I offer you an escape, and you abuse my weakness for you to release my toys and then my daughter." The dropping temperature in the hallway wasn't as severe as the tone in Anton's voice, and it was plummeting so quickly that ice formed along the walls. "My love is right. You are a leech."

"*Our* daughter, you said," Takashi gasped through the pain. More tendrils sought his limbs, and he fought to keep them from trapping him. He was losing the struggle. "She is part of me, and I cannot leave her in this hell."

"You were rude! Filling my head with longings for you when I should have known this was all a trick." Anton clenched his fist, and the tendrils tightened as one. "Everything you are is a lie."

"You saw into my mind!" Takashi cried out. "You saw the deepest parts of me before anyone else. What did you see, Anton? What did you truly see when you plunged into the depths of my soul? Am I a liar? Or are you so willing to blind yourself to the terrible truths about Seamus that you'll forsake what you know?"

"He is my *love*," Anton snarled.

"Why?" Takashi demanded. "Why defend him like this? Are you so afraid that no one else will love you that you will destroy everything for one bastard who does not see you as an equal?"

"You don't know us!" Anton roared.

"I walled away my heart because I feared letting anyone into it," Takashi said. "You have built a fortress around your feelings for Seamus, but it is a house of cards. You hate any wind because it would send his lies and his manipulations flat against the ground. And what you hate most of all is that I am right."

"Enough," Anton declared. "You will not come between us. Soon, nothing will ever hurt us again."

A tendril twisted around Takashi's neck and squeezed. Unable to hold himself up, he collapsed to his hands and knees, the shadows pulling ever tighter.

"Fulminis!" Katie shouted, and a streak of blue lightning soared over Takashi.

With a wave of his hand, Anton brought up an invisible shield, and the lightning bolt crashed against it. Blue sparks cascaded down. As Katie continued to blast the blot forth from her wand, it brightened the hallway.

The shadows lessened. As the light was pouring over Takashi, the tendrils couldn't keep their strength. He broke free of them.

Katie was panting from the effort of maintaining her spell, and Takashi could feel how she was pulling power from him. They wouldn't last like this.

Takashi surged forward, going for the low right side. Either the shield wasn't there, or Anton couldn't keep him out.

For all Takashi's hope that Anton might flourish into a

better man without Seamus in his life, there was none now. He rose to his feet behind Anton.

Anton half turned, calling on more shadows, but that divided his attention, and his shield cracked. Takashi struck at him, and though Anton countered, each move took a bit more focus. Pulling as much speed as he could, Takashi attempted to land his blows over and over. Anton continued to slide away, continued to counter, and began to slip.

But Takashi's energy was also fading.

With a last, desperate scream, Takashi shoved his hand toward Anton's chest with every ounce of his fury. His hand punctured his flesh, going through his ribs, and closed around his heart. He ripped it clean from Anton's body.

Anton dropped, his shield dissipating as he fell. The lightning bolt knocked Takashi back against the far wall beside the window, Anton's heart falling to the floor beside him as he did.

"Holy shit, I'm sorry!" Katie ran to Takashi's side. She glanced at Anton. "Is he … is he dead?"

"Do you have a fire spell?" Takashi groaned.

"Yeah."

Takashi nodded at the heart.

Katie pointed her wand at it. "Ignis!"

An orange flame lit the heart and quickly turned blue, then green. The blaze caught the wall on fire. Katie aimed her wand at the stray flame.

Takashi pushed himself off the floor. Every fiber of his being ached, and they had yet to make their escape. "Let it burn."

"Are you sure? Zack is still—"

"Zack will make it out," Takashi replied. *I pray he is himself when he does.* He threw the window open. "We have to leave."

Katie nodded and hurried out the window. As Takashi waited for her, his gaze lingered on Anton's body. No red mist emerged, even as the heart on the floor beside Takashi's foot crumpled into itself, and he remained handsome. He should have turned gray and lifeless; a flood of red mist should have escaped someone so old.

Had Anton managed to find true immortality? Would he hunt down Takashi if he survived?

Guilt swept over Takashi as he dropped out of the window and to the dark garden below. *If we're lucky, the fire will finish him off.* Takashi took Katie's hand, and they ran toward the western fence. Flames flickered in the window they'd left open, and the sounds of clashing enemies echoed out into the night.

CHAPTER 57

Kill, his mind demanded. *Kill, kill, kill.* He trod down the stairs, his feet heavy and fighting him, and spun the dagger in his hand. The silver glinted in the dim light of the halls, and the runes provided extra illumination. They were the shade of blood, the shade he was hoping to coat it in.

He tracked heartbeats and the noises of weapons meeting flesh until he found a group fighting in one of the parlors. A few combatants had spilled out into the hall. Some had familiar black uniforms; the others were dressed in black as well. They were living—or unliving in the case of the vampires—creatures. Targets ripe for destruction.

Blurring between the ones in the hall, slashing throats, and burning out hearts with his blade was laughably easy. In a few seconds, there were three dead bodies. The blood on his blade seeped into the runes, and a rush of warmth spread up his arm and into his chest. He strode into the room.

There were a dozen or so struggling in here. He danced through them, carving through veins as he went. Several fell down with a cry, though none of his blows had been killing ones this time. The vampires were healing. The humans were holding their wounds. They smelled delicious, and he bared his fangs in a wide smile.

A young black girl swung a baseball bat covered in silver nails at his head. He leaned out of the way. She redirected, swung again, and he dodged the other way. She wasn't fast like him, but she didn't hesitate between her strikes either. Another vampire came at him, and he reached out and broke the attacker's neck. She continued, nearly hit him that time.

How many could he kill while evading her? He blurred, stabbing one of the uniform-clad vampires, and destroyed the creature's heart. She chased him down.

The others were beginning to run. When he went to chase after one mortal, the black girl zoomed in front of him, actually catching him off guard with her movement. Laughing, he let her take more swings at him. She was spending energy; he was barely using any.

Or, at least, he thought he was hardly tapping into his strength. The longer he looked upon her face, the slower he seemed to get.

Enough games! Kill her and come to me! the voice in his head declared.

He ducked a wilder swing from her and grabbed the bat closer to her hands. Growling, he ripped it from her. She struck him in the solar plexus with her fist. Ribs crunched, and he coughed. He tossed the bat off to the side and dodged her fist again. This one grazed his nose. He was ... slowing down ... because ... because something was wrong. With him.

Kill.

He shook his head once and grabbed the girl's wrist during her next attempt. After snapping her arm, he followed up with a punch. He struck her again, driving her up against the wall.

The smell of smoke wafted in through the open door. She started to step away from the wall, so he pushed her roughly by the shoulder. He brought his dagger back, ready to drive it into her heart.

She closed her eyes and tilted her head back as if believing she could flatten herself into the wall and survive. Bloody tears ran from the corners of her eyes. She was so young. So incredibly young. Like Amber, his sister.

Amber. He had a sister named Amber, and he wanted to see her again.

Kill!

He started to bring the blade in, but the girl whimpered, and the sound tugged on his memory. He ... he had seen her like this before ... he knew her. How?

Detroit, his rational mind provided. *Janiyah Williams, age fourteen. Missing three weeks, last seen outside a library.* A missing person's page filtered through his inner mind. He had researched her. Seen her on a dark street on a rainy night with smoke on the air. She had been running. From ... from hunters.

I didn't want to kill her then. I don't want to do it now! Zack screamed, the frustration of his lust for death combating his inner self. He couldn't pull his blade back from where it was. He still wanted to drive it forward too badly.

"Zack!" Thomas shouted.

"D-dad?" Zack managed to turn his head.

Thomas had an arrow notched in his favorite bow. Zack's mom had always claimed it was too slow of a hunter's tool, that there was no point teaching archery to the kids. And so Zack hadn't learned his father's skill. "Let her go, Zack."

"I ... I can't." Zack tried to move his arm, but it was like pushing on a door that only opened with a pull. His body believed that was the wrong direction.

"Please," Janiyah whispered. "You let me go before."

"Before?" Thomas asked.

"Detroit." Zack clenched his jaw as his hand slid another

centimeter forward. Much more and he would pierce her skin. "Dad, you have to stop me."

"I don't want to hurt you," Thomas replied.

"If you don't, I'm going to kill her and then you," Zack cried. "Please, Dad!"

Resolution hardened Thomas's expression, and he raised the tip of his arrow. "I love you."

"I love you, too, Dad." Tears streaked down Zack's cheeks. "But hurry, I'm losing control."

Thomas loosed the arrow, and it sailed through the air. Zack closed his eyes, expecting pain in his chest. Instead, he had a splitting headache and then darkness as Janiyah snapped his neck.

CHAPTER 58

"I should have killed you centuries ago," Seamus said.

"We all make mistakes," Roger replied. Keeping Seamus talking provided him an opportunity to weigh his possible strategies but also let Seamus heal. Bastian's fire dome wouldn't last forever. If Roger couldn't kill Seamus, he at least had to injure him enough that he couldn't prevent the retreat.

The upside of the fire was that Seamus was limited in space; the downsides were that Roger was in that space, and the light from the flames made the shadows nearly nonexistent. The touch of them was too distant, and Roger wasn't about to sacrifice any power in trying to grow them in spite of the light.

"You have made plenty of them," Seamus taunted. "So many great loves turned to join you in immortality, and yet not one still stands beside you."

Seamus was attempting to goad him into an attack, to strike out in rage without calculation. But Seamus's words didn't ding Roger's mental armor. After all, three of those relationships had died because of Seamus's actions; James had left because of Roger's cowardice, and Phoenix had barely been a lover. Both James and Phoenix were out in the world, living their lives, Quinn's and Roger's first sirelings were dead, and Ezra was madly in love at long last.

Roger didn't rise to the bait.

But maybe he will.

"Remind me how many homes you've had?" Roger asked. "Not individual houses—you abandon those almost as often as you drain your entire collection. But we had to leave Devil's Cove because you were scared of the English Navy and then Southern France because you couldn't control your hunger. Paris because you killed a hunter and pissed off his family. London for nearly the same reason. Virginia was a scant time, and then there was New York. I almost thought we'd make it in New York. Then you insisted that we move here."

"To protect my ungrateful spawn from the chaos that continuously embroils that domain."

Roger grinned wider. "And I am going to make certain that no place in this city will protect you."

"I am the master. The coven will obey me," Seamus growled.

Roger laughed at him.

Seamus lunged, but Roger was ready for him. He pivoted and sliced out with both daggers as he spun farther away from Seamus. Blood sprinkled the ground. Playing defense, Roger countered Seamus's next attack, parried the one after that, and then kicked him hard enough to send him against the far side of the circle. Seamus's back erupted in flames when he touched the wall. With a howl, he staggered forward. Roger threw a blade at his heart, but Seamus knocked away.

After a second, the flames extinguished on their own. A regular vampire wouldn't be able to pull off that feat without smothering the fire, but Seamus only held his head and shouted until the flames stopped. The acrid smell of burnt flesh coupled with torched wood and decay.

"I've managed to rob you and destroy your home with the ragtag resources I've managed to cobble together in a few weeks," Roger said loudly. "You might be surprised how motivated people are in ending your life."

Seamus laughed with a disturbing malice. "I have turned your loyal pet into my diligent son. In fact, he nn—" Suddenly, Seamus put a hand to his temple. "What have you done to him?"

Roger steadied his stance. "I've been here."

"Take responsibility for your people," Seamus demanded. "What did they do to my son?"

I pray nothing. Roger flung both his daggers at Seamus, one right after the other, aiming for his chest and his knee. Seamus caught the one going for his heart but failed to move out of the way of the one to strike his knee.

The flames flickered. The dome at the top was beginning to come down. Bastian's spell was running its course.

Roger pulled his last two daggers and launched himself at Seamus. The tip of one blade sliced Seamus's shoulder, then missed his target. Seamus blurred with speed to avoid the next two strikes.

Then the circle dropped. Roger flung one dagger at Seamus and leapt upward with all his might. He grabbed onto the chandelier.

His team had formed a semicircle near the door, and with the flames no longer obscuring Seamus, they unleashed their ammunition upon him. Arrows, spells, and silver bullets pummeled Seamus.

The sudden change of light might have played tricks on Roger's sight, but he could have sworn that Seamus was becoming gaunter, that he was more inhuman as he took the damage. Seamus made a motion with his hand, and his blood rose from the floor to form a shield in front of him. He used it to block the bullets more than the wood flying in his direction.

Rage burning in his eyes, Seamus shot one last look up at Roger and then took off deeper into the mansion.

Roger dropped to the ground as a cheer went up and kept his gaze on the corridor Seamus disappeared through. He noticed that Lee, Bastian, and Lacey kept their focus on the battle instead of cheering, too.

"Roger!" Thomas shouted.

Thomas and Janiyah were carrying Zack between them, one of his arms over each of their shoulders. An arrow stuck out of either side of Zack's skull, and the fletching matched the ones in Thomas's quiver. He'd put an arrow in Zack.

"Was it an accident?" Roger hurried to take Zack from them, sweeping him up into his arms.

"We had to knock him out," Janiyah said.

"He was begging us to," Thomas added. "There was something wrong with his eyes. They were like ink and fire. He was cutting through everyone he came across but managed to hold off from killing Janiyah. She must have triggered his memory."

"You know him?" Roger asked as he strode toward the broken front doors. His team swept out ahead of him. No sounds of fighting was a good thing at this point. He rushed toward his truck.

Janiyah blurred ahead and opened the back door for him.

"Apparently, they met in Detroit," Thomas said tensely. "Something she could have mentioned."

"Your family killed the nest that made me," Janiyah replied. "I'm glad, but I'm not stupid enough to think you were going to spare me a second time."

"But Zack did," Roger murmured.

"He was trying to, yeah," Janiyah said, softening.

"Then whatever Seamus was doing couldn't have been permanent." Roger climbed into the back and held Zack in his arms. Holding him was a comfort, but he couldn't fully relax. Not until he knew where Takashi was.

Thomas climbed into the driver's seat, and Janiyah took the front passenger. As Thomas put the truck into gear, Janiyah took her phone out of her pocket.

"Is Takashi safe? Did he make it out?" Roger asked.

"Hold on. There are a lot of check-ins," Janiyah muttered.

Thomas pulled off to the side of the driveway, knocking into one of Seamus's obscene statues of a mortal offering themselves up. The reinforced front held, and the statue teetered on its plinth, eventually falling over. When Bastian started to slow his vehicle, Thomas gave him the signal to go ahead, and the other cars took off.

"Vincent has him and a girl," Janiyah said.

Without waiting, Thomas moved the truck back onto the driveway and took off after the others.

Roger spared one glance behind him. Several parts of the mansion were aflame, the blazes brightening the area more than the coming dawn for the moment.

He'd done it. He had actually faced Seamus and lived. He'd outmaneuvered the bastard and drove him off. Not only that, but he had Zack in his arms, and Takashi was free.

Though they weren't yet to the safe house, a tidal wave of relief like he'd never known before crashed over him. The taxation of the battle began to creep up on him, but he wouldn't sleep until he knew if Zack had reclaimed his mind. Until then, he'd hold him close and hope.

CHAPTER 59

"He wasn't feral. It was something more focused than that," Takashi murmured. He sat atop a dresser in the shabby bedroom. The trip to the safe house had been quicker than he'd expected. They weren't in Chicago but in one of the suburbs closer to Seamus's mansion than Takashi was comfortable with. Roger assured him the mages and warlocks working the illusions to protect the place could hold their magics for forty-eight hours, which would be enough time for the surviving forces that had rendezvoused to dissipate.

"Seamus attempted to use his vampiric manipulations when I initiated my fight. He only focused on the vampires. I wonder if he was doing that to Zack and that was taking a portion of his strength," Roger mused.

Roger had changed into a red long-sleeved T-shirt and a pair of dark gray sweatpants. Despite his short, horribly dyed hair, he looked better than he ever had. His confidence was enticing; his mannerisms were brusquer, but not in a bad way. This was Roger without pretenses, without putting on a show.

Takashi felt like he was seeing his lover for the first time and falling for him all over again.

Zack was on the bed. They had found enough rope and belts that he was tied down so tightly that he shouldn't be able to move anything besides his head. The arrow through his skull had kept him knocked out, his body healing around the wood but unable to restore where the arrow remained. Roger had removed the arrow a couple of minutes ago.

Sluggishly, Zack opened his eyes, and they were steel gray except for a ring of red around the center. He blinked heavily, then tried to move. He glanced down to see the ropes and belts. "Oh, that's probably smart."

With a laugh of relief, Takashi moved from the dresser to sit beside Zack. Roger sat on the other side so that Zack was between them. When Takashi reached to undo the first belt, Roger caught his hand and held it.

"Let's give him a minute," Roger murmured. He stroked Zack's hair. "You seem better, but—"

"But I went full psycho killer." Zack groaned, then tried to sit up with alarm. "Wait, my dad—"

"Thomas is fine. As is Janiyah," Roger said.

"Janiyah should play baseball." Zack snorted, then laughed harder. "I can't believe I just suggested a vampire play baseball."

Takashi laughed, too, and stretched out alongside Zack.

"What's so—oh. That movie." Roger rolled his eyes. "I try to forget you made me watch it."

"Well, now I can make you watch it *forever*," Zack chided.

"You can," Takashi said softly.

Zack met his gaze, and his beautiful eyes held a tender regret. "Takashi, I am sorry about—"

"You weren't yourself," Takashi replied.

"What happened?" Roger asked.

"Seamus got in my head. Suppressed everything but the desire to kill," Zack said. "I don't feel him like I did before, but he's still *there*."

"Then he survived," Roger said.

"Survived what exactly?" Zack asked.

"We set the mansion on fire," Roger replied.

Zack attempted to sit up again, actually managing to wriggle up a little. "Roger! There was a priceless library! Medieval texts! Lore books that I had only heard about before! Tell me you didn't burn that collection!"

The statement was so perfectly Zack that Takashi started laughing and couldn't stop. Roger began as well, not nearly as heartily, and yet Takashi only laughed harder, tears forming in his eyes. The relief was profound, made tender by having his lovers with him.

"You are yourself." Roger began to untie Zack, and at that impetus, Takashi helped him.

"I had a bag on me," Zack said. "And my dagger."

Takashi pointed to where they lay on the dresser. "Katie had similar purses stuffed full with jewelry and video games."

"Ah, I didn't think about selling those. Probably not worth as much as she thought," Zack replied.

"You were going to run away?" Roger asked.

"I didn't know a rescue was coming," Zack said.

"Well, it did." Takashi leaned up and kissed Roger. "Thank you."

"Always," Roger promised. He kissed Zack. "I love you both."

"I love you both, too," Zack said with a handsome smile.

Takashi decided to kiss each of them and let them feel his love that way instead.

After they untied Zack, Zack and Takashi slipped into changes of comfortable clothes. Takashi would have preferred to sleep in his underwear, but there were too many other people in the house. Without any clue when someone was going to disturb them, Roger pushed for modesty. Too many mortals or some nonsense like that.

When they lay down on the bed together, Zack insisted

that Takashi be between them. Exhaustion greater than the drowsiness of dawn pulled on him. With Roger's arm around him and Zack lightly stroking his arm, Takashi drifted off, content in ways he couldn't remember being before.

Waiting for Roger and Takashi to fall asleep was brutal. Zack struggled to keep his eyes open as the minutes crawled by. Takashi nodded off pretty quickly. Roger kept sending him lazy smiles, which Zack did his best to return, and staying awake despite the massive bags under his eyes. But Roger did fall asleep.

You will come back to me, Seamus demanded. His voice was more distant than it had been, like he was shouting across a ravine, but the fact that it was still there meant Zack remained connected to him. And if they were connected, Seamus could use that to track him down. Or worse, force him to do what he wanted.

Until Zack found some way to break it, he was a danger to the ones he loved.

He sat up and took a long moment to appreciate the view of his lovers in front of him. Takashi had his back up against Roger's front, and Roger had looped his arm over Takashi. They were nestled in together like they'd never been apart, and that brought a genuine smile to Zack's lips. Roger's hair was horrible, but the rest of him was the same handsome vampire that Zack had first seen.

They won't be alone. They have each other. And I'll come back to them, I will. Zack dared to kiss Takashi's forehead, then Roger's. He waited to see if either stirred. When they didn't, he slipped out of bed.

Roger had thought of everything for their corner of the safe house. There was another outfit, which included one of Zack's favorite hoodies and a pair of sneakers. Silently, Zack changed into the more practical outfit and took his dagger and the purse off the dresser. Then he snuck out of the room.

The rest of the safe house was in a recognizable chaos. Zack hadn't been on any family missions since Detroit, but he'd been home when everyone else arrived from one. Some of his early childhood memories included creeping down the stairs from where he was sleeping at his grandparents' to find his mom or dad. Usually, they sent him right back to bed, but getting to see that they were all right calmed him enough to do that.

Zack could try to find Thomas or Amber in the mess. He'd have to explain that he was leaving, and he wasn't sure they'd let him. *I'll call once I get away.*

Stealing a set of keys was almost too easy, and he made his way through the house to the garage. Once he shut the door, he was alone. The larger garage door was already open, and out beyond, there were cars in the driveway and a few on the street. He had to hope the keys he'd taken were for one of the cars that wasn't blocked in.

Dawn had given way to day, and sunlight poured in through the open door. The line of shadow on pavement seemed like the edge of an abyss. In theory, Zack stood a chance at surviving in sunlight. After all, he was supposedly a super-strong vamp. But extremely old vampires became more susceptible to sunlight, so he might be screwed.

"Only one way to find out," Zack muttered to himself. He took a deep breath and shoved his hand out into the light.

Immediately, his hand burst into flames.

Swearing, Zack yanked his hand out of the light and put the flame out with his other sleeve. "Fuck!"

"Problem with your escape plan?" Thomas drawled.

Zack jumped and spun to see his dad coming out of the house to join him in the garage. Thomas was older than Zack remembered. Gray hairs at his temples had been there for years, but there were more of them. More lines around his eyes, too.

Zack swallowed around the knot in his throat. "Dad, I can explain."

"You're worried that your bond to your sire means he'll be able to use you or find you, and you want to get away before dark to put as much distance between you and him as possible," Thomas said. He motioned upward. "And you want to do it before your boyfriends join you or talk you out of it."

"Not just them," Zack said. "I have to protect you and Amber."

"Zack—"

"I read your letter." Zack zoomed forward and hugged his dad tightly. He tried to hold in his tears when Thomas put his arms around him in return. "I love you, too. I can't put you in danger."

Thomas kissed the top of his head. "That isn't how being a father works. If you're in danger, I should be doing everything I can to help."

"Dad, I have to go." Zack withdrew from Thomas's hug and tapped his temple. "I can hear Seamus calling to me. I can't stay in Chicago. Maybe running will be a good thing. He'll be distracted, and you and Roger can carry on the war and—"

"You just caught on fire in the sunlight, Zack. You're not going anywhere," Thomas said. Zack opened his mouth to argue, but Thomas continued. "Unless someone else is driving."

"You'd do that? For me?" Zack asked. "What about Amber?"

"Lacey's here. Amber'll be pissed about this, but I never should have let her get this close to this much action in the first place. There's being in the field, then there's being in a war zone. She's too young. You are, too, but you don't have a choice anymore."

His dad was willing to drop everything and just run with him. No questions asked, no hesitation. Thomas wouldn't let him go through with his escape on his own.

Zack brushed away his tears. "I don't know why I'm crying. It's fucking stupid."

"Hey, no it's not." Thomas stepped forward and pulled him into another hug. "You've gone through a lot."

"Understatement," Zack managed.

He might have remained in his father's arms, crying his eyes out, but there was a yelp, followed by another yelp, and then the door to the house opened again. Vincent stumbled out, not looking ahead but behind. "What the fuck is wrong with you, Lee?"

A gray-striped tabby cat sat just inside the house. He fixed his gaze upon Thomas. "I take it you two intend to run."

"Did the cat just speak?" Zack asked. He looked to Thomas and Vincent. "You heard that, right?"

Vincent looked as shocked as Zack felt.

Thomas was calm, like he *knew*, and Zack knew his dad well enough to know that, yeah, somehow, Thomas had known before that moment that the cat spoke. "Lee's not a cat. He just looks like it right now. And yes, Lee, we're making a run for it."

"Great. Rousting the apprentice was hard enough. I wasn't about to wake Bastian if I didn't have to," Lee replied.

"Lee, you're not coming."

"Oh yes we are." Lee stood, tail swishing. "The apprentice needs to learn how to control his power before he unintentionally levels a city block, Bastian gets restless, you could use the magical protection, and I fucking hate Chicago."

Thomas puffed up. "Lee—"

"You owe me a favor, Tommy boy. Consider this it," Lee replied. Then he stalked off into the house.

"Wait, Bastian as in Bastian Stone?" Zack asked. "That guy's a legend."

"He is?" Vincent said.

Zack swung his attention from Thomas to Vincent and did a double take on Vincent. Though Vincent's hair was an unkempt mess, his pale complexion was less gray and more white guy who never went outside. He was still scrawny, but he looked like he got to eat and sleep regularly. He looked good.

"Yeah," Zack said, blinking so he didn't zero in on Vincent's pulse. "Phenomenal exorcist, proficient battle mage. He's—is he your mentor? Are you a mage?"

"Apprentice, and likely warlock because I think having to pay for the privilege of being called a mage is stupid." Vincent folded his arms over his chest and lifted his chin. "I already have a wand."

"He's on his second wand," Thomas murmured. "The first one blew up."

"Channeling magic is tough, okay?" Vincent replied. "It's not like biting a neck."

"That only looks easy," Zack said. "You slice a vein wrong and you can kill a person in seconds."

"If I don't focus my magic right, I'm going to blow off my hand."

"Well, if I don't get some distance, Seamus might take control of my mind and make me murder everyone!"

"I have to—"

"Boys, boys, please, for the love of God, do not bicker about who is the bigger time bomb," Thomas grumbled. "It's 8:00 a.m. I've been up all night, and we have to get on the road as soon as possible. Vincent, grab whatever you've got in the house and help Lee wake up Bastian. Poke him with a broom at a distance, if you can. I need to talk to Lacey. Zack, is there anything you need before we leave?"

Zack bit his bottom lip, tugging on it gently so he didn't pierce it with his fang. "Got any paper? I need to write a letter."

CHAPTER 60

Roger stretched, sleep having done its work of restoring his energy, and cuddled up against Takashi. He reached out to touch Zack but didn't find him. Frowning, he opened his eyes and leaned up. Just enough light was coming from under the crack of the door to provide illumination for him to see.

Where Zack's head should have been on a pillow, a folded piece of paper was waiting.

"What's wrong?" Takashi asked as he yawned.

"Zack isn't here, and this is." Roger plucked the paper off the pillow and unfolded it.

Roger, Takashi,

I thought about asking you to come with me, but you're safer without me in town. Think about it, if Seamus was livid that Roger was missing, he's going to actually lose his mind if he can't find me.

Both of you have risked so much for me. I am sorry, Takashi, that Seamus used what I told him against you. I should have known he'd do something terrible.

All my life, I've tried to be what other people told me I should be. A hunter. A researcher. Even you two have pushed me towards what you wanted for me, though you wanted what you thought was good for me. Now I'm not technically alive. I'm a vampire. And Seamus had a plan for my new life, one that I think I was sliding into without meaning it. His voice is quieter in my head, but it's still there.

Right now, what I need to do is learn to be okay with being me. I love the two of you. I love what we have together. I just need a second to breathe—well, not actually breathe. I just need time. What's awesome is that we will have forever if we want it, so I hope you can forgive me for skipping out for a few months, especially since this should take some heat off you.

I'm not on my own. Dad insisted on coming with me. He says he has a lot to make up for and that he loves me no matter what. Thank you, Roger, for making him own up to his bullshit like you showed me mine. I have my dad back because of you.

Lee, Bastian, and Vincent will be coming with us, too. Apparently, Vincent's arcane powers are a bit explosive at the moment and Lee hates the city. So I get to travel with them. Yay? Dad's already scolded Vincent and me once for bickering.

Honestly, it felt kind of nice. Almost normal.

I love you both more than I can say in words, more than I have time to write right now.

Zack

P.S. Dad's email is on the bottom of the page. He promised me it's a new one Mom doesn't know about, so it's secure from the rest of the shit-head hunters.

P.P.S. Did you know Lee can talk? Dad says he's not actually a cat. Lee said something about Dad owing him a favor, so maybe he's really a fey? Will tell you more as I find out.

. . .

Unable to speak, Roger handed the letter to Takashi. He noticed that Zack's dagger and the purse from the mansion were gone. That confirmed what Zack had written more than his absence from the bed.

Takashi finished reading the letter and leaned into Roger. "He left. To protect us."

"Can't fault his logic," Roger murmured, though his heart stung.

"I think I hate his logic right now," Takashi replied.

"Me too."

"I'm not going to wake and suddenly find that you need a break from us, am I?" Takashi asked.

Roger kissed Takashi's cheek. "No. I've missed you too much."

Takashi snuggled into him. "And you've missed him."

"I have." Roger held Takashi close. "But he has a point. He deserves some time."

"I hope he doesn't take long," Takashi whispered.

"Me too." Roger did his best to relax into his cuddling with Takashi. "We'll have to make a home for him to come back to."

They lay together for a long, quiet moment. Then Takashi said, "Sounds like an idea. When do we start?"

~

Zack, Roger, and Takashi will return in Midnight War. Be sure to join my newsletter for updates and an exclusive story!

AFTERWORD

Hey there, reader peeps! Hopefully you've enjoyed *Wicked Games* as much as I enjoyed writing it! Don't worry, the next one is on the way. If you loved—or even if you hated—this book, I hope you'll consider doing a review on your fave site so other readers can know the joy/agony you've felt. Readers sharing their opinions is how I've found many a book to read myself. It's fun to share!

If you're eager for more of my stories, check out my Patreon along with my Amazon profile page. You'll find plenty of sweet, spice, and adventure in my tales and I can't wait to share them with you!

Happy Reading!
JS "Jace" Harker

ACKNOWLEDGMENTS

Whew, this book was a *long* one, wasn't it? My initial thanks have to go out to my family on this one. 180k inside of six months is no easy task, and my fam has been super supportive, even when they wished I'd finally finish so I'd stop saying I had to finish it.

Big shout out to Sue again, though this is unfortunately the last time! She's a great friend and a great teacher. This world setting and story has gained so much depth from her encouragement.

Another thanks goes out to a friend who's helped me develop bigger, badder bad guys.

My sister deserves a round of thanks for helping me roll a bunch of dice to determine who got into trouble during the investment firm caper.

As always, thanks to my online buds who help cheer me on, and for those who said "if the story's meant to be that long, let it be that long."

And a final thanks to you, reader peep. This job's really not much of anything without you all reading. I hope you've enjoyed the ride and will join us for *Midnight War*, if not before then ;)

ALSO BY JS HARKER

ABOUT THE AUTHOR

JS Harker loves stories. She was one of those kids who constantly had a book in her hands and spent countless hours adventuring with her siblings. These days she wanders into her imaginary worlds and conjures up tales of magic, passion, and happily-ever-afters. She currently lives in the part of the Midwest that makes Tatooine look interesting by comparison (not that she's ever obsessively thought about becoming a Jedi or anything).

Follow her on Facebook or go to www.jsharker.com and sign up for her newsletter to receive updates!

Want more of her stories *now*? Be sure to join her Patreon!

Milton Keynes UK
Ingram Content Group UK Ltd.
UKHW021518080824
446561UK00005B/6

9 781959 146063